FOLK TALES OF INDIA

FOLK TALES OF

INDIA

Adapted by Lee Wyndham

EDITORIAL CONSULTANT

JEANNE CHALL, Ph. D.

Associate Professor of Education,
the City College of New York

THE **BOBBS-MERRILL** COMPANY, INC.
A SUBSIDIARY OF HOWARD W. SAMS & CO., INC.
Publishers • INDIANAPOLIS • NEW YORK

DRAWINGS BY EMILIO FREIXAS

Library of Congress Catalog Card No. 62-19337

Contents

About This Book

A FOLK TALE is a story that is so ancient no one knows who told it first. Storytelling is the oldest and most popular form of entertainment as well as of teaching. Today our storyteller often is the television set in our home. It "tells and shows" at the same time. Our storyteller might be someone who reads to us. When we read a book, the printed words are our "storytellers."

But hundreds and even thousands of years ago, before people had books or could read, storytellers went from village to

7

village, from castle to palace. They always found a welcome, for everyone, always, has loved to hear a story.

Traveling storytellers, merchants, adventurers, explorers, soldiers, gypsies, slaves—people who got about from place to place—carried stories with them. In this way the stories of one country found ready listeners in another. Sometimes these retold stories took on different titles and characters, a different situation or a different background, as people fitted them to their audience. After some time these imported stories became so familiar that everybody in a country seemed to know them, and people believed that these stories were originally told in their native country.

This is what happened to the folk tales, fairy tales and fables of India. Scholars have found that some of the oldest and most popular of these in the rest of the world were first told in India. Even some of Aesop's famous fables can be traced back to Hindu sources.

Sometimes the idea behind the story was entertainment. But more often than not, a story was told to teach a lesson or point up a moral. The *Panchatantra*, or The Five Books, is the oldest collection of stories in Hindu literature. It is believed that they were written down about 200 B.C., although they were told among the people long, long before that. These wonderful stories were collected by a wise Brahman—a priest-scholar-teacher—named Bidpai. Their purpose was to teach young princes of the land to understand all kinds of people, rich and poor, and therefore to rule more wisely.

Originally, it is thought, there were twelve books in this collection. But by the time the outside world discovered them, only five were left. The stories were so enchanting that they were translated into Persian, Arabic, Syrian, Greek, Latin, Chinese, Hebrew—so many languages, in fact, that now there exist more than two hundred different versions of these tales, retold in more than fifty languages.

How close they are to the original folk tales is anybody's

guess, but it really hardly matters. The main point is that these stories are still interesting to reàd. Those in this volume were selected especially for today's boys and girls.

Some of these appeared originally in the *Panchatantra*. Others are from the *Jatakas*, The Book of Buddha's Birth-Stories. Buddha was an Indian religious leader and founder of the Buddhist faith. He lived five hundred years before Christ. The Birth-Stories are legends which tell how he was born again and again in different animal forms until he became the Enlightened One. This kind of rebirth is called reincarnation, and was believed in widely at one time.

The fairy tales, in which the good always triumph, the wicked are punished, the innocent, the weak and oppressed and the hard-working are rewarded, were probably told much, much later by village storytellers sitting under trees. Later they were told by ayahs—Indian nursemaids—to their English charges, and were remembered and written down for others to read. Several of the stories in this collection were told to me, and I am passing them on to you.

The India all these portray is not today's progressive and independent country. Instead, they are set in a time when fairy tale adventures "could have happened," when animals talked to men and to each other—and often behaved like people, as you shall see. Then magic and magicians worked wonders and mischief that aided or hindered brave heroes. These folk and fairy tales are your magic carpet to an ancient yesterday. And yet, as you read these marvel-filled stories, you will find many thoughts, needs and emotions expressed which are no different now from what they were hundreds of years ago.

I have had many hours of happy work upon these stories. Here's happy reading for you!

Lee Wyndham

You'll want to know about these...

CASTE: one of the classes into which the people of India have been divided from the earliest times. A person was born into a certain caste, or class, and never could change this. The work one did was determined by his caste. Marriage outside one's caste was forbidden. In the new India these things are being changed. The main castes were:

> BRAHMANS: the priests
>
> KASHATRIYAS: the military
>
> VAISYAS: farmers and merchants
>
> SUDRAS: laborers
>
> "UNTOUCHABLES": the lowest class.

These main castes, however, had many other grades or divisions of social position within them. That is why in the stories here you will find at one point that a Brahman is a saintly person (*The Tiger, the Brahman and the Jackal*), and at another (*Harisarman*), the Brahman is a bit of a scoundrel.

FAKIR: a Hindu monk, a religious man who lives by begging for his daily needs. Sometimes these men practiced magic, as you'll see in *The King and the Fakir*.

HINDU: a native of Hindustan or India.

RAJAH: a king or prince.

RANI: the wife of an Indian king or prince. Also a reigning queen or princess.

Harisarman

IN A CERTAIN TOWN in India there once lived a Brahman whose name was Harisarman. He was poor and rather foolish, and never could hold on to any job for long. Often he was reduced to begging in the streets in order to provide food for his wife and children.

However, through a stroke of luck, he was taken into the service of a very rich man named Saradwata. Harisarman's duty was to live close to his master's home and to take care of his lawns and gardens. His sons were to tend the cattle of the rich man, and his wife was to prepare the meals for the household.

One day a great celebration was held in honor of the marriage of Saradwata's daughter. Harisarman's mouth watered all day at the thought of the fine food prepared for the feast. But no one in the household remembered the Brahman or his family. None of the delicacies came their way.

This made Harisarman very angry. That night, as he went to bed, he said to his wife, "Our master, Saradwata, has treated us this way because he thinks I am stupid. But I will change this. I shall make him believe that I have magic power, and then he will respect me."

"That is all very well," said his wife. "But you have no magic power, have you?"

"Not right now," grumbled Harisarman. "But I'll think about it and then I'll have some."

While his wife slept, the Brahman spent the night thinking. Shortly before dawn an idea came to him. He rose from his bed and hurried to his master's stables. There he took the horse of Saradwata's new son-in-law and hid it some distance from the main house. Then he returned to his bed.

Next morning, while the friends of the bridegroom searched for the horse, Harisarman said to his wife,

"Go to our master and tell him that although he is not aware of it, your husband is skilled in magic science. Tell him that you are sure I can return the horse—if he asks me properly."

"Very well," said his wife, much awed by her husband's grand manner.

She did as she had been told and soon Saradwata summoned Harisarman into his presence.

"Ah," said Harisarman. "Yesterday you forget me, but to-day, now that you have had the horse stolen, you remember me."

"Forgive me," Saradwata answered humbly. "I was not

aware of your wisdom. I beg you, tell me who has stolen my son-in-law's horse and where is it?"

Harisarman nodded in silence. Then he drew some lines on the floor and sat down to meditate. After remaining for some time in what appeared to be deep thought, he said, "At this moment the horse stands tied to a tree near the waterfall that lies one league beyond your house. The thieves plan to take it away when night falls."

As soon as he heard these words, Saradwata sent his servants to the waterfall. They promptly returned with the animal, and Saradwata could not say enough in praise of Harisarman. He also rewarded the Brahman generously and heaped honors upon him.

Time passed, and then one day a report came from the Rajah's palace. A great quantity of jewels, gold and silver had been stolen. Since the thief could not be found, the Rajah asked Harisarman to come to his aid, for the Brahman's knowledge of magic had spread throughout the land.

There was nothing for Harisarman to do but allow himself to be led to the palace. Putting on a bold manner before his sovereign, the Brahman said,

"O, Rajah, I will answer your question tomorrow."

Actually, he was only trying to gain time. Perhaps some miracle would happen and the jewels would be found—and he would not be exposed as the fraud he was.

But the Rajah, believing firmly in the Brahman's reported wisdom and knowledge of magic, had a splendid room prepared for him in the palace. Harisarman moved into it, but with no joy in his heart.

A palace servant named Tonga had stolen the jewels. Alarmed by the presence of Harisarman, she went at midnight to peer through the keyhole of his room.

At that moment, the false wizard was cursing his tongue for getting him into trouble. "What have you done, tongue, what have you done? Evil one, you'll soon get the punishment that you deserve!"

On hearing these words, Tonga thought that Harisarman was saying her name instead of tongue. Terrified at being discovered, she burst into the Brahman's room and kneeling before him cried,

"Brahman, I am Tonga whom you have discovered. I am the thief of the Rajah's treasure. It is hidden in the palace garden, as you no doubt know, under the pomegranate tree. I beg you, do not denounce me, but accept the little gold that I possess as a token of my gratitude."

After his first surprise, Harisarman recovered his wits quickly. "Leave me!" he thundered. "Indeed I know all that you have told me. I know the present, the past and the future. But I will not denounce you, for you are a miserable creature who has begged for my protection. However, you may leave the gold that you mentioned as a token of your gratitude."

Vastly relieved, the girl poured her gold into the Brahman's hands and then scurried from the room.

Harisarman tucked the gold away into his pockets. "Such is fate," he murmured. "It has decided that I am to be known as a wise magician. Though I have been one step away from death, all has gone well with me. While I cursed my tongue, Tonga the thief threw herself at my feet. I wonder how many crimes does fear uncover!"

Happy in his thoughts, Harisarman had a good night's sleep and arose refreshed. When he was brought before the Rajah, he made some strange movements with his hands, closed his eyes, and then declared that the stolen treasure was in the garden, under the pomegranate tree. He also added that the thief had escaped with part of the treasure.

"No matter, no matter," the Rajah declared as he gazed upon his jewels once more. Then he showered the highest praises upon the wise Harisarman. "What is more," he exclaimed, "I will make you governor over three towns."

Harisarman was overcome by the thought of his good luck. But the Chief Minister of the Rajah whispered into the royal ear.

"How is it possible for a simple Brahman to possess magic power that can only be had after many years of study? Perhaps he has been working with the thieves who stole your treasure, and therefore knew what he knew. Before you give him charge of all those towns, might it not be wise to put him to a test, right here and now?"

The Chief Minister had always given the Rajah good advice. So now the great man nodded and agreed to the test. Taking a porcelain cup, he filled it with water and slipped a tadpole into it. He then covered the cup with a cloth and presented it to Harisarman. "Tell me, Wise One, what is underneath this cloth?" he asked.

In an instant, Harisarman felt his luck slipping away from him. He closed his eyes, thinking that his final hour had come. Then, remembering how his father used to call him when he had behaved badly, he murmured,

"Where are you, you miserable tadpole?"

The Rajah and his court burst into applause, marveling at the speed with which the Brahman had guessed what was under the cloth. For good measure, the Rajah added a few more towns to those he had already given to the Brahman. He also presented him with a bagful of money and a trunkful of fine clothes.

And so it was that thanks to the likeness of one word to another, a frightened thief, and the fact that his father had once called him a tadpole, Harisarman became one of the richest men in India. His near-misses of misfortune taught him caution. With time and comfort at his hand, he applied himself to learning. And in the end he governed the Rajah's towns faithfully and well.

Why the Fish Laughed

A WOMAN SELLING FISH was approaching the palace when the Rajah's wife stepped out on her balcony.

"Come closer and show me your wares," the Rani called.

As the woman came near her, one of the fish in the basket jumped up, showing its silvery underside.

"Is it a male or a female?" the Rani asked. "I wish to purchase a female."

On hearing this, the fish burst into loud laughter.

"It is a male," replied the fishwoman, and melted into the crowd.

The Rani, very much annoyed, went back into her room. By the time the Rajah came to see her, she was furious.

"What is the matter?" he asked. "Are you ill?"

"No, but I am angry at what a fish has done. A fishwoman passed in front of the palace and when I asked her if the fish that had jumped in her basket were a male or a female, the fish laughed."

"A fish laughed?" The Rajah showed his surprise. "My dear, that is absolutely impossible!"

"I am not mad, my Lord. I tell you what I have seen with my own eyes and heard with my own ears," the Rani replied.

"There, there, dear," the Rajah said soothingly. "This is all very strange. I shall make inquiries about it at once. Don't you fret."

The Rajah informed his Grand Vizier of what had happened to his wife and ordered him to investigate the matter. The investigation proved fruitless. Not only was the Vizier unable to find the fishwoman, but there was no one who had seen or heard what the Rani claimed to have seen and heard.

This report made the Rajah angry and the Rani furious! The more ill-tempered she grew, the angrier the Rajah became. Finally he summoned his Grand Vizier and declared that he would give him six months in which to get to the bottom of this ridiculous business of a fish daring to laugh at the Rani.

"And if you fail," the Rajah finished darkly, "you shall be beheaded."

Trembling, the Grand Vizier assured his prince that he would not fail. However, five months of searching and questioning turned up nothing. Even the wisest of the realm's wise men could not find a logical explanation of a fish's laughing. The Vizier knew that his own end was very near. He made all the necessary preparations to die. He told his only son to leave the kingdom at once and travel until the Rajah's wrath had cooled.

The young man put on plain clothing, embraced his father and bade him farewell. A month before the deadline fixed by the Rajah, he set out on his wanderings with his father's blessing.

After some days on the road, he met a merchant who was also going in the same direction. He asked if he might join him and the merchant, liking the looks of the young fellow, agreed.

After a while the young man said to the merchant, "Don't you think that if we helped one another, now and then, the trip would be more entertaining?"

The merchant stared at him. "This young man must be out of his mind," he thought.

Soon after they came to a field of wheat that was ready to be harvested. Pausing for a moment, the son of the Vizier asked his companion,

"Is that wheat already eaten or not?"

Not knowing how to answer such a strange question, the merchant shrugged.

A few hours passed and the two men arrived at a town. The young man took out a knife and, giving it to the former, said,

"Friend, go and buy us two handsome horses with this, but don't forget to return it, for I hold it in great esteem."

Half amused and half angry, the merchant grumbled under his breath that either his companion was mad or he was trying to appear so. The son of the Vizier showed no sign of having heard the words of the merchant.

An hour later the two arrived at a town beyond which was the merchant's house.

As they passed through the busy market place, no one gave them a greeting, or offered them rest or refreshment.

"What an enormous cemetery!" the young man exclaimed.

The merchant frowned. Why should his companion speak of this bustling town as a cemetery?

When they came out of the town, they passed close to a cemetery. Several people there were praying for the souls of the dead and giving alms and food to anyone who passed by.

"What a splendid town!" the young man exclaimed.

Now there was no doubt in his companion's mind. The young man was mad! "Let us see what he will do now," the merchant said, half aloud, to himself. "Without doubt he will call the water, land and the land, water. He will say that shadow is light and that light is shadow."

Just then they came to a river which it was necessary to wade. The merchant took off his shoes and crossed it bare-footed. But the young man went into the water with his shoes still on.

"In all my life I have never seen the like of this!" said the merchant to himself.

Nevertheless, as the young man appeared to be harmless,

he thought it might be amusing for his daughter to meet him. So he begged his companion to accept the hospitality of his home, for as long as he wished to stay.

"Thank you very much," answered the son of the Vizier. "But before I accept, I would like to ask you if the foundations of your house are sufficiently strong."

The merchant threw up his hands. "Sit here in the courtyard under the tree and I'll go in and find out," he said and went into his house, laughing.

"I have brought a friend who seems to have taken leave of his senses," he told his daughter, who came running to greet him. "Before accepting my hospitality, he asked me if the foundations of my house were sufficiently strong."

"My father," said his daughter quietly. "This man is not mad."

The merchant listened to her attentively, for she was an unusually wise young woman.

"If he asked you that question," she continued, "it was to know if you could offer him your hospitality without putting yourself out. In other words, if you could afford to keep a guest in your house."

"Why of course!" exclaimed her father. "How clear you make it, Sakoontala. Perhaps you can help me to puzzle out the other riddles he set before me. At the beginning of our journey together he told me that if we were to help each other, the trip would prove more amusing."

"That is very simple, my father," Sakoontala replied. "What your companion meant was that if you told each other stories, the trip would have been made more pleasant."

"True! True!" the merchant cried. "What a clever girl you are, Sakoontala. Now tell me—as we passed by a wheat field, he asked me if the grain had already been eaten. What did he mean by that?"

His daughter smiled. "He wanted to know if the owner of that field owed money to anyone. If he did, then the money for the sale of the wheat would end up in the hands of the people to whom it was owed. In other words, though the wheat were not yet harvested, it was, in fact, already eaten."

"My daughter, I marvel at your wisdom. Now I will tell you another of his riddles. As we came to a town, he gave me a knife and told me to get two good horses, but warned me that he wanted the knife back."

Sakoontala's laugh tinkled merrily. "That is also simple, my father. Are not two good sticks an excellent help in walking? Could we not call them the poor man's horses? When he gave you the knife he was telling you to cut two sticks and to do it with care."

"Magnificent! What a mind you have, my daughter. Now —as we went through the town no one invited us to sit or refresh ourselves. And yet, as we passed the cemetery those who were praying there gave us food and had us rest with them. My companion called the town a cemetery and the cemetery, a town."

Sakoontala sighed lightly before she answered. "We think of a town as a place where we may obtain everything we need. On the other hand, we think of those who do not practice hospitality as worse than dead. Although filled with living people, the town to you was worse than a cemetery. Yet it was in the cemetery, where the dead are, that you found warmth and hospitality."

"It is true!" exclaimed her father in astonishment. "I will tell you the last thing my companion did. As we came to the river, instead of taking off his shoes, he went into the water wearing them. What think you of that?"

"I admire his good sense," replied the young woman. "Many times I have seen people cross the river after taking their shoes off. As you know, dear father, the river is full of sharp stones. Often the pain of stepping on a stone is such that a person loses his balance. Thus, instead of merely wetting his shoes, all his clothes are soaked and whatever he carries is spoiled. That friend of yours is a wise man. I should like to see him and speak with him."

"I will fetch him directly," the father promised, hurrying out the door.

"Be sure to tell him that the foundations of this house are strong," his daughter called out. "In fact, I will send him a gift to let him know that we are rich enough to grant him hospitality."

The young woman called a servant and sent the visitor a gift consisting of a cup of sweet oil, twelve tarts, a jug of milk and this message, "The moon is full. Twelve months make a year. The sea overflows with water."

On the way out to the courtyard, the servant met one of his sons. He saw what his father carried and he asked for some of it. The servant was foolish enough to give his son what he wanted. When he found the young man, he gave him what was left of Sakoontala's gifts and the message.

The son of the Vizier accepted all this, saying, "Return to your mistress and tell her that the moon is in its third quarter. The year has only seven months, and the tide is receding."

Not understanding the meaning of the message, the servant carried it back to his mistress. But the young woman understood it instantly and punished the dishonest servant severely.

The son of the Vizier was then welcomed into the house and treated with great courtesy. At the end of a splendid dinner, he told the story of the fish that had laughed.

"Perhaps, Sakoontala, since you solved my riddles so swiftly, you can tell me what this one means. It is a matter of the greatest importance."

"Indeed it is," Sakoontala agreed. "Were the matter not so close to your heart, you would have solved the riddle yourself. But your concern clouded your reason. Hear this, then. The laughter of the fish means that in the palace there is a man who wishes to kill the Rajah."

"Of course!" exclaimed the young man, leaping to his feet. "You need not finish. I understand it all now. There is no time to be lost. Let us return to my country at once, save my father's life and remove the danger from the Rajah's also."

"At once, at once!" cried the merchant, and ran out himself
to arrange for the swiftest transportation for the pair.

When the two young people arrived at the home of the
Vizier they told him the reason for the fish's laughter. The
poor man, who was now a mere shadow of himself, gathered
up his strength and ran to the Rajah's quarters. There he
repeated what he had just learned.

"It is impossible!" exclaimed the Rajah.

"It is the truth, my Lord," insisted the Vizier. "And to
prove that I do not lie, let us make a test. Summon all your
female slaves and make them take turns jumping the width of
this carpet. We shall soon find out if there is such a man
among them."

This was done, and all the female slaves failed to jump over
the carpet, except one. This slave turned out to be not only
a man, but the "fish woman," in still another disguise! The
Rajah had him beheaded on the spot.

Thus it was that the Rani was satisfied, the Rajah made
safe, and the Vizier kept his life.

As for his son, he married Sakoontala, and became one of
the Rajah's most valued ministers.

The Rajah's Son and
the Light Princess

A RAJAH who ruled over an important province of India had
but one son, who loved to hunt every day. Each morning,
before the young man started out, his mother, the Rani, would
say, "You may hunt to the north, to the east and to the west,

my son. But do not even think of going toward the south."

She told him this because she was certain that if her son were ever to go in that direction, he would surely hear of the beautiful Princess Labam. Then there would be no holding him. He would go in search of the young beauty, and perish, like many another suitor for her hand.

Being a dutiful son, the Prince obeyed his mother. But one day, finding nothing to test his hunting skill in the north, the east, or the west, he turned his horse to the south. His mother's warning came to his mind and he paused, scanning the jungle before him.

He saw nothing out of the ordinary, except for an enormous flock of parrots. So, dismissing the Rani's warning, he spurred his horse toward the south. And, for lack of choicer game, the young Prince let fly a few arrows at the parrots. With a whir of wings, the birds flew off and hid in the tallest trees.

Actually, however, not all of them had fled. Old Hiraman, their king, unable to keep up with the younger birds, remained on the branch and served him as a throne. Now, in a voice cracked with age, he shouted to the others, "Do not leave me alone to serve as a target for the Prince's arrows! Return at once or I shall tell Princess Labam of what you have done!"

No sooner had the birds heard these words than they sped back to their sovereign, full of humble apologies.

The Rajah's son was greatly surprised by all this talk. And then his curiosity was aroused. He rode closer to the king parrot's tree and asked, "Who is this Princess Labam, and where does she live?"

Hiraman ruffled his feathers and glared at the Prince. "Do not bother your head about her," he grumbled. "You will never be able to reach the place where she lives."

No matter how the Prince pressed for a more direct answer, it was useless. The king of the parrots would tell him nothing. At last the Prince wheeled his horse about and sped back to his palace. But he could not get the Princess Labam out of his mind.

Her name haunted him constantly, awake and asleep. Finally, he strode into the chambers of his parents. "I have heard of the Princess Labam," he announced, "and I cannot rest until I find her. Tell me where she lives."

The Rani wrung her hands in grief, but the Rajah answered quietly, "We do not know, my son, except that it is somewhere to the south."

"Then I will search for her," the Prince declared.

"No, no," exclaimed his father. "You are our only son. Do not leave your home on this fruitless search, for you are likely to perish as others have before you. The Princess Labam is so well guarded, no one can get to her."

"I must try," the young man insisted stubbornly.

There was nothing to do but bid him farewell. The Rani wept. The Rajah gave his son a magnificent horse, and a bow which could shoot arrows as far as a thousand feet. He also gave him a well-filled money bag.

Just before the Prince mounted his horse, the Rani embraced him tenderly and pressed a small package into his hands. "Here are some of your favorite sweets," she said.

The young man kissed her, slipped the package into his tunic and leaped upon the back of his horse. "Do not worry about me," he told his parents. "I shall not perish like the others. I shall return, and bring the Princess Labam with me!"

His bold words only sent his mother into fresh torrents of tears as the Prince rode out into the unknown country to the south.

After many hours of riding through thick jungle, the Prince came upon a pond of clear water. Wishing to refresh himself, he took off his garments and bathed. Then he lay in the shadow of a tree and reached for the package of sweets his mother had given him.

As he took out the first sweet, he saw that an ant was on it.

On the second one he also found an ant. He put the sweets on the ground and looked into the bag. It was full of hungry ants.

"Ah well, it does not matter," he murmured. "Let the ants have them."

The queen of the ants heard him and, leaving her subjects, spoke to him. "You have been kind to us, Prince. If ever you find yourself in danger, think of me and I will come to your aid."

The Rajah's son thanked her courteously and, mounting his horse, continued his search.

He rode out of one jungle only to enter another, more dense than the first. There he came upon a tiger roaring with pain.

"What is wrong?" the Prince asked. "Why do you roar in such agony?"

"Twelve years ago a thorn buried itself in this paw," answered the animal. "In all this time it has never stopped aching. That is why I cry out from the time the sun is born in the east to the time it dies in the west."

"I think I can help you," said the Prince, "but you must promise me that when you are rid of the thorn you will not eat me."

"I will not eat you," the tiger said. "I beg you to free me of this terrible pain."

The son of the Rajah drew out a sharp dagger and with a quick thrust and turn pulled out the thorn. The thorn was so deeply sunk in the paw of the beast that as it came out, it made the tiger roar more loudly than ever. His mate heard the sound and, fearing that something dreadful had happened, rushed toward him.

Seeing her coming, the tiger quickly hid the Prince, for fear she would think the Prince was harming him.

"Who has wounded you?" asked the tigress.

"No one," replied the tiger. "That roar was one of happiness. The Rajah's son has just removed the thorn which has bothered me these twelve years."

"Where is he? I must see him at once," declared the tigress.

"If you promise not to kill him, I will call him," the tiger said.

"I swear not to do him the least harm," the tigress assured her husband. "I wish only to thank him."

The tiger then called the young man, and the two animals spoke to him with great kindness. They then served him an excellent meal. The Prince remained with them for three days and each morning he attended to the wound in the tiger's paw. When it was completely healed, he said that he must continue on his way.

As he mounted his horse, the tiger said, "If ever you are in danger, think of us and we will rush to your aid."

"Thank you, dear friends, I'll remember that," the Prince told them, and spurred his horse.

Now he came to a third jungle. Here he found four thieves whose leader had died, leaving behind four valuable objects. One was a bed which would take whoever sat on it anywhere he wanted to go. The second was a purse which would give to its owner whatever he wished—jewels, food or clothing. The third was a stone cup with the gift of filling itself with water no matter how far its owner was from a waterhole. The fourth object was a stick and rope to which all that had to be said was, "Beat all men who are here, except me." The stick then would proceed to thrash one enemy after another, while the rope followed and tied them up.

The four thieves were quarreling over these four objects. One would say, "I want the bed!"

Another would immediately exclaim, "Ah, but it cannot be. I want the bed."

So it went, without any of them agreeing on anything for even a moment.

The Prince listened to their noise with some amusement for a while, then he rode boldly into their clearing. "I can settle

your problem quite easily if you will let me," he said pleas-
antly. "I will shoot four arrows. He who brings back the first
one will have the bed. The one who brings the second arrow
will get the purse. The stone cup will belong to the one who
brings back the third arrow. And he who brings the fourth
will be given the stick and rope."

The thieves agreed to abide by these conditions. When the
first arrow was shot, the four of them went running after it.
When the first arrow was brought back, the Prince shot off the
second.

Instead of remaining behind, with his bed, the thief who
had brought in the first arrow rushed off with his fellows, hoping to be first again. Thus each time an arrow was shot off,
all four men greedily raced after it. The Prince saw that their
problem would never be solved. As soon as they came back
with the fourth arrow they would start quarreling again.

On finding himself alone with the thieves' ill-gotten treasures for the fourth time, the Rajah's son let his horse go free.
He seated himself on the bed, took the stone cup, the purse
and the stick and the rope and said, "Bed, I wish to be taken
to the land of Princess Labam."

The bed rose through the air and flew straight as directed.
Then it descended in a green field not far from the palace
belonging to Princess Labam's father.

The Prince left the bed and walked to a small house where
he saw an old woman working in her garden.

"Who are you and where do you come from, noble sir?" she
asked.

"I come from a far country, lady," answered the Prince,
bowing respectfully. "I beg you to let me pass the night under
your roof."

"That I cannot do," said the woman regretfully, "for our
King has forbidden us to give shelter to foreign people."

"At least let me remain in your house till dawn, then," the
Prince urged. "It is very late now and if I were to sleep in

the jungle, I would be in danger of the wild beasts there."

"True, true." She sighed. "Very well, you may stay. But you must leave tomorrow, and early. If our King were to find out that I gave shelter to you, he would have me thrown into his dungeon for the rest of my life."

The good woman then went into her house with the Prince and made ready to prepare supper. The Prince, however, stopped her, saying,

"Do not be bothered with preparing food, dear lady. It will be I who will serve you." And reaching inside the magic purse he said in a low voice, "Purse, give me supper."

Instantly the purse brought forth the tastiest foods the old woman had ever seen, with everything served on golden plates.

When they finished eating, the woman rose to get some water to drink and wash their hands. The Prince again stopped her, saying,

"Do not trouble yourself, kind lady. You shall have all the water you wish." And taking the stone cup out, he ordered, "Cup, give me water."

The cup filled immediately with the fresh, sweet water, which the Prince poured into all the pots about the house. When they were filled, the Prince ordered the cup to cease giving water and it immediately became empty.

By this time it was night. The Rajah's son looked about the house but nowhere did he see a lamp or a candle. "Have you nothing with which to make a light?" he asked.

The old woman smiled. "It is not necessary. You see, as soon as it gets dark, our Princess Labam goes out on her balcony. Such is the brightness she sheds that her light is as the sun's rays, lighting our streets and houses."

She had barely finished speaking when the Princess stepped out on her balcony. Her gown was made of moonbeams, woven by the gods who watched over her beauty. Around her throat, her head and her body there were long strands of pearls and diamonds. In one magic instant, the night became bright as day.

The Prince watched from the doorway of the old woman's house, almost breathless in his delight over so much beauty. At midnight, when all the people of the nation had gone to their beds, the Princess also returned to her rooms. As her curtains were drawn, there was night once more in the kingdom.

The young Prince waited until he thought the Princess would be asleep. Then, going to the bed which he had hidden in the field, he sat on it, saying, "Bed, I wish you to take me to the room where Princess Labam sleeps."

The bed obeyed instantly and the Prince found himself in the chamber of the lovely Princess. The Prince then took out his magic purse and said, "I want you to bring me a golden basket of the rarest fruit from my country."

In a moment basket and fruit were at his hand. He set the basket on a low table beside the Princess. Then he went back to his magic bed and returned to the old woman's little house.

Next morning, neither the Princess nor her servants could explain where the rare fruit or the beautifully woven gold basket had come from.

In the meantime, the old lady awakened the Prince and told him sadly that he must leave her house at once.

"I cannot, dear lady," said the Prince. "I feel strangely ill. Please allow me to stay until tomorrow morning."

"Very well." The old woman agreed, for she had become fond of the young man.

That day they ate what the enchanted purse gave them. And when night came, the Princess, on her balcony, once more lighted the kingdom. All the time she remained on her balcony, the Prince stayed within the door of the little house and never took his gaze from her.

At midnight the Princess retired to her room, and shortly

thereafter, the Rajah's son sat on his magic bed and asked to be taken to see his beloved.

Once in her room, he told the purse to give him the most beautiful shawl in the world. As usual, the purse obeyed.

The shawl was made of the blue of the night sprinkled with little stars fallen from the heavens. The Prince took it and covered the beautiful Princess with it. Under the shawl she appeared more beautiful than ever. He could scarcely bear to leave her to return to the old woman's cottage.

When the Princess wakened and saw the shawl she ran with it to her mother, the Rani. "Surely this must be a gift from the gods," she said.

"It must be, indeed," agreed the Rani. "Human hands could not have woven such a marvelous thing."

At the very same moment, the old lady was saying to the Prince, "Now you must leave, noble sir. Every moment you stay, my danger increases."

"Please," begged the Prince, "let me remain a few more days. I am not yet well. I promise I shall not leave the house and no one will see me."

The old lady smiled fondly at her guest. "So be it," she said.

That night, as usual, the Princess was out on her balcony and the Prince gazed upon her, his heart filled with love for her. At half-past-midnight, he sat on his magic bed and had himself carried to her bedchamber.

Once there he took out his magic purse and ordered it to produce the most beautiful ring in the world.

The ring was made of midday sun and set with a midnight star. The Rajah's son placed it gently in the Princess' hand. As he closed her slim fingers over it, the girl wakened.

"Who are you?" she asked, her eyes large with fright. "What are you doing here?"

"Do not be afraid, O beautiful Princess," the young man

pleaded. "I am not a thief, but the son of a powerful Rajah. Hiraman, the king of the parrots, in the jungle where I hunt, spoke of you. I no sooner heard your name, than I had to find you. I no sooner saw you, than I loved you."

The Princess looked deep into his eyes, then down at the ring in her hand. "You must be the son of a powerful Rajah, indeed," she said. "Did you give me the marvelous shawl and the wonderful fruit, also?"

The Prince bowed low before her. "Will you be my wife?" he asked softly.

The Princess Labam blushed prettily. "I will tell my parents that I wish to marry you," she answered.

This made the Prince so happy that as his magic bed was flying him back to the old woman's house, he had it turn over and over in the air. It was a miracle that he didn't tumble out.

The next morning the Princess ran to her mother, the Rani, saying, "There has come to this country the son of a most

powerful Rajah, and I wish to marry him. I beg you to tell
this to my father."

"Oh she does, does she?" the Rajah said to the Rani, when
she told him. "I shall have no objections—if this Prince proves
himself worthy of our Labam. He must first do what I tell
him. If he fails, I will have his head. How did he ever get
into my kingdom in the first place, without my knowing? He
may find that was more simple than the task I have for him."

In the meantime, the Prince had waited until the old
woman awakened. He had not been able to sleep a wink, so
full was he of his happiness. The moment she stirred, he burst
out with his plans to marry the Princess Labam. "And, dear
lady," he finished, "I shall get you a lamp, or a dozen, for I
shall take my Princess of Light back to my own land with me
as soon as we are wed."

"Leave the country at once and forget the Princess!" cried
the old woman. "Many Princes have come here to ask for the
Princess' hand and the King has ordered them killed. To all
those who try to marry his daughter, he gives such impossible
tasks that there is no one who can perform them. If you try,
you will surely die like the rest."

Even though the advice of the old woman was sound, the
Prince refused to listen to it. He was young, he adored the
Princess and nothing could stop him.

Shortly before noon, a messenger arrived at the old
woman's house and invited the Prince to follow him back to
the palace. Once there, the King gave the young Prince one
hundred pounds of mustard seed.

"Extract every bit of oil from this seed," he directed the
young man, "and bring it back to the palace tomorrow at this
time. He who wishes to marry my daughter must do all that
I require of him. If he is unable to do it, I must have him beheaded. It is a rule I have made. Therefore, if you are unable
to extract the oil—every last drop of it—I will have to have
your head cut off."

Disheartened, the Prince gazed at the large bags of seed. He had no idea how he could extract the oil. But, since he could do no less, he took the seed and carried it to the old woman's house. There he sat and stared at it, without being able to decide how to proceed. All at once he remembered the queen of the ants. No sooner had he thought of her than she appeared before him.

"What makes you so sad, kind Prince?" she asked.

The Rajah's son pointed to the heap of seeds. "How can I take the oil out of these seeds? Yet I must do it by morning, or my head will be cut off by order of the Rajah of this country."

"Don't give it another thought," exclaimed the queen of the ants. "Go to your bed and rest. In the meantime my subjects and I will attend to the work."

In no time at all the oil was extracted.

The next day the Prince went to the Rajah's palace and presented him with the results of the work done by the industrious ants. But the Rajah only frowned.

"You cannot yet marry my daughter. It is necessary that you fight with my two monsters and that you slay them. It is a rule I have made. If you do not slay them, however, it will not be necessary to have you killed. My monsters will have attended to the matter—very thoroughly too. Show him the monsters, so that he may prepare to do them battle," he ordered the officers of his court.

Some years before, the Rajah had managed to trap two terrible monsters. He kept them as curiosities, locked in a triple cage, one cage set inside the other.

When the young man saw the two monsters he was upset. How in the world could he kill such frightful beings? Suddenly he remembered something.

"Leave me!" he ordered the officers who were showing him the monsters' dungeon. "And be quick about it!"

No sooner had they left, than his two tiger friends from the second jungle appeared.

"What is your trouble, O kind Prince?" asked the tiger.

"The Rajah of this country has ordered me to fight these two monsters and kill them," the Prince replied. "How can I do such an impossible thing?"

"Do not worry," the tigress said. "We will attend to the matter."

With that the two jungle beasts ripped apart the triple cage and devoured the monsters in two gulps.

Having thanked his tiger friends, the Prince returned to the Rajah. He dusted his hands off and informed the monarch that the deed was done.

"Impossible!" roared the Rajah. "Officers, go to the monsters' dungeon and tell me this man lies."

The officers sped away. When they returned they were white as ghosts. "The-the m-monsters are g-gone, your Majesty," they stammered. "Their cage was ripped apart and we found nothing there but their bones. W-we think this man *ate* them!"

"Imbeciles!" shrieked the Rajah, who saw his daughter slipping away from him. "I will see for myself, and I will have your heads if you lie!" He rushed away, shouting at the top of his voice.

He returned very quietly, keeping a cautious distance between himself and this would-be son-in-law. Yet he was not quite ready to give up his beautiful daughter.

"That was very good," he said, grudgingly, "though I don't know how you did it. No, no! Don't show me," he added hastily as the Prince made a slight movement with his hands. "Still, I cannot give you my daughter until you pass another test. It is a rule I have made." He kept a sharp eye on the Prince, but the young fellow appeared to be listening dutifully. "High in the heavens I have suspended a huge drum. It is necessary that you reach it and strike it so that I can hear it in the palace. If you cannot do this, you know what to expect!"

But the young man at once thought of his magic bed. Without losing a moment, he ran to the field where he kept it, leaped upon it and cried, "Bed, take me to where the Rajah's great drum is."

The bed obeyed instantly, and in a few minutes a tremendous BOO-OOOM! came from the great drum.

The people of the kingdom were almost deafened by the sound. The Rajah, himself, was still rubbing his ears when the Prince returned. Still the stubborn man would not give up his daughter.

"There is one last test," he said.

"What—another!" exclaimed the Prince. But he must remain courteous to his future father-in-law, the Prince told himself. "What is it, sire?" he asked politely.

"Come with me," said the Rajah, leading the way to the palace garden. He stopped before the black stump of a huge tree. It looked more like rock than wood to the Prince.

"This stump has been annoying me for a long time," said the Rajah. "Tomorrow morning I want you to split the thing in two so that my gardeners can dispose of it. I'll be on hand to see you do it, by the way," he added. This time the Rajah wanted to make sure no one was helping the Prince. "And— I want you to use this axe, and no other."

The Prince stared at the axe the Rajah gave him. It was made of wax!

"Well, I'll leave you now to think about your task." The Rajah went off, well pleased with himself. This was a very well-brought-up young man, he thought. He would not dare defy him—or do anything silly, like trying to run away with his daughter. In fact the Rajah wished the Prince's heart were set on someone else's daughter. In that case the Rajah would have been delighted to speak highly of this young man to his future father-in-law. As it was, he would be rather sorry to chop the young fellow's head off tomorrow. For of course he would not succeed.

This time the young Prince was very sad. He saw no way to accomplish this last task, especially with the Rajah right there, watching him. He was so sure that the next day he would be beheaded that he decided to say farewell to Princess Labam. So he went to her chambers on his magic bed.

"I have come to bid you good-by, my Beloved," he told her sorrowfully. "Tomorrow your father will have my head rolling in the dust."

"Oh, no!" the Princess cried out. Her hands flew to her heart, for she had grown to love this Prince, and to admire him for his brave deeds. "Tell me, what has happened?"

The Prince told her of the great black stump and showed her the wax axe her father had given him.

"Is that all!" The Princess threw her lovely head back and laughed, and it was as if a dozen nightingales had begun to sing in the room. Then she stood up on tiptoe and kissed the Prince. "Do not worry, my Beloved," she said. "I want to be your wife, and between us we are more than a match for my dear father. Take this strand of my hair and place it along the edge of the axe. Tomorrow, make sure no one overhears you. Then order the tree stump to let itself be split by this hair, and the order of Princess Labam."

The next day, with the whole court watching, the Rajah's son followed the Princess' instructions. No sooner had the strand of hair touched the stump than it split in two.

Astonished at the wonder of it, the Rajah at last gave in, saying, "You have won my daughter and you may marry her."

The feasts and rejoicing that accompanied the marriage of the royal pair lasted many weeks. When the celebrating was over, the Prince said to his wife, "Would you like to come with me to the country of my father?"

"Of course," said the Princess. "Where you want to be, there I wish to go also."

When he was informed about this, the Rajah put on a long face. But since the Prince, whom he secretly liked very much, was his daughter's husband now, there was nothing he could do. So he gave the young couple many camels and horses loaded with rupees and gifts of gold and jewels and fine cloth. He sent an escort of soldiers and servants, and tried to keep the tears out of his eyes as he kissed his daughter good-by.

Then his son-in-law leaned from his horse and placed a hand on the Rajah's shoulder. "See the magic bed there, sire, strapped on to the camel? That can bring us to you in a matter of minutes. Fear not. You will be able to see your daughter often."

"My son!" cried the Rajah, and embraced the Prince so hard he almost fell off his horse. "Truly, I have always liked you, but now I love you," declared the Rajah. "How well we understand each other!" And he sent them off, beaming broadly.

So the Prince took good care of his magic bed, which became a family heirloom. He kept the cup and the purse in a safe place. He kept the stick and the rope, too, but he never needed them. He lived in peace and harmony all his life and never had to use this last of his magic possessions.

The Tiger, the Brahman, and the Jackal

ONCE UPON A TIME, a tiger was caught in a trap. In vain he tried to break the bars of his cage. Finally he gave up and roared mightily in his despair.

A Brahman happened to be passing by and the tiger, seeing him, cried, "Good Brahman, help me out of this cage!"

"I'm sorry, friend," replied the Brahman. "If I were to let you out, you'd probably eat me."

41

"No, no!" the tiger assured him. "On the contrary, I shall be forever grateful to you. I will be your devoted slave."

The Brahman was still doubtful. But the tiger shed so many tears and made so many promises that the holy man was moved with pity. Without giving the matter another thought, the Brahman opened the cage.

The tiger leaped out, then turned upon the Brahman. "What a stupid fellow you are to be taken in by a few promises. What is to prevent me from devouring you this instant? Prepare to die!"

"But this is most unjust," the Brahman said, and began to plead for his life.

At last the tiger grew tired of listening to him. "Very well," he said. "I shall agree to the decision of the first three judges you ask regarding the justice of my eating you. If they decide that my action would be unjust, then I will not devour you. But let's not waste too much time on this nonsense."

The Brahman was not greatly reassured. But any delay was better than nothing. So, with the hungry tiger at his side, he went to a banyan tree and stated his case.

But the tree shook its branches. "What are you complaining about?" it said. "Do I not give shade to the weary shepherds? And do they not in return for my kindness break my branches off to feed their cattle? Men are an ungrateful lot. Why should a tiger be expected to behave differently?"

The Brahman sighed deeply as he went on. The tiger smacked his lips as he looked forward to his feast.

They came to a buffalo who was turning the wheel of a well. The Brahman told his story, but this second judge proved no kinder than the first.

"You are a fool if you trust in gratitude," she said. "Look at me! While I gave milk they fed me till my sides bulged. Now that I am old and unable to give it, they have tied me to this wheel where I shall end my days. Men are an ungrateful lot. Why should a tiger be expected to behave differently?"

Now the tiger smacked his lips more noisily than ever. The Brahman had little heart for stating his case again. But they had come to a road, and so he asked it to give an opinion.

"You are a poor foolish fellow to expect anything else but this sad fate which awaits you!" exclaimed the road. "Here am I, useful to all, yet rich and poor alike trample upon me and give me no thought whatever. The wheels of their wagons make deep ruts in me. They throw the leftovers from their meals on me. Men have no gratitude, so why should a tiger be different?"

"Well now," the tiger exclaimed, "you have had your three opinions. Is there any further reason why I should not eat you this instant?"

The Brahman was about to bow to his fate when a jackal trotted into view.

"Whatever is the matter, good Brahman?" asked the jackal, stopping short. "Why do you look so sad? And what is this tiger doing at your side?"

Sadly the Brahman explained what had happened to him.

"What a confusing story!" the jackal said, wrinkling his brow. "Would you mind repeating it all to me so that I fully understand what has happened?"

The Brahman repeated his story while the tiger walked around him and the jackal impatiently. As he listened, the jackal kept nodding and nodding. But when the Brahman finished, he shook his head.

"This is very strange," he said. "It all seems to go in one ear and straight out the other! Perhaps if we return to the place where all this started I'll understand what you have been trying to tell me."

"It's all perfectly clear," snarled the tiger. "But since you are so stupid, I suppose we'll have to go back to where the trap was and explain it all to you."

So they did, and the Brahman once more told his sad tale.

The jackal shook his head. "What a dull-witted fellow I am," he said. "But it's coming clearer to me now. Let me see, Brahman, you were in the trap when this tiger appeared suddenly—"

"Idiot!" roared the tiger. "I was the one in the trap!"

"Oh, of course. Now I understand!" the jackal exclaimed happily. "I was in the trap and . . . No. It was not I! I don't seem to have a brain at all! As I see it, this tiger had fallen inside the Brahman and when the cage arrived on the scene. . . No, not that either!"

"Of course not!" roared the tiger. "I will show you exactly how it happened. *I* am the tiger. You do understand that, don't you?"

"Indeed I do, noble tiger," the jackal assured the enraged beast.

"*This* is the Brahman," the tiger snarled.

"Yes, yes," the jackal repeated eagerly.

"I was inside the trap. *I*. Do you understand?"

"Yes . . . No . . . not really." The jackal blinked at the tiger helplessly.

. . "WHAT!" howled the tiger. "What don't you understand?"

"Well, could you explain to me just how you got into the trap?"

"How? In the usual way, like anyone else!" screamed the tiger.

"In the usual way . . . oh noble tiger . . . how magnificent you are. But my head is spinning. How does one get into a trap in the usual way?"

"LIKE THIS!" shrieked the tiger, his patience exhausted. With one great bound he leaped into the trap. "Now do you understand how it was?"

"Perfectly," said the jackal, as he slammed the trap's door shut and locked it. "And now we will leave things as they

were. Go your way, good Brahman, while this ungrateful
tiger reflects upon the evils that come from broken promises."

The Prince with the Moon on His Forehead and the Star on His Chin

IN NORTH INDIA there once lived an unhappy King. He had a beautiful palace, great wealth, several wives—as was the custom in his land—but he had no son.

One day, while he was walking through his garden, he stopped at the sound of merry female laughter. Peering through some bushes, he saw his gardener's daughters clustered around their eldest sister, Dorani. She was a lovely girl, with great dark eyes and black silk hair, skin white as milk, with the blush of a pink rose upon her cheeks. At that moment she had flung out her lovely arms and was saying,

"You may laugh all you want, sisters. But when I marry, I know I shall have a son who will have a moon on his forehead and a star on his chin."

Laughter tinkled all around her again, but the heart of the King leaped with joy. To him, Dorani's words were a sign and a promise.

Wasting no time, he sent for his gardener and asked him for Dorani's hand. The marriage was celebrated a few days later.

A year passed, and Dorani told her husband that she would have a child. The King embraced her, showered her with jewels, and gave orders that his other four wives should take good care of Dorani, and show her every sign of affection. As for himself, he was too restless to stay in one place for long. He could scarcely wait for his glorious promised son to be born. So day after day he rode out to hunt, while his other wives visited with Dorani.

Outwardly, of course, they were polite and attentive to the young favorite. But their hearts were eaten with envy. The eldest wife felt especially spiteful.

"Our Lord the Rajah is away a great deal," she remarked, one day, her voice dripping honey. "He should remain close by, for the infant might be born any time now. Don't you think so, dear sisters?" she asked, turning to the other wives.

"Yes. Yes, indeed," they replied. They knew that the eldest wife was up to something.

That night Dorani told her husband what the other wives had said.

The Rajah took her fair face in his two hands, saying, "I do not want you to worry, but I am too impatient now to stay in the palace. When I go out to hunt tomorrow, I shall leave with you a special drum. If you feel ill or if you should need me, sound the drum. Wherever I am, I shall hear it and will come to you at once."

When the other wives saw the drum, they asked Dorani what it was for, and she told them.

"Make it sound to see if your husband will really hear it," said one.

"I dare not," Dorani said. "He might be angry if I call him needlessly."

But the other wives insisted that she test the power of the drum, and at last Dorani struck it.

Within half an hour the King hurried into his wife's room. "What is wrong, my Dorani?" he asked.

"Nothing, my Lord. I only wanted to see you," Dorani replied.

The Rajah smiled. He kissed his wife and told her not to sound the drum without need. She promised that she would not. But the next day, as soon as the King had left, the other wives insisted that she sound the drum.

"No, no!" Dorani exclaimed. "My husband would be very annoyed with me."

"He loves you too much to be annoyed with you," the eldest wife told her in a silky tone.

"I don't want to do it!" Dorani said.

"Oh, come now, strike the drum. Then we will see if the Rajah will give up his hunt for you."

The other wives teased so much that finally young Dorani struck the drum. The King heard the sound just as he was about to let an arrow fly. He dropped his bow, wheeled his horse about and raced for the palace.

"What has happened? Is my son about to be born?" he demanded, rushing into Dorani's room.

"Oh, no," she replied. "I merely wished to know if you really loved me."

"And just for that you interrupted my hunting?" The King's face darkened with anger and his brows drew together in a terrible frown. "In the future do not play games with the drum!" With this the Rajah stomped out of the room, leaving Dorani trembling and in tears.

About the middle of the next day Dorani felt ill. She summoned one of her slaves and ordered her to sound the King's drum. In the forest the King heard it plainly enough, but thinking that this was another of his wife's whims, he paid no heed.

As he rode deeper into the forest, Dorani gave birth to a beautiful baby boy, with a moon on his forehead and a star on his chin.

The other wives of the Rajah, who were filled with envy, took the infant and put him in a box. They then ordered a slave to bury the box in the garden. When the slave had left, they placed a stone in the golden cradle. And, when the Rajah returned late that night, they told him that the stone was the son that his wife had given him.

Torn by rage and grief, the Rajah ordered his young wife from her rooms, and commanded that she be given the lowliest chores in the kitchen.

The slave, meanwhile, had buried the boy as she was ordered. But Shankar, the Rajah's dog, saw her. When she left, the animal dug the box out. Nuzzling it open, he saw the beautiful baby boy in it. He instantly recognized him as the promised Prince. And, to save him from further harm, Shankar swallowed the baby.

At the end of six months, the dog went deep into the forest and took the boy out. The little Prince was more beautiful than ever. Shankar kissed him with his long tongue and let the baby play with his ears. Then he swallowed him once more and returned to the palace grounds.

Another six months passed and the dog again went deep into the forest. Once more he produced the boy with the moon on his forehead and a star on his chin. Again he kissed him with his tongue and played with the one-year-old and let the baby tug and pull at him. Then he swallowed him again.

Unfortunately, the guardian of the King's dogs had followed Shankar into the forest. What was more unfortunate was that he saw everything that happened. Now he hurried back to the palace and reported it all to the wives of the Rajah.

"And inside the Rajah's dog Shankar, there is a boy with a moon on his forehead and a star on his chin," he concluded breathlessly.

Hearing this, the four wives were almost frightened to death. But they recovered their wits soon enough. They tore their clothes and ran to the Rajah, saying,

"Your dog, Shankar, has turned vicious. See what he has done to us while we were walking in the garden. You must have him killed."

"Very well," said the Rajah. "He shall die tomorrow."

The dog happened to overhear his own death sentence. Fearing for the life of the Prince that he carried, he decided to find someone else to care for him. This was the cow, Suri, who was in the palace stables.

"Listen to me, Suri," he told her. "I would like you to keep something very precious for me, for tomorrow the King will have me killed."

"I am sorry to hear this, Shankar," the cow said, "but the King's word is our law. Show me whatever it is you want me to keep."

The dog then showed the little Prince and the cow mooed with amazement at his beauty. "I will keep him gladly," she declared, and after kissing the boy, she swallowed him.

The next day Shankar was killed by the guardian of the Rajah's dogs, and the wives of the Rajah breathed more easily.

At the end of a year, Suri the cow, wishing to see the little Prince again, brought him out. He was more charming than ever. To protect him from harm, she swallowed him again. Thus she kept him for ten years. This was possible, of course, because Suri was no ordinary cow, and the Prince was no ordinary boy.

Unfortunately, one day the guardian of the cow stable saw her with the boy and ran to the Rajah's wives with the story.

The four wives of the Rajah almost fainted with fright. Then, after ripping their clothes and rubbing mud on each other, they sought out their husband.

"Your cow, Suri, attacked us while we were walking near her meadow," they wailed. "It is a miracle that we escaped alive. She must have gone mad."

The Rajah shook his head sadly. "She was a good cow. But tomorrow I will have her killed."

It so happened that Suri overheard some talk among the grooms and thus learned of her fate. The good cow, thinking only of the Prince, broke out of the stable that night and went to the special quarters where Katar, the wild horse was kept.

"Listen to me, Katar," she said. "I am to die tomorrow, but I would like you to keep something safe for me."

"I am sorry to hear this, dear Suri," the horse said. "Show me what it is you wish to keep safe."

When he saw the glorious Prince, Katar did not seem surprised, for he was an enchanted horse. Instead, he bent his knee and bowed before the boy with the moon on his forehead and the star on his chin.

"Go in peace," he said to the cow. "Your treasure shall be safe with me. In truth, I have been waiting for him."

The young Prince threw his arms around the cow's neck and bade her farewell. Then he turned to the horse and ran his hand over the sleek sides. And this was a marvel to see, for the stallion was thought to be so wild and fierce that those who were in charge of him lived in constant terror of the creature.

Now this horse kept the Prince for five years. Every six

months he would take him out of his stomach to enjoy his beauty and to give him special instructions. One of these times the boy was seen by the royal guardian of the stables. Filled with awe, he ran to tell of his discovery to the four wives.

The four wicked wōmen were at their wits' end when they heard the news. Could nothing destroy the Prince! If the Rajah were to see the boy, he would recognize him instantly, and their lives would be in danger. There was no time to lose.

Again they tore their clothing, rubbed mud on each other, and even smeared themselves with pigeon blood. Then they limped and groaned into the Rajah's chamber and complained of the horse, Katar.

"The vicious beast broke out of his paddock and would have trampled us to death if the grooms had not saved us. You must destroy that animal before he destroys us."

The Rajah frowned. "Katar is a very valuable horse, but I cannot deny that he is fierce, and therefore dangerous. I will have him killed tomorrow. As for you, ladies, please stay within the palace so that no more harm comes to you and I shall not need to destroy any more valuable animals."

The Queens tossed their heads a bit, but since they had gotten what they were after, they left quietly enough. The King was too busy thinking about his horse to notice that none of them limped or groaned now.

Since the horse was so fierce, the Rajah did not dare send a lone archer against him. Instead, he ordered a hundred soldiers to stand ready to shoot their arrows into the animal as soon as he left the stable. He, himself, armed with a bow, stood in the foreground.

But Katar, being a magic horse, knew at once what was afoot. Taking the Prince out of hiding, he said to him, "Go into that room to the right. In it you will find a saddle which I want you to put on me. You will also find some princely garments, a sword and golden armor. Put them on and come to me."

The Prince did exactly as he was told, then he mounted the horse and waited. Outside, the archers were ready. But before they could fit the arrows to their bows, the stable doors burst open and out galloped Katar with the Prince on his back. So swift was his pace, and so strong the rush of wind he made, that the lines of soldiers fell over like toys. Even the Rajah tumbled over backward.

Since the King himself had been outwitted, he did not punish his archers. And, to avoid the embarrassment of confessing his defeat, he said nothing about it to his wives. They, thinking the horse, and therefore the Prince, dead, breathed more easily.

But the Prince was very much alive and galloping through the world on the back of Katar. His gold armor flashed in the sun, and his sword sparkled with a hundred gems. Thus they galloped without pause for many days. At last they came to the walls of a rich city and Katar stopped and pawed at the ground. Crowds of people streamed past them toward the great open gates.

"What is this place, and what is happening here?" asked the Prince.

"This is the city of Calcutta, the most beautiful in all of India," answered Katar. "I have brought you here so that you may take part in a great contest which is about to take place. The winner will marry Princess Geeta, the most beautiful among the beautiful."

"But I don't know how to fight," replied the Prince.

"You will, when the time comes," Katar assured him. "The sword you carry is a magic sword. It will teach you, and you shall defeat all who try their luck against you."

So the Prince with the moon on his forehead and the star on his chin rode boldly into the city and into the arena where the contest was to take place. All who saw him marveled at his beauty. As for the Princess Geeta, she fell in love with him at once and wished with all her heart that he would win over all her other suitors.

There were three hundred of them, from all parts of India, and even some from Egypt and Arabia. With the aid of his magic sword the young Prince performed marvels. In minutes, those who opposed him lay in the dust. At last only one opponent remained—an enormous Arab who was armed with a magic axe.

So the fight was completely even. It was Katar who decided the contest by throwing the other horse to the ground with a powerful thrust from his great shoulders. The Arab was disarmed and at the mercy of the Prince. But the young man with the moon on his forehead and the star on his chin spared the life of his enemy with a royal gesture. Then he turned toward the place where the Princess Geeta was sitting and bowed low before her.

The Rajah of Calcutta gave his daughter to the winner and the wedding took place the very next day. The rejoicing lasted for three months. At the end of that time, Katar said to the Prince,

"Now you must visit your father and pay your respects to your mother." Then he told the young man with the moon on his forehead and the star on his chin the story of his birth and remarkable life.

The Prince was very upset and cried out, "It is my mother I must seek out and restore to her rightful place."

"Yes, indeed, my Lord," said the Princess Geeta, her lovely eyes brimming with tears. "Let us go at once."

And they did, mounted on the back of the great Katar, who flew like the wind to Northern India.

The Rajah, informed of the visit of the son-in-law of the King of Calcutta, ordered a great celebration in his honor.

When the Prince with the moon on the forehead and the star on the chin appeared in the hall where the feast was to be held, everyone fell back before the wonder of his beauty. The Rajah stared at him as if thunderstruck, and his heart turned over within him. Could this be? Was it possible?

Before he could speak, the young Prince said, "Is all of your court present?" and his voice was like ice.

"All," answered the Rajah in little more than a whisper.

The Prince turned his proud head this way and that. "Is not the daughter of your gardener missing? She was your wife once."

Now the Rajah knew for certain who the young man before him was. A hot wave of shame swept over him. "True," he said in a low voice. "She shall be brought here at once, and with full honor."

He then gave orders to his servants to fetch Dorani from the kitchen. This they did, and after bathing and perfuming the much-wronged Rani, they dressed her in rich garments and brought her into the great hall.

"My dearest mother," cried the Prince with the moon on his forehead and the star on his chin as he fell to his knees before her.

"My dearest and most respected mother-in-law," cried Princess Geeta, also falling to her knees before the Rani.

"O my wife," said the Rajah, bowing before Dorani, "can you ever forgive me the wrong I have done you?"

"I have always loved you, my Lord," Dorani said softly.

At these words, the magic sword of the Prince flew out of its scabbard. *Whing, whang, whisk, woosh!* Off flew the heads of the four wicked wives who had stood frozen with terror through all this. The servants carted off their bodies and the magic sword returned to the Prince's scabbard. The celebration which then took place lasted for a full year.

At the end of the year, the Rajah of Calcutta died and his kingdom was then united with that of the Rajah of North India. In time, the Prince with the moon on his forehead and the star on his chin became the King of this mighty nation and ruled over it wisely and well.

As for Katar, the magic horse of heaven, he vanished from the royal stables, since his mission was done. Only when a prince is born in the kingdom does he reappear to pledge his loyalty and love to the family.

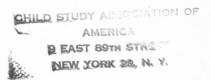

The Brahman's Dream

THERE ONCE LIVED a Brahman whose name was Savarakipana, which means "born to be poor," and this he was. One day, as he was begging for his daily food, a kind man gave him a bag of barley meal. When the Brahman had used a portion of this for his supper, he found that there was enough left over for the next day, and perhaps the next. To keep it safe, he put the barley meal into a clay pot and hung the pot from a nail on the wall above his head.

While he prepared for sleep, he could not keep from looking at the pot of meal, since it was most unusual for him to
have any food left over. The thought was so exciting that he
began to daydream.

"If there were famine in this country," he said to himself,
"I could easily get one hundred rupees for this pot of barley
meal. With this money I could buy a couple of goats, male
and female. Every six months my goats would bear some
kids. In a few years I would have a whole flock of goats.

"By selling the kids, I would get enough money to buy a
bull and a cow. With the money that I would get for the little
calves they would bear, I would buy water buffaloes. With
the offspring of the buffaloes, I would buy horses. With what
I would get for the colts, I would very soon be rich!"

The Brahman's eyes glittered as he continued to gaze at the
wonderful pot of barley meal hanging over his bed. "Once
rich," he went on, "I would buy myself a large house. I would
furnish it magnificently. I would then plan a splendid feast.

"To the feast I would invite the richest man in the city.
He would find me so gracious and entertaining that he would
want me to marry his daughter, after giving her a rich dowry,
of course.

"In due time we would have a son whom I would name
Soma-sarman. When my son would be old enough so that I
could bounce him on my knee, I would take the boy and—"

The Brahman was so carried away by his dream that he
flung up one leg to cross over the other. His foot struck the
clay pot hanging over his head and smashed it. In a moment
he was covered with white meal from head to foot. Not only
was his dream spoiled, but his precious barley meal as well.

In India, those who wish to point to the moral of this tale
say, "He who spends wealth before he has it is like the Brahman and the barley meal."

But you have probably heard your parents or your grand-parents say, "Don't count your chickens before they are hatched," which means the same thing.

The Valiant Chattee-Maker

ONE NIGHT a violent storm raged around a small village in India. Lightning ripped the clouds. Thunder boomed and crashed. The wind tore through the trees, while rain poured down in never-ending streams.

A tiger, caught out in the open, sought shelter beside the wall of an old woman's house. The old woman was very poor, and her house was a tumble-down hut. Her roof was full of holes and the rain leaked in, *drip, drip, drip*, everywhere at once. What little she possessed would be soaked in no time and this bothered her very much. She ran from place to place, dragging first one thing and then another out of the way of the leaks, and talking to herself all the while.

"Oh dear, oh dear. If this rain keeps up, I'm sure the roof will cave in. If an elephant, or a lion or a tiger were to walk in here, he wouldn't frighten me half as much as this constant *drip, drip, drip*."

The tiger, crouched outside, heard what she said, and he thought, "This is most extraordinary. The old woman says she would not be half as frightened of an elephant, or a lion or even a tiger as she is of this constant *drip, drip, drip*. What in the world can it be?"

Hearing her dragging her bed and other things about the room again, he said, "What a terrible noise. It must be this *constant drip, drip, drip* that is making it."

At this moment, a potter, or chattee-maker, came staggering down the road in search of his donkey, which had strayed away. He had stopped at the home of a friend before getting this far, and had eaten and drunk much more than was good for him. At this point he scarcely knew what he was doing. In this muddled state he saw, in a flash of lightning, a large animal crouched beside the wall of the old woman's hut. Mistaking it for his lost donkey, he ran up to the tiger and seized him by one ear.

"You wretched creature!" he exclaimed, and began to kick the tiger and beat him with all his might. "Is this a proper way to serve me—making me come out on a night like this to search for you! Get up this instant, or I will break every bone in your worthless body."

By this time the fellow had worked himself up into a terrible rage. He continued to thump and scold the tiger and yank at him this way and that.

Such a thing had never happened to the tiger before. He did not know what to make of it, and he began to feel quite frightened. "This must be the *constant, drip, drip, drip,*" he thought to himself. "No wonder the old woman said she was more afraid of it than of an elephant, or a lion or a tiger. It gives dreadfully hard blows and makes a terrible screeching noise besides."

By this time the chattee-maker had made the tiger get up, for he still thought he had found his lost donkey. Climbing on the animal's back, he forced him to carry him home, kicking and beating the tiger the whole way. Once in his own courtyard, he tied the animal's forefeet and his head firmly together and then tethered him to a post. Having done this, he staggered to his bed and fell asleep, leaving the tiger a trembling mass of nerves.

Next morning, when the chattee-maker's wife got up she

looked out the window. And what did she see but a huge tiger tied to the post where her husband usually tethered the donkey! Very much surprised, she ran to her husband and shook him awake. "Do you know what animal you brought home last night?" she asked as soon as he opened his eyes.

"Of course, I do! My donkey," he replied crossly.

"Come and see," she said, pulling him toward the window.

When the chattee-maker saw the great big tiger tied to his donkey-post he very nearly fainted. "Quick! See if I am wounded, or if a leg or an arm is missing," he told his wife as soon as he recovered his breath.

"You are safe and whole," she told him after a brief inspection. "But I wish you could explain to me how you got this tiger home."

"I guess I rode him," the chattee-maker said feebly. "I seem to remember something of the sort."

News of his deed soon spread through the village. People flocked to the courtyard to see the tiger and to hear the chattee-maker tell how he had captured the beast and ridden it home. He didn't bother to mention that he wasn't quite himself at the time.

His neighbors thought the thing so wonderful that they sent a message to their Rajah. A man, a potter in their village, had captured a great tiger, alone and unarmed, and had tied him to a post in front of his house.

When the Rajah read the message he also was very much surprised. He decided to go in person and see this astonishing sight and meet the chattee-maker. He ordered horses and carriages, and in fact his whole court, to go with him.

Now, this tiger was a very large beast. What is more, he had been the terror of that countryside for many years. Up to now, no one had been able to trap him or hunt him down. Yet here he was, meek as a donkey tied to a post, and he trembled with fear each time the chattee-maker came within sight.

Such a man must be rewarded, the Rajah thought. So he

gave every possible honor to the brave chattee-maker. He gave him houses and land and enough money to fill a well. He made him a lord of his court and gave him command over ten thousand horsemen.

Since the tiger was the reason behind all this honor, the chattee-maker had a comfortable cage built for him and saw to it that the beast was well fed. As for the tiger, he was quite happy to be in a strong cage. He liked the idea of having those stout bars between himself and the old woman's terrible *constant drip, drip, drip,* for he was convinced that was what the chattee-maker was.

Shortly after the village potter was settled in his new home, a neighboring ruler declared war upon the Rajah's kingdom. News came of an enormous army marching upon the Rajah's palace.

The Rajah at once sent for his generals and asked each one to take command of his forces. But the generals, one after another, said they would not dare oppose the powerful army marching upon the kingdom. It would mean certain defeat. "It would be better, sire," they advised, "to make peace with our enemy. Peace at any cost."

The Rajah turned him back upon his generals. Then some of his people made a suggestion. Only lately, they said, the Rajah had given command of ten thousand horsemen to the brave chattee-maker. A man who had caught a tiger single-handed and tied him to a post like a donkey could be afraid of nothing. Why not make *him* commander-in-chief of the royal army?

"The very thing," said the Rajah, and summoned the chattee-maker to him.

"I place the safety of our kingdom in your hands," he told the fellow. "Yours is the power to command all our forces, and to put our enemies to flight."

The chattee-maker's knees turned to water, but he dared not show his fright. "Very well, your majesty," he replied with a deep bow. "But before I lead our whole army against the enemy, I think I should spy upon them and check their strength."

To this the Rajah agreed, and the chattee-maker returned home to his wife. "The Rajah has made me commander-in-chief of the royal army," he told her. "It is a most difficult post for me to fill. I shall have to ride at the head of the army and as you know, my dear, I have never ridden anything but a donkey in all my life. I know I would fall off a horse and disgrace myself."

"You have ridden a tiger, O valiant chattee-maker, and you did not fall off then," said his wife.

Her husband shuddered. "Please don't remind me of that. I assure you, this is quite different. Anyway, I have gained a little delay, for the Rajah has allowed me to go alone and spy upon the enemy. What I want you to do now is go out and find me a nice, gentle pony, as much like a donkey as possible. I will then ride out tomorrow morning and see what is to be seen of the enemy."

But before his wife could get out the door, the Rajah sent over a magnificent horse. He also sent a message asking the chattee-maker to ride the animal on his spying mission.

The sight of the creature almost frightened the chattee-maker out of his life. The Rajah's horse was big and spirited. It pranced about and whinnied and snorted. The poor man was certain that if he ever managed to climb on its back, it would not be for long. But of course he could not refuse the royal gift, for fear of hurting the Rajah's feelings. So he sent back a message of thanks and then turned back to his wife.

"How will I ever ride that beast!" he wailed.

"Don't worry," she told him. "All you need do is get up on his back. I will then tie you firmly in the saddle so that you cannot possibly fall off. If you start out at night, no one will see that you are tied on."

"Very well," said the chattee-maker.

That night his wife brought the horse to the door. The

chattee-maker stared up at it doubtfully. "I can never get up into that saddle," he said. "It is much too high."

"You must jump," said his wife. "I have seen it done. It does not seem too difficult."

The chattee-maker tried several times to jump into the saddle as she directed, but without success. "When I am jumping I forget which way to turn," he said.

"Your face must be toward the horse's head," she told him.

"To be sure, to be sure," he exclaimed. Making another great effort, he jumped into the saddle. Unfortunately, his head was toward the horse's tail.

"This won't do at all," said his wife and helped him down again. "Try to get on without jumping. Put your foot in here."

Her husband frowned. "I can never remember when I get my left foot into the stirrup, what to do with my right foot. That is, where to put it."

"It must go into the other stirrup," she answered.

After trying it many times, and tumbling off just as many times, the chattee-maker finally did manage to get into the saddle with his head and the horse's head pointing in the same direction. "Wife! Wife!" he shouted. "Tie me on quickly. I know I shall jump down again unless you do!"

The good woman had the necessary ropes ready. Swiftly she tied his feet into the stirrups, and fastened the stirrups ·one to the other, under the horse's belly. She looped a rope around his waist and tied another loop around his neck, and fastened them to the horse's body, neck and tail.

When the horse felt all these ropes about him he could not imagine what peculiar creature had gotten up on his back. He began to rear and kick and prance. And then with a wild cry he set off at full gallop, straight across the fields.

"Wife! Wife!" screamed the chattee-maker. "You forgot to tie my hands."

"Never mind," she shouted after him. "Hold on to him by the mane."

So he caught hold of the flying mane and hung on for dear life. Away went the horse, and away went the chattee-maker. Away, away, over hedges and ditches, over rivers, over plains, away, away. The horse was like a flash of lightning, darting this way and that. On, on! gallop, gallop, gallop! until they came in sight of the enemy's camp.

The chattee-maker did not like his ride at all. And when he saw where they were heading, he liked it still less, for surely the enemy would catch him and most likely kill him on the spot. He decided to make one last desperate effort to free himself from the horse. As his steed was about to shoot past a young banyan tree, he stretched out his hand, grasped it with all his might, and hoped that the ropes which bound him would snap. But they held. The horse was going at full speed, and the soil around the roots of the young banyan tree was loose. Therefore, when the chattee-maker caught hold of the tree and gave it such a violent pull, it came up by the roots! On rode the chattee-maker as before, only now he held a tree in his hand. And, as its bottom dragged along the ground, it raised a tremendous cloud of dust.

The soldiers in the enemy camp heard the thunder of the horse's hooves. They ran out to see who was coming. When they saw the chattee-maker riding toward them at full speed and holding a tree in his hand, they thought that he was the leader of a great army which must be riding directly behind him in the cloud of dust.

"Look! Look!" they shouted. "See this giant of a man riding upon a gigantic horse. He rides toward us in such a rage that he tears up the trees in his path. If the others that follow him are as terrible as he, we will all soon be dead."

They rushed to their king and cried out, "Our enemies are coming! They are all giants, riding giant horses and tearing up the trees in their path. We can fight against man, but we cannot hope to defeat such monsters."

By this time the chattee-maker was almost at the camp.

Now others rushed to their king, shouting, "It is all true. They are coming, and they are terrible. Let us all flee for our lives."

And the whole panic-stricken camp, their king included, took to their heels, their horses, or whatever was handy. But before he fled with the rest, their king managed to write a letter begging for peace. He even managed to sign it and stamp it with his royal seal.

Scarcely had all the enemy left the camp when the chattee-maker and his horse came thundering into it. Just as they reached the enemy king's tent, the ropes which had held him broke, and the chattee-maker fell to the ground. Almost completely worn out, he lay like one dead, the banyan tree still clutched in his hand. The horse stood still beside him, too tired from his long run to go any farther.

When the chattee-maker recovered his senses, he was very much surprised to find himself still alive and in one piece. He was even more surprised to find the camp deserted, with rich arms, clothing, food and weapons left everywhere. In the royal tent he found the letter addressed to his Rajah, telling of the retreat of the invaders and begging for peace at any price.

The chattee-maker took the letter and returned home with it as fast as he could. He led the horse all the way, however, for he was afraid to mount him again.

He reached his own house at about nightfall, and his wife ran out to meet him. "Ah wife," he said, "since I saw you last, I feel as if I had been all around the world and had many wonderful and terrifying adventures. But never mind that now. Get a messenger and send this letter quickly to the Rajah, and send this horse back to him also. He will see by the condition of the animal what a long and hard ride I've had. And, if the beast is sent on beforehand, I shall not be obliged to ride him to the palace tomorrow. Such a thing would be most tiresome, since I probably would fall off him.

Truly, if I remember correctly, it was more comfortable to ride my tiger."

So his wife sent a messenger with the letter and the horse, and informed the Rajah that her husband would wait on him early in the morning.

The next day the chattee-maker set off for the palace. When the people saw him, they said, "What a modest man is our hero. Having put our enemies to flight, he walks to the palace like any ordinary person, instead of riding in state, as another might." They had no idea that although the chattee-maker had ridden a tiger, he was terrified of riding a horse!

Their Rajah came to the palace door himself, to greet the brave potter. He paid him all kinds of compliments and showed him great honor. The peace terms were arranged between the two countries and war was never waged between them again. The chattee-maker was rewarded for what he had done by being given twice as much rank as he had before, and twice as much wealth. He lived happily the rest of his life, and so did his tiger—with the stout bars between them.

The Ungrateful Sons

A VERY RICH MAN, believing that he was about to die, called his three sons to him and divided his wealth among them.

He did not die, however. When he recovered from his illness, he found that his sons no longer showed him the attention that they gave him when they expected to get a bigger share of his fortune than he had told them they would. In fact, they treated him quite badly, and let him know openly that they now thought him nothing but a burden and an expense to them.

The poor man was heartbroken. One day he met an old friend and told him what was happening. The friend, greatly moved, promised to help find a solution for this sad state of affairs.

A few days later the friend arrived at the man's house, followed by ten servants, each carrying a heavily loaded sack.

When the two old men were alone, the friend said, "In these sacks I have brought a quantity of stones. When I leave I am sure your sons will come to find out what I have brought you. Tell them that I came to pay an old debt, and that you are now richer than you ever were. I will be back soon to see how things turn out."

When this good friend returned after a few months had passed, he found the old father surrounded by his sons. They were looking after him with the greatest care. And this they continued to do until he died ten years later. Only then did they discover that their hoped-for wealth consisted of ten sacks of worthless stones.

The Magic Ring

THERE WAS ONCE a merchant who had a son who was a great trial to him. He simply could not master the art of trading. One day the merchant gave the young man, whose name was Sudhin, three hundred rupees and told him to go to some other country and try his fortune there.

Being an obedient son, Sudhin set off at once. A few hours from home, however, he came upon a group of men fighting over a dog. One of the fellows wished to kill the dog and the others were trying to prevent him from doing so.

"Please do not kill the dog," the kind-hearted Sudhin pleaded. "I will give you one hundred rupees for it."

The foolish offer promptly stopped the fighting. The money

was accepted and Sudhin and the dog he had purchased were on the way again. Soon after, the young man came upon men who were about to kill a cat.

"Do not kill it," Sudhin begged, "I will give you one hundred rupees for it."

The offer was accepted immediately and the young man received the cat in exchange for his gold. On he went, with the two animals at his heels, until he reached a crowd of people who were about to kill a great snake.

"Do not kill that serpent," the son of the merchant exclaimed. "I will give you one hundred rupees for it."

Of course the offer did not have to be repeated, and Sudhin found himself the owner of three useless creatures. Since he did not have any money left, he decided to return to his father's house.

The father, seeing how his son had spent the money, exclaimed, "You are more than a fool; you are mad! You shall never enter this house again. Go and live in the stable, and think about your foolishness."

Sudhin did as he was told. He made himself a bed of hay that was cut for the cattle. And thus he lived, with the dog, the cat and the serpent, for which he had paid so dearly. The three creatures loved him with all their hearts and never left his side for a moment. At night the cat slept at his head, the dog at his feet, and the serpent coiled on his chest.

One day the serpent said, "Master, I am the daughter of the king of serpents. I had gone out to breathe some fresh air when I was captured by those men who wanted to kill me. I should like my father to meet you. He would be most happy to know the man who saved his daughter's life."

"Where does he live?" Sudhin inquired. "I should like to meet him also."

"I will show you," replied the serpent. "At the foot of that mountain in the distance, there is a sacred well. By jumping into it we will come to my father's kingdom. Once there, I know he will reward you richly." The serpent paused for a moment, thinking. Then she said, "Listen to me well. When he asks you what you desire, tell him you want the enchanted ring, and the magic spoon and bowl. With these three things in your possession you will never lack for anything. The enchanted ring has the power to give you a beautiful home, furnished with all the comforts. The spoon and bowl will give you all the food you can eat."

So, accompanied by his three friends, the young man arrived at the well and made ready to jump in. Seeing this, the dog and the cat said, "What will become of us without you? Where shall we go?"

"Wait for me here. I am not going far and therefore will not take long." Having said this, the young man and the snake leaped into the water and disappeared from sight.

As soon as the young man and the serpent were discovered in the snake ruler's kingdom, messengers were sent to announce their arrival. The king ordered that his daughter and the stranger be brought to him. But the serpent princess refused to obey until Sudhin freed her, for she had become his slave the moment he had saved her from death.

Sudhin had never thought of her as his slave and he freed her at once. On hearing this, the king went out to meet the young fellow himself and put all of the palace at his disposal. The merchant's son thanked the king for his kindness and spent several days in his company. When he left, he had in his possession the magic ring, the spoon and the bowl.

As he came out of the well, he was happy to find that his cat and dog had, indeed, waited for him. Together they started back toward his father's home. But along the way they came to a river of great beauty. Sudhin decided to put the magic ring to a test. He grasped it firmly and asked for a house.

In a moment a beautiful little house appeared. In the doorway stood a girl, lovely as a princess. Her hair was golden, her teeth like pearls and her lips red as rubies. She said that

her name was Neela, and when she spoke her voice was like birds singing.

Sudhin fell in love with her on the spot and married her as soon as was possible. The bowl and spoon provided their wedding feast. The young couple then lived in the charming little house in happiness and content.

One day, while Neela was combing her hair, a few of the golden strands fell into a box made of mother-of-pearl. The box was lying on the window sill, and as Neela turned, she brushed against it. The lid dropped shut, and the box slid out the window and fell into the river.

As luck would have it, the box came into the hands of a prince who lived many leagues away, down river from Sudhin's little house. Curious to see what the small box contained, he opened it. And, from the moment he saw the golden strands of hair, he fell madly in love with the woman to whom they belonged.

Sick with love, the prince locked himself in his room and would neither eat nor drink—nor sleep, for that matter. His father, the Rajah, became terribly worried about him. His greatest fear was that the young man would die, leaving him without an heir to his kingdom. At last he decided to ask help from his aunt, who was a very accomplished witch.

The old woman hastened to the palace and assured the Rajah that she would find the cause of his son's unhappiness. Once she found out what had happened to the prince, she turned herself into a bee. Then, after smelling the strands of golden hair, she followed the scent up the river until she came to the house of the beautiful Neela. There she again turned into an old woman and presented herself at the door.

"My darling Neela," she cried when the young woman answered her knock, "I am your grandaunt. I have been living in a far country since you were a little girl and that is why you do not recognize me. But you are so like your mother, my dearest niece, I would have known you anywhere." She then wept and kissed and embraced the lovely young woman. And Neela was soon convinced that this lady was, in truth, a long-lost relative.

"Dearest grandaunt," she said, "remain with us as long as you please. This house is yours and I am but your servant."

The witch smiled, well pleased with herself. "I have fooled her," she thought. "Soon I shall do as I like with this girl."

By the end of three days she knew all about the ring and its powers. "My dear," she said, "your husband wears it all the time, even when he goes hunting. He might lose it. Think what that would mean, if the ring were to get into the wrong hands. You must ask him for it so that you can keep it safe."

Neela followed her advice and asked for the ring, and her husband gave it to her at once.

The witch waited one more day before asking to see the beautiful jewel. Without suspecting anything, the young wife gave her the ring. The witch immediately turned into a bee and flew off with the ring to the palace of the prince.

She flew straight to his room, turned into herself again, and exclaimed, "Weep no more, my beloved grandnephew. The young woman you love will appear before you the moment you wish. Here is the magic ring that will make it possible," and she explained to him how it worked.

The prince clasped the ring tightly and asked it to bring Neela to him. There was a great peal of thunder, and then the little house with the beautiful Neela descended into the palace garden.

The prince hurried into the house and, kneeling before the girl, asked her to be his wife. Too frightened by what had happened, the princess did not dare tell him that she was already married, and very happily, too. Instead, she clasped her little hands tightly and asked him to wait a month before she would give him her answer. The prince was so delighted to see her that he agreed to the condition.

In the meantime, Sudhin, who had been out hunting, returned to find both his lovely wife and the little house gone.

His heart was torn with grief, and he thought of throwing himself into the river, when his dog and cat appeared at his side. They had run away and hidden in the bushes when they saw the house fly away. Now they said to him,

"Master, we know how great your sorrow is. But please, do not do anything foolish. Give us a month's time and we promise to undo the evil that has been done to you. We shall rescue your Neela and bring back your house as well. Please trust us."

Sudhin pulled himself together. "Very well," he said. "I do trust you, dear friends. And, since there is nothing that I can do about this, I will leave the matter to you."

The cat and the dog then hurried away in the direction in which the house had flown. At the end of several days of traveling, they came to the Rajah's palace.

"Wait for me outside," the cat told the dog. "I will go in

and try to find our Neela. Since I am smaller than you, I can slip in and out unnoticed."

The dog agreed, and the cat jumped the high wall that surrounded the palace gardens. It did not take him long to find the sad Neela of the golden hair. When she saw the cat she embraced him and told him what had happened. "Is there any way for me to escape from here and return to my beloved husband?" she asked.

"Yes," answered the cat. "Tell me where the ring is. Once I have it, we can get out of here."

"The witch keeps the ring in her stomach," Neela told him sadly.

"Don't let that trouble you," the cat said. "I will have that ring this very night."

Taking leave of his mistress, the cat descended to the palace basement. After sniffing around carefully, he found a certain mouse hole. Then he lay down beside it and pretended that he was dead.

It so happened that on this particular night, a marriage was being celebrated. The son of the king of the small rats was being married to the daughter of the queen of the mice. The hole where the cat waited was the place where they would come out. As soon as the cat saw them, he followed the plan he had made. Pouncing on the prince of the little rats, he grasped him firmly.

"Let me go, let me go, please," screamed the little animal in terror.

"Do please let him go," pleaded the other little rats and mice while the bride fainted. "This is his wedding day."

The cat only took a firmer hold of the little prince. "If you wish me to let him go," he said, "you will have to do something for me."

"Anything!" the mice promised. "What do you wish us to do?"

"I want you to bring me the ring that the witch has in her stomach. If you bring it, I will let your prince go. Otherwise I shall eat him."

"I will bring it to you," said a white mouse. "I know where the witch lives. Besides, I saw her swallow the ring."

The little white mouse ran through thousands of hidden mouse-passages until he reached the witch's room. After making sure that she was asleep, he jumped on the bed. Then putting his long tail inside her mouth, he caused her to cough violently. As she did so, the ring came up and rolled to the floor.

Not losing a second, the mouse grabbed the ring and raced back through all the hidden passages to the palace basement. Once there he gave the ring to the cat. The cat, faithful to his promise, let the prince of the little rats go. The little prince went joyfully to his tiny bride and dried her tears, while the cat raced back to the dog.

"I have the ring," he announced breathlessly. "Let us return to our master."

"Good!" cried the dog. "Now you had best jump upon my back, for I can run faster than you."

For three days the dog ran, without taking a moment to rest. At last, panting and heaving, he fell exhausted at the feet of his master. The cat leaped toward Sudhin and gave him the ring.

Another moment or two, and then the magic power of the ring brought back the beautiful Neela of the golden hair, and the little house as well.

From that day on, the couple lived happily together. Never again did they part, and they kept the magic ring in a very safe place. The dog and the cat went on living with them as their beloved pets. Now and again an enormous serpent came to visit them all. She wore a diamond-studded crown on her head, and when she came there was much laughter and talk in the little house.

As for the witch, she died of rage when she found the magic ring gone. And as for the prince, when he found out who Neela really was, he came and apologized to her and to her husband. Having recovered his senses, he wooed a suitable princess in a neighboring kingdom, and won her without the use of magic. He, too, lived happily ever after.

The Talkative Tortoise

THE GRAND VIZIER of a certain young Rajah in India was a
man who possessed great wisdom and good sense. But the
Rajah whom he served with love and devotion had one great
fault. He talked too much. There was much yet that the
young man could learn if he ever gave his ears a chance to
hear what others, wiser than he, had to say. And, for that
matter, there were many private things he said which would
much better have remained unsaid. This troubled the good
Vizier.

One day, while he and the young man were strolling
through the palace gardens, the Vizier managed to get a few
words in edgewise, as the saying goes, while the Rajah was
taking a breath. "Would you like me to tell you a story, your
Majesty?" he asked.

"A story! Of course. It might be something I'd care to repeat," the Rajah exclaimed. "Proceed!"

The Grand Vizier started at once, before his Majesty should change his mind and tell *him* a story instead. "Many years ago," he said, "there lived a handsome young tortoise in a small pond that lay in the Himalaya Mountains. Two wild ducks which had come down on the pond for a rest made friends with the tortoise, and one of them said to him,

" 'The place to which we are going is called Lake Beautiful. It is a fine place to live. Why don't you go there with us?'

" 'How could I go with you?' the tortoise asked. 'I cannot fly.'

" 'We can take you,' replied the ducks. 'But you will have to remember to be silent and not speak a single word along the way.'

" 'That should be simple enough,' the tortoise said.

" 'Very well, then. Hold this stick tightly in your mouth. My friend and I will pick it up on each end. In this way we can carry you easily and safely, as long as you keep your mouth shut.'

" 'N,mmmm mummmm ummm,' muttered the tortoise, clamping tightly the stick.

"The ducks grasped the ends of the stick in their bills and soared up into the sky, with the tortoise hanging from its middle.

"Thus they flew mile after mile, until they came to a village. 'Look!' shouted the children as they stopped their play and stared up into the sky. 'What are those ducks carrying?'

" 'Can it be a rock?' one of the villagers asked.

" 'No, it looks more like a wheel of some kind,' remarked another.

" 'What a funny sight, whatever it is,' shouted a third.

"This was more than the tortoise could bear. 'Stupid people!' he cried, 'Can't you see I'm a tortoise? And if my friends choose to carry me this way, what business is it of yours?'

"No sooner had the tortoise started to say these words, than he lost hold of the stick. Down he fell to the ground, and as he spoke the last word—SMASH—he was dashed to pieces on the hard earth.

"In truth I must say, your Majesty," the Vizier concluded gently, "those who know not how to control their tongues, no matter how great their other qualities are, end up like the tortoise in this old, old tale."

The young Rajah made no answer but stared at the ground thoughtfully for a long, long time. From that day on he spoke much less, listened a great deal more and all went well in his kingdom.

The King and the Fakir

AN INDIAN KING who had no son to inherit his kingdom once went to a wonder-working fakir about his problem.

"Here I am, a king. I command thousands of men. I have wealth, I have power. But all these years I have lived without the joy of hearing the laughter of a son of my blood, a son whom I could train to rule after me."

"What would you give me if you were to have a son?" the fakir asked.

"All that you asked for," the King replied.

"I do not need jewels or gold," said the fakir. "I will make a prayer and thereafter you shall have two sons. One of them must be for me." Saying this, the old man took out two small cakes from inside his tunic and gave them to the King.

89

"Give these cakes to two of your wives and soon you shall have what you wish for. And in a year, I shall return to see you. Remember, one of the two sons who are to be born belongs to me."

"Of course," said the King, and the two men parted.

While the King was returning to the palace he began to think of his promise to the fakir. Actually, it hinged on his having two sons. If he had only one, there would be no need to give *him* up to the wonder-worker. So, he gave a cake to only one wife, and threw the other cake away.

But, instead of bearing only one son, the Rani bore twins! This upset the King very much. Not only would the fakir now demand one of the boys, but even if the King succeeded in outwitting the fellow, there was trouble for the kingdom in the future. Twin sons meant dividing the kingdom, and sometimes this was not done peacefully.

Greatly troubled, the King was pacing in the palace garden when the fakir appeared before him.

"Show me your sons, O Rajah," said the fakir, "that I may choose one for my own."

"Certainly," said the King, thinking fast. "I shall bring them to you myself."

When he returned, he carried two boys, but they were not his own twins. He had taken the sons of one of the slaves.

The fakir looked the babies over. Then he said, "Have a fire built for me so that I can roast one of these boys and eat him right here."

The King was about to give the order, when the fakir stopped him, saying, "These are not your sons, O Rajah. If they were, you would not have allowed me to eat one of them. Have your true sons brought to me at once or they shall both die within the hour."

With tears in his eyes, the King had his own little boys brought to the garden.

The fakir examined them carefully. "Twins," he said. "You planned to deceive me all along. It would serve you right if I took them both. But you have been a good ruler of your people. No doubt you will train your son to follow in your footsteps. You may keep this one. The other will be mine."

He was about to leave with the boy he had chosen, when he turned back to the King. "I see how dearly you love this one, also," he said. "Fear not for him. He, too, shall grow to be a King—and will inherit a full kingdom, not only half a one."

The fakir called his Prince Ram Singh, and loved him dearly. For fifteen years the boy lived with the wonder-worker, who taught him all he knew. He showed him how to make gold and precious stones, how to change water into wine, stones into bread, dogs into horses, ants into men and men into trees. When the old fakir died, the Prince was ignorant of nothing that was known to the wise men of India. Armed with this knowledge, and dressed in the garb of a fakir, he set out to see the world and its wonders.

Some time later he arrived at the capital of a country which was under siege of an invading army. The Prince slipped into the city and found that the people were on the point of dying from starvation. Even their dogs, which their religion kept them from killing, were nothing but skin and bones.

"Who rules this country?" the Prince asked an old warrior.

"Princess Jali," the man replied. "Her father died at the beginning of this war and she has kept on with it. But we are at the end of our strength. To make peace, our Princess will have to marry the King of our enemies."

"Take me to the Princess," Ram Singh ordered. "I wish to help her."

The warrior obeyed, though he could not see what a young fakir like this could do for the Princess.

Not even in his dreams had the Prince seen a more beautiful young woman. "What is it you wish, saintly man?" she asked, thinking him to be a fakir. Her voice was like gold and silver bells.

"I wish to help you, O beautiful Princess," cried Ram Singh.

"How can you help me?" she asked sadly. "Nothing can be done now. You managed to enter this city because you are a fakir. The enemy dared not stop you. But I have no friend left who can help me. And today I have given out the last bread in our stores."

"Have one hundred thousand stones brought to me," said the Prince.

The Princess obeyed. When the Prince had the stones before him, he murmured some magic words over them, and instantly they turned into bread.

"Now order that one thousand jugs of water be brought to me," said the Prince.

When the jugs were before him, the Prince said more magic words over them, and the water was changed into wine.

Thus strengthened, the warriors and the townspeople gathered before the palace and thanked the fakir for saving them from certain death.

"Tell them to bring me one hundred thousand ants and five hundred thousand dogs," the Prince then directed the Princess.

The order was carried out. Again through the magic taught him by the fakir the Prince turned the ants into men and the dogs into horses.

This enormous army easily defeated the enemy.

"What shall I do with these thousands of soldiers and their horses?" asked Princess Jali when the battle was over. "My kingdom is much too small for so vast an army. I could not possibly feed them all."

"Do not worry, beautiful Princess," replied the Prince. "I have noticed that your enemies destroyed the whole country and left it without a single fruit tree. To remedy this I shall turn all the soldiers into trees. Their horses I shall give away to your subjects so that they may labor in the fields with them."

This he did, and since that day the kingdom of the Princess Jali has had the most remarkable fruit trees in all of India.

As for the Prince, he married the Princess after telling her who he really was. They lived happily for many years governing the kingdom together.

Old histories tell that bread never failed to be plentiful in that country. They also say that the gold and precious stones which Prince Ram Singh gave to his wife made it necessary to build a marble palace in which to keep their enormous treasures.

Punchkin, the Wicked Wizard

ONCE UPON A TIME there was a Rajah who had seven beautiful daughters. They were good, industrious girls. But the youngest, named Balna, was more clever than the rest. Their mother, the Rani, had died when the girls were very young.

Since the King feared that his enemies might poison him, the seven princesses took it upon themselves to prepare his food.

At this time the Grand Vizier died, leaving a wife and daughter. Thereafter each day, while the seven princesses prepared the food for the Rajah's table, the widow came and visited with them. Before leaving, she always asked them for some burning coals for her own kitchen.

For some reason, Balna began to distrust the woman. "We should not allow her to come here and visit us all the time," she told her sisters. "If she wants coals for her fire, let her stay in her own home and tend them. I feel certain that she means us some harm."

The other princesses were astonished by the words of their usually gentle sister. "Hush, Balna. Do not talk this way," they said. "What have you against this poor widow? What does it matter that we give her a few coals from our fire? We are rich and this can do us no harm."

In vain the youngest sister tried to explain her strange feeling about the widow. Her older sisters did not listen.

But Balna was right. Whenever the widow came to visit, she waited for the moment when no one was watching. It was then that she would slip a bit of sand into one of the dishes being prepared for the Rajah.

The King, who loved his daughters dearly, was greatly puzzled when he found sand in his food. No one but the princesses was allowed in the kitchen. The sand must have found its way into his food through some accident, he decided, and did not scold the girls.

However, when this happened day after day, the King wanted to see for himself just what went on in his kitchen. Hidden in the next room, he was able to watch his daughters through a peephole he had made in the wall. He saw how carefully they washed the rice and prepared all the other things for his meals. Shortly after, the widow of his Grand Vizier arrived. After some polite chatter, she asked for some coals for her kitchen. As before, the older sisters put the glowing embers into the woman's copper pan.

As the sisters turned to speak to Balna, the Rajah saw the widow put a handful of sand into a pot bubbling on the fire.

Angered by this, he ordered his guards to hold the widow

and bring her into his presence. When the woman was brought in, she fell on her knees saying,

"My Lord, I did what I did in order to be able to speak with you." She went on and talked so cleverly, with such charming little airs, that the King not only forgave her, but fell in love with her.

In no time at all, the two were married. The new Rani came to live in the palace and brought her daughter with her.

She forgot the kind way in which the King's daughters had treated her, and she now did her best to make life miserable for them. She allowed them to eat only bread, and not much at that, and a little water, which was not very fresh. Before long the poor girls had scarcely any strength left. So great was their unhappiness that they crept to their mother's tomb and fell to weeping before it.

"Oh mother, mother!" they sobbed. "Can you not see how unfortunate we are, and how badly treated? The new Rani seems determined to starve us to death."

While they wept bitterly, an orange tree began to grow next to their mother's tomb. In a few moments it blossomed. Fruit appeared and ripened before their astonished eyes. The girls' tears dried as they picked the fruit and ate it. From then on, the marvelous little tree satisfied their hunger, and the seven princesses refused the mean food offered to them by their stepmother.

The Rani could not understand it. "I don't see how these girls, who appear to eat nothing, can look so well fed," she told her daughter. "They are growing more beautiful, too. Much more beautiful than you are. I want you to watch them. Tell me all they do, and if anyone feeds them."

The next day the daughter of the Rani followed the seven princesses and saw them picking the oranges.

Balna, who happened to notice her peering at them from behind another tomb, warned her sisters at once. "Our step-mother's daughter is spying on us," she said. "Let us leave this place, or at least hide the oranges, otherwise she will tell her mother about them."

"Do not talk this way," replied the others. "Our young stepsister cannot be so evil as to do a thing like that. As a matter of fact, we should offer her some of this fruit."

Saying this, the eldest sister called out to the daughter of the Rani and gave her two oranges. No sooner had the girl eaten them, than she ran back to the palace to tell her mother what had happened.

The Rani at once ordered her servants to pull up the orange tree by the roots and destroy it, and the tomb of the first Rani, as well. Not content with this, the next day she pretended to be terribly ill. When she saw how concerned the Rajah was over her condition, she told him that it was in his power to save her life.

"There is only one cure for my illness," she whispered, "but I already know that you will not bring it to me. So I am prepared to die."

"No, no!" exclaimed the Rajah. "Whatever it is you want, I swear I shall bring it to you. Tell me what it is."

"Very well," she said. "The only cure for my illness is the blood of your seven daughters. You must kill them and then put some of their blood on my forehead, the palms of my hands, and the soles of my feet. Their death will then be my life."

The Rajah fell back in horror at her words. Yet, having sworn to bring her what she needed, there was nothing he could do. He went in search of his daughters and found them weeping beside the ruined tomb of their mother.

Seeing their youth and beauty, and recalling his love for them, he realized that he could not kill them. So now he comforted them as best he could, but his promise hung over him heavily. How could he save his daughters and yet satisfy the Rani? At last he hit upon a plan, and invited the girls to go with him into a nearby jungle.

Once there, he helped them make a fire. Then they all sat around it till long after dark, talking of the old days. At last the girls grew sleepy. Finally, they dozed off.

Tears dimming his eyes, the King stole away, saying to himself, "It is far better to have my poor daughters die here than to have their stepmother cruelly murder them."

He then shot a deer, and taking some of its blood carried it to the palace. There he dabbed the blood on the Rani's forehead, her hands and the soles of her feet. She, believing this to be the blood of her hated stepdaughters, pretended to be cured immediately.

Back in the jungle, the princesses awakened. Their fire had died down to a few glowing coals. It was still night, and they were all alone. Surely their father could not have left them in such a place, they thought. He must be somewhere nearby. The girls began to call him, softly at first, then louder and louder.

It so happened that the seven sons of the Rajah of a neighboring country had gone hunting in that same jungle that very day. Now they were on their way home.

Suddenly the youngest prince raised his hand and cried, "Halt, brothers!" And when they had reined their horses, he said, "I thought I heard someone crying for help."

The young men listened. Soon they all heard the cries. Spurring their steeds, they galloped toward the sound.

When they appeared out of the night, their torches blazing and their steeds snorting and pawing the earth, the girls screamed in terror. They thought that they were being surrounded by evil jinni. The young men leaped off their horses and quickly explained who they were. Then the seven princesses told them their own sad story.

When they finished speaking, the eldest prince glanced at his brothers. He knelt before the eldest princess and asked her to be his wife. At almost the same moment all the other princes knelt, also, each selecting the right princess for himself. The youngest and handsomest of the seven asked the beautiful Balna to be his wife.

The young women agreed to marry them as soon as they were all better acquainted. The princes scooped up their ladies, set them before them on the saddles, and galloped home as fast as their steeds could carry them.

Their parents were delighted to see the lovely girls their princes wanted to marry. They made them welcome, and soon arranged a magnificent wedding feast for the seven brides of the seven brothers. The whole kingdom rejoiced, and celebrated the happy event for many days.

At the end of a year, the beautiful Balna had a baby boy. The princes and the six other princesses loved him so dearly that it seemed he had not two parents, but fourteen!

Several months after the baby's birth, the seventh prince, Balna's husband, went out hunting and failed to return. Greatly alarmed, his six brothers rode out in search of him, and they did not return either.

The seven princesses could think nothing but that their seven husbands had somehow met with death. If it were not for the precious baby in the palace, they could not have borne their grief.

One day, in the midst of their sorrow, an ancient fakir came to the doors of the palace begging for alms.

"You may not enter," the servants told him. "The Rajah's seven sons are believed to have died. We therefore cannot trouble their wives with your begging."

The fakir would not be put off. "I am a saintly man," he insisted. "Therefore you must allow me to enter."

Since this was so, judging from his appearance, the servants permitted him to enter. What they did not know was that this was no fakir, saintly or otherwise. This was an evil wizard called Punchkin, in disguise. What is more, he knew very well what had happened to the seven princes.

Punchkin now went straight to the room where Balna was rocking her little son in his cradle. Singing to her baby, she appeared more beautiful than ever. Throwing off his disguise, Punchkin asked her to be his wife.

Balna stared at him as if she thought he was mad. Then she said, "It is true that I fear my husband is dead. But my son is still very small and I wish to remain with him and teach him to become a worthy man. Besides," she looked the wizard up and down, "I do not wish to marry again."

Her glance, as much as her words, enraged the wizard. Muttering some magic words he returned to his disguise as a fakir. At the same instant he transformed Balna into a small puppy. Lifting the puppy in his arms, he said, "Since you do not wish to come with me of your own free will, I will take you by force."

And so it was that the poor princess was taken out of the palace, without a chance to sound an alarm. As Punchkin approached the palace doors, the guards asked, "Where did you get the little dog?"

"One of the princesses gave it to me as a gift," he replied, and slipped out the door and was gone.

Soon after this, the other sisters heard their little nephew crying in his cradle. They ran to see what was the matter and found him all alone. A search through the palace failed to produce their sister. They then questioned the servants and learned about the fakir and the little dog he had taken away with him. Then they guessed what had happened.

Soldiers and servants were sent out in search of the false fakir and the little dog. But all returned without finding any trace of either.

There was nothing more they could do. The six princesses

lost all hope of ever seeing their husbands or their sister alive again. They now devoted themselves to the care and education of their small nephew, Prince Ranga Singh.

When he reached the age of fourteen, his aunts told him the story of what had happened to their family. The boy was at once seized with a burning desire to go in search of his parents and uncles. From that moment he thought of nothing else.

His worried aunts tried to persuade him to give up the idea of such a search. But the youth told them clearly that he would not, could not. "If they are still alive, I will find them," he vowed, "and I shall bring them back."

He left on the next day, and searched vainly for months, riding through many parts of the kingdom.

He traveled many leagues and arrived at a strange jungle. It was full of stones and old trees. In the center of these there rose a huge castle with a tall tower. Not far from the castle stood the hut of a woodcutter.

The wife of the woodcutter saw the prince and came running to meet him. "Who are you, my son?" she inquired, "And how is it that you dare come to this dangerous place?"

"I am Ranga Singh, the grandson of a Rajah," replied the youth. "I am searching for my father and uncles. They disappeared many years ago. I am looking also for my mother, who was bewitched by an evil wizard."

The wife of the woodcutter shook her head sadly. "That castle and all this country belong to a powerful magician," she said. "All who displease him are changed into stones or trees. All of the rocks and trees that you see here are people, bewitched by the wizard." She thought a moment. "Yes, I remember. Years ago the son of a Rajah came here and was changed into a stone. Then his six brothers came, and they, too, suffered the same fate. And in yonder high tower there is a beautiful princess. She is held prisoner because she refuses to marry the wizard."

Prince Ranga Singh heard all this with tremendous excitement. At last he knew what had happened to his family. They were not dead! He then begged the old woman to let him stay in the woodcutter's hut while he planned what to do next.

She agreed, but advised the youth to dress like a woman. "In that way you will not arouse the suspicions of the wizard," she told Ranga Singh.

The prince saw the wisdom of this and put on the sari that the woman gave him. Then they agreed that he would pretend to be her daughter.

The next day, while strolling through his garden, the wizard saw what he thought was a pretty girl. "Who are you, my child?" he asked.

Making his voice sound like a girl's the prince told him that he was the woodcutter's daughter.

"You are a charming creature," said the wizard. "Tomorrow I shall have you take some flowers to the beautiful princess who lives in the tower."

Ranga Singh could scarcely keep a shout of joy from bursting out of him. Somehow he managed to walk away from the wizard, appearing enough like a girl not to arouse the evil one's suspicions.

When he reached the woodcutter's hut, he told the old woman of his good luck. Then he showed her a ring on his finger. "It was given to me at birth by my mother," he explained. "My aunts had it made to fit me as I grew older. My mother should recognize the ring and know me for her son," he finished in great excitement.

"True, true," the old woman agreed. "But be cautious. Be sure that the wizard suspects nothing, or you know what your fate will be." The prince shuddered and the old woman nodded. "He keeps a strict watch on the princess. Be careful," she repeated.

The next day the wizard called the woodcutter's "daughter" to him and gave her the flowers for the princess in the tower. Ranga Singh then slipped the ring over one of the blossoms as he handed the bouquet to his mother.

She recognized the ring at once and realized the "girl" before her was no other than her beloved son. In a voice that shook with emotion, she asked for news of her sisters, and then told him of her cruel imprisonment. "I shall never be able to escape," she finished sadly. "The wizard is much too powerful. Return home, my dearest son, and forget about me," she begged him.

"Never!" Ranga Singh declared. "I shall be most careful, dearest mother, and I shall rescue you. First we must find the source of the wizard's power, for I wish to rescue my father and my uncles, also. You may not know it, but they are there, below your windows, turned either to stones or trees."

Poor Balna would have cried out, but her son stopped her quickly. "Listen, mother. So far you would have nothing to do with the wizard. Now I want you to pretend that you feel more kindly toward him. Tell him that you were deeply touched by his gift of flowers. That now you feel it is foolish for you to spend the rest of your life in this tower. Your husband is surely dead, and you now consent to becoming his wife. Then do everything possible to find out what the source of his power is. Also, discover if he is mortal or not. If he is mortal, it may be possible to kill him in some way."

Balna promised to do everything her son advised. The next day she sent for Punchkin. What she told him delighted the wizard so that he begged her to marry him at once.

The princess smiled and put him off, saying that since they had been enemies for so long, they should spend a little time getting acquainted. This sounded reasonable to the wizard and he scarcely left the princess during that whole day.

In the evening he had a wonderful supper sent up to the tower. Afterward, he lay back on the cushions.

"Tell me," murmured Balna, "are you really immortal? Will death never touch you?"

"Why do you ask?" Punchkin asked.

She smiled at him. "Having been widowed once, is it any wonder I wish to know this? If you are mortal, then I want to know of everything that might harm you, so that I can help guard against it."

The wizard was so pleased by her answer that he told her everything then and there. "You need not fear of ever being widowed again, delight of both my eyes. In truth, I am not as other men. Far away, in the center of an enormous jungle, there is a clearing surrounded by palm trees. In the clearing are six chattees—pots—filled with water. They stand one on top of the other. Under these pots there is a cage with a green parrot in it. My life depends upon the life of this parrot. If he should die, I shall also die. However, my beloved, it is most unlikely that this can happen. For you see, besides the fact that it is impossible to get through this jungle, the clearing is protected by an army of my magical creatures. These jinni would kill anyone who attempted to get near the place."

Now that she was no longer a prisoner, Balna went down to the garden the next day. When the woodcutter's "daughter" appeared, the two strolled about and seemed to have a pleasant conversation.

Actually, Balna told her son what Punchkin had said. Then she begged him to forget about the parrot. "You could never get near him, and if you did, I cannot bear even to think of what would happen to you," she added.

Ranga Singh, however, would not give up his idea. "I must get this parrot," he declared. "Otherwise you, my father and my uncles will forever be the prisoners of this evil one. Do not fear for me. I promise I'll return. In the meantime, postpone this marriage with all kinds of excuses."

The prince left immediately. He traveled many leagues
and finally came to a thick jungle. Surely this was the one
Punchkin had told his mother about. But how he would ever
get through it was another matter. It grew thick and strong
as a fence. The prince decided to rest, then think about it.
He lay under a huge tree and fell asleep at once. He was
awakened by a rustling sound. And, glancing about him, he
saw a large serpent climbing up the trunk of the tree. In the
top of the tree was an eagle's nest with two young birds in it.

Realizing their danger, the prince whipped out his sword and killed the reptile. At that instant there was the beating of eagle wings above his head. The parent birds had returned and had seen what he had done.

The female swooped low, saying, "This cruel serpent has been devouring our young for many years. We are deeply grateful for what you have done. If you ever have need of us, call, and we shall rush to your aid. As for the eaglets, they are ready to leave the nest. Take them to be your servants."

Ranga Singh thanked the parent birds for their gift. "I could use the wings of eagles," he said wistfully.

No sooner were the words out of his mouth, than the eaglets flew down from the nest. They crossed their wings, making a seat for the prince.

"They will take you wherever you wish to go," the parent birds said.

So the prince left his horse under the tree, and seated himself on the eaglets' wings. The birds soared off into the air, as one.

"Take me to the clearing that lies in the center of this jungle," the prince directed. And almost in the wink of an eye he was circling over the area.

Below, the six chattees of water stood exactly in the center of the clearing. It was midday, and the steamy jungle heat was suffocating. Around the clearing the many jinni were dozing, snoring and wheezing in their sleep. Yet to walk past them would have been madness and certain death.

But, thanks to the eaglets, Ranga Singh was able to descend so quietly that not a snore nor a wheeze was interrupted. Toppling the water chattees, the prince grabbed the parrot's cage and soared off into the air again, just as the awakened jinni leaped to their feet. There was nothing they could do but start to wail.

The eaglets returned with the prince to their parents' tree and set him down on the ground once more.

"I return your sons to you," Ranga Singh told the eagles. "They have done me a great service. If ever again I stand in need of your aid, I shall call you."

"Be sure to do so," the female urged. "Now, before you leave, let me tell you something important. As you know, the life of the wizard Punchkin depends on the life of the parrot you carry in that cage. But if you wish to make Punchkin's power useless, all you need do is cut the claws on the right leg. In this way you will have nothing to fear from the wizard and you will be saved the trouble of having to kill him."

The youth thanked her for the advice, mounted his horse and sped back to the wizard's castle.

He rode slowly round the castle, dangling the parrot cage, until Punchkin saw him from one of the windows and hurried down.

"Boy," he called out, "where did you get such a beautiful bird? I beg you to make a gift of it to me."

"I couldn't do that," Ranga Singh exclaimed. "I have had him many years and he has brought me good luck."

"In that case, sell the bird to me. What price do you want for it?"

"I do not wish to sell it," the youth answered firmly.

Punchkin became frightened, for he knew very well what bird this was. "Ask any price you want," he begged. "No matter how high it is, I shall pay it. If you wish something else, besides money, ask for that, too."

"Ah!" said the prince. "That is more like it. I want no money. But first I want you to restore to their human shape the seven sons of the Rajah, whom you bewitched some fourteen years ago."

The wizard muttered some words and waved his right hand. In that instant the seven princes were restored to their natural shapes.

"It is done!" cried the wizard. "Now give me the parrot."

"Not so fast," he prince said. "Now restore to life all the

other people whom you have bewitched into rocks and trees."

The frantic wizard did this also, again waving his right hand as he muttered the magic words.

"Now!" he panted, stretching his hands toward the cage.

"One moment," Ranga Singh said. "First I wish to take one precaution, since I do not trust you. You would be quite capable of changing all these people just restored to life into rocks and trees again." And, before the wizard could prevent it, the prince cut the claws on the right foot of the green parrot.

Punchkin fell senseless to the ground, so strong was the shock of his being left without magic power. Before he could recover, the thousands of prisoners, with Balna and her family at the head of the caravan, were miles away.

When Punchkin did sit up and discover what had happened, he fell into such a fury that he grasped the parrot and wrung its neck. Thus the wicked wizard killed the bird and himself at one and the same time.

The Timid Rabbit

ONCE UPON A TIME there lived a rabbit in a jungle near the west coast of India. He was so timid that every light and shadow made him tremble. He was so fearful that he always expected the worst to happen.

One day, as he sat under a coconut tree, a dreadful thought came to him. Suppose the earth should cave in! What then would happen to him?

At that moment a large coconut fell from the tree. It made a hollow THUMP as it struck the soft earth. The next moment an alert monkey picked the coconut up and ran away with it.

The sound of the THUMP froze the timid rabbit with fear. As soon as he recovered a bit, he whirled about. By this time both monkey and coconut had disappeared. But, where the great nut had struck the earth, there was a shallow hole in the ground. The rabbit's eyes bulged. It was happening! The earth was caving in!

With a great hop he ran from the spot as fast as he could go.

"Where are you going so fast?" another rabbit called after him.

"Run!" shouted the timid rabbit. "The earth is caving in behind us. Run for your life!"

Without thinking, the second rabbit started to run, too. As he ran, he repeated the dreadful news to another rabbit and another, and another. Soon several hundred rabbits were running in a terrified pack, shouting the terrible news for all to hear,

"Run for your lives! The earth is caving in behind us!"

A family of monkeys, swinging through the trees, heard them. And they, too, began to scurry from tree to tree, chattering with fright. Then a fox picked up the news and passed it on to a deer, who told a wild boar, who told a wild ox, who told a camel, who told a jackal, who told a tiger. As all these animals thundered past, the tiger told an elephant.

This elephant was a bit slow-witted. It took him a while to grasp the meaning of the dreadful news. But once he did, he too started to run after the pack. In fact, fear gave him so much speed that in no time at all he was leading the stampede, trumpeting wildly as he went, "The earth is caving in! The earth is caving in!"

Now a wise old lion heard all this commotion and came out of his cave to see what was the matter. He saw the hundreds of terror-stricken animals rushing headlong through the jungle with a huge elephant in their lead.

The king of beasts leaped down from his rock, and taking a short cut got ahead of the pack. With a mighty roar he made all the animals stop in their tracks. "What is this all about?" he asked the elephant. "And what was that I heard you trumpeting just now?"

The elephant peered nervously behind him. "Your majesty," he told the king of beasts, "run for your life! The earth is caving in."

"Where?" the lion asked. "Where is it caving in?"

"Back there!" The elephant waved his trunk.

The lion peered into the distance. The world appeared

perfectly normal to him. "Did you see this yourself?" he asked.

"Well, no," admitted the elephant. "The tiger told me."

"The jackal told me," said the tiger.

"And the camel told me," said the jackal.

"The wild ox told me," the camel said.

"And the wild boar told me," said the wild ox.

"The deer told me," said the wild boar.

"The fox told me," said the deer.

"I heard it from the monkeys," said the fox.

"And we heard it from the rabbits," said the monkeys.

"And we heard it from HIM," said the rabbits, pointing to the timidest one among them.

"Well, now," said the lion towering in all his majesty above the trembling little rabbit. "Who told *you?*"

"Nobody," the timid rabbit replied. "I saw it."

"You saw it!" exclaimed the lion. "Where?"

"Back there. In a grove of coconut trees," the rabbit said.

"Show me," ordered the lion.

"No, no!" The timid rabbit began to tremble more violently than ever. "I dare not. I'm afraid."

"When I am with you, you need not be afraid of anything," the lion said. "Jump up on my back and we'll go together. The rest of you, please stay here until we return."

So at last the timid rabbit showed the lion the shallow hole in the ground, where he thought the earth had started caving in. Just then another coconut fell from the tree, making a hollow THUMP as it hit the soft ground.

The lion looked at the rabbit.

"But there is no coconut in this hole," the timid rabbit said.

The lion batted the coconut out of the hollow it had just made. A monkey caught it as the nut rolled away. "Thank you, your majesty," he exclaimed. "That's my second one today, from this same tree, too." And he scampered off into the jungle.

Now the timid rabbit stared at one hole and then the other. "I guess the earth is not caving in after all," he remarked in a small, small voice.

"Shall we go and tell the others?" the lion suggested gently.

"Do we have to?" the rabbit asked.

"Yes, we do," the king of beasts answered. "Come."

When the two returned to the spot where the other animals were waiting, the timid rabbit hopped off the lion's back. "The earth is not caving in," he told the other rabbits.

"It is not," said the lion firmly.

So the rabbits told the monkeys, and the monkeys told the fox, and the fox told the deer, and the deer told the wild boar, and the wild boar told the wild ox, and the wild ox told the camel, and the camel told the jackal and the jackal told the tiger. But when the tiger went to look for the elephant, to tell *him*, the elephant was gone.

He had time to think and to recover his wits. No one had to tell him that the earth was not caving in. He knew it. So he went home without wasting any more time.

As for the timid rabbit—well, he didn't get brave all at once. But he kept trying, and after a while, thinking brave became a habit. And then he was.

The Son of the
Seven Queens

AT ONE TIME, in India, there lived a Rajah who had seven wives and yet had no children. This was a great sorrow to him, especially when he remembered that at his death, no heir of his blood would sit upon his throne.

Now it happened that one day a fakir—a wise and holy man—came to see the Rajah. "Your prayers have been heard," he said. "One of your wives will bear a son."

The King was delighted. He immediately ordered a golden cradle and everything else for the baby's needs. Then he gave instructions for the celebration that would take place on the day of his son's birth.

In the meantime all seven of his wives lived in the greatest luxury in their own palace. They were attended by twice as many servants and slaves as before and fed on the rarest foods of the kingdom.

On a certain day of the month, the King prepared to go hunting, as was his custom. As he was about to leave, a messenger ran up to him with a letter from the seven Queens.

"Our dearest Lord," it said, "may it please you not to go hunting today. We have had disturbing dreams all the night and we fear that some evil may befall you."

The King smiled over the message. How like his dear Queens it was to worry over him. He hastily wrote a message back to them.

"The nobles and gentlemen of my court have been looking forward to this hunt. I cannot call it off because of dreams, dear ladies. Fear not for my person. All will be well."

However, it was not a successful hunt from the first. No matter in what direction they rode, and in spite of the servants' best efforts, no game was found. The King grew more and more annoyed. "Let us return to the palace," he shouted.

Suddenly he saw a beautiful doe, with shining golden horns and silver hoofs, standing on a rise of ground. She was white as snow and lovely as a goddess. She looked straight at the King for a moment, then like a flash of light, vanished in the thicket.

"I must capture that doe!" the King exclaimed. "Never have I seen anything so gloriously perfect."

The King's men knew how to go about such things. They formed a wide circle around the area, and began to close in on the doe. The King could see her, panting, as his men drew closer and closer. Just as he thought they had her, the doe gave such a mighty leap that she appeared to fly through the air. She leaped right over the Rajah's head and escaped into the mountains.

Without waiting for his companions, the Rajah set spurs to his horse and wheeled about in chase.

On and on he galloped, higher and higher into the mountains, always thinking that he saw the white doe in the distance. At last, too weary to go farther, he lost hope of ever overtaking the beautiful creature.

Searching about for a suitable place to rest, he saw a wretched little hut at the side of a steep cliff. Slowly he rode toward it. Dismounting, he entered to ask for some water.

An old woman, sitting on a rickety chair before a spinning wheel, nodded to his request. Then, turning away from him, she called to her daughter. The girl who stepped out of another room was so beautiful that she took the Rajah's breath away. Her skin was white and smooth as a rose petal, and her hair glowed like precious gold. She was graceful as a dancer, with delicate hands and feet. The King could not imagine how so rare a jewel could be found in so miserable a hut.

The young woman handed the Rajah a goblet filled with water. At the moment he lifted it to drink, she tossed her lovely head and looked full into his eyes. The Rajah was sure at once that here, in fact, was the white doe which he had been following.

Her beauty so bewitched the King that he fell on his knees before her and begged her to be his wife. Even though he suspected she was a witch, it did not matter. The girl stared at him for a moment, then laughed. "Are not seven wives enough to manage?" she asked.

"I want only one Queen," he replied. "You!" And straight away he forgot his love for the others. He even forgot that one of them was to bear the heir for whom he had longed for so many years. He continued to plead with the girl, to beg, to implore. He did not in the least resemble the proud ruler who had ridden out of his palace that morning. He promised this girl anything that her heart desired, anything.

At last the doe-witch said, "Very well. Bring me the eyes of the seven Queens and perhaps then I may believe that you mean what you say."

So bewitched was the King that without hesitation he started back for the palace at full gallop.

To the horror of all, he ordered the Queens' eyes to be taken out. The King's word was law, and the terrible thing was done. Still under a spell, the King ordered the poor Queens to be cast into a dungeon. Then, taking the casket into which their eyes had been placed, he sped back to the hut in the mountains.

"Here is that which you asked for," he told the doe-witch.

She lifted the lid of the casket and her lips turned up in a cruel smile. "Take this, mother," she said, handing the casket over carelessly. "Keep it somewhere while I'm at the palace."

Then she allowed the Rajah to take her back with him, and married him at once. He gave her the seven Queens' palace, their jewels, all their royal garments, and slaves and servants.

Shortly after the unfortunate Queens were thrown into the dungeon, one of them bore a son. She called the boy Ramdas. At first the other six were jealous of the seventh. However, before long, they all loved the baby so dearly that each seemed to be the child's mother. All were equally concerned for his welfare.

As an infant, they loved the boy for the joy he brought into their cheerless, sightless lives. As he grew older, he returned their love and made himself useful in every way to the poor prisoners. Each of the seven blessed the hour of his birth.

Soon after he was able to walk, the young prince dug a hole

in the wall. He made it larger and larger, until one day he was able to crawl through and leave the dungeon. At the end of an hour he returned, not only safe, but carrying a quantity of fine food in his little arms. This he divided equally among his seven mothers.

When the Queens had satisfied their hunger, they asked where he had gotten the food. "From the palace kitchen," he told them. "A servant gave it to me."

"Did she ask you no questions?" his seven mothers asked.

"Oh, yes," the little boy said. "I told her about us. She took me in her arms and kissed me and wept over me. I do not know why. And then she gave me the food and told me to come back tomorrow."

"I wonder who she can be?" one of the Queens wondered uneasily.

"She said her name was Shukoo," the little prince said.

"Oh, Shukoo! She was our favorite waiting woman," the seven Queens exclaimed. "We can trust her."

And so the little prince and the faithful servant, Shukoo, kept the seven Queens supplied with food and other bare necessities. Otherwise the poor things would have died of the small amounts of poor food the dungeon keeper thrust in every day through a narrow hole in their cell door.

When Ramdas grew into a young man, he made himself a bow and arrows and went out to hunt. He soon had several pigeons to take back to his mothers. As he passed close to the palace of the white doe-witch, she saw him and immediately recognized him as the Rajah's son. Her heart filled with such hatred for the lad that she was terrible to see. She vowed to destroy him, for if the Rajah were to see the boy, her own power over the King would end. Ordering one of her slaves to bring the lad to her, she asked him to sell her one of the birds he had killed.

"I cannot," the young man answered. "The pigeons are for
my seven blind mothers who live in the dungeon. They would
die if I were not to take care of them."

"Ah, yes," the doe-witch exclaimed. "I have heard of them,
poor things. And, having seen their son, I want to help them.
If you give me the pigeons, I will send you to the place where
you may find their eyes."

On hearing this, the prince at once made a gift of the birds
to the doe-witch. She, in turn, swiftly wrote a message, sealed
it and gave it to him.

"*Kill the carrier of this at once and turn his blood into morning dew*," it said.

"Take this to my mother, the Black Witch of the Mountains," she directed, "and she will at once give you the casket
with the eyes of the seven Queens."

Happily, Prince Ramdas took the message and set off with
all speed toward the mountains.

In the course of the journey, he came to a country where he found the whole population extremely sad. "Tell me, good people," he asked, "what is the cause of your sorrow?"

"The only child of our Rajah, his daughter, refuses to marry. Thus, when he dies our country will find itself without an heir to the throne," an old man told him.

"Moreover," a second man added, "the princess has stated that if she does marry, it must only be the son of seven mothers. This, of course, is unheard of."

"Just the same," a third chimed in, "our King has commanded that all strangers arriving in the city must immediately report at the palace for questioning. You had better go at once, young man. Our King is very strict about his orders."

So Ramdas had to go to the palace. Once at the gates, he was immediately conducted into the presence of the Rajah and the Princess Tara.

The moment the Princess saw him, she turned to her father. "Grieve no more, O my father," she said. "This is the man I shall marry, for he does, indeed, have seven mothers."

Never had so few words caused so much happiness. The whole country burst into wild celebrating.

But Prince Ramdas, though charmed by the Princess, explained that he could not marry her until he had completed his trip. Then he told her his story and showed her the Rani's sealed letter. The Princess was deeply touched by the story. She was also strangely troubled by the sealed letter. However, she made no mention of this.

Instead, she urged Ramdas to bathe and refresh himself, before going on with his journey. While the young man was bathing, Tara opened the Rani's letter and read it. Its words made her blood run cold. She was a very wise and clever girl. Now she imitated the wicked Rani's handwriting and set down another message, destroying the original afterward.

Her message said, "Take good care of this young man and give him all he desires. He has served me well."

This done, and with the young prince rested, she allowed him to continue on his way.

The Prince soon arrived in the mountains and before long found the hut of the Black Witch. "I have come for the eyes of the seven Queens," he told her, and gave her the letter he carried.

The old woman stared at him. Then she read the message. The words were right there, and the handwriting was certainly her daughter's.

"They're somewhere about," she grumbled, getting up from her spinning wheel.

After poking through piles of this and that, she finally found the casket, hidden in a dark corner. "Here," she said thrusting it into Ramdas' eager hands.

The Prince bade her a polite farewell and set off on his homeward journey at once. When he arrived back at the dungeon, the seven Queens were waiting for him anxiously. He had never been away so long before.

"Wait till you see what I have for you!" he exclaimed as they kissed and embraced him. Then he gave back a pair of eyes to each one of them.

The Queens laughed and cried with joy. They could not stop looking at or admiring the handsome son before them.

"Dearest mothers," he told them, "I shall go now to be married. But the servant, Shukoo, and I shall continue to care for you. One day there will be a way to make you free again."

Having said a fond farewell to them all, he set off for his own Princess. But, as he passed the Rani's palace, he saw some pigeons on the roof of her tower. Without thinking twice about it, he whipped out an arrow and shot a bird.

The Rani heard the arrow whistle by and looked out from her balcony. There, to her great astonishment, she saw the prince, who was very much alive.

With an angry shout she summoned a slave and told him to bring the young man up. Once in her presence, she asked him how he had managed to return so quickly.

"I did not waste any time," he answered, "and your mother was very kind."

"Oh she was, was she?" the Rani muttered under her breath. She could not imagine what had gone wrong. Now, however, she pretended to be very happy over the success of his trip. "And, I see that you have shot another pigeon," she exclaimed. "I am very fond of them, cooked just right. Won't you give this one to me? In exchange I'll give you a wonderful cow, whose milk never ceases to flow. Think what a help she would be to your mothers!"

The young prince was delighted with the exchange.

"Of course," the doe-witch added, "you will have to go back to my mother and ask her for the cow. I'll give you a message so that she will surely give it to you."

What the message really said was, *Kill the carrier of this letter without fail, and turn his blood into morning dew.*

But the Prince, all unknowing, set off happily on his second trip. On the way he stopped at the Princess' palace, to tell her that their wedding would be delayed a bit. "This cow would mean a great deal to my mothers," he told her.

"Of course it would," she agreed.

Then the clever young woman managed to get the second letter and read it. Again she changed the message, and sent her trusting young Prince on his way.

In the heart of the mountains, the Black Witch could not understand what had come over her daughter. She also could not imagine what service this young prince could have done her to deserve so rich a prize as the wonderful cow. But she did as her daughter asked, and the Prince left her hut, leading the cow behind him.

The seven Queens were delighted with the cow. Her endless supply of milk not only kept them well fed, but now they were able to sell the milk, with Shukoo's aid. They also made butter and cheese, and in no time at all they had earned a good deal of money.

Seeing that his mothers were now well off, the Prince decided to return to his Princess, whom he now loved very much. But, as he passed the Rani's palace, he could not resist shooting one of the fat pigeons flying around her tower. It landed on the window sill of her room. The Rani, looking out, almost fell from the window when she saw the Rajah's son, safe and sound once more.

Again she sent for him and barely managed to hide her anger as she questioned him. When she found out that the old witch had given him the cow, she almost fainted with rage. But she controlled herself and again asked for the pigeon he had shot.

"In exchange," she said, and her eyes glittered with hate, "I shall give you a grain of wheat which will bear a million seeds that will grow overnight."

The Prince was delighted, and went off to the witch of the mountains, armed with the usual letter. This time the message said, *"Kill this young upstart at once. Do not fail, and turn his blood into morning dew."*

As had happened before, Princess Tara changed the message. The Black Witch, although almost beside herself with anger, gave the magic grain of wheat to the young Prince.

Now the young Prince went back to his Princess and their marriage was celebrated at once. With the magic grain of wheat in his possession, he soon became the largest wheat grower in the country. In a few months he was the richest man in India, not even counting his wife's great fortune.

The young couple was happy enough. Yet both were troubled by the thought of the seven Queens who still spent their lives in their dungeon. By law, only the Rajah, their husband, could release them. But the Rajah was still under the spell

of the white doe-witch. He never thought of the seven
Queens, nor did he know of the son who had been born to him.

"I do not really have any magic power," Princess Tara told
her husband, "but I have thought of a way to lift the wicked
spell from the Rajah, your father."

So she had an exact copy of the palace of the seven Queens
built in her own royal park. Then she sent an invitation for
a state visit to Prince Ramdas' father.

Now the Rajah had been hearing of the Prince and Princess
of the neighboring kingdom and he had long wanted to meet
them. The invitation suited him perfectly. He prepared for
a state visit and commanded his Rani to go with him. The
young Prince had never mentioned the Princess, or his coming marriage. And he had never reappeared since she had
sent him for the grain of wheat, so the wicked Rani thought
that at last he was dead. She never suspected that she was
preparing to visit him and his bride in their own kingdom.

The royal company arrived after dark, so the new palace
in the park was not visible. However, as they were led into
the entrance hall, the Rajah was amazed to see how like his
own Rani's palace this was. The next moment a handsome
young man came forward to welcome him. The Rajah stood,
his eyes fixed on the face of Prince Ramdas. A strange feeling came over him—a sense of gladness, and at the same time
a sadness so great, he wanted to burst into tears.

Beside him, the Rani also stood, thunderstruck. "YOU!" she
exclaimed. "I am undone!"

"Come," said Prince Ramdas to the visitors, "my wife and
my mothers wish to greet you also."

"Mothers!" mumbled the King, trying to remember something very important.

"*Mothers!*" shrieked the Rani beside him. She would have
turned and run. But two enormous slaves appeared at her
side. Holding her arms they forced her to move forward with
the King.

Now two great doors opened, and the seven Queens, dressed as befitted their rank, together with their beautiful daughter-in-law, rose to greet the visitors.

"These are my seven mothers," Prince Ramdas said proudly, "and my wife, Princess Tara."

The Princess threw herself at the Rajah's feet. "Your majesty, the seven mothers before you are in truth seven Queens. They are your own seven wives who have lived in a dungeon all these years."

"But how can this be?" the King asked, for the black magic still held his mind. "Why would my wives be in a dungeon? And if they were, how came they here? Only I could release them."

"I know, your majesty," the Princess said. "My husband and I took them from the dungeon without your permission."

"Kill her! Kill them all!" screamed the doe-witch Rani. "They have broken the King's law."

"Your majesty," the Princess jumped to her feet. "Look at my husband! This is Prince Ramdas, the son you have waited for all these years. And these are his seven mothers."

The Rajah stared at the Prince. Suddenly all the darkness that the wicked magic of the white doe-witch had spun in his mind melted away. "My son!" he exclaimed, and clasped Prince Ramdas to his breast.

Then he turned to the Queens, his face filled with shame and sorrow. All at once he remembered everything that had happened. "I do not know what to say." He bowed before them.

"Say nothing, your majesty," the seven Queens spoke as one. "You were bewitched. You knew not what you were doing."

"I am not bewitched now!" the Rajah exclaimed, turning upon the wicked Rani.

But she was so overcome with rage and terror that she sud-

denly burst into flame. In a moment she was reduced to
nothing but a heap of ashes.

"Sweep her out," Princess Tara told a slave.

From that day no one ever spoke of the white doe-witch.
The seven Queens returned to their rightful palace and lived
out the rest of their days happily. Their son governed the
kingdom he inherited with great wisdom—and the people
there never lacked for bread on their tables.

1

"Phew, what is that? It smells like someone died in here," Lainie Yeager said loudly—which was the way she said almost everything. She stood in the kitchen doorway and wrinkled her nose.

Franny Yeager, her elder sister, who was standing next to her, grimaced—at both the smell and Lainie's voice, which was still reverberating in her eardrums. She'd been hoping that, for once, the house would be quiet this afternoon. Lainie was supposed to be at her dance class, but she'd decided to cut, telling Franny on the bus ride home from school that the teacher was a wimp. Franny had listened without much sympathy. Lainie was always calling various teachers wimps. "Lainie has a problem with authority figures," a school psychologist had once told Mrs. Yeager, who'd wor-

riedly told Franny and Mr. Yeager. Mr. Yeager had had a different explanation. "Lainie's a brat," he'd said in his terse way. Franny tended to agree with him.

"Phew," Lainie said again.

Mrs. Yeager, whose back was to the girls, whirled around. "How many times have I told you two not to shove leftovers to the back of the refrigerator?" she asked in a voice that matched Lainie's decibel for decibel. "Look at this."

The sisters crossed the room and peered at the plastic container their mother was holding. A lurid red-and-green mold nestled inside it.

"Yuck! What is—I mean, was—that?" Lainie shrieked.

"I don't know. Do you?" asked her mother.

"No," Lainie said.

Franny shook her head. She'd planned to have a snack before settling down with her homework, but now she'd lost her appetite.

Lainie, on the other hand, seemed to have held on to hers. She grabbed a handful of chocolate chip cookies out of the jar on the counter.

"I thought you had a dance class today," Mrs. Yeager said to her.

"I decided not to go," Lainie said, daring her mother to ask why.

Instead, Mrs. Yeager just sighed and began to scrape the gook out of the container.

"Why are you doing that? Why don't you just throw out the whole thing?" Lainie demanded.

Franny knew just what Mrs. Yeager was going to answer. And she knew that Lainie knew too.

"And waste a perfectly good container? Money doesn't grow on trees," their mother replied on cue.

"It doesn't grow in moldy containers either," Lainie retorted.

Mrs. Yeager didn't respond. She was filling the now-empty container with soapy water.

There was a pause. Franny shifted awkwardly, wriggling her shoulders. Her book-filled backpack was heavy, but she didn't take it off. She wasn't sure she wanted to stay in the kitchen much longer.

"Well, then, by now you must've saved enough money from saving enough of those things to give me the increase in my allowance I've been asking for," Lainie said.

Franny sighed. Now she knew she didn't want to stay in the kitchen. Still she lingered.

"Lainie, we've been through this already," Mrs. Yeager said. "You know we can't afford to raise your allowance. We pay for your clothes and extra classes already. All you have to pay for is your entertainment."

"And just how am I supposed to entertain myself on five dollars a week?"

"Lower your voice," Mrs. Yeager said, raising hers. "If five dollars isn't enough, why don't you get a job?"

5

"A job? Now there's a brilliant idea! You can't imagine how many places are just dying to hire a fourteen-year-old girl."

"You could baby-sit. The Beltramis asked about you just the other—"

Lainie cut her off. "Actually, come to think of it, I know a place that *would* hire me. The Gay Paree Massage Parlor. Maybe I'll go there. That would take care of both my money *and* my entertainment."

Franny sighed again. Lainie had about as much firsthand experience with sex as she did with interstellar travel. But "dirty talk," as their mother called it, got Mrs. Yeager annoyed. And that was something Lainie liked to do.

"Very funny," Mrs. Yeager responded.

"I'm not trying to be funny," Lainie said. "I'm dead serious."

Franny'd had enough. "Mom, is Grandma upstairs?" she interrupted.

"What? Oh, yes. She was taking a nap. I don't know whether or not she still is. But if she is, don't wake her."

"I won't," Franny said. As she left the kitchen, she heard her mother say, "I don't know what's wrong with you, Lainie. You used to be such a sweet child. Now you have such a fresh mouth."

Franny shook her head and thought about the fickleness of her mother's memory. As a child Lainie

had been cute and bright—and just as fresh as she was now.

"Franny never had such a fresh mouth," Mrs. Yeager continued.

"That's because Franny's *perfect*," Lainie replied sarcastically.

Franny winced and fled up the stairs.

Franny's door was closed. Not sound came from behind it. Grandma's probably still asleep, Franny thought. She and her grandmother had shared a bedroom since Franny was a baby. For most of her life Franny hadn't minded that. She loved her grandmother. In fact, she often thought Grandma was the sanest member of the family. But lately Franny'd begun to resent not having her own room. She had no place to bring her friends. And, more importantly, no place to be alone. She wondered why and how Lainie'd managed to get her own room and told herself, for the hundredth time, that she ought to ask their mother. Feeling irritated, she quietly opened the door, expecting to see her grandmother lying in bed.

Instead, she saw Grandma sitting in the rocking chair, plunging a hypodermic needle into her leg.

Franny averted her eyes, not because the sight sickened her—she was used to her grandmother's insulin injections—but because seeing Grandma so vulnerable made Franny feel guilty about resenting her.

7

Then Grandma's soft voice with the slight Russian accent said, "If I knew I was going to live this long, I would've taken better care of myself."

And Franny, even though she'd heard the joke many times before, had to chuckle.

Grandma looked up at her and smiled. "There," she said, breaking the disposable syringe and tossing it and the empty insulin vial into a wastebin. "Hmmm. I need more of this stuff."

"Do you want me to get you some more, Grandma?" Franny asked promptly.

"That would be nice, Lainie." There was a pause. Then Grandma tapped her skull. "I mean Franny. Oy, I'm such an *alter kocker*," Grandma said.

Franny smiled again. Ever since she could remember, Grandma was always calling her Lainie and Lainie Franny. Sometimes their parents did that as well. But more often Mr. and Mrs. Yeager came out with some amalgam such as FraLainie. When Franny and Lainie were younger they considered forming a singing group with that name until Lainie screamed that she was not going to sing backup even though Franny had the better voice for lead.

"So, how was school today?" Grandma asked.

"Okay." Franny shrugged. Then, after a moment, she said, "My English teacher handed out a funny thing for us to read and discuss."

"What was it?"

"Do you want me to read it to you?"

"Sure."

Franny fished a piece of paper out of her book bag. She cleared her throat and began, " 'Once Chuang Chou dreamed that he was a butterfly. He did not know that he had ever been anything but a butterfly and was content to hover from flower to flower. Suddenly he woke and found to his surprise that he was Chuang Chou.' " She paused, then went on, " 'But it was hard to be sure whether he was Chuang Chou and had only dreamed that he was a butterfly or was really a butterfly and was only dreaming that he was Chuang Chou.' " Franny looked up. "It's funny, isn't it?"

Grandma nodded. Then she asked, "Well, which do you think he was—a man or a butterfly?"

Franny suppressed a laugh. Grandma often missed the point of things she read to her, but somehow it didn't matter. "I don't know," she answered. "Someone in class said the passage means that people and butterflies are the same—they have the same spirit or soul. And someone else said it means that all life is a dream."

Grandma said nothing, so Franny went on. "This kid said good stuff, bad stuff, it's all the same: an illusion. So we shouldn't get too excited or too upset by anything."

"Sounds like good advice for your mother and your sister," Grandma said wryly as Lainie's and Mrs. Yeager's voices came screeching up the stairs:

"Lainie, where are you going?"

"Out—to an orgy."

"You're so fresh!"

Bang! The front door slammed, echoing through the house.

Franny grimaced. She wondered what it would be like to live in a home where the only sound was beautiful music.

"You mother's too hard on that girl," Grandma said, shaking her head.

Franny looked at her but didn't say anything. Personally, she thought Lainie was just as hard on her mother.

"I wonder if I was that hard on Irene," Grandma went on, referring to Mrs. Yeager. She thought about it, then shrugged. "I can't remember." She smiled at Franny. "I think I'll go downstairs for a cup of tea. Do you want to join me?"

"Not now," Franny answered. Not when the house is finally quiet and I can have my room to myself, she thought. Feeling another twinge of guilt, she added quickly, "I've got to do some homework. And then I'll go to the drugstore for you."

"All right," Grandma said. She got up slowly and made her way to the door. Just before she went out, she said, without turning, "You're a good girl, Franny."

Franny watched the door close behind her. "Am I?" she whispered. "Am I really?"

2

"So there's this lull, and I'm boxing the burgers when I hear this buzzing at the counter, but I ignore it because those silly girls are always buzzing about something or other. Somebody tells me I've got a customer on my line. She says it with a giggle. I roll my eyes and go up to the counter. 'Can I help you?' I say, except it comes out 'Can I help you-whoo!' because standing in front of me is the most gorgeous guy I've ever seen. Thick blond hair and baby blues, just the way I like 'em. Tall, well built. He's wearing this cool jacket, and he's smiling this sexy smile. 'Can I help you?' I ask again, thinking about long walks in the moonlight, dancing in the dark, and similar stuff.

"He smiles again and pauses to study the menu, which is on the wall over my head. A line's beginning

11

to form behind him, but I don't care. I like a man who takes his time. I wait, happy just to be looking at him. 'Come on, buddy,' the guy behind him mutters. But he doesn't pay any attention. Finally, he finishes studying the choices: regular, cheese, double cheese, chili, or bacon. He opens his mouth to speak. I hold my breath.

" 'Ain't ya got any Chicken McNuggets?' he says in a voice like my dentist's drill with a Brooklyn accent. 'I want some Chicken McNuggets.'

"It takes me a few seconds to respond. 'No, sir, we don't.' I don't bother to tell him he's in Burger Bonanza, not McDonald's.

" 'Ya sure?' he asks.

" 'I'm positive,' I answer.

" 'Aw, man. I really wanted some Chicken McNuggets,' he says, and walks out the door.

"And there, Franny, you have yet another example of He Opened His Mouth and It Was All Over from the ever-colorful life of Susan Brandenberg."

Franny was trying not to laugh too loudly and disturb all the customers in the pharmacy, where she and Susan were standing on line. Susan had been entertaining Franny with her stories for over four years—ever since seventh grade, in fact. Franny was happy they'd run into each other today at the pharmacy, because she needed a dose of entertainment after the unpleasant scene in her house.

"Who's next?" the pharmacist asked.

"I am," Susan said, plunking some roll-on deodorant on the counter.

"Will that be all?"

"Yes. At least until tomorrow." Susan turned back to Franny. "I sweat so much in that place, I use up one of these every day."

Franny smiled at Susan's exaggeration, but she knew that Burger Bonanza was sweaty—and greasy too. That was why she'd decided not to take a job there even though there'd been an opening and, God knew, she could use the money. She hadn't told Susan that, though. Instead she'd made up a feeble excuse about being afraid she'd gain too much weight there. But she suspected Susan guessed the real reason. I ought to check out some of the other places and see if they're hiring, Franny told herself. Like the yarn shop or the bookstore or, better yet, the crafts gallery. She co⟩ see herself behind the cash register at Artistic Te perament, ringing up a sale for a beautiful vase or a pair of gorgeous earrings. . . .

The pharmacist interrupted her thoughts. "And what can I get for you, Franny? Does Mrs. Gallinsky need more insulin?"

"Yes—and more syringes."

"Right." The pharmacist went to get them.

"How is your grandmother?" Susan asked, putting the deodorant into her purse. She liked Mrs. Gallinsky a lot. She often spent time chatting with her when she visited Franny.

"Fine," Franny answered, thinking that that was a dumb thing to call someone who had diabetes.

"I'm sorry I haven't been able to see her for a while—or you very much, for that matter. But between this job and school . . ."

Franny nodded. She understood. But it made her a bit sad. They didn't even have lunch period together this term. In fact, the only period they did share was history, and Mrs. Coleman didn't brook any socializing during her class. So they had to make do with occasional Sundays (when they weren't overloaded with homework), telephone conversations (always difficult because there was only one phone in Franny's house, and that was in the kitchen), and unplanned encounters like today's. If I'd taken that job, I would see her a lot more, Franny thought with some guilt.

"How's the rest of your family?" Susan asked.

"All right. Mom and Lainie had another argument today, so I guess things are what you might call normal," Franny said wryly.

Susan shook her head. "Why don't you tell them to shut up?"

"Sure. That would go down really well."

"I mean it, Fran."

Franny looked at her friend and realized she was serious.

"Tell them they're driving you nuts, and if they have to argue, to do it when you're not around," Susan continued.

14

Franny didn't answer. She was annoyed that Susan'd suggested something so ridiculous.

The pharmacist returned then and said, "I'll add these to your bill." He smiled and put Grandma's things into a bag.

Franny thanked him and took the package. She and Susan walked out of the store toward Burger Bonanza. Franny hoped Susan was going to drop the topic of how she should deal with her mother and Lainie.

Susan did. "Maybe we can get together this Sunday," she said, "if Coleman doesn't ask for another essay like the last one. 'Slavery—Why Did It Work So Well.' God, that thing took me six hours to write."

"That's because you were watching a football game at the same time," Franny reminded her.

"True. But I couldn't resist. I love football—and besides, those players have the cutest butts I've ever seen. Whoo-whee!"

Franny laughed. "Well, I won't disagree with you about that."

They reached the fast-food restaurant. "You want to come in for a Coke or something? If Short Nose isn't looking, I won't have to charge you."

"No. It's almost dinnertime. I'd better get home."

"Okay. Listen, Franny. Essay or not, let's definitely plan on Sunday. I can visit your grandma after we do something socially significant—like some serious butt watching at the mall."

Franny laughed again. "Sounds good," she said.

15

Susan blew her a kiss and went into the restaurant. She turned and waved to Franny through the plate-glass window.

Franny waved back and went on her way. As she strolled home, she thought of Susan's story and giggled. She wished she could tell stories like that. For Susan, life was a book—one she was in the process of writing. No, that wasn't right. It made her sound like an observer, when in fact she was an active participant. A highly active participant.

She smiled with good humor, then realized she was walking too slowly and picked up her pace. Being late for dinner caused problems in the Yeager household, because if there was anything Mr. Yeager demanded, it was having dinner on time.

Franny turned a corner quickly. The daylight was waning rapidly. Ugh, she thought. November. It gets dark so early.

As if in response, the streetlights snapped on. Franny passed under one of them. Something brushed against her cheek and slid under her collar. She carefully removed it. It was a moth. "Rather late in the year for you to be around, isn't it?" she said. "Or are you really a person who is dreaming he's a moth?" The moth flew away uncertainly.

"Whoo-whoo!" A sharp whistle made her start. She turned her head and frowned. A trio of boys was heading toward her. She braced herself for more whistles and crude remarks. Then she realized they

16

weren't looking at her. She followed their stares and swallowed back her own exclamation.

Right between the boys and Franny a girl was leaning against a lamppost. Her arms were above her head and her breasts and hips were thrust out provocatively. She looked like a streetwalker from some corny old film—except that instead of a dress and heels, she wore jeans, a sweatshirt, sneakers, and a slouch hat pulled down over her face.

"Hey, baby. You looking for a good time?" one of the boys yelled.

"How about it, baby? You sure look ready, don't she, Al?"

The girl didn't budge. The boy called Al answered, "She must be stoned."

"That's okay with me," the first boy replied.

Why doesn't she move? Franny wondered, not moving either. What's wrong with her? She felt a mixture of embarrassment, fascination, and revulsion toward the girl.

"Ah, leave her alone. She might be an undercover cop," Al said.

"An undercover cop? You're nuts. She's too young," the first boy responded. "Isn't she, John?"

"Yeah," said John, sounding less than certain. Then, with forced casualness, "Hey, we going to Burger Bonanza or not?"

"Yeah. We're going," the first boy said with palpable relief.

17

"Well, let's go."

The boys moved off rapidly. When they were safely up the block, they turned and whistled at the girl again, then disappeared around the corner.

Franny might have laughed at them if the girl had been gone too. But the girl was still in her pose. Suddenly Franny wanted to get past her as quickly as possible. She strode up the street and was almost by the girl when a raspy but familiar voice called out, "Hey, honey, got a cigarette?"

Franny whipped her head around.

The girl at the lamppost had removed her hat. The light shone on her grinning face. It was Lainie.

3

"Have you gone crazy?" Franny said tightly. She was furious. She rattled the bag from the pharmacy as if it were Lainie's neck.

"Not that I've noticed," Lainie answered, smoothing back her long auburn hair and replacing the hat on her head. Lainie was a "looker," as Uncle Mike put it, and she knew it.

A wave of jealousy hit Franny, making her even angrier, this time with herself. "You looked like a hooker," she blurted out.

"It was just a joke," Lainie responded. "I saw you leaving Burger Bonanza. I ran on ahead of you to the lamppost. Damn, you were slow."

Franny gritted her teeth, trying to rein in her emotions. "Those boys . . . You could've gotten hurt," she

19

said, trying to sound more concerned than irate.

"No, I couldn't have. And you sound just like Mom."

Franny flushed and bit her tongue. She'd just received Lainie's ultimate insult.

They walked for several blocks in silence. Franny was still seething. She wasn't sure why she was so angry. It had been a joke and nothing bad had happened. Settle down, she told herself. Or you'll end up screaming just like Mom.

After several more quiet blocks she began to calm down. She hoped she could make it all the way home without any more arguments or even conversation.

But Lainie, who could never stand silence for very long, thwarted Franny's desire. "How do you like my hat?" she asked, pulling the fedora down over one eye.

So much for that, Franny thought. She glanced at Lainie. "Very chic," she answered politely.

Lainie snorted. "You always say that when you don't like something."

Franny didn't respond, especially since the observation was true. Instead, in an effort to maintain the peace, she asked, "Where'd you get it?"

"At a new thrift shop on Grosvenor."

"You went all the way to Grosvenor?" Franny's voice rose in surprise, and she winced. I really do sound like Mom, she thought in disgust.

However, Lainie charitably let that one go. "So, how's Sue?" She changed the topic.

20

"Oh, she's fine," Franny answered gratefully.

"She hasn't been over much lately."

"No. She's been busy."

Lainie nodded. "Did she tell you any good stories today?" Lainie was also a big fan of Susan's stories.

"As a matter of fact . . ." Franny repeated Susan's story, trying to tell it the way Susan had.

Lainie's only response was "How come she likes those beefy blond types?"

"They're not beefy, the guys Susan likes. Big yes, but not beefy," Franny answered, annoyed that her narrative abilities had flopped once again.

"That last guy she was dating sure looked like a rump roast to me," Lainie said.

Even though she thought her sister's description of Eddie Porter was fairly accurate, in defense of Susan Franny refused to laugh.

They turned a corner. One of their neighbors waved at them from his car. Lainie waved back.

"Does Sue like working at Burger Bonanza?" she asked after the man disappeared.

"She likes the paycheck."

"The pay's lousy there."

"How do you know that?" Franny asked.

"Everybody knows that."

"You mean you wouldn't work there if you could get a job?" Franny said.

"I'd probably work *anywhere* if I could get a job," Lainie answered straightforwardly.

Surprised at the genuine frustration in Lainie's voice, Franny asked with equal straightforwardness, "How come you don't baby-sit? You like kids and you could make some dough doing it."

Lainie sighed. "I know I could. It's just—I don't want to deal with Mom's friends."

Or Mom's smug satisfaction if you took a job she suggested, Franny added silently. She could understand how Lainie felt. Their mother was an awful I-told-you-so.

Then Lainie asked, "How come *you* don't have a job yet?"

"I'm still looking," Franny answered defensively. The truth was she hadn't been job hunting for the past several weeks, but the last thing she wanted to do was tell Lainie that.

"I thought there was an opening at Burger Bonanza."

She *would* know about that, Franny thought. "There was," she said carefully, "but I decided not to take it."

"Too low-class, huh."

Franny stiffened. "I'm looking for something that . . . pays more."

"Oh. Well, maybe *you* should try Madame Fifi's."

Very funny, Franny was about to say. She caught herself in time. "Maybe I should," she declared.

Lainie's eyes widened in astonishment. Then she broke into a wide grin.

Franny grinned back.

They turned another corner onto their own street.

"Well, here we are. The Happy Home," Lainie announced as they reached the driveway. "Uh-oh."

"What's the matter?" Franny asked.

"Look." Lainie had stopped dead and was pointing at their father's car.

"Dad's home already." Franny looked at her watch. "But it's okay. We're not late for dinner."

"Look," Lainie insisted.

"What am I supposed to be looking at?"

"The taillight."

"The taillight?"

"It's busted. And the rear end is crumpled."

"It wasn't broken before?"

"Franny, how come for somebody who's supposed to be so smart, you sound like you've got your head screwed on backward? No, it wasn't broken before. Not yesterday. Not this morning. That means sometime between eight A.M. and five P.M. this car was smashed into."

"Oh, God," Franny said.

"He ain't gonna help. He isn't a mechanic. Come on. Let's get it over with." Lainie took Franny's arm and pulled her up the steps into the house.

"So, Franny, tell your father how you did on your history test."

Franny closed her eyes. She'd been concentrating on her drumstick, praying that they would somehow

23

escape the dinner table without a blowup.

Grandma had eaten earlier and retired for the night. Franny wished she could've done the same thing.

When Franny and Lainie had entered the house, Mrs. Yeager had met them in the hall and whispered frantically that some kids fooling around in the plant parking lot had smashed into the rear end of their dad's car. The police hadn't caught them yet. "Your father's very upset, so for heaven's sake, don't say anything to get him even more upset," Mrs. Yeager had said, staring right at Lainie.

"You mean like 'Well, we need a new car anyway'?"

"That's exactly what I mean. Keep your mouth closed for a change, Lainie." She went into the kitchen.

After a pause, Franny said, "You're not going to say anything that'll start him up, are you?"

"Do you think I'm a jerk?" Lainie answered.

Yes, Franny thought, but she shook her head.

Now she shook her head again. "I didn't have a history test, Mom," she answered.

"I thought you were studying for a history test last night," Mrs. Yeager said, an edge of panic in her voice.

"No, I was studying for a chemistry test."

"Oh." Mrs. Yeager breathed a sigh of relief. "Tell your father how you did on that."

Franny looked at her father. Dark-haired, dark-eyed, with beetle brows, bags under his eyes, and a perpetual scowl, Mr. Yeager had been what her mother called a "good catch." Besides being handsome, he

24

was hardworking and clean living. Drugs, student protests, and the war (thanks to his high blood pressure) had passed him by. True, he didn't have a college education, but the auto-parts business he was in was booming. No one could have guessed that twenty years later the bottom would fall out of it, and that he and his family would be worrying all the time.

Franny thought she could recall a time when he'd smiled more often, been more affectionate. She wished she remembered it more clearly. She wished even more he'd be that way again.

Angry and tired, he looked back at her now. "So, how'd you do?" he asked.

"All right, I guess," she answered.

Mrs. Yeager beamed. It was the first thing he'd said all evening. But her smile quickly died when he asked, in a voice raspy from the cigarettes he chain-smoked despite her nagging and the doctor's warning, "You guess? What do you mean, you guess?"

Franny silently cursed herself for qualifying her remark. "I mean I'm pretty sure I did well, but we don't get our grades until Friday."

"Oh," Mr. Yeager grunted. He went back to his chicken.

Rather than letting the conversation die there, Mrs. Yeager said, "Chemistry's interesting, isn't it? You liked chemistry in school, didn't you, Gene?"

"No," he answered without looking up.

"I thought—But—Didn't you tell me you did? You

were even thinking of becoming a chemical engineer."

Mr. Yeager swallowed a mouthful of dark meat. "You must be confusing me with one of your other boyfriends," he said.

For a second Mrs. Yeager didn't respond. Then she realized her husband was finally rewarding her efforts with a joke. She laughed—too loudly.

Franny dutifully joined in.

"How many boyfriends did you have, Ma?" Lainie asked when they stopped laughing. It was the first thing *she'd* said since they'd sat down to eat.

"Oh, dozens and dozens," Mrs. Yeager tossed off lightly.

"Ha," said Mr. Yeager.

"Ha yourself, I did have quite a few. One of them, Arnie Roth—you remember him, Gene? He went to your school. He was very rich. He picked me up for a date in a brand-new Jaguar. That was some car. . . ." She stopped when she realized what she was saying and cast a stricken glance at her husband.

Franny looked at him too. A muscle in his cheek was twitching. He threw down his fork, and it clattered on the plate, sending up a spray of gravy. Without a word he stomped out of the room.

Mrs. Yeager sighed. There was a long silence; then Lainie said, "I guess Dad didn't like Arnie Roth."

Franny closed her eyes. It was happening again. She couldn't stand it. Shut them out, she told herself. This is only an illusion.

Mrs. Yeager threw up her hands. "Shut up, Lainie!" she said.

"Don't yell at me!" Lainie shouted. "Yell at him! You're always tiptoeing around him like he's a god-damn king."

"Go to your room!"

"With pleasure," Lainie spat back, and stomped out.

"Oh, God," Mrs. Yeager said, turning to Franny. "Your sister's impossible."

Franny didn't answer her. An illusion, she was re-peating to herself like a mantra.

"I better go talk to your father. . . . Oh no, look at all the dishes!"

Mechanically, Franny rose and began to gather and stack them in the sink.

"Oh, Franny, I didn't mean that you should do them. It's Lainie's turn. You must have homework to do. Leave them—I'll finish them later."

"It's all right, Mom," Franny said. "I'll do them."

Mrs. Yeager sighed. "Why can't your sister be more like you?" She left the room.

"Lainie's an illusion," Franny said. A little smile played across her lips as she began to do the dishes.

4

"You came to bed late last night," Grandma said, examining her feet.

"I had to finish an essay," Franny told her. She pulled a sweater over her head.

"Why didn't you write it up here?"

"You were asleep. I didn't want to wake you."

"I wasn't asleep. And you wouldn't have awakened me if I had been."

Franny didn't say anything. She didn't want to explain that she hadn't felt like going to their room. She hadn't wanted to see her grandmother or anybody. So she'd gone down to the basement.

The Yeager basement resembled the town dump. It was filled with mildewed books, outgrown clothes,

old toys, broken furniture, television sets that hadn't worked for years, and other assorted things. There was also a workbench covered with dusty tools Mr. Yeager never used and a good-smelling cedar closet where winter coats were stored. When she was younger, Franny spent a lot of time in the basement, sifting through the piles and boxes to see if there were any treasures to be found. Sometimes Lainie joined her. One year the two of them made a secret hideout down there out of some worn tablecloths and a couple of broken chairs. They called it the Crystal Cave and conducted magic ceremonies inside. The ceremony Franny remembered best involved mixing salt with sand and rose petals in a bowl and waving a magic wand, made of a Chinese backscratcher with a piece of sea glass tied to it, over the mixture. She couldn't recall what magic they were trying to work, only how fanciful the whole thing was.

As Franny got older, she lost interest not only in the Crystal Cave, but in the basement too. It had been a long time since she'd puttered around in it—until last night. Last night it had been the only place in the house that offered the privacy she'd needed.

Grandma stopped examining her feet. "Franny, you're growing up," she said gently. "You're too big to share a bedroom."

Franny started guiltily. This time she said quickly, "Oh no, Grandma. I don't mind sharing a room with

29

you. There are only three bedrooms in this house, and I'd much rather share one with you than with Lainie."

"But you could have Lainie's room and Lainie could move in here for a while. That would be fair. After all, Lainie's had her own room for years."

Franny blinked. Grandma was saying exactly what she herself had thought many times. My own room. Yes! Let Lainie suffer for a while. Oh, Franny, what a horrible thing to think. You're not suffering. You love Grandma. And she loves you. Besides, Lainie would make a horrible roommate. She's not used to tiptoeing around. I mean being quiet, sharing her space. "You trying to get rid of me, Grandma?" Franny joked.

"You bet," Grandma kidded her back.

"Well, you can't." Franny turned and looked at the clock on her night table. "Whoops! I've got to hurry or I'll be late."

"Don't rush off without eating your breakfast. Bad to start the day without a meal."

"I'll eat something, Grandma." Then, giving her a mock scolding, "You eat something too. You had dinner hours ago."

"You're right. And now I could eat a horse. Well, at least a pony. Come, let's have some breakfast together."

"Oh, Grandma, I really will be late."

30

"So I'll give you a note."

Franny chuckled. "Okay, you win. Let's go."

Franny was chewing her sandwich and thinking about that morning's breakfast with Grandma. By a stroke of luck they'd had the kitchen alone for a short time. Grandma'd fixed French toast, while Franny'd made the tea. They hadn't talked much. They hadn't needed to. For a change Franny'd left for school with a warm and full belly.

"Yeager, you eating or meditating?" a male voice asked. It was accompanied by the strong scent of cologne.

Franny coughed slightly and blinked. Eddie Porter, Susan's former beau, was standing next to her, a tray in his hand. Next to him was Larry Lefferts. Larry was almost as big as Eddie, but not quite as blond. Franny'd gone out with him a couple of times—double-dated with Susan and Eddie. They'd even fooled around a bit in the backseat of Eddie's car. But Franny didn't get much of a zing from Larry, and they shared the same taste in hardly anything.

"Both," Franny said to Eddie.

"Oh. Well, mind if we watch?"

She laughed. "Go right ahead." She got a kick out of Eddie. Even if he did look like a rump roast and wore too much cologne, he was smart and funny. He and Susan sometimes outdid each other with one-

31

liners. She wasn't sure why Susan had broken up with him—but then she was never sure why Susan broke up with any of her many boyfriends. "Carol and Greenie are sitting here too, as soon as Mr. Motta's finished talking with them," she told Eddie and Larry.

"That'll be sometime next week," Eddie said, referring to the college advisor's habit of talking his students' ears off.

"Wrong. Here they come now," said Franny.

"Well, that's okay. We can be big about these things. We will allow them to join us. Right, Larry?"

"Sure," Larry said. He wasn't paying much attention to Eddie. He was busy looking at Franny.

When she looked back at him, he winked.

He still likes me, Franny thought. Too bad I can't reciprocate.

"Hi, Franny. Hi, Eddie. Hi, Larry," Carol said.

"Hi, all," said Greenie.

Franny greeted them both. They were nice girls. She'd become friendly with them in gym class. She knew they'd never be close friends—not like Susan. But she thought they'd do for lunchtime companions.

"So what did Mr. Motta have to say for himself?" Eddie asked.

"Nothing," Carol answered.

"Nothing? My God, this is a Historical Day— November tenth, the Day Mr. Motta Was Struck Dumb."

"It isn't funny. Paula Rodriguez was in his office

crying her eyes out. He had to deal with her, so he never got to talk with us."

"Why was Paula crying?" Franny asked. She didn't know Paula well. Franny's father and Mr. Rodriguez were co-workers.

"Because her father said she couldn't go to college."

"That doesn't make sense. Paula's always been in the academic program."

"He said he couldn't afford to send her now that he'd been laid off. Mr. Motta tried to reassure her that she has almost two years before she became a freshman and her dad would surely have a new job by then. But if not, there were always scholarships and . . ."

Franny had stopped listening. Two words were reverberating in her head, the two words that the Yeagers lived in fear of: *laid off*. "They're talking about laying more people off," Mr. Yeager would say ominously.

"But you've been working there for twenty-one years," Mrs. Yeager would say. "They can't lay you off."

"Oh no? I'm one of the last people doing my job. They can lay me off. Me, John Rodriguez, who's been there almost as long as me, just about anybody now."

Franny leaped to her feet, bumping the table as she did so. Apple juice splashed out of Larry's cup onto his tray. "Excuse me," she said, and hurried out of the cafeteria.

33

She walked swiftly down the hall, trying, as she went, to slow down her rapid heartbeat. Finally she reached the pay phone and fumbled with the buttons until she got the numbers right. The phone rang once, twice, three times before her mother picked it up.

"Hello," Mrs. Yeager said.

"Hello, Mom. It's Franny."

"Franny? What's wrong?"

Franny paused. Her mother sounded concerned— but only about her. "Um, nothing, Mom," she answered.

"Nothing? Then how come you're calling from school? You are in school, aren't you?"

"Yes. Lunch period."

"Are you sick? Did you eat?"

"No. I mean, yes. I mean, no, I'm not sick. And yes, I ate." She took a deep breath. "Mom, is Dad all right?"

"Dad? Sure. I just talked with him, as a matter of fact."

"Oh. Good. He's at work?"

"Of course he is. Franny, what is all this about?'

Franny inhaled again. Her father still had his job. And he hadn't told her mother about John Rodriguez. Or else he didn't know yet. Should I tell her? Franny wondered. "I . . . uh . . . heard some rumors," she said slowly. "About people being . . . uh . . . laid off at the plant."

34

"You thought your father was laid off?" Mrs. Yeager asked.

"Well, uh, yes."

"Oh, poor Franny. You shouldn't have to worry about these things. You're only sixteen. You should be thinking about your schoolwork. And dating. You don't get out enough."

Franny didn't reply.

Her mother was silent a moment too. Then she asked, "These rumors, did Dad's name come up?"

"No."

Franny heard her mother give a sigh of relief. "See? You shouldn't worry. Now, go finish your lunch."

"Okay, Mom." Franny hung up. She stood still a moment. Then she turned and started slowly back down the hall. Today's the day, she told herself. Today's the day I'm going to get a job.

5

Franny's feet hurt. She'd been walking in and out of shops for the past two hours with no results. Oh, she'd filled out applications in four places, but nobody had been very encouraging about hiring her.

She sat down on a bench at a bus stop, slipped off her shoes, and rubbed her toes. Well, she thought, at least I've saved the best for last. She put her shoes back on, stood up, and headed for Artistic Temperament.

Hire me, hire me, hire me, she chanted silently, as she dragged her aching feet there. Please hire me. Please . . . "Oh!" In the window of the small gallery was an ornately lettered sign that said HELP WANTED. "I don't believe it!" Franny gasped. She hurried to the door, then stopped herself. Be cool, she warned.

36

Be calm. Be collected. She straightened her spine and sauntered inside.

There were more salespeople than customers inside. Two, in fact. A tall, slender young woman with gorgeous blond ringlets and a tall, slender, young woman with gorgeous red ringlets. Franny was wondering if someone had forgotten to remove the HELP WANTED sign when the blonde quickly approached her.

"May I help you?" she asked. "We're having a sale today on hand-dyed silk scarves and these mugs and candleholders." The saleswoman picked up a candleholder from a stand near Franny and held it out to her. It reminded Franny of something Ebenezer Scrooge might have on his night table.

"It's very nice," she answered politely, "but I—"

"It's only twelve ninety-nine today," the blonde went on. "Or you might prefer one of these mugs instead. Hand-thrown porcelain."

Franny glanced at the mug. It wasn't porcelain at all, but earthenware.

"Are you looking for a gift or something for yourself?"

"Something for myself," Franny said. "I'm looking for a job."

The saleswoman didn't hear her. "The scarves are beautiful. We have a blue-and-purple one that would look good with your—"

"I'm looking for a job." Franny cut her off loudly.

The other saleswoman and single customer turned to stare at her. In a lower voice, she said, "I saw the sign in the window."

The blonde frowned slightly. "Oh," she said. "You'll have to talk to Mr. Gerber. He owns the gallery." She started to walk off toward the scarf display.

"Is he here now?" Franny called, hating to raise her voice again.

"Yes."

"Would you tell him Franny Yeager is here for an interview?"

"Oh, all right," the blonde said irritably. She moved off to the back of the store.

Franny waited awkwardly in the same spot. It was several minutes before Mr. Gerber emerged. He was a portly, middle-aged man, wearing a bright sweater that Franny thought was a little bit too youthful for him.

"Hello, can I help you?" he asked. His eyes flicked rapidly over her.

She felt him take in her pony-tailed brown hair and short, not-so-slender shape. Uncomfortably, she said, "I've come about the job."

"Ever worked in a gallery before?"

"No, but I'm very interested in crafts. In school I've made pots and—"

"How old are you?"

"Sixteen."

Mr. Gerber nodded. "I'm afraid I'm looking for someone a bit older and more experienced. Someone who really knows crafts."

Like what's porcelain and what isn't, Franny thought. But she didn't say anything.

"Tell you what, though. I'll give you this application to fill out. If nobody else satisfactory shows up, I'll give you a call."

Franny had the urge to crumple the application and throw it in his face. But she forced herself to take out a pen and fill it out. Mr. Gerber instructed the blonde to collect the form from Franny, and then he disappeared back into his office.

Franny was nearly finished with the application when a tall, slender, young woman with gorgeous black hair (minus the ringlets) appeared. "I'm here about the job," she announced.

The blonde smiled at her. "Go right into Mr. Gerber's office. He's expecting you."

The brunette smiled back and went to the rear of the gallery.

When she disappeared, the blonde called to the redhead, "There's your replacement, Sasha." Then she turned to Franny. "Are you finished?" she asked impatiently.

With as much dignity as she could muster, Franny answered, "Yes, I am." She handed the application to the blonde and walked slowly out of the store.

It wasn't until she was four blocks away from there that she allowed herself to cry.

"That's disgusting! You should call the Better Business Bureau and bring that creep up on charges of job discrimination." Susan was indignant over the telephone.

"I don't think I—or they—would be able to prove anything," Franny said in a low voice. "He didn't refuse to hire me because of my sex or race."

"Well, you have to do something. At least go bawl him out. People like that think they can get away with anything if nobody lets them have it."

"It wouldn't help me get a job there."

"You don't want to work for a creep like that."

"Maybe he isn't such a creep, Sue. Maybe he just thinks that 'decorative' saleswomen sell more than ordinary-looking ones."

"That's sexist and disgusting," Susan reiterated firmly.

Franny paused, then said, "You're right. But what am I going to do for a job?" She was immediately sorry she'd asked that question.

After a slight hesitation, Susan said, "Well, there's another opening at Burger Bonanza."

Things aren't that desperate, Franny thought. She recalled her father's anger and fear at dinner when he'd talked about John Rodriguez and her mother's anxious glances at him and at Franny. Yet, she added

silently. "I think I'll try a few more places tomorrow," she said carefully. "If nothing turns up, maybe I'll be your fellow Burgerette."

"Okay, Franny," Susan responded. "But listen, if you need any help in getting Gerber or whatever the bum's name is, count me in."

"Thanks," Franny said, and hung up the phone.

She left the kitchen and went up to her room. Grandma was there soaking her feet in a plastic washtub. She looked lost in thought. She blinked when Franny closed the door. "I'm sorry, Grandma. Did I startle you?"

"No. I was just remembering."

"Do your feet hurt?"

"A little," Grandma said, lifting them and patting first one, then the other with a towel.

"Must be in sympathy with mine."

"Why do your feet hurt?" Grandma began to put on socks.

"I did a lot of walking today." She repeated her job-hunting story in a shortened form.

Grandma clucked her tongue. "Oh, Franny. What a nasty experience. You must feel just awful."

Although she'd described her experience more dispassionately to Grandma than to Susan, Franny found herself suddenly weepy again. When Grandma said, "Come here," and opened her arms wide, she blundered into them, bumping the washtub and sniffling.

Grandma shoved the tub out of the way and patted

41

Franny's back the way she always did when her grand-daughter got upset. "Some people should be taught a lesson," she said.

"That's what Susan just said," Franny responded, blowing her nose.

"How is Susan? I haven't seen her in a long time."

"Well, you're in for a treat. She's coming over on Sunday."

Grandma's wrinkled face lit up. "She is? Good. I'm glad."

"Me too." There was a pause; then Franny asked, "What were you remembering just before?"

"Oh." Grandma smiled. "I was remembering the apartment we used to live in before we moved out here, into this house. Do you remember it, Franny? You were very young."

"Sure I do. It was nice. Small, but nice. There were just three rooms. I slept in a crib in Mom and Dad's room until Lainie was born, then I got to sleep on the sofa bed with you. You used to tell me what it was like to live in Russia when you were a kid. And we'd both talk to the pair of pigeons that roosted outside our window."

"Do you remember what we called them?"

Franny thought, then smiled. "Yes. Bill and Coo."

"Right. What else do you remember about Eleven-oh-eight Grand Avenue?"

"Was that the address? I don't think I ever knew that. Let's see . . . Oh, I know. There was a great bath-

tub with feet there. And a wonderful old stove too."

"Not so wonderful. It almost exploded in my face one day."

"Oh no. Really? Where was I?"

"Out with your father. He'd taken you to the movies. He used to take you out somewhere almost every Sunday afternoon."

"He did?"

"Yes. You don't remember that?"

Franny frowned. "No, I . . ." She didn't finish the sentence, because suddenly there she was, a small, pale, timid three-year-old, sitting in a movie theater, perhaps on the very day Grandma had just described. On the screen soldiers were running, screaming as shells whistled and burst around them. She began to scream too. But someone took her hand and patted it. Her father.

"Shh, Franny. It's only a movie," he said. "They're not really shooting at them. It's only a movie."

She snuggled against him, burying her face in his nubbly sweater. It smelled like cigarette smoke. All his sweaters did.

"Shh. Shh," he kept saying as he stroked her hair. Finally, because she was still crying, he said, "This isn't a very good movie anyway," and hand in hand they left the theater.

Franny sighed. She was back in her bedroom. The memory had made her sad—not for what had been, but for what was gone.

43

Then her grandmother said, "Do you remember the elevator?"

Franny smiled again. "The elevator. I rode it by myself, up and down, up and down. And it always smelled like . . . garlic!"

Grandma laughed. "Mrs. Fell. She was always cooking."

Franny laughed too, then asked curiously, "Why were you thinking about the apartment, Grandma?"

"Oh, it just came up. It's one of my happy memories, living there."

"It was a good place. I wonder how Mom and Dad found it."

It was Grandma's turn to look surprised. "They never told you that?"

"No. Why? Is it a good story? Or a bad one?"

"Neither. I mean, it isn't much of a story. It was my apartment."

"Yours?"

"Yes. Mine and your grandfather's, may he rest in peace."

Franny's eyes widened. "You mean you didn't move in with Mom and Dad? They moved in with you?"

"Your father did. Your mother was already living there."

"Did you mind—his moving in?"

"No. I was happy Irene was getting married."

Franny didn't reply, and after a few moments

Grandma said, "Are you going to do your homework now?"

"I guess that's a good idea. Maybe I can do it while I soak my feet."

"I'll get you some fresh hot water."

"No, Grandma, I was only kidding." Franny protested.

But Grandma was already halfway out the door.

Hours later Franny couldn't sleep, whether from being overtired, depressed, tense, or all three, she wasn't sure. She got up, put a robe over her nightgown, and opened the bedroom door as quietly as she could. The hall was dark and quiet. Her parents were asleep. Lainie probably was too, Franny thought. Her door was closed and no light shone from under it.

Franny shut the door with a faint click and padded down two flights of stairs to the basement. The basement was partitioned into four rooms, one housing the boiler, the other three containing the Yeagers' accumulated junk. Franny flicked on the switch near the doorway, walked all the way to the back room, pulled the cord to turn on the light there, returned to the doorway and flicked off the switch, then went to the back room again. By the light of the single dusty bulb she wiped off a wobbly stool with an old blouse she found in a bag and sat down, surveying the space. In one corner were several risers with boxes on them

45

to keep them off the sometimes damp floor. A rug was rolled up on top of the boxes. Against the wall opposite Franny was a bunch of bags, boards, and metal mesh carriers, the kind milk cartons are transported in. They'd made temporary bookshelves for her room until she'd gotten real wooden ones. The rest of the room was filled with more bags and boxes, none of which were labeled. Franny got up and poked around in a few of the bags. One contained Barbie dolls and clothes. Another held lengths and scraps of material. Franny recognized a piece of expensive purple suede that Lainie had brought home with the loud announcement that she was going to make a vest. Needless to say, she never had. In a third bag, Franny found photographs: Polaroids, their colors faded and strange; black-and-white snapshots from somebody's defunct Brownie; artistic prints that Franny had attempted with her father's 35mm. At the bottom of these was a small stack of sepia portraits on stiff paper. Franny lifted one out to look at. It showed a family— father, mother, two boys, and a small girl, in suits and high-necked dresses, posed formally on and around a sofa. Everyone looked very solemn, except the little girl, who couldn't help grinning. There was engraved printing at the bottom of the photo. Franny tried to make it out and realized it was in Russian. She turned it over. On the back was more Russian, handwritten, and one word in English letters, inscribed by a child's hand: Anna.

"Grandma," Franny whispered. She turned over the picture again and stared at the face of the irrepressible little girl. She ran her finger down her cheek and started. At that age, Grandma had looked just like Lainie.

Franny slid it and the other photographs back into the bag and yawned. She left the room, repeating the same process with the lights in reverse, tiptoed up one flight of stairs, and froze. Someone was coming in the front door. "Who's there?" she whispered. "Who is it?"

"Aah! Oh God, Franny, is that you?" Lainie stepped forward, the door clicking loudly behind her.

"Lainie, what were you doing out at this hour?" Franny demanded, trying to keep her voice down.

"I couldn't sleep, so I went for a walk. What are you doing down here at this hour?"

Franny exhaled, and her body relaxed once more. "I couldn't sleep either," she admitted.

Lainie came closer and sat on the stairs. "I had this dream—"

"I thought you said you couldn't sleep," Franny interrupted.

"The dream woke me up, and then I couldn't fall back to sleep."

"What was the dream?"

"It was weird. I was in my room, trying on a dress. It was a kid's dress, and it was way too small for me, but I wore it anyway. In fact, everything in the room

47

was too small for me. Then I went downstairs. Mom and Dad were at the dining room table, all dressed up in a tuxedo and a ball gown, with a bunch of guests I didn't recognize. They were all dressed up too. I sat down on a chair and it was way too big for me. I was beginning to feel like Alice in Wonderland. Then you and Grandma walked in. I said hello to you, but I guess neither of you heard. You both sat at the table too. Nobody said anything. We all just sat there until a maid came in with a big soup tureen. She ladled out soup. When she got to me she said, 'Pass or fail.' " Lainie paused.

"What did you say?"

"I said, 'Pass.' " Lainie started to giggle.

"Then what happened?"

Lainie kept giggling. "I . . . didn't . . . get any . . . soup."

Franny snorted and clapped her hand over her mouth.

Suddenly they heard a door upstairs open and Mrs. Yeager's voice called, "What's going on down there? Lainie, is that you?"

Franny put her hand over Lainie's mouth before she could answer. "It's me, Mom," she answered.

"Franny? What are you doing out of bed?"

"Getting some . . . seltzer."

"Seltzer? You have an upset stomach or something?"

"No, I'm fine. Now."

48

"Then go back to bed."

"I will, Mom."

The bedroom door closed.

After a moment Lainie said, "You know what I think my dream means?"

"What?" asked Franny.

"Damned if I do and damned if I don't."

"Do or don't what?"

"I'm not sure. But I think it has something to do with growing up."

Franny didn't say anything. After another pause she started up the stairs. "I'm going back to bed. If you walk up with me, Mom won't know it's both of us."

"Okay," said Lainie.

The two of them climbed to their rooms together.

At her door Lainie said, "Good night, Franny. And thanks."

"You're welcome," Franny replied, and slipped into her bedroom.

6

"I'd rate that one a five. It's too wide and too flat," Susan said. "What do you give it?"

Franny glanced at the blue-jeaned butt moving away from her past a colorful display of potted chrysanthemums. "A five," she agreed. "The one with him's an eight."

"I'd say a seven. Nice shape, but too high up."

Another boy passed from the opposite direction. The seat of his jeans was baggy and wrinkled.

"A three," Susan and Franny said simultaneously, and laughed.

A group of kids walked by, then a fat middle-aged man.

"Jeez, not much around here today," Susan complained lightly. "We might as well find some other

form of amusement. Want to try on dresses at Salyer's?"

"Not really. I can't afford anything there."

"Neither can I, but it's fun to look at the stuff anyway."

"Not for me." Franny frowned. "Not these days."

"Did your father talk to his boss?" Susan asked quietly.

"He talked to the foreman. The foreman told him not to worry—he's too valuable to be laid off."

"That must've made him feel better, and you, too."

"Not really, because the foreman also told John Rodriguez a few weeks ago that he was too valuable to be laid off."

Susan nodded sympathetically. She and Franny fell silent a moment; then she snapped her fingers. "I know what we can do. Let's go over to Grosvenor. There's a great new thrift shop there that even *we* can afford."

You went all the way to Grosvenor? Franny's own voice echoed in her brain. To Susan she said, "Lainie got a hat there the other day."

Susan nodded again. "They've got great hats, and lots of other stuff."

Franny wasn't fond of thrift shops. She didn't like to wear other people's clothing, especially when each piece seemed to have some story behind it, one she'd never know. But she didn't want to nix another idea of Susan's, so she agreed to go.

The two girls rose from the low brick wall they were sitting on. It encircled a display of stuffed turkeys, donated by a local taxidermist, standing amid some shrubs.

"Poor things," Susan said, looking at the turkeys. "They're almost enough to turn me into a vegetarian. Almost, but not quite. Then again, if Burger Bonanza's burgers don't do that, nothing will."

Franny chuckled as she and Susan headed for the exit.

Grosvenor was a short street consisting of a few houses and a bunch of small stores that were constantly changing. Franny wasn't sure why shops opened and closed there with such frequency. She tried not to get attached to any place there because it couldn't be counted on to be around two months later. The store that had been there the longest was an ice-cream parlor. It held the record of ten months. On its first anniversary the whole street should have a party, Franny thought.

"Here it is," Susan said. "Cheap Frills."

They went inside the store and poked around, Susan enthusiastically, Franny half-heartedly. Susan found a beaded top from the 1950's. "Just perfect for the Christmas dance," she said as the cashier rang up the sale.

She was still bubbling about it when they left the store. "These sequins are fantastic. Must have been a

52

lot of work for someone to sew them on."

"Yes," Franny said, trying to share her friend's delight.

Suddenly a tall young man stepped out of a doorway some twenty feet ahead of them.

They didn't see his face—he'd turned too quickly. But they caught a good back view of the rest of him, clad in black pants and a black jacket with a blood-red dragon embroidered on it.

"Wow!" said Franny.

"Wow!" echoed Susan.

"A perfect ten!"

"What are we standing around here for? Let's follow him."

Before Franny could nix the idea, Susan was off, with Franny at her heels.

They reached the corner a few moments after the boy had turned it and looked down the street. He was nowhere to be seen.

"Where'd he go?" Susan asked. "He couldn't have disappeared into thin air."

"Maybe he went into one of these houses," Franny said.

"Or was abducted by a couple of other sex-starved women."

"Other?" said Franny.

Susan ignored her. "Or maybe he did disappear into thin air. A hunk like that couldn't really exist. He was probably a mirage."

They turned slowly back to Grosvenor.

"I wonder which shop he came out of," Susan said casually.

"I thought you just said he was probably a mirage," Franny teased her.

"I take it back. That tush was all too solid."

Franny raised an eyebrow at Susan and said, equally casually, "I think it was this one." She stopped in front of a shop, then gave an exclamation of pleasure. The shop was a florist's. It was called Petals. Franny'd never seen it before. She stared admiringly at the window. In it was a solitary flower arrangement made of crab-apple branches and mums in a low bowl. It looks Oriental, she thought. Japanese. I wonder who made it. The owner or some salesperson? Her mind did a little skip. God, it would be lovely to work in a flower shop.

"He couldn't have come out of here," Susan interrupted her thoughts. "It's closed." She pointed to the record store next to it. "It must've been this one."

"Hmmmm. I guess you're right."

"Oh well. He's gone. *C'est la vie.*"

Franny didn't reply. She was still looking at the flower arrangement. She could see herself inside the store. A dozen roses? Yes, sir, Would you like a card sent with that? Irises? We have two kinds—purple or white. The arrangement in the window. Yes, we do sell arrangements like that. I'll let you speak to—

"Franny, there's the bus!" Susan yelled, grabbing her hand. "Let's catch it!"

Franny gave her head a little shake. "Okay," she said.

The two of them dashed to the bus and made it up the steps just before the doors closed. They plopped into seats. Franny glanced out the window as the bus pulled away. I could've sworn he came out of there, she thought. Then the bus chugged ahead and the shop was no longer in view.

7

The TV set was loudly proclaiming the pleasures of some beer when Franny and Susan entered the Yeager house. Franny led Susan into the living room. "Hi, Mom. Hi, Dad," she said.

Her parents looked up from the TV. Mr. Yeager nodded at the girls and turned back to the set. Mrs. Yeager greeted them with "Hi, Franny. Hello, Susan. Nice to see you again."

"Nice to see you, too," Susan said.

The beer commercial ended and an automobile one began.

"That car's got the lousiest transmission on the market," said Mr. Yeager.

"Did you have a good time at the mall?" Mrs. Yeager, ignoring him, said to the girls.

"Yes. We went to Grosvenor, too."

"Grosvenor?" Mrs. Yeager made a face. "I don't like that area of town."

"Why not? It isn't dangerous," Susan said.

"It's . . . it's neither fish nor fowl."

"You mean it hasn't figured out what it is yet."

"Exactly."

"But that's what makes it sort of fun, don't you think?" said Susan. "Every time you go there, it's different."

"I don't enjoy that. I like things to stay the same."

Susan didn't reply to Mrs. Yeager's remark, and Franny was glad. She wanted to get away from the living room. Whenever she was in it—especially on Sunday afternoons with the TV blaring away—she wanted to curl up and fall asleep. "Where's Grandma?" she asked.

"Upstairs," her mother replied.

Franny sensed her grandmother didn't much like the living room either.

"And Lainie's out with friends." She frowned. "You should see how she was dressed. And all that makeup . . ."

Franny stifled a yawn. The commercial ended and the football game came back on. "Well, we're going up to see Grandma—" she began.

Susan cut her off. "Oh, it's the Jets and the Rams. Who's winning?"

"The Rams," Mr. Yeager said without taking his eyes off the television set.

"Too bad."

"You like football?" Franny's father asked, a bit surprised.

"Oh, yes, I think it's a game of staggering proportions."

Before Mr. Yeager could ask Susan what she meant by that, Franny said firmly, "We're going up to visit Grandma," and nearly dragged Susan out of the room.

"Staggering proportions?" she whispered as they headed up the stairs.

"Well, you must agree the proportions of just about everything on those guys are pretty staggering."

Franny giggled, and Susan joined in.

They composed themselves before they opened the door to Franny's room.

Grandma was in her chair, examining her feet again. The same washtub she'd used the day before was on the floor in front of her. She looked up with a start. "Oh, Franny and Susan. Oh my, what a way to greet guests." She reached for her socks.

But before she could get them on, Susan walked right over and hugged and kissed her. "Hello, Grandma Gallinsky. How are you?"

"Not bad for an old lady," she said.

"Grandma, are your feet still bothering you?" Franny

asked. She'd never seen her grandmother soaking her feet so often.

"A little. It's nothing much really."

"Here," Susan said, kneeling down beside her. "Let me massage them. I'm really good with feet. Even my mom thinks so."

"Oh no, Susie. You're a—" Grandma began.

But Susan already had hold of Grandma's right foot and was massaging the sole and arch. "Feels good, doesn't it?" she asked.

"I could've used you on Friday," Franny joked. "How come you're never around when I need you?"

"Now you just relax," Susan said, ignoring Franny. She rubbed and stretched Grandma's toes gently. When she finished with the right foot, she set it down and started on the left, repeating the same technique. She'd just reached the toes when Grandma stopped her. "Thanks, Susan. That was wonderful."

"I haven't finished yet."

"That's all right," Grandma said, trying to withdraw her foot. "You're my guest. We should go down and have some tea."

But Susan wouldn't release her foot. "What's this?" she asked, peering between Grandma's big toe and the one next to it.

"That? Oh, it's a sore. Don't worry about it." Grandma succeeded in removing her foot from Susan's grasp. She reached for her socks again.

59

"Have you had it a long time?" Susan asked.

"Not too long," Grandma said.

Franny knew instantly that she was lying. "Let me see, Grandma," she said.

"Now, Franny. You and Susan didn't come to look at my ugly feet."

"Let me see," Franny insisted.

Reluctantly, Grandma let Franny take her foot.

Carefully, Franny pried apart the toes and peered down at the sore. It was red, swollen, and oozing. "Grandma, that looks infected. Have you called Dr. Carver? I think he should look at this."

"Oh no, it isn't serious," Grandma said. "It's much better than it was. The soaking is helping it."

Franny looked doubtful, but Susan said, "Have you tried marigold cream on it? It's wonderful for sores. My mother uses it."

"No, I haven't tried that." Grandma smiled.

"I'll lend you Mom's. She won't mind. I'll give it to Franny tomorrow."

"That's very sweet of you."

"I still think you ought to show that to Dr. Carver," Franny said.

"I'll tell you what, Frannele. If it isn't better by the end of the week, I'll call your boyfriend, Dr. Carver. Okay?"

Franny knew she wasn't going to get any further with this discussion, so she just nodded.

Grandma quickly put on her socks. "Now, enough

about my feet. What did you girls do today?"

"Looked at butts in the mall," Susan replied swiftly.

"Oh, *tuchuses!*" Grandma said. Then, with a twinkle, "And did you see any nice ones?"

"Well, there was a really good one on Grosvenor Street, but it disappeared. We think it was a mirage, right?"

"Right." Franny's mouth was twitching with laughter.

"How do you mean mirage? Like a ghost?"

"Sort of, but not really," Franny explained.

"I saw a ghost once. In fact it was twice," Grandma said.

"You did?" said Susan. "I saw one once too."

"What was yours like?"

"You tell your ghost stories first. Then I'll tell mine."

For the next half hour Grandma and Susan swapped ghost stories, each one funnier and more exaggerated than the last.

Franny listened and laughed, but during the last story her mind drifted off. She pictured the three of them, herself, Susan and Grandma, on brocade cushions, sipping tea out of china cups and nibbling biscuits in a sunny, elegant dining room. On a satiny sideboard was a bowl of gorgeous flowers. Irises and forsythia, Franny's favorites. Grandma wore her best black dress. Susan was in red. And Franny had on a purple kimono covered with pale-blue butterflies.

"To our health," Susan toasted with her teacup.

61

"To our health," Grandma agreed.

Franny graciously nodded at them both.

When the tea party was finished, they all rose gracefully to retire, each to her own separate room.

"Franny! Franny! Susie, I think we put her to sleep," Grandma's voice was saying.

Franny blinked. "Oh. Oh, I'm sorry, Grandma, Susan. I was daydreaming."

"I bet I know about what," Susan said. "Dragon Boy."

"Dragon Boy?"

"The mirage," Susan explained. "He had on a black jacket with a red dragon on the back."

"I saw a real dragon once too," Grandma said.

"You're kidding!"

"Yes. I am," Grandma replied, deadpan.

Susan laughed. Franny joined in.

"Well, I've got to get home for dinner." Susan rose.

"Oh, my, we never even got to have tea and cookies," said Grandma.

"I did," Franny murmured, but neither Susan nor Grandma heard her.

8

The crab-apple-and-mum arrangement was no longer in the window. It had been replaced by a more elaborate yet still spare one of strange tufted grasses and twisty branches Franny couldn't identify. In fact the only thing she did recognize among the plants was a single orchid. It should have been terribly out of place there, but it wasn't. It was perfect.

Franny stepped back from the window toward the door of the flower shop. Then she stopped. The memory of her humiliation at Artistic Temperament rose up. What if the same thing happens here? she asked herself. Maybe I ought to give up on the whole idea. She turned to go. But another thought came to her. I can go into the shop and look around, pretend I'm a customer. That way I can check out the salesgirls

or assistants and maybe even the owner before I ask about a job.

Taking a deep breath, she turned back and, as nonchalantly as possible, stepped into the shop.

The scent of lilies greeted her. A big vase of them, white with blood-red spots and dangling anthers, stood on a shelf nearby. Their odor was so rich Franny felt a little woozy. She moved over to a vase of Dutch irises that had no smell at all.

She admired their shapely purple blooms for a while, and then glanced around the shop. It was quite small, with twelve or so vases of flowers on little platforms, several groups of house plants on stands and in hanging baskets, and a glass-doored cooler with more flowers inside. There were no people in the place—neither customers nor salespersons. Where is everybody, anybody? Franny thought. She glanced at the counter. A single vase stood there, near the cash register, with a pine branch and two roses in it. Next to the vase was a silver bell with a small sign underneath that read RING FOR ASSISTANCE.

Franny looked at the door, then back at the bell, and frowned. Here goes nothing, she told herself. In one fluid movement she strode to the bell, picked it up, and rang it.

As she waited for "assistance," she studied the vase on the counter. The pine branch was drooping heavily over the side. Without thinking, Franny moved it slightly. Better, she thought, and looked up to see a

short, sturdy woman with gray hair and remarkable gray eyes watching her.

Franny flushed with embarrassment. Great, she thought. I might as well leave right now. "I . . . um . . . sorry . . . the flower arrangements . . . uh . . . who does them?" she stammered.

"I do," the woman answered tersely, still watching Franny.

Worse and worse. "They're . . . uh . . . beautiful." Franny wanted to turn and run out of the store, but the woman's eyes held her. Their color was striking enough, but it was the *wiseness* in them that transfixed her.

The woman smiled, reached into her pocket, and pulled out a slim pair of shears. "Here." She offered them to Franny.

"I beg your pardon," Franny said, confused.

"In Japan it is traditional for the host to invite the guest to alter an arrangement any way she or he sees fit."

Franny's flush deepened. "Oh, I'm so sorry. I didn't mean to touch this. I—"

The florist walked around the counter and took Franny's hand. "Come," she said, leading her outside the shop. She stopped in front of the window. "So, how would you change this?"

"I wouldn't. It's perfect the way it is," Franny replied.

"Nothing's perfect—at least not from one moment

to the next," the woman said matter-of-factly. "So how would you change it?"

"I'd snip some of that branch off the left side."

"All right," the woman said, leading Franny back into the shop. She slapped the shears into her hand.

Franny nervously slid down the catch that locked the shears. She approached the arrangement and very carefully cut off a bit of a branch. Then she turned to the florist.

"Thank you," the woman said.

"Thank you," Franny responded. She handed over the shears and asked, "Do you teach that kind of flower arranging?"

"No. But I don't think that's why you came here, is it?"

"No, it isn't. Well, it is, but it isn't the main reason." Franny's voice cracked a little. "I came to ask about a job."

"All right, you're hired."

"I haven't worked before, but I—what did you say?"

"I said you're hired. I could use some help around here."

Franny blinked. Had she really heard what she thought she had? "You could?" she said. "I mean, you could! That's great! When do I start?"

"Don't you want to discuss your salary first?"

"No, I mean, yes, certainly."

"I'll pay you minimum wage for the first month. Then we'll see what you're worth. I'll need you Mon-

day through Friday from—when do you get out of school?"

"Two thirty."

"From three to six and all day Saturday. We're closed Sundays. Yes, I know it's a big shopping day, but it is *my* day of *rest*, and that's more important to me than making a lot of money."

Franny nodded. Then, with a little apologetic laugh, she repeated, "When do I start?"

"How about right now?"

"Oh, yes!"

"Splendid. Let me tell you what your duties will be. You'll sweep the floor, receive deliveries, pack the flowers, water the plants, change the water daily in the vases, throw out dying material, make bouquets and corsages, tie ribbons, and ring up and wrap purchases." She ticked the things off on her fingers.

Franny nodded at each duty.

"Good. What's your name?"

"Franny. Frances. Yeager."

"Which do you prefer, Franny or Frances?"

"Franny."

"Then Franny it is. I'm Lillian Morrison—Lillian to you. Don't call me Lil, Lily, or Mrs. Morrison."

Franny nodded again.

"Okay, now that we've got that straight, here's your first job." She took off her tunic and pitched it at Franny. "Hang this up on the hook in the back room. I'm going out for an ice-cream cone."

67

Franny was smiling out the bus window. She'd been smiling for the past three hours, all through the sweeping, watering, and answering the phone in the flower shop. Now a song Grandma sometimes played on the stereo came into her head. Something about how things were looking up. She hummed the tune, trying to remember the lyrics.

"George and Ira Gershwin," a gravelly voice across from her said.

She turned her head.

The white-haired man sitting in the seat opposite her repeated, "George and Ira Gershwin wrote that. You're a girl with good taste."

"I'm a girl with a job," Franny answered jauntily.

"Congratulations. What is it?"

"I'm assistant to a florist."

"Well, your landscape really is covered with four-leaf clover."

"I beg your pardon?"

Without any hesitation or visible embarrassment, the man began to sing in a gravelly but tuneful voice:

"Things are looking up!
I've been looking the landscape over
And it's covered with four-leaf clover.
Oh, things are looking up
Since love looked up at me."

Franny smiled again and blushed.

The man went on, and sang all the way to the end of the song.

The other passengers on the bus applauded. Franny just kept blushing and smiling.

Then the bus braked at a corner.

"Oh, this is my stop," Franny said.

The man saluted her. "Good luck." He winked.

Franny grinned at him and hopped off the bus. She ran up the street to her house, flung open the door, and went straight to the kitchen, where she expected to find her mother cooking dinner. She was nearly bursting with her news. The friendly man on the bus had heightened her giddiness.

"Mom! Mom!" she called. Then she stopped short. Her mother was in the kitchen, but she wasn't cooking. She was sitting at the table, staring into space.

Franny's excitement died swiftly. "Mom, what is it?" she asked cautiously.

Mrs. Yeager looked up. "Oh, Lainie, I mean Franny— What time is it?"

"Six thirty."

"That late?"

"Yes."

Mrs. Yeager got up slowly. "Your father called and said not to put up dinner yet. He said there was going to be a union meeting after work today. Mr. Maney is going to speak to them."

Franny's stomach seized up. Mr. Maney was the

69

owner of the plant. As far as Franny knew, he never spoke to anybody. But she said, "Well, maybe it's a good thing. Maybe he'll have something encouraging to say."

"Maybe," Mrs. Yeager said, but she didn't sound very convinced. Then she asked, "How was your day? You're home late."

"Yes." Franny no longer felt eager to tell her mother her news. "I got a job."

"A job? That's good, Franny. That's very good. What is it?"

Franny told her, but she didn't think her mother was listening very well. "I rang up three sales today. And Lillian—she's the owner and the designer, that's what a florist is called—Lillian got some big phone orders, one for a wedding, another for a bar mitzvah. Lillian says that's how she makes most of her money— doing flowers for parties. The shop itself doesn't get a lot of customers during the week, she says. But on Saturdays and holidays it can be pretty crowded. And the rest of the time there's plenty of work to do too. That's why she hired me as her assistant. Her first assistant. She's never hired anybody before, except for the delivery boy."

"That's nice, dear," Mrs. Yeager said distractedly. She glanced anxiously at the phone.

"Well, I guess that's about all I have to say about the job for now," Franny finished awkwardly.

There was a tense silence in the room until Grandma and Lainie came in.

"Grandma was teaching me how to embroider," Lainie said, "so I can embroider one of my blouses."

"You?" Franny said, without thinking.

"Yeah, me. What's so odd about that?"

Franny tried to correct her tone. "Nothing. It's just I never thought you were very craft oriented."

"You think you're the only one with talented hands in this house?"

"Franny doesn't think that," Grandma interrupted. "And you should show her what you did. It's very good."

"I'd like to see it," Franny said politely.

Mollified, Lainie said, "Okay, I'll go get it." She stood up, but before she left she looked at her mother. "Hey, Ma, where's Dad? Aren't we eating soon?"

"I don't know when we're eating," Mrs. Yeager answered tensely.

"Dad's at a meeting," Franny explained.

She and Lainie locked eyes. Lainie immediately read the concern in Franny's. "Oh. Well, I'm not that hungry yet anyway," she said.

Franny thanked her silently for being agreeable. "Let's go upstairs. You can show me the embroidery in your room."

The two sisters had just started up the stairs when they heard the front door open.

71

"Dad," Lainie said in what, for her, was nearly a whisper.

Franny froze next to her. Her happy day was slipping away from her, along with her father's job. Please, please, please, no bad news. Not tonight, she prayed silently.

The two girls stood there and listened to their father's footsteps tread heavily into the kitchen. They heard his voice rumble something, but they couldn't tell what it was. Their mother's lighter voice answered him, but again the words weren't clear.

"Franny, Lainie!" Mrs. Yeager suddenly called, and both of them jumped. "Come in quickly."

Franny and Lainie looked at each other helplessly, then went back to the kitchen. They stood uncertainly in the doorway.

"Tell them, Gene," Mrs. Yeager said.

They turned to their father. "Get your coats," he said. "We're all going out to dinner."

"What?" Lainie yelled.

"We're going out to *dinner*?" Franny asked, equally incredulous. The last time the Yeagers had gone out to dinner was nearly five months ago.

"Yes. Dinner. You know, that meal we have in the evening," Mr. Yeager said dryly, but there was a twinkle in his eye.

"Mr. Maney told the men there'd be no more layoffs. Your father's job is safe!" Mrs. Yeager said, smiling widely.

"Hallelujah!" cheered Lainie.

"Thank goodness!" said Franny.

"So we're going out to celebrate." Mrs. Yeager paused, remembering something. "Franny, we can celebrate your job too."

"You got a job?" Mr. Yeager and Lainie said simultaneously.

"Yes. Yes, I did," Franny said, the excitement of the day flooding back to her.

"Congratulations, Frannele," Grandma said. "You can tell us all about it while we *eat.*" She patted her stomach and smacked her lips.

Franny grinned at her.

The Yeager family all went out to get their coats.

As Franny got into hers, the song came back to her. " 'Things are looking up,' " she sang under her breath. Then, being a Yeager, she added, "Maybe."

9

By Thursday Franny was beginning to believe the good times really might be here to stay. Her father's scowl was gone. Her mother had stopped bowing and scraping around him. And even Lainie was quieter.

One night the four of them, and Grandma, went bowling together. Lainie knocked down exactly one pin in ten frames. Franny didn't do much better, with a final score of twenty-two. They laughed themselves silly. Mr. Yeager proclaimed them the Pinheads, which Lainie changed to the Gutter Girls. Their mother declared that that sounded like a punk rock group.

"Hey, yeah," Lainie agreed. "Good-bye, FraLainie. Here come the Gutter Girls. We're mad. We're bad. We rock and roll . . ."

74

"But we can't bowl," Franny joined in, and everyone laughed some more.

Yes, things were definitely better in the Yeager family.

As for Franny's job, the only word for that, as she told Susan, was "fabulous." With Thanksgiving only a week away, Petals was incredibly busy with orders for bouquets, centerpieces, and floral decorations, especially from local restaurants. Lillian already had Franny working on the bouquets and corsages. "You have a real feel for flowers," Lillian told her. Franny was thrilled. In her opinion Lillian was a master, and to be complimented by her was high praise indeed.

Most of the decorations and arrangements Lillian provided were in what she called the "Western" style—lavish, symmetrical bunches of flowers with colors harmonious to the American eye. Her Japanese arrangements, which Franny had learned were called *ikebana*, she rarely sold. They were more for herself, Lillian said.

Franny understood that, although she couldn't see why other people didn't want to buy or order them when they were so much more exquisite, in Franny's opinion, than the "stuffed vase" kind. She was hoping that Lillian would teach her the Japanese art, but so far the florist hadn't offered to. However, that Thursday afternoon, while Franny was getting some carnations from the large cooler in the back room, she

75

noticed a book lying on the small desk near it. *Ikebana: Zen Flowers* was its title. Unable to resist, Franny began to look through it.

Life is change, she read. *Day turns to night. The tide ebbs and flows. The flower blooms and dies. So it is with Man. He is here—he is gone. If he has lived his life well, it is with the knowledge that this is so. All things must pass. All but the soul, which is immortal. To know this and to live serenely, in harmony with nature, is to be enlightened.*

Enlightenment is the destination, but many roads lead to that point. One path is through the contemplation of the flower. Flowers are among the most fleeting of life forms. But the soul of the flower never dies. That is why the masters of ikebana say, "Flowers may be cut, but not killed." In ikebana you must become one with the flower. You must understand its soul. Thus you may understand your own.

"There you are," Lillian said.

Franny looked up with a start. "I'm sorry, Lillian. I . . ."

Lillian waved away the apology. "I see you found old Kizu."

"Kizu?"

"The author of the book you're holding. He's not bad, although a bit *florid* for my tastes, if you'll excuse the pun. You can borrow that if you want to."

"May I really?" Franny asked excitedly.

"I wouldn't have said you could if I didn't mean it," Lillian said, sounding cranky and overworked.

Franny ignored the crankiness. "Thank you, Lillian. Thanks a lot."

Lillian waved her hand again. "Now, where are those carnations?" she demanded.

"Right here," Franny said, snapping to attention.

"Good. Now let's go work on another vase stuffer."

On the bus ride home Franny was so caught up in the book that she nearly missed her stop. She floated toward her house, her head filled with strange new words: *moribana, shoka, nageire*; *shin, soe, tai*; *mizagawa.* She was especially enthralled by the word—and idea of—*tokonoma*, the meditation alcove or shrine found in every traditional Japanese home. In each tokonoma was a scenic or floral scroll that was changed each season, an incense burner or treasured art object, and a flower arrangement. It wasn't just the aesthetics that intrigued her, but the idea of harmony with nature, with the world, with oneself, through art—an art involving something as lovely as flowers.

She was still thinking about all those ideas when the Yeagers sat down to dinner.

"What're we having?" Mr. Yeager asked.

"Tuna casserole," his wife answered.

"Tuna casserole? We had that a couple of days ago."

"I know, Gene, but there was a big sale on tuna at the Save More, so I stocked up."

"A growing man needs steak, Irene, not tuna fish," Mr. Yeager bantered.

"It depends on which way he wants to grow," Mrs. Yeager countered.

Mr. Yeager patted his stomach. "Nothing wrong with my weight. I still wear the same size pants I did when we were married."

"In the length maybe—but not the waist."

Mr. Yeager gave his wife a fish-eyed stare. Then he said, "Anyway, we can afford a little more meat on this table now that things have settled down at the plant."

"Then maybe we can afford an increase in my allowance, too," Lainie spoke up.

A silence fell over the table. Mrs. Yeager shot Lainie a warning look. If she'd been paying any attention, Franny would have found herself growing tense. But she wasn't, so she didn't react—not even when her father said, "We'll talk about it later," in what for him was an encouraging tone. Nor did she notice her mother's shoulders relaxing or Lainie grinning into her casserole.

"Who wants some more salad?" Mrs. Yeager said happily. "Franny?"

Franny didn't reply.

"I think she's off in dreamland," Lainie said.

"Or coming up with plans to soak her old man for money too," said Mr. Yeager jovially.

"Frannele, are you okay? You're not touching your food," Grandma said.

Franny blinked and looked up. Her whole family was staring at her. She stood up.

"Where are you going?" her father asked.

"Isn't it . . . uh . . . it's my turn to clear the table, isn't it?"

"You doof, nobody's finished eating yet," Lainie said good-naturedly.

"Oh," Franny sat back down. "Sorry." Then, seeing her dinner for the first time, she forked some casserole into her mouth.

"What's with you?" Mr. Yeager said. "Didn't you get enough sleep last night?"

"You okay, Franny?" asked her mother. "Your job and school and all, it isn't too much for you?"

"She's probably just stoned," Lainie said.

"Lainie!"

"You don't have to yell at me, Ma. It was just a joke."

"I'm fine, Mom," Franny said, "I was just thinking about a book I was reading. Lillian lent it to me."

"Lillian." Mrs. Yeager shook her head. "I know you said she asked you to call her that, but it sounds so impolite."

"What kind of book?" Grandma asked.

Franny turned to her gratefully. "It's on ikebana."

"Ikebana? What's that?"

"Sounds Jap to me," Mr. Yeager put in.

Franny winced. For the past few years her father'd sounded as though it was nineteen forty-two and the Japanese were the enemy. Franny knew it had to do with fear for his job, but she couldn't stand his attitude just the same. "It is Japanese," she said. "Japanese flower arranging."

"Flower arranging. How nice! My mother used to do that when I was a girl," Grandma said.

"Damn Japs. Ruined the auto industry," Mr. Yeager muttered, viciously spearing a lettuce leaf.

"Have some more salad, Gene," Mrs. Yeager said, quickly lifting the bowl. "Guess who I saw at the supermarket today?"

Mr. Yeager ignored her.

And Grandma asked Franny, "How is Japanese flower arranging different from American flower arranging?"

Franny's face lit up. "Well," she said excitedly, "I'm only just learning about it, but . . ." She described some of the things she'd read. She was so enthusiastic, her family couldn't help listening.

"It sounds interesting," Grandma said.

Franny beamed.

"It sounds like typical Jap mumbo jumbo to me," her father said. "Watch out—they'll find a way to wreck the flower industry too. Use fewer flowers, sell the stuff cheaper, and *bang*, you'll be out of a job."

80

Lainie began to giggle. "The fl-flower industry!" she choked out.

"What's so funny, Miss Yeager? You think they wouldn't like to corner every market they can?"

Oh, Dad. Franny sighed. Why did he have to disappoint her again when he'd been so much more pleasant lately? She stood up. "Excuse me. I've got to go to the bathroom," she said, leaving the kitchen.

Lainie's giggles and her father's annoyed exclamations followed her all the way up the stairs.

It was three o'clock in the morning and Franny had just sneezed twenty times. She was covered with dust and sweat. Her pajamas were clinging to her and she had to use the bathroom. But her eyes were gleaming. In the back room of the basement, where before there'd been nothing but bags and boxes, there was now a shrine—or at least the beginnings of one. Franny had cleared out the space, made two low shelves with the boards and milk crates, beaten out a rug, and placed it over two old cushions for a seat. She'd found an old poster, a still life with fruit and flowers, from the Metropolitan Museum of Art. Her aunt had sent it to her years ago, and it had hung in Franny's room until they'd decided to paint the walls. She hadn't remembered where the poster'd gone and was delighted to find it, even if it was slightly wrinkled and ripped on one corner. Along with the poster she'd uncovered a

81

small brass candlestick. She'd placed it on one shelf and next to it laid the small incense burner she'd kept in her dresser drawer but never used.

Franny sat on her seat and stared at her handiwork. It's a real tokonoma, she thought. All it needs now is one thing: a flower arrangement. I'm going to learn ikebana. If Lillian won't teach me, I'll learn it from a book. But I *will* learn it.

She nodded her head firmly and sneezed three more times.

10

"So given that information, if Lincoln hadn't been assassinated, what would the Reconstruction period have been like in the South? Ms. Yeager?"

In response, Franny let out a dainty snore.

The class laughed.

"Well, I see that my teaching is not as inspiring as I thought it was," Ms. Coleman said.

Susan poked Franny.

"All things are positive and negative," Franny said clearly.

The class laughed again, and Franny's eyelids shot open. She realized with a start she'd been asleep in history class, and she turned red. "I'm sorry, Ms. Coleman," she said, mortified. "I didn't sleep much last night."

"Then it's fortunate that you have the weekend to catch up," the teacher said, and focused on another student.

Franny lowered her head and her eyes. She was still embarrassed. She'd never conked out in class before, especially history, where in order to pass Ms. Coleman's rough exams you had to be alert all the time. If I'm going to work on my tokonoma, I'll have to do it earlier, she thought.

History ended a few minutes later, and Franny tried to ignore her classmates's friendly teasing as she left, with Susan at her heels.

"What were you doing that you didn't sleep last night?" Susan asked as they walked to their next classes.

"I was building a shrine," Franny said.

"To whom? The all-too-fleeting memory of Dragon Boy?"

"No. It isn't a shrine to anybody. It's just a place to sit and . . . uh . . . meditate."

Susan raised one eyebrow. "Since when do you meditate?"

"I'm thinking of starting. Ikebana's related to Zen."

"Ikebana?"

"Japanese flower arranging."

"Oh," Susan said, nodding. "Is Lillian teaching you that?"

"Not yet—but soon, I hope."

"That's great, Franny." They reached Susan's class-

room. "Oh listen, before I forget, do you want to double-date Sunday afternoon?"

"With whom?"

"Me, of course, and Eddie and Larry."

This time Franny raised her eyebrow. "You're dating Eddie again?"

"Just this Sunday," Susan said defensively.

"Of course," Franny replied wryly.

"So, how about it? Larry still likes you."

I know, Franny thought. Too bad I don't feel the same way. But it wouldn't hurt to get out more often. And besides, I'd get to be with Susan. "Okay," she said.

"Great!" Susan responded, and zipped into her room.

As Franny headed for hers, she felt a funny knot in her stomach—the kind she got when she made plans she didn't really want to keep.

Then the late bell rang. "Damn!" Franny swore aloud and sped toward her class. "This just isn't my day."

That feeling continued at Petals. Franny accidentally hung up on an important customer, knocked over a vase, and dropped a bag of decorative pebbles. The vase didn't break, but the bag did split, scattering the pebbles all over the floor. Lillian slipped on one of them and nearly fell down.

Franny kept apologizing profusely until Lillian had

85

to tell her that one "I'm sorry" was enough. It's obviously not the right day to ask her about teaching me ikebana, Franny thought. She resolved to go to bed early that night and get to work early the next day too. Then I'll ask her, Franny said to herself. With that thought, she picked up a watering can and promptly tipped it all over a shelf. "Oh, Lillian, I'm so . . ." she began.

Lillian gave her a baleful look.

"Sociable. I'm very sociable," Franny finished. "Don't you think?"

Lillian snorted. "I can think of another word for you." But she patted Franny's back and went to get a sponge.

The next day, well rested, Franny was ten minutes early for work. Today I'll ask her about ikebana, she thought as she headed into the store.

Lillian came out from the back carrying a brand-new arrangement for the window, a Japanese version of Thanksgiving, Franny thought, with bittersweet, orange mums, and yellow-spotted acuba. "Good morning," the florist greeted her.

"Hi," Franny said. Then, casually, "I've been reading that book you lent me."

"Oh, which one was that?" Lillian asked, grunting as she bent to place the arrangement in the window.

"The one on ikebana."

"Oh, yes. It's pretty good. But don't believe everything you read."

Franny didn't ask her what she meant by that. Instead, she said, "The moribana form is very lovely, isn't it? So is the nageire. But the shoka, that's the true test of the artist, isn't it?"

"No," Lillian answered. "Would you start clipping the bottoms of those roses? Make 'em last a little longer."

Deflated, Franny obeyed.

The shop was busy all morning. Franny didn't have the chance to bring up the topic of ikebana again until lunchtime.

"You go out first," Lillian told her. "And make sure to eat. You're a growing girl."

Franny smiled. For just that moment, Lillian reminded her of her grandmother. Then she said, "You know, I *am* sorry I was so clumsy yesterday. But it was because I was tired from Thursday night." She waited for Lillian to ask her what had happened Thursday night. When the designer didn't, she was forced to go on. "You see, I was up till past three in the morning. I was making a tokonoma."

Finally, Lillian did speak. "What's a tokonoma?" she asked.

Franny was taken aback. Was Lillian joking? "It's a place to meditate. Every Japanese home has one. There's a scroll in it, and an incense burner and flower arrangement."

"Oh, yes. Is that what they call it?"

Two customers walked into the shop. Lillian greeted them and, out of the corner of her mouth, said to Franny, "You'd better take that lunch break now while you still have the chance."

Disappointed once again, Franny left.

It was nearly closing time. Franny was frustrated. She'd tried twice more to ask Lillian to teach her ikebana and failed. Now she was in the back room putting some irises into the cooler. She looked over at the desk, on which sat an empty low bowl. The bowl was a beautiful, glossy green. Franny'd never seen it before. She ran her fingers around the rim. Then she noticed that inside was a *kenzan*, a round metal form with needle-sharp points sticking up from it to hold flowers and branches in place. Franny looked at the irises in her hand and impetuously began sticking them into the kenzan.

"Take out two of them," Lillian said.

Franny whipped her head around. "Oh, Lillian. I'm so . . ."

"Yes, I know, sociable. Sociable Franny. Take out two of them."

"Which ones?" Franny asked hopefully.

"These two." Lillian pointed.

"Why?"

Lillian smiled. "I see I'm going to have to teach you some ikebana after all."

"Oh! Oh, Lillian, would you? Would you please.

88

I've been trying all day to ask you. When can I have my first lesson?"

"How about tomorrow?"

"Tomorrow? But it's Sunday, your rest day."

"So? Ikebana is very restful."

"What time?"

"Not too early. Say ten thirty?"

"Oh, yes. Ten thirty's fine."

"Good. Now it's closing time, so scrammez-vous," Lillian said.

"Okay," said Franny. "See you tomorrow." As she glided out of the shop and waited at the corner for the bus, it seemed to her that the auto lights were like shining chrysanthemums and the air was sweet with their perfume.

11

"Ouch," Franny said. She was washing her hair and had just gotten soap in her eyes. She'd awakened early and thought she'd have plenty of time to get to her lesson, but Lainie had hogged the bathroom for forty-five minutes, so now she was having to hurry.

Franny reached out from behind the shower curtain for the towel she kept nearby. But she didn't find it. Her eyes still blurry and stinging, she drew aside the curtain, whose plastic hooks squeaked horribly on the metal shower rod, and stumbled out of the tub in search of the towel rack. Hands outstretched, she shuffled forward and grabbed something. At the same moment Franny realized it didn't feel like terry cloth, a sharp voice yelled, "Hey, watch it. That's my new shirt."

90

"Lainie? Give me a towel, for Pete's sake," Franny demanded. Lainie tossed one into her hand. She wiped her eyes with relief. When she could see again, she looked at her sister, who, with Franny's missing towel draped around her neck, was putting on eye shadow. How come I never lock the door the way she does? Franny thought. "Lainie, what are you doing in here again?" she said aloud. "Wasn't forty-five minutes enough time?"

"My eye shadow wasn't right," Lainie answered calmly.

"Why didn't you fix it in your room? You've got a vanity there." To Franny's dismay, her voice was rising.

"The light is better here. Relax, Big Sis. I'll be out of your way soon. You got a hot date or something?"

"I have a lesson at ten thirty. What about you? Do you have a hot date?"

Lainie paused before she answered. "Maybe."

"What does that mean?"

"It means yes, if I pick up some hunk."

"You're going out to pick up boys?"

"What's wrong with that? You and Susan go butt watching, don't you?"

"Yes, but . . ." But we only watch, we don't touch, Franny almost said. She was glad she didn't, because 1) it wasn't completely true—especially in Susan's case; 2) Lainie, as far as she knew, didn't touch either. She was all talk and no action.

Franny got back into the shower to finish rinsing her hair. "I forgot to ask you," she called. "Did you ever get that raise in your allowance from Dad?"

"Yes. A measly three bucks," Lainie said. "And it doesn't start until next month. Still, it's better than nothing. And to tell you the truth, I was surprised Dad gave it to me, especially after I laughed at him the other night. He's such a racist. What I wouldn't give to bring home a Japanese boyfriend!"

Anything to start an argument, Franny thought. But she didn't say anything, just shut off the shower, got out of the tub once more, and wrapped a towel around her body and another over her head.

"Done," Lainie said. She turned to Franny and batted her lashes.

"Lovely," Franny, who rarely wore makeup, said.

"What do *you* know?" Lainie sniffed, and tossing her towel on the floor, sashayed out of the bathroom.

Shaking her head, Franny picked up the eyeshadow–dusted towel and dropped it in the hamper.

When Franny arrived at ten thirty-seven at Petals, Lillian wasn't there yet. The store was locked and the "Closed" sign was hanging in the door. We'll leave the sign up, Franny thought, so no one bothers us. She smiled to herself, then tapped her foot. Where's Lillian? she wondered, impatient to begin her lesson. She looked up and down the street. There was no sign of the woman. I know. I'll study this arrangement in the

92

window so I can ask her questions, Franny thought.

Five minutes later she tapped her foot and looked up and down the street again. Hooray! There was Lillian at last. Franny waved.

Lillian waved back and ambled up to her. "You're very punctual," she said, unlocking the door and ushering the two of them in.

"I can't wait to get started. Which will you teach me first, shoka, nageire, or moribana? Or how about free style," Franny babbled. "I was reading up on the shin, soe, and tai lines, and I think I understand the basic idea." She talked on and on. Lillian didn't say a word until they got to the back room. Then she commanded, "Sit down, Franny, and take a deep breath."

Confused, Franny did so.

"Good. Now throw all that stuff you just spouted out of your head and listen to me. Don't talk, just listen—and breathe."

The bowl and kenzan Franny had played with the day before were still on the desk. From the cooler Lillian took three gladioluses. She snipped the stems of two of them, so the three were now of varying heights. "Heaven." She held up the tallest. "Man." The middle one. "Earth." The shortest. "For now, you will use these three lines. In moribana you take your pinholder and divide it into quarters. You place the flowers in one, two or three of those quarters. But you always leave one quarter free. Got that?"

Franny nodded.

"When you look down at the plants, their tops should form a triangle. Okay, here are the gladioluses, plus two more you can use as 'filler.' Here's some shears if you need them. Let's see what you can do."

Franny swallowed hard. "All right," she said, and began to work.

An hour and a half later, after trial and error, Franny had made two simple arrangements, which Lillian had taken apart and redone to show her what was correct. Lillian also explained more about line, form, and placement. Finally, the florist said, "Okay, that's enough for today."

"Oh no," Franny said. "One more, please."

Lillian smiled. "You sure have stamina. Okay. We'll get a little more complex now. I'm going to give you three types of plants. You create a moribana arrangement with them while I go out and get us some sandwiches." With that, she left.

Franny picked up the eucalyptus branch Lillian had handed her. Turning it this way and that, she finally placed it in the kenzan. "Heaven. Shin," she said. Next she reached for a tall spider mum. She measured it against the eucalyptus, cut it down, and measured it again. Satisfied, she fixed it in front of the branch. "Man. Soe." Then, trimming them too, she added a second and third mum. Last, she put a cedar twig behind the eucalyptus. "Earth. Tai," she murmured, and sat back to admire her work.

"Ugh!" she exclaimed, took apart the whole thing, and started all over.

She'd just finished when she heard a sound in the doorway. "Lillian, what do you think?" she asked, looked up, and gasped.

The figure in the doorway was not Lillian. He was a boy, perhaps a year or two older than Franny, dressed all in black—and he was the handsomest boy she'd ever seen. He had black hair that fell across his forehead; dark, almond-shaped eyes; high cheekbones; a flat nose; and full lips. He looked Japanese.

It took Franny a moment to speak. "We're . . . we're closed," she said.

The boy didn't answer, only smiled slowly.

"How did you get in? The door was locked."

The boy kept smiling. Insolently, Franny thought. She didn't know whether or not to be afraid. The boy was so handsome, but so strange.

"Look, whoever you are, you'd better go." She moved her hand, and her fingers touched the shears. Please, don't let me have to use them, she thought.

"Where is Lillian?" the boy asked. His voice was low and musical.

"Getting our lunch. She'll be back any minute."

"Then I'll wait."

"No, you won't!" Franny's hand closed on the shears.

The boy moved back, startled by her outcry. "All right. Then I won't wait," he said. He walked backward toward the door.

Franny followed him, the shears in her hand. When he got to the door, he turned and fled.

It was then Franny saw that embroidered on the back of his jacket was a fierce red dragon.

12

Franny splashed some cold water on her flaming cheeks. Dragon Boy. He was here. He was gorgeous. And I chased him away with a pair of shears, she thought. How stupid can you get? She patted her face with a paper towel. Then again, he did act weird. Maybe he is weird. Just because he's gorgeous doesn't mean he isn't a thief or something.

But she knew she didn't really believe he was. Well, I'll never find out. He won't set foot in this place again, she thought ruefully. Then she remembered—he'd asked for Lillian. Does that mean he really knows her—and that she knows him? And if she does . . . Franny's cheeks reddened again. Suddenly she was nearly bursting with impatience for Lillian to return.

The phone rang. Franny ignored it. The shop was

officially closed, and the answering machine would take any messages. She heard the click that signaled that it was doing its job.

Stop thinking about Dragon Boy, she told herself, and concentrate on your ikebana. Are you satisfied with this arrangement? Will Lillian think it's any good?

Suddenly, Lillian's voice pierced the air. "Franny, are you there? Pick up the phone, Franny."

With a start, Franny realized that Lillian was talking through the answering machine. She ran to the counter and grabbed the phone. "Hello, Lillian? It's me. I'm here."

"Franny, listen. There's been an accident. The man here at the deli cut his thumb rather badly while making our sandwiches. I'm going to drive him to the hospital. Don't know when I'll be back. Lock up. There's an extra key under the big bella palm. See you tomorrow."

"But my lesson—" Franny got out and was immediately embarrassed. The deli man's sliced thumb was a lot more important than her lesson.

"To be continued," Lillian said, and hung up.

Franny put down the phone. Her stomach rumbled with hunger, and that embarrassed her too. At least I didn't try to ask her about Dragon Boy, she thought, stroking her warm forehead.

She moved into the back room and looked at her moribana once more. I'll leave it here. Lillian will see it first thing tomorrow. Maybe she'll have time to give

me suggestions when I come in. Then Franny began to straighten out the desk, sweeping away leaves and stems into a wastebasket. She picked up the shears to wipe them clean and shook her head again. "So stupid," she murmured. "Wait'll I tell Susan—Oh, my God!" Her hand flew to her mouth. "Susan!" She looked at her watch. One twenty-five. In less than five minutes, she was supposed to meet Susan, Eddie, and Larry at the movie theater in the mall.

"Stupid!" Franny swore at herself as she struggled into her jacket, hauled aside the palm, found the key, locked the door, and dashed to the bus stop.

"There she is!" Eddie called.

"I know you wouldn't desert us!" said Susan.

"I'm sorry I'm late. I was having a lesson and I lost track of the time. . . ."

"A lesson? In what?" Susan asked.

"Ikebana."

"Oh, great! You got Lillian to teach you."

"What's ikubana?" Larry said, mispronouncing the word.

"Japanese flower arranging."

"Oh," he said, and didn't ask any further questions.

"Well, people," said Eddie. "What film shall we see? *The Crawling Dead*, *Sorority Summer Vacation*, or *Alligator Bundy*? My personal vote is for *Sorority Summer Vacation*." He wiggled his eyebrows.

99

"Mine's for *Alligator Bundy*. He's cute," Susan said, cocking her head at Eddie.

"The Crawling Dead," Larry said.

"Great. That's one, one, and one," said Eddie. "Franny, you get to cast the deciding vote."

Franny didn't want to see any of the three movies. What she did want to see was *Parfum*, a French film that was playing in one of the other cinemas there. She'd read somewhere that it was very beautiful and poetic. But as she looked at their expectant faces, she mumbled, *"Alligator Bundy."*

"All right!" Susan exclaimed. "The women win!" She put her arm around Franny's shoulders and whispered into her ear, "It doesn't matter what we see anyway, eh?" She nudged her and winked.

"Susan, I've got to talk with you . . ." Franny whispered back.

But Eddie cut her off. "Some women have no taste," he said. He put his arm around Susan and steered her toward the box office, leaving Franny standing there.

Larry came up to her and imitated Eddie. "Come on, woman!" he breathed into her ear.

Franny made a face, which he didn't see, and let him lead her into the theater.

The place was fairly crowded, because the movie was a popular one, but they were able to find four seats together in the middle of a row in the back. They stepped over six pairs of legs to get to them.

As soon as they were seated, Eddie said, "Anybody want any popcorn?"

"Sure," Susan said.

"How about you, Franny?" asked Larry.

Franny was starved, and she gratefully said yes.

The two boys got up and stepped back over the legs to the aisle.

"Susan," Franny said urgently as soon as they were out of earshot. "You won't believe what happened today. You won't believe who came into the shop."

"Who?"

Franny paused dramatically. "Dragon Boy."

"No! What was the front of him like?"

"A perfect ten." Franny sighed and told the story, blushing again as she admitted how dumb she'd been, but gratified because this tale definitely rivaled any of Susan's.

When she finished, Susan, eyes wide, said, "You've got to find out from Lillian who he is."

"I know," Franny agreed. "But Susan, I'm so embarrassed."

"Don't be. You didn't know who he was. He could've been a thief."

"He still could be."

Susan shook her head and voiced Franny's inner sentiment. "Not Dragon Boy. Oh, Franny, you can't let him get away."

Franny looked at her. "He *got* away."

"He'll be back. You've seen him twice. That means

you have to see him again. Things like that always come in threes."

"Who told you that?"

"My mother."

Franny laughed.

"I can just see you two now, sipping tea and slipping off each other's kimonos."

"Sue!"

"Excuse me, excuse me," Eddie's voice boomed out.

The girls looked up to see him and Larry returning with two jumbo pails of popcorn and four large sodas. They made it to their seats just as the house lights dimmed.

Franny took a big handful of popcorn and one soda, which she chugged half of, then set under her seat. The screen lit up with various announcements, followed by coming attractions and finally the feature.

Franny didn't pay much attention to it. She was munching popcorn and running over her encounter with Dragon Boy for the nth time, remembering details she thought she'd forgotten—the way his hair dipped over one eye; the jut of one hip as he stood in the doorway.

She was still thinking about him when Larry took the popcorn away and turned her head to meet his lips. Except now she saw Dragon Boy not in his black jacket and jeans, but in a black kimono with silver fans on it. And the doorway didn't lead to the flower shop,

but to a white-tiled room. Franny followed him into it. There was a big raised bath in the center, the kind Franny'd seen in movies about Japan. Dragon Boy smiled as Franny approached. She stood before him, wearing her butterfly kimono. He lifted his hands and slowly began to undo her sash. She did the same with his. They slid off the robes and stood before each other, naked. Then Dragon Boy led her into the steaming, fragrant bath.

"Oh, baby," he whispered, as she began to wash his back.

Oh, baby. Franny frowned. Dragon Boy wouldn't use such a crass expression. Suddenly her eyes flew open. She realized it wasn't Dragon Boy who'd spoken, but Larry. Larry, whose feet were all tangled up with hers and whose hands were snaking up underneath her shirt.

She pulled away from him. "I think we'd better stop," she whispered.

Larry reached for her again, but she bent down and fumbled under her seat for her soda. She found it and took a sip. Over Larry's shoulder she could see Eddie and Susan kissing.

"You want to go some place else where we'd be more comfortable?" Larry whispered back.

"Shhh!" someone in front of them hissed.

"Let's just watch the movie," Franny told him, and turned to the screen. Out of the corner of her eye

she saw him shake his head and fidget uncomfortably in his seat.

She blew out her breath and tried to focus on Alligator Bundy's adventures in the New York City subways. But she didn't succeed.

13

The Yeager house was dark and quiet when Franny arrived. She'd gone straight home after the movie, refusing a snack with the excuse that she'd spoil her appetite for dinner. It was a poor excuse—dinner was two hours away—and she thought her friends knew it. But she couldn't hang out with them anymore that day—especially with Larry. She was embarrassed to look at him. She'd gotten carried away—but not because of Larry. Because of Dragon Boy. She wished Susan hadn't said that thing about the two of them slipping off each other's kimonos. But she suspected she might have had that fantasy anyway, even without Susan's prompting. Dragon Boy was made for fantasizing.

Wondering where her family was, Franny walked

into the kitchen and flicked on a switch. Harsh fluorescent light flooded the room. ("Saves a lot of money," her mother had told her when she'd once asked why they didn't use the incandescent type.) There was a note stuck to the refrigerator with a starfish magnet. The starfish was real, with a chunk of metal pasted underneath it. Franny had given it to her mother as a Hanukkah present six years ago to replace the ugly plastic-daisy magnet she used to use. Sometimes Franny wished she had enough money to replace everything in the house.

The note said that Mr. and Mrs. Yeager had gone to a movie and would be back for dinner with takeout Chinese food. If Franny got hungry before then, there was plenty to nosh in the fridge, including cheese, fruit, leftover tuna casserole, etc. The note filled up an entire sheet of paper and was signed, "Love, Mom." Its length didn't surprise Franny—whenever her mother wrote anything to her, it was that long. But she was surprised that her parents had gone to a movie, and pleased as well. They're living it up, she thought, crumpling the paper and pitching it into the wastebin.

Then she went up to her room. It was dim and empty too. She turned on the light. Grandma must've gone with them, she thought. That means I have the house all to myself. She smiled and stretched out on her bed, luxuriating in the solitude. Then she wrinkled her nose. There was an odor in the room she'd never smelled before. It was faint, but Franny's keen

nose picked it up. She didn't know what it was, but it was nasty. Like decay, she thought. Maybe a mouse died behind the wall.

She got up and walked around, trying to pinpoint its source. But the odor wasn't coming from one spot. Even though it was chilly outside, she threw open a window. She stood near it for a while, inhaling the fresh air. When she began to shiver, she shut it and sniffed. The smell seemed to be gone. Taking Lillian's ikebana book from her night table, she lay down on her bed once more. She flipped through the pages, looking at the pictures of arrangements and wondering if she'd ever be adept enough to make anything like them.

Then she turned to a chapter near the end of the book.

It has been mentioned that Zen and ikebana walk hand in hand.

Here are some Zen teachings. They may help you in your art.

The mind is like a grasshopper, leaping from blade of grass to blade of grass. It must be stilled before we can understand what is the ultimate reality of life.

When the mind is still and empty, free of all images, illusions, delusions, emotions, desires, we know the joy of living in reality here and now. Then the "mind doors burst open." We achieve enlightenment.

To the unenlightened, flowers are just flowers, trees are just trees, people are just people. When the mind doors burst

open, we see that these are all illusions. They have no lasting reality. Then we are enlightened. And after this moment, to the enlightened, flowers are once again flowers, trees are once again trees and people are once again people. That is their Buddha nature.

Franny read the paragraphs over again. They were difficult to understand. What does it mean, to still the mind? Franny asked herself. What is a Buddha nature? Is everything really an illusion?

The questions buzzed around in her head until she shook it. "Ooh," she sputtered in frustration. She looked down at the book again and read, *You cannot reach enlightenment by thought or logic. The truth is communicated in silence.*

"Thanks a lot," Franny said aloud to the book. Then she heard the distant sound of the front door opening downstairs. She put down the book and listened, trying to guess who'd arrived. She hoped it wasn't Lainie.

In a few moments the bedroom door opened. Pink-faced and a bit winded, Grandma came in.

"Hi, Grandma," Franny said. "I thought it was you, by the footsteps. But I didn't hear the car pull up."

"The car?" Grandma said, plopping down in her chair.

Now it was Franny's turn to be confused. "Our car. I didn't hear it pull into the garage," she explained.

"That's because I didn't take the car. Your parents did."

"Didn't you go to the movies with them?"

"No. I went for a walk."

"A walk?" Grandma rarely went for walks. "By yourself?"

"Aren't I old enough?" Grandma teased.

"No," Franny joked back. Then she asked, "Where'd you go?"

"Just to that little park on Hilton. It's pretty there, even though the trees are bare. I like that little pond. I should go there more often."

"Were there any ducks there?"

"Yes. The ones with the green heads. What do they call them?"

"Mallards."

"Yes. I wanted to feed them, but I didn't have any bread. Oh well, next time." She paused. "Next time maybe we'll feed them together." She smiled at Franny.

Franny smiled back, guiltily. She suddenly realized she hadn't talked much with her grandmother since she'd gotten the job at Petals. Between that and her schoolwork and other things, she hadn't had much time. "That would be fun, to go to the park with you."

"Maybe we'll find a firebird," Grandma said.

This time Franny's grin was broad and wholehearted. Years ago, when she was much younger, the whole family took a day trip to Pine Lake. Franny had a fairy-tale book with her. On the long ride there, she read several stories. Her favorite, one her mother had read her before, told of a fabulous bird, golden as the flames it was said to have sprung from.

109

When they reached their destination, the Yeagers quickly took over a picnic spot. Mr. Yeager began to barbecue. Mrs. Yeager took Lainie for a swim. Franny wanted to sit under a tree and read. But she overheard a conversation between two people with binoculars. "First time I've ever seen a green heron," one was saying. "And I've only seen goldeneyes and buffle-heads a few times before. You were right about this place—it's great for birding."

Green heron. Goldeneyes. Buffleheads. Franny's ears pricked up. I bet there's a firebird here, she thought, and asked Grandma if she would like to take a walk and look for it. Grandma happily agreed. They set off on a path they thought would encircle the lake.

They took their time, scanning the trees and the bushes, listening for chirps and warbles. Franny didn't know what the firebird was supposed to sound like, but she guessed it would be something resembling the oboe her friend Helen's mother played, although she couldn't say why. They saw a few little dun-colored birds, some blue jays, and a pretty red cardinal, but nothing that could be called a firebird. Franny was very disappointed, but since they'd been walking for quite a while, she nodded when Grandma said they ought to call it quits. It was then they realized they were no longer trailing around the lake—that they were, in fact, lost.

"Don't worry," Grandma said. "We just have to find the water again. That shouldn't be too hard."

110

But it was. And Franny, who was getting tired, began to whimper a little.

Then, suddenly, a bird flew up out of a pine tree in front of them. It wasn't a big bird—robin-sized, perhaps—and it sounded nothing like an oboe, but its wings flashed a pure, bright gold. "Look, Grandma! Look. A firebird!" Franny exclaimed.

"I see it! I see it!" Grandma answered, just as excited.

Franny ran after it, with Grandma following as swiftly as she was able. The bird disappeared as quickly as it had arrived. But in front of them was the lake.

They got back to the picnic site soon after, only to be confronted by Franny's distraught parents and an envious Lainie. "Where were you?" "What happened to you?" "Why didn't you take me?" they demanded. "You've been gone for nearly two hours!"

Upset that they were upset, she told them the truth. "We were looking for the firebird and we got lost."

"The what?" Mr. Yeager asked.

"The firebird. . . . It was all gold, just like fire. And you know what? We saw it!"

"There's no such thing as a firebird," said Mrs. Yeager.

"There is. Grandma saw it too, didn't you, Grandma?"

"I saw it," she confirmed.

But Mrs. Yeager insisted the firebird was a myth. Franny got sadder and sadder and began to doubt

that she and Grandma had actually seen the fabled bird.

That night in her room, just before she fell asleep, Grandma whispered, "Thank you for a special day, Franny. It's not every day I get to see a firebird."

Franny paused, then said, "It really was a firebird, wasn't it, Grandma?"

"What else could it have been?" was her reply.

It wasn't until two years later that Franny found out there was no such thing as a firebird—and that Grandma had known it.

Now Grandma smiled again, then shivered a little. "It's cold in here. Is the heat off? Or is it just my old bones?"

"I had the window open before. To air the room out. Would you like a sweater?" Franny stood up.

"No. It's all right. A little cold is good for the soul."

Franny sat back down. There was a silence; then Grandma said, "How was your lesson today? Your employer was going to teach you how to arrange flowers like the Japanese do, no?"

"No. I mean, yes. She was. She did. I need a lot more lessons."

"Didn't it go well?"

"It went fine. But it's hard. How can something that looks so easy be so difficult?"

"Ah, that's how I've always felt about baking pies," Grandma joked. When Franny still looked pensive, she asked, "Are you discouraged?"

"Oh, no. It makes me want to work harder."

"That's my Frannele." Grandma beamed. "You never give up."

Franny smiled back. Her mother often told her the same thing. She told Lainie just the opposite. "How come you never finish anything? Why can't you be more like Franny? She never gives up." Franny the Finisher. Lainie the Quitter.

"So, tell me what you like about this flower arranging," Grandma said.

Franny was pleased to be asked. "Well, the flowers are beautiful. It's nice to design them by shape, line, color. It's like sculpting. You can cut, twist, turn, bend the plants, pull off petals and leaves, even break stems. You have to concentrate very hard to see how everything should flow together. I like concentrating like that. It's very . . . soothing."

Grandma nodded. "That's how I feel about embroidery. It lets my mind be still for a while."

Something pinged inside Franny's skull. She blinked. "What did you just say?"

"I said I like embroidery."

"No, the other thing."

"It lets my mind be still."

"Grandma, have you ever studied Zen?"

"Zen? You mean the philosophy?"

"Yes."

"Oh. No, I don't think I've ever studied it."

"Then maybe you learned it by not learning."

113

"Huh?"

"Nothing." Franny smiled.

Grandma smiled back.

Franny felt a wave of affection rise in her. It was tinged with a little sadness and more guilt. I love her. I really should spend more time with her, she thought.

"So, did you spend all afternoon with your flowers?" Grandma asked.

Franny shook her head. "No. I went to the movies with Susan and, uh, a couple of guys, Eddie and Larry." She blushed as the scene in the cinema came back to her.

"Which one was yours?" There was a decided twinkle in Grandma's eye.

"Larry."

"You like him?"

Franny picked a piece of lint off her sweater. "He's okay."

"Only okay?"

Franny didn't know what to say. There were a lot of things she could talk to her grandmother about, but what had happened with Larry (and Dragon Boy) wasn't one of them. "He's nice," she finally said. "Not really my type, though."

"Well, you might change your mind. I didn't think your grandfather was my type either when I first met him. But he grew on me. He used to try to give me all these fancy presents—orchids, lace handkerchiefs, earrings—and I wouldn't take them. Finally he got

114

the idea and stopped. Not giving me presents—just fancy ones. One day he brought me a bucket of raspberries he picked himself. You know how hard it is to pick a bucket of raspberries? All those thorns! Well, that was it. I think I told him that day I'd marry him."

"I didn't know you liked raspberries that much," Franny teased.

Grandma's smile faded. "I miss . . . raspberries," she said.

Franny knew what she was really missing was Grandpa. Franny thought about him for a moment. She'd never met him; he'd died before she was born. From his photos, she knew he was a short man with a shock of dark hair and glasses that magnified his eyes. Her mother said he'd had a good sense of humor. Franny was sorry she'd never known him.

"Well," Grandma said, standing up and moving to her dresser. "I think it's time for me to shoot up." She'd gotten that phrase from some TV movie about drugs. Mrs. Yeager hated when Grandma used it, but Franny and Lainie always laughed.

Grandma took out her insulin and a syringe. As she closed the drawer, something rolled off the dresser and landed at Franny's feet. Franny picked it up. It was the marigold cream Susan had lent Grandma.

"How's your foot? Did this stuff do you any good?" Franny asked, realizing she hadn't questioned Grandma about it at all.

"Let's see. Where shall I stick this today?" Grandma said.

"Grandma, I said, how's your foot?" Franny repeated, and her stomach rumbled.

Holding up the hypodermic, Grandma turned to look at Franny. "Did you eat any lunch?" she asked with mock sternness.

"I had some popcorn," Franny answered lamely.

"I thought so. Go down and fix yourself a snack."

"But dinner's soon," Franny protested, and this time it was true. "Mom and Dad are bringing home Chinese food. And you know how they hate it if I don't clean my plate."

"So have an appetizer. Tomato juice. Pickled herring. A hot fudge sundae. Go on. Now."

"Well, maybe I could have some celery and a couple of olives."

"Okay. Then leave the hot fudge sundae for me," Grandma said, filling the syringe.

"Will do," said Franny, and she went downstairs.

14

Lillian wasn't in the front of the shop when Franny arrived, burning to ask her about Dragon Boy and, at the same time, wondering how to bring him up.

"Lillian?" she called, as she went into the back room to hang up her coat.

Lillian was sitting at the desk with Franny's flower arrangement in front of her. She didn't look up.

Franny stopped thinking about Dragon Boy. She crossed behind the florist, then stood awkwardly, waiting for Lillian to pass judgment on the moribana.

"This is good," Lillian said at last. "It has the right feeling."

Franny sighed with relief.

But Lillian went on, "I would suggest moving this"—she lifted up the cedar twig—"over here." She fixed

it in its new place. "And these two mums here . . . see? Now they're talking to each other."

Franny sighed again, this time out of the knowledge that she was such a novice. "I see that it looks better that way," she said. After a pause, she asked, "Is that a Zen idea—the flowers talking to each other?"

"I don't know. I don't speak Zen."

Franny once again had the feeling that the woman was teasing her, but she didn't pursue the topic.

"You take this home and look at it for a while," Lillian told her. "Bring the bowl back on Sunday for your next lesson. Barring any accidents—and, by the way, Mr. Meachem from the deli is fine—we can have three uninterrupted hours."

The mention of Mr. Meachem brought Dragon Boy whooshing back to Franny. Ask about him, she told herself. Ask now. Just plunge right in. That's what Susan would do.

Lillian stood up and stretched. "Well, we'd better get back to work. Got to do that centerpiece for Farrell's today. It'll be picked up first thing tomorrow morning. I want you to do the nosegays."

Lillian, the oddest thing happened while you were taking Mr. Meachem to the hospital. I heard this sound and I looked up, thinking it was you. . . . No. Lillian, do you know what a perfect ten is? Well, yesterday, while you were supposed to be getting us lunch, the perfect ten showed up and . . . . No.

"Thank heavens I talked them out of those God-

118

awful turkeys this year. The ones with middles that look like orange accordions. Ugh!" Lillian headed for the door.

"Lillian!" Franny blurted out. "Who's Dragon Boy?"

Lillian turned and looked quizzically at her. "Dragon Boy?"

Franny flushed scarlet. "This . . . uh . . . boy showed up while you were gone. He asked where you were. I told him you were getting us lunch and you'd be right back."

"What did he look like?"

Franny turned an even deeper red. "He was . . . uh . . . good-looking. Tall, with dark hair and almond-shaped eyes. I think he was Japanese. He wore black pants and a black jacket with a red dragon on it. That's why I, uh, called him Dragon Boy."

"Ah. I see. Why didn't he wait for me?"

"I, well, you see, I didn't know who he was and I told him to go away. I'm afraid I was very insistent."

"How?"

"I waved my shears at him."

"Ah," Lillian repeated. "Well, that was quick think-ing on your part. I know for certain this shop is safe in your hands. Now, to that centerpiece . . ." She kept walking to the front of the shop.

Franny followed her. "But, Lillian," she squeaked, then cleared her throat. "Lillian, do you know who he is?"

"I can't be positive, of course, without having seen

119

him, but from your description, I'd say it sounds like Ren."

"Ren," Franny repeated, the name rippling off her tongue like a bird's song.

"Yes."

Franny didn't know quite what to ask next. But who *is* he? How do you know him? How can I meet him? Cautiously, she said, "Does he come here often?"

"Sometimes. Sometimes he'll show up every day— and then not for weeks."

"Well, I'm glad he wasn't a thief or something. I was kind of startled when he appeared, because I thought the door was locked."

"It was."

Franny's brow furrowed. "Then how did he get in?"

"With a key."

"He has a key?"

Lillian nodded, and the phone rang. She answered it.

At the same time a customer walked in, and Franny saw to her.

The customer was followed by another, then a third. By the time Franny turned to Lillian again, the florist was immersed in the centerpiece.

Franny knew Lillian hated to be disturbed when she was designing, so she started on the nosegays.

The phone rang again, and with a sigh Lillian answered it. "Yes? Yes. Yes." She looked at her watch. "Not tonight. How about Wednesday?" She glanced

at Franny. "Yes. She might. I'll ask. Okay, I'll tell her to leave her shears at the shop. Good-bye." She hung up. "So," she said.

"So." Franny swallowed. "That was Ren, wasn't it?"

"Yes. He's invited himself for dinner Wednesday night. He requested your presence. So how would you like to join us? I'm a plain but decent cook."

"He asked me to come? For dinner? I don't know. Do you want me to? I don't want to impose."

"Of course I'd like you to come. I wouldn't have asked otherwise, regardless of what Ren wants."

"Oh, you do? Well, I . . . Well, all right. I'll come."

"Good. It'll be just the three of us. I don't like big dinner parties. It's impossible to have a conversation with more than two other people at one time."

Franny nodded in agreement.

"All right then, next time the phone rings, *you* answer it and tell whoever it is I'll get back to them in an hour. I've *got* to finish this thing now."

Franny nodded again and went back to her nosegay. She put three bronze-colored mums into it and smiled. Dragon Boy once. Dragon Boy twice. Dragon Boy a third time. Wednesday night. Over dinner.

"I don't understand how anyone could possibly want to have a dinner party the night before Thanksgiving," Mrs. Yeager was saying as she dished out some goulash, one of Franny's least favorite dishes. "To cook that much two days in a row is beyond me."

"It's going to be a small party," Franny said.

"How small?"

"Three people. Me and Lillian and a . . . friend of hers."

Franny'd hesitated only slightly before the word "friend," but Mrs. Yeager, whose ears were sharper than Mr. Spock's on any given *Star Trek* episode, said, "A *boy*friend?"

"Oh no," Franny said, with a nervous giggle. "I don't think so." But don't ask me what kind of relationship they do have, she thought. "He's around my age, a year or two older." She gritted her teeth, waiting for her mother to say, "Why would somebody your grandmother's age have a teenager for a friend?"

But her mother surprised her. "Oh. You mean she's fixing you up on a blind date and she's acting as chaperone. That's nice." She beamed.

Franny didn't tell her that it wasn't a blind date at all. Far from it. I've seen him, Mom. And he's the most gorgeous boy. I think he's Japanese . . . Oh, no. She looked at her father. How could I have forgotten?

But Mr. Yeager was unconcernedly winding noodles around his fork.

"A chaperone," Lainie said. "What do you think they're going to do, Ma, that they need a chaperone, jump on each other the minute they're introduced?"

"Lainie!"

"Jeez, from the way you talk, it's like it's a hundred years ago. Ma, you were around in the swinging six-

ties. What were you doing, hanging out with nuns or something?"

"Of course I wasn't hanging out with nuns. I'm Jewish."

Lainie burst out laughing. Even Mr. Yeager smiled.

But Mrs. Yeager frowned at them. "There's nothing funny about what I just said. Even in the sixties not everybody was running wild. I wasn't brought up that way."

"Is that true, Grandma?" Lainie asked, swiveling in her seat. "Did you really tell Mom she couldn't go out on dates without a chaperone?"

"Lainie, you know very well that's not what *I* said about your sister," Mrs. Yeager protested. "I said I thought it was nice that Lillian—Mrs. Morrison—is acting as chaperone, not that she had to or that Franny needed one. I just said it was—"

"She's not acting as chaperone," Franny announced, a bit too loudly, surprising herself.

Both her mother and Lainie stopped talking and looked at her.

In a lower voice, she said, "I'm her friend and Ren's her friend and she's invited us both to dinner."

There was a brief silence. Then Mr. Yeager asked curiously, "Ren? What kind of name is that?"

What is this, the third degree? Franny wanted to burst out. You haven't grilled me about my other dates, not that I've gone on many. "I . . . uh . . . don't know," she said.

123

"It's unusual. It sounds . . ." Her father paused. She felt her stomach seizing up as usual. "Swedish or something," he finished.

"I don't know," Franny repeated weakly.

"It doesn't sound Swedish to me," Lainie said. "It sounds Japanese."

Franny clenched her hand into a fist. She could feel it pummeling Lainie's guts.

Mr. Yeager gave Lainie a dirty look.

"Whoever he is, I'm sure he's nice," Mrs. Yeager said, wanting to end the questioning she'd started.

"Japanese boys are supposed to be nice," Lainie went on. "Very polite. Very proper. Except when they're slicing through bricks with their hands or rolling around with a geisha girl or two."

"Lainie!" Mrs. Yeager exclaimed.

"You know, you're not too old to be spanked," Mr. Yeager rapped out.

"Yes I am—by you. But maybe not by someone else."

"Lainie!"

"You little—"

"Slivovitz."

They all stopped talking and turned their heads to Grandma.

"What did you just say?" Mr. Yeager asked.

"I said I could use a glass of Slivovitz."

"But Mom," said Mrs. Yeager, "you don't drink."

"Oh, don't I? Well, maybe it's time I started." She

124

rose slowly. "Come on, Franny. Why don't you join me?"

Franny smiled a little. "All right, Grandma," she said.

The two of them walked out together.

Franny was unable to sleep again. The dinner "conversation" had jangled her nerves. And on top of that her bedroom smelled foul, the way it had the day before. But this time she couldn't open the window.

Finally she got out of bed and went down to the tokonoma. She lit a candle in the back room, as well as some incense, and sat down on the cushions. The pungent odor of sandalwood cleared her nostrils of the bedroom's odor. Breathing deeply, she gazed at the altar. The moribana was in its place of honor just below the poster. She'd hidden it in the yard until everyone had gone to bed, then smuggled it in. She'd wanted to show it to Grandma, but it was too risky. Someone else might have seen it, and then she wouldn't have been able to put it in her secret shrine.

"See? Now they're talking to each other," she could hear Lillian saying. "Look at it for a while. . . ." She stared at it for a long time. Her breathing slowed down and her nerves stopped jangling. Then a little voice in her head said, Look, Ma, I'm meditating, and she giggled.

A while later her eyelids began to droop. Better go to bed, she told herself. She yawned, stretched, blew

out the candle, and made her way back upstairs.

She opened the bedroom door softly and tiptoed in. The room still reeked. She lay down on her bed with the top sheet over her nose and mouth. Closing her eyes, she began to drift off.

"Oh, no! No! Back! Take me back!"

Franny sat bolt upright in bed. Someone was yelling. Someone in the room. Grandma! She threw off her blanket and ran over to her.

"No! No! Please!" Grandma shouted, arms and legs flailing.

Franny shook her gently, then harder. "Grandma, wake up! You're having a bad dream."

Grandma shuddered. Her eyes opened wide. "Where . . . where am I?"

"You're here. In our bedroom. You were dreaming."

"Oh. Oh, that's right. Dreaming." Her chest rose and fell rapidly.

Franny sat next to her grandmother on the bed, holding her hand until her breathing was normal again. Then she asked, "What was the dream about, Grandma?"

"The dream? Oh, it was . . . silly," she said slowly. "You and I were standing in a train station, watching people get on a train. We didn't know where it was going. The doors closed and the train started to pull away. And then, all of a sudden, I was on the train and it was taking me away and I didn't know where,

but I knew it was far and I didn't want to go. Silly, no?"

"Very silly," Franny said, patting her hand.

"I didn't mean to wake you up."

"Just close your eyes and relax," Franny said. "A girl your age needs her beauty sleep."

"That's true." Franny could hear the smile in Grandma's voice.

The bedroom door opened. "What's going on in here?" Lainie croaked, stumbling into the room.

"Oh, Lainie, sweetheart, I woke you up too. I'm sorry."

"What?"

"She was having a nightmare," Franny explained.

"Oh. Are you okay now, Grandma?"

"Yes. But if you give me a good-night kiss, I'll be even better."

Lainie staggered over and kissed her. The white of her nightgown shone in the dark room. Franny knew the gown had little pink rabbits all over it. Lainie'd had it since she was eleven, and even though it was shrunken and faded, she still wore it. "I love you, Grandma," she said, and staggered back out of the room.

She's sweet when she's half asleep. Maybe we should drug her or something to keep her that way all the time, Franny thought. She kissed her grandmother too and got back into bed.

15

"Oh, brother!" Lillian said, locking up the shop. "I'm glad Thanksgiving's over."

"But it isn't," said Franny, confused. "It's tomorrow."

"I mean as far as Petals is concerned."

"Oh. But next we'll have Christmas."

"Don't remind me," Lillian groaned. "Poinsettias. Evergreen swags. Jerusalem cherries. And those hideous spray-painted white branches I can't get out of carrying."

"I sort of like that stuff—minus the branches," Franny said timidly.

"Actually, I do too. I'm just doing my 'Bah, humbug' act. And don't be afraid to tell me what you like and what you don't like."

They rounded a corner. "Where do you live?" Franny asked.

"Right here," Lillian said, leading Franny to the back of a small split-level house.

"Oh, that's convenient. Oh! Then he did disappear into a house."

"What?"

Franny flushed. "Uh . . . See, my friend Susan and I were around here one day and we saw Ren. I mean, we saw the back of his jacket. He turned this corner before we did. When Susan and I got here, he was gone."

Lillian didn't comment. She opened the back door, flicked on a light, and ushered Franny inside.

Franny found herself in a bright kitchen with gleaming white appliances. The walls were painted a pleasing light coral. The color was repeated in subtle stenciled designs on the white cabinets that encircled the room. A glass-topped round bamboo table and four chairs stood in the center of the room, the only furniture there.

"This is such a friendly room!" Franny exclaimed. "So light and airy."

"I'm glad you think so," Lillian answered her. "The people who lived here before me had dark-green cabinets and the most hideous ochre wallpaper you can imagine. You walked in here and felt you'd wandered into someone's nasal passages."

Franny burst out laughing. The image was hilar-

iously gross, especially coming from Lillian. It sounded more like something Susan would say. Franny committed it to memory to tell it to her.

"Sling your coat on one of those chairs," Lillian went on. "I'll hang it up for you later. I've got to start on this stuff right away or we won't eat until midnight." She began to take things out of the refrigerator. "Ren'll be here in a while. Why don't you explore the apartment till then. I can't concentrate on company and cooking at the same time."

Franny knew she was being dismissed, and she didn't mind it in the least. She was eager to explore Lillian's home, but she would never have been so impolite as to have asked to do so.

As she walked out of the room, Lillian called, "If you run into Miss Priss, let her sniff your hand before you pet her. Otherwise she turns into a real harridan."

Unsure as to exactly what manner of being Miss Priss was, but guessing her to be of either the canine or feline variety, Franny emerged into the living room, where the inviting plush chairs and sofa were deep-blue velvet flecked with red, a real contrast to the light furniture in the kitchen. But the contrast worked. There was a remarkable red-and-black lacquered cabinet set against one wall, all tiny drawers with brass pulls, and an equally striking coffee table with a procession of kimono-clad ladies carved into the wood under a sheet of protective glass. How perfect, Franny thought, running her hand over the latter. If I had

my own place, this is just how I'd furnish it.

She wandered next into a hallway where there were three doors. Two of these were open, revealing, respectively, a bathroom and Lillian's bedroom. The bathroom didn't hold much interest for Franny, and much as she wanted to, she didn't feel right about going into the bedroom. She was trying to decide whether or not to open the closed door when it opened by itself and a large long-haired white cat came out and stared balefully at her.

"Miss Priss, I presume," Franny said, squatting down and extending her hand for the cat to sniff.

Miss Priss took Franny up on her offer. Her pink nose twitched and her whiskers tickled Franny's skin for a good minute before she inclined her head so that Franny could scratch between her ears. Franny's position let her look through the half-open door into the room the cat had just vacated. She could see that the walls were lined with shelves and shelves of books, except for one alcove that had no books at all. Instead, it had a single shelf on which stood a graceful flower arrangement beneath a hanging scroll. "A tokonoma!" Franny exclaimed, standing up so suddenly, Miss Priss hissed and backed away.

Stepping into the room, Franny took in more details—an incense burner, a statue of Buddha, a meditation bench on the floor, a group of cushions near a tiny table. "What's a tokonoma?" she remembered Lillian asking, and she shook her head and smiled.

She studied the flower arrangement for a while, then glanced over the bookshelves. They held many types of books, but one block was devoted entirely to works on Eastern philosophy. Franny sighed, thinking that at that moment the old cliché "I felt like I'd died and gone to heaven" fit her exactly. She didn't know which book to pull out first, then noticed that there was one lying on a cushion near her feet. She sat down, cross-legged, and picked it up. A slim, sharp-pointed brass bookmark rested inside. Opening to the page with great care, she removed the bookmark and, holding on to it in one hand, read aloud, *"Form is emptiness and emptiness is indeed form. Emptiness is not different from form; form is not different from emptiness. . . ."*

"What is form, that is emptiness; what is emptiness, that is form," a male voice finished with her.

Franny looked up, startled.

Ren was standing there in the doorway, looking just the way he had in the shop, only this time he had on a dazzling white shirt that set off his dark hair and tawny skin. "Hi. I'm Ren," he said. "Ren Tanazaki."

It took Franny a moment to speak. "Ohayo," she finally said, having spent both her study hall and lunch periods reading up on Japan and the Japanese language.

"No. California," Ren responded.

"I beg your pardon?"

"That's where I was born. Not Ohio. And you're

not going to chase me with that lethal-looking book-mark, are you?"

Franny dropped the bookmark to the floor and blushed furiously. "No, I . . . I'm sorry. *Ohayo* does mean hello in Japanese, doesn't it? My accent's probably terrible."

"I wouldn't know if it was. I don't speak Japanese."

"You don't?" Franny said, surprised.

"No. My father does a little. He was born in San Francisco." He moved into the room and sat on a cushion next to her. "You haven't told me your name yet."

"Oh, I'm sorry. It's—"

"No, wait! Let me guess." He put his index and middle fingers against his brow and hummed. Suddenly, he waved his hand in the air. "I've got it!" he shouted. "It's . . . Flossie!"

Franny shook her head.

"No? How about . . . Fern!"

She began to giggle.

"Wrong again, eh? Well then, let me try once more." His eyes danced and, in his low, musical voice, he crooned, "Franny. Franny Yeager."

"Lillian told you." Franny giggled again.

Ren smiled that insolent smile. "You don't believe in my psychic powers, eh?"

"Not really," she answered, and blushed.

Ren laughed, leaning back against the cushions and

133

stretching out his long legs in front of him. Miss Priss bounded into the room and, with a meow, leaped on him, sprawling across his thighs. He didn't bother to offer her his hand to sniff, but immediately began stroking her back, all the while watching Franny and saying nothing.

Finally she said awkwardly, "This book . . . you must have read it a lot of times to have . . . uh . . . memorized it."

"I haven't read it at all," he replied. "I just know that particular passage because Capra quotes it in *The Tao of Physics*. He uses it to explain how subatomic physics can resolve the paradox of quanta existing as both particles and waves." When Franny looked blank, he said, "Sorry. Physics-major talk."

"You go to the college," Franny said, thinking, What will he think of me, a lowly high school junior?

"Uh-huh. Braddington. I'm a lonely freshman far away from home." He grinned, still stroking Miss Priss, who was purring loudly.

Then Lillian appeared in the doorway. "Okay, you two. It's now safe to enter the kitchen."

"Thank you, Julia Child," Ren said. He set Miss Priss gently on the floor and rose in one fluid motion, offering his hand to Franny. It was warm and soft, except for the tips of his fingers, which were rough and callused.

She began to follow him and Lillian out, then realized she still had the book in her hand, but not the

bookmark. "Excuse me," she said, awkwardly returning to the cushions, searching for the fallen bookmark, and replacing it in the volume. By then Lillian and Ren had already gone into the kitchen, and Franny was breathless when she caught up with them.

"So, have you apologized to Franny for scaring her out of her wits the other day?" Lillian asked, taking dishes out of the cabinet.

Ren flashed his wicked grin at Franny. "Did I really leave you witless? You seem witful enough to me. But let's try a foolproof test. Quick, why did the chicken cross the road?"

"To get to the other side?" Franny asked in response.

"See, what did I tell you? No dimwits here."

"Here," Lillian said, handing a stack of dishes with silverware on top to Ren. "Make yourself useful and set the table."

"Can I do anything to help?" Franny asked.

"Yes. You can sit and watch Ren and make sure he doesn't break anything." She swiveled a chair around and motioned Franny into it.

"Lillian! Are you accusing me of being a klutz?" he asked. "Just because I smashed that prize flower arrangement of yours doesn't mean I'm clumsy." He winked at Franny and slipped a plate onto the table behind her.

"You smashed one of Lillian's ikebana arrangements?" Franny was horrified.

135

"She was taking it to a show, and she asked me to put it in the car. It slipped out of my hands right onto the sidewalk. I tried to fix it up in a new bowl, but unlike you I'm no good with flowers."

"How terrible!"

"Yes. She hasn't forgiven me yet," Ren replied. He laid the knives and forks in place.

"I have," Lillian corrected him. "I decided Buddha was teaching me a lesson."

"What kind of lesson?" Franny asked eagerly.

"Not to ask anyone to carry my flower arrangements out to the car."

Ren snorted. "Which glasses do you want to use?"

"Wine." She didn't ask Franny if she was allowed to drink, and Franny didn't tell her that half a glass was her limit before she got totally silly.

"Be careful with those wine glasses," Lillian warned.

"Yes, madam."

"*Voilà!*" he exclaimed when he finished setting the table. He planted himself in front of Franny. "I didn't break a single thing, did I?"

"No. You were very good," she answered, as though he were a small boy.

They both laughed.

"Perfect timing. Soup's on," Lillian said.

Ren sat down, and Franny turned her chair around. She was feeling more relaxed now, although every time Ren smiled at her, she still felt as though she'd stuck her finger in an electric outlet.

Lillian began to dish out the food, spaghetti and meatballs, and Ren to pour the wine. "So," he asked, taking Franny's glass, "what's it like working for Lillian here? She a good boss?"

"She's very good," Franny said honestly. "Very patient. Very kind."

"Really? That doesn't sound like Lillian at all."

"Hand me your plate," Lillian said tonelessly to him.

"Do you want to be a florist too?" Ren continued to question Franny.

"A florist?" she answered, startled. A florist. Did she want to be a florist? It certainly was something that interested her. But it was a long way off. Post-high school and college. And besides . . . "My mother wants me to be a teacher," she said. "She thinks that's a good steady job for a woman."

"And what do you think?" Ren stared at her intently.

Franny looked down at her plate. "I don't know. I haven't thought about it." I've just assumed a teacher's what I'll be, she finished silently. Then she looked up at Ren again. "Are you going to be a physicist?"

"Uh-uh. A pilot. It's the closest I'll ever get to being a dragon." He laughed.

"What?" Franny's eyes widened.

"You know—soaring in the sky, feeling the wind in my wings, spitting fire. The whole bit."

"Right now you're spitting spaghetti," Lillian said, wiping her cheek.

"Sorry. And I want to own my own little single-engine so I can really feel part of the sky. Have you ever flown in a single-engine plane?"

"I've never flown at all."

"Never? I'll fix that as soon as I get my license. I'll take you for a ride you won't forget. I'm going to be a great pilot, right, Lillian? Tell Franny she'll be totally safe in my hands."

"He's going to be a great pilot," said Lillian. "But I won't vouch for the latter statement."

"Pah," Ren said. He looked back at Franny. "You would like to fly with me, Franny Yeager, wouldn't you?" he asked, his voice low and sexy.

Franny stared at him, then lowered her eyes. It was a moment before she answered, "Yes."

"This is a nice street," Ren said, turning onto Franny's block. He'd offered to drive her home and, her heart hammering in her chest, she'd accepted. "Prettier than where I live."

"Where do you live?" she asked.

"Over on Marley. I've got one room in a house there."

"You don't live with your parents?" Franny asked, realizing that, with all the subjects they'd discussed, they'd hardly talked about their families at all. Which was fine with Franny, concerning her own. But Ren's interested her.

138

"No, they live in San Francisco. . . . Is this your house?" he asked, pulling up in front of it.

"Yes."

"Nice."

There was silence for a moment. Franny waited for him to say something else. When he didn't, she bit back discouragement. "Well, I enjoyed meeting you," she said formally, reaching for the door handle. "Good night and thanks for the—"

He laid a hand on her arm. "Wait. I want to say a few things." He suddenly sounded a little less sure of himself. "First of all, I really do owe you an apology for scaring you last Sunday. You looked so cute and serious, I couldn't help teasing you. I guess I did deserve being chased out."

No, you didn't, Franny was about to say. I'm the one who's sorry. But instead, to her surprise, she said, "That's true. You did deserve it. You scared me."

"I know. And I do apologize." He chuckled. "You were pretty fierce, though. You reminded me of a tiger."

"A tiger? Me?"

"Yes. You," he said softly.

After a pause, she said, "What else did you want to tell me?"

"That I want to see you again. Soon. How about Friday night?"

"Friday night? Okay." Her heart was pounding again.

"And Saturday night. And Sunday afternoon," Ren went on, not taking his eyes off her.

"You're teasing me again."

"No. Not now."

She got goose bumps from the way he said it. "All right," she whispered.

Then he kissed her—a tender, unhurried kiss. It took her breath away.

"Hmmm," he sighed, stroking her hair. "My grandmother has impeccable taste in assistants."

Franny blinked. It took her a moment to speak. "Your grandmother? Who's your grandmother?"

"Why, Lillian, of course. Didn't she tell you?"

"No, she didn't. But I don't understand. How—"

"Simple. Her daughter—my mother—married my father."

"Then your mother isn't Japanese?"

"Not the last time I looked."

"I wonder why Lillian didn't tell me."

"Maybe she thought it wasn't important. Or maybe she was teasing. Lillian is a great teaser. In case you haven't noticed, it runs in the family." He smiled at her.

"I've noticed." She smiled back.

Then he peered over her shoulder. "Looks like someone's waiting for you."

Franny turned her head. Someone was indeed peeking out the Yeagers' front door. It looked like

her father. Franny's stomach did a nosedive. "I'd better go in," she said, willing her voice to keep steady.

"Okay." He opened the door, walked around to her side, opened her door, and helped her out of the car. "I'll pick you up at Petals on Friday after work," he said. "We can have dinner and then go to a movie."

"I'd like that."

"Well, good night, Franny."

For a moment she thought he was going to kiss her again, but he just touched her cheek with his hand, got back into the car, and drove away.

Franny stared after him until he was out of sight. God, she thought. Lillian's grandson. How crazy. *I'm* crazy. I'm crazy about him and I'm crazy for being crazy about him. She walked slowly up the path to her front door. It was unlocked. She went into the hall. The TV was blaring away as usual in the living room. "Mom? Dad?" she called, walking into it.

Her father was sitting there alone.

"Hi, Dad," she said. "I'm home."

He glanced at her briefly. "Good," he said.

She waited to see if he'd ask about her evening, but he didn't. She was relieved, but also curiously disappointed. "Where's Mom?" she asked.

"Upstairs with your grandmother." There was something a bit odd in his voice.

"Is something wrong?"

"Your mother's upset."

"About what?"

141

"Your grandmother's foot."

"Grandma's foot? Oh. She had a sore on it. But she said it was better."

"It isn't better," her father said.

"It isn't?"

"No. She went to the doctor today. More bills."

Franny grimaced. Did her father always have to relate everything to money. "Well, how is she now?"

"Not good," he said.

When he didn't continue, Franny frowned at his back and hurried up the stairs.

"I don't understand. Why didn't you tell me sooner. Why didn't you call Dr. Carver sooner?" Her mother's voice rose from behind Franny's bedroom door.

She threw it open. The stench in the room almost overpowered her. She coughed and covered her nose and mouth.

Her mother and grandmother looked up at her. Grandma was sitting in her chair; her bare foot lay raised off the floor on several pillows. And Franny knew without a doubt the smell was emanating from it.

"Your grandmother is a very foolish woman," Mrs. Yeager said, her voice choked with anger and tears. "Look at this."

"Irene, stop it. Frannele, go outside . . ." Grandma began.

But Franny entered the room, forcing herself not

to retch. She went over and stared at Grandma's toes. They were black. Black and rotten.

"Wh-what is it?" Franny murmured.

"Don't you know?" said her mother. "It's gangrene. This foolish woman has gangrene."

16

"So this guy wants to know the meaning of life, right?" Uncle Mike was talking and chomping his cigar at the same time. "And he travels all over the world, visiting gurus all over the place. Nobody can tell him the answer. Finally, he hears there's this great swami up on a mountaintop. But it's a tough journey. It'll take six weeks, and the last leg has to be done on his hands and knees. But he decides to do it. He climbs and climbs for six weeks, and he finally comes to the swami's hut. He goes inside. This little old man is sitting there. The guy goes up to him and says, 'Oh, great swami, I've come to ask you an important question. I want to know: What is the meaning of life?'

"The swami closes his eyes. He doesn't say anything

for a long time. Finally, he opens his mouth and four words come out: 'Life is a fountain.'

"For a moment, the guy doesn't speak. Then he shouts, 'Wait a minute. Wait just one damn minute. I traveled halfway across the world. I climbed up this mountain on my hands and knees to find out the meaning of life. I finally get here and you tell me, "Life is a fountain." What kind of cockamamie answer is that? Life is a fountain! Jeez!'

"The swami is quiet while the guy rants and raves. Finally, the guy stops, exhausted. Then the swami cocks his head at him and says, 'You mean it isn't?'" Uncle Mike took his cigar out of his mouth and laughed so heartily, he began to choke and Aunt Myrna had to slap him on the back. "Isn't that a riot? The guy crawls on his hands and knees to find this swami and the old guy doesn't even know what he's talking about!"

Mrs. Yeager laughed along with her brother. So did Cousin Marcy and Cousin Allen. Lainie laughed too, but not at the joke.

"You're not laughing, Gene," Uncle Mike said to Mr. Yeager. "Don't you get it?"

"Ask Franny if she does—she's the one who's into swamis these days."

"Yeah? You got a guru?" Uncle Mike turned to her.

"Franny doesn't have a guru. She has an employer who's also teaching her Japanese flower arranging," her mother said.

145

"Oh, is that so? Flower arranging, huh? Very nice. Very nice. This one of yours?" He pointed to the centerpiece on the table.

"No," Franny said quietly. "It's Lil—It's my boss's."

"Very nice. But it should have something Thanksgivingish in it. A turkey or something. Which reminds me of the one about the pilgrim who . . ." And Uncle Mike was off and running again.

Franny looked at him, then at all the others around the table. Last of all she focused on her grandmother and her insides gave a wrench. Grandma was listening, too, with a warm smile on her face. She looked just the way she always did. In fact, she wasn't acting any different either. Last night she'd apologized to Franny for causing any worry and for not calling Dr. Carver sooner. Then she'd told Franny not to worry about her. "I'll be all right," she'd said.

Franny had assured her she would be, but she really wasn't so sure. And she was disturbed by the way everyone was pretending nothing was wrong. Not that she wanted them to have a big conversation about the topic either. She didn't want a conversation at all. Or a bunch of stupid jokes from Uncle Mike. She wanted to do two things—call Susan and then sit in her tokonoma, alone.

"And then he says, 'So who told you?' " Uncle Mike finished, roared, and slapped the table.

Everyone who'd laughed before laughed again.

When the guffaws died down, Franny said, "May I be excused?"

"Sure," her mother said.

"Such a polite girl," she heard her aunt say as she left the dining room.

Once out of sight, Franny darted into the kitchen and hurriedly dialed Susan's number. The phone rang four times before Susan answered. "It's me," Franny said. "I hope I'm not interrupting your dinner—"

"Dinner schminner. Give it to me straight, girl!" Susan shouted. "How was it? How was *he*?"

Franny took a deep breath. "He was—he was . . . Oh, God, Susan! I'm in trouble."

"What do you mean? What are you talking about?"

"I'm supposed to go out with him tomorrow night, Saturday night, and Sunday afternoon. He . . . I've never met a guy like him." She described the evening, how Ren had asked her dozens of questions, wanting to hear her opinion about everything. "And here's the punchline: He's Lillian's grandson."

"What!"

"Yes. He and Lillian, they like each other a lot, too. And I think they like me."

"Oh, Franny, I'm so happy for you."

"And I'm so scared."

"But why?"

"Don't you see? I shouldn't be dating him at all. If my parents find out, they'll be furious."

"Why?"

"Because he's Japanese. Only part Japanese. But that part would be enough for them."

"I don't understand."

"Don't you remember what I told you about my dad's feelings toward the Japanese? He thinks they ruined the American auto industry and that his job's in danger because of them."

"But his job's secure now, right?"

"I think so."

"So he can't feel that way anymore."

"Susan, you know my dad better than that."

"Look, Franny, Ren sounds like a prize. I bet even your dad will like him. And if he doesn't, that's too bad for him."

"You mean it's too bad for me."

"No, I don't. This is *your* life, Franny Yeager. You have to live it for yourself and not for your parents."

Franny didn't respond for a long moment. Then she said, "There's something else. That sore on Grandma's foot."

"Isn't it better? I thought she told you it was, that the marigold cream had helped."

"No. It's not better. She's got . . . gangrene."

"Gangrene? I thought you only got that from gunshot wounds that were left untreated."

Franny didn't feel like delivering the lecture her mother had given her privately that morning about

how diabetics have poor blood circulation and how easily a sore on a diabetic's foot can get infected. So all she said was "No."

"Jeez, that's awful. Your poor grandmother. How are they treating it?"

"With antibiotics." Franny didn't mention what would happen if the antibiotics failed. "I should spend more time with her. If I go out with Ren all weekend, I won't see much of her."

"Why don't you bring Ren to meet her? She'd love that. And he'd love her," Susan suggested.

"I can't do that, even if her foot didn't sm—I mean, I can't and I just told you why."

"And I've just told you why you should do it."

There was a tense silence. Susan finally broke it. "I'm sorry about your grandmother," she said in a gentler voice. "I wish I could come over and see her this weekend myself, but I've got to work and then I'm going out with Eddie."

Normally, Franny would've teased her friend: "Eddie, huh? But you saw him *last* weekend." But she was still feeling upset. "I understand," she said tightly.

"Listen, Franny, there's something my mother says, but I think it's true: 'Don't spit in the face of happiness.' Did you hear me, Franny? Are you still there?"

"I'm here. I heard you."

149

"I love you, Franny. You're my best friend. I'm only telling you what I really believe is best for you."

"I know."

Lainie walked into the kitchen with a stack of dirty dishes.

"I've got to go now," Franny said.

"Okay. Talk to you later." Susan hung up.

"Who was that?" Lainie asked, depositing the dishes in the sink.

"Susan," Franny answered.

Lainie nodded, turned on the taps, and filled a dishpan. "You dry, okay?" she said.

Franny glanced longingly at the doorway, then back to the sink. "All right," she said with resignation. The tokonoma would have to wait.

"Uncle Mike's really a jerk." Lainie growled, scrubbing at a greasy platter. "He took Mom aside and I heard him tell her that he and Uncle Jack were prepared to help with all of Grandma's medical expenses, especially if they have to operate. They're so stupid. Grandma's taking antibiotics. She's not going to have to have her leg cut off."

Franny shuddered. Why did Lainie have to be so blunt? Once again she looked at the doorway.

Lainie didn't notice. "And I can't stand the way Aunt Myrna whispered to me that she doesn't want Marcy to know about Grandma's 'little problem.' She's a jerk too."

150

When Franny didn't say anything, Lainie finally turned to her. "So anyway, I didn't get to hear about your 'little' dinner party last night. Is Ren a 'dirty Jap' after all?" she joked.

Franny flinched. "Lainie . . ." she began, then stopped. "No," she said. "No, he's not."

"Oh. Too bad. That would've made things more interesting. Well, is he at least hot?"

"No," Franny lied, turning red.

"No? So how come you're blushing?"

"It's warm in here, that's why."

"Sure it is." Lainie laughed. "Oh, I almost forgot. While you were out with the not-so-hot Ren, some guy named Larry called. He thought I was you and boy, did he burn my ears. You must've had one hell of a time at *Alligator Bundy* the other day."

Franny's blush deepened. Damn it, she thought. I wish I could wear a mask.

"He was very entertaining. I was sorry I finally had to tell him the truth, that I wasn't you. He sort of laughed embarrassedly and said to tell you he called and he'd call again soon. So, message delivered."

"Thanks," Franny said, almost inaudibly.

"Don't mention it." Lainie handed a bowl to Franny to dry.

Franny took it and wiped it briskly.

"You know, for such a polite girl you live a pretty colorful life," Lainie said amiably. "Hot boys with

151

strange names. Sinful scenes in the cinema. I'm beginning to think there's more to you than meets the eye, Big Sis."

Franny dabbed at a spot of water remaining on the bowl and didn't say a word.

17

Saturday night at Barger's, a tiny bar near Braddington University, was crowded, noisy, and smoky. Wedged
into a minuscule booth, a nearly empty wine glass in
front of her (Ren had gotten the drinks without explaining how), Franny didn't care. Nor did she care
at that moment that her parents would be furious if
they knew she was out for the second night in a row
with this American auto industry destroyer named
Ren Tanazaki.

After spending most of Thursday night in the tokonoma, Franny had decided she would go out with
Ren on Friday and only Friday, telling him there were
problems at home and she wasn't sure she could see
him again. But when Friday night came and he strode
into Petals, so enthusiastic to see her, she couldn't say

a word. And by the end of the exhilarating evening, his soft good-night kisses still on her mouth, she felt that being with him Saturday and Sunday wouldn't be nearly enough time.

Franny picked up her glass and downed the last few drops of wine. "Delicious," she said. "Good wine for a bad girl. And believe me, I'm a very bad girl. You do believe me, don't you?"

"Sure," Ren said. He was pressed against her in the booth, one arm wrapped tightly around her shoulders.

"No, you don't. You think I'm a good girl. Just like everybody else does. But I'm not. I'm bad."

"Want to dance, bad girl?" he asked.

"Okay."

The deejay was spinning a fast song as Ren led Franny out onto the diminutive dance floor. Comfortable with his body, he was a very good dancer. Franny wasn't—at least not usually. She could follow the beat well enough, but she was too inhibited to cut loose. But tonight, with the glass of wine waltzing through her veins, she was rocking.

"Yeah!" she yelled, shaking her hips.

"Awww," she said, when the song ended.

The second record was a slow one. "Come here," Ren said, taking her into his arms. "I have a surprise for you tonight," he murmured into her ear.

"What is it?" she asked.

"You'll see."

"Will I like it?"

"I hope so." He laughed.

When the dance ended, Ren took Franny back to the booth.

"No more dancing?" she said.

"It's time for the show to begin," he told her.

"Oh. What show?"

"A live band."

"Oh. I'm thirsty. Can I have another glass of wine?"

"Sure." Ren disappeared into the crush, reappearing, after what seemed a long time to Franny, with her wine and another beer.

Over his mike, the deejay announced, "And now, Barger's is proud to present Braddington University's hottest new band. The one . . . the only . . . the Physicists."

Four young men ran out onto the stage. *Bom-bom-bom, bom-bom-bom, bom-bom-bom*, the bass player began. The lead guitarist joined in, followed by the drummer. Then the lead singer, whose gravity-defying green hair stood nearly six inches high, grabbed the mike and began to belt out the Pointer Sisters' tune "Neutron Dance."

Franny wiggled her shoulders to the beat. I'm a bad girl, she thought. And it feels good.

The Physicists were into Thomas Dolby's "She Blinded Me With Science" when Franny lifted her glass. How do you like polite little Franny Yeager now, Aunt Myrna? She took a big swallow and giggled.

Beedle-boddle, beedle-boddle, bop-boom. The Physicists' drummer did a roll on the snare. There was loud applause. The lead singer held up his hands. "Thank you, thank you. At this juncture, the Physicists would like to introduce a special guest . . ."

"Oooh," said Franny. "I love special guests."

Ren smiled. "I hope you really love this one," he said with a candid smile.

"Rock star, pilot, fellow physicist—and he dabbles in brain surgery on the side . . ."

Ren stood up.

"Where are you going?" Franny asked, her voice very loud in the hushed room.

"Performing his own composition entitled 'Relativity,' our own Buckaroo Banzai, Renshaw Tanazaki."

"Renshaw? Who's—Huh? Oh!" Franny gasped as Ren blew her a kiss and ran up to the stage.

The bassist handed him a guitar. "One. Two. One, two, three, four!" *Thwang!* Ren smashed down on the guitar. *Flinga-flanga-thwap! Bebompadoo.* Ren finished the opening riff and began to sing.

"Well, you can run. You can take flight.
You can approach the speed of light.
Go back in time.
Go off in space.
Or even leave the human race.
It don't matter,

You soon will see,
Because you'll never get away from me.
Oo-whee—
Relativity."

"Yeah!" "All right!" yelled several members of the audience, clapping along with the beat. In the background, the Physicists chanted, "E equals M C squared." And Franny, face flushed, eyes wide, palms sweating, clutched her wine glass without drinking from it and stared at the stage.

"Well, you can swim, or take a train.
Move to Siam, or maybe Spain.
Go underground.
Go overboard.
Or even join a Mongol horde.
It don't matter,
On land or sea.
You will never get away from me.
Oo-whee—"

Ren bumped his hips, then pointed a finger straight at Franny.

"Oh-whee," she breathed.

"Relativity." Wang wangadang. Wanga wanga danga danga dang. Ren's guitar squawked and yowled as he wiggled and shimmied across the stage to playful squeals and cheers.

"Play that thing!" someone shouted.

"Shake that thing!" yelled someone else.

Franny was too stunned to say anything at all.

"Well, you can hole up in your bed.
Or take a trip inside your head.
Leave all your folks.
Leave all your friends.
Go to extremes to reach your ends.
It don't matter,
'Cause wherever you'll be,
You'll never ever get away from me.
Aw, don't you see—
Relativity.
I said baby, baby, baby, baby, don't you see.
Oo-whee!
Relativity!"

Ren jumped in the air and crashed down the final chord on his guitar.

The crowd screamed and stomped and pounded on the tables for an encore. Ren obliged. When he finally finished, he got off the stage and headed for the booth. It was slow going because people kept patting him on the back, offering him drinks or flirting outrageously. But at last he got there. "Well, what did you think?" he asked, flushed and eager. "Did you like the song?"

"Yes," Franny said. "But I like the performer even better."

"What?" He stooped to catch her words.

Tugging him down beside her, she kissed him.

"I guess you liked it," he said with a laugh.

Franny laughed too. She was intoxicated in every sense of the word.

She hummed and clapped throughout the rest of the Physicists' set, leaning into Ren's arm, unable to stop grinning.

Then the Physicists, plus two young women, came over to join them.

"You was wailing tonight, Buckaroo." Darryl, the lead singer, praised Ren in a put-on voice.

"No rust on your pipes either," Ren kidded back.

"What'll you have, Buckaroo?" Johnny, the bassist, asked.

"I'm set," Ren said, holding up the second beer, which he hadn't had time to drink. "Do you want anything, Franny?"

Franny gulped down the rest of her wine. "Another one of these."

After Johnny went to get the drinks, Franny said to Darryl, "How come . . . how come you all call him Buckaroo?"

"You never saw the movie *Buckaroo Banzai*? He's this half-Japanese guy who's a rock star, a race-car driver, a neurosurgeon, a scientist, and an all-American hero."

"Oh. Nope. Never saw it. But I saw a good movie last night. *Parfum*. I liked the ending. Ren didn't. He made me argue about it with him. We argued for

159

hours. I used to hate arguing, but not with Ren. With Ren it's fun. With Ren everything's fun."

"I think this woman likes you, Renshaw." Darryl winked.

"Renshaw? First you call him Buckaroo, now Renshaw. Stop confusing me."

"Renshaw's my full name," Ren told her, brushing a wisp of hair out of her eyes.

"Doesn't sound Japanese," Franny slurred.

"It isn't. It's old English. It means 'from the trees black with watchful ravens.' "

"Yeah?" said Darryl.

"Beautiful," Franny said, staring into Ren's eyes. Her own crossed. "Where's my wine?"

Ren chuckled. "I think maybe you've had enough wine tonight."

"Oh no I haven't."

"You know, Ren," the lead guitarist, whose name was Fritz, said, "anytime you want to become a full-time Physicist, you're in."

"Thanks," Ren said. "But I think I'm going to be too busy." He grinned at Franny and stroked back her hair again. Then he asked Fritz, "So, where's Gina tonight?"

"Her mom's sick again. She's taking care of the kids."

"Gina's got the patience of a saint," Darryl's girl-friend, Peggy, said.

Franny didn't know Gina at all, but she suddenly

pictured her, pale and thin, sitting by her mother's side, with four fat kids running around the room. Gina was smiling a beatific smile at them all. "She's a good girl," Franny said, aloud.

"Yeah, unfortunately," said Fritz.

"I'm not. I should be home with my mother—I mean, my grandmother."

Everyone laughed.

"It's not funny," Franny said, louder. "I *should* be home with my grandmother." She stood up. "Excuse me. I have to go to the bathroom." She made her way, not too steadily, to the double-stalled rest room at the back of the bar. Once inside, she sat on a toilet and leaned her head against the wall. What am I doing? she thought. What am I doing? She sat that way for a long time.

"Franny?" a voice asked. "It's Peggy. Ren asked me to find out if you're okay. Are you okay?"

"I'm okay," Franny said.

"Can you come out?"

Franny didn't answer her. But after a few moments she unlocked the stall and stepped out.

Peggy smiled at her.

Franny walked over to the sink and began to wash her face.

"You're really lucky to be dating Ren," Peggy told her. "I know at least ten girls who'd give anything—and I mean anything—to go out with him. But he's been looking for Ms. Right. And I guess that's you."

Franny dried her face and walked out the door. Peggy followed her.

The Physicists were tuning up for their second set, so Ren was alone in the booth. "Franny, are you okay?" he asked, concern all over his face.

"Ren, will you take me home?" she said quietly.

He didn't argue with or question her. "All right," he said. "Good night, Peggy. Tell everybody else I'll catch them later. And thanks." He eased Franny into her jacket and escorted her out of the bar.

She said nothing on the ride home, and he didn't press her to speak. When they reached her house, he opened the car door and helped her out. "Are you really all right?" he asked.

"I guess I'm not very good at being bad," she answered.

He smiled.

"Ren, I can't go out with you tomorrow."

His smile faded. "Why?"

"My grandmother. She *is* sick, and I *do* have to be with her. I'm sorry."

"Do you have to be with her the whole day? I thought we could go out to Pine Lake. But maybe we could go someplace nearer for an hour or two—"

"I have to spend the whole day with her."

He tried to squelch a sigh of disappointment, but it slipped out anyway. "Well, I'll call you then. At least we can talk on the phone."

"No, don't do that. My . . . my parents don't want me to . . . to tie up the line."

"Oh," he said, sounding as if he didn't quite believe her. After a moment he asked, "Well, when am I going to see you again?"

"I don't know." Never. Always. "Next Friday?"

"Next Friday? That's six days away. I'll never make it till then," he said lightly.

Neither will I, she thought as he embraced her. Neither will I.

18

For the fourth time, Franny adjusted the flowers in the vase on the dresser. To her increasing annoyance, they kept slipping out of place. It had taken Franny nearly two hours to do the arrangement. She'd had to pay for the vase and beg Lillian to teach her the nageire form, the style appropriate for that container, so that she could bring an arrangement home to Grandma. The other arrangement she'd made (and once again hidden in the yard) was for her tokonoma—and her eyes alone.

She guessed the nageire was amateurish, but it pleased her anyway. The stocks were lovely, and their perfume was strong enough to mask the putrescent odor that clung to the bedroom, even though Grandma's foot was bandaged with gauze and Mrs. Yeager

kept spraying air freshener all over the place whenever she thought anyone wasn't looking. Franny had excitedly carried the arrangement up to present it to Grandma. She'd looked forward to telling her about the nageire style. We'll have a good time together, she'd thought. I won't miss Ren that much. I won't think about him.

But when Franny got to her room with the flowers, Grandma was asleep—and now, an hour later, she was still sleeping. Franny resented it. She's ill. She needs to sleep, she said to herself. But inside another voice, a nasty little voice, murmured, How dare she sleep! I gave up my whole afternoon with Ren to be with her. Maybe I could call him, she thought. Maybe he's at home (moping, the nasty voice added) and it's not too late to—

"Hunnnnhhh," Grandma groaned.

Franny turned to her. The elderly woman's eyes were half open. She looked frail against the pastel-striped pillowcase. "Frannele, is that you?"

"It's me, Grandma."

"What time is it?"

"Three forty."

"Oy vay, how long have I been asleep?"

"I'm not sure, Grandma. At least an hour. You were asleep when I came home."

"I think it's this drug the doctor gave me. It makes me so tired."

How could it? It's just an antibiotic, Franny almost

165

said. Instead, she agreed. "Maybe it does. But sleep is good for you. It'll help you get better faster."

Grandma didn't say anything, which surprised Franny. She'd been so quick to assure Franny, everyone in fact, on Wednesday and Thursday, that she was going to get better. But on Friday and Saturday she'd been much more subdued—something Franny hadn't noticed because she'd hardly been around to see her.

"I brought you a surprise, Grandma," Franny said cheerfully. Too cheerfully. "You have to tell me honestly what you think of it."

"What is it?" Grandma asked, sitting up partway and blinking.

Jeez, the flowers of course. There's nothing wrong with your eyes, is there? said the nasty voice. Franny was so upset she said nothing for a moment. Then, with the same strained cheerfulness, "This flower arrangement."

"Oh," Grandma said, squinting at it. "Nice. Very nice."

"They're stocks—the flowers, that is. And the green stuff, that's Scotch broom. The style's called nageire. It means 'thrown in.' See, the flowers have to look as though they've been tossed into the vase and they landed just right." She paused, expecting Grandma to ask her how long it took her to "toss" the flowers, or something to that effect, but Grandma just repeated, "Very nice," so Franny had to go on. "It took

me almost two hours to do." Her voice sounded whiny to her and she hated it.

"I think it's time for my shot," Grandma said. "Would you mind getting me the syringe and insulin. In fact, would you mind filling it for me?"

"I don't know how to, Grandma. I've never done it before."

"Haven't you? No, I guess it's Lainie who has."

"Lainie? Lainie's filled your syringe?"

"Yes, maybe six, seven times. She wanted to learn how. She even gave me the injection once."

"*Lainie* did?"

"Yes. That was when she wanted to be a nurse. Remember?"

Franny didn't. Lainie's career phases came and went with as much frequency as all her other interests.

Franny handed Grandma the hypodermic and insulin.

When Grandma finished with them, she smiled wanly at Franny. "So, I haven't seen much of you for a few days."

Franny felt as though she were wallowing in guilt. "I know, Grandma. I'm sorry."

"Don't be sorry. I guess Larry turned out to be more than just okay, no?"

On Friday morning Franny had told her mother she had a date that night. She hadn't said with whom. But when her mother had said, "I'm glad you're getting out. Larry's a nice boy," Franny hadn't bothered

167

to correct her. Grandma and Lainie had been in the kitchen at the time and had heard the whole exchange. Lainie'd given Franny a funny look, but for once she hadn't said anything. Grandma hadn't said anything either.

Now Franny looked at her and wanted to tell her the truth. Maybe telling the truth would make this afternoon come out right. And maybe talking about Ren would soothe some of that terrible yearning to be with him. "Grandma, I didn't—" she began.

But she didn't get any further because the bedroom door opened and her mother came in. "Time to change your bandages, Mom," she said brightly. After Wednesday night's outburst, Mrs. Yeager had decided to be relentlessly upbeat. "Oh, what lovely flowers! Did you arrange them, Franny?"

"Yes," Franny answered flatly.

"Very nice. Maybe you could bring home one or two more and really fill up the vase. . . . Now, Mom. You slide that cover off and I'll have you done in a jiffy."

The last thing in the world Franny wanted to do was stay and watch (and smell) Grandma's foot being un- and rewrapped. Which was exactly why she did. It was penance for the nasty voice, for the two glorious evenings with Ren, for the lies she'd told her family.

Mrs. Yeager chatted all through the bandaging, chatted and complained about her favorite topic,

Lainie. "She's at the mall now, and I know just what she's doing. Trying to pick up boys."

"All the girls go to the mall. Even Franny goes," Grandma said, smiling at her granddaughter.

"Not to pick up boys, she doesn't. Franny knows better than that," Mrs. Yeager said, as if Franny weren't even in the room. "And the boys she goes out with are from school. Or . . ." She suddenly remembered something and turned to her daughter. "How was that boy Lillian introduced you to? The one with the strange name?"

Franny paused a moment before she lied coolly. "Nothing special."

"Oh, well. There'll be others. There. You know, I think it's looking a little better. Of course, Dr. Carver will tell us for sure. You have an appointment with him the day after tomorrow."

Grandma nodded vaguely. Her eyelids were drooping again.

Mrs. Yeager picked up her wastebasket. "I'll dump this and bring it right back," she said to no one in particular, and left.

Franny sat quietly a minute, then said, "Grandma? Can I get you anything?"

"No, Frannele. I think I need to sleep some more. Why don't you get some air? Go to Hilton Park. It looks nice and sunny out. . . ." Her voice trailed off.

Franny still didn't budge until her mother returned with the bin.

"She's sleeping again," Mrs. Yeager said. "Let's leave her alone."

Franny didn't want to leave. It's my room too, she felt like yelling. But she got up and went, out the door and then out of the house, telling her mother she was going to take a walk.

It was sunny out, but the sun didn't gladden her. Not even the mallards in the pond at the park did. She sat down on a bench and closed her eyes.

In a few moments Ren was sitting next to her, his hands turning a wheel, working some controls. "Fasten your seat belt," he said.

She did. There was a hum of engines. The hum swelled to a roar. The plane began to move. She leaned back in her seat as it zoomed faster and faster down the runway.

And then they were airborne. Clouds and sky rushed to meet them.

"Oh!" She sighed. "Oh, we're free. Free!"

"Yes. At last," Ren said.

Then something soft touched her face. Franny opened her eyes. A withered leaf was clinging to her cheek. She brushed it away and sighed again. "Free," she murmured, shaking her head. Then she got up and headed for home.

19

"Uh-huh. And are there white, cottony deposits? That sounds like mealy bugs. We have an insecticide that you could purchase . . . What's in it? Hold on, please." Shaking her head, Franny rested the receiver on the counter and went to get the insecticide. At least every other day somebody called up about mealy bugs.

"You know the Bible story of the ten plagues God sent?" Lillian had said the first week Franny worked for her. "Well, whoever wrote that book left out the eleventh plague: mealy bugs." She'd taught Franny how to recognize them and advise customers on them, as well as introducing her to the florist's other foes—scale, white fly, aphids, and spider mites.

Franny looked at the back of the spray can and, picking up the phone once again, read the ingredients

off to the caller. She hung up, wondering whether he was planning to mix up his own batch of the stuff.

"Excuse me, ma'am, where do you want this here plant?"

Franny looked up, startled by the gruff voice that didn't sound like the delivery boy's. "Ren!" she exclaimed.

He was standing in the doorway, his arms full of grape ivy, grinning at her.

"What are you doing here? I mean with the plant?"

"Delivering it," he answered in his normal voice. "Marco's sick today, so Lillian pressed me into emergency service. It didn't take much pressing." He grinned again.

She smiled back shyly. She was thrilled to see him, but not sure she had the right to be. "The plant goes over there." She pointed to an empty hook hanging from the ceiling.

Ren carried it there. "Man, you can practically see these things grow," he said. "These little tendrils, they just shoot out so fast, they—Help!" He grabbed at his throat with one hand. A strand of ivy lay across it. "Help! They've got me! The deadly tendrils! I'm being strangled by a wild grape ivy!" He wrestled with the vine. "Take that! And that!"

Franny laughed out loud. His act was hilarious.

"What the hell's going on out here?" Lillian demanded, striding in from the back room, where she'd been paying bills.

172

"Good grief, Lillian. You said this job was safe. You neglected to tell me about the man-eating plants. This place is a regular Little Shop of Horrors!"

Lillian shook her head. "I ought to dock you for interrupting my assistant's work day, except that I'm not paying you anyway."

"That's right. I'm nothing but your slave." Ren got down on his knees and shuffled across the floor toward Lillian. "Beat me. Kick me. Lock me in my room without any supper. I'm yours—unless . . ." He shuffled over to Franny, who was giggling. "Unless *you* buy me and set me free. You would set me free, wouldn't you?" He gazed up at her. "Or would you keep me for yourself?"

Franny blushed. The boy had no shame.

Ren got gracefully to his feet just as the door opened and a customer came in, asking for Lillian.

"I'm Lillian Morrison," the florist said, walking toward her. "Can I help you?"

"I hope so. My friend Linda Bonner says you did those lovely arrangements for her daughter's wedding. My daughter's getting married in February, and I'd like you to do the flowers."

"Fine. Why don't we step into my office and talk about it?" Lillian led the woman to the back room.

Franny picked up a watering can and took it over to the grape ivy.

Ren followed her. "I missed you yesterday," he said in a low voice, leaning close to her as she watered the

173

plant. "I spent the whole afternoon virtuously studying thermodynamics. Have you ever studied thermodynamics? No? Then you don't know just how virtuous I was."

Franny moved over to a dieffenbachia to give it a soaking, but Ren took the watering can from her and turned her around to face him.

"I don't feel like being virtuous tonight," he said. "Do you?"

"I have to do homework tonight," Franny said.

"Damn. You do want to be virtuous. All right. Tell you what, let's be virtuous together. I'll come over to your house and we'll both do our homework."

"No! Not my house!" Franny said, too quickly and loudly. When she realized that he was taken aback, she said more quietly, "It's my grandmother." She hated having to use Grandma as an excuse. Her insides twisted with sadness and self-disgust, made worse by the look of concern on Ren's face.

"She's still sick?" he asked.

Franny didn't want to talk about Grandma. "Yes," she answered, hoping he'd drop the topic.

He didn't. "What's wrong with her?"

"She's a diabetic." No more questions, Ren, please.

"Hmmm. I don't know much about diabetes, but can't it be controlled with insulin?"

"She has . . . complications," Franny answered stiffly.

Ren caught the stiffness and decided this time not

to pursue the topic. Instead he suggested, "Well then, how about you coming over to my place? You're not really going to make me wait until Friday to see you, are you?"

Ren's place. Ren's den, thought Franny. A place smelling of dragon musk and freedom instead of overripe flowers and decay. Grandma didn't need her at home. She was still spending most of the time sleeping. Her parents didn't need her either. But . . . "I don't think I—" she began.

"That's just what I had in mind." Linda Bonner's friend interrupted her as she and Lillian emerged from the back room.

"Good," Lillian responded, walking her to the door. On her way, she gave Ren a look.

He gave her a sheepish one back and headed out the door to unload the rest of the plants.

As Lillian strode toward the rear of the store once more, Franny stopped her. "I'm sorry. I know I'm not supposed to be fooling around at work."

"No, you aren't. After work is a more appropriate time." Her eyes had an amused glint in them.

"I really like him," Franny said in a low voice. "A lot. But . . ." All at once, Franny wanted to pour everything out to her. But she couldn't. Ren's her grandson, she thought. How can you expect her to have sympathy when you tell her you can't bring him home, shouldn't even see him, because your parents wouldn't

approve? "But feelings, emotion, Kizu says they're not real, that we have to *transcend* them. That's the Zen way."

Lillian was quiet a moment. When she finally spoke, it was with a seriousness and a gentleness Franny hadn't heard from her before. "You can't transcend what you don't understand," she said. "First you have to get to know your feelings, Franny. Maybe even indulge them. Then you can worry about transcendence."

Franny didn't understand exactly what she meant, and before she could ask, Ren came in again with a box of poinsettias and Jerusalem cherries.

Lillian disappeared into the back room. Franny took up her watering can again. Ren set the plants down, left the shop, and reentered twice more. After he brought in the last batch, he went over to Franny, stuck his finger in the spout of Franny's watering can, and said, "You haven't answered me about tonight. Will you come over to my place?" His eyes held her. "I really want your company."

Say no, Franny, her conscience told her. She pulled a strand of grape ivy off his jacket and tossed it on the floor. "Yes," she said.

Marley Street was an old block of row houses. Franny found the one Ren lived in with little difficulty. But her legs felt funny, tight and rubbery at the same time, as she walked up the stoop. She couldn't believe she

was doing this—going to a guy's place, and on a school night. She was unhappy about having lied to her parents, telling them she was going to Susan's to study. At the same time, she didn't want to turn back. She took several deep breaths before she rang the bell.

A short red-haired guy opened the door.

"I'm here to see Ren," she told him. "He's expecting me."

"Upstairs. Third room on the left," the guy said.

Franny climbed the stairs and found the room. There was a drawing of an airplane on the door, the kind Franny imagined preadolescent boys did. Sure enough, Franny discovered, beneath Ren's signature in the lower right-hand corner, the inscription "Age 10." She smiled, then knocked.

Quick footsteps. The door swung open and Ren stood there, smiling. "Hi," he said. "Welcome to my humble abode." He ushered her inside.

The first things she noticed were books. Piles and piles of them, in every corner, on every piece of furniture. Ren took her backpack and jacket from her, set them on his desk, and said, "Now, let me give you the Grand Tour. Here we have my desk and books. My chair and books. My bureau and books. My bed and books."

She giggled, both out of amusement and nervousness.

"And on the walls, posters of two of my idols, Albert Einstein and Amelia Earhart, and the plane I'd give

my left brain to own. A Piper Warrior. Gorgeous, isn't it?"

Franny looked dutifully at the plane. It didn't look particularly gorgeous to her, but then, planes never did. What caught her attention was the painting next to it, a fanciful scene of a dragon and a tiger confronting each other on a cliff. "That's wonderful," she said.

"Last year's birthday present from Lillian."

"What did you get from your parents?"

"A lot of grief," he said, sitting on the bed.

"You don't get along with your parents?" Franny asked, perching on the single chair across from him.

"Oh, they're okay. But last April when I got my college acceptances and told them I was coming here, they got upset. Especially my mother. She wanted me to stay in San Francisco—that's where they live. I'm her baby, you see. And my dad, he wanted me to stay in San Francisco too, but not for the same reason. He thinks Stanford is better than Braddington. He thinks if I'm going to be a serious physicist, I should go there. He's wrong. Braddington isn't as well known as Stanford, but it's got an excellent science department. And anyway, I'm not going to be a serious physicist. I'm going to be a serious pilot. And he can't understand that. So on my birthday, he gave me a card. Inside was a picture of that Warrior with a check and a note that said, 'Here's the first installment. Four more will

178

follow, one for each year you complete at Stanford.' "

"But that's bribery."

"Yeah. And that's what I told him, but he didn't see it that way. He said the plane was an 'incentive'— he likes to use words like that—and that if I didn't want the plane, he'd give me something else. I wanted the plane all right, so much I thought I'd die. So I agreed. I said yes to Stanford. My folks were ecstatic. Correction, Mom was ecstatic. Dad was pleased. That's what he told me. 'Son, I'm pleased.' Very emotional, my father," Ren said sarcastically.

"Well, he's Japanese," Franny put in, and was immediately embarrassed. "I mean, in Zen, you—"

But Ren snorted. "My father doesn't know Zen from voodoo. He was raised Baptist. Anyway, it didn't work. The closer it got to the semester starting, the more I knew, Warrior or no Warrior, I couldn't be the good son, live at home, and go to a university I didn't want to go to. So I wrote to Braddington and asked if they'd still have me. When they said yes, I kissed my parents and my Warrior good-bye. I guess I'm more willing to give up my left brain for it than my freedom. Lillian's being here has helped a lot. She thinks kids have to get away from their parents—and sometimes parents from their kids." He paused, then said, "How about you? Do your folks get on your case? Do you want to get away from them?"

For a moment, Franny didn't know what to say;

179

then she replied self-consciously, as if she'd memorized the words, "Sometimes. But they've done a lot for me and I've got to be grateful."

Ren waited for more. When Franny remained silent, he said, "I'm grateful to mine too. But the problem is that gets mixed up with guilt. You owe your birth to your parents, but not your whole life." He thought of something and laughed. "Some people who believe in reincarnation think you may not even owe them that. They say it's you, or rather your spirit, that chooses the body to enter and the parents you want in each lifetime."

"Really?" Franny was fascinated. "But what about them? I mean, don't the parents have any choice?"

"Well, if I've got this right, which I probably don't, they attract you, the reasons having to do with karma, working out stuff you—and they—didn't work out in previous lifetimes."

"If that's the case, I'd hate to see what my past lifetimes were like," Franny thought, then realized she'd spoken aloud.

Ren laughed, and so she did too. Then they sat quietly gazing at each other.

"I think we'd better start studying now," Franny said after a pause. "I've got a French test tomorrow."

"Really? Do we have to?"

"Yes, we have to."

"Quel dommage," Ren said. But he slid back against his headboard and flipped open a book.

180

Franny turned her chair around, unzipped her pack, took out her French text and began to read it.

At first it was hard to concentrate with Ren behind her on his bed, but he was quiet and focused, and soon she was able to study too.

She wasn't aware of how long they'd been working until he grunted. She looked over her shoulder at him.

"What do you think about the fact that we can use calculus to compute a planet's trajectory or position from knowing its acceleration, plus a few other things?"

"I'm not following you," Franny answered.

"I'm not sure I'm following myself. Want some coffee? I need a break."

"Okay."

"There's always a pot brewing in the kitchen. I'll be right back." He left the room.

She stood up, stretched, and walked around, looking at the few knicknacks, plucking the strings of the guitar leaning against the wall. On the top of Ren's bureau was a small model of the solar system. There was a switch on the side. Franny flicked it. The model began to hum, and slowly, majestically, the little planets started to orbit around the bright, golden sun. Franny was enthralled. She watched it make one complete revolution, trying to remember how many solar years Saturn's orbit took. Then she focused on the other planets and realized something was wrong. One of them was missing. Which one is it? she wondered.

Let's see, there's Mercury. That's that little one. Venus. Earth. Mars. Jupiter, right, the big one. Saturn, of course. Then . . . what's the next one, Neptune or Uranus? Whichever it is, it's the other one that isn't here. . . .

At that moment Ren returned with two mugs of coffee.

"Which planet comes after Saturn?" Franny asked him.

"Uranus."

"Then Neptune's missing."

"What?" Ren set down the mugs and crossed over to her.

She pointed to the empty space where the planet should have been.

"Damn!" he said. "Where'd that go?" He bent down and searched under and behind the bureau, but Neptune didn't turn up.

"Maybe it rolled into the closet," Franny said.

Ren opened the closet door and squatted. And there, on the floor, near one of his shoes, was the missing planet. "Eureka!"

Franny gasped. She was not reacting to finding the planet or to Ren at all. She was looking past him at the kimono hanging in his closet. A black kimono with silver fans, just like the one Ren had been wearing in her fantasy.

"What's wrong? Did we just lose another celestial

body? Maybe I can compute its trajectory and figure out where it went."

"No. It's that . . . that kimono."

He looked back over his shoulder.

"Nice, isn't it? Another birthday present from Lillian. I like to wear it when I'm studying. It makes me feel scholarly. Want to try it on?" He slipped it off the hanger and held it out for her.

Without saying anything she put her arms into the long, silken sleeves and tied the sash around her waist. He adjusted the collar for her. "Look," he said, drawing her in front of his mirror.

She giggled a little. The kimono was way too big. The hem drooped on the floor. The sleeves extended at least half a foot past her fingertips.

"Hmm. Who's your tailor?"

Franny giggled again. She took the kimono off. Then, shyly, she asked, "Will you put it on?"

"All right." Franny lowered her eyes as he took off the bulky sweater he was wearing, as well as the shirt beneath it. He got into the robe, tying it over his pants.

Franny looked up at him and swallowed hard. Even with the jeans peeking out at the bottom, the kimono had transformed him into the Dragon Boy of her dreams.

For a moment they held each other's eyes. Then they were embracing, kissing. Franny didn't know how they got on his bed, but there they were, entangled

183

amid the fat books and crumpled papers. Ren, his sash undone and the kimono gapping open, was kissing her throat, unbuttoning her shirt. And she was running her hands along his arms and spine.

Stop. You should stop, her conscience told her. But she didn't want to stop.

Now Ren was lying on top of her, his kimono spread out over them like dragon wings, his bare skin warm against hers. Murmuring his name, she stroked the nape of his neck, then wrapped her arms tightly around him.

Abruptly he pulled away from her onto his back.

She lay there, unmoving. She didn't know what had happened, what she'd done wrong.

For several minutes, Ren didn't speak or move. At last he said, "Look, Franny. I don't want this to happen. I mean I do, but not yet, not so fast. You're special to me. Very special. . . . There was another girl a couple of years ago. She was special, too. But things happened too fast and she got scared. I don't want to scare you away like that. So I've got to slow down. Which is hard because I'm not much good at taking things slow." He moved his head from his pillow to her chest, clutching hold of her as if she'd brake his speed.

Feeling a strange combination of relief, disappointment, and lingering desire, she silently stroked his tousled hair.

In a lighter voice he said, "Maybe I should court

184

you. Come to your house in a suit and tie for dinner. Flatter your mom. Call your dad 'Sir' and ask politely if I might date his daughter. Then we could take one of them or Lillian along as a chaperone. What do you think? Think that would teach me patience?"

Franny shuddered at the thought.

"Are you cold?" he asked, leaning up on one elbow.

"A little," she lied. "I think I'd better go home now."

"I'll take you." He got up, stripping off the kimono and putting his shirt and sweater back on.

She froze midway in fastening her shirt. She'd told her parents she was going to be at Susan's—just a brief walk from her house. If she arrived in a car, which they'd be bound to hear pulling up, they'd know she'd lied, even if they didn't see Ren and know the full extent of the lie.

"Uh . . . well . . . okay. But drop me off at my friend Susan's. I have to pick up a book from her and go over an assignment before I go home."

Ren looked at her and his brow furrowed. He had the sense that she wasn't telling him the truth. He started to say something, thought better of it, and just nodded.

Franny gathered her books into her pack and slipped it on over her jacket. She started for the door, but before she could open it, Ren took her by the shoulders, turned her around, and pulled her tight against him.

"Don't get scared of me, Franny. Don't run away from me."

"I'm not scared of you," she murmured. But she didn't tell him what she was scared of, and he didn't ask.

20

The bell had barely finished ringing to end Ms. Coleman's class before Susan, gripping Franny's elbow tightly, steered her out the door and against a row of lockers in the hall.

"Okay, Ms. Yeager, just what are you up to?" she demanded.

"What do you mean?"

"I called your house last night. Your mom answered and said, 'Why, hasn't Franny reached your house yet? She left fifteen minutes ago.' "

Franny clapped her hand over her mouth. "Oh, God," she said. "I . . ." She stopped, puzzled. Her mother had said nothing to her last night or this morning either, so she couldn't have found out the truth. "What did you tell her?" Franny asked.

"Lucky for you I'm a fast thinker. I said, 'Oh, I think I hear her now. Yes, there she is. I just wanted to remind her to bring her history notes.' Then I hung up. You were out with Ren last night, weren't you?"

Franny nodded.

"Thanks for not telling me. I'm only your best friend."

"I'm sorry. I should've called you. I didn't think you'd call. I guess I didn't want you to have to lie for me too. I mean, my own lying's bad enough."

"So, tell them the truth."

Franny pursed her lips. They'd been through this already. "I won't ask you to cover for me in the future," she said tightly.

Susan shook her head. "That's not the point. You know I don't mind covering for you. I just think in the long run the truth is better for your health." Then, her tone softening, she said, "So are you going to tell me where you went with him last night?"

Franny paused a moment before answering. "His room."

It was Susan's turn to look surprised. "Wow. What was it like?"

"Cluttered, but comfortable."

"Not his room. Him. Being with him. What did you do?"

"Susan, we're going to be late for class."

"So we'll be late. Come on, Franny! You can't deprive your closest friend of a vicarious thrill by clam-

ming up about your sex life. It's unfair!"

"We . . . uh . . . fooled around some. But he didn't want to rush things."

"He didn't? *He* didn't? My God, you mean the guy's not only got looks, brains, talent, taste, and a beautiful butt, but he's noble to boot? If I were you, I'd marry him tomorrow. No, don't even wait until tomorrow. Do it tonight!"

"Susan!" Franny smiled. But she quickly grew serious again. "Last night I . . . I didn't want to stop. It was as if my body just took over. My mind wasn't thinking at all."

"Hmmm. That sounds like the Zen state you told me about. You know, I once read about some people who practice meditation through sex. It's called something like tantrum. I remember thinking, now there's a type of meditation I could go for." She grinned, then went on soberly, "Franny, you're in love with him, aren't you?"

"I don't know. We just met last week. But, well, I think so."

"That's wonderful. Don't you see? Let it be wonderful."

"But—" Franny began and broke off. She didn't want to say the same things she'd said before and get another lecture from Susan. Then she realized Susan wasn't listening.

"Holy cow!" Susan said, staring over Franny's shoulder.

Franny turned around and there, in an outrageously short and tight pink miniskirt and a black shirt unbuttoned over an equally tight pink tank top, was Lainie. Franny couldn't remember ever having seen her sister in an outfit like that before, didn't remember her wearing it this morning. Mom would have a fit, she thought.

Lainie spotted her and Susan and strolled over.

"That's some outfit," Susan said.

"Like it? I think it shows off a few of my strong points."

"It definitely does that."

"So, did you two study hard last night?" Lainie gave her sister a smirk.

Franny felt a sudden chill go up her back. She knows. I don't know how, but somehow she knows.

"Sure," Susan said nonchalantly.

"Glad to hear it. You know, Mom was saying just last night that you work too hard. She's glad you've been going on dates more often, especially with nice guys like *Larry*."

Franny said nothing. Mercifully, the late bell rang. "I'll see you later," she flung out at both her sister and her friend, and ran to class, swearing to herself the whole way there.

After her last class ended, Franny, on her way to Petals, worried about Lainie. Just how much did she know? Would she tell their parents? Why was she so

190

mean? She was glad when she finally arrived at the store and plunged into her work. And there was plenty of it. The Christmas season had descended like a blizzard on the flower shop—and Lillian warned Franny that things were only going to get worse, especially on Saturdays, when customers looking for the perfect, or even not so perfect gift, would pack the place.

At a quarter to six, with half of the latest delivery still unpacked and a bunch of decorations to be put up, Lillian asked Franny if she could work an extra hour. "I'll pay you time and a half," Lillian told her.

"Well, I'll have to call my mother," Franny replied. She didn't tell Lillian about the way her parents, especially her father, got upset if she was not on time for dinner. But Franny didn't want to let Lillian down, and she thought she could play on her folks' sense of "work ethic" to escape their wrath.

She dialed her number, pumping up her confidence as she did so. Her mother answered. "Hi, Mom. It's Franny," she began. "It's very busy here, and—"

Mrs. Yeager cut her off. "Oh, Franny. I was just about to call you."

"What? You were?"

"Yes. Now, listen. Don't get upset," her mother said, saying the words carefully, as if she thought they might break. "Your grandmother saw Dr. Carver this afternoon, and he thinks it's best for her to go into the hospital."

The room grew flat and unreal. "The hospital?"

Franny said hollowly. "You mean . . . you mean . . ." They're going to amputate her leg, she thought. But she couldn't, didn't want to say the words. "I thought she was better." No, you didn't. You knew she was worse. But you didn't care. You could have stayed with her last night. But you went to Ren's room instead. You chose him over her. You even forgot she had a doctor's appointment today.

"They're going to try intravenous antibiotics there. Dr. Carver says they work better than the oral kind. He says he has high hopes they'll do the trick."

Trick. It's a trick. Once they put you in the hospital, you never come out better, just smaller.

"Anyway, the hospital just called and said there's a bed available, so we're going there right now. Lainie's not here yet, so I'd like you to be around to tell her where we've gone and that we'll have dinner later. I didn't want to just leave her a note. It seemed too . . . cold."

"Cold," Franny repeated in a whisper.

"What? Franny? Are you still there?"

"I'm here."

"Well, you can visit Grandma tomorrow and bring her some flowers. Maybe some of those tall ones with all the blossoms—what are they called, gladiolas?"

"Gladioluses."

"Right."

Neither of them could hang up.

"She'll be fine, Franny," Mrs. Yeager reassured her once again.

"Sure."

Another moment went by. Finally, her mother said, "Well, we've got to go."

"Good-bye," said Franny. She set down the phone. "I can't work late," she told Lillian woodenly. "I've got to go home."

"All right," Lillian responded. She didn't ask Franny why, and Franny didn't tell her.

The living room was as dark and depressing as ever, but it seemed to Franny the right place to wait for Lainie's return. She couldn't bear her room, the tokonoma was out of the question, and the kitchen, with its fluorescence and formica, was too harshly bright to suit the occasion.

Lainie was late. It was already past seven o'clock. Franny wished she'd show up already. Not that she wanted to see her, but she didn't want Lainie to come in after their parents returned and cause a fight on top of everything else. She leaned back into the scratchy dirt-brown sofa and wondered why God (or Buddha or whoever) had given her this family or if she'd really "chosen" it herself. She wasn't sure she'd have picked these parents or Lainie, regardless of what she hadn't worked out in a past life. But Grandma, I know I'd pick Grandma, she thought, and her lips trembled. It

isn't fair. Why should Grandma be suffering now? She's kind and sweet and never hurt anyone. Why not Lainie, for God's sake? "Not that I want anything to happen to her," she aloud, quickly, fearfully. But why not some dictator? Or that Mafia guy who just got acquitted? Why don't they suffer? Karma. That was the word Ren had used. She'd read up on it in study hall. It was the idea that whatever you did wrong in one lifetime you'd pay for in the next one. Or whatever you'd left unresolved, you'd have to work out next time around. So maybe if the dictator or the Mafia don didn't suffer this time, they would later on. But then what about Grandma? Was she suffering now for something bad she'd done in *her* last life? Franny didn't find the idea comforting at all. In fact, she found it infuriating. She began to shake with anger.

Stop it, she commanded herself. You're letting your emotions take over. She breathed deeply and, for a moment, calmed down. But then a voice in her head said, And if we're supposed to transcend our emotions, why do we have them in the first place? Why'd God do that, huh? Huh? "How come, God?" she said out loud.

Then she heard the front door open. She took a great gulp of air. Immediately, everything, all the fury, shrank to a small spot of cold fire in her chest. She heard Lainie pad into and out of the kitchen, then head upstairs and down again. She pictured the smirk

on her sister's face slowly fading as Lainie grew more and more bewildered by everyone's absence.

"Hello? Hello? Hey, where is everybody?" Lainie finally came into the living room. She was wearing jeans and the black shirt, now buttoned almost to the throat. "Franny? Is that you?"

"Yes."

"What's going on?" Her thick brows winged together in worry. "Where're Mom and Dad and Grandma?"

Why, are you disappointed that they're not here to yell at you, so you could scream back and have a real lung buster of a fight? Franny wanted to say. But instead, tonelessly, she answered, "They're at the hospital. Grandma's being admitted."

Lainie's eyes widened in distress. "Oh, no. Oh, no," she said. "They're not . . . But they said. The doctor said she'd be better. The antibiotics . . ." she stammered, sounding like Franny had before on the phone with their mother.

"They're going to try new ones. Intravenous," Franny said. Her voice was still brittle, and she was beginning to feel more brittle inside, too.

"Oh," said Lainie. "Oh. Then they're not going to—"

"Not yet."

Some color came back to Lainie's cheeks. "Good. That's good. She'll be all right, then. Intravenous drugs work faster than oral ones or even shots. And at the

hospital they can monitor the dosage," Lainie spouted doctor talk as well as her mother. Then she said, "It's so dark in here."

Franny didn't say anything. Lainie walked over to the lamp and flicked the switch to the highest wattage of the three-way bulb in it. Mrs. Yeager never let them do that when she was around unless they had company. "Burns too much electricity," she'd say. For good measure, Lainie flicked on another lamp too. Then she went over to the radio and turned it on, spinning the dial at a rapid clip.

Franny sat still as a stone, watching her, the cold fire still glowing inside until Lainie tuned in a station that was playing some old rock tune. "Hey, remember this? Dad has this record. He used to play it for us all the time when we were little. It's prehistoric." She began to sing along with it.

Franny remembered. And she remembered something else too. She and Lainie had decided to write a song sort of like it. It was going to be FraLainie's big hit.

Suddenly, in mid note, Lainie clicked off the radio and sang,

"We kissed in the movie show,
My angel baby and me,
And the name of the show
I will never, ever know.
Oh gosh,

Oh gee,
My baby and me.

Come on, Franny, what's the next verse?"

"He held me oh so tight
Till they turned on the theater light—"

"That's it! That's it!"
Together the two sisters finished the verse:

"Everybody was looking our way,
We didn't know what to say.
Oh gosh,
Oh gee,
My baby and me."

"What's the rest of it?" asked Lainie.

"There isn't any rest of it," said Franny. "That's as far as we ever got."

"You're kidding. Some songwriters we'd make," Lainie said. She sat down next to Franny on the couch and shook back her long hair.

Franny felt a sadness and a longing replace the anger inside her. She wanted to stroke her sister's hair the way she used to when they were small. She wanted them to be small once again. She saw herself standing by Lainie's crib, patting the fine red down on her head. "Here, Franny, why don't you tie this ribbon in your sister's hair?" she heard their mother say. "You tie such nice, neat bows." Tears came to her eyes.

197

"Hey, look at this." Lainie brought her out of her reverie. She was holding a book in her hand. *"Forbidden Encounter,"* she read aloud.

"What? Where'd you find that?"

"Here. In the couch just now. Stuck between the cushions. It must be Mom's." She flipped through it. "Woo-woo. Listen to this. *'The temple was sacred to the Chinese goddess of love,' he murmured into her shell-like ear. He smelled like musk. She felt herself grow hot with longing. She turned to him. The sight of his smooth black hair, slanting brown eyes, and high cheekbones filled her with desire. She could almost taste his kisses on her tongue. 'But he's a half-breed,' she remembered Letitia sneering. She took a step back. He caught her and crushed her in his muscular arms, raining fiery kisses on her lips, her neck, and her heaving bosom. As they sank to the jade floor, she answered Letitia in silence, But he's* my *half-breed.* Oh, my God!" Lainie cackled. "I didn't know Mom read this stuff. This romantic crap! *My half-breed.* God, and it's racist too!"

Franny's face reddened.

Lainie looked at her. "This is *Mom's*, isn't it?" she said, with more impishness than malice.

But Franny snapped, "Yes, it's Mom's," and then, with self-disgust, saw Lainie smirk at her.

"Well, well. You sure have a lot of interesting secrets lately. Like what are you really doing when you claim you're dating Larry?"

Unwillingly, Franny found herself saying, "What do you mean 'claim'? What makes you so sure I'm not dating Larry?"

"Because *I* am," said Lainie.

21

The curtains around the bed were drawn, but the stench proclaimed that Franny'd found the right room. Clutching the bouquet of roses she'd brought, she called softly, "Grandma?"

A blond nurse stuck her head out from the curtains. Her white cap had an odd black smudge near the peak, and Franny was struck with the peculiar idea that it, not Grandma's foot, was rotting and giving off the foul smell. "We're almost finished in here," the nurse said cheerily, and disappeared.

Finished with what, Franny didn't dare ask. With the roses against her nose, she walked nervously toward the window and nearly bumped into a large elderly woman getting out of the bed next to it.

"Hello, little girl," the woman said in a rumbling voice.

"Hello," Franny answered, accepting the idea that she was little compared to the woman. "I'm sorry. I didn't know anyone else was here."

"That's all right. I was just going for a walk." She belched. "That your grandma in the next bed?"

"Yes."

"Nice woman. Very nice. Too bad about her foot." Franny nodded.

"Must be especially rough because of what she was. I must admit I never heard of her myself, but I've never been one for much culture. I'm a farmer's daughter and a farmer's wife." She belched again. "Sorry. Gall bladder," the woman apologized.

Before Franny had time to ask or even wonder what she meant about Grandma, there was a clatter of rings on the curtain rod and the nurse announced, "Here she is." The nurse picked up a bedpan and trotted briskly out.

Swallowing the hard lump in her throat, Franny smiled and walked over.

Grandma, in a blue nightgown, was propped up against several pillows. A needle was attached to her arm and a tube to the needle, leading to a small bottle that dripped its contents steadily into her veins. She looked as pale as when Franny had seen her last, yesterday morning, but more alert. She smiled a smile

201

of both welcome and embarrassment that Franny found almost too much to bear.

"Frannele, you didn't need to come here. I'll be home soon. You could've waited."

"No, I couldn't have," Franny replied, with what she hoped was lightness. She hugged Grandma and handed her the roses.

"Beautiful. Did you see my beautiful roses, Mrs. Parker?" Grandma said to her roommate as the woman lumbered past.

"Yes. They're lovely."

"But my granddaughter's even lovelier, don't you think?"

"She certainly is. Have a good visit now." Mrs. Parker waddled her way out of the room.

Franny watched her go, then looked back at Grandma. She stood there awkwardly, then asked, "Shall I put those in water for you?"

"Yes, thank you. I think there's a vase in this drawer."

Franny found the vase, filled it with water, and set the roses in it. Her movements were as crisp as the nurse's had been, and she wondered if the hospital air had some strange component that made anyone who wasn't a patient act that way. She put the vase on Grandma's night table. "I didn't have time to make an arrangement," she explained. "The Christmas rush is on."

Grandma reached out and touched the petals of the blossom nearest her. "Roses have always been my

favorite. They used to shower me with them."

"Who did, Grandma? Your boyfriends?"

"My public."

Franny laughed, too loudly, at the joke.

Grandma didn't laugh with her. She furrowed her brow slightly, then asked, "How was school today? Did you read anything interesting in your English class?"

Franny sat in a chair near the roses. "Not today. Today we diagramed sentences. Mr. Jonas said most of our last papers showed original thought and the worst grammar he'd seen in a long time for an honors class." Franny paused, then went on. "The big thing in school today was this Christmas dance everybody's excited about. The rumor is some really good band is going to play, but nobody knows which one."

"Are you going to it?"

"I don't think so."

"I remember a dance at Christmastime. I wore a red dress. It was considered very daring."

Franny smiled.

"You should go, Frannele. Get that boy you're seeing to take you. What's his name again? Larry?"

Franny's smile faded. Larry. Larry and Lainie. How Lainie had gloated yesterday, triumphantly exposing Franny's lie and stealing a former beau in one fell swoop. She'd expected some big reaction in return, but Franny'd refused to give her one. She'd simply left the room, her insides roiling. But she knew Lainie wasn't about to let the matter drop.

Now Franny pictured Ren, stunning in tux, leading her, quite passable in a floaty red dress, out onto the dance floor. Everyone was staring at them in admiration or envy—except for Lainie, on Larry's arm. Lainie's eyes glittered like those of a detective who's finally solved her case and is about to turn in the culprit for retribution. Franny shuddered.

"Are you all right?" Grandma asked.

"What? Oh, yes. Yes, Grandma. I'm fine. I was thinking about the dance. I'm such a . . . a bad dancer, I don't think I'd enjoy myself."

"A bad dancer? Impossible," Grandma said. "Not Anya Gallinsky's granddaughter."

Her tone was so haughty that Franny smiled. "Well, Grandma, I guess the dance gene bypassed me."

Grandma opened her mouth to say something else and was interrupted by two doctors who rustled in and proceeded to examine her foot.

Franny went over to the window again as they did. A terrible sadness was swelling in her chest. She was afraid she might suddenly burst into tears.

Then she heard Grandma say, "Toe shoes. That's what ruined my feet. Those terrible toe shoes."

"I see," responded one of the doctors.

Franny shook her head. Grandma was remarkable. Making jokes about her horrible disease. Maybe she really was getting better. Franny turned to smile encouragement at her.

But then Grandma added, "I was the greatest bal-

lerina in all of Russia," and her tone took Franny aback. Grandma hadn't said the words as though she were joking. She'd said them as though she believed them.

When the doctors left, Franny returned to her side.

"So," Grandma said. "How's Lainie? Your mother said she might visit me tomorrow, but I don't think she should come here. It's not a good place for her to visit."

"She's okay," Franny said. Then gently, "Grandma, you really had those doctors confused. They really believe you were a ballerina." She held her breath.

"Of course they do. Because I was. I danced before the crowned heads of Europe. They showered me with roses."

Franny felt as though a hand had reached inside her and squeezed her heart. "Grandma, I think maybe you're a little mixed up."

"No, I don't think so," she answered matter-of-factly. "So, what about Susan? How's she doing?"

"F-fine," Franny stammered.

"Good. Maybe she'll pay me a visit when I get home." She laughed, and Franny got even more tense.

"Why're you laughing?" she asked, not certain she wanted to hear the answer.

"I was just remembering Susan's story about the wet ghost that turned out to be her Aunt Hannah."

Relieved, Franny said, "I'm not sure I remember that one."

"I think you were daydreaming when she told it. Let's see if I can repeat it. . . ." She did, with as much panache as Susan must've given it.

Franny laughed, but her mind reeled with questions. How could Grandma be lucid one moment and mixed up the next? Was it from the drugs they were giving her? Or did her illness affect the brain too?

Then, as the visit went on and Grandma said nothing else strange, Franny began to doubt first her hearing, then her own mind. By the time she departed, she was wondering if she'd imagined the whole thing herself.

On the following day, when Franny entered Grandma's room, Uncle Mike and Aunt Myrna were there.

"Mom, what are you talking about?" Uncle Mike was saying. "You never studied at the Kirov."

The word was vaguely familiar to Franny, but she couldn't remember what it meant. Then Uncle Mike spotted her.

"Well, if it isn't my favorite niece!" he said heartily. "Still studying Chinese flower arrangement?"

"Japanese," Franny corrected. "And yes, I am."

"Great. Did you arrange those?" He pointed to the roses. "Nice job. Well, Aunt Myrna and I were just about to leave." He kissed Grandma. "Bye-bye, Mom. Don't do anything I wouldn't do."

"You can be sure of that," Grandma replied.

Uncle Mike and Aunt Myrna hustled out. To Franny they seemed eager to go.

"How was school today?" Grandma asked, as usual.

"Okay." Franny didn't want to talk about school. She was far more excited about something else. Lillian had asked her if she wanted to attend a lecture on Zen at the university the following night. The speaker was to be George Henkin, a Zen master and friend of Lillian's. Ren was coming along too. So, leaving out any mention of Ren, Franny told Grandma about it, finishing with, "I looked up Master Henkin in the library. He's written several books on Zen. The library had one—*Light Before Your Eyes*—but it wasn't on the shelf."

"*Light Before Your Eyes*. When I danced, there was always a big spotlight on me."

Franny's excitement died. Oh, no, she thought. It's happening again. She's talking weird again. "Grandma," she blurted out, "why do you say these things about being a dancer? You were never a ballerina. You know that. Are you just trying to tease me?"

"But I *was* a ballerina," Grandma said. "The greatest in all of Russia. Everyone knows that. They've even asked me to dance again. But I can't right now."

"Oh God," Franny moaned, her hand in front of her mouth. "Oh, Grandma."

Grandma just smiled in response.

———

207

At dinner that night, Franny was very quiet. So was the rest of her family, even Lainie, who, so far, hadn't attempted extortion or told their parents about Franny's lie. Afterward, as Franny was helping her mother with the dishes, she said slowly, "Mom, have you talked with Grandma's doctor?"

"Yes," Mrs. Yeager answered. "Today."

"How is she doing?"

Mrs. Yeager hesitated, then said, "There hasn't been the improvement they'd hoped for in her foot."

"They're going to operate?"

"They're not certain yet. They'll know within the next few days."

"Um . . . what about her mental health?"

Her mother looked sharply at her. "Why do you ask that?"

"Because Grandma's been acting a little . . . uh . . . confused."

"How?"

"She thinks she was a ballerina."

Mrs. Yeager's face crumpled. She quickly forced it back into shape. "Yes. I was hoping she wouldn't . . . Well, I noticed that myself, and I asked the doctor. He said she was suffering from delusions, but that they were probably a result of depression rather than something like schizophrenia."

"But she doesn't act depressed. At least, not now."

"No. I think he said this is how she's coping with depression. I don't know. At any rate, he said that

once she stops being depressed, the delusions will stop. Of course, surgery might prolong the condition." Her face collapsed again, and this time she couldn't put it back in place. "Oh, Franny. I know how upsetting this is. Things have been so difficult. First your father worrying about his job, and now Grandma. I'm sorry you and your sister have to be exposed to it. All I ever wanted is for us to be a healthy, happy family. I don't understand why we can't be." She sounded so sad and bewildered. Franny put a hand on her shoulder.

Mrs. Yeager gave a little shake and composed her mouth into a parody of a smile. "Anyway, we mustn't get too grim. We have to stay cheerful. Grandma's still with us and—"

"She's losing her mind along with her leg." Franny hadn't meant the words to come out, but they did.

Her mother whipped her head around with an expression of shock and distaste. "Lainie!" she snapped.

Franny set down the dish she was holding. "Franny," she corrected quietly.

22

"So let me leave you with a short poem by a far more enlightened soul than I—Master Bankei. It's called 'New Year's,' which I think is fitting for this season:

'What does it matter, the new year, the old year?
I stretch out my legs and all alone have a good sleep.
Don't tell me the monks aren't getting their instruction.
Here and there the nightingale is singing: the highest Zen!' "

George Henkin bowed to the audience, which applauded him warmly.

Franny didn't applaud; she was thinking about the poem and other things the man had said. Many of his anecdotes and jokes had been coarse and funny. He'd started his talk with a story about a Zen master who, when a disciple asked the question "How can I become

enlightened?" dropped his pants and peed. Franny was a bit shocked. What kind of Zen master is this? she thought. But the rest of the audience seemed to find the tale both hilarious and instructive. Master Henkin enjoyed his stories the most of anyone, laughing with big braying guffaws like a donkey. In fact, Franny thought he looked a bit like a donkey (if donkeys could be attractive), which was not the way she expected a Zen master to look.

"George is a great speaker, isn't he?" Ren, sitting next to her, said.

Franny nodded, even though she wasn't exactly sure she agreed.

"And he's good-looking too, eh, Lillian?"

Franny, hearing the teasing note in his voice, looked first at him, then at his grandmother.

Lillian's eyes were sparkling and there was a faint blush on her cheeks. But all she said was "We'll wait until this crowd disperses before we say hello to him."

Which was what they did. And it took a while. The enthusiastic audience swarmed around the man, asking him questions, seeking guidance. One bone-thin woman monopolized him for a full five minutes. At last Lillian stood up and led Franny and Ren over to him.

"Lillian, my flower lady." The Zen master smiled fondly. "What do you think—have I lost weight?" He patted his small paunch.

"A little," Lillian answered.

"And Ren, my God, you've grown at least a foot since I saw you last. And you're so handsome. You must be devastating to the ladies."

"Definitely." Ren grinned at Franny.

"George, this is Franny. She's studying ikebana," Lillian said, leaving out "with me."

"Pleased to meet you, Franny." He extended his hand.

Shyly, Franny shook it. "I thought your talk was very interesting, Master Henkin."

"But?" He said the word for her.

Franny blushed. She'd thought she'd kept her voice neutral. Now she had no choice but to explain herself. "Well," she said slowly, "you told a lot of funny stories. But I always thought that Zen was serious."

"It is. And it's also the most ridiculous thing in the world. Because we humans are the most ridiculous creatures in the world, don't you think?"

"I guess we can be pretty silly sometimes. But the master who answered the student's question by . . . uh . . . urinating. What was his point? Was he trying to make fun of the question or the student?"

"Oh no, not at all. He was saying that enlightenment is about everyday things—like eating, drinking, pissing. But the trick is to piss with total concentration." He brayed. "Can you do that yet, Lillian?"

"On occasion," she answered.

They both laughed.

"Well, shall we continue this discussion over some coffee?" George asked.

212

Before either Franny or Lillian could say anything, Ren spoke up, "Not tonight, George. Franny and I have some plans."

"Oh well. Another time then. What about you, Lillian?"

"I'll join you."

Good-byes were said, and Ren led Franny away. She was disappointed, even angry. What was Ren doing? They hadn't made any plans, and she wanted to talk with George Henkin some more.

She was silent until they reached the quad. "What plans do we have?" she asked at last, unable to keep the irritation out of her voice.

"We don't. I said that to give them the chance to spend the rest of the evening alone together. They haven't seen each other in quite a while."

Franny's annoyance ebbed. "Are they close friends?"

"They're lovers."

"What!"

"Yeah. It's the great Morrison family scandal. Lillian and George met in a Zendo, a meditation center, during something called sashin or sesshin—I can't remember—but it's a week of intense meditation when no one's allowed to socialize or even talk. By the time sesshin was over, everybody was ready to party. Someone threw a big blowout. Lillian and George went to it, and *wham!* Lillian was still married to Robert—Grandpa—at the time. When she finally came home, she told him that she still loved him, but that she also

loved George. Robert couldn't take it. He busted up the house. Then he told her to get out and he got a divorce. Lillian and George lived together for a while, until she decided to split and come here."

"How long ago did they meet?" Franny, shocked by the story, asked.

"About ten years ago," Ren answered. "I didn't really understand what was going on at the time. I was too young. My older brother, Chris, explained it to me a couple of years afterward."

"Ten years ago! But she was already in her fifties then!" Franny exclaimed, and was immediately ashamed. So what if Lillian had been in her fifties? Was that supposed to be too old for sex? Too old for love? "Sorry. That was a stupid remark."

Ren chuckled. "I said the same thing to Chris when he told me."

Franny paused a moment, then asked, "Was your family upset about it?"

"Oh yeah. Everybody sided with my grandfather except for my mother. She defended Lillian—at least in public. But in private she let Lillian have it too. And they all blamed Zen."

"Zen!"

"Uh-huh. Said it made Lillian irresponsible. Hey, we're at my place and I didn't even ask you if you wanted to come here. Do you?"

"Yes."

They went into his house and up to his room. He

threw off his jacket, picked his guitar off the bed, sat down, and began to strum it softly.

Doffing her jacket, Franny sat next to him. "Is your family still angry at Lillian?"

"No. Not since Robert died a couple of years ago. They still think she's weird, though."

"It must have been hard for her when they were angry."

"Lillian's pretty tough. She thought it was mostly their problem. I think she was right, but not completely. I understand how my grandfather must've felt. I've got his bad temper and a big possessive streak in me, too. That girl I told you about? She stopped seeing me and started going out with another guy. I saw them together and kicked in a door." He put down his guitar. "You know, you haven't told me much about your family. Any juicy scandals there?"

"Uh-uh," Franny said tersely. She plucked a blank sheet of paper from the bed and began to fold it.

"No black sheep? No outcasts?"

"No," she said, the paper turning into a bird in her skillful hands.

"Clean-living types, huh? Well, we won't tell them about my scandal-ridden roots when you bring me home for dinner."

The bird's wing tore. Damn, she swore silently.

Ren took the mangled origami from her and turned her face up to his. "Listen," he said gently. "Maybe this is my imagination, but it seems like whenever I

mention your family, you get tense and clam up. Especially if I say anything about meeting them. Am I imagining things?"

"I . . . I don't like to talk about my family. Things are a little . . . difficult with them," she answered haltingly.

"How? How are they difficult? Is it your grandmother or something else? I'm your friend. More than your friend, I hope. Talk to me, Franny."

When she didn't say anything, he frowned and picked up his guitar. "I'm screwing up again, aren't I?" he said, half to himself. "Except this time I don't know how."

"You're not screwing up," she said quietly.

He put down the guitar. "No?"

"No. I like you. A lot. I want to be with you. I just can't talk, Ren. Not right now."

He sighed. "Okay. Okay, I won't push you."

They sat in silence. She reached out and laid her hand on his cheek. He closed his eyes as she caressed him. Then he took her hand, kissed her palm, and licked the spaces between her fingers.

"You taste like flowers," he said. "Lilacs?"

Smiling, she shook her head. "They're out of season."

He brought her other hand to his mouth. "Roses?"

She shook her head again.

He kissed her lips. "Gardenias. Just beginning to open," he whispered.

216

They kissed again, deeper.

Franny sighed, pressing herself against him. He held her tightly for a moment, then he drew away gently. "I think we ought to take a walk. It's getting kind of hot in here." He pulled both of them to their feet.

Damn, Franny swore to herself for the second time that night. Damn, damn, damn.

23

"How was the lecture last night?" Mrs. Yeager asked.

"Interesting," Franny said noncommittally, her mouth full of toast. She was gobbling down her breakfast because she'd overslept and couldn't afford to be late for work today, three Saturdays away from Christmas.

Yawning, Mr. Yeager shuffled into the kitchen. He hadn't slept well. There were mutterings again down at the plant that all was not as secure as Mr. Maney had assured them a few weeks before.

"What did you say it was about?" said Franny's mother.

"Zen."

Her father made a derogatory noise and dropped into his seat. His wife quickly placed a cup of black coffee at his elbow.

Franny grimaced into her cup of tea.

Lainie appeared then, her hair uncombed, her eyes bleary. She slumped at the table. Mr. Yeager put down his coffee and stared at her, obviously not liking what he saw. "What the hell were you up to last night?" he said.

"Gene," Mrs. Yeager warned.

"Wouldn't you like to know," mumbled Lainie.

"What was that?" her father demanded.

Lainie squinted at him. "I went to the movies," she answered.

"And where'd you go afterward, Mooney's Bar?"

"I went to the Bonanza Burger afterward. The spice in their chiliburgers packs a real wallop."

"Don't get smart with me, Lainie. If I find out you've been drinking . . ."

Glad that she had a solid excuse to escape, Franny rose. "Mom, I've got to work late tonight—holiday rush. I won't be able to visit Grandma today." She tried to keep the relief out of her voice. She dreaded going to the hospital again, but she didn't want her mother to know it. She barely wanted to acknowledge it to herself.

"Oh, well. I'm sure Grandma will understand. What about dinner?"

"I won't be home for dinner. I've got a date."

"Oh? Who's the lucky guy?" asked Lainie.

"Susan," Franny replied through gritted teeth.

Her father shifted his attention from Lainie to her.

"What is this? You're not eating here again tonight? All week long we've had to eat late because of you, when you care to show up."

Franny took a step backward to get away from his anger.

"Gene," Mrs. Yeager said. "The only time Franny can visit Mama during the week is after work. You know that." Her voice was strained, and the last words came out with an impatience and irritability she usually hid from him.

"What I know is that there's a lack of discipline in this household. These kids are doing whatever they want to do whenever they feel like it."

No one answered him. Franny held her breath, fearing that he was going to forbid her to go out tonight, maybe even forbid her to go to work.

But instead he said, "You're burning those eggs, Irene."

Mrs. Yeager leaped to rescue them.

"I've got to go," Franny said, scurrying out of the room.

The day was long and exhausting, with a never-ending flow of customers. They were still arriving at eight o'clock when Lillian locked the front door. She let the remaining customers out one at a time.

"Go home," she waved at the faces that kept peering and gesturing through the glass, mouthing, "Are you open?" even though the sign in front of their

faces clearly announced *Closed*. "Shoo! Scat!"

Franny laughed. " 'Deck the halls with et cetera, et cetera . . . ' " she sang lightly.

"And you shut up," Lillian said.

Franny laughed again. She was tired, but she also felt good. She'd done her work well, and it had taken her mind off everything else.

There was another rap on the glass.

"Beat it!" Lillian scowled, then said, "Oh, it's you." She opened the door and let in Ren.

"How're my two favorite working girls?" he asked.

Lillian grunted in reply.

"Tsk tsk. What's the matter? Wasn't George good to you last night?"

Lillian didn't answer him, but a blush crept over her cheeks. "I'll see you tomorrow, Franny, for your lesson."

Franny nodded and left with Ren into the chilly night.

"Are your friends meeting us for dinner or at Barger's?"

"Barger's, at nine thirty," Franny replied. She hadn't really lied to Lainie this morning—she did have a date with Susan, and with Eddie. They were going to meet Ren.

Throughout dinner at a small Chinese restaurant, she told Ren Susan stories. She hoped Susan would be something of a substitute to him for the family she couldn't introduce him to. And when Ren said he

couldn't wait to meet her, she glowed and said, "Oh, I know you'll like each other a lot."

By the time they arrived at Barger's, she was eagerly anticipating the gathering. The place was even more packed than the last time they'd been there. But as luck would have it, the sole empty booth was the same one they'd sat in before.

"This must be our booth," Ren said.

"Maybe we should put a plaque over it," Franny joked. " 'Permanently Reserved for Renshaw Tanazaki and Frances Yeager.' "

They slid into it and Franny asked, "Are you going to do 'Relativity' again?"

"Yeah—and I've got an encore, too."

"You wrote a new song?"

"Uh-uh. I didn't write this one. . . . I'm going to get a beer. Want a glass of wine?"

"I think I'll stick to Coke tonight," said Franny.

"With or without rum?" asked Ren.

"Without."

"Shucks. You mean I can't get you sloshed and ravish you?"

"You can ravish me sober," Franny said lightly. If the hospital makes me brisk, this place makes me reckless, she thought.

"Oh yeah?" He grinned, then grabbed and kissed her, refusing to let her up for air until she beat on his back.

222

They looked up to see Susan and Eddie laughing at them.

"Uh . . . uh . . . Susan, this is Ren. Ren, Susan. Susan, Eddie. I mean, Reddie . . ." Franny giggled.

"Well, that was one hell of an introduction," said Susan. "Say, Reddie, I want a beer. Are they gonna ask for i.d.'s in this place?"

"Yes," said Eddie.

"I'll get them," said Ren. "They don't hassle me here—I'm part of the entertainment."

He went to get the drinks. When he returned, Susan gave him the once-over. "Well, Ren," she said. "Franny's right. The front side of you is as good as the back."

"Thanks," said Ren. "I think there was a compliment somewhere in there, but I'm not totally sure."

Susan kept ogling him until Eddie put his hands over her eyes and said to him, "So, I heard you want to be a pilot. I'm interested in flying myself. My uncle owns a Piper Cherokee. I've been up in it a few times."

"Yeah? That's a great little plane," Ren responded.

While the two young men got into an enthusiastic discussion about aviation, Susan wiggled her eyebrows and made kiss faces at Franny behind her hand to tell her what she thought of Ren.

Smiling, Franny kicked her gently under the table.

Soon the Physicists arrived onstage and began to tune up.

223

"Wow. They should sponsor a contest," said Susan, watching them. "Guess how many cans of mousse that guy uses per day on his hair and you win a year's supply of shampoo. You think he'd let me touch it?"

"He would, but his girlfriend might not," Ren bantered.

The Physicists went into their set. It was the same one Franny'd heard last time, but perhaps because she was now sober, it sounded different to her, and even better.

Six songs later Darryl introduced Ren. Susan, Eddie, and Franny yelled, stomped, and applauded.

He slammed into a dazzling version of "Relativity." During it, Susan leaned across the table and shouted in Franny's ear, "He's the hottest thing since jalapeños."

"Shut up," Franny said jovially.

The song over, Ren announced his encore. "I'd like to dedicate this song to a special person—Franny Yeager."

"Awww," Susan and Eddie teased.

Ren sat on the edge of the stage and, a cappella, in a sweet, clear tenor, sang,

"When an irresistible force such as you
Meets an old immovable object like me,
You can bet as sure as you live
Something's gotta give, something's gotta give, something's gotta give . . ."

Watching him, Franny wished the night wouldn't end.

He sang the whole song through without any accompaniment. The audience was totally silent before bursting into appreciative applause. Ren smiled broadly at Franny and did an encore of the encore with the band behind him. When the audience finally let him off the stage, Susan squeezed Franny's hand and said seriously, "He's super. I could listen to him all night."

"He really is good," agreed Eddie.

"Yes" was all Franny could say. She glanced up to note Ren's progress across the room and did a double take. Oh, no. No, it couldn't be.

"Hey, it's Larry and your sister," Eddie announced.

"Where?" asked Susan.

"Heading toward us. Ren's right behind them."

"Oh, no." Franny moaned aloud, and stood up.

Susan grabbed her hand again. "It'll be okay," she said just before Lainie, smirking and clinging to Larry's arm, descended upon them.

"Well, hello. Fancy meeting you here," she greeted them. Noticing their drinks, she said, "Hey, how'd you get served? How about getting your dear sister a drink?"

"Someone else got them for us," Franny said, her voice tight.

"Hello, Franny," Larry said softly, his eyes flicking over her face.

"Hello," Franny barely croaked out. "Have you been here long?"

"Long enough," Lainie answered sweetly.

"We just got here," said Larry.

Lainie frowned at him.

And then Ren joined them. "Whew, I need a beer . . ." he started, and stopped. "Hi." He looked from Lainie and Larry to Franny, awaiting an introduction.

"Hel-lo," cooed Lainie, casting a triumphant look at Franny.

"My sister, Lainie. Larry Lefferts."

"Your sister? Well, this is—" Ren began.

Franny cut him off loudly. "This is Ren—Renshaw Tanazaki. We met once at my boss's house. It is nice to . . . uh . . . see you again, Renshaw. You sing very well," Franny said stiffly.

"What?" he said, with an expression that said he didn't know whether or not she was joking.

"Yes. . . . Oh . . . Dar— someone's calling you over."

Ren turned and saw the lead singer beckoning.

"Maybe we'll run into each other again. Thanks for coming over," Franny finished.

Ren faced her. "What the hell are you talking about?"

"Excuse me. I'm not feeling well." Clapping her hand over her mouth, Franny fled to the ladies' room.

She sat in the stall for a long time, thinking humorlessly that she seemed to be spending more time in Barger's bathroom than anywhere else in the place.

This time it was Susan who came to fetch her. "You can come out now. Lainie's gone," she said. Then,

226

after a hesitation, she added, "Ren's gone too."

Franny came out of the stall. "Will you and Eddie take me home?"

"Sure. But—"

"Don't say it, Susan. Just don't. Please." Franny walked out of the room without seeing Susan shaking her head behind her.

24

Franny couldn't get the branch to stick in the pin-holder. She jabbed and jabbed at it until her hand slipped and the sharp points pierced her fingers. She refused to cry out. I deserve it, she thought, watching a drop of blood fall onto the table.

"Better wash that," Lillian said calmly. "You don't want to get blood poisoning."

Or gangrene, Franny added silently. Why not? Wouldn't that be poetic justice? But she got up and washed her hand.

When she returned to her seat, Lillian picked the branch and notched the bottom with her clippers. "Look. When you have tough material like this, you do this and then you can slip it right into place." She stuck the spruce branch into the kenzan. "Got it?"

Franny nodded.

"Now, where are you putting the euonymus?"

"Here. No, here." She rubbed her face and neck. She was stiff, a result of falling asleep in her tokonoma instead of her bed. She'd spent the night there, trying to shut off her brain. She succeeded for a while. But she couldn't shut off her dreams. They were filled with anonymous angry faces and voices yelling, "Bad, Franny. Bad girl. What have you done? What have you done?" She was on trial, for what crime she didn't know. In the last dream she was pronounced guilty and led away in a tumbrel. In the distance she could see a guillotine. When she got to it, the executioner made her put not her head but her feet on the block. "Let the punishment fit the crime," he said. "Then take out my heart," she answered just before he dropped the blade.

She'd awakened whimpering and immobile. It was several moments before she was able to get up and leave, praying she wouldn't run into any of her family. For three hours before her lesson, she walked the streets and tried in vain not to think about Ren and what she'd done to him the night before.

"All right. And the carnations?" Lillian asked.

"Here. No, there . . . No . . . I don't know."

"Franny, don't waste my time today. And don't waste your own," Lillian said sharply.

Franny started. Oh, God. She's mad at me too. Why did I come here today? If Lillian knew what I did to

229

Ren, she wouldn't want me here. Oh God, maybe she does know. "I'm sorry," she said. "I didn't—"

Lillian cut her off. "You want to pick up the circular movement. So use the carnations to complete that. Now tell me where you're putting them." She was perfectly calm again.

Franny stopped trying to figure out what Lillian knew or didn't know and forced herself to look at the arrangement again. "There and here. And the third one here."

"Good. That's good. Now take this home and study it. Next week we'll begin shoka."

"Shoka!" Franny exclaimed. She'd been eager to learn the subtle formal style for weeks, but Lillian had said she needed to understand moribana first. Today she'd failed miserably at moribana and Lillian was offering to teach her shoka. It didn't make sense.

"Shoka," Lillian repeated. "You said you wanted to learn it, didn't you?"

"Yes, but—"

"We'll begin it next week." The woman stood up and stretched.

Silently, Franny began to clean off her desk. She picked up the arrangement, then set it back down. She turned to the florist, who was wiping her clippers. "Lillian, can I leave this here? I'm not going straight home."

"Okay. You have a key."

"Thanks."

There was a pause; then Franny said tremulously, "Lillian."

"Yes?" She looked up.

"I . . . I . . ." I'm sorry, sorry, sorry, she wanted to cry out. I'm a lousy student, a lousy Zen Buddhist, a lousy person. Why does Ren have to be your grandson? I can't talk to you about him. Can't talk to anybody. "I'll see you tomorrow," she said.

"Right." Lillian went back to wiping her clippers.

The roses on Grandma's night table were dropping their petals. Two were lying on Grandma's shoulder as she slept. " 'Flower petals fall though we love them. Weeds grow though we hate them. That's just the way it is,' " Franny murmured the words that George Henkin had recited the other night. She picked the petals off gently.

Grandma opened her eyes. "Lainie. I mean Franny. I was just thinking about you. I was wishing I'd brought along that lovely shawl you made me for Hanukkah last year."

"I'll bring it for you tomorrow."

"That would be nice." Grandma began to chuckle. "Hanukkah guilt."

"What?"

"You don't remember that? When you were five or six, you asked me why anybody would want to give somebody guilt for Hanukkah."

"Guilt?"

"*Gelt.* Money."

"Oh. Right."

From the bed next to Grandma's came the sounds of sniffling intermingled with voices from the TV: "I love you. How can I stand never seeing you again?" "You'll see me in your dreams."

"Are you all right, Mrs. Parker?" Grandma called.

"I'm okay. This is my favorite movie." She let out a loud sob.

"Is that the one where the actress is dying of a brain tumor?"

"No. In this one she's dying of lung cancer."

"Grandma," Franny said, kneading her hands, "I need to talk to you."

"I was in a movie once. I played a dying ballerina. I died beautifully. You know, they're asking me to dance again. But I think I'm a little too old."

"Grandma, I need to talk to you," Franny repeated louder.

Grandma blinked. "About what, sweetheart?"

"About . . . about a boy," Franny said in a lower voice.

"A boy? Is Larry giving you problems?"

"No, not Larry. This is a different boy." She stopped.

"A boy you like?" Grandma prodded gently.

"Yes."

"Does he like you?"

"Yes."

"What's wrong then?"

232

Franny's mouth worked, but nothing came out of it. "Mom and Dad," she finally squeaked.

Grandma waited for her to go on.

Then two doctors came in. Franny recognized them as the two who'd examined Grandma a few days before.

"Well, Mrs. Gallinsky. Let's see how your foot's doing today," one of them said.

"Fine," said Grandma. She turned to Franny and, in a stage whisper, said, "They're going to chop it off."

Franny recoiled.

"Mrs. Gallinsky," the doctor said, "you know you're scheduled for surgery tomorrow, don't you?"

"Yes," Grandma answered.

"No!" Franny bit down on her sore finger.

"The prognosis is good. We may be able to save your knee."

"Oh, good," said Grandma.

Franny bit down harder. They were going to amputate Grandma's leg and they were all discussing it as calmly as if they were in a butcher shop talking about cuts of meat.

When the doctors finally left, Grandma said, "Nice young men. The tall one looks just like Nureyev. I would've danced with him, but he wasn't good enough. Now, what were we talking about before? This boy of yours, Larry. No, not Larry—"

"Here she is," Uncle Mike's voice boomed out, star-

tling both Grandma and Franny. "With my favorite niece."

Franny turned her head and saw him, Aunt Myrna, and her parents advancing on them.

"Franny, when did you leave the house this morning? Did you have any breakfast?" asked Mrs. Yeager.

"Never mind breakfast, are you going to grace us with your presence at dinner tonight?" her father demanded.

"I'm afraid there are too many visitors in here. Only two are allowed at once," said a nurse, pushing through them with a bedpan.

Voices. Loud voices. Angry voices. Franny watched their mouths opening and shutting like fish.

She turned from them to Grandma. Next time I see her she won't be whole. She grabbed Grandma's hand.

"Some of you will have to leave," the nurse insisted.

"So, what about dinner?" said Mr. Yeager.

"What about lunch? She must be starving now," her mother put in.

"Why only two people? That's ridiculous!" Uncle Mike argued with the nurse.

"Hospital rules."

Releasing Grandma's hand, Franny stood up. Without a word, she walked out stiffly, as if she were trying to keep all her body parts firmly in place.

Petals was locked up tight when she arrived there. Franny was glad. She no longer felt like talking to Lillian. She didn't feel like talking to anyone—not even Susan. All she wanted to do was be alone in her tokonoma, thinking nothing, feeling nothing. Good things, bad things, whatever happened, the answer, Franny said to herself, was to accept them and feel nothing. " 'Flower petals fall though we love them. Weeds grow though we hate them. That's just the way it is,' " she repeated aloud as she poured the water out of her flower arrangement, then wrapped wet paper towels around the bottoms of the plants in the pinholder. She slipped container and pinholder into a plastic bag, turned off the light, and plodded to the front door.

Ren was on the other side of it. They stared at each other through the glass.

Oh God, Franny thought, feeling a dull pain in her chest. Last night came back to her full force.

Unlocking the door, Ren let himself in. "Lillian said you might be here," he said.

"I came to get my arrangement."

He nodded, then searched her face.

She looked down at the bag in her hand. There was a small rip in it. I hope it doesn't tear further, she thought. I don't want the bag to break. She concentrated on worrying about the rip and avoided Ren's eyes.

235

"Look at me, Franny," he said. "Look at me and tell me why you did that last night. Why'd you pretend you hardly knew me?"

"I'm sorry."

"I don't want an apology. I want to know the reason."

"I didn't want my s-sister to know that we're . . . we're going out together," she said to the rip.

"Why? Are you ashamed of me?" His voice had a crack in it.

Involuntarily, she lifted her eyes to his. "No. No, I'm not ashamed of you."

"Then why? Why don't you want her to know? Why are you keeping me a secret?"

Franny looked away from him again. "I can't talk about it now. I have to go home."

"Franny, don't do this to me. To both of us."

"I'm sorry." She tried to move past him.

He grabbed her arm. "Stop saying that and just tell me what's going on."

The pain in her chest grew sharper. She had to get away from him before it cut her in two. "Please, Ren. Please. I can't talk now."

He eased his grip. "All right, then, when? When can you talk? Give me a date and time."

"Ren . . ."

"A date and time, Franny."

"All right. To-tomorrow night at eight."

"Where?"

"I'll . . . I'll come over to your place."

"Promise me. Look at me and promise you'll show up."

He was staring hard at her. Franny thought he might give her a kiss or a slap.

"Promise me," he demanded again. His fingers tightened once more on her shoulder.

"I promise," she vowed at last, staring back at him.

He nodded once and dropped his hand.

"I've got to go," she said.

He moved aside to let her pass. "I'll lock up," he said.

She nodded and opened the door. She was not quite halfway down the street before she began to wonder what lies she could tell him this time.

25

Susan caught up with Franny on the way to history class. One look at her face told Franny that her friend knew about Grandma.

"I just ran into Lainie," Susan said. "She's pretty upset."

Franny nodded. Lainie'd been so upset last night, she'd stayed in her room, refusing to come down for dinner, and even Mr. Yeager hadn't insisted she do so. Franny had picked at her own food, then excused herself too. She'd thought about calling Susan, but couldn't bring herself to.

Susan didn't chide her about it now. She just took Franny's hand and squeezed it. "I don't feel like going to this class today," she said. "Do you?"

Franny looked at her. "No," she said.

"Then let's cut. Let's go to the mall."

Franny hesitated. She'd never cut class before. But the idea of sitting and listening to a lot of stuff about the impeachment process was suddenly unbearable. "All right," she agreed. "But we'd better hurry up before Ms. Coleman sees us."

They walked rapidly up the hall, down the stairs to the basement, and out the side entrance. Franny glanced at her watch. Eleven oh five. Were they through with Grandma already? Or were they just at that moment sawing off her leg? A wave of nausea hit her and she had to lean against a wall.

"Are you okay?" Susan asked.

Franny took several deep breaths. The nausea subsided. She nodded, then quickened her pace across the football field.

They caught the bus at Holliwell. Franny was quiet and Susan let her be. Then Franny said, "I'm going over to Ren's tonight."

"You are?"

"Yes. He came into the shop yesterday while I was there. He wanted me to explain why I acted the way I did on Saturday night. I couldn't tell him then, so he made me promise to tell him tonight."

Susan's face lit up. "And you're going to? Oh, I'm so glad."

"I'm going to tell him that Lainie tries to steal all my boyfriends and that's why I lied about him to her."

Susan frowned. "Oh, Franny. Not another lie."

"That's what I'm going to tell him, Susan."

Susan sighed and tried a different tack. "Okay, let's say you tell Ren that and he buys it. How are you going to explain why you still won't introduce him to your folks? And as for your folks, what are you going to tell *them* when Lainie starts asking about him at dinner some night soon? 'How's that cute Japanese boy?' " she mimicked Lainie perfectly. " 'The one you introduced me to the other night. What was his name, Ren? Have you seen him lately? If you don't want to, I will.' "

Franny sighed. Susan was voicing all her doubts. Franny knew that Lainie couldn't have been taken in by her act. Lainie's memory was sharp, and right off she must've recalled her sister's lies about Ren's not being Japanese or sexy. She'll either definitely try to blackmail me now or do just what Susan said, Franny thought. As for Ren . . . "Oh, God," Franny moaned and rubbed her forehead. Neither she nor Susan said anything else for the rest of the bus ride.

At the mall, they got out and drifted into Salyer's, the big department store there. Festooned with fake greenery, twinkling lights, and big red satin bows dripping from the ceiling, the store was relatively empty. "I haven't bought a single present yet," Susan said. "Every year I swear I'll do all my shopping early, and every year Christmas Eve arrives and like an idiot there I am, being pushed and shoved by all the other idiots who haven't bought their presents either. I don't

240

know what I'd do if we gave each other gifts for Hanukkah the way we're supposed to. That's usually even earlier than Christmas."

"You can buy some gifts today." Franny spoke reluctantly. She still didn't feel like talking.

"Yeah, I could—except for one thing. I didn't bring any money." She fingered a pair of earrings at the jewelry counter. "Maybe I should take up shoplifting. What do you think?"

"I think you'd be lousy at it."

"Yeah. I'm too honest. That's my problem. What about you? I bet you did all your shopping and gift making weeks ago, Early Bird."

It was a running joke between them. Franny, a perpetual early bird in everything, sometimes had her presents ready by Thanksgiving. So when she said with a frown, "No, I haven't," Susan was surprised. "Really?" she said.

"I sort of forgot about them this year. I bought some yarn to knit booties for Grandma . . ." She stopped, swallowing hard.

"Well, never mind," Susan said kindly. "There's always bubble bath and after-shave. In fact, you don't even have to buy them. My parents got so many bottles of the stuff from me, they'd be glad to give it away."

Blinking her brimming eyes, Franny rattled a string of pearls hanging in front of her and said nothing.

After a moment, Susan tapped her shoulder. "Hey, let's go up to the fifth floor."

241

"The fifth floor? That's Santaland," Franny said dully.

"Yeah, I know. I want to sit on the old man's lap and give him a reason for having those red cheeks."

Franny looked at her and barked out a laugh.

"Come on!" Susan tugged her to the elevator.

They emerged into a gaudy world of silver-sprinkled cotton and tinsel and walked slowly down the aisle, alternately admiring and laughing at the reindeer with the red light-bulb nose, the fluffy-tailed squirrels, and the mechanical elves all clad in red and green velvet.

Approaching the entrance to the "North Pole" Franny said, "You're kidding. You're not really going to sit on his lap, are you?"

"You bet I am. Why don't you do it too? Then we'll really give him a thrill."

"Not on your life!"

"Then at least come watch." She grabbed Franny's hand and pulled her into line, which today consisted only of a pair of twin boys, aged three or four.

They could see the roly-poly red-suited man seated on a thronelike chair. "And who's next?" he called.

"Go ahead in," the twins' mother shooed, following behind them.

Franny and Susan watched as the boys climbed onto Santa's lap.

"Ho, ho, ho! Merry Christmas! Have you been good little boys?"

The pair nodded solemnly.

"And what can Santa bring you this year?"

"A tricycle," said one.

"A great white shark," said the other.

"Ha, ha. I mean, ho, ho. That might be a little hard unless you live in the ocean. How about this nice Santa Claus doll?"

"No. I want a great white shark," the boy said matter-of-factly.

"Well, I'll see what I can do," said Santa. "In the meantime, here's a lollipop for each of you."

The first twin took one.

"No, thank you," said the second. "It's bad for my teeth." He opened his mouth wide as a shark's.

"Ho, ho, ho. Next," Santa called.

The twins' mother ushered them out and Susan entered the room with Franny in tow. "Hi, Santa," she said. She bounced up to him and settled herself in his lap.

Standing at the back of the room, Franny saw his eyes widen under bushy white cotton brows. "Ho, ho, ho. Aren't you a little old for this sort of thing?" he said.

"Aren't you?" Susan smiled sweetly at him.

"Well, um, Merry Christmas. Ho, ho, ho. Have you been a good lit— big girl?"

"Not in the least."

Santa coughed. "Well then, I, uh, can't bring you any presents, can I?"

"You can't? You really can't? Oh, no." Susan began to cry convincingly.

Franny began to giggle.

"Well, maybe I can," Santa said quickly. "How about one of these Santa Claus dolls?"

"How about Santa Claus himself?" She tweaked his beard.

"Next," Santa yelled, his cheeks considerably redder than the rouge on them accounted for.

Franny bolted outside and was laughing hard when Susan came out. "Oh, Susan," she gasped. "You're too much."

"Well of course I am," said Susan. "That's why you love me."

It wasn't until the bus ride home that Franny got depressed again. Susan's antics had taken her mind off things. Petals was so busy there'd been no time to think at all. But alone once more, she thought about Grandma. She pictured her asleep in the recovery room, the remains of her left leg swathed in bandages. When she awoke, would she still babble about her dancing career? Or would she be sane again? Another thought struck Franny and made her shiver. Perhaps Grandma would be worse. Maybe she'd decide she had to go into training for the marathon. Maybe she would no longer know her own name or recognize anyone. Suddenly, with immense horror and guilt, Franny realized that not only didn't she want to visit her grandmother in the hospital anymore, but that

she didn't want to see her again at all. She bit the soft skin near her thumbnails until they bled.

Then she remembered Ren. Oh, help. God. What am I going to do about him? Tell him the truth, she heard Susan's voice saying. He loves you. You love him. Don't spit in the face of happiness. The truth. It would be so good to tell him the truth. Talk to me, Franny, he'd said. I'm your friend. More than a friend, I hope. All right, she said. I will. The truth is I haven't introduced you to my parents because they're racists who'd hate your guts and forbid me to see you ever again. . . . Oh, God! I can't tell him that. I can't. She moaned.

"Are you all right?" the plump woman next to her asked.

She lowered her hands. "Yes. Just a headache." She stumbled off the bus at a stop a half mile from her house, her mind battling itself all the way home.

Her mother was in the kitchen, pacing the floor. She looked up when Franny entered. "That sister of yours, where in the world is she? Your father's having another meeting at the plant. But he should be back soon, and he's going to be mad as anything if she isn't here."

"I don't know, Mom," Franny answered, pronouncing the words carefully.

"God, if it's not one thing, it's another." Mrs. Yeager opened the oven door, peered inside, and shut it. Then she pulled a pack of cigarettes out of her apron

pocket. Shaking one out, she lit it and puffed hard.

Franny was dumbstruck. "What are you doing?" she said when she finally found her voice.

"What does it look like?"

"But . . . but you don't smoke."

"I did before you were born. I haven't forgotten how."

Franny knew she should ask about Grandma, but she couldn't. She just sat there, watching her mother sucking in smoke and exhaling it through her nose until it made her cough.

Mrs. Yeager stabbed out the butt in the sink. "They were able to save her knee," she said.

Franny nodded.

"You'll be able to visit her in a few days."

Franny nodded a second time.

"The doctors said there are some good artificial legs now. Very lifelike. When she's wearing pants, you can't tell the difference."

Franny didn't point out that Grandma never wore pants.

Her mother sighed, checked the oven again, and said, "Where is that girl?"

As if in response, the front door slammed. But instead of Lainie, it was Mr. Yeager who shambled into the kitchen with a glazed look on his face.

And his wife was immediately transformed. "Gene, you're home," she said brightly.

246

"Yeah. Home," he said.

"Dinner's warming up. We can eat in just a minute."

"Eat," he repeated.

Franny, who'd been watching him, felt her stomach begin to churn. Something's very wrong, she thought.

Mrs. Yeager noticed it too. "Gene, are you all right? You look a little peaked. I hope you're not coming down with the flu, are you?"

"The flu?" He gave a short, bitter laugh.

"Please, Gene. Tell me what's wrong."

"Can't you figure it out, Irene? I bet Franny can. She's the smart one in this family." He looked around. "Where's the other one? The brat."

"She'll be home any moment now."

"Like hell she will. Some family we've got. Some family, some country."

"Gene, I don't understand."

"Tell her, Franny. Go on. You know. GO ON!" he shouted.

Franny shrank back into her seat. "You . . . you got laid off," she whispered.

"Give her an A."

"But that's impossible. Mr. Maney promised you your job was safe," Mrs. Yeager's voice quavered.

"Yeah. And today the bastard told me it's gone. My job. Joe Burke's job. Harry Lederer's job. Everybody's goddamn job. Why? Because the whole goddamn plant is closing. Got that? Closing. Thanks to Mr. Honda,

247

Mr. Nissan, Mr. Mitsubishi, Mr. Toyota and all those goddamn foreigners!" he spat out. Then, suddenly, he collapsed heavily into his chair.

Mrs. Yeager put her hand on his shoulder.

"Leave me alone, Irene," he said in a leaden voice. "I want to be left alone."

She dropped her hand as if stung and left the room.

Shaking, Franny got up too. Her legs weren't working right, but they got her downstairs and into her tokonoma. She sank onto the cushions. It was a while before she no longer trembled, and more time after that before a welcome numbness began to grow inside her. The world is awful, but I don't care, she thought. That's the highest Zen, George Henkin. The highest Zen.

26

The numbness was nice. More filling than a meal. More comforting than a lullaby. It was no worries, no thoughts, no feelings. It got her through the night, the next morning, the whole day at school. It got her through Ren, who was waiting for her outside Petals when she finished work.

"What happened last night?" he said angrily. "You made me a promise."

"I couldn't keep it," she answered dully.

"Why not?"

She shrugged.

"I don't get it. I thought you really cared about me. You let me kiss you, touch you. You'd let me inside your body, wouldn't you? But not inside your head. Oh, no. Not inside your head . . . Look, if you don't

want to see me again, tell me now. To my face."

"I don't want to see you again," she uttered tonelessly. And she saw his face fall instantly.

"Damn," he said. "Damn, damn, damn." He closed his eyes, but tears squeezed out of the corners and began to run down his cheeks. He punched the wall, hurting his hand, and punched it again.

"Ren, don't!" Franny said, more sharply than she'd intended. His pain had slashed her.

He stopped. "Give me a reason not to," he pleaded.

But she gathered the numbness around the wound. "Because. Because if you break your hand, you won't be able to play your guitar."

He stared at her for a long moment. Then, tears still falling, he choked, "Thanks very much for the good advice." Spinning on his heel, he tore down the street.

Franny watched him go. It's better this way, she told herself, checking for any rents in the numbness. It was still intact, and she carried it home with her.

It got her through dinnertime there, with her father slumped and silent at the table, her mother staring hauntedly at him, and Lainie going on and on about the Christmas dance that she was going to with Larry at the end of the week.

"Larry?" Mrs. Yeager asked, allowing herself to be distracted from her attentions to her husband. "Larry who?"

"Larry Lefferts."

"But he's Franny's boyfriend, isn't he?" She turned to her older daughter.

"No, he isn't," Franny said flatly. She stared at Lainie, challenging, *Go ahead. Tell them. This is the moment you've been waiting for. So go ahead and do it. It doesn't matter anymore.*

But Lainie regarded her knowingly and said nothing.

Later that night—and for the next few nights—Franny, twisted into an uncomfortable lotus position that gave her legs pins and needles, nurtured her numbness in her tokonoma. It was easy to slip down there now. Her parents were too preoccupied with their own misery to pay attention to her, and Lainie was out a lot, presumably with Larry.

By the end of the week, on the evening of the Christmas dance to which she wasn't going, Franny was numb enough to visit Grandma. From the little her mother had said, Franny understood that physically Grandma was apparently doing all right, but that emotionally she wasn't faring as well. So Franny had prepared herself for more delusions. *Whatever she says, whatever she believes, it doesn't matter because life is all one big illusion anyway,* she told herself.

When she got to Grandma's room, the first thing she noticed was the smell—or lack of it. The stench that had surrounded Grandma for weeks was gone. The second thing was Grandma herself, on her back,

251

under the blankets, staring up at the ceiling. She didn't turn to look at Franny when she entered. She didn't respond to her greeting or the pot of pretty, almost cloying narcissuses she'd brought, or ask, "So how was school today?" She just lay there, unmoving, her diminished body well hidden from view.

"She's been like that since they brought her back in here," Mrs. Parker called from the other bed. "Hardly eats. Doesn't want to do her exercises. Hasn't said a word to me in days. The nurses are worried about her. I heard them talking."

Franny felt a thin blade of sadness scratch at her heart. Grandma was numb too. Except she didn't appear to have reached the highest Zen. She looked like a zombie. Franny wanted to say something, to make *her* say something, even if it was to proclaim that she'd been the pinup queen of World War II or the president's secret flame. Anything that smacked of life, feeling, spirit. But Franny had done too good a job on her own numbness, and she couldn't say anything at all. She sat in silence at Grandma's side while Mrs. Parker kept up a running commentary until visiting hours were over about Grandma's operation, information gleaned from the bits and snatches of doctor/nurse talk she'd heard.

When Franny got up to leave, she kissed Grandma and thought she saw tears in her eyes, but it might have been just a reflection from the light.

Instead of taking the bus home, she decided to walk. The temperature had dropped sharply below freezing, and a stiff wind chilled the air even further. Franny had left her hat and gloves at Petals, and she was shod only in sneakers, but she didn't care. Numb inside, numb outside, she told herself.

Halfway there, her feet so cold she could barely feel them, she was suddenly exhausted. Each step was like slogging through honey. Frozen honey. There was a busted-up bench at a nearby bus stop and she sank onto it, shoving her hands deep into her pockets, huddling into her coat. She was thinking about stretching out full length on the bench and falling asleep when a car pulled up to the curb.

The window rolled down and a male voice called, "Franny? Franny, is that you?"

"Of course it's her. Don't you think I know my own sister?" The car door opened and Lainie, in her mother's good coat open over a sequined dress, got out and stood, legs akimbo, in front of her. "What are you doing here? This isn't near that flower shop you work at."

"I went to the hospital," Franny said thickly.

"This isn't near the hospital, either."

"I decided to walk home."

"In weather like this? Are you nuts? Come on, get in. We'll drive you home. Come on." She tugged at Franny's arm.

Thinking that Lainie sounded a lot like their mother,

253

Franny let herself be pushed into the backseat of the car.

Larry looked over at her. "Are you all right?"

"Fine. I'm fine," she answered with a yawn.

"She's not fine. She's crazy. She was walking home in this weather. She's got no hat or gloves on and no boots either."

"It's not that guy, is it? You're not upset because of him? That Ren? Eddie and I can take care of him for you. Just say the word," Larry offered ardently.

"I'm not upset about anything," Franny said, yawning again. She didn't see Lainie's injured glance at Larry, followed by a spiteful one at her.

"Come on, Larry," Lainie said. "Let's take her home so we can get to the dance and then on to *other things*." She made the last two words sound extremely lewd.

With one last long look at Franny, Larry started the car and drove to the Yeager house.

"Okay. Home, sweet home. Out, sister dearest. Christ, she's asleep."

"I'll get her inside."

Lainie and Larry's words buzzed faintly like little bees in Franny's head. She felt Larry lift her out of the car and prop her on her feet. She was half walking, half being carried as he steered her to the door.

"Can you get in by yourself?" he asked.

"Uh-huh."

"Come on, Larry," Lainie shrilled from the car.

"Uh, Franny. About Lainie and me. I . . . Listen,

254

I'm only going out with her because . . . because I thought it would make you jealous."

"Uh-huh."

"I guess it hasn't worked though, has it?"

"Uh-huh. Uh-uh." Franny yawned a third time and leaned back against the doorbell. The loud noise startled both her and Larry.

"Larry!" Lainie yelled again.

"Well, I'll see you around," he said, leaping over the neat row of azalea bushes down the lawn to his father's car.

Simultaneously, the front door opened and Mrs. Yeager, jaundiced by the amber porchlight, said, "Franny! Where were you? Your father and I were beginning to worry."

"Bus broke down," Franny lied, without batting an eyelash. She stepped inside the warm house, and her feet immediately began to prickle as the feeling flowed back into them.

"Your dinner's been warming so long it's probably dried out by now. How was Grandma?"

"Fine. I think I'll skip dinner, Mom. I'm kind of tired." Without another word, Franny stumbled up to her room and tumbled onto the bed. She thought she'd fall asleep at once but she didn't. Instead she lay for hours staring up at the ceiling. And inside her, the numbness began to stretch and wear thin—a sheet of cellophane over a geyser.

27

"She's grieving," the social worker said, looking at each member of the family in turn. They were all gathered in their living room, discussing Grandma, who'd come home the day after Christmas.

"Grieving? For what? Nobody died," Mr. Yeager said.

"She's grieving for her leg. That's why she's not speaking to anybody or making any effort to leave her bed."

Mr. Yeager looked skeptical.

"Well, how can we help her?" asked Mrs. Yeager.

"Talk to her. Be encouraging. Be understanding. And give her time." On the last sentence, the social worker's eyes lighted on Franny.

She shifted uncomfortably in her seat. She was trying

to be as impervious to the woman's and her parents' comments as she'd been to everything a few days before, but she was no longer succeeding. Go home, she told the social worker silently, so I can get out of here. The social worker did leave shortly after.

"Time!" Mr. Yeager said as soon as she was out the door and his wife returned to the room. "Time is money. Which we don't have."

"Don't worry. Mike and Jack have promised to help."

"I'll believe that when I see it. Christ, grieving? She lost her leg, but—"

Not her life or, worse, her job, Franny could almost hear him finish.

"How'd you feel if you lost yours?" Lainie hurled, which forced him back into his own sullen brand of grief.

Franny mumbled something about homework—even though she was on vacation—and disappeared into the basement. She couldn't bear to be with them or with Grandma. She slept in the tokonoma every night now and left the house every morning before anyone else got up. She spent the time in between working at Petals. The routine was soothing, and she dreaded the disruption in it that Sunday would bring. After her ikebana lesson, she'd have to come home. Against all of Franny's attempts to dissuade her, Susan had insisted she was going to pay Grandma a visit. It would be unforgivably rude of Franny not to be there too.

Why can't you all go away? Franny thought, folded

into her lotus position. She stared at her first clumsy attempt at a shoka arrangement and wished Sunday wouldn't come.

But Sunday did come—and it proved to be even worse than Franny had anticipated. Her lesson went well enough. She'd succeeded in creating a fine shoka this time, and she allowed herself a small frisson of pleasure at the idea of smuggling it into her toko-noma. But at the lesson's end, Lillian said, "Please don't leave just yet, Franny. I have a few things to say to you.

"First of all, I've decided to take a short vacation this week. Petals will be closed from New Year's Day until the following Monday."

Franny pressed her hands together. No work for the rest of my vacation? Where will I go? What will I do?

"I was going to ask you to feed Miss Priss, but Ren will be back by then from San Francisco, and with great reluctance, he's agreed to do it." Lillian paused, and it was clear she was choosing her next words carefully. "Ren was reluctant because he's afraid of running into you. He told me you 'dumped' him— his word, not mine—with no explanation. He's hurt. Very hurt. Franny, I don't like to meddle in people's lives. But Ren is very dear to me. I think you should at least talk with him."

With a trace of hostility in her voice, Franny said, "I thought the Zen way is silent."

Lillian took a while before answering. "There are several kinds of silence. There's the silence when your heart is at peace and you know yourself well. Then there's another kind—when your heart is squeezed shut. Think about which kind you're keeping."

"I have to leave now, Lillian" was Franny's response. Hurriedly wrapping her shoka, she bolted out of the store, which, because of Lillian's "meddling," had suddenly become a place to escape from rather than to. Ahead of her lay the bleak afternoon with Grandma. "Oh, God," she muttered.

When Franny arrived in the kitchen, having first, as usual, sneaked the flower arrangement into the basement, Susan was already there, sipping tea with Mrs. Yeager.

"Hi, Franny. I'm a bit early," Susan said.

"Have you gone upstairs yet?"

"No, I haven't seen Grandma Gallinsky yet."

"I'm sure she'll be happy to see you, Susan," said Franny's mother. "You always perk her up."

The eternal optimist, Franny thought bitterly.

"Well, she perks *me* up." Susan rose from the table and moved toward the door. "Come on, Franny," she said, when she noticed her friend wasn't following.

Oh, hell.

They headed upstairs.

Grandma was on her side, turned toward them, eyes open.

"Hi, Grandma Gallinsky," Susan greeted her.

259

Grandma didn't respond.

"How are you feeling today?"

No answer.

"I'm sorry I haven't come to see you in a while, but between school, work, Christmas shopping, and Eddie Porter, I've been awfully busy. Have I told you about Eddie? He's my boyfriend? Yes, that's right. You heard it first, Grandma Gallinsky. Susan 'I Refuse to Be Tied Down' Brandenburg has finally decided to go steady." She grinned at Franny.

Franny managed only the smallest of smiles back. The scene was driving her crazy—Susan talking normally as if Grandma were paying attention, and Grandma just lying there like a lump.

"See, last week he introduced himself to my mother as my boyfriend and I threw a fit. Told him he had no right to call himself that, and as far as I was concerned, he'd have to take a flying leap into a vat of lime Jell-O before I'd ever call him my boyfriend. Well, Saturday night, after a normal date at the movies, he took me to this house on Lakeland.

" 'What are we doing here?' I asked.

" 'I'm going to make you keep your word' was all he said.

"A woman I never saw before opened the front door. 'Mr. Porter?' she said. 'It's all ready.' She let us in, pointing out the door to the basement. I followed Eddie down there. In the center of the room was a hot tub—the kind you see in movies about California.

Next to it was a ladder. Eddie started to take off his clothes.

" 'Hey, wait a minute . . . ' I said.

"But he motioned me to a chair and kept stripping down to a bathing suit. Then he climbed the ladder.

" 'Eddie, what the hell's going on?' I yelled.

" 'I'm about to meet your condition for becoming your boyfriend,' he said, and jumped into the hot tub.

" 'Eddie!' I screamed, racing over to him.

"He stood up in the tub, squishy, slimy, and decidedly green. I swear to you—cross my heart and hope to die—the thing was filled to the brim with lime Jell-O!" Laughing, Susan looked at Grandma for her reaction.

But Grandma didn't react at all. And Franny, watching her, felt a horrible tightness in her chest.

Susan didn't give up, though. She launched into another story about dumb Christmas presents she'd received.

In the middle of it, Grandma suddenly made a sound in her throat and Susan stopped speaking. "Did you say something, Grandma Gallinsky?" she asked.

In a voice that sounded rusty from disuse, Grandma replied, "I said do you want to see my stump?"

"Well . . . okay," said Susan dubiously.

"Oh, God," choked Franny, and fled down to her tokonoma. She stayed there until well after Susan had gone.

Later that night Susan called. "I know it upset you,

261

what your grandmother did. But I think it was a good sign. I think she's coming to terms with what happened to her and I'm sure she's going to be okay. But frankly, I'm worried about you. You're so withdrawn. I know you're feeling bad about your grandmother, your father's job, and Ren. You should be yelling, crying, talking a blue streak about all of it, but instead you're keeping everything inside."

"Don't worry about me. I'm all right," Franny said, wanting to get off the phone.

"But I am worried. Jeez, Fran, you disappeared this afternoon. Where'd you go? You weren't wandering the streets again, were you? Larry told Eddie and me what happened the night of the dance, how he and Lainie found you sprawled on a bench at a bus stop."

"I wasn't sprawled," Franny said coldly.

"Sprawled, schmawled. Whatever you were doing on it, you could have frozen to death," Susan persisted. "You can't do anything about your dad or your grandma, Franny, but you can stop hurting yourself. For God's sake, go to Ren, tell him what's been going on, and get back together with him."

Oh, God. First Lillian. Now Susan. Why don't they all shut up? "Shut up," she snarled into the phone. "Just shut up." She slammed it down, her hands shaking.

28

"Isn't this lovely, the family spending New Year's Eve together?" Mrs. Yeager said, taking a sip of the single brandy Alexander she allowed herself each year to toast the holiday. She glanced around the living room, smiling brightly at Mr. Yeager, Franny, and Grandma, the latter bundled in an armchair.

"Lainie's not spending it with us," Mr. Yeager pointed out irritably. He was on his fourth drink, two more than either Mrs. Yeager or Franny had ever seen him have, and the effects were clearly visible.

"Well, she had a date. That's what girls do on New Year's Eve—go out on dates," his wife said placatingly, then cast a worried look at Franny, who had no date, whose boyfriend had been "stolen" by her sister.

Franny looked away from her. Her blank face be-

trayed nothing of the craziness she was feeling inside, a craziness that had been steadily building, building, building for days. Three hours. We've been sitting together for three hours in front of the TV, she thought. When her mother had learned that she wasn't going out, she came up with the idea of a "family party." She bought some cheap caviar, even though no one liked the stuff, and made some fancy little sandwiches. "You can even have a brandy Alexander tonight," she told her daughter. "Just one, though. We don't want you to stagger into the New Year."

It looks like Dad's the one who's staggering in, Franny almost said aloud now.

"Girls are supposed to do what their parents tell them to," he said.

Nobody responded to him, but Grandma shifted audibly in her seat.

"Are you comfortable, Mama?" Mrs. Yeager asked her.

"I'm all right," she answered slowly. She was still not talking much, but there was a definite change from her former catatonic state.

"Look at that bozo up there," Mr. Yeager commented, pointing at the host of a TV variety show. "No brains, no talent. Makes five million a year doing nothing but showing off his capped teeth. If he ever had to work a day in his life, he'd drop dead on the spot."

264

The host disappeared as a commercial came on. The clock in the room chimed the hour. "Ten," Mrs. Yeager said enthusiastically. "Just two hours more until midnight and a whole new year. It's going to be a lot better than this one."

"Don't count on it," said Mr. Yeager. "Last year I had a job."

"You'll find another one, Gene. I know you will."

"Doing what? Being an emcee like that jerk?"

"I think I'll go to bed now," said Grandma.

"Oh, Franny and I will help you, Mama." Mrs. Yeager jumped to her feet.

Franny stood up and took Grandma under one arm. Her mother took the other. Carefully they steered her out of the living room to the stairs. It was harder work getting her up than it had been helping her down. When the hell will she learn to use her crutches? Franny thought. The image of a lifetime of hauling Grandma up and down stairs came into her head, and she swallowed back a curse.

They tucked Grandma into bed, then Franny and her mother went back downstairs. Mr. Yeager was polishing off his drink.

"Thank God," he said.

"Thank God what, dear?" his wife asked, taking her place next to him on the sofa.

"Thank God she decided to go to bed. She depresses the hell out of me."

265

Franny went white. Her father had just said what she'd been thinking, hated thinking. The craziness in her began to dance and gibber.

Mrs. Yeager was too shocked to say anything for a few moments. Then, her voice strained, she said, "She's a lot better than she was, Gene. The social worker—"

"Social worker," he spat. "Listen, why can't one of your brothers take her in for a while?"

"She's my mother, Gene."

"She's their mother too. We've had her long enough."

"Gene, I can't believe you're saying these things. Mama, she let us live in her apartment when we couldn't afford another place."

"You mean when I couldn't afford it. That's what you mean, isn't it? Mr. Lousy Provider here. The guy who had to rely on his mother-in-law to give his family a roof over their heads." His voice rose.

"You were just starting out—"

"And now I'm finished. Finished."

Franny stood up so swiftly, she knocked over her untouched brandy Alexander. It splashed over her leg and onto the rug, but she didn't bother to clean it up. I can't stand it anymore. I can't. Got to get away. She fled to the basement. Nearly tripping in the dark, she reached her tokonoma and, without even turning on a light, flung herself onto her cushions.

"Ouch" came from the body she'd crashed on top of.

Franny gasped, leaped up, and pulled the light cord.

266

Lying rumpled and mussy-looking was Lainie.

"What are you doing here?" Franny's voice, low and deadly, lashed out.

"Escaping New Year's Eve with the folks," Lainie answered.

"You had a date."

"That's right, I did, didn't I? Well, I got tired of him. He could only talk about football, and he thinks foreplay is what you do while you're waiting for the kickoff."

"What are you doing here?" Franny repeated through gritted teeth. Fury rose in her. My space, defiled. She's defiled it, she thought.

"I already told you. What are *you* doing here? I thought you'd be out with that hot Japanese guy you did a number on at Barger's. He is your boyfriend, isn't he? Mom and Dad would flip if they knew. . . ."

And suddenly, everything Franny had been holding back poured out. "Well, why don't you just tell them then?" she screamed, so suddenly and loudly that Lainie jumped. "Tell them! That's what you've been wanting to do all along, isn't it? Go on. Go upstairs and tell them that Miss Perfect isn't perfect at all. That she's in love with a goddamn half-breed." Her face red and contorted, she stood over her sister, clenching and unclenching her fists.

For the first time in her life, Lainie was afraid of her. "I . . . I wouldn't tell them that. I . . . You're my sister. I wouldn't rat on you."

"Liar! You little liar." Franny grabbed her by the shoulders and shook her violently. "I'm your enemy. You hate me. Hate, hate, hate me!"

"Stop it, Franny. Stop it. You're hurting me."

Franny thrust her sister away from her, whirled to the shelves, and with one sweep of her hand knocked the Buddha and incense burner to the floor. "Damn you," she yelled, ripping down the still-life poster and tearing it into little pieces. Then she seized her beautiful shoka. "Damn all of you!" she shrieked, and with tremendous force hurled the shoka against the wall. It shattered at once, splattering water, leaves, and flower petals everywhere. Snatching Lainie's coat from the cushions, Franny pelted through the basement and out the back door into the night.

She raced through the streets, oblivious to the cold and the drunken revelers weaving in and out of her path, a reeling crazy amid the crazies. "Happy New Year. Happy damn New Year," she muttered over and over.

On she ran until she found herself on a vaguely familiar street. It took her a moment to realize it was Lillian's. And there was her house, with a light burning inside.

"Lillian. Oh, Lillian," Franny panted. "Help me, Lillian." She hurried to the door and rang the bell, stamping her feet and shivering as the cold hit her at last.

The porch light went on and the door opened. But it wasn't Lillian who stood behind it. It was Ren, dressed in his kimono. He said nothing, only stared at her, waiting.

She stared back. Then, with a sob, she fell into his arms. Tears gushed from her, splotching the fine silk of his robe. He guided her through the kitchen into Lillian's library, helped her down onto the cushions, and held her against him as she wept and wept.

When her tears subsided, she looked up at him. "I'm ready to talk now," she said soberly.

He wiped her face with his fingers. "I'm ready to listen," he said.

Slowly, painfully, she poured it out—her grandma's illness, her father's job loss, her sister's nastiness, her mother's cringing. As she talked, Ren didn't speak, but his expressive face reflected the anguish she felt. When she finally told him why she'd kept him a secret from her family, she had to look away. "I'm such a coward. Such a horrible coward. I still don't know how I'm going to face them after tonight, how I'm going to tell them I . . . I love you." She said the last words so softly they were scarcely audible.

But Ren heard them loud and clear. Gently he turned her face to his. "We'll find a way together to tell them," he said firmly. "Because I love you, too."

She reached for him, and as they kissed, car horns blared outside, and there came the faint *pop pop pop*

269

of a string of firecrackers someone had just set off.

"Happy New Year," he murmured, nuzzling her cheek.

She leaned against him, her eyes alighting on the tokonoma. She began to cry again.

"What is it?" he asked as a tear dropped on his hand.

"My shoka. I smashed it to bits."

"You'll make another one."

"Yes," she said after a moment. "I will."

They sat quietly, listening to each other's breathing, the creaking of the house, and the occasional blast of a horn until Franny began to sniffle.

"More tears?" Ren said kindly.

"I really wanted to go to the Christmas dance with you. And now, now it's too late."

He kissed her hair. "That's okay. Come June you can ask me to the prom."

Franny smiled for the first time in many days. "That's a promise I'll keep," she said.

29

"Franny, is that you?" Pale-faced, still in her dress, Mrs. Yeager came out into the front hall.

"Yes," Franny answered, hanging Lainie's coat in the closet. It was nearly three in the morning. Ren had driven her home.

"My God, where were you? Lainie said you'd had a fight and that you ran out of the house. I was so worried, I called Susan, but she's not home. Then I tried the police, but they said they had their hands full tonight and they couldn't do anything until you'd been missing a lot longer. I was just about to try and wake your dad so we could take the car and look for you. He's out cold and I didn't know where to look

by myself. Where *were* you? Why did you run off like that?" She twisted the bottom of her sweater in her hands.

"Lillian's house," Franny answered calmly.

"Lillian! I should've thought to try there. . . . But why didn't you call? You could've at least told us."

"Mom, I wasn't in any shape to call."

"Lillian could've called for you. She's a responsible adult."

Franny hesitated, then said, "Lillian wasn't there."

"What? I don't understand. Do you have a key to her place?"

"Lillian wasn't there, but her grandson was. I was with him."

"I still don't understand. Do you know this boy? You've never mentioned him. Is he a friend?"

"Yes, he's a friend."

Mrs. Yeager fumbled with her sweater again. "Well, that's good. But why didn't you tell us you were going to see him? And why haven't you talked about him?"

"Mom, I want to answer your questions, but not now. Soon. But not now."

"Well, it is late. We can talk tomorrow. Would you like some hot milk before you go to bed? I'm going to have some."

"No thanks." She turned toward the stairs.

"Franny, things will get better. I know they will."

272

"I know they will too, Mom," Franny said. This time she believed it.

As her mother headed for the kitchen, Franny walked up the stairs and down the hall. Lainie was standing in her doorway. "I heard you come in. I had to tell Mom you left like that. Congratulations—you scared me pretty good."

"I'm sorry."

"No, you're not," Lainie said matter-of-factly.

"You're right. I'm not," Franny answered with equal straightforwardness.

They fell silent, neither moving.

At last, Lainie said, "You know, I really liked Larry. I didn't that much at first. I went out with him because, well, because I thought he was yours. But then I really started to like him. And I thought he really liked me too. Until right before the Christmas dance when we picked you up. That's when I began to guess the truth. But I told myself I could still get him to be mine. Then tonight we were fooling around and he called me by *your* name. That was the last straw. I started yelling, so he told me the truth, that he'd just been using me to make you jealous and he thought we ought to stop seeing each other. I ran out of his place and ended up in our basement. I guess you think it serves me right, huh?"

Franny said nothing for a moment, then, gently, impulsively, she reached for and clasped her sister's hand. "I did. But I don't now."

Lainie squeezed her hand once in return and said, "Thanks."

"I've got to go to bed now," said Franny.

"Me too. It's been a long night." Lainie backed into her room and closed the door.

Franny ran her hand over its surface, pitted here from a book Lainie'd thrown at it, there with tack holes from a long-gone Miss Piggy poster. Changes, she thought. How large, how lasting, it was too early to tell. Will Lainie and I have a permanent truce? Will my parents listen to what I have to say? Will I even be able to say it? The future loomed hazy and disturbing. But then another of George Henkin's quotes came to her mind: "A journey of a thousand miles starts with your own feet." And the comforting truth of it brought tears to her eyes.

She went into her room, closing the door quietly, undressing in the soft darkness. She slid into bed and was nearly asleep when Grandma said, "Is it morning?"

Franny opened her eyes. "No, not yet," she answered, a little befuddled.

"Are you sleeping here tonight?"

"Yes, Grandma. I am."

"Good."

There was a long silence, then Grandma said, "Happy New Year, Frannele."

"Happy New Year, Grandma."

Another silence. Then Franny heard Grandma's

snores. "There's someone I want to introduce you to, Grandma," she told her sleeping form. "Someone you'll like and who'll like you. He's my boyfriend, Grandma. His name is Ren." She tried out the words in a whisper over and over. They sounded exactly right.

About the Author

MARILYN SINGER is the author of a number of books for children and young readers, including THE COURSE OF TRUE LOVE NEVER DID RUN SMOOTH, GHOST HOST, LIZZIE SILVER OF SHERWOOD FOREST, TARANTULAS ON THE BRAIN, IT CAN'T HURT FOREVER, and four Sam and Dave mystery stories. She lives with her husband, three dogs, several cats, and a parakeet in a Brooklyn brownstone. She has studied Japanese flower arranging at the Brooklyn Botanic Garden for several years.

C.1

FIC
SIN

Singer, Marilyn

Several kinds of
silence

$13.89

DATE		
08 FEB 2008		

Several Kinds of Silence

Many thanks to:
Bill Aronson
Dena Aronson
Michael Bernstein
Renee Cafiero
Nora Chavooshian
Leslie Kimmelman
Taro Meyer
Terry Moogan
Hopi Morton
Joe Morton
Linda Ottiger
Fonda Sara
Shirley Singer
Sandi Williams
and most especially to
my ikebana teacher, Mildred Lipton

To Steve, who saw me through this one, too.

The publisher gratefully acknowledges the following organizations: Warner Bros. Music for permission to reprint a portion of the lyrics of "Something's Gotta Give" by Johnny Mercer. © 1954 WB Music Corp. All Rights Reserved. Used by Permission.

Chappell/Intersong for permission to reprint a portion of the lyrics of "Things Are Looking Up" by George & Ira Gershwin. © 1937 by Chappell & Co., Inc. Copyright Renewed. International Copyright Secured. All Rights Reserved. Used by Permission.

Grove Press, a division of Wheatland Corporation, for permission to reprint "New Year's" from *Bankei Zen*, copyright © 1984 by Peter Haskel and Yoshito Hakeda. All Rights Reserved. Used by Permission.

Several Kinds of Silence

Typography by Joyce Hopkins

2 3 4 5 6 7 8 9 10

Library of Congress Cataloging-in-Publication Data
Singer, Marilyn.
    Several kinds of silence.

    Summary: Faced with her beloved grandmother's illness and her own attraction to a boy her parents would disapprove of, Franny tries to shut off her feelings completely.
    [1. Family problems—Fiction.   2. Grandmothers—Fiction]   I. Title.
PZ7.S6172Se   1988   [Fic]   87-45304
ISBN 0-06-025627-3
ISBN 0-06-025628-1 (lib. bdg.)

Several Kinds of Silence

Marilyn Singer

HARPER & ROW, PUBLISHERS, NEW YORK
Cambridge, Philadelphia, San Francisco, St. Louis,
London, Singapore, Sydney

Also by Marilyn Singer

Several Kinds
of Silence

1

Introduction: Debating the Assumptions of State-Led Nation Building in Ukraine

Paul D'Anieri

In the decade since Ukraine attained independence from the Soviet Union, questions of national identity have dominated the study of Ukrainian politics and society. This focus has been justified for several different reasons. First, it seemed clear to observers of Ukraine that ethnic, linguistic, and regional divisions in the country called into question its ability to persist as a unified independent state. Second, the relationship between regional, linguistic, and ethnic identities in Ukraine was unclear and needed to be better understood. Such study promised a better understanding not only of the situation in Ukraine but also of national identity formation more broadly. Third, for the Ukrainian government and for those who would influence it, there were serious policy questions and political disputes over what sort of policies concerning language and national identity the new state should adopt.

Despite the considerable debate on the nature of cleavages in Ukraine, scholars on various sides of the debate seem to share the assumption that Ukraine's identity cleavages constitute a potential source of societal conflict and hence endanger the new state in some way. Dominique Arel and David Laitin, on one side, have seen Ukraine's Russian/Ukrainian language divide as a likely source of conflict.[1] Hence some scholars have advocated state policies explicitly embracing the Russian language, as a way of avoiding alienation of Russophone Ukrainians. An opposing school of thought, epitomized by the work of Taras Kuzio, sharply disagrees with the notion that Ukraine should accept the post-Soviet linguistic status quo. In Kuzio's view, accepting that status quo is dangerous, because it is an obstacle to building a stable and unified nation-state and an obstacle to generating the political consensus needed to undertake economic and political reform.[2] Moreover, accepting the status quo is morally repugnant to some, who see that as endorsing the de-Ukrainianization policies of the Tsars and the Soviets. These opposing views share two overarching assumptions. First, national identity matters immensely to contemporary Ukrainian politics.

Second, state policies can profoundly influence national identity, for better or worse.

Thus, beyond debates over the actual state of identity politics in Ukraine and beyond normative preferences for various programs, there is an underlying agreement that the state has an essential role to play in identity politics in Ukraine. That role, however, has been assumed much more often than it has been examined, such that a number of crucial questions have been given much less treatment than they merit. The goal of this volume is to begin to address systematically the role of the state in Ukrainian identity politics. The chapters in this volume have a range of perspectives and contend with a variety of issues, but all are connected to the fundamental but underresearched questions concerning the state's role in national identity formation.

While these chapters cover a variety of specific topics, they all grapple with the question of state-led promotion of national identity in Ukraine. Rather than beginning with a single unifying perspective and then elaborating it, this volume begins only with a common set of questions. Rather than seeking to produce a single coherent viewpoint, the chapters express a series of profound disagreements and contradictions. We leave it for the reader and for future research to judge the merit of the various contentions advanced in these chapters. More important than arriving at a unified conclusion, however, is establishing these issues as questions to be debated theoretically and studied empirically, instead of as assumptions to be made casually and left unexamined.

Within this broad question about the state's role in identity politics, several constituent questions need to be dealt with. First, is it true, as often assumed, that overcoming Ukraine's current cleavages is a prerequisite for holding the country together or for reforming it? Second, how have the legacies of history constrained the ability of the state to tackle such a project, and what lessons can be learned from Tsarist and Soviet efforts to alter Ukrainian national identity? Third, what are the natures of the cleavages that need to be overcome, and what sort of national identity might provide the most solid foundation for the construction of an overarching Ukrainian national identity? Finally, and most importantly, how has the Ukrainian state sought to build national identity over the last ten years, and what have been the results?

These are big questions, and the chapters in this volume certainly will not end discussion of them. But the chapters in this volume do seek to push the debate forward. Despite all the discussion of identity divisions in Ukraine, there has been little systematic attempt to evaluate the premises of such policies or to evaluate the results. After ten years of these policies, such an evaluation is overdue. The findings will be relevant well beyond Ukraine. In all of the other societies in the former Soviet Union and elsewhere that are divided on questions of national identity, it is important to examine the implications of these kinds of divisions for the survival and prosperity of their states. The rest of this introduction shall explore these four basic questions in greater detail and show how they relate to the rest of the book.

THE THREAT OF IDENTITY DIFFERENCES AND THE ROLE OF THE STATE

The first section of the book examines how Ukrainian national identity arrived at its current state and addresses the implications of the historical legacy for nation building today. These chapters focus on linking events in the past to the policy problems of today, and while much has been written about the Russian and Soviet legacy in Ukraine, crucial questions have been neglected. First among them is the question of establishing a status quo, a state of affairs that can be considered normal for Ukrainian national identity.

It is widely asserted that Ukraine's domestic divisions—regional, ethnic, and linguistic—undermine various fundamental state goals. To the extent that this is true, it is easy to conclude that the state should do something about it. Most profoundly, many have argued that the country simply does not cohere and is prone to fragmenting along the lines of one cleavage or another. Raised most provocatively by William Zimmerman's article title "Is Ukraine a Political Community?" the notion that Ukraine is likely to fragment, probably with significant violence, is shared from academic circles to the CIA.[3] The argument is relatively straightforward. If many of the country's citizens consider themselves Russian, national self-determination implies that they might seek to be governed by a Russian state rather than a Ukrainian one. This is even more likely, many conclude, to the extent that the Ukrainian state adopts an ethnic notion of Ukrainian national identity that excludes those who define themselves as ethnically Russian. Equally problematic, in this view, are efforts to force Russian speakers to speak Ukrainian instead.

This notion is critiqued by Taras Kuzio, who is a partisan of a very different notion of Ukrainian national identity. From Kuzio's perspective, the danger is not that Russians will seek to secede from Ukraine, a tendency for which we see very little evidence, but rather that Russians will remain in Ukraine but continue to maintain distance from the Ukrainian national identity. Along with Alexander Motyl, Kuzio asserts that only a political community can reach the consensus and commitment to undertake the changes that Ukraine so desperately needs, and that such a community cannot succeed until damage done in the past is undone. The notion of a Ukrainian national identity, Kuzio fears, is undermined by the continued use of the Russian language in Ukraine, and more broadly by the prevalence of Russian literature, media, and culture in Ukraine, a subject discussed further by Mykola Riabchuk.

Kuzio disagrees with those who criticize as "illiberal" efforts to promote a single homogeneous national identity, asserting that critics are simply uninformed about the reality of national identity construction throughout history. Few states, Kuzio points out, are ethnically homogeneous, all have ethnic as well as civic components to their national identities, and all of the successful ones have at some time promoted a specific national identity through state policies. For Ukraine to do the same is normal, Kuzio argues, and historically justified. In short, then, Kuzio's chapter provides a clear statement of the view that state promotion of a Ukrainian national identity is important to Ukraine's future development.

THE HISTORICAL LEGACY

As Georgii Kasianov shows, there tends to be an assumption that Ukrainian national identity has some teleological end-point, and that only artificial interference has prevented that end-point from being attained. If Kuzio and others are to contend that affirmative action is justifiable to overcome the discrimination that Ukrainian language and culture suffered in the past, then it is essential to generate some notion of what situation would obtain had not that discrimination taken place. Hence the search for a historical Ukrainian "state of nature" from which to infer the goal of present policy. The highlighting of Russian and Soviet efforts to undermine Ukrainian language, as well as the search for the roots of the Ukrainian nationality, forge not only the justification for today's nation-building efforts, but also the content, as Jan Janmaat's chapter shows.

But the discussion of Tsarist and Soviet language and identity policy has a more fundamental connection to the problems of contemporary Ukraine. If we want to know something about how state-led efforts to shift linguistic and national identity work in practice, the Tsarist and Soviet efforts could provide valuable insight. Two conclusions seem possible based on a cursory examination, and both should be considered by today's nation builders. First, as the chapter by Riabchuk emphasizes, such policies were in part successful: by being able to provide certain incentives, Soviet authorities induced many to abandon the Ukrainian language and a Ukrainian identity. Moreover, through Tsarist and Soviet times, the stigmatization of Ukrainian as a peasant language has at least in part taken on a life of its own. In that sense, state efforts to nationalize worked (though to the disadvantage of Ukrainian).

What is equally striking, however, about Tsarist and Soviet nationalization efforts is how incompletely they succeeded given the resources put into them. From the time of the Ems Ukaz, and even earlier, the Tsarist government implemented extremely repressive policies to eradicate the Ukrainian language, and used autocratic methods to enforce those policies. Yet the Ukrainian language and national identity were not eradicated, and in some cases may have strengthened in response to the repression (an outcome that is not surprising according to the literature on protest and repression). Similarly, Stalinist policies after 1930 provided powerful economic incentives to speak Russian and physically eliminated a great number of Ukrainian speakers. While physical repression waned after Stalin's death, substantial economic incentives continued to prompt Ukrainian speakers to adopt Russian. But while many did, many others did not. It is worth asking how the Ukrainian state today, which is much weaker than its predecessors, much more democratic, much less able to repress, and much less able to provide economic incentives, is going to promote a shift potentially more substantial than what could be accomplished by two of the most repressive regimes in history.

WHICH VERSION OF UKRAINIAN NATIONAL IDENTITY SHOULD BE PROMOTED?

Apart from the question of how to promote a Ukrainian national identity is the question of what type of Ukrainian national identity the state should be promoting. This issue touches on the broader debate over the nature of identity patterns in Ukraine, which has received a great deal of attention. It also is connected to normative concerns concerning liberalism and historical justice.

To many authors and observers, it is obvious how the Ukrainian national identity should be defined. It should be defined in terms of Ukrainian ethnicity and language, and in distinction from Russian ethnicity and language. This is made clear in Kuzio's chapter. An opposing view is that the Ukrainian language is not any more widely spoken than Russian in Ukraine, and that a substantial minority of Ukrainian citizens define themselves as ethnically Russian. From this perspective, some advocate a "hands off" policy that would tolerate Russian as well as Ukrainian. To the liberal argument in favor of toleration of ethnic and linguistic pluralism (and hence acceptance of the Russian language, perhaps even as an official language), two responses are made. First is the argument, discussed earlier, that a single identity is required for the state to thrive, and that construction of such an identity is the historical norm. Second is an argument concerning historical justice: For the Ukrainian state to now adopt a liberal policy that freezes in place the results of past Russification efforts is to reward past oppression and to ensure its success. On the contrary, it is argued, historical justice requires that the oppression be reversed.

At some point, arguments over the proper content of Ukrainian national identity become circular: Those who see Ukraine as a naturally mono-ethnic and mono-lingual society tend to support establishing such a Ukraine as state policy. Those who see Ukraine as naturally bi-ethnic and bilingual argue for that view. In the end, these are political questions, which can be studied by scholars but not in any way resolved by them. Scholarship can, however, investigate the empirical situation in Ukraine and offer some indications concerning what type of national identity might be successfully constructed in Ukraine (as well as what sort of national identity may be difficult or impossible to construct).

The second section of the book is in many respects the most significant, because it seeks to investigate several related issues on which assertions are common but empirically investigations are rare. Craig Weller's chapter leads us to question the validity of a basic assumption in much of the literature—that ethnic difference will lead to conflict and undermine reform. Relying on data from three nationwide surveys, Weller finds that Ukrainians have remarkably low expectations of ethnic conflict. He finds low expectations of conflict even among groups one might expect to be most aggrieved, such as Russian speakers and residents of Crimea, on the one hand, and Ukrainian speakers from western Ukraine, on the other. Another finding perhaps indicates why: ethnic Ukrainians and ethnic Russians in Ukraine do not perceive themselves to be very different from one another, and even when they do, they do not see this difference as a source of conflict. To the extent Weller's findings are correct, we must wonder whether much of the concern over ethnic differences is overblown. This notion is consistent with a casual observation of politics in Ukraine, which reveals many reasons more important than national identity to explain the utter lack of reform in the country.

The chapters by Stephen Shulman and Lowell Barrington both investigate national identity through the lens of foreign policy. Since much of the debate on Ukrainian national identity concerns connections with Russia—in identity as well in economy and politics—it makes sense that popular attitudes toward Russia would reflect perceptions of national identity.

Barrington's concern above all is to sort out the three cleavages often identified in Ukraine: linguistic, ethnic, and regional cleavages. His research represents the progress that has been made since the early 1990s, when most researchers tended to assume that those three issues were simply different manifestations of a single cleavage. By showing that regional cleavages in Ukraine are more salient than ethnic or linguistic cleavages, Barrington's research raises some difficult questions. First, it makes us wonder whether, in identifying the problems of Ukrainian national identity as problems of ethnicity and language, we have not missed the most important component of the problem. Perhaps, for example, the discussions of history should focus less on linguistic repression than on geographic division to identify the most powerful legacy of the past. More practically, if the barrier to a coherent Ukrainian national identity is regional rather than linguistic or ethnic, we must wonder whether government policies, both actual and suggested, to build a single identity by closing language and ethnicity gaps are misguided. If the problem is regional, how will language policies fix it?

For advocates of a Ukrainian national identity based on an ethnic and linguistic definition of Ukraine, and based on the distinctions between Ukrainians and Russians, Stephen Shulman's chapter raises even more provocative questions. Shulman, also using survey data on attitudes toward relations with Russia, shows that there is a tension between the key components of the typical Ukrainian nation-building agenda. If the goal is to define Ukrainian national identity in such a way that it creates political consensus (on which reform can then be built), Shulman argues, then that identity should not be defined in a way that emphasizes the distinction between Ukrainians and Russians or tends to exclude ethnic Russians and Russophones. Instead, Shulman finds that the easiest national identity to establish, given the current distribution of attitudes, would be an "East Slavic" identity focused on the closeness rather than the distinctiveness of Ukrainians and Russians. Rather than seeing national identity as something that must overcome historical injustices, Shulman takes the past as given, and asks where consensus today can most easily be built. If Shulman is correct, those who believe both that Ukraine needs a cohesive national identity and that this identity should emphasize the differences between Ukraine and Russia may face agonizing tradeoffs, for Shulman's research implies that an effort to establish a Western-oriented national identity will be less likely to succeed than one aimed at an East Slavic identity.

NATION BUILDING IN PRACTICE

If much of the debate concerning the promotion of Ukrainian national identity has occurred in the abstract, these chapters investigate specific efforts to advance Ukrainian national identity and evaluate the question of what sort of identity will be easiest to build. Advocates of "Ukrainianization" or "affirmative action" for the Ukrainian language and of a particular "Ukrainian national historiography" seem to take it for granted that such efforts will succeed over time. Similarly, opponents of such plans seem to think that these efforts will inevitably lead to conflict. Both of these propositions should be subjected to empirical scrutiny rather than assumed, and this section of the book takes up that task.

Andrew Fesiak's chapter on nation building in the military and Jan Janmaat's chapter on textbook changes get to the heart of the matter. The programs to increase Ukrainian national consciousness in the military, which Fesiak evaluates, represent of one type of approach to nationalization: given a relatively captive audience, focused education efforts are used to readjust attitudes and even identities of the individuals involved. Janmaat investigates the longer-term route to increasing national identity, the broad inculcation of a view of Ukrainian history that emphasizes the deep historical roots of the Ukrainian nation and the distinctness of the Ukrainian and Russian peoples. Interestingly, both studies find mixed results. Fesiak finds that in many instances the military program has increased tensions rather than reducing them, supplying some credence to the "backlash" hypothesis advanced by opponents of Ukrainianization. Similarly, Janmaat shows how difficult it is to build a history curriculum that promotes Ukrainian nationhood and statehood without presenting Russia as an "other," and hence alienating precisely that portion of the Ukrainian citizenry that the program seeks to engage. These two issue studies are not necessarily definitive, but they highlight the difficulties involved in state-led programs to promote national identity in Ukraine.

SUMMARY

In different ways, all of these chapters weigh in on crucial questions concerning the role of the state in promoting Ukrainian national identity. Some assert both the need for state-led national identity development and the practicality. Others question one or another of those suppositions. Still others accept the idea in theory, but question whether the particular national identity being promoted by the Ukrainian state will find a base of support in society broad enough to ensure the program's success. By raising these questions, and by seeking to answer them, these chapters seek to take a substantial step forward in the study of national identity in post-Soviet Ukraine. To this point, empirical work has focused largely on identifying and characterizing public attitudes on Ukrainian national identity. The potential for state policies to influence those attitudes has been widely suggested but not thoroughly investigated. These questions, however, are of vital importance both for the future of Ukraine and for scholars' understanding of the process of nation building. This volume aims to begin that crucial discussion.

NOTES

1. Dominique Arel, "Ukraine: The Temptation of the Nationalizing State," in Vladimir Tismaneanu, ed., *Political Culture and Civil Society in Russia and the New States of Eurasia* (Armonk, NY: M. E. Sharpe, 1995), pp. 157–188; and David Laitin, *Identity in Formation: The Russian-Speaking Populations in the Near Abroad* (Ithaca, NY: Cornell University Press, 1998), especially pp. 178–180.

2. Taras Kuzio, *Ukraine: State and Nation Building* (London: Routledge, 1998), Chap. 7; Taras Kuzio, "Defining the Political Community in Ukraine: State, Nation, and the Transition to Modernity" in Taras Kuzio, Robert Kravchuk, and Paul D'Anieri, eds., *State and Institution Building in Ukraine* (New York: St. Martin's, 1999), pp. 213–244; and Alexander J. Motyl, *Dilemmas of Independence: Ukraine after Totalitarianism* (New York: Council on Foreign Relations, 1993), pp. 67–70.

3. William Zimmerman, "Is Ukraine a Political Community?" *Communist and Post-Communist Studies*, vol. 31, no. 1 (1998), pp. 43–55. For predictions of Ukraine's collapse, see, among others, "Ukraine: The Birth and Possible Death of a Country," *The Economist*, 7 May 1994; Eugene B. Rumer, "Letter from Eurasia: Will Ukraine Return to Russia?" *Foreign Policy*, no. 96 (Fall 1994), pp. 129–144; P. Klebnikov, "Tinderbox," *Forbes*, 9 September 1996, pp. 158–164; and F. Stephen Larabee, "Ukraine: Europe's Next Crisis?" *Arms Control Today*, vol. 24, no. 6 (July/August 1994), pp. 14–19.

2

The Nation-Building Project in Ukraine and Identity: Toward a Consensus

Taras Kuzio

This chapter has two arguments. First, the promotion of a Ukrainian national identity through a nation-building project is necessary, and normal and can be undertaken in a liberal manner without conflict. Treatment of national identity and the nation-building project in Ukraine is often inconsistent, and what is often described negatively in Ukraine ("nationalizing state") can be defined in a positive manner or sidestepped elsewhere ("nation building"). Second, the four components of the nation-building project are a unitary state, identity, language, and historiography. I critically engage the published literature on contemporary Ukraine in each of these four areas by placing the discussion within a theoretical and comparative perspective.

The chapter is divided into two sections. An outline of the nation-building project and its four areas are placed within the first section of the chapter. The second section outlines five areas where elite consensus has emerged with regard to Ukraine's nation-building project. These are state and institution building, borders and territorial integrity, federalism and regionalism, pragmatic state nationalism, national integration and foreign policy. Most other scholars in this field have tended to stress disunity, not consensus. In contrast, this chapter argues that in the second half of the 1990s Ukrainian elites reached a consensus on the three areas of the nation-building project outlined in the first section of the chapter.

THE NATION-BUILDING PROJECT

Nation building in Ukraine has to overcome over two centuries of colonial rule.[1] Nation and state building are usually synonymous processes: "It might be argued that state building and nation-building can be separated only conceptually but that both processes have gone and are going hand in hand."[2] These two factors should be treated as distinct processes while recognizing that they are also interlinked through the armed forces and the media, historical myths and symbols, national anthems and folk culture. The state may create institutions, such as a Ministry of Education, but the curricula it will direct schools and higher education to teach will be reflected in the nation-building priorities of the state leadership.

The two processes of state and nation building are going hand in hand (together with democratization and marketization) in Ukraine. Yet, simultaneous state and nation building is a difficult task for the following reasons:

First, Ukraine inherited a "quasi-state" from the former USSR. This state and the institutions it incorporated were insufficient to run a modern state.[3] Ukraine's inheritance of a quasi state gave it a better launching pad for state and nation building than in 1917 but by the late 1990s, nearly a decade after the USSR disintegrated, Ukraine is still a "weak state" and exhibits elements of immature stateness.[4]

Second, postcolonial states, such as Ukraine, did not inherit modern nations. As Robert Jackson pointed out in relation to former Western colonies, "very few new states are 'nations' either by long history or common ethnicity or successful constitutional integration."[5] Some scholars, using the model of Rogers Brubaker (see later), have been reluctant to place Ukraine's post-Soviet transition within a postcolonial framework. One can argue that such a framework would make affirmative action a perfectly natural and just course of events.

Third, Ukraine did not inherit a uniform level of national consciousness throughout its territory. Due to the different history of Western Ukraine, a modern nation was allowed to develop in the Austrian era prior to 1918, a factor which was helped along from 1918 to the 1950s by war and conflict with "others" (Poles, Hungarians, Romanians, and Soviets). In Eastern and Southern Ukraine, on the other hand, modern nation building was suppressed by the state on two occasions, first in the late Tsarist era and again in the 1930s.[6] A modern Ukrainian national consciousness does not therefore exist in Eastern and Southern Ukraine.

Nation building in post-Soviet Ukraine therefore must undertake two processes. First, nation building must occur in areas where this had previously not been allowed (Eastern and Southern Ukraine). Second, an overarching political community must be developed that unites all of the inhabitants within independent Ukraine. Scholars remain divided over whether such a political community is emerging in Ukraine.[7] Nation building has never been evenly undertaken (as it is not in Ukraine). Thus, "different sectors of the polity at any one time are in different stages of the passage."[8] The media, education system, and armed forces are important vehicles for the inculcation of mass values during this process (see the chapters by Jan Janmaat and Andrew Fesiak). The role and place of women in the nation-building project are usually ignored, but nation builders, while they support national and human rights, are not always sensitive to the liberation of women from traditional roles and duties.

Nation building in Ukraine is taking place unevenly at three levels:

- *Micro level:* In regions where national consciousness is low (e.g., Eastern and Southern Ukraine) the revival of Ukrainian identity, culture, and language is an uneven process that seeks to partly overcome the colonial legacy. As in most postcolonial states (e.g., Ireland), it is unlikely to completely remove this legacy.

- *Macro level:* A new Ukrainian political community is being created that exhibits loyalty to the state's borders, institutions, constitution, political system, and other citizens within the civic nation. Such an overarching community identity can coexist with both regional differences and polyethnic rights in the private sphere.

- *International level:* Ukraine is both accepted as an independent state (all of Ukraine's borders were legally codified by 1999) and regarded as different to "others" (principally Russia). A new Ukrainian national identity on this level competes with allegiances in some regions (e.g., the Donbas and Crimea) to both the East Slavic and Soviet cultural-political spaces (see the chapter by Stephen Shulman).[9]

Unitary State

I have argued elsewhere that the debate in Ukraine on federalism has been a "non-debate" and support for it has been again highly exaggerated by Western scholars.[10] The majority of Ukraine's elites reject both "extremes"—federalism (favored by some sections of the left) or a unitary state (favored by nationalists)—as not suited to Ukraine's period of transition. Instead, they favor what is enshrined in the constitution (for example, in article 140): a devolved unitary state that lies midway between these unitary and federal proposals. This centrist policy acknowledges Ukraine's inherited regional diversity while, at the same time, rejecting a federal option which would simply freeze it and prevent state and nation building to remove some (but not all) of the colonial legacy.[11] During the Kravchuk era the most radical supporter of federalism was the Labor Party, which had strong links to what were termed the Red Directors based in Donets'k.[12]

Ukrainian scholars and officials see the introduction of federalism when the state and civic nation are still weak as preventing the consolidation that Ukrainian leaders proclaim as a goal. A 1993 study by the influential National Institute of Strategic Studies declared that federalism "is the way to ruin of Ukrainian statehood." The study linked those in favor of federalism to the left who desire a return to the totalitarian past and an end to Ukrainian statehood.[13] In other studies it is negatively assessed as likely to lead to the growth of regional clans, as premature and as leading to the creation of "regionocracies."[14] The former mayor of Kharkiv, Yevgenny Kushnariov, who went on to become head of the Presidential Administration in 1997–1999, did not support any autonomous status for Slobidska Ukraina, the old name for the Kharkiv region, or a federal Ukraine.[15]

A close correlation of views has emerged between those within Ukraine and Western scholars, such as Andrew Wilson and Gwendolyn Sasse, who seek to define federalism in Ukraine as a liberal solution to Ukraine's regionalism by preventing "nationalizing policies." This would freeze the inherited postcolonial status quo,[16] "as the *de jure* recognition of the existence of the specific ethnolinguistic, economic, and cultural nature of the territory of Ukraine." Vladimir Grynev, leader of the Russophile Inter-Regional Bloc of Reforms party, does not conceal that his support for federalism is to prevent the creation of "any kind of state ideology," including an overarching national identity. In other words, federalism would freeze Ukraine's inherited postcolonial situation.[17]

Federalism, in Sasse's view, "is *de facto* inscribed in Ukraine's regional diversity" and the Crimean autonomous region "perforates" the unitary state. Although Ukraine lacks federal structures, this "does not preclude the existence of a 'federalized society', which is the basis of every regionalism and expresses itself through different economic, political, social, cultural, religious, national or historical interests and institutions."[18] Ukraine is not unique in possessing a unitary state which is "perforated." France, the archetypal unitary nation-state, has granted Corsica a degree of autonomy in a bid to thwart its separatist movement.

However, there is little evidence indicating that federalism has widespread support in Ukraine.[19] In a February 2000 poll by SOCIS-Gallup, the number of supporters of a bicameral parliament (which, because its members would be the governors of regions, is seen as a step toward federalism) proved to be only 39% with 25% resolutely against and a large number (34%) who could not answer the question. Those opposed to a bicameral parliament believed that it would lead to the growth of separatism and a weakening of central government.[20] On the eve of the 16 April 2000 referendum two polls gave figures of only 45% and 39% in favor of a bicameral *Rada*.[21] The high support of 82% allegedly given to this question in the 16 April 2000 referendum cannot be portrayed as conclusive support for bicameralism due to highly biased media coverage and strong suspicion of ballot rigging.

In most studies of interethnic questions in contemporary Ukraine the focus has been on ethnic Russians. Few studies have dealt with smaller minorities, such as Poles, Romanians, and Hungarians. Jewish-Ukrainian relations have also been dealt with by only a small number of studies, perhaps because of the rare occurrence of anti-Semitism and the small number of Jews remaining in Ukraine.[22]

Ukraine's policies, stability, and good interethnic relations have been noted by scholars and government officials alike but few have sought to analyze why predictions of conflict have not materialized (see the chapter by Craig Weller).[23] This is despite the fact that from 1991 to 1995 Western scholarly and journalistic studies argued that Ukraine was likely to face widespread interethnic conflict up to, and including, civil war and separatism.[24]

Yet, the lack of interethnic discord was reflected in a poll conducted by SOCIS-Gallup and the Institute of Sociology, Academy of Sciences, which asked, "Are there in Ukraine nationalities toward whom you harbor antipathy or negative feelings?" Fifty-one percent replied that there were none and another 31% were apathetic toward the entire question. Only 15% admitted that there were such nationalities (3% could not answer).[25]

As is noted later in this chapter, the strategic outlines of the nationality policies of the Kravchuk era have been continued without any negative impact upon Ukraine's stability or interethnic relations. On the contrary, ethnic relations have remained stable, are good, and are improving. In polls between 1994 and 1999 conducted by the Kyiv International Institute of Sociology, interethnic relations were not seen as a problem by those polled (see Table 2.1). SOCIS-Gallup also found that there was little public perception of discrimination against Russians in Ukraine that, if it existed, could be the basis for poor interethnic relations (see Table 2.2).

Table 2.1
Which of the Ukrainian Problems Concerns You Most (Interethnic Relations)? (in percentages)

Year	Yes	No	Other Answer/ Difficult to Say
1994	-	3	5
1995	-	2	7
1996	-	0	3
1997	5	3	5
1998	4	5	6
1999	3	7	8

Source: State of Security: Dynamics of Public Opinion in Ukraine (Kyiv: Center for Peace, Conversion and Security Policy of Ukraine, October 1999).

Table 2.2
Have You Witnessed Discrimination against Russians? (in percentages)

Year	Yes	No	No Answer
1994	8.6	85.7	5.7
1995	9.5	90	0.5
1996	9.3	90.1	0.6
1997	7.4	92.2	0.4
1998	8.8	90.2	1.0
1999	8.5	91.4	0.4

Source: State of Security: Dynamics of Public Opinion in Ukraine (Kyiv: Center for Peace, Conversion and Security Policy of Ukraine, October 1999).

Several questions about interethnic relations in Ukraine arise, given the view that federalism is necessary to avert conflict:

- Despite all the predictions by scholars, policy makers, and journalists, interethnic conflict has not occurred. Why has Ukraine not proved to be fertile ground for ethnic strife?
- Why has mobilization along ethnic lines not taken place among either Russians or Ukrainians?[26]
- Why did Crimean separatism collapse so quickly in early 1995? Was Crimean separatism ever that powerful a force?[27]
- What is the role of the Crimean Tatars in the Crimean conflict?[28]
- Why did separatism only occur in Crimea?
- Why did Ukraine's national democratic and national communist leaders promote internationally acclaimed nationality policies?

- To what degree can those defined as ethnic Russians in the 1989 Soviet census be regarded as such?[29]

Identity

All civic states require the creation of a public (societal) culture or an overarching national identity to which all citizens are expected to pay homage, at least in the public sphere. This societal-public culture or national identity draws on the political culture of the dominant ethnic group and its symbols, historiography, myths, ceremonies, language, and folk culture. When a state becomes an independent entity, such an overarching identity is usually absent; hence, the necessity of undertaking nation building to forge a societal culture that will seek to provide the ethnocultural solidarity that all civic states need. This will define the "we" in contrast to "others."[30]

Pure civic states, where citizens would only pay patriotic homage to institutions, the rule of law, the constitution, and the territory exist only in theory. In practice, pure civic states are insufficient to create the solidarity that liberal democracies require for societal trust. The ethnocultural core of the state and the national identity that is developed from it give the state the depth that otherwise would be lacking. Such an identity, or in Miller's words "nationality," does not have to be tantamount to cultural homogenization. Nevertheless, a pluralistic state that tolerates different cultures and languages in the private sphere and respects cultural groups would still require the creation of an overarching identity that provides solidarity (e.g., multicultural policies in Canada and Australia take place alongside the promotion of overarching Canadian and Australian identities within the public domain).

National identity refers then to a variety of factors which unite a population within a given territory. These factors are similar to those discussed earlier when defining nations and include:

- a sense of a political community
- common institutions
- a single code of rights and duties
- a united economy
- a demarcated bounded space with which the citizens feel they belong (the "homeland")
- common mass public culture
- shared historical memory and common ancestry
- shared religion
- common language[31]

These nine elements of national identity include both state (e.g., common institutions, legislation) and national factors, thereby reflecting how liberal democracies are composed of both civic and ethnocultural attributes. The factors that we would describe as part of the state, such as the judiciary, a demarcated boundary, and institutions, can be established relatively quickly (although their public acceptance, functional efficiency, and ability to implement policies can take far longer). Many of these state functions were established in Ukraine during the 1990s. By the end of the decade Ukraine had two constitutions (Ukrainian and Crimean), recognized borders, and emerging institutions. Nevertheless, Ukraine still remains a "weak state," and state and institution building are an ongoing process.[32]

Language

Many Western scholars are especially critical of the demands of nationalists in Ukraine to prioritize its "core, indigenous peoples" (ethnic Ukrainians). In their view, national democrats hold contradictory policies whereby they back civic liberalism as well as ethnic supremacy. However, nation and state building in Europe has always prioritized the "core" culture and language and hence the ethnic supremacy of the core ethnic group. There are no pure civic states because all inclusive liberal democracies exhibit a mixture of both civic and ethnic elements. Western Europe's civic nations are, at the same time, based on the cultures, traditions, and languages of the dominant, core ethnic group. The problem that Western scholars fail to grapple with in dividing nationalism into civic (liberal) and ethnic (illiberal) varieties is that historically *both* have sought to homogenize internally and differentiate their societies externally during their nation- and state-building projects.

Critics of the official recognition of a core, titular nation (ethnic Ukrainians) and the legal codification of only one state language (Ukrainian) idealize the civic West through a "mixture of self-congratulation and wishful thinking." The Western-civic/ Eastern-ethnic dichotomy "itself reflects a considerable dose of ethnocentrism"[33] Liberal democracies have been realized only within national communities, with a shared culture and memories and where civil society and the civic nation are coterminous. Scholars who view Ukraine as a "nationalizing state" have pointed to Western "civicness" as a better non-nationalizing alternative without understanding the very essence of liberal democratic "civic states," which are themselves nationalizing.

As a supporter of the inherited status quo and in opposition to affirmative action, Wilson consciously does not use the term *Russification* in his study. Use of *Russification*, which in his view is a loaded term, "assumes loyalty to Ukrainian language and culture which may not have existed. Many Russophone Ukrainians have indeed been deprived of access to their native language and culture; others have always existed in a Russophone environment." Therefore, the term *Russification* was avoided by Wilson, "because it implies a prior loyalty to Ukrainian language and culture which may not necessarily have existed."[34]

Whether one uses the term *Russification* or not, it is nevertheless beyond a shadow of a doubt that both the Tsarist Russian and Soviet regimes have used homogenizing policies that favored the Russian language. During the Tsarist era Ukrainians and Belarusians were not treated as separate ethnic groups from "Great Russians." Homogenizing policies in these two territories were therefore perceived by the majority of Russian political parties as the elevation of provincial, backward peoples to the higher language and culture of what was the core

Great Russian ethnic group within the *Rus'kij* (Russian) nation. In this manner, Ukrainians and Belarusians were merely perceived analogously to Bretons or Alsatians who should be homogenized in favor of the core French national identity and language.

It is somewhat inconsistent for Western scholars to argue *against* affirmative action in favor of Ukrainian language and culture while promoting the same policies as liberals in Western democracies or other postcolonial or post-apartheid states (e.g., South Africa). Russification was a policy consciously carried out by the Soviet authorities, particularly during the Nikita Khrushchev and Leonid Brezhnev eras, following the near total annihilation of the Ukrainian intelligentsia in the 1930s and 1940s. The policy of Russification by the Soviet authorities affected the Belarusians and Ukrainians to a degree greater than other non-Russians of the former USSR. If Ukrainians and Belarusians could be assimilated into Russians this would accomplish two factors. First, Russians would maintain their majority in the USSR in the face of the rising Muslim populations. Second, the three eastern Slavic peoples would form the core of the emerging Soviet nation around which the non-Slavs would be expected to coalesce.

Given that undermining the Ukrainian language was a key part of efforts to eradicate Ukrainian national identity, it makes sense that affirmative action in favor of Ukrainian language and culture would be therefore a key policy for any Ukrainian leadership in an independent state committed to building a state-nation.

Historiography

Historiography, myths, and legends have long been recognized as important to nation building. As Anthony Smith argues, "The modern nation, to become truly a 'nation', requires the unifying myths, symbols and memories of pre-modern ethnie."[35] Civic states are founded on ethnocultural core(s) which include national histories. Anthropologists are more willing than historians or political scientists to point out "that history is not a product of the past but a response to requirements of the present."[36] Anthropologists, such as Catherine Wanner, see the use of history and myths as a normal process common to all civic states.[37]

Scholars working on these themes in Ukraine have often treated them as a peculiar, unnecessary phenomenon which have only been introduced because of the intransigence of Ukrainophone "nationalists." Three problems arise in this question. First, this argument fails to explain why history and myths are common to all civic states. As the Council of Europe has complained, "virtually all political systems have used history for their own ends and have imposed both their version of historical facts and their defense of the good and bad figures of history."[38] An objective history may be what historians should strive to write but, in reality, objective history is as much a myth as states being wholly civic.[39] Second, the argument against "nationalist historiography" ignores the continuity in the introduction of a national history, myths and legends between the Kravchuk and Kuchma eras. Third, opposition to the introduction of such a history comes *not* from a linguistic group (i.e., Russophones) but from an ideological perspective (i.e., communists) who see it as undermining Soviet myths and identity (which, of course, it is meant to do).

History and myth making is important to state-nation builders for three reasons. First, regime change usually involves some "form of confrontation with national history." This process is inevitably painful because not only the ancien regime is rejected but also its "national experience" (i.e., Soviet identity).[40] Tsarist nationality policies denied that Ukrainians constituted a separate ethnic group; they were merely a Little Russian regional group of Russians. The entire Ukrainian past was usurped by Great Russians. Soviet nationality policies also monopolized the past on behalf of Russians (i.e., the Kyiv Rus' legacy was transferred to Muscovy and then Russia). Ukrainians were portrayed as a nation that came into existence by chance (i.e., due to the Tatars, Lithuanians, and Poles having broken up "Russian" unity); hence, their only goal was to reunite with Russians at the first available opportunity. In both Tsarist and Soviet historiography Ukrainians had no future (and little of a usable past).[41] As Kolsto and Janmaat have concluded, a Russophile historiography could not be continued in an independent state because such states always attempt to trace their historical roots as far back as possible in history in order to provide a basis for their legitimation in the present and future.[42] The revival of national historiography in Ukraine therefore plays a central role in debunking these Tsarist and Soviet nationality policies which denied Ukrainians a past, present, or future.[43]

Second, it is impossible, David Miller believes, for an overarching national identity to be established without some recourse to myth making.[44] The process of forgetting is as important as that of remembering. Liberal democracies traditionally homogenized their citizens around shared values, symbols, myths, and ideas which were incorporated into the public culture of the state. It is through golden ages, symbols, ceremonies, and myths that nations are created and celebrated.[45] During this process of deconstructing the old myths and historiography and reconstructing new ones, increased pride in one's identity among the majority ethnic group (i.e., the titular nation) may be offset by anguish among national minorities.[46]

Third, historians and politicians in all states, including Ukraine, "have taken great pains to demonstrate that their nations are really very old, although they were usually created in the nineteenth century."[47] Politicians, literati, academics, and journalists become archaeologists in the quest to legitimize their state by showing that they have a long history of struggle and statehood and to prove that their territory was always controlled by their ethnie (i.e., the right of first settlement). From the nineteenth century archaeologists and nation builders have proved to be uneasy allies who both had an interest in tracing their country's history, "back into the mists of the prehistoric past."[48]

In the Ukrainian case this aspect of history making is important in two ways. The chapter by Georgii Kasianov divides Ukrainian historians into two groups, one which he defines as primordialists because they seek to trace Ukrainians as an ethnie or nation as far back as possible into the premodern era. These historians claim that Ukrainians have always held title to the lands located within their boundaries. Second, Ukrainian history making allows them to assert themselves as an "old nation" vis-à-vis Russians, whom Tsarist and Soviet nationality policies had depicted as the "elder brother" of the eastern Slavs.[49] Who "owns" the medieval state of Kyiv Rus' is therefore crucial in defining the national identity of Ukrainians and Russians. Consequently, the Ukrainian question plays a vitally important defining role in Russian national identity.

ELITE CONSENSUS AND THE NATION-BUILDING PROJECT[50]

The majority of scholars have stressed problems and difficulties within Ukraine's state-nation-building project. Undoubtedly, this approach has merits because it has highlighted many of the fundamental legacies that Ukraine has to overcome in building a coherent, consolidated state-nation. Nevertheless, it largely ignores the growing consensus among Ukraine's elites about the parameters of the state-nation-building project.

This section points to five areas where the Ukrainian elites have reached a consensus within nation building. These five areas include: state and institution building, borders and territorial integrity, federalism and regionalism, civic state nationalism, and national integration. Consensus at the mass level is still far from secured, and this section of this chapter therefore only focuses on consensus at the elite level.

Some scholars have written of such a consensus emerging from Ukraine's Tsarist and Soviet legacies that force it to adopt a nation-building strategy that lies between the two extremes of the homogenizing French nation-state model of Latvia and Estonia,[51] on the one hand, and the Russian nationalizing state of Belarus, on the other. Such a middle path is the result of the strength of national consciousness (which prevents Ukraine from becoming another Belarus) and linguistic divisions within Ukraine's titular nation (which prevent it from becoming Latvia or Estonia). Scholars have dubbed this the Ukrainian consociational nation-building model or a Creole amalgam of Ukrainophone-Russophone identities (see the chapter by Mykola Riabchuk in this volume).[52] Riabchuk defines this Creole *mishanyna* as follows:

In political terms, it is quite "Ukrainian," that is, quite supportive of state independence, territorial integrity, and many historical myths and symbols, shared with Ukrainophones. In cultural and linguistic terms, though, it is rather "Russian" in nature, that is, unsympathetic to Ukrainophones . . . and strongly biased against Ukrainian culture and language. Unlike "true" Russian nationalists, they never completely deny Ukrainian culture and language. Their approach is rather "archaeological:" they recognize that the Ukrainian language is beautiful but it has disappeared and will never be revived.[53]

Riabchuk may be too pessimistic about the cultural component of the emerging Ukrainian state-nation. Without an ethnocultural component the Ukrainian state would be hard pressed to define itself as different from Russia; after all, this is precisely why Belarus is finding it difficult to maintain itself as an independent state. As Weiner points out, in postcolonial states the norm is to adopt a mixture of policies (i.e., *mishanyna?*) which balance uniformity with compromise.[54]

Although Riabchuk is correct to argue that Ukraine's Creolic elites prefer elements of a cultural (but certainly not economic!) laissez-faire, this is *not* tantamount to freezing the inherited postcolonial status quo. As this chapter points out, a state-nation-building project is underway in Ukraine that is disturbing the inherited status quo. Because it cannot go as fast as the cultural intelligentsia would like does not mean that it is not progressing. This is precisely why the state-nation-building project is still criticized by those who do advocate the preservation of the status quo (e.g., communists and cosmopolitan liberals, such as the Inter-Regional Bloc of Reforms). Therefore, the fact that Ukraine's state-nation-building project is a Creolic compromise borne out of its inherited postcolonial legacy does not imply that the project preserves the status quo.[55]

We now turn to the five elements of this state-nation-building project where elite consensus has emerged.

1. *State Building*: All political forces within Ukraine support state and institution building. Even Unionist parties, such as the communists and the progressive socialists, would not accept the transformation of Ukraine into a *gubernia* within the Russian Federation. Ironically, their wish to support both sovereignty and a new union is similar to the confederation of Soviet sovereign states that national communists in Ukraine supported prior to 24 August 1991. During the 1990s Unionist forces had therefore evolved from imperial to the national (sovereign) communism of pre-August 1991 national communists. This evolution of Unionist political parties toward pre-August 1991 national communism is likely to continue in the new millennium as the possibility of reviving the USSR over time becomes increasingly unrealistic.

2. *Borders and Territorial Integrity*: Votes in the *Rada* in response to either territorial claims on the Crimea or against separatist tendencies by Crimean leaders have always been passed by more than two thirds of deputies (i.e., a constitutional majority). Such a majority consensus is rare in Ukrainian parliamentary politics. Ukraine's leaders (i.e., Russophone Kuchma as much as Ukrainophone Kravchuk) have always adopted a tough, nonviolent line on the Crimea through the use of economic, judicial, military, and political pressure. In Eastern Ukraine, separatism has not manifested itself in any manner whatsoever (including in elections) and Russian nationalists have been unable to find fertile ground for support in Ukraine. In the Crimea, where separatism existed for a brief period, it rapidly disintegrated after 1995 because Russian ethnic nationalism is a "minority faith" in Ukraine. The largest party on the peninsula, the communists, always backed Ukraine's territorial integrity and were instrumental in adopting the nonseparatist Crimean constitution in October 1998 (ratified by the *Rada* in December). After the adoption of the June 1996 Ukrainian constitution, Crimean regional parties had to re-register either as all-Ukrainian ones or as regional branches of existing Ukrainian parties. This undercut them and forced formerly separatist parties to defend Russian speakers and Unionist, pan-eastern Slavic policies, but not separatism (for example, the Russia Bloc became the Union party). Support for separatism was further undercut after the Russian executive recognized Ukraine's borders in May 1997, a recognition ratified by the lower and upper houses of the Russian parliament in December 1998 and February 1999, respectively.

3. *Federalism and Regionalism*: Ukraine's elites—including those on the left—hold a broad consensus against federalism, because it would prevent national consolidation and policy implementation by the center in the regions. Kuchma's backing for a bicameral *Rada* is not tantamount to backing federalism, because it would not actually devolve power from Kyiv. Poland, Ireland, the Netherlands and the United Kingdom all have bicameral parliaments but are not federalist. During the discussion over a new constitution between 1994 and 1996 center-right and extreme right-wing parties also backed a bicameral parliament with regional decentralization.[56] At the same time, Ukraine's elites also recognize Ukraine's regional diversity and the reality of Crimean autonomy. Elite consensus therefore supports the current centrist policy of rejecting both federalism and a unitary state in favor of a decentralized unitary state.

4. *Civic Nationalism*: Ukrainian independence was achieved through a combination of pressure from the bottom up by national democrats and top down by national communists. Since 1992 civic nationalism has evolved into a widespread phenomenon throughout Ukraine's elites. This has occurred through the spread of the national idea from national democrats to centrists (where many of the former national communists, such as Kravchuk and Kuchma, ended up[57]) and then gradually into the moderate left (for example, the Socialists) political spectrum. The defeat of Kravchuk in 1994 was not therefore a defeat for nationalism because Kravchuk and Kuchma have both been state or civic nationalists. State civic nationalist ideology is common to the ruling elites of all civic states, including Ukraine.

5. *Nation building and Consolidation*: This is the most difficult area for Ukraine's elites to have reached a consensus as it touches upon how the national idea is to be defined and what is being built in Ukraine. Under Kuchma, the nation-building project was not halted—as it was under President Alyaksandr Lukashenka in Belarus after 1994. The 1996 constitution and 1997 national security doctrine continued to outline nation building as a state objective. The 1996 Ukrainian and 1998 Crimean constitutions also signaled a watershed of no going back to the USSR; something symbolically confirmed when Soviet passports became invalid in January 1998. Ukraine's nation building project seeks to strike a balance between the Baltic nation-building and Belarusian nation-rejecting paths. This centrist path between two polar opposite projects thereby leads to dissatisfaction on the part of both national democrats (who support a faster state-nation-building project) and pro-Russian forces, such as the Inter-Regional Bloc of Reforms (who support the maintenance of the inherited postcolonial status quo). The more abrasive nationality policies of the Kravchuk era were "pragmatized" (i.e., moderated) in the Kuchma era because Russophone Ukrainians would not accept a radical and swift nation-building project. Ukraine's national symbols have not been challenged by any political forces, except the extreme left.

The language question did not influence the outcome of either the 1998 parliamentary or 1999 presidential elections. There is declining support for Russian to become a second state language (with virtually no support, again except on the extreme left, for Russians to be a second titular nation). The Russian language has been removed from education and public life in Western Ukraine, where nationality policies resemble those implemented in the Baltic states. Elsewhere in Ukraine it is unlikely that the Russian language will become "foreign." Ukrainianization of the education system has continued under Kuchma and has spread to most regions, except the Donbas and the Crimea.[58] Between the 1990–1991 and 1997–1998 school years the proportion of school children instructed in Ukrainian rose from 47.9 to 62.8%. Meanwhile, the proportion of pupils instructed in Russian declined from 51.4 to 31.7%. In pre-schools, 25.3% of children are taught in Russian and in higher education 35% of students are taught in Russian.[59] In higher education the proportion of students instructed in Ukrainian rose from 36.8% (1992–1993) to 51.2% (1995–1996).[60]

The Ukrainian authorities continue to uphold the view that the proportion of pupils educated in a language should approximate the proportion of the corresponding ethnic group within the population.[61] In December 1999 the Constitutional Court issued a ruling that explained the language provisions of the 1996 constitution (such as state administrators using Ukrainian) as applying throughout Ukrainian territory. In January 2000 the Ukrainian Presidential Council on Language Policy Issues approved a government program, "On Additional Measures to Expand the Use of Ukrainian as the State Language," which came into force in a government program in June of that year. It called for all officials to be checked for their Ukrainian language proficiency, for the de-Russification of the sports and cultural spheres, and for the use of taxation to regulate the import of publications. The following month Ivan Drach, the well-known former head of Rukh and head of the Congress of Ukrainian Intellectuals, was appointed chairman of the State Committee on Information Policy, Television, and Radio. The new language program would be monitored throughout the regions in order to halt "the hindering and localizing of the process of promoting the state status of Ukrainian."

Ukrainian elites agree that an independent state needs a state language as an attribute of identity, pointing to Belarus as an example of a country that lost its independence because of a weak national consciousness. Nevertheless, as in all postcolonial states, Ukraine will never be able to completely remove the colonial linguistic legacy of Russification and bilingualism. Outside Western Ukraine use and acceptance of the Ukrainian language will grow, but it will not remove Russian from Eastern and Southern Ukraine (just as English was never removed from Ireland). Whereas the Russian language has lost out in Western Ukraine to Ukrainian the Ukrainian-Russian language contest over public and private space will continue in the remainder of the country.

Despite concerns by some that a "nationalist historiography" (i.e., the Mykhailo Hrushevs'kyi schema) would not be accepted by Russophones,[62] the chapter by Jan Janmaat shows to what extent the same historiography is taught throughout Ukraine's education system. Meanwhile, Georgii Kasianov outlines the weak influence of Russophile historiography on contemporary Ukrainian national history making.

There is also consensus on the provision of polyethnic rights and inclusive citizenship, which are backed by all political parties except the extreme right. Support for polyethnic rights by national democrats makes them more liberal (and not nationalist) than standard center-right parties in liberal democracies who usually argue that rights should be provided on an individual—not a group—basis. National democrats always backed the national revival of minorities. The problem in this field has always rested not on national minorities as such, but on the Russian question. Should Russians be treated as a national minority (in the manner, for example, of Poles or Jews), or are they a second titular ethnic group? The Russian question is made all the more difficult by the fact that not all the 12 million "ethnic Russians" from the 1989 Soviet census are really "Russians." Upward of half of them are from mixed marriages and may re-identify themselves as "Ukrainian" (Ukrainian internal and foreign passports do not have an ethnic entry, unlike their Soviet counterparts).

CONCLUSION

The first section of this chapter argued that the Ukrainian nation-building project is an important aspect of its post-Soviet transition and that when placed within a theoretical or comparative perspective it is a normal process. This section discussed four aspects of the nation-building project—a unitary state, identity, language and historiography.

The second section argues that during the Kuchma era of the second half of the 1990s Ukraine's elites established a consensus on state-nation building and thereby stabilized the domestic political environment. This consensus in state-nation building in five strategically important areas—state and institution building, borders and territorial integrity, federalism and regionalism, civic state nationalism, and national integration—strengthened after Ukraine entered the new millennium. In Kuchma's inauguration speech he defined his defeat of the communist candidate in the second round of the November 1999 presidential elections as a second referendum on Ukrainian independence.[63] In the new millennium state-nation building will continue to play a vitally important role in Ukraine's quadruple transition from Soviet rule to a modern state-nation.

NOTES

1. Orest Subtelny, "Imperial Disintegration and Nation-State Formation: The Case of Ukraine" in John W. Blaney, ed., *The Successor States to the USSR* (Washington, DC: Congressional Quarterly Inc., 1995), pp. 184–195; and Roman Szporluk, "Ukraine: From an Imperial Periphery to a Sovereign State," *Daedalus*, vol. 126, no. 3 (Summer 1997), pp. 85–120.
2. Juan J. Linz, "State and Nation-building," *European Review*, vol. 1, no. 4 (1993), p. 356.
3. Far less has been published on state—in contrast to nation—building in Ukraine. See Taras Kuzio, Robert Kravchuk, and Paul D'Anieri, eds., *State and Institution Building in Ukraine* (New York: St. Martin's, 1999). See also Timo Aarrevaara, "Ukrainian Cities: Weak Soviets and Strong Mayors," *The Journal of Post Communist Studies and Transition Politics*, vol. 10, no. 4 (December 1994), pp. 55–70; Adrian Campbell, "Regional and Local Government in Ukraine," in Andrew Coulson, ed., *Local Government in Eastern Europe* (Aldershot, England: Edward Elgar, 1994), pp. 115–127; Judy Hague, Aidan Rose, and Marko Bojcun, "Rebuilding Ukraine's Hollow State: Developing a De-

mocratic Public Service in Ukraine," *Public Administration and Development*, vol. 15, no. 4 (October 1995), pp. 417–433, Alexander J. Motyl, "Structural Constraints and Starting Points: The Logic of Systematic Change in Ukraine and Russia," *Comparative Politics*, vol. 29, no. 4 (July 1997), pp. 433–447; and Marc Nordberg, "State and Institution Building in Ukraine," in Taras Kuzio, ed., *Contemporary Ukraine: Dynamics of Post-Soviet Transformation* (Armonk, NY: M. E. Sharpe, 1998), pp. 41–56.

4. See Kuzio, Kravchuk, and D'Anieri, eds., *State and Institution Building*; and Paul D'Anieri, Robert Kravchuk, and Taras Kuzio, *Politics and Society in Ukraine* (Boulder, CO: Westview, 1999), pp. 90–140.

5. Robert H. Jackson, *Quasi-states: Sovereignty, International Relations, and the Third World* (Cambridge: Cambridge University Press, 1990), p. 41.

6 . See T. Kuzio, "Ukraine: Coming to Terms with the Soviet Legacy," *The Journal of Communist Studies & Transition Politics*, vol. 14, no. 4 (December 1998), pp. 1–27.

7. William Zimmerman, "Is Ukraine a Political Community?" *Communist and Post-Communist Studies*, vol. 31, no. 1 (1998), pp. 43–55; George Liber, "Imagined Ukraine: Regional Differences and the Emergence of an Integrated State Identity," *Nations and Nationalism*, vol. 4, no. 2 (April 1998), pp. 187–206; and Catherine Wanner, *Burden of Dreams: History and Identity in Post-Soviet Ukraine* (University Park: Pennsylvania State University Press, 1998). For a more pessimistic view see Andrew Wilson, *Ukrainian Nationalism in the 1990s: A Minority Faith* (Cambridge: Cambridge University Press, 1997); and A. Wilson and Valeriy Khmelko, "Regionalism and Ethnic and Linguistic Cleavages in Ukraine," in T. Kuzio, *Contemporary Ukraine*, pp. 60–80.

8. Arnold van Gennep, *The Rites of Passage* (Chicago: University of Chicago Press, 1961), quoted in Ilya Prizel, *National Identity and Foreign Policy: Nationalism and Leadership in Poland, Russia and Ukraine* (Cambridge: Cambridge University Press, 1998), p. 340.

9. Vasily Kremen, "The East Slav Triangle," in Vladimir Baranovsky, ed., *Russia and Europe: The Emerging Security Agenda* (Oxford: Oxford University Press, 1997), pp. 271–288; and T. Kuzio and Marc Nordberg, "Nation and State Building, Historical Legacies and National Identities in Belarus and Ukraine: A Comparative Analysis," *Canadian Review of Studies in Nationalism*, vol. 26, nos. 1–2 (1999), pp. 69–90.

10. See T. Kuzio, "Center-Periphery Relations in Ukraine: Regionalism, Federalism and National Integration," in Jurgen Rose and Johannes Raut, eds., *Federalism and Decentralization in Eastern and Central Europe* (Frankfurt and New York: Carl Lang Verlag, forthcoming).

11. See the views of the influential oligarch close to President Kuchma in O. M. Volkov, *Politychna Ideolohiya* (Kyiv: Stylos, 1999), p. 129.

12. F. M. Rudych et al., *Politychni Struktury ta Protsesy v Suchasniy Ukraiini* (Kyiv: Naukova Dumka, 1995), pp. 115–116.

13. V. O. Parahons'kyi, *Natsional'nyi Interesy Ukraiiny (dukhovno-intelektual'nyi aspekt)* (Kyiv: National Institute of Strategic Studies, 1993), p. 32.

14. Leonid Shklar, "Ethnonational Aspects of National State Development in Ukraine," *International Journal of Sociology*, vol. 29, no. 3 (Fall 1999), p. 56. The authors of the Rudych et al. volume also remained opposed to federalism. See Rudych et al., *Politychni Struktury*, p. 197.

15. A. Lieven, "Russkoyazychnye Regiony Ukrainy: Troyanskyi Kon'?" in D. E. Furman ed., *Ukraina I Rosiya: Obshchestva I Gosudarstva* (Moscow: Prava Cheloveka, 1997), p. 243.

16. Wilson, *Ukrainian Nationalism*, pp. 71, 111, 130, 143, 163–168; and Gwendolyn Sasse, "Constitution-Making 'From Above:' Crimea's Regional Autonomy," in Theofil Kis and Irena Makaryk, eds., *Toward a New Ukraine II: Meeting the New Century* (Ottawa: University of Ottawa, 1999), pp. 83–102.

17. V. B. Grynev, *Nova Ukraiina: Iakoiu ia ii Bachu* (Kyiv: Abrys, 1995), p. 41.

18. Sasse, "Constitution-Making," pp. 97–98.

19. Victor Chudowsky points out that "by the time of the Constitutional vote in 1996, Ukrainian federalism was a dead issue, as most elites seemed to agree that a strong central government was necessary to carry out reforms and maintain control over areas such as Crimea." See his *Ukrainian Foreign Policy in the Kuchma Era*, Ph.D. diss. University of Connecticut, 1998, chap. 6.

20. "Public opinion in Ukraine: February 2000," Center for Peace, Conversion and Foreign Policy of Ukraine, Kyiv, Ukraine. 2000.

21. The first poll was by the Center for Economic and Political Research and the second by Socis-Gallup. Oleg Varfolomeyev, "Taming the Tamed," *Transitions on Line*, July 1999 (www.tol.cz/jul99/specr03005.html).

22. The only study is by Vicki L. Hesli and Arthur H. Miller, William M. Reisinger and Kevin L. Morgan, "Social Distance from Jews in Russia and Ukraine," *Slavic Review*, vol. 53, no. 3 (Fall 1994), pp. 807–828.

23. Tamara J. Resler, "Dilemmas of Democratization: Safeguarding Minorities in Russia, Ukraine and Lithuania," *Europe-Asia Studies*, vol. 49, no. 1 (January 1997), pp. 89–106.

24. Wilson's volume, published in 1997, also argued that the continuation of nationalizing policies would lead to conflict between Ukrainophones and Russophones. See Wilson, *Ukrainian Nationalism*.

25. *Den'*, 28 August 1997.

26. Graham Smith and Andrew Wilson, "Rethinking Russia's Post-Soviet Diaspora: The Potential for Political Mobilization in Eastern Ukraine and North-east Estonia," *Europe-Asia Studies*, vol. 49, no. 5 (July 1997), pp. 845–864; and T. Kuzio and David Meyer, "The Donbas and Crimea: An Institutional and Demographic Approach to Ethnic Mobilization in Two Ukrainian Regions," in Kuzio, Kravchuk and D'Anieri, *State and Institution Building*, pp. 297–324.

27. Ian Bremmer, "Ethnic Issues in Crimea," *RFE/RL Research Report*, vol. 2, no. 18 (30 April 1993); Tor Bukkvoll, "A Fall From Grace for Crimean Separatists," *Transition*, vol. 1, no. 21 (17 November 1995); Jane I. Dawson, "Ethnicity, Ideology and Geopolitics in Crimea," *Communist and Post-Communist Studies*, vol. 30, no. 4 (1998), pp. 427–444; Maria Drohobycky, ed., *Crimea: Dynamics, Challenges, and Prospects* (Lanham, MD and London: Rowman and Littlefield Publishers and the American Association for the Advancement of Science, 1995); T. Kuzio, *Ukraine-Crimea-Russia: Triangle of Conflict*: *Conflict Studies 267* (London: Research Institute for the Study of Conflict and Terrorism, 1994); T. Kuzio, "The Crimea and European Security," *European Security*, vol. 3, no. 4 (Winter 1994), pp. 734–774; and Edward Ozhiganov, "The Crimean Republic: Rivalries for Control," in Alexei Arbatov et al., eds., *Managing Conflict in the Former Soviet Union: Russian and American Perspectives* (Cambridge, MA: MIT Press, 1997), pp. 83–135.

28. Edward Allworth, ed., *The Tatars of the Crimea: Return to the Homeland: Studies and Documents* (Durham, NC: Duke University Press, 1998).

29. I. Bremmer, "The Politics of Ethnicity: Russians in the New Ukraine," *Europe-Asia Studies*, vol. 46, no. 2 (March–April 1994), pp. 261–283; E. Golovakha, N. Panina, and Nikolai Churilov, "Russians in Ukraine," in Vladimir Shlapentokh, Munir Sendich, and Emil Payin, eds., *The New Russian Diaspora: Russian Minorities in the Former Soviet Repubics* (Armonk, NY: M. E. Sharpe, 1994), pp. 59–71; Paul Kolstoe, *Russians in the Former Soviet Republics* (London: Hurst & Co., 1995), pp. 166–199; and Neil Melvin, *Russians Beyond Russia: The Politics of National Identity. Chatham House Papers* (London: Royal Institute International Affairs, 1995), pp. 78–99.

30. The theoretical literature on national identity is huge. See Parekh Bhikhu, "Discourses on National Identity," *Political Studies*, vol. 42, no. 3 (September 1994), pp. 492–504; "The Concept of National Identity," *New Community*, vol. 21, no. 2 (April 1995), pp. 255–268; A. D. Smith, "The Problem of National Identity: Ancient, Medieval and Modern?" *Ethnic and Racial Studies*, vol. 11, no. 3 (July 1994), pp. 375–400; and David Miller, *On Nationality* (Oxford: Clarendon Press, 1995).

31. Smith, *National Identity*.

32. D'Anieri, Kravchuk, and Kuzio, *Politics and Society*, pp. 90–140.

33. Bernard Yak, "The Myth of the Civic Nation: A Critical Review," in Ronald Beiner, ed., *Theorizing Nationalism* (New York: State University of New York, 1999), p. 105.

34. Wilson, *Ukrainian Nationalism*, pp. 214, 256.

35. Anthony D. Smith, "The Myth of the 'Modern Nation' and the Myths of Nation," *Ethnic and Racial Studies*, vol. 11, no. 1 (January 1988), p. 11. See also his "The Nation: Invented, Imagined, Reconstructed?" *Millennium, Journal of International Affairs*, vol. 20, no. 3 (Winter 1991), pp. 353–368 and "Gastronomy or Geology? The Role of Nationalism in the Reconstruction of Nations," *Nations and Nationalism*, vol. 1, no. 1 (March 1995), pp. 3–24.

36. Thomas H. Eriksen, *Ethnicity and Nationalism: Anthropological Perspectives* (London: Pluto Press, 1993), p. 71.

37. Wanner, *Burden of Dreams*. Further anthropological perspectives are provided by Jonathan Friedman, "Myth, History and Political Identity," *Cultural Anthropology*, vol. 7, no. 2 (May 1992), pp. 193–209; and "The Past in the Future: History and the Politics of Identity," *American Anthropologist*, vol. 94, no. 4 (December 1992), pp. 837–859.

38. Recommendation 1283 (22 January 1996). Document 7446, Committee on Culture and Education, Council of Europe. Copy in the possession of the author.

39. Friedman, "Past in the Future," p. 837. See also David M. Potter, "The Historian's Use of Nationalism and Vice Versa," *American Historical Review*, vol. 67, no. 4 (April 1962), pp. 924–950. Norman Davies writes that "Distortion is a necessary characteristic of all sources of information. Absolute objectivity is absolutely unattainable." In *Europe: A History* (Oxford: Oxford University Press, 1996), p. 5.

40. Geoffrey Pridham, "The International Dimension of Democracy: Theory, Practice, and Inter-regime Comparisons," in G. Pridham, Eric Herring, and George Sanford, eds., *Building Democracy? The International Dimensions of Democratization in Eastern Europe* (Leicester: University of Leicester Press, 1994), p. 26.

41. See Marta Dyczok, *Ukraine: Movement without Change, Change without Movement* (Amsterdam: Harwood Academic Press, 2000), p. 8; and T. Kuzio, "History and National Identity Among the Eastern Slavs," *National Identity*, vol. 3, no. 1 (2001).

42. See Jan G. Janmaat, *Nation-Building in Post-Soviet Ukraine: Educational Policy and the Response of the Russian-Speaking Population* (Amsterdam: Netherlands Geo-

graphical Studies, 2000); and Pal Kolsto, *Political Construction Sites: Nation-Building and the Post-Soviet States* (Boulder, CO: Westview, 2000).

43. Kuzio, *Ukraine: State and Nation Building* (London: Routledge, 1998), pp. 198–229.

44. Miller, *On Nationality*.

45. See Anthony D. Smith, "Ethnic Myths and Ethnic Revivals," *Journal of European Sociology*, vol. XXV (1984), pp. 283–305; *Nations and Nationalism in a Global Era* (Cambridge: Polity Press, 1996), pp. 63, 150; "The 'Golden Age' and National Renewal," in Geoffrey Hoskings and George Schopflin, eds., *Myths and Nationhood* (London: Hurst, 1997), pp. 36–59; and *Nationalism and Modernism* (London: Routledge, 1998), pp. 40–41. See also Barny Schwartz, "The Social Context of Commemoration: A Study in Collective Memory," *Social Forces*, vol. 61, no. 2 (December 1982), pp. 374–402.

46. Will Kymlicka, *Multicultural Citizenship* (Oxford: Clarendon Press, 1996), p. 189.

47. Eriksen, *Ethnicity and Nationalism*, p. 72.

48. Philip L. Kohl, "Nationalism and Archaeology: On the Construction of Nations and the Reconstruction of the Remote Past," *Annual Review of Anthropology*, vol. 27 (1998), pp. 223–246. See also Helen Parkins, "Archaeology and Nationalism: Excavating the Foundation of Identity," *Nations and Nationalism*, vol. 3, no. 3 (November 1997), pp. 451–458.

49. See T. Kuzio, "Borders, Symbolism and Nation-State Building: Ukraine and Russia," *Geopolitics and International Boundaries*, vol. 2, no. 2 (Autumn 1997), pp. 36–56, and "National Identity and Foreign Policy: The East Slavic Conundrum," in Kuzio, ed., *Contemporary Ukraine,* pp. 221–244.

50. This is based on a talk presented by the author entitled "Nation and State Building in Ukraine: Progress and the Emerging Consensus," given at the Kennan Institute, Woodrow Wilson International Center for Scholars, Washington DC, 9 November 1999.

51. In the Kravchuk era (December 1991–July 1994), some scholars believed that Ukraine did in fact adopt the Latvian/Estonian approach of a "nationalizing" French nation-state. See Dominique Arel, "Ukraine: The Temptation of the Nationalizing State," in Vladimir Tismaneanu, ed., *Political Culture and Civil Society in Russia and the New States of Eurasia* (Armonk, NY: M. E. Sharpe, 1995), pp. 157–188; and T. Kuzio, "Nationalizing States or Nation-building: A Review of the Theoretical Literature and Empirical Evidence," *Nations and Nationalism*, vol. 7, part 2 (April 2001).

52. See Arunas Juska, "Ethno-political transformation in the states of the former USSR," *Ethnic and Racial Studies*, vol. 22, no. 3 (May 1999), pp. 524–553; and Mykola Riabchuk, "Queen Without a Court: On the Current state of Ukrainian Culture," unpublished paper in the possession of the author; and "Behind the Talks on 'Ukrainianization:' Laissez Faire or Affirmative Action?" in Kis and Makaryk, eds., *Towards a New Ukraine II*, pp. 135–142.

53. Riabchuk, "Behind the Talks on 'Ukrainianization,' " p. 139.

54. Myron Weiner, "Political Integration and Political Development," *Annals of the American Academy of Politics and Social Science*, vol. 358 (March 1965), pp. 52–64.

55. Ibid., p. 140.

56. The Congress of Ukrainian Nationalists (KUN) proposed a draft constitution in late 1994 prepared by its experts. The draft constitution envisaged Ukraine as a presidential-parliamentary republic where the president was to have been head of the executive

with the right to dissolve parliament. The Supreme Council would have become the National Assembly elected on a proportional system and divided into two houses (Upper Senate and Lower House of Representatives). The current territorial system would have been transformed into seventy-five "lands" which would obtain wide self-government. See *Shliakh Peremohy*, 22 October 1994. Clearly, KUN did not regard a bicameral parliament as introducing federalism, which nationalist groups, such as KUN, traditionally abhor.

57. By their very nature, national communists were pragmatists as they deserted communism, leaving it in the hands of ideological, imperial communists. Hence, the ideological rigidity of the revived Communist Party of Ukraine after October 1993.

58. See Viktor Stepanenko, *The Construction of Identity and School Policy in Ukraine* (Commack, NY: Nova Science Publishers, 1999).

59. Figures provided by Yuriy Bohuts'kyi of the presidential administration ("Russia Afraid of Ukraine's De-Russification," *RFE/RL Poland, Belarus, Ukraine Report, 15 February 2000*). In Ukraine, 1,195 Russian language newspapers are published, the Ukrainian Foreign Ministry pointed out, in comparison to none in Ukrainian for the second-largest national minority of the Russian Federation, Ukrainians. See "Russian Language in Ukraine: Surrealistic Notes," *Research Update, Ukrainian Center for Independent Political Research, Kyiv*, vol. 6, no. 161 (21 February 2000).

60. J. G. Janmaat, "Language Politics in Education and the Response of the Russians in Ukraine," *Nationalities Papers*, vol. 27, no. 3 (September 1999), pp. 475, 478. Roman Solchanyk gives official figures showing a decline from 76.6% to 34% (higher education), 50% to 34% (school) and 48.8% to 25.3% (pre-school) in students taught in the Russian language between the 1990–1991 and 1998–1999 school years (*The Ukrainian Weekly*, 5 March 2000).

61. V. Kremen', Dmytro Tabachnyk, and Vasyl' Tkachenko, *Ukraiina: Alternatyvy Postupu. Krytyka Istorychnoho Dosvidu* (Kyiv: Arc-Ukraine, 1996), pp. 756–757. The January 2000 program "On Additional Measures to Expand the Use of Ukrainian as the State Language" proposes "bringing the system of educational institutions into line with the ethnic composition of the population" (*RFE/RL Poland, Belarus, Ukraine Report*, 15 February 2000).

62. A. Wilson, "Myths of National History in Belarus and Ukraine," in Hosking and Schopflin, eds., *Myths and Nationhood*, pp. 182–197; "National History and National Identity in Ukraine and Belarus," in Graham Smith, Vivien Law, Andrew Wilson, Annette Bohr and Edward Allworth, *Nation-building in the Post-Soviet Borderland: The Politics of National Identities* (Cambridge: Cambridge University Press, 1998), pp. 23–47.

63. *Holos Ukraiiny*, 2 December 1999.

3

Rewriting and Rethinking: Contemporary Historiography and Nation Building in Ukraine[*]

Georgii Kasianov

Since the early 1990s the number of works devoted to the Ukrainian nation and every conceivable aspect of its existence has multiplied at a catastrophic rate. Increasingly, philosophers, historians, ethnographers, literary specialists, archaeologists, political scientists, economists, and others are being drawn into the creation or "revival" of a new "imagined community" that claims the desired title of a European nation. The basic questions pertaining to research on the history of Ukrainian nation formation are: "How, when, and where?" Since Ukrainian society has cast off the ideological uniformity of the Soviet period, while the variety of research topics has broadened considerably, one might expect the answers to these questions to be rather diverse.

In fact, however, we hear the voices of representatives of various disciplines—pitched at various intellectual and cultural levels and, indeed, belonging to different generations—blending into a rather harmonious chorus. This chorus is ever more resolutely intoning a motif familiar to us from the development of patriotic historiography, especially in periods of national self-assertion. Discordant notes are heard only when intellectual interests, specific areas of research (thematic, geographic or chronological), or external (generally Western) influences clash with the immutable rigidity of patriotic discourse or challenge the generally accepted canon that has rather precipitately and mechanistically displaced the official Soviet stereotype.

This chapter concerns the efforts of contemporary Ukrainian historians to rethink the development of the Ukrainian nation within the general context of the "nationalization" of Ukrainian history that has been going on for the last decade. As we shall see, whatever the subjective intentions and desires of these historians, objectively their efforts have become ensnared in the current political and ideo-

---

[*]This chapter was written at Monash University (Melbourne, Australia) during the author's tenure as a Ukrainian Studies Foundation of Australia Visiting Scholar. The chapter was translated by Myroslav Yurkevich.

logical agenda, most notably the problem of establishing the historical right of the Ukrainian people to a state of its own and the need to develop arguments legitimizing the existence of the present-day Ukrainian nation and state. Accordingly, the rethinking of Ukrainian history all too often culminates in a reversion to the methodological principles of the past: history is rewritten according to the classical dogmas of patriotic historiography as practiced in the nineteenth century. The following analysis of the scholarly and methodological aspects of this subject, attempts to show how the scholarly discourse is changing and how these changes are conditioned by cognitive developments and the shifting political situation. The way in which the scholarly discussion is beginning to feed back into politics and society is a separate question worth exploring in its own right.

In this discussion, the competing images of the nation currently taking shape in Ukrainian social science are presented in terms of a debate between "primordialists" or "perennialists" on the one side and "modernists" on the other. These labels are of course employed merely for analytical convenience.

THE "PRIMORDIALIST" ACCOUNT

As was only to be expected, the primordialist account of the formation of the Ukrainian nation has become the most popular one in current scholarly treatments (at the level of popular history and school curricula, it is simply taken for granted). The problem of the development of the Ukrainian nation is generally analyzed in the context of ethnogenetic or "ethnicist" conceptions based on the linkage of "ethnos, people, and nation," with the first term understood as generative and usually identified with the second and even the third. Here, for example, is a rather typical formulation:

A people in its capacity as an ethnos brings together within itself all the features that define it as a distinct society possessing a set of stable characteristics developed over the course of history. Accordingly, ethnoses are peoples either at the tribal stage of development or at the national stage, i.e., when an ethnos becomes a people/nation. Thus, *"ethnos" is a generative concept for any stage of the civilizational development of one people or another.* Considered as a nation, a people is characterized—aside from such properties as language, character, etc., inherent in its anterior stages of historical development—by national consciousness and a stable political order that gives expression to its national interests.[1]

The axiomatic account of nation formation (or, more precisely, ethnonation formation) runs generally as follows: Ukrainians (as an ethnos/people and/or as a potential nation) have existed since the most ancient times. In the period of Kyiv Rus', they gave rise to an ethnocultural (in other accounts, an ethnosocial or even ethnopolitical) society that subsequently attempted to constitute itself as a political or sovereign national entity (mainly in the sixteenth and seventeenth centuries). Following a period of latent existence within imperial structures, that entity underwent a national renaissance in the nineteenth century, resulting in the formation of the "modern Ukrainian nation." To be sure, the latter term implies the previous existence of a premodern Ukrainian nation with which, in turn, the concept of a Ukrainian people is sometimes identified.

Let us note that this analytical scheme generally resembles the account of nation formation elaborated by Western "ethnicists" (and moderate "primordialists"), most notably Anthony Smith, John A. Armstrong, and Paul Brass, which may be reduced to the following basic axioms:

1. Nations are not created ex nihilo, but ARE formed on the basis of ethnic associations, whether real, constructed, or invented.
2. Ethnogenesis is associated with nation formation by means of certain elements of cultural continuity (symbols, myths, traditions).
3. These elements of cultural continuity undergo qualitative change, particularly during the period of nation formation, when they acquire instrumental significance.

On the analytical level, however, the concepts of *ethnos*, *ethnic group*, and *ethnogenesis* are usually distinguished from the concepts of *nation* and *nation formation*.

The similarity in the approaches of Ukrainian and Western analysts may be explained either by the use of the latter's theoretical constructs by the former (still a rarity, as access to Western social-science literature remains limited in Ukraine) or by the circumstance that the analysis of similar phenomena evokes similar associations. Even so, there are considerable disparities in these approaches that often reduce such analogies to purely formal terms.

Present-day Ukrainian social scientists who profess the primordialist, ethnogenetic account of nation formation generally do not acknowledge that a nation may be constructed or invented, considering it a natural formation. Some insist on an unbroken anthropological and biological continuity in the process of ethnonational development. The notion of the "organic nature" of elements of cultural continuity is quite popular, and in some accounts it turns into a complete rejection of the "instrumentalist" approach. As noted earlier, the concepts of *ethnos*, *people*, and *nation* are quite often identified with one another. Finally, the element of continuity in ethnonational formation is exaggerated or absolutized, so that the Ukrainian people as an ethnically autochthonous body is empowered to claim many centuries or even many millennia of unbroken existence on a particular territory. The primordialist accounts have the further advantage of making it possible to concentrate primarily on cultural factors of ethnogenesis and nation formation or even on anthropological and biological factors, an important consideration when the nation lacks a history of sovereign statehood.

Let us cite some specific examples. The first of them may be characterized as a sociobiological variant of primordialism. The archaeologist Leonid Zalizniak maintains that

present-day Ukrainians are *genetically* linked with the population of Southern Rus', unlike most Belarusians and Russians, who belong to another anthropological type. According to basic defining criteria of ethnicity (culture, language, ethnic territory, mentality, self-identification, anthropological type, etc.), Ukrainians of the sixteenth to eighteenth centuries were direct *genetic* descendants of the population of Southern Rus' of the tenth to fourteenth centuries. The Rus' of the middle Dnipro region, Volhynia, Galicia, and Podilia *were proto-Ukrainians according to ethnic criteria.* (emphasis added)[2]

This "ethnocultural continuity" is of course intended to establish a subsequent historical link with the national renaissance of the nineteenth century, twentieth-century Ukrainian statehood, and so on.

A culturalist variant of primordialism (or, to employ Smith's term, *perennialism*) is advanced by Anatolii Ponomariov. According to him, the Ukrainian ethnos was transformed into a nation by means of protracted historical evolution. This process was reflected most particularly in changes of names that the ethnos applied to itself. "The stage of the formation of the Ukrainian ethnos," writes Ponomariov, "is associated with the ethnonym 'Rus',' while that of the formation of the Ukrainian nation is associated with the name 'Ukrainians.' " In chronological terms, the first stage encompasses the historical period up to the twelfth century, while the second begins in the twelfth century, that is, "from the time when the ethnos established a state."[3]

Of fundamental importance to nation formation, notes the author, is the subjective factor. Among the principal elements of the nation that constitute its foundation and manifest its inner essence are national interests, which "are set in motion by the maturing of a national idea around which an ethnos crystallizes." The existence of a national idea is manifested by the rise of national consciousness among the people, "which may find expression in a heightened interest in national roots, ethnic history, and native language." This becomes the basis for the formation of a "national culture" and a nation-state, which, for some reason, Ponomariov terms an *external attribute.*

On this basis, Ponomariov goes on to advance the following "conception of nation formation" (let us note that he identifies the concept of "ethnogenesis" with that of "nation formation"):

Ukrainian ethnogenesis should be sought in the Kyivan Rus' strata. However, the process of nation formation was interrupted at that time and resumed in the sixteenth and seventeenth centuries. On a wave of *national enthusiasm*, catalyzed by the Steppe, which threatened Ukrainians with physical extinction, Polish *national* subjugation, and internal treason, all the characteristics of the *Ukrainian nation*, concocted on Cossack soil, took shape. . . . To be sure, the geographic borders of the genetic process that gave rise to Ukrainians expanded rapidly, for the *national idea* took hold of the entire population of Ukraine, as did the *national spirit*, which was basically common to all Ukrainians (all emphases added).[4]

Over time, writes Ponomariov, the process of nation formation "matured" in the course of several stages known as the cultural and national renaissance: "Having begun in the sixteenth century as a military and political renaissance, it developed toward the end of the nineteenth century in the sphere of culture and spirituality and in the 1920s as a wave of national enthusiasm that encompassed every important sphere in the life of the Ukrainian ethnos."[5]

We have taken the liberty of quoting at such length for the sole purpose of demonstrating the obvious terminological underdevelopment that results in a chaotic accumulation of categories pertaining to a variety of analytical levels. The archaization of the term *national*, the identification of nation formation with ethnogenesis (along with concurrent efforts to distinguish one from the other); the lack of criteria for the definition of these and other terms (it remains unclear in what sense the author employs the concepts of national spirit, national enthusiasm, and even national itself)—all these are not merely flaws in the approach of a particular author, but a reflection of the general state of social science in Ukraine. Our main interest, however, lies elsewhere: Ponomariov attempts to solve the problem of continuity and discontinuity in Ukrainian nation formation by referring mainly to subjective factors, which indeed have been and still remain most useful for that purpose. In this instance, Ponomariov typifies the approach most commonly adopted in current Ukrainian social-science research.

Finally, it is worth mentioning yet another variant of primordialism/perennialism that may provisionally be termed the politico-genetic account of Ukrainian nation formation. In the opinion of the L'viv historian Iaroslav Dashkevych, a nation called Rus' already existed in the period of Kyiv Rus'. "The process of the formation of Rus' as a political and ethnic nation in the ninth and tenth centuries," he asserts, "corresponds to the principles of ethnicity that are advanced by ethnosociology with respect to nations—in the period after the French Revolution, to be sure."[6] In this account, Kyiv Rus' is regarded as a "state/empire with a multi-ethnic population." This empire, continues Dashkevych, was established by the elite of a single political nation that was initially formed on the basis of several ethnic elements. Of these, the one that prevailed was the "initial East Slavic substratum, which was thus transformed into a superstratum that assimilated Normans and Iranians, adopting the name of Rus' for its national state/empire and creating an already homogeneous nation, not only in political but also in ethnic terms, bearing the same name."[7]

Dashkevych defines ethnonational unity by means of the following parameters:

1. *Sociocultural unity* (a single pagan pantheon, and subsequently a common Christian religion "of the Slavic rite with a single ritual Church Slavonic language, which also played a unifying role as the language of a single Rus' literature" and as the language of the elite;
2. *Unity of historical and contemporary experience* (the struggle with the Steppe and its tradition; territorial conquest from the ninth to the eleventh century);
3. *The notion of a common origin*;
4. *Collective identity* (a distinction between "one's own" and "foreigners" established, according to Dashkevych, on the basis of ethnic and religious characteristics) and even "a highly developed feeling of *national consciousness* and national pride;"
5. *A feeling of solidarity* (most notably within the elite of the "political nation").

To these elements, Dashkevych adds the *factor of politics and statehood* (the existence of a state with a more or less established border and a center in Kyiv),

the *socioeconomic factor* (a particular form of social stratification specific to Kyivan Rus'), and the formation of "regional markets" (clearly, what is meant is
something along the lines of unity of economic life, but here the author expresses
himself incomprehensibly); and the *cultural and ideological factor* (the existence
of a single Rus' culture).[8]

In commenting on this account of nation formation, let us note its obvious re-
semblances to the scheme put forward by Smith in his *Ethnic Origins of Nations*:[9]
we find an "ethnic nucleus" of the lateral type—Rus', around which the nation
coalesces; the "bureaucratic incorporation" of subject ethnoses proceeds under the
aegis of the state. This also has its resemblance to Ivan L. Rudnytsky's analytical
scheme of *narod* (people) and *natsiia* (nation) as successive formations.[10] Let us
return nevertheless to Dashkevych's own argument. If one takes his views to their
logical conclusion, then Kyiv Rus' witnessed the development of processes similar
to those of the formation of "nations before nationalism" in France, England and
Spain. This leads to another conclusion: the history or roots of Ukrainians as a
nation go back to the times of Kyiv Rus' itself.

If the views of the L'viv historian are taken to constitute a hypothesis based on
the theoretical constructions of Smith and Rudnytsky,[11] then that hypothesis is
interesting, if hardly novel in theoretical terms, and clearly gratifying to patriotic
sentiments. If one attends to Dashkevych's specific arguments, then obvious methodological flaws and contradictory conclusions become apparent. In the first place,
the nation is once again identified with the ethnos and the state (although not in
every case), and the term is of course archaized, as is the concept of the ethnic and
political nation. Secondly, doubts arise concerning Dashkevych's arguments about
the existence in the Rus' nation of some of the unifying elements on his list: the
"notion of a common origin," "collective identity," "national consciousness" (an
obvious anachronism), and a "feeling of solidarity." Even if all these subjective
factors are ascribed to the political and intellectual elite of Kyiv Rus' (the political
nation), it is difficult to establish their existence beyond reasonable doubt. Finally,
we encounter once again the underdevelopment of categories and concepts: the
interchangeability of different terms has already been mentioned, and we may also
note that the nation-state and the state/empire seem to be equivalent notions in
Dashkevych's usage, which seems methodologically unacceptable.

Solidarity with Dashkevych's views is expressed by another L'viv historian,
Iaroslav Isaievych, although the latter refers directly to Smith's *Ethnic Origins of
Nations* as the theoretical source of his views. Pointing out that ethnic groups
(Isaievych uses the term *etniia* as a calque of *ethnie*) and nations at an early stage
of development exhibit a number of common characteristics, including symbols,
self-concepts, and notions of the future, Isaievych draws the following conclusion:

the assertion that modern nations are so different from the ethnic formations of earlier times
that the same term cannot be employed for ancient and modern societies is not so undeni-
able. . . . [S]ince the beginnings of statehood, since the appearance of ethnic consciousness,
one may discern certain traits of self-identification that were perpetuated throughout the
following 1,000 or 1,500 years. . . . I am rather persuaded by the view that the principal

factor in nation formation were [sic] events of millennial antiquity, and not the political movement of the late nineteenth century, which fostered consolidation but by no means initiated it.[12]

The primordialist accounts of Ukrainian history produced in recent years can certainly be considered classical examples of the formation or, more precisely (taking into account the achievements of pre-Soviet historiography), the renewal of the national(ist) historical myth. Its basic constituents may be defined as follows:

1. The absolutization and even the canonization of historical (cultural, linguistic, at times even biological or political) continuity in the development of the nation (which is most often identified with the ethnos in this connection);
2. The presence of a "territorial syndrome": the historical boundaries of the ethnic (national) territory are extended as far as possible and the "autochthonous" roots of the people and nation and the stability of their ethnic territory are stressed in every possible way;
3. The absolutization of the stability of certain "genetic traits" (biological, anthropological, cultural) of the ethnos and nation;
4. The desire to extend the history of one's own ethnos and nation as far into the past as possible;
5. The unconditional identification of the ethnos and nation with a certain language that is also supposed to have existed since the most ancient times;
6. Prior claims to the exclusive possession of the "joint historical legacy" of the Slavic peoples (i.e., Kyivan Rus')—the "cradle syndrome."

As the Russian scholar Viktor Shnirelman persuasively argues, these and other characteristics of historical myths of ethnogenesis are common to the East Slavic peoples. In that context, the official thesis of Soviet historiography on the "common historical destiny of the fraternal Slavic peoples," an irksome myth in the Neopanslavist style, turns into an ironic paradox and an intellectual farce: myths incorporating common features are now exploited as evidence of separate identity.

Nevertheless, in contemporary Ukrainian primordialist mythologems an unbiased analyst of the problem will readily discern features in common with analogous historical accounts of the so-called "continuous" nations (in Hugh Seton-Watson's terminology) or "historic" nations (to employ Hegel's term). As is well known, every national historiography undergoes a period of formation of national myths, a considerable portion of which becomes an inalienable element of national consciousness, long established in the pages of school textbooks. The only difference here is that Ukrainian historiography once again finds itself obliged to engage in such myth making at the end of the twentieth century, while the "historic" nations managed to accomplish it in the second half of the nineteenth.

The Modernist "Alternative"

Given the undoubted dominance of primordialist accounts of Ukrainian nation formation, the accomplishments of those scholars whom we shall provisionally describe as modernists is somewhat more modest in quantity, but more interesting intellectually. Let us note that the modernist camp is more international, as it consists largely of Western scholars, who are less preoccupied with substantiating the historical rights of the Ukrainian nation.

The development of the modernist trend in contemporary Ukrainian historiography was attended by circumstances of a rather particular kind. In the Ukrainian SSR, works dealing with any aspect of Ukrainian nation formation were necessarily based on orthodox Marxist methodology. Thus, in purely formal terms, they may be classified as modernist. The growth of the nation was associated with the transition from feudalism to capitalism, the rise of the bourgeoisie, specific socioeconomic developments, class struggle, and so on. Given that in the years immediately following Ukraine's attainment of formal independence most historians remained strictly within the confines of orthodox Marxist discourse (other modes were simply unknown and inaccessible to them at the time), any work devoted to nation formation was precast—formally, at least—in a modernist tonality.

The first work to concern itself directly with the making of the Ukrainian nation is symptomatic in this respect. Valerii Smolii and Oleksandr Hurzhii[13] note that their monograph employs "the traditional conceptual framework accepted by most of the country's scholars. The authors depart from the premise that nationality is the product of the feudal mode of production and that it is characterized by such features as a common language, territory, economy and culture, as well as by evidence of particular types of economic ties and ethnic consciousness. In the process of transition from the feudal to the capitalist order, these features crystallize and become more strongly marked, acquiring broader qualitative content, that is to say, nationality develops into the higher form of ethnosocial community that constitutes a nation."[14]

As we see, this analytical scheme is the traditional one inherited from Soviet Ukrainian historiography: it is based on a class-conscious approach, entailing principles of economic determinism along with elements of "formative teleology," as well as the standard definition of the "nation obligatory for any scholar whose intellectual formation included a course in scientific communism." The theme, by contrast, is nontraditional: the development of the Ukrainian nation is posed as a historical problem in its own right (moreover, the authors refer to their predecessor, Kost Huslysty, who attempted in the late 1960s to investigate the problem of Ukrainian nation formation within the framework of official methodology). The fact that "official" historians were now addressing themselves to this problem was unusual as well: in some measure this was a reply to the parascholarly versions that began to multiply on a catastrophic scale as Ukraine embarked on an independent existence. Novel elements were also apparent in some of the authors' approaches. In particular, they formally acknowledged the multifaceted and contradictory nature of the economic and social developments that contributed to the making of the nation, a process the authors deemed "complex and protracted." It was therefore inappropriate, in their judgment, to specify a period of time within which that process fluctuated. Yet that did not prevent them from venturing to establish chronological limits and concluding that the Ukrainian nation took form in several stages extending from the seventeenth to the nineteenth century, or, to employ terms then still unfamiliar to most Ukrainian historians, the early modern and modern era.

The most significant account of Ukrainian history written under the patent influence of the Western modernist concepts of nation formation is *Narys istorii Ukrainy* (An Outline of Ukrainian History) by the L'viv historian Iaroslav Hrytsak (the subtitle of his book, *The Formation of the Modern Ukrainian Nation*, is rather eloquent). Basing himself on an analytical distinction introduced long ago by Ivan L. Rudnytsky, Hrytsak considers that one may speak of the existence of two types of nations, pre-modern and modern (the failure to grasp this accounts, in Hrytsak's view, for the misunderstandings between primordialists and modernists). Accordingly, when it comes to the formation of the modern Ukrainian nation, it is crucial to analyze developments of the nineteenth and twentieth centuries, while the pre-modern or early modern nation pertains to the sixteenth and seventeenth centuries.

Hrytsak proposes an account of national history in which elements of the primordialist or perennialist versions may be reconciled with the modernist view. Ukrainian history, considered precisely as the history of the nation's development, fits perfectly into the West European context at a certain point.

In Hrytsak's view, the formation of modern nations in Europe (including the Ukrainian nation) had its origins in the period that saw "the gradual transformation of agrarian society, with its low level of literacy and mobility, into industrial society, which was educated and mobile, with broad political rights and economic freedom for all its members, not only for the elite."[15] Hrytsak maintains that the formation of the modern Ukrainian nation proceeded in synchrony with analogous developments in Western Europe, that is, beginning as early as the sixteenth century. The religious movements and Cossack wars of the sixteenth and seventeenth centuries were Ukrainian analogues of general European trends: "the ecclesiastical movements and Cossack wars of the sixteenth and seventeenth centuries are Ukrainian analogues of the West European process that gave rise to a new form of collective identity (national consciousness), and the national renaissance of the nineteenth century was a transformation that corresponded to new conditions and to the spread of that consciousness among the masses."[16] Accordingly, the national renaissance of the nineteenth century consisted in the transformation and mass dissemination of that form of consciousness under new conditions. Thus the starting line in the development of the Ukrainian nation is pushed back to the early modern period, which, naturally enough, aligns the Ukrainian nation with the historic nations, legitimizing its claims to the possession of a national history.

Let us note that the author is unambiguous in formulating the operational principles on which his conception is based. First of all, the history of the Ukrainian nation is to be regarded as an integral part of the universal (or all-European) historical process. The history of Eastern Europe (and thus of Ukraine), asserts Hrytsak, "does, after all, conform to the periodization of world history as a whole."[17] Secondly, Hrytsak revises the notion of the "backwardness" and "non-historicity" of the Ukrainian nation: Eastern Europe, including Ukraine, was "among the first" regions that set out to overtake the "developed" West and replicate its technical and social achievements.

The idea of backdating the origins of Ukrainian "national" history to the so-called early modern period has become highly popular precisely among those scholars who seek a compromise between primordialism, so familiar, attractive and reassuring to any Ukrainian historian, and modernism, so unaccustomed and repulsive to the "true patriot." Those scholars have invented (more precisely, borrowed) the philosopher's stone that makes it possible to turn intellectual lead into vastly more agreeable gold (as yet, no one is particularly concerned to determine whether it is pure gold).

Let us cite the most outstanding example of the way in which the thesis of Ukrainian nation formation in the early modern period has been embodied in actual research or, rather, *reinterpretation*. The historians Valerii Smolii and Valerii Stepankov have formulated the concept of a seventeenth-century "Ukrainian National revolution." The capitalization of the word *national* is itself a clear indication of the authors' ideological aspirations. As lack of space precludes lengthy citation, the essence of their conceptual framework may be reduced to the following points:

1. A national revolution took place in Ukraine in the mid-seventeenth century (more precisely, between the years 1648 and 1676);
2. That revolution gave rise to the formation of a *nation-state* that perished, but whose remnants continued to exist into the 1780s;
3. In the course of the revolution, there arose the "idea of a nation-state," which became "an unwritten testament for successive generations of Ukrainians in the struggle for independence;"[18]
4. The "idea of a nation-state" provided the stimulus for the formation of a new political elite and for the development of *national* consciousness, most notably an "ideology of elitist nationalism;" it "aroused the will of the nation to self-assertion and self-expression in the form of an independent sovereign state;"[19]
5. The Ukrainian national revolution of the seventeenth century was analogous to the revolutions that took place in the Netherlands, England, Germany, and France in the sixteenth and seventeenth centuries; hence it was an event of all-European significance and thus an integral part of European history.

As we see, these quasi-modernist formulations (the term *early modern* is unknown to these authors, as is the standard terminology of modernist historiography in general) evince an overt attempt to "archaize" the terms *nation, national,* and *nationalism*. Unlike some of their Western colleagues (e.g., Frank Sysyn and Teresa Chynczewska-Hennel), who apply the term "nation" only to certain elite strata of the seventeenth century, Smolii and Stepankov fall prey to the (by now traditional) confusion of "nation" (*natsiia*) with "people" (*narod*) and employ the former term with reference to the *masses*, considering national consciousness to have been a *mass* phenomenon in the seventeenth-century Ukrainian lands. Smolii notes that "unlike the nobility of the Commonwealth, which considered itself alone the Polish political people [*narod*; the intended reference is probably to the political nation] Cossackdom viewed itself as constituting only a portion of the Ukrainian people, which also included the nobility, clergy, burghers, and even peasants."[20] The authors' subsequent discussion makes it apparent that they consider these strata and social orders to have constituted a nation complete with a national elite.

In Stepankov's view, the *Ukrainian masses* were already imbued with a "sense of nationalism" in the seventeenth century; indeed, citing Dashkevych, he goes so far as to posit the existence of an ideological level of national consciousness. Noting Dashkevych's thesis that "nations rose to the struggle for national liberation—ordinary peasant masses without an elite ideology, but with an entirely nationalist attitude to their national oppressors," Stepankov concludes that "national consciousness was nourished by feelings of hatred for Polish rule," thus clearly following Dashkevych in identifying nationalism with xenophobia.[21]

In some respects, to be sure, these scholars are unoriginal and merely continue the traditions of the early twentieth century, when the activists of the national renaissance of the day wrote about the "Ukrainian national movement of the seventeenth and eighteenth centuries," the "Ukrainian national and cultural movement of the sixteenth and seventeenth centuries,"[22] and so on (being true positivists, however, they were not so bold as to discover nationalism among seventeenth-century Ukrainians). In this case, of course, the problem is not merely one of the inappropriate use of terms or their archaization. Unlike Hrytsak and the "true" modernists, Smolii and Stepankov regard the events of the seventeenth century as evidence not of the beginnings of Ukrainian nation formation, but of the nation's existence as a fait accompli. Unfortunately, Smolii and Stepankov do not explain what they mean by the term *nation* and semantically related terms. In context, as we have seen, it would appear that they tend toward the identification of *nation* with *people* characteristic of Ukrainian primordialists and ethnicists.

It is equally apparent that Smolii and Stepankov are favorably inclined toward the notion of continuity (in every sense of the word) in Ukrainian nation formation. Hence they find themselves in the modernist camp not because they consider the Ukrainian nation a modern or early modern phenomenon, but as a result of *déformation professionnelle*, so to speak, given their specialization in seventeenth-century history.

A TACIT UNDERSTANDING

There was never any reason to expect an outright intellectual confrontation between the Ukrainian primordialists/perennialists and modernists, since differentiation between them presupposes a society accustomed to intellectual pluralism (Ukrainian intellectual space is still dominated by the habit of erecting monistic structures). In Ukraine today, modernists of every stripe invariably seek compromise with the primordialists/perennialists, if only because of the unchallenged dominance of the ethnogenetic approach to interpreting the origins of the Ukrainian nation, to say nothing of the pressure of political circumstance, lack of methodological awareness, the drastic underdevelopment of the social sciences in Ukraine, and so on. Significantly, it is the West that has become the principal supplier of modernist dissidents to the Ukrainian social-science community. The authors of the best-known modernist accounts and interpretations of Ukrainian nation formation either are based at Western universities (George Grabowicz, Andreas Kappeler, Roman Szporluk) or, if they reside in Ukraine, have taken over the corresponding analytical frameworks from Western social science. The same applies to practitioners of the early modern approach (Sysyn, Zenon Kohut, Chynczewska-Hennel), many of whose works in fact appear to represent a compromise between the adherents of the primordial past and modernity.

Granted, one might cite an instance of direct and rather heated confrontation between representatives of these divergent trends. The Second International Congress of Ukrainian Studies, which took place in L'viv in August 1993, featured a roundtable discussion on "The Formation of the Ukrainian Nation: History and Interpretation." Symptomatically enough, those Ukrainian participants who favored the modernist tendency or criticized primordialism/perennialism (primarily for its teleological subtext) were decidedly in the minority (Hrytsak and Oleksii Tolochko),[23] and were supported by colleagues from the West. The efforts of Tolochko, a specialist in medieval history (who would therefore seem destined to find his niche in the primordialist camp), to draw attention to episodes of discontinuity in Ukrainian nation formation and to the intellectual attractiveness of such an approach met with concerted opposition from partisans of millennial continuity in tracing the existence of the Ukrainian ethnos/nation.

The polemic following upon Mark von Hagen's essay "Does Ukraine Have a History?" may be construed as an echo of the L'viv debate, though in a different context.[24] For present purposes, a remark by the Ukrainian academician Isaievych is especially significant. Responding to von Hagen's perfectly sound observation that in present-day Ukraine the leading principle of historiography is "an overly nationalistic rewriting of the past that posits a sovereign, national state as a teleological outcome of history," Isaievych poses the equally apt question, "Is not a teleological approach typical for *any* patriotic textbook of *any* national history?"[25] Isaievych goes on to account for the natural dominance of ethnogenetic approaches to the problem of Ukrainian nation formation by citing specific features of that process (lengthy periods of statelessness, stability of ethnic territory, cultural continuity) and the historical material that is available to modern historians as a result. True enough, Isaievych attributes a teleological approach only to textbooks of Ukrainian history, but the examples cited above make it abundantly clear that most scholarly treatments of the subject suffer from the same flaw.

Perhaps the ideal instance of complete agreement between the primordialists/perennialists and the modernists is the concept of national renaissance, which has not yet undergone revision. The thesis that the late nineteenth and early twentieth centuries witnessed a national renaissance in the Ukrainian lands is universally accepted. The latest academic series intended to present a new view of Ukrainian history to a mass audience includes a volume on the national renaissance, and its exposition follows the classical scheme of the late nineteenth and early twentieth centuries.[26] The very term *national renaissance*, an obvious borrowing from the Italian *Risorgimento* that was widely used in Ukrainian political writing of the early twentieth century, has been adopted as an analytical category in current scholarly discourse. Yet its cognitive burden remains the same as it was a century ago: if the nation underwent a renaissance in the nineteenth and early twentieth centuries, then it clearly must have existed earlier.

The judicious modernist Hrytsak also makes use of this term, though with a number of nuances. Unlike most Ukrainian historians, who have revived the concept of the national renaissance on the strength of its use in the classical Ukrainian historiography of the 1900s and 1920s, Hrytsak predicates his view of the renaissance on an analytical distinction between modern and premodern nations. Moreover, Hrytsak eschews the classical populist tradition, drawing instead on the analytical scheme advanced by the Czech historian Miroslav Hroch. Hrytsak acknowledges the instrumentalist context of the Ukrainian national renaissance, distancing himself from the generally accepted organicism of that phenomenon, although he does not question that it was historically determined. Understandably enough, the cognitive utility of the term also is not put into question.

The only systematically revisionist account of the Ukrainian national renaissance produced to date is Szporluk's article "Ukraine: From an Imperial Periphery to a Sovereign State."[27] Here, the term *national renaissance* is itself replaced by *nation-building*, and the notion of a Ukrainian project, that is, a consciously created image of the nation, is advanced. There is, however, no attempt to negate the organic elements deliberately employed by the Ukrainian intelligentsia for the realization of its project.

It may thus be asserted that there is something in the nature of a tacit understanding among the representatives of various approaches to the analysis of Ukrainian nation formation. Under its terms, certain ideas and concepts are simply accepted as given without further analysis. Consciously or not, most Ukrainian historians incline toward the organic version of nation formation, in which the rise of the Ukrainian nation is seen as an objective necessity and a manifestation of historical justice, and all that impeded it is dismissed as mere happenstance. Similarly, the continuity of ethnic/national history is presented as natural, while episodes of discontinuity, if noted at all, are regarded as accidental consequences of external factors.

CONCLUSION

On the basis of our previous citations from the works of practicing Ukrainian social scientists, we may now formulate a summary response to the question, "How, when, and where did the Ukrainian nation take shape?" This in turn will give us an idea of how the social sciences are creating a new image, or restoring an old one, of the Ukrainian "imagined community." The answer to the first part of the question is as follows: the development of the nation was a process of *organic* evolution, but its organicity was compromised by external factors and obstacles (foreign intervention and rule, assimilation, elite "treason," etc.). The prevailing conviction is that the Ukrainian nation developed on the basis of a homogeneous ethnic nucleus and related ethnic and subethnic groups that existed from ancient or even prehistoric times, retaining certain constant cultural traits throughout the centuries while resisting external ethnic influences and assimilation, as well as maintaining their specific character, geographic base, and "nation-creating potential." The existence of this nucleus and its ancillary components ensured continuity in the millennial formation (and, at some points, the very existence) of the Ukrainian nation. If some scholars accept the view that nationality or national consciousness can be constructed (but not artificially), ethnicity is nonetheless considered a wholly organic natural component.

Although the answer to the question *where* is less unanimous, it also presents no great diversity of ideas. Whether consciously or not, most scholars seek to fit the Ukrainian nation into the European geopolitical and historical space in order to show that Ukrainians constitute a European nation. On one hand, this is clear evidence of the provincial or postcolonial status of Ukraine, which was formerly a province of Moscow and now has prospects of becoming a province of Europe (in other words, Ukraine is at once a western province of the East and an eastern province of the West). On the other hand, this approach manifests the characteristic aspiration of so-called non-historic nations and their attendant national movements to attain full membership in the world community and establish their cultural and historical legitimacy. Understandably, one of the dominant nationalist myths is that of centuries-old or millennial territorial continuity in the history of the Ukrainian ethnos/people/nation. Moreover, unlike in the past, Ukraine's location at the crossroads of culture can now be cited as a positive factor, and not as one that traditionally led to cultural and political assimilation.

Deviations from this pattern usually take the form of a rather common stereotype, "Ukraine between East and West," which admittedly offers a much broader scope for interesting interpretations.[28] Some scholars with a penchant for postmodern wit deliberately scoff at this analytical matrix, placing Ukraine "between one thing and another."[29]

Finally, the question *when* reveals a concerted general effort to push the historical origins of the Ukrainian nation as far into the past as possible, to establish the starting point of Ukrainian nation formation as early as possible, and to present the history of the nation as a natural continuation of the history of the ethnos.

Whether directly or indirectly, all this is meant to confirm the historical necessity of the emergence of independent Ukraine, thereby legitimizing the right of the Ukrainian nation to statehood and to a place of honor in world civilization. This "legitimation syndrome" should not, of course, be taken literally and treated merely as an expression of the current demands of political and cultural elites. The subjective factors that lead Ukrainian social scientists to draw certain conclusions and not others may be of various kinds, ranging from a conscious desire to respond to current political imperatives all the way to the search for true, objective history. It is also worth taking into account that the *national* history of Ukraine was treated for decades as the history of a people striving at all costs to rid itself of its national characteristics and merge with a new historical community, the Soviet people. Understandably, the taboo on national history in the Soviet period has prompted a compensating reaction in independent Ukraine: in the works of social scientists, the millennial dream of reunification has been transformed into a no less ancient desire for independence.

Finally, let us note the influence of yet another factor, that of historical rehabilitation, on the social sciences. The restoration to intellectual respectability of the names of eminent historians, ethnographers, and anthropologists of the past and the canonization of certain figures has led to the enshrinement of their views. Citing Hrushevs'kyi has become widely accepted as a way of clinching an argument, and his views are often employed as the basis of new conceptions. Accordingly, Ukraine is witnessing the intellectual renaissance of accounts of nation formation now almost a century old, originally generated by the same need for legitimacy.

To be sure, when it comes to evaluating the efforts of contemporary Ukrainian social science in the sphere of nation building, there is little point in moralizing and offering superficial criticism of its methodological backwardness and political engagement. *Backwardness* is, after all, a highly relative term. It requires no more than one generation of students to enrich Ukrainian social-science methodology with new approaches and theories. It should be recalled in this connection that many "new" achievements in Western (or, let us say, Anglo-Saxon) sociology, which has traditionally been regarded as a source of new methods of research on problems of nations and nationalism, have amounted to nothing more than the reinterpretation of neglected concepts. But that is a subject in itself. It is also worth noting that certain "backward" or "antiquarian" approaches to nation formation currently popular in Ukrainian social science seem extraordinarily pertinent to Western sociology itself as it undergoes a rather sweeping revision of modernist notions and a true resurgence of primordialist or perennialist accounts of nation formation.

At present, then, Ukrainian social science is quite intensively engaged in the process of nation building, which is the decisive factor in shaping the account of national history that now holds sway. As noted above, this tendency is strengthened by a number of specific intellectual, philosophical, and historical circumstances affecting the outlook of Ukrainian social scientists. The ever more frequent debates occurring among them[30] show that some scholars have already gone beyond the confines of patriotic discourse as such, raising the prospect of a greater variety of approaches to the problem of creating the national image, and thus to ways of shaping that image in current discussion.

NOTES

1. B. V. Popov, V. O. Ihnatov, M. T. Stepiko, et al., *Zhyttia etnosu: sotsiokul'turni narysy* (Kyiv: Lybid', 1997), p. 170.

2. Leonid Zalizniak, *Narysy starodavn'oi istorii Ukrainy* (Kyiv: Abrys, 1994), pp. 147, 148.

3. V. Ponomariov, *Etnichnist' ta etnichna istoriia Ukrainy* (Kyiv: Lybid', 1996), p. 178.

4. Ibid., p. 179.

5. Ibid.

6. Iaroslav Dashkevych, "Natsiia i utvorennia Kyivs'koi Rusi" in Iaroslav Hrytsak and Olena Dzhedzhora, eds., *Formuvannia ukrains'koi natsii: istoriia ta interpretatsii. Materialy kruhloho stolu istorykiv Ukrainy* (L'viv: Naukove Tovarystvo im. T. Shevchenka, 1995), p. 14.

7. Ibid., pp. 11⁻12.

8. Ibid., pp. 12⁻15.

9. Anthony D. Smith, *The Ethnic Origins of Nations* (Oxford: Oxford University Press, 1986).

10. Ivan Lysiak-Rydnyts'kyi, "Formuvannia ukrains'koho narodu i natsii," in his *Istorychni ese*, 2 vols. (Kyiv: Osnovy, 1994), vol. 1, pp. 11⁻27.

11. Smith, *Ethnic Origins of Nations,* and Lysiak-Rudnyts'kyi, "Formuvannia ukrains'koho narodu i natsii."

12. Iaroslav Isaievych, "Etnichne korinnia ukrains'koi natsii," in Hrytsak and Dzedzhora, *Formuvannia ukrains'koi natsii,* pp. 17, 21, 22.

13. V. A. Smolii and O. I. Hurzhii, *Iak i koly pochala formuvatysia ukrains'ka natsiia* (Kyiv: Naukova dumka, 1991).

14. Ibid., p. 7.

15. Ibid.

16. Iaroslav Hrytsak, *Narys istorii Ukrainy. Formuvannia modernoi ukrains'koi natsii XIX–XX st.* (Kyiv: Heneza, 1996), p. 15.

17. Ibid., p. 15.

18. Valerii Smolii and Valerii Stepankov, *Ukrains'ka natsional'na revoliutsiia XVII st. (1648–1676 rr.)* (Kyiv: Al'ternatyvy, 1999), p. 338.

19. Ibid.

20. Valerii Smolii, "Natsional'no-vyzvol'na viina v konteksti ukrains'koho derzhavotvorennia," in *Natsional'no-vyzvol'na viina ukrains'koho narodu seredyny XVII st.: polityka, ideolohiia, viis'kove mystetstvo* (Kyiv: Heneza, 1998), p. 21.

21. Valerii Stepankov, "Ukrains'ka natsional'na revoliutsiia XVII st.: prychyny, typolohiia, khronolohichni mezhi (dyskusiini notatky)," in *Natsional'no vyzvol'na viina ukrains'koho narodu seredyny XVII st.: Polityka, ideolohiia, viis'kove mystetstvo* (Kyiv: Heneza, 1998), pp. 31, 40.

22. See "Ukrains'ke pytannia" in *Ukrains'ke pytannia,* comp. Mykola Tymoshyk (Kyiv: V-vo im. Oleny Telihy, 1997), pp. 64⁻70. This is a Ukrainian translation of Mykhailo Hrushevs'kyi's brochure *Ukrainskii vopros,* published on the eve of World War I. See also M. Hrushevs'kyi, *Kul'turno-natsional'nyi rukh na Ukraini v XVI-XVII vitsi* (Kyiv and L'viv: n.p., 1912).

23. Hrytsak and Dzhedzhora, *Formuvannia ukrains'koi natsii,* pp. 43⁻83.

24. Mark von Hagen, "Does Ukraine Have a History?" *Slavic Review,* vol. 54, no. 4 (Fall 1995), pp. 658⁻673.

25. Iaroslav Isaievych, "Ukrainian Studies: Exceptional or Merely Exemplary?" *Slavic Review,* vol. 54, no. 4 (Fall 1995), p. 705.

26. Vitalii Sarbei, *Ukrains'ke natsional'ne vidrodzhennia* (Kyiv: Al'ternatyvy, 1999).

27. Roman Szporluk, "Ukraine: From an Imperial Periphery to a Sovereign State," *Daedalus,* vol. 126, no. 3 (Summer 1997), pp. 85⁻119.

28. For a more detailed discussion, see Serhy Yekelchyk, "The Location of Nation: Postcolonial Perspectives on Ukrainian Historical Debates," *Australian Slavonic and East European Studies,* vol. 11, nos. 1–2 (1997), pp. 161–184.

29. Oleksii Tolochko, "The Good, the Bad and the Ugly," *Krytyka* (July–August 1998), pp. 24–31. The alternative title "Ukraina mizh chymos' i chymos'" appears on the cover.

30. I shall note only a few of them: a discussion initiated by Iaroslav Hrytsak in L'viv in the spring of 1998 on postmodern historical accounts; a debate on nationalism in contemporary Ukraine at the Kyiv Mohyla Academy in the winter of 1999; and a discussion at the Fourth International Congress of Ukrainian Studies (Odesa, summer 1999), in the course of which patriotic discourse in historiography was criticized by a number of speakers (who, of course, found themselves in the minority).

4

Culture and Cultural Politics in Ukraine: A Postcolonial Perspective

Mykola Riabchuk

The collapse of the Soviet empire brought with it a large number of problems which resemble both those of some other postcommunist countries of Eastern Europe and those of the more numerous postcolonial countries of the developing world. In Ukraine, the ultimate results of this social, political, cultural, and economic experiment are hardly predictable.

Ukraine is undertaking a difficult triple transition—from a dictatorship to a democracy, from a command economy to a free market, and from an empire to statehood. Kuzio, however, points to an additional transitional process that further complicates the entire endeavor: "evolution from a country possessing an uneven national identity to one with a civic, unified nation and political culture,"[1] in other words, nation building.

Ukraine has historically emerged as a *Kulturnation* rather than a *Staatnation* and a "genuine" Ukrainian identity has been mostly defined in ethnolinguistic terms; the cultural approach to the quadruple transition just described is therefore important to bear in mind. It is quite clear that each of the four transitional processes has its own separate impact on culture and cultural politics in contemporary Ukraine. On the other hand, it is also apparent that culture (broadly understood as a "whole way of life"[2]) significantly determines the character, the speed, and the very direction of the quadruple transition. The four-pronged transition can thus be described, from the cultural perspective, as a dual process of decommunization and decolonization, largely, but not exclusively, meaning desovietization and de-Russification.

In this chapter, culture and cultural politics in contemporary Ukraine hence will be considered primarily within the context of the twin legacies of communism and colonialism, and of rather incoherent attempts to overcome them. This incoherence stems from the general incoherence and inconsistency of the "Ukrainian revolution" of 1991 and the so-called reforms adopted later. The ambivalent character of political and economic system of contemporary Ukraine which is neither totalitarian nor democratic, neither "communist" nor "capitalist," "neither European nor Soviet" (Sherman Garnett) has been described in detail in numerous works within a broad framework of postcommunist "transitology."[3] The cultural ambivalence, however, draws less attention—partly because the sphere of culture seems to be less important for many scholars, partly because the Ukrainian case does not fit the patterns of cultural transition in Russia (which is a major concern for most "transitologists") and needs a rather uncommon (for most experts on postcommunism) postcolonial approach.

In this chapter I argue that the postcommunist ambivalence and ambiguity of Ukrainian politics and economy match the postcolonial ambiguity of the cultural situation. This ambiguity is conceptualized through the notion of a Creole state; that is, a state that belongs primarily to the descendants of Russian settlers as well as to those indigenes who had eventually assimilated into the dominant (Russophone) urban culture. Such a state, however, profoundly differs from the traditional Creole states of America, Australia, South Africa, and so on. First, the culture and language of settlers happened to be unusually proximate to those of indigenes. Second, the indigenous culture was and still is capable of competing against the culture of colonizers not only in the realm of folklore and traditional art but also in virtually all modern, professional genres. This makes the Ukrainian case very peculiar and, as this chapter will propose, open to a great variety of possible developments. Some tendencies and phenomena of the ongoing processes will be analyzed at the end of the chapter.

The only secure, legitimate, and generally acceptable way of development is that of gradual "Ukrainianization," that is, of the very moderate but consistent policy of affirmative action, or state protectionism, on behalf of Ukrainian language and culture. Even though the Ukrainian state seems to be too dysfunctional now to pursue any coherent policy, it does not mean such a policy should not be elaborated and promoted by the both state and society. The Ukrainian state will be dysfunctional as long as it remains Creole, that is, neither Ukrainian nor Russian but, rather, Soviet. Ukrainianization thus, under peculiar post-Soviet circumstances, is by and large a synonymous word for desovietization.

THE UNFINISHED REVOLUTION

The Ancien Regime, Democrats, and State-Nation Building

As many observers have noticed,[4] neither an anticolonial nor an anticommunist revolution in fact ever happened in Ukraine. If we understand "decolonization" to mean that "which sets out to change the order of the world, is a program of complete disorder"; "a violent phenomenon"; and "a total, complete, and absolute substitution." (Frantz Fannon), then decolonization did not take place in Ukraine.

What happened in Kyiv in 1991, when central power in Moscow collapsed, was a compromise between the ruling pro-Moscow communists and oppositional anti-Moscow national democrats. The communists agreed to abandon Moscow's overlordship, while democrats agreed to accept the ancien regime as a renewed one (supposedly decommunized and decolonized). In fact, the compromise reflected and legitimized two mutually dependent processes that had occurred in Ukraine during perestroika. On one side was the evolution of the pro-imperial, heavily Russified *nomenklatura* toward local patriotism and, hence, civic nationalism (or, rather, bureaucratic statism). On the other side was the evolution of the rather weak democratic and nationalist opposition toward pragmatism.

The positive results of this historical compromise are well known: independent Ukraine emerged as a legal continuation of the Ukrainian Soviet Socialist Republic; its withdrawal from the USSR was carried out by constitutional bodies of the ancien regime; and the new state, from the very beginning, defined itself as a territorial jurisdiction rather than as a ethnolinguistic entity ("people of Ukraine" rather than "Ukrainian people").[5] This secured acceptance of the new state's independence by hitherto loyal Soviet citizens, and, at the same time, prevented the rise of rival claimants to power from among opponents of communism or opponents of Russian/Russophone dominance. It also helped to avoid a war with Russia or the former metropolitan center. [6]

The drawbacks of the compromise are also well known, at least in the spheres of economy and politics. The old, formally "departized," *nomenklatura* remained in power, successfully hampering much-needed economic and political reforms. A corporatist economy dominated by organized crime and corrupt officials gained foothold, hyper-inflation and hyper-corruption reigned supreme, and the "bread-basket of Europe" became, in the words of *The Economist*, a "waste-basket." Social stability, which was claimed to be the major achievement of the 1991 compromise between communists and national democrats, led to stagnation.

However, in the cultural sphere the pitfalls of the 1991 arrangement are less evident. On its face, Ukrainian culture seems firmly secured by the very existence of the Ukrainian state where ethnic Ukrainians make up 73% of the entire population and where Ukrainian officially enjoys the status of state language since 1989. The number of pupils instructed in Ukrainian has gradually increased from 48% in 1990/91 to 63% in 1997/98;[7] some measures (or, rather, half-measures) have been undertaken to introduce Ukrainian into the Soviet-turned-Ukrainian army, state apparatus, and higher education.[8] The cultural institutions of the Ukrainian SSR have largely survived, dominated by communists-turned-democrats, yet new institutions have also emerged, and members of the anticommunist, national democratic opposition have been incorporated en masse within the new-old cultural establishment.

Is Ukraine a Ukrainophone or Russophone "Nationalizing State"?

It is hardly surprising, then, that many Western scholars and journalists who never bothered to learn Ukrainian or spend more time in Kyiv than in Moscow reported eagerly on Ukraine as a nationalizing state which tends to oppress and denationalize minorities, particularly the largest and most vociferous one, the Russians. Such reports have been largely supported by Russophone activists who claimed that Ukrainian nationalists obtained the upper hand in the country, launched forceful Ukrainianization, destroyed the national economy through corruption and incompetence, and began adopting a pro-Western, pro-capitalist, anti-Russian and anti-Soviet orientation.[9]

Ironically, many Ukrainophone activists perceive the situation in the same way, although the oppressors and, therefore, the recipes for salvation are said to be the opposite. In 1995, for example, a long and emotional *Manifesto of the Ukrainian intelligentsia* appeared in a number of Ukrainophile periodicals, signed by some notable Ukrainian writers, scholars, and cultural activists. In very strong words the *Manifesto* claimed that:

there has re-emerged the centuries-old policy of "Ukraine without Ukrainians"—a policy aimed at the destruction of the Ukrainian nation. . . . A part of this policy is the intensi-fied devastation of Ukrainian culture. . . . On the fifth anniversary of independence Ukrainian book publishing is dying—only 3 per cent of books written in Ukrainian are published. . . . Ukrainian kindergartens and schools are being closed; and documentation in many branches of government, including the highest ones, is not conducted in the state language. In many areas attempts to open new Ukrainian cultural centers are blocked, Ukrainian newspapers and journals are closed down or their circulation forcibly stopped, and Ukrainian culture is excluded from radio and television. . . . Scholars, scientists, teachers, doctors, and cultural researchers are struggling for survival. . . . Ukrainian pa-triots are being dismissed from the army and left without work. Everything is being done in the training of cadres to attain a "critical mass" of those who hate Ukraine in the state apparatus. . . . In fact, anti-Ukrainian ethnic cleansings are already being conducted in Ukraine.[10]

No doubt, the *Manifesto* loses a great deal by its exalted, apocalyptic tone, especially when it compares the ongoing de-Ukrainianization to that of the 1930s, "when the Bolsheviks destroyed virtually every activist in Ukrainian culture, scholarship, and science." It sees a conspiracy aimed at Ukraine's de-struction where there may be none. In many Third World countries the oligar-chies act in a similar self-interested manner without incitement from Moscow. And finally, the authors of the *Manifesto* urge the government to rely more on the "true" Ukrainian patriots to effectively promote state building. However, they do not specify how these "true" patriots should be selected and, the crucial question remains, why the allegedly anti-Ukrainian government should bother itself with such a selection.

All these faults notwithstanding, the document aptly reflects the confusion, despair, and hysterical search for a solution or, rather, for scapegoats by the marginalized postcolonial intelligentsia. It tells us little about the essence of the current situation but quite a lot about the way it is perceived by many Ukraino-phones disappointed with developments in postcolonial Ukraine.

Of course, 1995 was a peculiar year, when the worst expectations of the Ukrainian intelligentsia seemed to become a reality. Leonid Kuchma, who won the presidential elections in July 1994 under the slogans of strengthening ties with Russia and making Russian the second official language in Ukraine, stated that the "Ukrainian (national) idea had not worked." Kuchma's remark was un-derstood by the predominantly Sovietophile and Russophone bureaucracy as a signal to halt "Ukrainianization" (in reality, it had never been treated seriously anyway). In summer 1995 the mass funeral of the Patriarch of the Ukrainian Orthodox Church (Kyiv Patriarchate) was physically attacked in Kyiv by pre-dominantly Russophone special police. Two prominent Ukrainian intellectuals, Dzyuba and Petro Talanchuk, who had respectively led the Ministries of Culture and Education, were dismissed and replaced by dull Soviet functionaries. In neighboring Belarus, the newly elected President Alyaksandr Lukashenka, perceived commonly as Kuchma's double, launched an extensive anti-Belarusian campaign of further sovietization and Russification.

The years that followed have not changed the situation dramatically for the worse, as was expected in 1995, but they have hardly improved it, either. Kuchma's policy in virtually all spheres proved to be a continuation of those of the Leonid Kravchuk era. The new president and his highly corrupted clique have not sold their chiefdom to Moscow as many experts predicted and many Ukrainophiles worried, but neither have they done very much to appease the indigenes on the territory they luckily happened to privatize. A Ukrainian publicist complains:

Again, as ten years ago a child could be derided by other children in the yard just because he or she speaks Ukrainian. The print of Ukrainian publications is miserable. Ukrainian books are virtually absent in book stores. And more than one third of Ukrainian citizens comes out against national independence.[11]

Another Ukrainophone activist adds:

The state has been called "Ukrainian," but nothing has changed, besides phraseology. . . . The state power, the state authorities are the same. Ukrainian language and culture, and culture in general, have always been alien for the Soviet *nomenklatura* which still rules the country. . . . Lack of national will at the top gives a carte blanche to a predominantly Ukrainophobic bureaucracy which still lives with old stereotypes of intolerance. . . . The linguistic situation in Ukraine reflects the social situation. The Ukrainian people have always been wretched in Ukraine—and they still are.[12]

The Ambiguity of a Dysfunctional State

It is probably much easier to understand why the Russians are dissatisfied with the independent Ukraine than why the Ukrainians are. Russians, in Kuzio's words, "have been such privileged immigrants, that any nationally-minded government in Kyiv is bound to try to redress the balance by restoring state support for Ukrainian language, culture and education, thus provoking easily manipulable fears of Ukrainianization, whether justified or not."[13] As the Ukrainian scholar, Kulyk, wrote:

Despite the fact that the sphere of Russian usage had not grown smaller and Russian speakers retained all their opportunities to exercise their traditional cultural rights—the pro-Russian and left parties made use of the opportunity to frighten the electorate in the east and south with "Ukrainianization," when, in fact, it had not even begun there. Under these conditions the demand for the legislative confirmation of bilingualism was a demand for a guarantee against future Ukrainianization. . . . They were not demanding a legalization of the obligation of Ukrainian-speaking citizens to know Russian (they know it), but the right of Russian speakers not to know Ukrainian.[14]

We should face however the more profound truth that Ukraine is a dysfunctional state which cannot satisfy anybody.[15] The ruling *nomenklatura* is largely a-national and non-ideological, and pursues, in fact, no comprehensive policy in *any* sphere except self-profit and day-to-day survival. To achieve this paramount goal it pays lip-service to both communist and nationalist symbols, flirts with both Russophone and Ukrainophone leaders, sends mixed messages, and deliberately contributes to the total confusion, aptly called a "social schizophrenia."[16] There is no coherent, consistent cultural policy in Ukraine that could be interpreted as either a radical desovietization, decommunization, or decolonization (unlike in the Baltic, Central, and East European states) or a further sovietization and colonization-creolization (like in Belarus). Ukraine remains stuck between these two models.

On the surface, however, it may look as an odd mixture of laissez-faire policy, which irritates the Ukrainophones, and a very weak, incoherent, and inconsistent affirmative action, which provokes Russians' anxiety. The word *Ukrainianization* (like democratization and economic reforms) seems to become discredited long before any real Ukrainianization (democratization, economic reforms) begins. This results, rather naturally, from the overall governmental impotence and dysfunctionality, as well as from incompetence and basic indifference to all those things cultural and Ukrainian[17] (reformative, democratic, and so on).

The confusing eclecticism of Ukrainian life and Ukrainian cultural (and any other) politics results from the ambivalent nature of Ukrainian society, which is divided along regional, cultural, ethnic, linguistic, religious, generational, and many other lines. The victorious referendum of 1 December 1991 that had brought both Ukrainophones and Russophones together in the nearly unanimous 90% vote for Ukrainian independence hid the outcome of the presidential elections held on the same day. Only one-third of the voters supported the noncommunist candidates (i.e., a definitive break of the nascent nation with the Soviet legacy and a firm orientation toward a European way of development). Two-thirds of the voters supported the Soviet presidential candidate (Kravchuk) as a guarantee that relatively minimal cultural, political, and economical changes would occur and that the Soviet way of life would be largely preserved. An American scholar commented on those developments:

Political borders were quickly redrawn following the failed coup, but cultural barriers are not so easily dislodged. In spite of widespread support for an independent Ukrainian state, many living in Ukraine are less supportive of the cultural changes that have followed new state formation. . . . Having acquired a state, nationalist leaders have tried to forge a link between individuals and the state via a national culture. This link has been inadvertently challenged by the residual appeal and habit of seeing oneself as Soviet. . . . Practices and values spawned by the Soviet system and nostalgia for the security of a Soviet way of life persist and compete with a nationalist redefinition of self and society by providing alternative, non-national points of orientation for individuals reassessing their values and identities. Thus the process of institutionalizing a national culture must operate within the confines of tenacious aspects of a Soviet way of life and the allure of local allegiances.[18]

THE LEGACY OF COLONIALISM

Ukraine as a Postcolonial Creole State

The pervasiveness and persistence of the colonial status quo in Ukraine infuriates many Ukrainian intellectuals and makes them define the independent Ukraine that emerged in 1991 as a kind of Creole state, that is, a state dominated by the descendants of Russian settlers and by Russified Ukrainians.[19]

This results from the fact, recognized by many historians, that the twin processes of modernization and urbanization in Ukraine coincided with large-scale Russification.[20] A huge gap between things Ukrainian and modern emerged in the nineteenth century, something that has largely persisted to the present day. Not only did the indigenous population (Ukrainophone Ukrainians) become the oppressed majority (that tends to become a minority) in their own country vis-à-vis dominant Russophones, but also the Ukrainophone world became firmly associated with village backwardness and "bumpkin-ness." In fact, this world became a kind of inner colony, a local Third World of *kolkhoz* slaves that provided the First World of the higher (Russophone) civilization with lower-class employees.[21] Today, according to some sociological data, almost twice as many people possess higher education among Russians than among Ukrainians,[22] and perhaps ten times more among the (mostly urban) Russophones than (mostly rural) Ukrainophones. In nine years of Ukrainian independence, neither civic nor numerical equality have made Russophones and Ukrainophones genuinely equal in cultural and linguistic practices in everyday life.

The proposed conceptualization of contemporary Ukraine as a Creole state may provide a good explanation of why the numerical preponderance of Ukrainians gives them few if any advantages in independent Ukraine, especially compared with the much smaller preponderance of Latvians and Estonians in Latvia and Estonia, respectively. First of all, one should remember that the real hallmark of identity in the heavily Russified Ukraine is cultural and linguistic rather than ethnic. This means that the numerical preponderance of ethnic Ukrainians over ethnic Russians in Ukraine is much less relevant than the (approximate) numerical equality of Russophones and Ukrainophones: each group makes up 45% to 55% of the entire population. (The precise figure is not available because the identity of bilingual Ukrainians often proves to be very hazy, and there are no methods to unequivocally define it.)

According to the 1989 Soviet census, however, over 80% of ethnic Ukrainians claim Ukrainian to be their native language ("mother tongue"). This figure is questioned today by many sociologists who claim the term *native language* is imprecise and should be replaced with the less equivocal term *language of convenience* or *language of everyday usage*. Still, even if we take the census results at face value, and accept the number of Ukrainian speakers in Ukraine to make up over 60%, we cannot ignore the fact that most of these people live in villages and small towns (or else in economically marginal Western Ukraine) and represent therefore the socially marginalized strata of society, barred from adequate cultural, educational, and financial resources and dispossessed from appropriate levers of political and economic influence. In a sense, they represent a kind of rural "blacks" vis-à-vis urban, predominantly Russophone "whites." Or, as Edward Said may have put it, they originated from "a lesser world, populated with lesser people." This seems to be the most relevant fact for making sense of any—cultural, ethnic, linguistic, regional, social—division of contemporary Ukraine.

Ukrainophones, indeed, were subjected to open "linguistic apartheid" in the Tsarist empire and to more sophisticated discriminatory measures in the USSR. In both cases they were exposed to an arrogant—if not "racist"—attitude on the part of the dominant Russophones, something encouraged by both empires. Those few Ukrainophones who resisted linguistic apartheid in everyday urban life and stubbornly upheld their ethnolinguistic identity were perceived as nationalists, as impudent and crazy dissidents who dared to publicly challenge behavioral conformity:

> Language use has a potent symbolic quality in a politicized linguistic environment: it immediately assigns the user to one of two sides of the ideological barricade. . . . The use of Ukrainian, they realized, is tantamount to opposition to the Soviet state. . . . Although no laws forbid deviations from this behavioral norm (as one Soviet Ukrainian representative once told me, no one "is holding a gun to their heads"), non-Russians in general and Ukrainians in particular appear to understand that insistence on speaking one's native language—especially among Russians—will be perceived as rejection of the "friendship of peoples" and as hostility to the "Soviet people." Few Ukrainians are audacious enough to risk such unpleasantness as public censure, loss of employment, or even jail for the sake of linguistic purity. As a result, they signal their loyalty to the state and sidestep chauvinist reactions by speaking Russian.[23]

The question remains, however, and needs to be answered: why, nearly a decade into Ukrainian independence, has the state ended such behavioral conformity? And, consequently, why are both Ukrainian language and culture still perceived as inferior to Russian—not only by virtually all Russians but also by many Ukrainians?

Dysfunctional Culture

As early as 1987, on the eve of perestroika, Ivan Dzyuba, a prominent Ukrainian dissident writer and author of the well-known 1965 *samvydav* book *Internationalism or Russification?* published an extended article entitled "Towards a Conceptualization of Ukrainian National Culture as a Complete System."[24] Having examined various aspects and levels of the functioning of Ukrainian culture, Dzyuba concluded that it is a dysfunctional culture, with many genres, trends, institutions, and phenomena underdeveloped or missing, and many indispensable vertical and horizontal links badly weakened or forcefully interrupted. "Ukrainian culture is a culture with an incomplete structure," Dzyuba bemoaned.

For the first time in the official media the Soviet propagandistic myth on the thriving and flourishing of ethnic cultures in the USSR was challenged. Moreso, the strongest taboo on any reference to Russification was rebutted. "The Ukrainian language," Dzyuba argued, does not fulfill all of its social and cultural functions, and national language is, after all, the backbone of a national culture. Even non-verbal art forms are linked to a language through imagination which is formulated via language and even through its sounds. . . . And since entire social stratas, the non-humanitarian intelligentsia in particular, and the urban population in general, began to abandon the Ukrainian language, all the sphere of Ukrainian language usage has shrunk dramatically, and the entire Ukrainian discourse, its intellectual and spiritual content, became badly impoverished.[25]

At the time, Dzyuba had probably not been aware of the polemics between George G. Grabowicz and Ivan L. Rudnytsky, two prominent Ukrainian scholars in the West, who ten years earlier heatedly argued over Dmytro Chyzhevsky's concept of "complete/incomplete" literatures, cultures, and nations. Being rather preoccupied with political hypercorrectness, Prof. Grabowicz claimed that "the differentiation, and, necessarily, evaluation of nations according to superior and inferior, historical and non-historical, complete and incomplete, is in the realm not of scholarship but of, say, political propaganda."[26] Professor Rudnytsky quite reasonably responded that completeness or incompleteness of any nation or culture reflects primarily its socially and politically determined structure, its ability to function, and has nothing to do with superiority or inferiority, in anthropological terms, that might well have racist implications:

What determines the completeness or incompleteness of a literature is not the presence or absence of certain features, but rather whether a literature can satisfy all the essential cultural needs of its own society during a given historical period. . . . This, of course, has nothing to do with the artistic value of individual works, but refers only to the social function of a literature as a whole.[27]

The dysfunctionality of Ukrainian culture, conceptualized in sociopolitical terms by Rudnytsky and later by Dzyuba, is a pervasive legacy of colonial subjugation and forceful Russification. Such a postcolonial framework has become rather commonplace in both scholarly and popular writing after Ukraine became an independent state. Such a positivistic approach, however substantiated, leaves little room to comprehensively explain the current "pervasiveness and persistence of a Russian-based sovietized culture," in the words of Wanner.[28] The sovietization and Russification of Ukraine still tend to be treated by scholars as an essentially social and cultural phenomenon—a sort of inertia, inherited, socially constructed, and imposed on society's way of life, thought, and behavior. Implicitly this suggests that, in the newly independent Ukraine, these old patterns could be rapidly, by simple administrative measures, replaced with new ones (i.e., through Ukrainianization and de-sovietization).

Some scholars, however, have challenged this view, pointing instead at the primarily psychological problem of people who had been "raped" for decades and, in order to survive, had to abandon their identity and to accept the alien one, imposed by the "rapists" (i.e., to accept the prolonged perverse relations with the "rapist" as a kind of voluntary quasi-marriage).[29]

The Collective Shadow

Such a breakthrough approach to the Ukrainian postcolonial reality seems to be paved by the American anthropologist Oksana Grabowicz, who delivered a paper at the International Congress of Experts on Ukrainian Studies in L'viv as early as 1993. Her purely academic presentation elicited enormous reaction and was published in the local daily newspaper *Ratusha*, then reprinted by the Warsaw Ukrainian weekly *Nasze slowo*, the *Berezil* monthly in Kharkiv, and the *Arka* quarterly in Kyiv.[30]

In her paper Grabowicz argued that centuries of colonial subjugation have led to a perverse impact on both the colonizers and the colonized. The former have gradually developed a superior attitude toward the "inferior" indigenous culture. Meanwhile, the latter have deeply internalized such an attitude, evolving inferiority complexes and accepting a stereotypical, "Oriental" view of themselves, imposed by the colonizers. Such a view of Ukraine was nothing new. The prominent Russian critic Vissarion Belinsky, who labeled Ukrainians as "cast iron headed," and his Ukrainian contemporary Mykola Hohol' (a.k.a. Nikolai Gogol'), who wrote rather sympathetically about "Little Russian" songs and dances, had something very important in common. Both considered Ukraine as an exotic, uncivilized borderland that used to have a glorious past and a great folklore which was naturally disappearing and doomed to be assimilated into a superior culture.

To disclose this mechanism of colonial subjugation, Grabowicz employed Carl Jung's concept of the collective shadow, defined as "a dark side of man, the unconscious, the negative, the destructive, and the self destructive tendencies and desires in the psyche." When the shadow is severely repressed, the negative contents of the unconscious are activated and forced out as projections on outside objects. Eventually, these projections come to be perceived as qualities of the "other"—the person, group or a nation. Hence, the collective shadow of the dominant society (its subconscious negative self-image) projected onto the oppressed group over a long period of time exerts a ruinous influence on the oppressed because the group begins to identify itself with such a projection. Ultimately, the oppressed group loses confidence in its own qualities (the qualities of its culture and society) and increasingly adopts the colonizers' views as superior: "The subordinated group at the end becomes a despised minority in their own native land."[31]

Ukrainian society shows a remarkable similarity with other colonized societies, in terms of patterns and syndromes already described and elaborated at length by Frantz Fannon, Volodymyr Odajnyk, and many other students of colonialism. In Ukraine the distinction between the two rival groups is basically cultural and linguistic, not racial. Therefore, the problem of the social inferiority of the aboriginal *kolkhoz* slaves is solved (or at least cushioned) in a manner unthinkable in Africa or America: by passing for white; in other words, by discarding the "lower" Ukrainian language and adopting the "higher" Russian one. As a result, Russification and cultural creolization of East Ukrainian rural aborigines may well continue, despite the formal national independence of Ukraine and even after the granting of official status to the indigenous language.

More often than not the converted aborigines are ashamed of their autochthonous background (e.g., Ukrainian-speaking parents) and are even less inclined than ethnic Russians to show any interest in Ukrainian culture, which they consider inferior. Despite the fact that Ukrainian culture of the twentieth century and particularly of the last decade has very significant, internationally recognized, achievements,[32] even the best Ukrainian books, magazines, films, or music are not much in demand in "Ukrainian" cities, whereas third-rate Moscow mass culture (or American, yet in Russian translations) is happily consumed by the aboriginal immigrants from the rural (so far, Ukrainophone) Third World areas. Paradoxically, the huge Russophone population of Ukraine (as well as of many other post-Soviet republics) has failed, so far, to produce any significant cultural artifacts—despite its hitherto cultural/social predominance in the country. On their part, Ukraine still remains "Little Russia," meaning a primitive supplier of cultural raw materials and a passive consumer of ready-made, second-rate, and obsolete cultural products supplied by the former imperial metropolis.

Many Ukrainian intellectuals therefore remain rather cautious about the future of Ukrainian culture and language and the plight of the Ukrainophone majority-cum-minority in Ukraine. "Neither culturally nor politically independent Ukraine (in the real sense of the word) seems to be possible for a long time on, even under the most favorable circumstances. For a long time, if not eternally, the Ukrainophones will remain a social and cultural minority in the Ukrainian state. Ukrainian language and culture, of course, will persist—but only as assets of a minority group," Hrabovs'kyi provocatively argued.[33]

UKRAINE: TOWARD A POSTCOLONIAL FRAMEWORK

The Power of Nationalistic Myths

The pessimistic forecasts, however substantiated by many aspects of Ukrainian reality, seem to be slightly at odds with some other aspects of Ukrainian historical and current developments. Particularly, they seem to underestimate the resilience of Ukrainian nationalism and Ukrainian identity, which survived for centuries under highly unfavorable circumstances. And they seem to ignore the ambivalent character of the Ukrainian Creole state which, paradoxically, tends to be more Ukrainian than Russian in many (if not all possible) terms.

One may argue, of course—and quite reasonably—that this state, dominated by the "white" Russophone minority, has successfully marginalized the "black" Ukrainophone majority, corrupted a significant part of the Ukrainophone elites, and legitimized its rule by coopting some Ukrainian symbols, heroes, ideas, and narratives. Yet it is not so clear why the Creole elite in Ukraine opted primarily for indigenous, nationalistic heritage rather than Soviet, quasi-internationalist—like the Creoles in neighboring Belarus did. In 1991, such a choice looked quite reasonable in both Ukraine and any other Soviet republics where the Soviet, predominantly Russophone (Creole) nomenklatura was looking for allies among the indigenous nationalists, and for emancipatory narratives elaborated by natives, in order to secede from Moscow and to legitimize independent statebuilding. Yet by 1994, as the Soviet republics-cum-independent states were successfully privatized by local postcommunist Creoles, the need for ideologically committed allies had vanished. It was especially clear in Belarus and Ukraine, where modern national identity has not been determined by race or ethnicity or religion but, rather, by common language and culture and a desperate struggle against Russification. It proved to be very difficult to cure historical injuries and to obliviate the fact that Russophones were on the other side of historical barricade, on the side of the oppressor, "rapist," and colonizer. Since independence both Russophones and native-speakers seemed to be unified by a common state, citizenship, territory, and history. But different cultural and linguistic identities still divide them and, moreover, significantly subvert the unifying effect of civic factors, giving both groups very different, if not opposite, ideas of their history(-ies), statehood(-s), geopolitical arrangement(-s), and desirable development(-s) for the future.

In both Belarus and Ukraine, the post-Soviet Creole elite had eventually broken ties with local nationalists and opted for overtly pro-Soviet, antinationalistic leaders. Kuchma, however, has not become a local brand of Lukashenka, despite a strong pro-Russian rhetoric, and promises to de facto preserve the colonial status quo by making Russian de jure the second state language in Ukraine. Of course, the indigenous nationalists in Ukraine proved to be much stronger than in Belarus, making it rather impossible for any Creole elite to simply ignore them. However, indigenous nationalists proved to be a minority both in 1991, when they managed to mobilize up to 30% of the electorate to support the nationalistic presidential candidates; and in 1994, when they succeeded to mobilize only 46% of votes against the assumed threat to Ukrainian independence embodied in the would-be pro-Russian candidate Leonid Kuchma.

How, therefore, could such a minority force, for nearly a decade, get the ruling Creole elites to accept Ukrainian as a language of official communication; to grant Ukrainophone leaders various positions in the state apparatus, including ministerial posts; to promote, however equivocally, the gradual Ukrainianization of education and state institutions; to gradually abandon Soviet symbols and narratives and to accept those of Ukrainian National Republic (1918–1920), of Ukrainian seventeenth-century Kozakdom, and finally, of Kyivan Rus'? Why do Ukrainian Creoles make so many concessions to the indigenes—unlike their Belarusian colleagues who seem to have found the "final solution" for the "Belarusophone problem?"

The only reasonable answer to these questions is that Ukrainian nationalistic myths are much more powerful than Belarusian, and therefore more attractive for local Russophones, at least in some, the most acceptable and adaptable parts (Kyivan Rus' and Kozakdom rather than OUN and UPA, Hrushevsky rather than Petliura, etc.). Ukrainian Russophones seem to be an even less homogeneous group than Ukrainophones;[34] many of them are actually bilingual: they speak more Russian than Ukrainian just because Russian is the common language in places where they live and work. In the Ukrainian environment they easily change their communication patterns, proving thereby that the sociological term *language of convenience* is probably as dubious as that of the *mother tongue*. In fact, the nearly 20% difference between the numbers of people who claim Ukrainian to be their native language (over 60%)[35] and who claim Ukrainian is their language of convenience (over 40%)[36] reflects, on one hand, the rather high attachment of many Ukrainians to their mother tongue and, on the other hand, rather low possibility to employ this tongue in their everyday life in heavily Russified (and rather unfriendly to Ukrainian speech) East Ukrainian cities. In a sense, the ambiguous linguistic identity of these people resembles the identity of many Ukrainian immigrants to the West who still claim their native language to be Ukrainian but find it much more convenient to communicate in English when living in Toronto or Philadelphia.

Another indicator of the relatively high attachment of many Ukrainian Russophones to things Ukrainian can be seen in the fact that nearly all of them agree that their children and grandchildren should be fluent in Ukrainian; nearly two-thirds of them confirm that they would not mind their children and grand-children to be instructed at school in Ukrainian.[37] This is an apparent sign that although many Russophones in Ukraine refuse (quite naturally) to be Ukrainian-ized themselves, are ready to accept the smooth Ukrainianization of their off-spring.

In Search of Appropriate Cultural Policy

In sum, we may conclude that Ukraine has not become and probably will not ever become another Belarus just because Ukrainian Creoles came to be at-tached to the indigenes' land both politically and culturally much more than their Belarusian siblings. According to sociological data, fewer than 2% of Ukrainian Russophones identify themselves with Russia politically; many more, however, do so culturally. But again, there is a significant difference between their prevailing orientation toward high Russian culture, versatile and rather ambivalent attitude towards Russian popular culture, and extremely low attach-ment to Russian traditional culture and folklore. Ukrainian Russophones per-ceive Ukrainian rather than Russian folklore as their own, consume rather sym-pathetically Ukrainian popular culture, and, as a rule, are eager to accept Ukrainian high culture as soon as they manage to discover it under the layers of colonial biases and postcolonial ignorance.

Such a biased, a priori negative attitude towards Ukrainian culture on the sig-nificant part of Ukrainian Russophones is not easy to overcome, of course. Yet, the local Ukrainian patriotism of virtually all Russophones, as well as the am-bivalent, latently sympathetic, however cautious and socially oppressed, attitude of many of them toward Ukrainian culture, provides Ukrainian activists with sufficient room to gradually subvert the negative stereotypes by appropriate, comprehensive, and coherent cultural politics.

The first attempt to systemically elaborate the cultural policy of the Ukrain-ian state was undertaken as early as 1994, by the Ministry of Culture of Ukraine, briefly headed at the time by Ivan Dzyuba. Under his auspices, a team of bright young experts analyzed the current cultural situation in Ukraine and produced some preliminary guidelines for the cultural policy to be pursued.[38] They con-sidered four major models of cultural politics defined as "European," "nativist," "wild-western," and "CIS" (Commonwealth of Independent States). In Ukraine, they argued, the economic conditions of mafia-style capitalism promote in fact no cultural policy but a "wild-west" laissez-faire, while the political conditions are rather supportive of a "CIS" cultural (under)development (i.e., neocolonial dominance by the former imperial culture, primarily through mass culture, and the further marginalization of Ukrainian culture and language). To alter this, they opted for the European model as a sophisticated mixture of free- market laissez-faire and various forms of state paternalism for national culture and support for the high arts. The nativist model, however, should not have been abandoned either, because in their view it may be rather effectively adopted in a postcolonial country to revive the formerly discriminated against national culture and language.

Within the framework of the European model, the young reformers suggested gradual transformation of the Ministry of Culture into a project-management and grant-distribution agency. They insisted on greater transparency and efficiency of state cultural institutions, and encouraged competitiveness among grant seekers. At the same time, in order to overcome the colonial legacy, they provided protectionist measures for Ukrainian culture which emphasized tax credits rather than direct subsidies for Ukrainian cultural products and activities. The major strategic goal outlined by the reformers was to promote by all means the modern, primarily urban, and youth-oriented image of Ukrainian culture.

The election of Kuchma and resignation of Dzyuba in July 1994 ended the courageous, yet quixotic, attempts to reform one of many post-Soviet bureaucratic strongholds in Ukraine from within. The negative cultural tendencies (wild west and CIS) remained dominant in Ukraine, although the positive (European and nativist) have not been completely abandoned either. Six years later, they still are noticeable in both public discussions and some government policies, however weak, incoherent, and inconsistent.

Society versus the State

The most if not the only significant change that occurred on the Ukrainian cultural scene within the last decade was the emergence of a relatively large, outspoken, well-educated and socially well-established group of intellectuals who have no illusions about Ukrainian state and its cultural or any other politics. As a rule, they tend to dissociate themselves from a highly corrupt and culturally incompetent government. They seem skeptical about their predecessors who, by and large, have opted for cooperation with a ruling regime (however limited, reserved, and equivocal), and accepted en masse diplomatic, governmental, and other posts through a romantic or, perhaps, self-deceptive belief in the ability to improve and, maybe, Ukrainianize the post-Soviet establishment from within.

At the same time, they are not prone to demonize the Ukrainian oligarchic state as anti-Ukrainian, and the ruling Creole elite as "Ukrainophobic." With a grain of philosophical irony, they claim that the Ukrainian state is very bad but so far this is the best state Ukrainians have ever had; it is almost as good as the Austro-Hungarian monarchy which ruled the western part of Ukraine throughout the nineteenth century. The Habsburgs, one may remember, provided virtually no support for Ukrainian culture and language, but, unlike Russians, they did not oppress them either. As a result, western Ukrainians, without any governmental support, developed their own civic and cultural institutions, and entered the twentieth century with modern national self-awareness while eastern Ukrainians had been arrested in their national and cultural development and largely preserved until present a premodern, quasi-medieval level of civic consciousness and national self-awareness.

Today, for the first time in their history, eastern Ukrainians have a government that does not kill them, starve them deliberately to death, deport them to Siberia, oppress their language, or impose censorship. One may complain that the government is not good enough, but it would be unwise to ignore the rare historical opportunity to successfully replicate what western Ukrainians did hundred years ago: promote national culture and self-awareness by the efforts of civil society rather than an alien or, at best, indifferent state. This belief is reflected in deeds and words of many Ukrainian intellectuals, for example, in the following statement of the prominent young artist Tibery Silvashi:

In the last decade, we have a very favorable situation for artistic activity. The state is not interested in us any more, it goes into various businesses, except ideology, thank God. Somebody becomes anxious about this, somebody keeps on begging for state subsidies. But the state guardianship over the arts usually proves to be too expensive for artists. . . . As long as there is freedom of artistic expression in Ukraine, there is no reason to emigrate. Emigration could be pushed only by persecutions, terror by the only and "true" ideology. We should be happy that our rulers have no ideology, so far.[39]

Such a philosophical attitude does not prevent, of course, Ukrainian intellectuals from sharply criticizing the ruling, highly corrupted, elite and the policies they pursue. "Our culture is oppressed, and our rulers lack culture," a leading Ukrainian writer of the younger generation, Yuri Andrukhovych, said, having withdrawn his candidacy for the (Taras) Shevchenko State Prize (traditionally presented by the President). Andrukhovych argued:

I don't know whether seven years [of independence] can be considered as a long period from the standpoint of eternity, but I know that national culture remains unfree, and the state leaves much to be desired in terms of cultural standards. . . . Our current political order is conveniently referred to as "transitional" (maybe eternally transitional). To me, it is personified by a steadily increasing "lumpenization"—what Shevchenko called the reign of stupid and thick-headed bureaucrats, complemented by mushrooming structures built in the Soviet baroque style and paid for by the *nouveaux riches*; by our decision to be like Africa, and by the lack of the will to be true to oneself—all of which reigns in Ukraine.

The sharp polemics with more "collaborative" predecessors and colleagues could be read behind the lines of Andrukhovych's statement:

How can one accept a government award against this backdrop? If I did, I would feel like an accomplice or maybe like one of those hear-no-evil speak-no-evil monkeys. I'm not a lackey and need no handouts. I don't want to be one of those that accept them and wake up the next morning morally castrated, resting on laurels made from a dying tree.[40]

Intellectuals versus the Intelligentsia

The profound disparity between the postmodern Ukrainian intellectuals and traditional populist intelligentsia has been embodied perhaps most graphically in the extensive conflict and eventual split within the official post-Soviet Writers' Union of Ukraine. In Autumn 1996, during the Union congress in Kyiv, a relatively small but notorious group of young and middle-aged writers left the organization and in March the following year founded an alternative Association of Ukrainian Writers with about 100 members.

There apparently were both generational and aesthetic reasons for the schism: the dissidents proved to be not only younger but also more Western-oriented, better educated, inclined to modern and postmodern cultural practices, adjusted to a free-market environment, more dynamic, and published, translated, and anthologized abroad, and rather skeptical about any ideology. In sum, they resemble more nonengaged West European intellectuals than the ideologically preoccupied East European intelligentsia, a dubious product of inner freedom and outer slavery.

The major discrepancy yet, although largely under the surface, was about the Soviet legacy and the Writers' Union reluctance to break with it definitely and unequivocally. Created by the Communist Party in 1934 as a kind of a "literati *kolkhoz*," the Writers' Union was heavily branded from the very beginning with servilism, mediocrity, state paternalism, preoccupation with ideology and propaganda, intrinsic nativism and anti-Westernism, authoritarianism, and intolerance. This legacy, from the dissidents' point of view, had not been duly overcome during the first years of national independence, prompting them to establish their own very loose professional association—partly to alter the seemingly mainstream literary process, partly to draw the public attention to desovietization problems.

For some observers, this episode has heralded a more general tendency of a gradual decline of the Ukrainian intelligentsia as a social stratum—with all its agendas, behavioral patterns, and discursive practices.[41] This would be matched by a gradual rise of independent intellectuals with a more moral than ideological basis, professionally rather than ideologically motivated. The problem, however, is that not only are the prospects for Ukrainian democracy unsteady, but the very future of Ukrainian language, culture, and Ukrainophones themselves remains unclear.

Therefore, many observers remain reserved about the "end of the intelligentsia" and the advent of a bright postcolonial freedom, nonpartisanship, and a firmly committed non-commitment to ideology. The Ukrainian poet Oksana Zabuzhko prematurely declared: "The 'New Wave,' the generation to which I belong, is actually the first one after the last six decades that has been freed from the obligation 'to save the nation.' "[42] Michael Naydan, an American Slavist, aptly remarked that she is only partly correct because

Writers like Zabuzhko, as well as hundreds of others, by writing in Ukrainian today continue that traditional line from Shevchenko. While they are not "obligated" to save the nation, they, indeed, do so. They are absolutely necessary for two primary tasks: (1) to promote the expansion of the usage of the Ukrainian language and culture within the borders of Ukraine; and (2) to establish an articulate voice for the nation as a bridge to the West and the rest of the world.[43]

As long as the Ukrainian language is endangered, any attempt to write in it, promote it, and make it thrive, is an essentially moral choice, a choice for the weakest species against the strongest, an act of solidarity with a marginalized culture against a dominant one. Or, as Zabuzhko has less pathetically put it, it's something "very much akin to being a masochistic occupation."[44] The common truth is that "in Ukrainian history the cultural has been inexorably linked to the political,"[45] something that has remained virtually unchallenged, Naydan believes:

With independence in 1991 the Ukrainian idea has been realized and, for the first time, Ukraine has control over its own destiny as a state. Yet over the course of over eight years of independence, that state has been defined by its own government not culturally, but rather only in geographic terms, with the same borders that had delineated it previously as a republic in the Soviet Union with the concomitant bicultural/bilingual remnants of imperialist Russian and imperialist Soviet rule. Thus, the cultural impetus that had sustained the Ukrainian idea over two centuries remains—but in reality only among a still relatively small number of cultural activists. While the government has declared Ukrainian as the official national language, with benign indifference it has failed to support the growth of the indigenous Ukrainian literary culture in virtually any way.[46]

The politically correct observations by an American scholar have probably little in common with the frantic *Manifesto of the Ukrainian intelligentsia*. And the sardonic style of Andrukhovych's *Eulogy* hardly resembles a highly discreet speech of Dzyuba, who claims:

Still, there is a dramatic lack of any coherent and reasonable cultural policy of the state, and there are heated arguments about its concepts in Ukraine. The further persistence of such a situation is fraught with serious consequences since the cultural problems evoke little comprehension in Ukrainian society while in some [upper] circles, including the ruling elite milieu, one may find overt counteraction against the development of Ukrainian national culture.[47]

Yet, at least one feature apparently brings all these texts together: their authors are highly uncertain to which degree (if at all) the "Ukrainian" state is Ukrainian and whether the natural rights of Ukrainophones to preserve and develop their language and culture are really affirmed in Ukraine's postcolonial environment.

CONCLUSION

Such an ambiguous situation may persist for an indefinite time because of a number of factors. First, while Russophones seem to have a numerical preponderance over Ukrainophones or at least stronger social positions in urban centers, Ukrainophones are far more active, vociferous, and committed to their cause. Second, neither Russophones nor Ukrainophones are unanimous in their cultural orientations. While many less educated Ukrainophones are inclined to

Russian (mass) culture, many educated Russophones are rather bilingual and sympathetic about Ukrainian culture. Finally, the culturally ambivalent and indifferent postcommunist elites in Ukraine are interested in preserving rather than resolving such a situation because it enables them to manipulate both sides and to effectively hold power.

Such a dysfunctional policy preserves a "bad peace," which is certainly better than a "good war." But, at the same time, such a policy makes any prospects for a "good peace" quite bleak. Neither a modern Ukrainian nation nor a civil society can fully emerge unless a modern national identity and civic consciousness are forged and accepted by the majority of the population. So far most of these people are neither Ukrainians nor citizens sensu stricto—because they are predominantly *Homo Sovieticus*. As long as desovietization and de-Russification are delayed Ukraine is doomed to political-economic stagnation. So far Ukraine remains at the crossroads in all possible terms—"undecided" in cultural direction, economic reforms, or geopolitical orientations. If the Russophone and Soviet culture persists Ukraine will resemble another postsoviet "Eurasian" republic, like Belarus. If Ukrainian (anti-Soviet) culture achieves the upper hand, then Ukraine will certainly take the European way of development, like its Baltic, Central, and East European neighbors.

The first scenario seems to be highly explosive—as the experience of Northern Ireland or Basque country graphically confirms. Modern Ukrainian (Ukrainophone) national self-awareness that emerged in the nineteenth century encompasses today at least one-third of the population, having its stronghold in Western Ukraine but recruiting supporters all over the country. This self-awareness may be counterweighted with modern Russian or, the most probably, premodern-cum-modern Creole (Ukrainian Russophone) self-awareness. So far there is no evidence anywhere that a modern national identity, once having emerged, would ever disappear. This means that the modern Ukrainian self-awareness can be contained, at the worst scenario, within its current boundaries of the 30% of the population. Ukrainophones would become a minority on their own territory, that is, a historically abused minority which would never accept a minority status as just and legitimate. It would certainly launch a protracted and probably endless struggle for its "natural," "God-given" rights.

The second scenario seems to be also difficult to complete, but, as the experience of Latvia and Estonia shows, it can be done if appropriate cultural and linguistic policy is supported by successful economic reforms. In Ukraine the economy is of paramount importance because any extension of modern Ukrainian national self-awareness largely depends on changes in the agricultural sector, on modernization of the rural/provincial environment where a majority of East Ukrainian Ukrainophones live. So far most of them have rather premodern, local self-awareness, and have virtually no civic consciousness being heavily dependent on the quasi-feudal *kolkhoz* system. Russophones in Ukraine, as was pointed out earlier, are prone to accept gradual "Ukrainianization" of their children because of a number of reasons. First, the Ukrainian language is not as alien for them as Latvian or Estonian and, at the same time, is not perceived as inferior to Russian as are the Central Asian languages. Modernization of the Ukrainian economy and promotion of modern Ukrainian culture may ultimately eradicate any biases against things Ukrainian. Second, most Ukrainian Russophones have not yet developed modern national self-awareness (of the Creole type) and, in these terms, are more susceptible to any properly arranged nationalization than committed Ukrainophones. Finally, even those Russians and Russophones who have firmly developed their national (Russian or Creole) self-awareness, as opposed to the Ukrainophone "other," would much more easily accept minority status than committed Ukrainians—just because they neither feel their demands are historically quite legitimate nor believe that Ukraine is the only place where Russian language and culture could be preserved and cherished.

One may suggest that there could be also a third scenario of peaceful coexistence of two cultures, two languages, and, actually, two nations (Creole Ukrainian and Ukrainophone Ukrainian) on the same territory.[48] The Belarusian experience shows, however, that in a post-Soviet state this is hardly possible: formal equality of two cultures and languages means in reality nothing more than preserving the odious colonial status quo. Yet, even if Ukraine (or Belarus) were an exemplary liberal democracy, it would not be so easy to practically equalize two languages, one of which has a reputation as international, empowered by centuries of imperial domination, while the other one is perceived as a local, stigmatized by centuries of colonial subjugation.[49] Even reputable "international" languages like German and French, or French and English, are not on a par in Bern or Ottawa, let alone in Brussels, where French is apparently much more "equal" in practical terms than Flemish. Still, in Ukraine there is one more problem, uncommon elsewhere: Ukrainophones and Russophones cannot be successfully "cantonized" (i.e., administratively separated and satisfied with relative cultural autonomy within certain native territory). For Ukrainophones, all the territory of Ukraine is native and they would hardly accept being ghettoized in rural regions—a sort of cultural autonomy the Russophones are eager to concede. Finally, the main question remains: as far as Creole (Russophone) identity is largely premodern, ambivalent, vague, and virtually based on no original culture, is it worthwhile to promote this identity into full-fledged national self-awareness while 30% of Ukrainians already profess a modern Ukrainian national self-awareness?

Although most experts recognize that the economy, in the Ukrainian case, is to play a crucial role, culture also remains an important battlefield. It has largely determined the context of Ukrainian national identity for decades and seems likely to determine it in the decades to come.

NOTES

1. Taras Kuzio, "Ukraine: A Four-Pronged Transition" in T. Kuzio ed., *Contemporary Ukraine: Dynamics of Post-Soviet Transformation* (Armonk, NY: M. E. Sharpe, 1998), pp. 165–180.

2. Raymond Williams, *Keywords: A Vocabulary of Culture and Society* (Oxford: Oxford University Press, 1983), p. 87.

3. For the relevant bibliography see, for example, Andrew Wilson, *The Ukrainians: Unexpected Nation* (New Haven and London: Yale University Press, 2000), pp. 320–321.

4. See, for example, Taras Kuzio, *Ukraine: The Unfinished Revolution* (London: Institute for European Defense & Strategic Studies, 1992).

5. Roman Szporluk, "Ukraine: From an Imperial Periphery to a Sovereign State," *Daedalus*, vol. 126, no. 3 (Summer 1997), pp. 85–120.

6. Roman Szporluk, "Introduction: Statehood and Nation Building in Post-Soviet Space," in Roman Szporluk, ed., *National Identity and Ethnicity in Russia and the New States of Eurasia* (Armonk, NY: M. E. Sharpe, 1994), p. 15.

7. Jan Germen Janmaat, *Nation-Building in Post-Soviet Ukraine: Educational Policy and the Response of the Russian-Speaking Population* (Amsterdam: Universiteit van Amsterdam, 2000), pp. 62, 113.

8. According to the same source (ibid., p. 115), the proportion of students instructed in Ukrainian in institutes of higher education increased from 37% in 1992–1993 to 51% in 1995–1996.

9. Just to cite a few random samples from Russian mass periodicals published in Ukraine which represent the opposite view: "Now, it is [Ukrainian] bureaucrats who reign supreme, determining language policy in the country. It is they, who, with a typical bureaucratic zeal, turned the support for Ukrainian language into a ruthless struggle against everything Russian." Pavel Smirnov, "V Ukrainye russkiy yazyk nye dolzhen chuvstvovat' syebya inostrannym," *Fakty*, 18 September 1999; "Expulsion of Russian language from the territory of Ukraine is underway. . . . Nobody respects the people who cannot defend themselves. Therefore we [Russians] should get organized. . . . The main goal of our organization is to protect the rights of Russians [in Ukraine] and to disseminate information about rights violations." Lyudmila Gordyeeva, "Russkiye s'yezdami bogatyeut," *Donyetskiy kryazh*, no. 25 (1–7 July 1999).

10. See Ralph Lindheim and George S. N. Luckyj eds., *Towards an Intellectual History of Ukraine: An Anthology of Ukrainian Thought from 1710 to 1995* (Toronto: University of Toronto Press, 1996), pp. 395–397.

11. Serhiy Hrabovs'kyi, "Ukrayina nasha sovkova," *Krytyka*, vol. 3, no. 9 (September 1999), p. 4.

12. Yevhen Sverstiuk, "Problema zaminy osnov kultury," in Theofil Kis and Irena Makaryk eds., *Towards a New Ukraine II: Meeting the Next Century* (Ottawa: Chair of Ukrainian Studies, University of Ottawa, 1998), p. 144.

13. Kuzio, *Ukraine. The Unfinished Revolution*, p. 9.

14. Volodymyr Kulyk, "The Search for Post-Soviet Identity in Ukraine and Russia and Its Influence on the Relations between the Two States," *Harriman Review*, vol. 9, nos. 1–2 (Spring 1996), p. 23. Putting it more theoretically, one may disclose here a typical "desire by the historically dominant culture to continue imposing its cultural norms on a changing society." Fred Bennett, "The Face of the State," *Political Studies,* vol. 47, no. 4 (September 1999), p. 678.

15. The concept was elaborated at length by James Mace in his conference presentation "Ukraine as a Dysfunctional State." See T. Kis, I. Makaryk, and Roman Weretelnyk, eds., *Towards a New Ukraine I: Ukraine and the New World Order, 1991–1996.* (Ottawa: Chair of Ukrainian Studies, University of Ottawa, 1997). To address the same phenomenon, Paul D'Anieri employed the term "weak state"— "where weak describes not the power of the state relative to other states but the ability of the government to adopt a policy and implement it in the society." "Ukrainian society is divided," he comments, "and its institutions do little to resolve those divisions. Indeed, the government may be even more divided than the society." See Paul D'Anieri, "The Impact of Domestic Divisions on Ukrainian Foreign Policy: Ukraine as a 'Weak State,'" in Taras Kuzio, Robert S. Kravchuk, and Paul D'Anieri, *State and Institution Building in Ukraine* (New York: St. Martin's, 2000), p. 84.

16. Ukrainian sociologist Yevhen Holovakha was perhaps the first who explored this

phenomenon in his article "Osoblyvosti politychnoyi svidomosti: ambivalentnist suspilstva ta osobystosti," *Politolohichni chytannya*, vol. 1, no. 1 (1992) pp. 24–39. See also "Post-Soviet Schizophrenia," *The Economist*, 4 February 1995, p. 27.

17. One of Ukraine's leaders visited the museum of Taras Shevchenko in 1999. Shevchenko is the greatest Ukrainian poet and a sacred figure in the Ukrainian national iconostasis. The top politician was highly surprised to know that Shevchenko was also a gifted artist, despite the fact that this is common knowledge and taught in schools.

18. Catherine Wanner, *Burden of Dreams: History and Identity in Post-Soviet Ukraine* (State College: Pennsylvania State University Press, 1998), pp. 46–48.

19. The concept was initially introduced in a couple of my articles published in 1997–1998 and eventually incorporated into my book *Vid Malorosiyi do Ukrayiny: Paradoksy zapizniloho natsiyetvorennya* (Kyiv: Krytyka, 2000), pp. 152–172, 227–229. For further discussion on this concept see Oleksandr Hrytsenko's and Serhiy Hrabov'skyi's articles in *Krytyka*, vol. 4, nos. 9–10 (September–October), 2000.

20. Chapter 15, "Socioeconomic Change" in Orest Subtelny, *Ukraine: A History* (Toronto: University of Toronto Press, 1988), pp. 260–278.

21. In this conceptual framework, the Soviet *propiska* system, largely preserved in post-Soviet republics and even strengthened in today's Moscow, can be interpreted as a system of visa surrogates which enabled the better-off urban "First World" to limit the influx of immigrants from the rural "inner colony." Not accidentally, these immigrants got a nick-name, *limitchiki*.

22. Ian Bremmer, "The Politics of Ethnicity: Russians in the New Ukraine," *Europe-Asia Studies*, vol. 46, no. 2 (March–April 1994), p. 266. See also Bohdan Krawchenko, *Social Change and National Consciousness in Twentieth-Century Ukraine* (Basingstoke, England: Macmillan, 1985). According to Krawchenko, the percentage decline of Ukrainians in the student population since the 1930s was a "direct consequence of the Russification policies which put Ukrainians at a natural disadvantage *vis-a-vis* Russians in the struggle for *vuz*-entrance." In particular, Germ Janmaat comments, Ukrainians proved to be less competitive "because of their low social origins (most of them had a working class or collective farm background), with insufficient means and skills to vie with the Russians and Jews, who disproportionately came from an intelligentsia or middle-class milieu" (Janmaat, p. 58).

23. Alexander J. Motyl, *Will the Non-Russians Rebel? State, Ethnicity and Stability in the USSR* (Ithaca, NY: Cornell University Press, 1987), pp. 100–101.

24. Ivan Dzyuba, "Chy usvidomlyuyemo natsionalnu kulturu yak tsilisnist?" *Kultura i zhyttia*, 24 January 1987. For an abridged English version see *Soviet Ukrainian Affairs*, vol. 2, no. 1 (Spring 1988), pp. 26–29.

25. Ivan Dzyuba, "Chy usvidomlyuyemo natsionalnu kulturu yak tsilisnist?" *Nauka i kultura: Ukraina*, vol. 22 (1988), p. 313.

26. George G. Grabowicz, *Toward a History of Ukrainian Literature* (Cambridge, MA: Harvard Ukrainian Research Institute, 1981), p. 88.

27. Ivan L. Rudnytsky, "Observations on the Problem of 'Historical' and 'Non-historical' Nations," in his *Essays in Modern Ukrainian History* (Edmonton: Canadian Institute of Ukrainian Studies, 1987), p. 39.

28. See Wanner, *Burden of Dreams*.

29. See in particular Oksana Zabuzhko, *Shevchenkiv mif Ukrainy* (Kyiv: Abrys, 1998) and *Khroniky vid Fortinbrasa* (Kyiv: Fakt, 2000).

30. For an English version see Oksana Grabowicz, "The Legacy of Colonialism and Communism in Ukraine: Some Key Issues," *Perspectives on Contemporary Ukraine*, vol. 2, no. 2 (March–April 1995).

31. Ibid., cited from the manuscript in the possession of the author, pp. 3–4.

32. While Oleksandr Dovzhenko's and Serhiy Paradzanov's films, Arkhypenko's sculptures, or Silvestrov's music are still categorized in the West as "Russian," Ukrainian writing (at least that in Ukrainian) escapes from this unfortunate labeling. A number of anthologies of contemporary Ukrainian literature have been recently published and received good reviews in the West. In particular, the American anthology *From Three Worlds: Writing from Contemporary Ukraine* (Boston: Zephyr Press, 1996) was reprinted in hardcover after the initial, rather unexpected, success of the paperback edition. A few more publications should be mentioned here: Yuri Andrukhovych's and Oksana Zabuzhko's prose, translated into many European languages (including Finnish and Hungarian), and Oleh Lysheha's poetry distinguished in 1999 with the American PEN-Club Award for the best translated poetry book.

33. Hrabovs'kyi, "Ukrayina nasha sovkova," p. 7.

34. As Andrew Wilson has aptly noticed, "when opinion polls are sensitive to the possibility of dual or situational identity and offer a broader choice of categories [than the rigid census questionnaire], the results can be very different." Wilson refers to the 1997 survey which revealed that 27% of the respondents identified themselves as "both Ukrainian and Russian," including "more Ukrainian than Russian" 7%, "equally Ukrainian and Russian" 14%, "more Russian than Ukrainian" 5%. Only 56% defined themselves as "Ukrainian only," and 11% as "Russian only"—against 73% and 22%, according to the census data, respectively. Wilson, *The Ukrainians*, p. 219.

35. Janmaat, pp. 19–20.

36. Valeri Khmelko and Dominique Arel, "The Russian Factor and Territorial Polarization in Ukraine," *The Harriman Review*, vol. 9, nos. 1–2 (Spring 1996), p. 86.

37. Ian Bremmer, "The Politics of Ethnicity: Russians in the New Ukraine," *Europe-Asia Studies*, vol. 46, no. 2 (1994), pp. 261–283.

38. See Oleksandr Hrytsenko, *Kulturna polityka: kontseptsiyi i dosvid* (Kyiv: Instytut derzhavnoho upravlinnya, 1994); and Oleksandr Hrytsenko, ed., *Kulturna polityka: metodolohichni, pravovi, ekonomichno problemy* (Kyiv: Instytut kulturnoyi polityky, 1995).

39. *Den'*, 11 November 1998.

40. Yuri Andrukhovych, "A Eulogy to Dead Laurels," *The Day*, 19–25 January 1998.

41. The split in the Writers' Union gives us the most graphical, but not the only, example, of how the nascent civil society tries to overcome the legacy of sovietism, etatism, and state paternalism. The old Soviet "creative unions," the Academy of Sciences, and some other institutions are still privileged by the post-Soviet state (all of them have been recently declared "National")—while the new institutions have no subsidies, wages, pensions, rent discounts, and tax exemptions. For a comprehensive analysis of similar problems in Ukrainian humanities, see Hryhoriy Hrabovch, "Sovietyzatsiya humanistyky," *Krytyka*, vol. 1, nos. 1–2 (Summer–Fall 1997); also Marko Pavlyshyn, *Kanon ta ikonostas* (Kyiv: Chas, 1997).

42. Oksana Zabuzhko, "Reinventing the Poet," in *A Kingdom of Fallen Statues: Poems and Essays,* Marko Carynnyk, trans. and ed., (Toronto: Wellspring, 1996), p. 87.

43. Michael M. Naydan, "National Identity for the Ukrainian Writer: Writing Into the New Millenium," in Kis and Makaryk, eds., *Towards a New Ukraine II*, p. 144.

44. Oksana Zabuzhko, "Poetry in Exile," *Partisan Review*, vol. 59, no. 4 (1992), p. 609.

45. Naydan, "National Identity for the Ukrainian Writer," p. 144.

46. Naydan, "National Identity for the Ukrainian Writer," p. 144.

47. Ivan Dzyuba, "Problemy kultury v nezalezhniy Ukrayini," in T. Kis, I. Makaryk, and Roman Weretelnyk, eds., *Towards a New Ukraine I: Ukraine and the New World*

Order, 1991–1996. (Ottawa: Chair of Ukrainian Studies, University of Ottawa, 1997), p. 120.

48. "In Ukraine there is great consensus on the need to build an inclusive nation around the civic features. . . . The problem is that such civic features are not likely to be sufficient to give great cohesion to the people of Ukraine. In part this is because civic features are inherently less likely than ethnic and cultural features to evoke an emotional attachment to the nation. Also, however, the fact that the Ukrainian state is young and its political institutions are not very effective and certainly not very well respected means that relying on civic components of national identity is likely not going to be sufficient to bind the citizenry together. Thus, nation-builders in Ukraine must rely heavily on ethnic or cultural factors to unite the population. And here there are two main options in Ukraine that are popular and potentially viable. One might be termed an Ethnic Ukrainian National Identity, and the other an East Slavic National Identity." See Stephen Shulman, "Nation-Building and Ukrainian Foreign Policy," in Theofil Kis and Irena Makaryk, eds., *Towards a New Ukraine III: Geopolitical Imperatives of Ukraine: Regional Contexts* (Ottawa: Chair of Ukrainian Studies, University of Ottawa, 2001), pp. 11–30. Despite the vague terminology (Ukrainophone and, respectively, Creole identities seems to be more precise in this case), the American scholar rightly stresses that any Ukrainian government "must choose between an East Slavic national identity and an Ethnic Ukrainian one," in order to unify the nation and to mobilize it for much-needed reforms. Shulman seems, however, to mistakenly believe that "there is no right or wrong answer here as to which of these choices is 'best'—these are purely normative questions that depend on the values of the observer." I am arguing here that the "Ukrainian" choice is better because it is more acceptable for the majority of the people and less prone to set about the endless conflict for the future.

49. In 1998, I failed to find any person in the French embassy in Kyiv able to communicate in Ukrainian. English, as a neutral language, was also boldly rejected. The only languages in use were French and Russian. The most astonishing thing was that nobody bothered to apologize for this. To the contrary, the young women in the consulate responded aggressively, with extreme arrogance.

5

Mass Attitudes and Ethnic Conflict in Ukraine

Craig A. Weller

With the collapse of the Soviet Union in 1991, 25 million Russians found themselves outside the Russian Federation. No longer were these Russians the majority ethnic group of the Soviet Union. Russians outside Russia found themselves in the new position of being part of ethnic minorities in countries renewing or beginning the complicated process of state building. The fate of these Russians, to what state they owe their allegiance, how they might figure or be manipulated in relations between Russia and her neighbors, and what impact they might have in the democratization processes of post-Soviet states are just a few of the issues that have become the object of intense interest among scholars.[1]

Of the over 25 million Russians living outside Russia, roughly 44% of them live in Ukraine. They number nearly 11.4 million and make up roughly 22% of the population.[2] They are by far the largest ethnic minority in Ukraine. Paul Kolstoe has determined that in Ukraine, "four out of every five non-Ukrainians are Russian."[3] These numbers, in and of themselves, are of interest to those studying the impact of large ethnic minorities on the process of democratic consolidation and transition.[4] Perhaps more worrisome for observers interested in the potential for ethnic conflict are the assertions of some scholars that there has been a growing perception in Ukraine, especially among Russians and Russophones, that the Ukrainian state since 1991 has embarked on a nationalizing course.[5]

This chapter, based on an examination of all-Ukrainian surveys conducted in 1993, 1995, and 1998,[6] addresses the question of to what extent the Ukrainian population believes in the likelihood of ethnic conflict. This chapter argues four points. First, attitudes of Ukrainians and Russians toward the likelihood of ethnic conflict have remained remarkably stable over time and are consistent with the low level of violent interethnic conflict in Ukraine since 1991. Second, possible perceptions of nationalizing tendencies by the Ukrainian state do not seem to be manifested in either Ukrainophone or Russophone attitudes toward the likelihood of ethnic conflict. Third, when the regional dimension is considered, polarization along the lines that we might expect from regional voting preferences is not powerfully reflected in attitudes towards ethnic conflict. Fourth, surveys indicate generally low levels of ethnic distance between Ukrainians and Russians, but even in regions where perceptions of ethnic distance are greatest, there is not an accompanying increase in percentages of respondents who believe there is bound to be conflict. While recognizing that Ukrainians and Russians do differ on important issues in Ukraine, this chapter argues against viewing these differences as evidence of a deep social cleavage along ethnic lines that is bound to lead to conflict. Instead, this chapter offers evidence of increased partisanship as a factor that might help explain the seemingly incongruous existence of both low expectations of ethnic conflict and the electoral divisions witnessed in 1994. In other words, the 1994 presidential elections might have been an indication that the voters of Ukraine were actually getting better at democracy—a pattern that seems to be confirmed by all-Ukrainian surveys conducted in 1998, as well as by the presidential elections of October–November 1999.

CIVIC AND NATIONALIZING STATE?

In 1991, there seemed to be no shortage of obstacles to the democratic consolidation of post-Soviet Ukraine.[7] Differences with Russia over the Black Sea Fleet, the status of the Crimea, and nuclear weapons were all issues that might have served as potential flashpoints. Add to these issues economic hardship, a large Russian minority, and a common border with the Russian Federation, and the ground in Ukraine seemed to be fertile for conflict along ethnic divisions. Thus far, the worst fears of outside observers have not been fulfilled. This is not to argue that there have not been incidents of ethnic conflict. Indeed, Ukraine has not been totally immune from violent conflict along ethnic dimensions.[8] Ethnic conflict in Ukraine is the exception, however, not the norm, and these incidents remain fairly isolated.

Scholars might be tempted to explain this relative absence of ethnic conflict by Ukraine's avowed commitment to define the state in civic rather than ethnic terms. The Ukrainian citizenship law, a variant of the "zero principle," is one of the most liberal citizenship laws of the post-Soviet states.[9] Moreover, other indicators of political discrimination based on ethnicity, including restrictions on political participation, election to office, and political association, appear to be mostly absent.[10]

Several studies, however, have questioned Ukraine's commitment to define the state in civic rather than ethnocultural terms. David Laitin metaphorically refers to Ukraine as "Dr. Jekyll and Mr. Hyde."[11] Laitin writes:

Ukraine presents to the world a civic agenda; but just below the surface seethes anger against, even hatred of Russians. The West sees the civic face of Dr. Jekyll; the Russians are beginning to see the enraged one, Mr. Hyde. Which half of the double personality will prevail is a question that is deeply worrisome to Russians now living in Ukraine.[12]

Some of Laitin's supporting evidence includes the threatening language by both radical and national democrats appearing in the Ukrainian-language press.[13]

Dominique Arel, as early as 1995, wrote on the perception that Ukraine had initiated a nationalizing agenda: "Despite official rhetoric that it [Ukraine] embraced a territorial, or civic, conception of the state, that is, one not favoring one national group at the expense of the another, after the 1991 independence a perception began to grow, particularly in the eastern and southern regions, that the Ukrainian state was being set on a nationalist course. The two most divisive issues revolve around language policy and Ukraine's relations with Russia."[14]

Arel goes on to argue that the "nationalizing intent" was not directed at any particular national minority but at a linguistic group, the Russophones. He concludes: "The state sent signals that Russian might be phased out of state institutions; decreed that the language of instruction in schools should be determined by an ethnic, rather than linguistic, criterion, and that all higher educational institutions will have to transfer to Ukrainian; and engaged in a hostile political discourse toward Russia based on an exclusive and victimized conception of Ukrainian versus Russian identities."

It is important, I think, to distinguish the differences between Laitin's and Arel's views. Laitin's language is much stronger and most powerfully expressed by the "Jekyll and Hyde" metaphor. Laitin suggests that Ukraine is Janus-faced, showing a civic side to the West and another side to ethnic Russians. He implies that just below the surface, many ethnic Ukrainians harbor angry, if not hateful, feelings toward ethnic Russians. Finally, he intimates that ethnic Russians recognize this and are increasingly apprehensive and perhaps fearful of it. If this scenario is accurate, one could reasonably expect it to be strongly reflected in attitudes towards ethnic conflict among both ethnic Ukrainians and ethnic Russians. Given Laitin's characterization, one might anticipate the expectation of ethnic conflict to be substantial among both groups.

Arel's views are more measured. Writing prior to 1995, Arel doesn't necessarily accept that Ukraine has embarked on a nationalizing course, but argues that this has widely been the *perception*, especially in eastern and southern regions of Ukraine, where there are significant numbers of ethnic Russians and Russophones. Perceptions are often more crucial in framing beliefs than reality. If there has been a perception that Ukraine has been instituting nationalizing policies, one might also reasonably expect this to be reflected in attitudes toward ethnic conflict, especially among Russians. Especially in the East and in the South we might anticipate higher expectations of ethnic conflict among ethnic Russians.

ATTITUDES TOWARD ETHNIC CONFLICT: THE ETHNIC GROUP AND LANGUAGE (NON-) FACTORS

Addressing first possible ethnic differences in attitudes toward ethnic conflict, neither the seething "anger and even hatred" of Russians by Ukrainians nor the Russians' unmasking of the "enraged" Mr. Hyde that Laitin alludes to are reflected in the attitudes of either ethnic Ukrainians or ethnic Russians toward the likelihood of ethnic conflict (Tables 5.1 and 5.2).

Table 5.1
Attitudes toward the Likelihood of Ethnic Conflict

	1993 $n = 2264$	1995 $n = 2260$	1998 $n = 2196$
Bound to be conflict	9.1%	10.6%	7.0%
Can get along	90.9%	89.4%	93.0%

In Table 5.1, when we look at the attitudes of all ethnic groups, we see consistently low percentages of respondents believing that there is bound to be ethnic conflict in Ukraine.[15] What is also notable is that the percentages are, in general, consistent from year to year. There is a slight increase in the percentage who believe there is bound to be conflict in 1995, but the percentage decreases to lower than 1993 levels in 1998.

Table 5.2
Attitudes toward the Likelihood of Ethnic Conflict by Ethnic Group

	1993 $n = 2124$		1995 $n = 2118$		1998 $n = 2087$	
	Ukrainian $n = 1645$	Russian $n = 479$	Ukrainian $n = 1614$	Russian $n = 504$	Ukrainian $n = 1593$	Russian $n = 494$
Bound to be conflict	8.6%	9.8%	10.5%	11.3%	6.7%	7.7%
Can get along	91.4%	90.2%	89.5%	88.7%	93.3%	92.3%
Difference Index	1.2%		0.8%		1.0%	

Again, in Table 5.2, when we look particularly at the attitudes of ethnic Ukrainians and ethnic Russians, we see very consistent low percentages of individuals who believe there is bound to be conflict. As in Table 5.1, we do witness in 1995 slight percentage increases of both ethnic Ukrainians and ethnic Russians who believe there is bound to be conflict, but those percentages diminish to lower than 1993 levels in 1998. The attitudes of both ethnic Ukrainians and ethnic Russians change by less than four percentage points in the three surveys. The final row of the table shows an index that measures the attitudinal differences between ethnic groups. This index is calculated by taking the sum of the differences between the proportions of each ethnic group giving a particular response and dividing by two. The resulting difference index (D.I.) ranges from 0 when the proportions are identical in both ethnic groups to 100 when no ethnic Ukrainian shares an opinion with an ethnic Russian on the given issue.[16] Although in each survey ethnic Ukrainians are less likely than ethnic Russians to believe in the likelihood of ethnic conflict, the D.I.s show the differences between the two groups to be negligible. The overall attitudes of both ethnic groups are almost precisely the same on the likelihood of ethnic conflict. The possible expectations from Laitin's "Jekyll-and-Hyde" characterization of Ukraine are not reflected in the attitudes of either ethnic Ukrainians or ethnic Russians toward conflict.

Yet what about the language dimension? Laitin's path-breaking book is more about language and identity than ethnicity, and it has already been noted that Arel is quite clear that he believes that the Russophones, not just the Russians, perceived the state to be embarking on a nationalizing course. The distinction is quite important. As Arel points out, language cuts across ethnic lines in Ukraine. Significant numbers of ethnic Ukrainians are Russophones. Arel argues that the *perceived* nationalizing tendencies of Ukraine therefore were also directed against ethnic Ukrainians. In fact, both Arel and Laitin argue that the state's nationalizing strategies were perhaps directed more against ethnic Ukrainian Russophones than against ethnic Russians.

Without attempting to diminish the significance of this point, there are reasons to believe that ethnic Russians might not feel the weight of this distinction. In the three all-Ukrainian surveys utilized in this chapter, the percentage of ethnic Ukrainians who spoke Russian at home was consistently around 30%. On the other hand, the percentage of ethnic Russians who spoke Ukrainian at home was only around 7% or 8%. Ethnic Russians might therefore view themselves to be more the targets of a nationalizing strategy. In any event, if Russophones of either ethnic group have perceived themselves to be the target of a nationalizing policy and discourse, one might reasonably expect it to be reflected in attitudes toward ethnic conflict. Table 5.3 looks at attitudes toward ethnic conflict by language at home.

Table 5.3
Attitudes toward the Likelihood of Ethnic Conflict by Language at Home

	1993 $n = 2221$		1995 $n = 2216$		1998 $n = 2147$	
	Ukrainian $n = 1187$	Russian $n = 1034$	Ukrainian $n = 1175$	Russian $n = 1041$	Ukrainian $n = 1162$	Russian $n = 985$
Bound to be Conflict	9.4%	8.5%	12.4%	8.7%	6.1%	8.2%
Can get along	90.6%	91.5%	87.6%	91.3%	93.9%	91.8%
Difference Index	0.9%		3.7%		2.1%	

The language variable does not seem to substantially alter the picture of attitudes toward ethnic conflict in Ukraine. Comparisons with Table 5.1 and Table 5.2 again underline both the consistency and the low percentages of those who believe there is bound to be ethnic conflict in Ukraine. We do see a slight increase in difference between Ukrainophones and Russophones in 1995, but by

1998 the percentages of respondents who believe in the likelihood of ethnic conflict drop down to lower than 1993 levels. Again, the D.I.s indicate that there are virtually *no* differences between Ukrainophones and Russophones on the likelihood of ethnic conflict. Interestingly, in 1995, where the D.I. is slightly larger, the Ukrainophones rather than the Russophones are more likely to believe in the likelihood of ethnic conflict. This is contrary to what we might expect if nationalizing policies were strongly felt by Russophones. Possible perceptions of nationalizing tendencies by the Ukrainian state thus do not seem to be manifested in language group attitudes toward the likelihood of ethnic conflict.

LOOKING AT THE REGIONAL DIMENSION

Regional differences have been widely explored by scholars seeking to understand post-Soviet Ukraine.[17] It is a dimension that encompasses a range of historical, economic, linguistic, and ethnic issues. The outcome of the June–July 1994 presidential elections has led some to point to a regional-linguistic polarization of the country.[18] A recent study of Ukraine's 1998 parliamentary elections concludes that "where people live in Ukraine is more important than who they are in determining values and political attitudes."[19] An examination of the regional dimension in Ukraine, then, might provide us with a more nuanced understanding of attitudes toward the likelihood of ethnic conflict.

The ethnic and linguistic makeup of Ukraine is well known. Neither ethnic Ukrainians and ethnic Russians nor Ukrainophones and Russophones are evenly distributed throughout the country. As in most other post-Soviet states, there are larger populations of ethnic Russians and Russophones in urban areas. Moreover, in Ukraine, the concentrations of ethnic Russian and Russophone populations are located in the East and the South. The Crimea, part of the Russian Soviet Federated Socialist Republic until 1954, is an area of particular concern. Ethnic Russians constitute more than 65% of the population of that peninsula, and more than 80% of the population are Russophones.[20] The issues surrounding the possibility of ethnic conflict in Crimea are complex ones and have received the attention of a number of scholars.[21] Most agree that Crimea poses the most threat to Ukraine's state-building and territorial integrity.[22] Given Arel's assertion that the Eastern and Southern regions most keenly perceived nationalizing tendencies by the Ukrainian state, we might expect attitudes in the East, West, and Crimea to reflect higher expectations of ethnic conflict.

Similar points can be made about the West. The percentages of ethnic Ukrainians are highest in the West, and there are correspondingly low percentages of ethnic Russians and Russophones. In the Western *oblast* of Ternopil' for example, ethnic Russians account for just 2% of the population.[23] Moreover, the western parts of Ukraine have a different historical legacy than that of Eastern Ukraine. Arel describes the West as the "heart of Ukrainian nationalism."[24] Similarly, Melvin views the West as a region of "fierce Ukrainian ethnonationalism."[25] One might expect this also to be reflected in attitudes toward ethnic conflict by region.[26] Table 5.4 attempts to capture the possible regional influence of attitude toward ethnic conflict.

Table 5.4
Attitudes toward Ethnic Conflict by Region

				1993			
	East $n = 594$	South $n = 121$	West $n = 415$	Center East $n = 204$	Center West $n = 611$	Kyiv City $n = 208$	Crimea $n = 111$
Bound to be conflict	11.4%	7.4%	8.9%	6.4%	8.3%	9.1%	9.0%
Can get along	88.6%	92.6%	91.1%	93.6%	91.7%	90.9%	91.0%
				1995			
	East $n = 700$	South $n = 253$	West $n = 380$	Center East $n = 200$	Center West $n = 476$	Kyiv City $n = 153$	Crimea $n = 98$
Bound to be conflict	10.6%	7.5%	8.4%	18.5%	13.2%	5.9%	5.1%
Can get along	89.4%	92.5%	91.6%	81.5%	86.8%	94.1%	94.9%
				1998			
	East $n = 673$	South $n = 229$	West $n = 390$	Center East $n = 175$	Center West $n = 490$	Kyiv City $n = 143$	Crimea $n = 96$
Bound to be conflict	6.2%	9.2%	3.6%	8.6%	7.3%	5.6%	17.7%
Can get along	93.8%	90.8%	96.4%	91.4%	92.7%	94.4%	82.3%

An examination of Table 5.4 is illuminating, more for what it says about a lack of regional polarization on attitudes toward ethnic conflict than for the regional differences that we observe. Looking particularly at the South and East, where there are large percentages of ethnic Russians and Russophones, regional influences on attitudes toward ethnic conflict remain mostly unrevealed. Singling out the Crimean region, if we look at the 1993 data we see that respondents in Crimea are in tune with respondents in the rest of the country. The 1995 data suggest that Crimean respondents were, perhaps not surprisingly, slightly *less* likely to believe that there was bound to be conflict between ethnic groups. However, in the Crimea in 1998 we do see a significant increase in the percentage of respondents who believe that there is bound to be conflict. It may at first seem a paradox that attitudes toward the likelihood of ethnic conflict were low and stable in 1993 and 1995 when the threat of separatist movements was greatest, and increasing in 1998, well after the separatist movements had collapsed. This, however, would be consistent with the growing hostilities between ethnic Russians and Crimean Tartars on the peninsula in the last four years. The Crimean Tartar leadership has been well organized in pressing for their legal rights and for protection against what they perceive to be discrimination by a Russian majority intent on preserving its economic and political advantages.[27] At the same time, there has been a disquieting trend among the younger radical Tartars to forward their agenda by violent means.[28] What actually might be manifesting itself, then, is not interethnic discord between ethnic Russians and ethnic Ukrainians, but rather discord between ethnic Russians and Crimean Tartars.

In the West, where Ukrainian nationalists are more likely to be found, the regional impact of attitudes toward ethnic conflict is not evident in any year. The same holds true for Kyiv City. In 1995, we do see a slightly increased percentage of respondents in the Center-West who believe there is bound to be ethnic conflict, and a more significant percentage in the Center-East who feel similarly. Sub-region examination reveals the largest percentage increases in the Sumy and Poltava *oblasti*. Unfortunately small sample size on the *oblast* level makes it difficult to explain with any confidence what factors may have led to this increase in those who believe there is bound to be conflict. Encouragingly, the 1998 responses do not reflect the same tendencies.

Still, even taking into account the Center-East figure in 1995 and the Crimea figure in 1998, the overall trend is clear. Expectations of ethnic conflict are generally low in all the regions in all three years.

ETHNIC DISTANCE AND ETHNIC CONFLICT

The eminent scholar on ethno-nationalism, Walker Connor, has written that: "ethnic strife is too often superficially discerned as principally predicated upon language, religion, customs, economic inequality, or some other tangible element. But what is fundamentally involved in such a conflict is that divergence of basic identity which manifests itself in the "us-them" syndrome."[29]

This "'us-them' syndrome," otherwise referred to in the literature as "ethnic schism" or "ethnic distance," has been examined by a number of scholars on both an all-Ukrainian and regional level.[30] Taras Kuzio concludes that, outside of Crimea, an "us-them" syndrome is largely absent from Ukraine along either ethnic or linguistic divisions. Ian Bremmer, while pointing out ethnic stereotyping differentiations in L'viv, Kyiv, and Simferopol, similarly believes that ethnic Ukrainians and ethnic Russians "exhibit a low sense of ethnic schism."[31] Liber, while stressing that ethnic distance perceptions do vary according to region, does not view these differences as insurmountable obstacles to Ukrainian state building because of the Ukrainian peoples' common longing for peace and stability. The following section attempts to explore some of these contentions.

Table 5.5 reflects responses of both ethnic Ukrainians and ethnic Russians when asked how much they have in common in their views and way of life with the Ukrainian ethnic group. A number of scholars have cautioned against viewing ethnic groups as monoliths and failing to take into account diversity and heterogeneity subsumed under broad ethnic labels.[32] It should not necessarily be assumed, then, that all ethnic Ukrainians believe they share common views and a way of life. However, the survey evidence suggesting that ethnic Ukrainians do indeed believe that they have a great deal or a lot in common with fellow members of their ethnic group is quite compelling on the all-Ukraine level. Roughly 99% of ethnic Ukrainian respondents believe they have a great deal or a lot in common in their views and way of life with other ethnic Ukrainians. It is apparent, as well, that ethnic Russians, at almost the same levels, also believe they have a great deal or a lot in common with ethnic Ukrainians. In fact, looking at the D.I. in each year, one can see that ethnic Ukrainians and ethnic Russian responses are almost identical.

Table 5.5
How Much Do You Feel You Have in Common—in Your Views and Way of Life— with Members of the Ukrainian Ethnic Group? (by Ethnic Group)

	1993 n = 2261		1995 n = 2298		1998 n = 2345	
	Ukrainian n = 1755	Russian n = 506	Ukrainian n = 1762	Russian n = 536	Ukrainian n = 1800	Russian n = 545
A great deal or quite a lot	98.6%	97.2%	98.9%	98.1%	99.1%	97.4%
Little or nothing at all	1.4%	2.8%	1.1%	1.9%	.9%	2.6%
Difference Index	1.4%		.8%		1.7%	

The similar responses can be interpreted in different ways. Following Connor's assertions, the ethnic distance perceptions of ethnic Russians are quite encouraging for the prospects of inter ethnic peace and are consistent with attitudes of ethnic Russians toward the likelihood of ethnic conflict. If ethnic Russians have felt themselves to be the target of nationalizing policies, it does not seem to be reflected in ethnic distance measures in any year. Still, some may see it differently. It is possible to argue that the ethnic Russian response is consistent with the legacy of Russian colonialism and the Russian view that ethnic Ukrainians are not a distinct people. This may or may not be true. The percentages do not reflect the responses of a dominant ethnic group within their empire; they reflect a minority ethnic group within a Ukrainian state. Second, the question in the survey is formulated such that it is asking respondents to comment on how much they have in common with ethnic Ukrainians, rather than asking the respondents to evaluate how much ethnic Ukrainians have in common with them.

Yet ethnic distance is not a unidirectional concept. It is important to examine how both ethnic groups view their differences. If ethnic Russians do not feel significant levels of ethnic distance from ethnic Ukrainians, then how much do ethnic Ukrainians feel that they have in common with ethnic Russians? Large differences in perceptions of ethnic distance vis-à-vis each other might lend support to those who believe that the low ethnic distance perceptions of ethnic Russians toward ethnic Ukrainians impede rather than aid harmonious interethnic relations between the two groups. In Table 5.6, we do see that there are differences between ethnic Ukrainians and ethnic Russians in their perception of ethnic distance from the Russian ethnic group. While ethnic Russians show the same levels of ethnic distance from the Russian ethnic group as they did from the Ukrainian ethnic group, ethnic Ukrainians perceive a greater degree of ethnic distance from the Russian ethnic group than from their own ethnic group.

Table 5.6
How Much Do You Feel You Have in Common—in Your Views and Way of Life—with Members of the Russian Ethnic Group? (by Ethnic Group)

	1993 n = 2245		1995 n = 2278		1998 n = 2333	
	Ukrainian n = 1740	Russian n = 505	Ukrainian n = 1742	Russian n = 536	Ukrainian n = 1790	Russian n = 543
A great deal or quite a lot	88.3%	97.4%	89.0%	98.3%	86.7%	98.5%
Little or nothing at all	11.7%	2.6%	11.0%	1.7%	13.3%	1.5%
Difference Index	9.1%		9.3%		11.8%	

Yet, despite the differences in perceptions of ethnic distance between each ethnic group, what stands out is that high percentages of ethnic Ukrainians feel they have a great deal or a lot in common with ethnic Russians. Ethnic distance perceptions between ethnic Ukrainians and ethnic Russians, then, are generally very low. The difference indexes remain fairly consistent from year to year with a slight increase in 1998. We will note from Table 5.2 that this slight increase is not accompanied by an increase in percentages of either ethnic group who feel there is bound to be ethnic conflict.

If we look at the same question by "language at home" instead of ethnicity, we see the same patterns emerge with only very slight variations. Table 5.7 shows extremely high percentages of both Ukrainophones and Russophones who believe they have a great deal or a lot in common with the Ukrainian ethnic group. The D.I.s range from just 1.2% to 2.2%.

In Table 5.8 we see that Ukrainophones and Russophones have different perceptions of commonality with the Russian ethnic group, yet the percentages of both groups who feel they have a great deal or a lot in common still remain very high. A comparison of Tables 5.6 and 5.8 will reveal slightly lower percentages of Ukrainophones than ethnic Ukrainians who feel a great deal or a lot in common with the Russian ethnic group. Consequently the difference indexes in 1993, 1995, and 1998 are greater in Table 5.8 than they are in Table 5.6. This is almost certainly a reflection of ethnic Ukrainians who speak Ukrainian at home feeling more distinct from ethnic Russians than ethnic Ukrainians who speak Russian at home.

Table 5.7
How Much Do you Feel You Have in Common—in Your Views and Way of Life—with Members of the Ukrainian Ethnic Group? (by Language at Home)

	1993 $n = 2362$		1995 $n = 2407$		1998 $n = 2415$	
	Ukrainian $n = 1284$	Russian $n = 1078$	Ukrainian $n = 1311$	Russian $n = 1096$	Ukrainian $n = 1317$	Russian $n = 1098$
A great deal or quite a lot	99.0%	96.8%	99.0%	97.8%	99.2%	97.7%
Little or nothing at all	1.0%	3.2%	1.0%	2.2%	0.8%	2.3%
Difference Index	2.2%		1.2%		1.5%	

Table 5.8
How Much Do You Feel You Have in Common—in Your Views and Way of Life—with Members of the Russian Ethnic Group? (by Language at Home)

	1993 $n = 2347$		1995 $n = 2384$		1998 $n = 2403$	
	Ukrainian $n = 1262$	Russian $n = 1085$	Ukrainian $n = 1289$	Russian $n = 1095$	Ukrainian $n = 1305$	Russian $n = 1098$
A great deal or quite a lot	85.5%	95.8%	85.0%	98.3%	83.2%	97.2%
Little or nothing at all	14.5%	4.2%	15.0%	1.7%	16.8%	2.8%
Difference Index	10.3%		13.3%		14.0%	

If we examine the same questions on a regional level, we see from Table 5.9 that high percentages of respondents in each region in 1993, 1995, and 1998 feel that they have a great deal or quite a lot in common with the Ukrainian ethnic group. What may surprise observers is that the percentages are nearly identical in six of the seven regions. Those who focus on East/West divisions in Ukraine might be surprised to see no variation on attitudes toward ethnic distance from Ukrainians in these two regions. As might be expected, the lowest percentages are in Crimea, yet, perhaps surprisingly, even these percentages do not fall below 91% in any year.

Table 5.9
How Much Do You Feel You Have in Common—in Your Views and Way of Life— with Members of the Ukrainian Ethnic Group? (by Region)

1993						
	East $n = 635$	South $n = 128$	West $n = 463$	Center East $n = 212$	Center West $n = 644$	Kyiv City $n = 207$	Crimea $n = 126$
A great deal or quite a lot	97.5%	97.7%	97.0%	98.1%	98.8%	98.1%	91.3%
Little or nothing at all	2.5%	2.3%	3.0%	1.9%	1.2%	1.9%	8.7%
1995						
	East $n = 728$	South $n = 280$	West $n = 427$	Center East $n = 221$	Center West $n = 533$	Kyiv City $n = 154$	Crimea $n = 112$
A great deal or quite a lot	98.6%	96.1%	97.9%	98.6%	99.2%	98.1%	94.6%
Little or nothing at all	1.4%	3.9%	2.1%	1.4%	.8%	1.9%	5.4%
1998						
	East $n = 726$	South $n = 278$	West $n = 439$	Center East $n = 239$	Center West $n = 525$	Kyiv City $n = 154$	Crimea $n = 108$
A great deal or quite a lot	98.5%	99.6%	98.6%	100%	97.3%	99.4%	93.5%
Little or nothing at all	1.5%	.4%	1.4%	0%	2.7%	.6%	6.5%

From Table 5.10, we do see more regional variation and variation from year to year in ethnic distance when respondents are asked how much they have in common in their views and way of life with the Russian ethnic group. In the

East and in the South, very high percentages of respondents feel they have a great deal or quite a lot in common with the Russian ethnic group. In the West, however, as might be expected from its different historical legacy and from its reputation as the heartland of Ukrainian nationalism, significantly smaller percentages of respondents believed they had a great deal or a lot in common with the Russian ethnic group. Moreover, while the percentages in the West were nearly the same in 1993 and in 1995, in 1998 we see the figure of those who believe they have a great deal or quite a lot in common with the Russian ethnic group drop to just over 62%.

Table 5.10
How Much Do You Feel You Have in Common—in Your Niews and Way of Life—with Members of the Russian Ethnic Group? (by Region)

1993						
	East $n = 635$	South $n = 128$	West $n = 444$	Center East $n = 211$	Center West $n = 642$	Kyiv City $n = 212$	Crimea $n = 126$
A great deal or quite a lot	97.0%	97.7%	72.5%	92.9%	91.0%	89.6%	93.7%
Little or nothing at all	3.0%	2.3%	27.5%	7.1%	9.0%	10.4%	6.3%
1995						
	East $n = 729$	South $n = 279$	West $n = 414$	Center East $n = 218$	Center West $n = 528$	Kyiv City $n = 154$	Crimea $n = 111$
A great deal or quite a lot	98.8%	95.0%	71.0%	89.0%	92.0%	94.2%	97.3%
Little or nothing at all	1.2%	5.0%	29.0%	11.0%	8.0%	5.8%	2.7%
1998						
	East $n = 726$	South $n = 276$	West $n = 431$	Center East $n = 236$	Center West $n = 524$	Kyiv City $n = 155$	Crimea $n = 109$
A great deal or quite a lot	97.7%	97.8%	62.4%	97.9%	89.5%	92.9%	99.1%
Little or nothing at all	2.3%	2.2%	37.6%	2.1%	10.5%	7.1%	.9%

Thus, an important point to arise from this study is that ethnic distance between respondents and the Russian ethnic group seem to be widening in the
West. In the Center-East, the percentage figures of those who feel they have a
great deal or quite a lot in common with ethnic Russians are high. In the Center-
West and in Kyiv City the percentages of those who feel a great deal or quite a
lot of commonality with ethnic Russians are also high in the three years under
investigation. Perceptions of ethnic distance between respondents and ethnic
Russians are low in Crimea as we might expect, and the survey trend indicates
that ethnic distance diminished in each year.

If we compare respondents' perceptions of ethnic distance from both ethnic
Ukrainians and ethnic Russians in the three years, several patterns emerge that
might reveal something about identities in each of the regions. In the East and in
the South, very high percentages of respondents felt that they had a great deal or
quite a lot in common with both ethnic Ukrainians and ethnic Russians. Ethnic
distance between ethnic Russians and ethnic Ukrainians, then, would appear to
be extremely low in these regions. A number of explanations might account for
this. It is possible that the long intermingling of ethnic Ukrainians and ethnic
Russians in this region has blurred ethnic boundaries and distinctions. It is also
plausible that a regional identity, based on a variety of social, cultural, and economic factors, is more powerfully felt than identities based on ethnicity. It might
be argued as well that what we are witnessing in these regions is actually the
legacy of a supra state Soviet identity that transcends ethnic boundaries (which
is reflected in polls where respondents describe their identity as Soviet). Without
attempting to delve deeper into which of these, or other explanations best account for ethnic distance attitudes in these regions, it does seem apparent that an
"us-them syndrome" based on ethnicity is absent in the East and in the South.

In the West, we see quite another story. There are significant differences
when comparing respondents' perceptions of ethnic distance from ethnic
Ukrainians and ethnic Russians. Very high percentages of respondents feel they
have a great deal or quite a lot in common with ethnic Ukrainians. On the other
hand, much lower percentages of respondents feel that they have a great deal or
quite a lot in common with the Russian ethnic group. This gulf in ethnic distance
perceptions suggests a much more powerful ethnicity-based identity in the West
in comparison with the other regions. It appears that these significant ethnic distance perceptions are unidirectional and probably exclusive to the majority
Ukrainian ethnic group which is overwhelmingly dominant in the region. It
should also be noted, however, that on average in the three years, over two-
thirds of the respondents believed they had a great deal or quite a lot in common
with the Russian ethnic group. Thus if we do see an "us-them syndrome" in the
West, it is not the dominant perception in the region and it is likely to be a perception of mostly ethnic Ukrainians.

The Center-East is a region that seems to have witnessed a slight change in
attitudes toward ethnic distance over the five years in which the surveys were
conducted. High percentages of respondents in this region have felt a great deal
or quite a lot in common with members of the Ukrainian ethnic group in the

three survey years. In 1993 and 1995, slightly lower percentages of respondents felt they had a great deal or quite a lot in common with the Russian ethnic group. This would suggest perhaps that a distinct ethnic Ukrainian identity, however weak, existed alongside an identity that transcended ethnicity. However, by 1998, the percentage of respondents who felt they had a great deal or quite a lot in common with ethnic Russians rose to 98%. This is in the same year that 100% of the respondents felt they had a great deal or quite a lot in common with ethnic Ukrainians. By 1998 then, we witness ethnic distance measures in the Center-East similar to those found in the East and in the South. The "us-them syndrome" seems completely absent.

Ethnic distance measures in the Center-West and in Kyiv City reveal patterns similar to those found in the Center-East in 1993 and in 1995. High percentages of respondents felt that they had a great deal or quite a lot in common with the Ukrainian ethnic group. Lower percentages of respondents felt that they had a great deal or quite a lot in common with ethnic Russians. There are low perceptions of ethnic distance between groups in these regions, although it seems likely that ethnic Ukrainians feel more distinct from ethnic Russians than ethnic Russians do from ethnic Ukrainians. The "us-them syndrome" appears to be at the most extremely weak.

Crimea is the only region where respondents feel a greater affinity toward the Russian rather than the Ukrainian ethnic group in each of the surveys conducted. This may not come as a surprise since Crimea is the only region in Ukraine where ethnic Russians constitute the majority population and where Russian ethnic identity is strongest. It might come as a surprise, however, that there are overall greater disparities in respondents' views toward ethnic Ukrainians and ethnic Russians in the Center-East in 1993 and 1995, and in the Center-West and Kyiv City in all three years, than in Crimea. In no year do fewer than 91% of the respondents feel that they have a great deal or quite a lot in common with the Ukrainian or Russian ethnic groups. Thus, while it may be argued that there is more of a Russian rather than Ukrainian identity in the region, there are still rather low perceptions of ethnic distance.

How do ethnic distance measures, then, relate to attitudes toward ethnic conflict? First, at an all-Ukraine level, there are extremely low perceptions of ethnic distance toward the Ukrainian ethnic group by both ethnic Russians and ethnic Ukrainians. The same holds true if we look specifically at Russophones and Ukrainophones. There are higher perceptions of ethnic distance toward the Russian ethnic group by both ethnic Ukrainians and Ukrainophones. Yet overall the ethnic distance measures are still low. If we were to accept Connor's paradigm that ethnic strife is often predicated on an "us-them syndrome," then we would find the low numbers of respondents on the all-Ukraine level who believe there is bound to be conflict consistent with low perceptions of ethnic strife. However, ethnic distance measures at the regional level might bring into question the efficacy of Connors assertion. We still find low and very low perceptions of ethnic distance in most regions, including Crimea.

Yet, in the West there does seem to be a significant and growing feeling among ethnic Ukrainians that they are distinct from the Russian ethnic group. Following Connor, we might expect this to be manifested in attitudes toward the likelihood of ethnic conflict at the regional level. However, looking at Table 5.4 we note that growing ethnic distance perceptions in the West are not accompanied by an increase in those who believe there is bound to be conflict. In fact, comparing Tables 5.4 and 5.10 we note that the greatest perception of ethnic distance in the West occurs in 1998, the same year where the lowest percentage of respondents in the West believe there is bound to be conflict. Liber's claim that ethnic distance measures are outweighed by an overall desire among the population for peace and stability seems to be supported.

A VIEW OF ETHNIC DIVISIONS

Thus far, this chapter has attempted to demonstrate that attitudes toward ethnic conflict have remained stable over time and that expectations on the inevitability of conflict based on ethnicity are low. This is also true when we look at language. A look at attitudes in the regions did reveal some regional differences in particular years, but overall attitudinal trends were mostly unaffected. Ethnic distance perceptions theorized as indicators of ethnic strife, are low in Ukraine at the mass level. Even where ethnic distance measures seem significant at the regional level, they seem weak predictors of attitudes toward ethnic conflict. If ethnic Russians and Russophones have seen the "enraged face of Mr. Hyde," or if they have had perceptions of a nationalizing strategy on the part of the Ukrainian state, it has not in any substantial way manifested itself in attitudes toward ethnic conflict or, for that matter, in perceptions of ethnic distance.[33] This is not to argue, however, the absence of divisions between ethnic Ukrainians and ethnic Russians over certain issues. Arel and Laitin both point to language as a divisive issue in Ukraine. Table 5.11, which reveals ethnic Ukrainian and ethnic Russian views toward language instruction in schools, confirms this.

From Table 5.11 we see deep divisions between ethnic Russians and ethnic Ukrainians on the issue of minority ethnic groups being taught in Ukrainian. The divisions occur in all three years, and the difference index increases from year to year. In 1993 and 1995 the ethnic Ukrainian responses were almost identical. In neither year did a majority of ethnic Ukrainians strongly agree or agree as opposed to neither agree nor disagree, disagree, or strongly disagree with the proposition that all minority ethnic groups should be taught in Ukrainian. A subethnic group analysis reveals that Ukrainophone Ukrainians in 1993 and 1995 were evenly split between the two categories, while only 19% to 25% of Russophone Ukrainians strongly agreed or agreed with the statement. Ethnic Ukrainians were slightly under 1.5 times more likely to neither agree nor disagree, disagree, or strongly disagree than to strongly agree or agree with minority ethnic groups being taught in Ukrainian. On the other hand, ethnic Russians in 1993 were over three times more likely to feel the same way. The division is more pronounced in 1995 where we see ethnic Russians five times more likely to have no opinion or disagree than to agree with the statement in Table 5.11. Deep divisions and interesting trends can be seen in 1998 as well. The percentage of ethnic Ukrainians who strongly agree or agree with the statement that all minority groups should be taught in the Ukrainian language increases to nearly 50%. The percentage of ethnic Russians who strongly agree or agree with the statement also increases from 1995, however ethnic Russians are still almost four times more likely to neither agree nor disagree, disagree, or strongly disagree with the statement. Comparing Ukrainian and Russian responses in each year, Ukrainians were about twice as likely as Russians to strongly agree or agree with minority groups in Ukraine being taught in Ukrainian.

Table 5.11
All Minority Ethnic Groups in This Country Should Have to Be Taught in Ukrainian (by Ethnic Group)

	1993 $n = 2117$		1995 $n = 2216$		1998 $n = 2241$	
	Ukrainian $n = 1632$	Russian $n = 485$	Ukrainian $n = 1683$	Russian $n = 519$	Ukrainian $n = 1711$	Russian $n = 530$
Agree or strongly agree	41.9%	23.3%	41.2%	16.2%	48.6%	20.2%
Neither agree nor disagree, disagree, or strongly disagree	58.1%	76.7%	58.8%	83.8%	51.4%	79.8%
Difference Index	18.6%		25.0%		28.4%	

We would be telling only a partial story if we failed to look at the language factor on the same issue. In every year there is a greater level of polarity between Ukrainophones and Russophones on this issue than the polarity exhibited between ethnic Ukrainians and ethnic Russians. One can readily see from Table 5.12 that the significant divisions between the Ukrainophones and Russophones occur in all three years. The difference indexes show the greatest divisions between Ukrainophones and Russophones to occur in 1995, before diminishing somewhat in 1998.

Slightly increasing percentages of Ukrainophones were more likely to strongly agree or agree than to neither agree nor disagree, disagree, or strongly disagree with the statement that minority groups should be taught in Ukrainian. Russophones do not replicate exactly the converse pattern. Although Russophones were significantly more likely to neither agree nor disagree, disagree, or strongly disagree than to agree or strongly agree in all three years, the differential did not increase in each year. In 1993 Russophones were over three times more likely to have no opinion or to disagree than to agree with ethnic minorities' being taught in Ukrainian. In 1995, Russophones were five times more likely to have the same attitude. By 1998, Russophones were just three times more likely to possess the same view. Comparing Ukrainophone and Russophone responses in each year, Ukrainophones were over twice as likely as Russophones to agree with minority groups' being taught in Ukrainian in 1993 and 1998. In 1995 Ukrainophones were three times more likely to agree with that same view.

Table 5.12
All Minority Ethnic Groups in This Country Should Have to Be Taught in Ukrainian (by Language at Home)

	1993 n = 2212		1995 n = 2310		1998 n = 2309	
	Ukrainian n = 1180	Russian n = 1032	Ukrainian n = 1240	Russian n = 1070	Ukrainian n = 1254	Russian n = 1055
Agree or strongly agree	49.8%	22.8%	50.7%	16.2%	55.5%	25.3%
Neither agree nor disagree, eisagree, or strongly disagree	50.2%	77.2%	49.3%	83.8%	44.5%	74.7%
Difference Index	27.0%		34.5%		30.2%	

A look at this question by region in the three survey years reveals some interesting figures (see Table 5.13). In the East, the percentage of respondents who strongly agree or agree with the statement that all minority groups should be taught in Ukrainian barely exceeds 25% in any of the three survey years. There is a significant decrease in the percentage who agree with the statement in 1995, but by 1998 the percentage returns to slightly below the 1993 figure. The figures might be consistent with Arel's view that there was a perception in the region, especially on the language issue, that the state was pursuing a nationalizing line. The drop in those who strongly agreed or agreed with minorities being taught in Ukrainian might have been a reaction to this perception.

However, the same trend does not seem to be evident in the South. In the South, the percentage of respondents who strongly agreed or agreed remained stable in 1993 and 1995. In fact, the 1995 figure is slightly higher than the 1993 figure. What is most surprising is that the 1998 percentage figure jumped to 38%. Thus, even though a minority of respondents in the South strongly agree or agree that minority groups should be taught in Ukrainian the numbers have swelled substantially since 1993.

The West is the only region where a substantial majority of the respondents in all three years strongly agreed or agreed that all minority groups in Ukraine should be taught in Ukrainian. In 1993, 57% of respondents in the West strongly agreed or agreed with this view. The percentage of respondents answering similarly increased to about 70% in 1995 and 1998. Thus there has not only been a significant increase in this view, but the view remained stable between 1995 and 1998.

Table 5.13
All Minority Ethnic Groups in This Country Should Have to Be Taught in Ukrainian (by Region)

1993						
	East $n = 598$	South $n = 115$	West $n = 450$	Center East $n = 185$	Center West $n = 586$	Kyiv City $n = 201$	Crimea $n = 123$
Agree or Strongly agree	25.4%	22.6%	57.3%	42.7%	36.3%	42.3%	11.4%
Neither agree nor disagree, disagree, or strongly disagree	74.6%	77.4%	42.7%	57.3%	63.7%	57.7%	88.6%
1995						
	East $n = 710$	South $n = 269$	West $n = 402$	Center East $n = 210$	Center West $n = 512$	Kyiv City $n = 148$	Crimea $n = 105$
Agree or Strongly agree	15.8%	24.9%	69.9%	44.3%	41.2%	29.7%	2.9%
Neither agree nor disagree, disagree, or strongly disagree	84.2%	75.1%	30.1%	55.7%	58.8%	70.3%	97.1%
1998						
	East $n = 710$	South $n = 256$	West $n = 426$	Center East $n = 203$	Center West $n = 515$	Kyiv City $n = 152$	Crimea $n = 100$
Agree or strongly agree	23.5%	38.3%	70.4%	30.5%	51.5%	52.0%	8.0%
Neither agree nor disagree, disagree, or strongly disagree	76.5%	61.7%	29.6%	69.5%	48.8%	48.0%	92.0%

The Center-East seems to have shown the opposite trend. Although a minority of respondents in 1993 strongly agreed or agreed with the view that all minority ethnic groups should be taught in Ukrainian, the percentage was about 43%, much higher than in the East and in the South. The percentage slightly increased in 1995, but in 1998 there was a substantial decrease in the percentage of respondents with this view. The Center-East, then, is the only region in 1998 that has shown a decrease in the percentages in comparison to 1995 levels.

The Center-West, on the other hand, has shown a steady increase in the percentages of respondents who strongly agree or agree that all minority ethnic groups should be taught in Ukrainian. The percentages in 1993 and 1995 were smaller than in the Center-East in those same years. However, by 1998, over a majority of the respondents strongly agree or agree with the view that all minority ethnic groups in Ukraine should be taught in Ukrainian.

Kyiv City is interesting because of the fluctuation from year to year. In 1993, a substantial minority of respondents strongly agreed or agreed with the view that all ethnic minorities should be taught in Ukrainian. This figure, however, dropped to below 30% in 1995. By 1998, however, a majority of respondents agreed with this view.

In Crimea, where 1989 census figures calculated the percentage of Russophones to be around 82%, we not surprisingly find the lowest percentages in all three years of respondents who strongly agree or agree that all ethnic minorities should be taught in Ukrainian. The pattern in Crimea strongly resembles the pattern in the East over the three years. In 1993, the percentage of respondents who agreed with ethnic minorities being taught in Ukrainian was only 11%. That percentage decreased to just 3% in 1995, before increasing slightly in 1998. The sample size in Crimea is quite small, so that trends should be viewed with caution. However, it is clear that the overwhelming majority in the autonomous republic neither agree nor disagree, disagree, or strongly disagree that all minority groups in Ukraine should be taught in Ukrainian.

What seems clear when we examine the views of respondents on the issue of minorities being taught in Ukrainian is that no overall trend holds true for all the regions. That is not to say that there have not been interesting attitudinal shifts on this issue. In 1993, only in the West could there be found a majority of respondents who agreed that all minority ethnic groups should be taught in Ukrainian. In 1998, a majority of respondents in three regions agreed with that view. Three regions, the East, Kyiv City, and Crimea, experienced sharp drops in the percentages, between 1993 and 1995, of respondents who agreed with minority ethnic groups' being taught in Ukrainian. In all three regions, the percentages increased, albeit by different degrees, in 1998.

Language instruction in schools has been a contentious issue in Ukraine. From the preceding tables we have, not surprisingly, seen differences between both ethnic groups and language groups on this question. There have been significant trends and fluctuations in particular regions on this issue as well. Despite these differences, it is also clear that these have not been strongly manifested in attitudes toward ethnic conflict, which have remained mostly stable over time.

ELECTORAL POLARITY

The previous section highlighted the ethnic and language division around the issue of language instruction in schools. Yet are ethnic divisions manifested in electoral politics? Arel makes the case that the 1994 presidential elections demonstrated a polarization in politics along a linguistic/regional dimension rather than an economic one. The following table attempts to present at voting preferences according to ethnicity. In Table 5.14 are outlined presidential voting preferences by ethnic group for the years 1993, 1995, and 1998.[34] Since respondents were not limited in their choice of candidates, candidates were loosely assigned into two camps.[35] The first camp, whose mainstay is Leonid Kravchuk, might be viewed as having a more nationalist orientation on issues such as language and relations with Russia than the second camp, whose mainstay is Leonid Kuchma. The grouping of candidates according to nationalist orientation might give us a better idea of how salient a dimension this is in influencing ethnic, linguistic, and regional electoral behavior. Grouping candidates according to this dimension is replete with difficulties. For example, Kuzio has argued that Kravchuk and Kuchma have had a great deal more in common than not on issues of defining the Ukrainian state, and that both "promoted the view that Ukraine needs political centrism in its current stage of state and nation-building."[36] Kuzio further asserts that far from donning the nationalist cloak, Kravchuk's policies were "pluralistic, multicultural, and liberal."[37] Yet, if there are broad areas of agreement between Kravchuk and Kuchma, their differences on certain national issues seem to have clearly been the focus in the 1994 presidential elections. These differences would been evident not only in the run up to the 1994 elections, but also before, when there were disagreements between the two in 1992 and 1993 on how closely Ukraine should integrate into the CIS.[38]

Another hazard in grouping candidates along one dimension is that it may obscure important differences along other dimensions. Relatedly, views, alliances, and defining issues may shift over time. The October–November 1999 presidential elections provide good examples of this. The *Zlahoda* bloc, which supported Kuchma's reelection bid, had among its members both Kravchuk and former Parliamentary Chairman Ivan Pluishch.[39] The "Kaniv Four" alliance, formed shortly before the October 1999 elections, consisted of Oleksandr Tkachenko, Yevhen Marchuk, Oleksandr Moroz, and Volodymyr Oliynyk— candidates with quite different reputations on nationalist issues. However, if the goal of this section is to shed light on the impact of ethnic, linguistic, and regional divisions on voting behavior, the 1999 shifts do not invalidate the 1998 candidate groupings. Rather, the 1998 data suggest that we should not have been surprised by the shifting 1999 electoral alliances, which transcended real or imagined nationalist/non-nationalist cleavages.

In Table 5.14, the trends seem fairly clear. In 1993 both ethnic Ukrainians and ethnic Russians preferred candidates who could be at least loosely characterized as having more nationalist views. It is important, however, to note the differences. Ethnic Ukrainians were slightly less than two times more likely to vote for nationalist candidates than for the other candidates. Ethnic Russians, on the other hand, were only marginally more likely to vote for the nationalist candidates in 1993. The difference index between the two ethnic groups in 1993 is just under 12%. In 1995, the difference index jumps to 25% and we see what appears to be clear and sometimes dramatic increased polarization along ethnic lines. When ethnic Ukrainian respondents were asked whom they voted for in the first round of the June 1994 presidential elections, a majority still preferred the Kravchuk grouping, albeit, interestingly, by a lesser margin than in 1993. Ethnic Russians, however, by a close to 3-to-1 margin claimed to have voted for candidates in the Kuchma grouping. Ethnic Ukrainians were almost twice as likely as ethnic Russians to vote for nationalist candidates in 1994. Ethnic Russians were more than 1.5 times as likely as Ukrainians to vote for a candidate who defined the state more in civic-territorial than in ethnocultural terms. In 1998, even considering the problems in grouping candidates, there appears to be an end to ethnic polarization. The difference index drops to roughly 9%, which is lower than the 1993 D.I. Both ethnic Ukrainians and ethnic Russians significantly preferred the Kuchma grouping of candidates, although ethnic Russians did so by a wider margin.

Table 5.14
Presidential Voting Preferences (by Ethnic Group)

Candidate Groupings	1993 (future) $n = 867$		1995 (past/1st) $n = 1722$		1998 (future) $n = 943$	
	Ukrainian $n = 686$	Russian $n = 181$	Ukrainian $n = 1340$	Russian $n = 382$	Ukrainian $n = 754$	Russian $n = 189$
Kravchuk (93, 95, 98) Chornovil (93) Pliushsch (93, 95) Lanovoi (95) Marchuk (98) Yuschenko (98)	64.9%	53.0%	51.2%	25.9%	37.3%	28.6%
Kuchma (93, 95, 98) Grinyov (93) Babich (95) Moroz (95, 98) Lazarenko (98)	35.1%	47.0%	48.8%	74.1%	62.7%	71.4%
Difference Index	11.9%		25.3%		8.7%	

It might be claimed that what is manifesting itself is actually the language divide. The percentages do indeed show a divide along the language dimension in 1993 and 1995. In 1993 the difference index in presidential voting preferences by language at home, at 16.5%, is greater than the 11.9% difference index in voting preferences by ethnicity in the same year. However, in view of the 1998 figures, the D.I. is smaller when in the comparison of Ukrainophones and Russophones than in the comparison of ethnic Ukrainians and ethnic Russians. We witness an end to polarization along a linguistic dimension in 1998.

An examination of the regional dimension of electoral preferences reveals several points. First, voter preferences differ significantly by region in 1993, 1995, and 1998. In 1993 all regions come out for the Kravchuk grouping although in varying degrees. In the 1995 surveys, regional voting polarization was consistent with the actual 1994 presidential election results, with the minor exception of the Center-West, which might be explained by a certain amount of recall bias. As we keep in mind the caveats about grouping candidates, the 1998 data show that with the exception of Kyiv City, which is split almost evenly, all regions would support a presidential candidate who possesses less of a nationalist (ethnocultural) than territorial (civic) perception of the state.

The discussion in this section is an attempt to highlight and confirm the existence of increased electoral polarity, at least reflected in the 1995 data, along an ethnic, linguistic and regional dimension. The existence of this split raised important questions about the future of Ukrainian politics and state building.[40] The splits along these divides, however, seem to have largely disappeared by 1998 if we attempt to group candidates by nationalist orientations. Moreover, alliances made prior to the 1999 presidential elections between candidates and political figures with conflicting views on such issues as language and Ukraine's relationship with Russia suggest that dimensions other than ethnicity and language were important in determining voting preferences. How ethnic conflict and other measures may or may not have been reflected in this electoral split is addressed in the next section.

COMPARING LEVELS OF ETHNIC AND LANGUAGE POLARIZATION

To glean a better understanding of ethnic and language divisions and how they may or may not have influenced voting preferences, Table 5.15 has been devised. The numbers in this table have been derived by maximizing the ratios of the responses of ethnic Ukrainians to ethnic Russians, or Ukrainophones to Russophones, found in the tables under the column headings. As an example, in Table 5.2, for 1993, the ratio between ethnic Ukrainians and ethnic Russians who believe there is bound to be conflict is 8.6/9.8 or 0.87. The ratio of ethnic Ukrainians to ethnic Russians who believe ethnic groups can get along is 91.4/90.2 or 1.01. The resultant ratio 0.87/1.01 can be otherwise expressed as 0.86. If ethnic Ukrainians and ethnic Russians had no differences in their views, then the number derived would be 1. The further away the derived number is from 1, the greater the differences between ethnic Ukrainians and ethnic Russians or Ukrainophones and Russophones. By performing the same operation for each of the tables, we should be able to see the more clearly degree of differences between groups, how the magnitude of those differences have changed over time, and, perhaps most important, the relationships between measures.

The main focus has been on ethnic conflict. What stands out are the minimal differences between ethnic Ukrainians and ethnic Russians on the issue of conflict and the stability of those views over time. Even when increased voting polarity by ethnicity occurs, such as between 1993 and 1995, we do not see that polarity reflected in views toward ethnic conflict, nor are deep ethnic divides over language use in school reflected in ethnic Ukrainian and ethnic Russian views toward conflict.

Table 5.15
Trends in Ethnic and Language Polarization

	Ethnic Conflict by ethnicity (Table 5.2)	Ethnic Conflict by language (Table 5.3)	Language in schools by ethnicity (Table 5.11)	Language in schools by language (Table 5.12)	Voting preference by ethnicity (Table 5.14)	Voting preferences by Language*
1993	0.86	1.10	2.37	3.35	1.64	2.04
1995	0.92	1.49	3.63	5.30	3.03	2.50
1998	0.86	0.72	3.77	3.67	1.40	1.21

*In 1993, 69.7% of Ukrainophones preferred candidates in the Kravchuk grouping, as opposed to 30.3% preferring candidates in the Kuchma grouping. In the same year, 53.2% of Russophones preferred candidates in the Kravchuk grouping, as opposed to 46.8% preferring candidates in the Kuchma grouping. In 1995, 54.8% of Ukrainophones preferred candidates in the Kravchuk grouping, as opposed to 45.2% preferring candidates in the Kuchma grouping. In the same year, 32.3% of Russophones preferred candidates in the Kravchuk grouping, as opposed to 67.7% preferring candidates in the Kuchma grouping. In 1998, 37.6% of Ukrainophones preferred candidates in the Kravchuk grouping," as opposed to 62.4% preferring candidates in the Kuchma grouping. In the same year, 33.2% of Russophones preferred candidates in the Kravchuk grouping, as opposed to 66.8% preferring candidates in the Kuchma grouping.

We see similar patterns when we look at the language factor and how it relates to ethnic conflict. Perhaps not surprisingly, considering the language makeup of Ukraine, we see especially in the 1993 and 1995 data, deep divisions among Ukrainophones and Russophones over language use in school. We do not, however, see the divide at anywhere near the same level in attitudes toward conflict.

We might infer other things as well from the table. If we do not find a relationship between voting preferences and ethnic conflict, we still might see a relationship between the "language at school" variable and voting preferences. For example, a comparison of the "language in school by ethnicity" column with the "voting by ethnicity" column possibly reveals a relationship between the two variables in an examination the trends in 1993 and 1995. Although differences between ethnic Ukrainians and ethnic Russians in voting preferences are smaller than the differences in views toward language in schools in 1993 and 1995, the magnitudinal change is quite similar. Interestingly, the same trends are not markedly evident when you look at these variables by language. An examination of columns 4 and 6 reveals that the magnitudinal change in language in schools by language is not concomitant with a similar change in voting preferences by language.

Patterns, when they exist, should be viewed cautiously. However, it does appear that voting polarization and differences in voting preferences by language and ethnicity have largely disappeared by 1998. While this seems consistent with measures of ethnic conflict, we know from the 1995 data the weakness of ethnic conflict measures against the reality of polarization. Moreover, differences between ethnic Ukrainians and ethnic Russians and Ukrainophones and Russophones on views toward language in schools in 1998 remain great. Measures other than the ones offered in this chapter may or may not better explain voting preferences and how they have changed over time. For example, Arel asserts that views on relation towards Russia might be a measure that could help explain changes in voting polarity between 1993 and 1995 (by 1997–1999 Russian-Ukrainian relations had stabilized after a treaty was signed and ratified). Another measure that might help us explain voting preferences and polarity might be the increasing partisanship of Ukrainian voters.

INCREASING PARTISANSHIP

Stephen Whitefield and Geoffrey Evans have made a strong case for the existence of increasing partisanship in Eastern Europe since 1991.[41] Their view is that despite all the difficulties encountered by post-communist states, such as "newness to democracy, the weak organizational links between parties and citizens, and the general social and ideological flux associated with the transition," there exist "well-structured cleavages underlying partisanship."[42] Whitefield and Evans argue that there are increasingly intelligible links between voters and parties, and presidential preferences. An examination of the survey data does demonstrate this increasing partisanship among the Ukrainian electorate. In answer to the question, Do you think of yourself as a supporter of any particular party? only 14.6% of respondents in 1993 answered positively. In 1995 this percentage increased to 22.0%. By 1998, 58.7% of respondents answered yes to the question.

More and more Ukrainian voters are identifying themselves with political parties. This increased identification would suggest that voters are becoming more politically savvy and better able to identify political preferences with parties and candidates. If in fact candidates are partly defining themselves or being defined in terms of how they stand on certain issues, we should expect this to be increasingly evident in Ukrainian voting preferences. If there was little to distinguish between candidates on economic issues in the 1994 presidential elections, differences on language issues or the fact that Kuchma chose to campaign in

Russian[43] naturally would not be lost on even the most politically naïve voter. It is likely that as Ukrainian voters become increasingly more sophisticated they will be better able to distinguish candidates and party views on issues important to them.

Not only are Ukrainian voters becoming increasingly more partisan, but they are also becoming more increasingly involved with the democratic process. In response to the question, If there were a presidential election tomorrow whom would you most likely vote for? 26.9% of the respondents in 1993 indicated that they would not vote. In 1995 this percentage decreased to 22.9%. By 1998, the number of respondents saying they would note vote decreased to 14.6%. This trend seemed to be confirmed by the first round of the Ukrainian presidential elections of October 1999. By most accounts campaigning was nasty and dirty. Under these circumstances we might expect a lower voter turnout from an electorate turned off by unsavory campaign tactics. Instead, voter turnout was higher than it was in 1994.

How might increased partisanship explain trends in Table 5.15? It might be argued that the polarity exhibited in 1995, compared to 1993, can at least be partially explained by partisanship. Voters in 1995 increasingly were able to identify where the candidates stood on issues. Thus issue cleavages, such as language, might have been reflected more accurately in voting preferences. The absence of polarity in 1998 might also be reflected by partisanship. Whitefield and Evans assert that ethnic divisions do not constitute the only axis of partisan polarity.[44] Perhaps another social or ideological dimension is more relevant to explaining voting preferences in 1998. The November 1999 second-round presidential results would seem to confirm this, because it offered a clear choice between two candidates—communist and anticommunist.

CONCLUSION

Attitudinal surveys in Ukraine show low expectations of ethnic conflict. This is true for ethnic Ukrainians and ethnic Russians as well as for Ukrainophones and Russophones. Moreover, with some exceptions, regional factors do not appear to have had a great impact on attitudes toward conflict. Attitudes toward ethnic conflict have remained stable, despite what we might have expected from real or perceived nationalizing policies and in the face of polarization manifested in the 1994 presidential elections.

How can the weakness of ethnic conflict measures against these expectations and realities be explained? Low perceptions of ethnic distance between ethnic Ukrainians and ethnic Russians may provide a partial answer. Yet, perhaps more important, it seems probable that both ethnic Ukrainians and ethnic Russians are seeking to address their differences through normal democratic processes rather than through conflict. This is manifested not only by the low levels of conflict that have occurred in Ukraine since the collapse of the Soviet Union, but also by the manner in which deep issue cleavages with an ethnic dimension have been addressed. Ethnic divisions on certain issues do not have to be an indication of ethnic cleavages along other dimensions. In Ukraine, there are a number of crosscutting cleavages, as we have seen with the language issue. The findings of this chapter caution against the notion that a nationalizing program is needed to hold the country together. Ethnic divisions on issues can exist in a society alongside low expectations of ethnic conflict. What may be more important are mechanisms for expressing differences.

That the citizens of Ukraine have been able to use normal democratic means to voice their preferences has in no small part been because of the inclusive citizenship policy and absence of political discrimination. Moreover, Ukrainians, rather than demonstrating apathy toward politics, are demonstrating increased participation and partisanship, which are sure to be reflected in their future political choices. Voter preferences will be important in determining how far a real or imagined nationalizing agenda can be pursued. This is not to rule out the possibility of ethnic conflict in Ukraine, but if Ukrainians continue on the path of democratic reform, the likelihood that differences will continue to be dealt with through the democratic process remains high.

APPENDIX: DETAILS OF THE SURVEYS[45]

The questionnaires contained approximately 300 items. They were pilot tested on 50 to 100 respondents in Ukraine prior to being finalized for use in the main surveys. Back-translation of the items took several months of iterative adjustment. It was facilitated by the presence of fluent Slavonic speakers in the British team, academic translators, and the helpful contribution of East European collaborators, who also provided additional information regarding the political salience of the issues being examined. All interviews were conducted face to face in respondents' homes. Interviewers were generally experienced and were also given special training for some of the more difficult aspects of the interview schedule. Local area supervisors carried out checks on interviewers. The reliability of responses was also checked using a follow-up study of 10% of the respondents, who were randomly selected and were reinterviewed a few weeks after the main surveys. This also allowed a check on whether interviewers had obtained the interview as claimed. Dr. Mykola Churilov, Director, Institute of Sociology, Ukrainian National Academy of Sciences, Kyiv, directed the fieldwork. The sampling frame consisted of the adult population (18+) drawn from the Housing Offices' residence list of individuals. The sample achieved in 1993 was 2,537, and in 1995 and 1998 the samples achieved were 2,500.

NOTES

1. See, for example, David D. Laitin, *Identity in Formation: The Russian-Speaking Populations in the Near Abroad* (Ithaca, NY: Cornell University Press, 1998); Jeff Chinn and Robert Kaiser, *Russians as the New Minority: Ethnicity and Nationalism in the Soviet Successor States* (Boulder, CO: Westview Press, 1996); Neil Melvin, *Russians beyond Russia: The Politics of National Identity* (London: Royal Institute of International Affairs, 1995); Paul Kolstoe, *Russians in the Former Soviet Republics* (Bloomington, IN: Indiana University Press, 1995); and the collected articles edited by Vladimir Shlapen-

tokh, Munir Sendich, and Emil Payin, *The New Russian Diaspora: Russian Minorities in the Former Soviet Republics* (New York: M. E. Sharpe, 1994).

2. These numbers are taken from Chauncy Harris, "The New Russian Minorities: A Statistical Overview," *Post-Soviet Geography*, vol. 34, no. 1 (January 1993), p. 4. Harris's source is *Goskomstat*, 1991.

3. Kolstoe, *Russians in The Former Soviet Republics*, p. 170.

4. See Juan Linz and Alfred Stepan, *Problems of Democratic Transition and Consolidation in Southern Europe, South America, and Post-Communist Europe* (Baltimore: Johns Hopkins University Press, 1996).

5. See Laitin, *Identity in Formation*, and Dominique Arel, "Ukraine: The Temptation of the Nationalizing State," in Vladimir Tismaneanu, ed., *Political Culture and Civil Society in the Former Soviet Union* (Armonk, NY: M. E. Sharpe, 1995), pp. 157–188.

6. The survey data presented in this chapter were commissioned as part of the Economic and Social Research Council's East-West Programme: Grant No. Y 309 25 3025, "Emerging Forms of Political Representation and Participation in Eastern Europe," awarded to Geoffrey Evans, Stephen Whitefield, Anthony Heath, and Clive Payne as well as from an INTAS Grant, "Ethnicity, Nationality, and Citizenship in the Former Soviet Union," awarded to Geoffrey Evans and Stephen Whitefield. The surveys were conducted in May–June 1993, April–May 1995, and in April 1998. I would like to thank Stephen Whitefield for his kind permission to use these data as well as for helpful comments on an earlier draft of this chapter. All errors and omissions are, of course, my own.

7. For commentators who have taken a less-than-sanguine view of Ukraine's prospects, see, for example Paul Klebnikov, "Tinderbox," *Forbes*, 9 September 1996, pp. 158–164; Eugene Rumer, "Eurasia Letter: Will Ukraine Return to Russia?" *Foreign Policy*, no. 96, 1994, pp. 129–144, and F. Stephen Larrabee, "Ukraine: Europe's Next Crisis?" *Arms Control Today*, July/August 1994, pp. 14–19.

8. For incidents of ethnic conflict in Ukraine see Laitin, *Identity in Formation*, pp. 179–180. Laitin acknowledges that ethnic conflict has been largely contained in Ukraine but claims that "extremist groups have brought areas of Ukraine to the brink of ethnic war" (p. 179).

9. For a detailed examination on Ukraine's citizenship policies see Lowell William Barrington's Ph.D. dissertation, *To Exclude or not to Exclude: Citizenship Policies in Newly Independent States*, University of Michigan, 1993. While the inclusiveness of the citizenship law is generally recognized as a positive aspect, Barrington notes that there exist both ethnic Ukrainians and ethnic Russians who feel that the law is too inclusive.

10. It might be argued that Ukraine has clearly set limits on political expression in Crimea. However, one should not confuse political discrimination of one ethnic group over another with limits on the political expression of territorial secession.

11. Laitin, *Identity in Formation*, pp. 99–102.

12. Ibid., p. 102.

13. Ibid.

14. Arel, "Ukraine: The Temptation," p. 158.

15. In all three surveys, respondents were more likely to believe that there would be conflict among workers, entrepreneurs, managers, the intelligentsia, and farmers than they were to believe that there would be conflict among ethnic groups.

16. This index and its calculation are taken from Richard Rose, *Governing without Consensus: An Irish Perspective* (London: Faber and Faber, 1971), pp. 200–201. I would like to thank Professor Rose for bringing his index to my attention.

17. See, for example, D. Arel and Valerii Khmelko, "The Russian Factor and Territorial Polarization in Ukraine," *Harriman Review*, vol. 9, nos. 1–2 (Spring-Summer 1996); pp. 81–91; Taras Kuzio, *Ukraine: State and Nation Building* (New York: Routledge, 1998), pp. 69–99; George Liber, "Imagining Ukraine: Regional Differences and the Emergence of an Integrated State Identity, 1926–1994," *Nations and Nationalism*, vol. 4, part 2 (April 1998), pp. 187–206; Neil Melvin, *Russians Beyond Russia: The Politics of National Identity* (London: Royal Institute of International Affairs, 1995), pp. 88–95; Grigory Nemiria, *Regionalism: An Underestimated Dimension of State-building in Ukraine*, Occasional Papers on Changes in the Slavic-Eurasian World, no.8 (Sapporo: Slavic Research Center, Hokkaido University, 1996), pp. 1–22; and V. Khmelko and Andrew Wilson, "Regionalism, Ethnic and Linguistic Cleavages in Ukraine," in T. Kuzio, ed., *Contemporary Ukraine: Dynamics of Post-Soviet Transformation* (Armonk, NY: M.E. Sharpe, 1998), pp. 60–80.

18. See Arel, "Ukraine: The Temptation," pp. 160–166; Arel and Khmelko, "The Russian Factor;" and Khmelko and Wilson, "Regionalism, Ethnic and Linguistic Cleavages."

19. A. Wilson and Sarah Birch, "Voting Stability, Political Gridlock: Ukraine's 1998 Parliamentary Elections," *Europe-Asia Studies*, vol. 51, no. 6 (September 1999), pp. 1039–1068.

20. Kolstoe, *Russians in the Former Soviet Republics*, pp. xi, 190.

21. See for example, Ian Bremmer, "Ethnic Issues in Crimea," *RFE/RL Research Report*, vol. 2, no. 18 (30 April 1993); Andrew Wilson, "Crimea's Political Cauldron," *RFE/RL Research Report*, vol. 2, no. 45 (12 November 1993); Kolstoe, *Russians in the Former Soviet Republics,* pp. 190–199; and Taras Kuzio, *Ukraine Under Kuchma: Political Reform, Economic Transformation and Security Policy in Independent Ukraine* (London: Macmillan, 1997), pp. 67–89.

22. See, for example, Kuzio, *Ukraine: State and Nation Building,* p. 82; and Kolstoe, *Russians in the Former Soviet Republics*, p. 190.

23. Kolstoe, *Russians in the Former Soviet Republics*, p. xi.

24. Arel, "Ukraine: The Temptation," p. 161.

25. Melvin, *Russians Beyond Russia*, p. 94.

26. The regional division I use is based on the division utilized by Arel, "Ukraine: The Temptation," p. 170. I do, however, in most cases treat the Crimea as a separate region because of its unique status as an autonomous republic and because of the perceived greater potential for ethnic conflict in the region. I also look at Kyiv City separately. Laitin suggests that a language shift and Ukrainianization of Kyiv might determine what kind of "national state [Ukraine] will become" (Laitin, *Identity in Formation*, p. 140). It might be important then to look at how a potential shift might be reflected in attitudes toward ethnic conflict. Otherwise, the East comprises of the Donets'k, Luhans'k, Kharkiv, Dnipropetrovs'k, and Zaporizhzhia *oblasti*. The South is made up of the Odesa, Kherson, and Mykolaiv *oblasti*. The West is constituted by the Volyn', Rivne, L'viv, Ivano-Frankivs'k, Ternopil', Chernivtsi, and Zakarpatia *oblasti*. The Center-East is made up of the Chernihiv, Poltava, and Sumy *oblasti* and the Center-West is made up of the Kyiv, Cherkasy, Zhytomyr, Kirovohrad, Vinnytsia, and Khmel'nyts'kyi *oblasti*.

27. *Forced Migration Monitor*, September 1996, no. 13. Online. 23 October 1999. Available: www.euronet.nl/users/sota/monitor.html.

28. See Michael Haxton and Anne Pitsch, *Russians of the Crimea in Ukraine*, 6 May 1997. Online. Minorities at Risk Project, Center for International Development and Con-

flict Management, University of Maryland. Internet. 23 October 1999. Available: www.bsos.umd.edu/cidcm/mar/ukrcrus.htm; and Taras Kuzio, "The Crimea: A Russian Nationalizing Republic," in Dominique Arel, ed., *The Ukraine List (UKL)*, no 44. Item 4. Published as "Next Ethnic Hot Spot: Crimea," *Foreign Report*, no. 2547 (10 June 1999).

29. Walker Connor, "Nation-Building or Nation-Destroying," in Walker Connor, *Ethnonationalism: The Quest for Understanding* (Princeton, Princeton University Press, 1993), p. 46. This chapter was originally published as Walker Connor, "Nation-Building or Nation-Destroying?" *World Politics*, vol. 24, no. 2 (April 1972), pp. 319–355. Connor's quotation was brought to my attention from reading Kuzio, *Ukraine: State and Nation Building*, p. 73.

30. See Kuzio, *Ukraine: State and Nation Building*, pp. 75–79; Ian Bremmer, "The Politics of Ethnicity: Russians in the New Ukraine," *Europe-Asia Studies*, vol. 46, no. 2 (March–April 1994), pp. 261–283; and Liber, *Imagining Ukraine*, pp. 187–206.

31. Bremmer, " Politics of Ethnicity," p. 264.

32. In the general ethnic conflict literature see, for example, Donald Horowitz, *Ethnic Groups in Conflict* (Berkeley: University of California Press, 1985), pp. 64–74; Milton Esman, *Ethnic Politics* (Ithaca, NY: Cornell University Press, 1994), pp. 14–15; and Ted Robert Gurr, *Ethnic Conflict in World Politics* (Boulder, CO: Westview Press, 1994), pp. 84–89. In the literature dealing specifically with the post-Soviet Russian diaspora see Graham Smith and Andrew Wilson, "Rethinking Russia's Post-Soviet Diaspora: The Potential for Political Mobilization in Eastern Ukraine and North-east Estonia," *Europe-Asia Studies*, vol. 49, no. 5 (July 1997), p. 854.

33. This chapter does not directly engage in the debate as to what degree Ukraine has pursued a nationalizing agenda or to what extent it should be regarded as a nationalizing state. I am, however, sympathetic to the view that characterizing Ukraine as a nationalizing state" in some areas underplays the importance of Ukraine's efforts to define the state in civic rather than ethnic terms. For a critique of Brubaker's nationalizing states paradigm and how it is applied to Ukraine see Taras Kuzio, "'Nationalizing States' or Nation-Building? A Critical Review of the Theoretical Literature and Empirical Evidence," paper prepared for the annual convention of the Association of the Study of Nationalities, Columbia University, New York, 15–18 April 1999.

34. Past vote was used in 1995 to better compare responses with actual voting results in the 1994 Ukrainian presidential elections. The first-round preferences were used because there were more candidates in the field. This would make for a better basis of comparison with 1993 and 1998 future preferences.

35. I would like to thank Dominique Arel for helping me with the groupings. However, as Arel has pointed out to me in personal correspondence, assigning candidates into clear-cut camps is a difficult business at best. Certainly my 1998 groupings are most open to question. Still, what I am looking for are general trends, and I would argue that grouping changes in 1998 would not terribly affect the point I am making.

36. Kuzio, *Ukraine: State and Nation Building*, p. 29.

37. Ibid., p. 172.

38. Andrew Wilson, *Ukrainian Nationalism in the 1990s: A Minority Faith* (Cambridge: Cambridge University Press, 1997), p. 143.

39. See Taras Kuzio's comments in *The Ukraine List (UKL)*, no 54, Item 4.

40. See for example Arel, "Ukraine: The Temptation," p. 181.

41. See Stephen Whitefield and Geoffrey Evans, "Electoral Politics in Eastern Europe: Social and Ideological Influences on Partisanship in Post-Communist Societies,"

in John Higley, Jan Pakulski, and W. Wesolowski, eds., *Postcommunist Elites and De-mocracy in Eastern Europe* (London: St. Martin's, 1998), pp. 226–250.

42. Ibid., p. 245.

43. Laitin, *Identity in Formation*, p. 140.

44. Whitefield and Evans, "Electoral Politics," p. 241.

45. Much of this information on the surveys is taken from Whitefield and Evans, "Electoral Politics," p. 247.

6

The Internal-External Nexus in the Formation of Ukrainian National Identity:
The Case for Slavic Integration

Stephen Shulman

Leaders of states seeking to develop and solidify the national identity of their populations have a wide array of tools at their disposal, including language policy, education policy, citizenship laws, power-sharing arrangements, and federal territorial-administrative structures. Another nation-building resource often overlooked by scholars and analysts is foreign policy. In Ukraine in particular, how leaders resolve the central foreign policy debate—whether they place priority on developing political, economic, and military ties with Europe and the West or with Russia and the Commonwealth of Independent States—will greatly influence whether a unified nation is built in Ukraine and what type of nation is built. This chapter explores in a systematic manner the main ways in which Ukraine's foreign ties influence its national identity, and on the basis of this analysis recommends how Ukrainian leaders can use foreign policy to maximize the success of the nation-building project.

Several previous works have investigated the internal-external linkage in the realm of identity in Ukraine.[1] One problem with many of these works is that the term *identity* is usually not clearly defined and explicated. Scholars routinely use the term as though there were general agreement on its meaning, but this is far from the case. Particular confusion surrounds the term *national identity*, since often it is not clear whose identity is being discussed—that of the Ukrainian ethnic group or that of all citizens of the Ukrainian state, an ambiguity resulting from the fact that both ethnic groups and states make pretensions at being (or representing) nations. Additionally, and most importantly, specific mechanisms by which foreign policy and national identity interact are usually not clearly laid out. For example, Ilya Prizel's long monograph on national identity and foreign policy in Ukraine, Poland, and Russia, contains no general theoretical statements on the relationship between national identity and foreign policy which are then empirically examined in the case studies.[2]

National identity is defined here as the feeling of solidarity and unity among the people living in a state. There are two components to national identity: strength and content. Strength refers to the intensity with which people feel solidarity and unity with one another and wish to live together in their own state. Thus, strength is the quantitative component of national identity. National identity is weakest in countries where individuals from different ethnic groups and regions feel a high degree of estrangement and hostility toward one another, separatist movements are strong, the population feels alienated from the state's political system and its leaders, or large numbers of citizens wish to terminate the independent existence of the state. Cultivating the strength of national identity entails measures by states to increase the "we-feeling" among its citizens and their desire for common statehood. This goal in itself is usually not controversial, except for those individuals and groups who seek to exit or terminate the state and therefore do not want to be part of the political community in the first place. A strong national identity is important because it legitimizes government, increases political stability, and assists policy makers in the formulation and implementation of coherent and effective policies.

Content of national identity, on the other hand, refers to the substantive or qualitative reasons by which the people in a state feel they form a community separate and distinct from other communities. Such content varies in accordance with the traits people in a state stress as unifying all or most of the population and distinguishing them from the populations of other states. In this sense, constructing the content of national identity is an act of self-definition, whereby state and non-state elites seek to alter the characteristics of the population and the state and manipulate symbols so that certain traits stand out as the basis for the population's special persona and image. This process is potentially highly conflictual, because different ethnic groups and regions in a state often have different visions of the basis on which national unity should be built. Content and strength of national identity are thus closely intertwined. The construction of some contents of national identity may be successful in strengthening national identity, while others may in fact weaken this identity, depending on the relative popularity of the contents and the domestic and foreign policies they require for their construction.

While national identity is affected by many domestic factors, this chapter focuses on how Ukrainian foreign policy influences both the content and strength of Ukrainian national identity. It argues that the content of national identity with the greatest ability to produce a strong national identity is an Eastern Slavic one, which can in part be pursued with a foreign policy placing priority on integration with Russia and other CIS (Commonwealth of Independent States) countries. In making this argument, this chapter pursues a strictly empirical analysis, eschewing the normative concerns that seem to underlie many approaches to the emotionally charged questions of Ukrainian national identity and foreign orientation.

STRENGTH OF NATIONAL IDENTITY AND FOREIGN POLICY IN UKRAINE

Foreign policy affects the strength of national identity in a state in two main ways. First, disagreement among the state's citizens over foreign policy is both a reflection of weak national identity and a source of it. Several scholars have pointed to common values as an important basis for national unity, though the precise values that are most important to national unity are not specified.[3] Disputes over which foreign peoples and states to associate with denote conflict over values in two senses, and thus represent a potentially powerful obstacle to strong national identity. First, they constitute conflict over values defined as preferences. Different individuals have different goals for the state's foreign policy orientation. Second, they constitute conflict over values defined as norms. Some states and peoples, because of their past behavior and culture, are liked and respected, while others are disliked and condemned. Furthermore, foreign policy debate in a state often reflects the different value placed by citizens on various contents of national identity, a linkage further explored below. If people disagree over what traits, ideas, and symbols should serve as the basis for unity in the state, then unity itself suffers, and this disintegrative effect is intensified when the debate finds expression in the foreign policy sphere.

In short, one's desire for association or dissociation with foreign states is a statement of one's values. Controversy over foreign policy makes apparent to citizens of a state their different values, and in so doing can feed feelings of alienation among them. When disagreement over foreign policy falls along ethnic and/or regional lines, then the threat to national identity is potentially very strong given the key role played by ethnicity and territory in the construction of national identity. Ethnic groups and regions will be more likely to see themselves as incompatible partners in the nation-building enterprise as a result of their disparate values.

A second way that foreign policy influences the strength of national identity relates to the degree of match between the foreign policy preferences of the population and the actual foreign policy pursued by the state. In the modern era, democratic ideology has very successfully promoted the principles of popular sovereignty and self-determination of peoples. Under the influence of nationalist ideology, states usually claim that they represent a nation that is the ultimate bearer of sovereignty and authority in the state. In this formulation, the state, as the agent of the nation it represents, is obligated to fulfill the latter's will. Where the state fails in its mandate to obey the values, preferences, and interests of its people, its respect and legitimacy suffer.[4] As a result, a potent symbol of national unity is weakened, and intra-national tensions can arise, since those members of the state whose values are ignored are likely to feel alienated not only from the state but also from the groups and individuals seen as responsible for state policy. National unity is especially vulnerable to state policies that violate the values of many or most of its people in the sphere of culture and identity. Ethnic and regional conflicts have repeatedly been catalyzed or exacerbated by language, educational, economic, migration, and other policies that retard or promote the culture and identities of various groups within a state.[5] Particularly in light of the link between foreign policy on one hand and culture and identity on the other (to be explored below), a state that pursues a foreign policy program that is at odds with the values of the majority of the population, or of particular ethnic groups and regions, risks weakening national identity. Conversely, a foreign policy that accords with the values of most of the population of a state will tend to intensify feelings of devotion to the state and its dominant group(s), and thus to the political community—the nation—as a whole.

To what extent do foreign policy issues in Ukraine affect the strength of national identity through the two paths discussed above? Tables 6.1 through 6.5 present data collected from the population of Ukraine on their views of foreign policy. The following analysis of the data in Tables 6.1 through 6.5 indicates that foreign policy preferences of the population vary substantially according to ethnicity and region, and, for large numbers of Ukrainians, differ from the foreign policy implemented by the state. The result is that Ukrainian national identity is weakened.

A mass survey conducted by the Ukrainian Institute of Social Research and the Social Monitoring Center in March 1999 reveals substantial dissension over foreign policy, particularly toward Russia.[6] One question asked is, Is an orientation of greater closeness (*orientatsiia na zblyzhennia*) with Western European countries important for the successful development of Ukrainian society? Table 6.1 shows the responses according to region[7] and ethnicity.

Table 6.1
Mass Views on Foreign Policy toward Western Europe by Region and Ethnicity, Respectively (in Percentages)

"Is an orientation of greater closeness with Western European countries important for the successful development of Ukrainian society?"

By Region

	West	Center	North	East	South	Crimea	Kyiv
Yes	73	53	61	58	45	27	78
No	7	14	17	22	29	39	9
Difficult to say	20	33	22	20	26	34	13

By Ethnicity

	Ukrainians	Russians	All
Yes	61	52	59
No	16	25	18
Difficult to say	23	23	23

The highest regional levels of support for closer ties with Western Europe are in Kyiv and the West, where 78% and 73% of respondents, respectively, answered yes to the question. In contrast, only 27% and 45% answered yes in the South and Crimea. The North, Center, and East register levels of support between these extremes. When categorized according to ethnicity, differences remain, though they are smaller than regional ones. Thus, 61% of Ukrainians and 52% of Russians think closer ties with Western Europe are important.

Another question inquired, Is unification (*ob''ednannia*) of the Eastern Slavic states—Ukraine, Russia and Belarus—important for the successful development of Ukrainian society? Here a higher degree of integration is being asked about than in the previous question. While not clearly defined, "unification" implies much greater contact and cooperation than "greater closeness." The regions of Ukraine express distinct positions regarding such unification (Table 6.2).

Table 6.2
Mass Views on Foreign Policy toward Russia and Belarus by Region and Ethnicity, Respectively (in Percentages)

"Is unification of the Eastern Slavic states—Ukraine, Russia and Belarus—important for the successful development of Ukrainian society?"

By Region

	West	Center	North	East	South	Crimea	Kyiv
Yes	16	56	53	69	59	81	34
No	61	21	30	18	17	7	50
Difficult to say	23	23	17	13	24	12	16

By Ethnicity

	Ukrainians	Russians	All
Yes	46	73	53
No	34	15	29
Difficult to say	20	12	18

The West, Kyiv, and Crimea again occupy the extreme positions, with 16%, 34%, and 81%, respectively, supporting Eastern Slavic integration. While the other regions also show varying levels of support, in each case a majority of respondents answered yes to the survey question. Further, as Table 6.2 shows, ethnic Ukrainians and ethnic Russians differ on foreign policy toward Russia and Belarus much more than they do for foreign policy toward Western Europe. Only 43% of ethnic Ukrainians support Eastern Slavic unification, while 73% of ethnic Russians do.

Other data on foreign policy preferences tell a similar story. In a survey conducted by the Kyiv International Institute of Sociology in November–December 1997, respondents were asked what kind of relations they want with Russia.[8] Three choices were given: "The same relations as with other states," "independent but friendly states," and "unification into one state." The last choice unambiguously refers to the eradication of Ukrainian statehood, and thus represents the most extreme form of integration with Russia. Table 6.3 shows the results according to a regional scheme that differs from that in the previously discussed survey.[9]

Large differences again manifest themselves, particularly with respect to the option of merging with Russia. Only 7% from the West want to end Ukrainian statehood, compared to 45% from the South and 50% from the East. Table 6.3 also shows how ethnic differences complement these regional ones, with 22% of those declaring themselves Ukrainian supporting this option, in contrast to 56% of Russians. Not surprisingly, the proportion of mixed Ukrainian–Russians who expressed a desire to end statehood falls between these extremes (43%).

Table 6.3
Mass Views on Status of Ukraine's Relations with Russia, by Region and Ethnicity, Respectively (in Percentages)

By Region

	West	West-Center	South	East-Center	East
Same relations as with other states	32	10	3	6	2
Independent but friendly states	54	57	50	56	45
Unification into one state	7	26	45	35	50

By Ethnicity

	Ukrainians	Ukrainian-Russians	Russians	All
Same relations as with other states	16	3	1	10
Independent but friendly states	55	52	41	52
Unification into one state	23	42	56	33

Finally, a survey distributed in what may be called the antipodes of Ukrainian society, L'viv and Donets'k, in September 1994–January 1995 indicates the degree of dispute over foreign policy among elites, not the masses.[10] A sample of approximately 1,000 elites in Donets'k and L'viv was presented with a list of six geographic regions of the world: the Near East, Russia/Belarus, all countries of the CIS, United States/Canada, Western Europe, and Eastern Europe (Table 6.4). The respondents were asked: Which two regions do you consider the most important partners for Ukraine?

In Donets'k, the two regions mentioned most often as desirable foreign partners are Russia/Belarus, chosen by 77% of the respondents, and all CIS countries, chosen by 38%. In L'viv, however, these regions fared much less well, beating out only the Near East. Instead, Western Europe (72%) and the United States/Canada (37%) were deemed the most important regions. Especially noteworthy is the fact that relatively tiny Eastern Europe (27%) surpasses the huge CIS (26%)—with which western Ukraine still has substantial economic ties. Large numbers of Donets'k elites chose Western Europe (36%) and United States/Canada (29%), while large numbers of L'viv elites chose the CIS (26%) and Russia/Belarus (21%). Thus there is a significant degree of overlap in preferences between the Donets'k and L'viv, and the degree of dissension over foreign policy in Ukraine should not be exaggerated, even in two cities as different as Donets'k and L'viv.

Table 6.4
Elite Foreign Folicy Preferences in Donets'k and L'viv (Percentage of Respondents Who Chose the Given Geographical Regions as Being the Most Important Foreign Partners for Ukraine; Relative Rank Given in Parentheses)

Geographic Region	Donets'k (n =496)	L'viv (n =487)
Near East (including Turkey)	3 (6)	15 (6)
Russia and Belarus	72 (1)	21 (5)
All Countries of the Commonwealth of Independent States	38 (2)	26 (4)
United States and Canada	29 (4)	37 (2)
Western Europe (including Germany)	36 (3)	71 (1)
Eastern Europe (including the Baltics)	9 (5)	27 (3)

However, this survey question does not indicate the relative strength of the pro-West and pro-East orientations of the cities. Another question from the same survey designed to ascertain directly the relative strength of a westward versus eastward orientation requested respondents to agree or disagree with the following statement:

Close international ties with Russia and Belarus are more beneficial for Ukraine than close international ties with Eastern Europe.

In Donets'k, 90% of the respondents agreed in some fashion (fully, basically, or somewhat). In L'viv, though, only 36% agreed with this statement—testimony to a strong cleavage between these cities, and likely Galicia and Donbas more broadly, over foreign policy orientation.

As argued earlier, such foreign policy dissension in Ukraine weakens national unity by underscoring value differences among its citizens. Russians and Ukrainians and inhabitants of the various regions are likely to feel less close to one another as a result of these differences over such an important issue. Is it possible to demonstrate more concretely that such a negative result ensues from the foreign policy debate? Strong empirical evidence that conflict over relations with Russia directly weakens national identity comes from the elite survey in Donets'k and L'viv. In Donets'k the survey asked respondents to agree or disagree on a six-point scale with this statement:

If someone in western Ukraine does *not* want to have close ties with Russia, it would be better if he simply emigrates to a country weakly tied to Russia.

In L'viv, this version appeared:

If someone in Donbas wants to have close ties with Russia, it would be better if he simply emigrates there.

The questions seek to discover whether conflict over foreign policy leads to an extreme form of alienation—the desire not to live in the same political community with those who disagree with one's position in the debate.

Donets'k elites who indicated their support for ties with Russia/Belarus and/or All Countries of the CIS were included in the analysis. Though the modal answer is to disagree fully with the proposition, 41% (189/463) of all respondents agree to one degree or another (fully, basically, or somewhat) that western Ukrainians who do not want close ties with Russia should leave their own country—the homeland of ethnic Ukrainians—in search of a state that is weakly tied to Russia. Nearly a fifth (19%) agree fully with this assertion. An even higher degree of alienation was expressed by L'viv elites toward those in Donbas with different foreign policy preferences. Included in this analysis are L'viv elites who chose neither Russia/Belarus nor All Countries of the CIS as the most important regions with which Ukraine should develop ties. The modal answer to the L'viv version of the survey question is agree fully, with 66% (176/268) of respondents choosing this option. And 88% of respondents agree to one degree or another (fully, basically, or somewhat) with the statement that those in Donbas who want close ties with Russia should emigrate there. These results suggest an extremely high degree of alienation felt by L'viv elites, the vast majority of whom are ethnic Ukrainians, toward eastern Ukrainian Russophiles, who compose both ethnic Russians and ethnic Ukrainians.

There is also evidence of a mismatch between the actual foreign policy implemented by Kyiv and the foreign policy preferences of significant portions of Ukraine's citizenry. The foreign policy pursued since independence is best described as "multi-vectored," to use the term popular in Ukraine. Presidents Kuchma and Kravchuk have each sought to develop Ukraine's ties with both Europe/United States and Russia/CIS without tilting much in either direction.[11]

This attempt to balance Ukraine's foreign policy orientation, however, leaves large numbers of Ukrainians with their foreign policy preferences unsatisfied. An insufficiently eastern orientation is likely to cause greater overall dissatisfaction with and alienation from the government in Kyiv—to the detriment of national identity—than an insufficiently westward orientation. This is because of the great overall popularity for extremely high degrees of integration with Russia/CIS, which outmatch in intensity the widespread desire merely for closer relations with Europe and the West. Additionally, the main obstacle to close ties with Europe and the United States is not policymakers in Kyiv, but the West itself (which is unwilling to let Ukraine into the European Union and NATO anytime soon) and the poor condition and lack of competitiveness of the Ukrainian economy. The main obstacle to strong integration with Russia and Belarus, on the other hand, is the government in Kyiv. National identity is likely to suffer under the latter circumstances precisely because representatives of the state are primarily seen as responsible for the gap between one's preferences and the state's implemented policy.

Survey data, especially at the aggregate level for Ukraine as a whole, indicate just how large is the unsatisfied contingent of Ukrainian citizens with Ukrainian foreign policy as a result of its failure to pursue a stronger eastern orientation. A survey from July 1999 asked respondents, "Do you favor close security relations primarily with Russia and the CIS or the U.S. and NATO?" Only 13% said the United States/NATO, while 58% said Russia and the CIS.[12] A large regional difference here appears, with 38% of Western Ukrainians wanting closer relations with the United States/NATO, and only 8% of respondents from all other regions. Additionally, according to Table 6.2, 53% of the population want unification of Ukraine, Belarus, and Russia, versus 29% against. Important here as well is the fact that majorities in every region except the West and Kyiv support such unification. And while ethnic differences in support for Slavic unification exist, as noted earlier, a plurality of ethnic Ukrainians favor such unification (46% for, versus 34% against). Another survey conducted in December 1995–January 1996 similarly finds that 59% think "Ukraine's interests would best be served if the government sought confederation with Russia, Kazakhstan, Belarus and other former Soviet republics," compared to 31% who desire that Ukraine remain "a sovereign and independent state."[13]

Most remarkable of all, a third of the country so desires close relations with Russia that they want to wholly terminate Ukraine's statehood (Table 6.3). This represents the greatest threat to the strength of Ukrainian national identity; these citizens want to eliminate that identity. A majority of Russians (56%) and near-majorities of the inhabitants of the East (50%) and South (45%) do not support the continued existence of a sovereign Ukrainian political community. Additionally, an enormous 23% of the country's titular ethnic group—ethnic Ukrainians[14]—wish to unify their country with a neighboring state. It is surely an anomaly with few parallels in world history for large proportions of both of the two largest ethnic groups in a state to wish to terminate its existence (Belarus also belongs in this rare club). Perplexing is the lack of attention many analysts of Ukrainian politics devote to this phenomenon, which should be seen as a crisis for Ukrainian national identity. For example, Taras Kuzio's otherwise fine account of national identity in Ukraine neglects even to mention figures on the lack of support for statehood, asserting instead that "Ukrainian society is largely united at a 'minimal' level through relatively high backing for statehood and sovereignty."[15] Relative to almost any other state in the world, the levels of support for independence, statehood, and sovereignty in Ukraine are extremely low.[16]

The preceding analysis reveals two somewhat contradictory patterns. On one hand, substantial ethnic and regional differences over foreign policy exist in Ukraine. But on the other hand, there is great *overall* mass support for a strong eastern foreign orientation. It is the western territories of Ukraine in particular that distinguish themselves as outliers against this general tendency. To understand how policy makers in Kyiv might strengthen national unity as much as possible in the face of ethnic/regional disputes over foreign policy and the gap between popular foreign policy preferences for a strong eastern orientation and state foreign policy, it is necessary to explore the content of national identity in Ukraine and how foreign policy constructs it.

CONTENT OF NATIONAL IDENTITY AND FOREIGN POLICY IN UKRAINE

The foreign policy debate in Ukraine has many sources.[17] There can be no doubt that citizens of Ukraine disagree about the economic and political consequences of integration with Russia/CIS and Europe/United States. Those who place priority on strong ties with the West believe not only that such an orientation is economically beneficial to Ukraine, but also that it will reduce Russia's ability to impose its will on Ukraine and threaten her security and sovereignty. Likewise, those who place priority on strong ties with Russia believe that this will improve the economy, while at the same not threatening the security of the people of Ukraine. Some scholars mistakenly assume that the driving force behind the desire in Ukraine for close ties with Russia is economic. For example, Zenovia Sochor writes that "it may very well be that the 'pro-Russian' position is based largely on economic considerations and a nostalgia for the 'good old days' rather than shared identities and values."[18] Kuzio argues that "Reintegration with Russia is only popular at the level of elites or at the level of the public at large as a substitute for economic reform to overcome the pain of the reform process."[19] Such analysis implies that as the economy strengthens in Ukraine the desire for close ties with Russia will wane rapidly, and national unity in Ukraine will increase.

The ethnic and regional basis for the debate suggests, however, that in addition to differences over the expected political and economic consequences of foreign ties with the West or the CIS, an additional important source is the consequence of foreign policy for content of national identity. Also, if economic motivations were paramount, one would have expected a marked decrease in Ukrainian popular support for integration with Russia after the crash of its economy in August 1998. However, there was no such decrease.[20] More generally, the experience of other countries demonstrates that there is no consistent relationship between the level of economic prosperity in a country and its level of national unity.[21] Often economic growth strengthens ethnic identities and conflict, and frequently secessionist movements arise or intensify in groups that are becoming wealthier (e.g., Quebecois in Canada) or are already wealthy compared to other groups in the state (e.g., Sikhs in India).[22]

Data from the 1994–1995 elite survey in Donets'k and L'viv provide further insight into the identity-related basis for the foreign policy debate. The survey sought to uncover the extent to which concerns about culture and identity underlay respondents' foreign policy preferences indirectly by asking respondents about the role economic and political factors play. Elites in Donets'k were asked to agree or disagree on a six-point scale with this statement:

I support Ukraine's development of strong ties with Russia and Belarus even if these ties were to bring *no* economic or political advantages to Ukraine.

Those who agree with this statement, it may be assumed, support ties with Russia and Belarus mainly because of considerations of culture and identity. Of course, the measurement is a blunt one, since it cannot determine the degree of support that results from consideration of culture and identity alone. Donets'k respondents were included in the analysis if they indicated in the previously discussed question on foreign policy preferences that either Russia/Belarus or all Countries of the CIS (or both) are among the two most important regional partners for Ukraine. Of these 464 Donets'k respondents, the great majority—81%—agree in some manner (fully, basically, or somewhat) with the statement. Indeed, 46% agree fully, while only 8% disagree fully. These figures suggest that noneconomic and nonpolitical factors alone are likely sufficient in explaining the high levels of eastern Ukrainian support for close ties with Russia and Belarus.

The survey asked L'viv elites to agree or disagree with the following analogous statement regarding their views toward Russia:

I do *not* support Ukraine's development of strong ties with Russia even if these ties were to bring economic or political advantages to Ukraine.[23]

This statement even more strongly than the previous statement taps into the concerns of the respondents over culture and identity. This is because it refers to their support for a foreign orientation that forgoes available political or economic benefits, while the Donets'k elites were asked about their support for a particular foreign orientation merely *in the absence* of political or economic benefits.

Included in the analysis were the 274 L'viv respondents who indicated that they consider neither Russia/Belarus nor all Countries of the CIS as among the most important foreign partners for Ukraine. A large majority—69%—of these respondents agree in some manner with the question (fully, basically, or somewhat) and thus do *not* want close ties with Russia/Belarus *even in the event that these ties are politically or economically beneficial to Ukraine*. The modal response is to agree fully with the statement in the survey (38%), with a total of only 31% of the respondents disagreeing in some form. Thus, while much of the ethnic Ukrainian nationalists' rhetoric and anti-CIS arguments are filled with assertions that integration eastward will hurt the Ukrainian economy and weaken Ukrainian statehood and sovereignty in the face of Russian attempts to reestablish imperial control, the results of the survey indicate that while these fears may be very real, they are not the sole source of nationalists' policy preferences.

This analysis suggests that an important element of the debate over foreign policy in Ukraine is the content of national identity. What are the main options for the content of national identity in Ukraine and how does foreign policy construct these contents?

The most fundamental choice for the content of national identity for a state has been conceptualized in the academic literature as one between a "civic," "political," or "territorial" nation on the one hand, or an "ethnic" or "cultural" nation on the other.[24] The primary basis for unity in a civic-territorial nation is, depending on the scholar, common rights and duties in the political system, living in common territory, shared belief in a set of political principles, or some combination thereof. The basis for unity in ethnocultural nations is common ancestry, culture, language, religion, and traditions, or some combination thereof. These are ideal types, and most states strive to develop an identity grounded in both, though states often stress one type of content more than the other.

A national identity based primarily on civic-territorial traits is likely insufficient to promote a high degree of positive affect and solidarity in Ukraine; that is, it is unlikely to promote a strong national identity. The political and legal institutions of the Ukrainian state are new and generally do not have much legitimacy and respect among Ukrainian citizens. Opinion polls show that of the major state institutions, only the armed forces enjoy a substantial degree of trust.[25] Most Ukrainians also do not believe that the elections conducted by the state are fair and honest, and they feel low levels of political efficacy in their capacity as citizens to affect the political process.[26] In addition, there is vigorous debate and disagreement over political ideology in Ukraine, especially with regard to the role the state should play in the economy and the proper institutional structure of the polity.[27] Finally, the historical fragmentation of the territory of Ukraine impedes the construction of a predominantly civic-territorial nation. The lands that constitute present-day Ukraine have been incorporated into several empires and states over the course of approximately 600–700 years: the Polish-Lithuanian Commonwealth, Russian Empire, Ottoman Empire, Austro-Hungarian Empire, Poland, Czechoslovakia, Hungary, Romania and the Soviet Union. Most important, different parts of Ukraine were subjugated by different states in a prolonged imperial tug of war.[28] As a consequence of this turbulent history, strong regional identities in Ukraine hinder attachment to the Ukrainian territory as a whole, whose present boundaries date only to 1954.[29]

Even if Ukraine did have a rich political and legal tradition, basic consensus over political ideology, and strong popular identification with its current territory, it is not clear that a primarily civic national identity would provide the emotional and psychological resonance that the Ukrainian state needs to weather successfully its economic difficulties, which will not be overcome anytime soon. Generally speaking, ethnocultural identities are superior to civic identities (and perhaps all other social identities with the exception of the family) in their great potential to mobilize people's passions and loyalties. Even the states that are often hailed as prototypical civic nations—the United States and France—achieved their unity and solidarity in good part because of common language and culture among their citizens. In any case, in Ukraine the issue of ethnocultural rebirth and identity is so salient that it is not clear how the government would be able to put this question on the back burner, so to speak.

Consequently, the historical and political reality in Ukraine is such that if the government in Kyiv is to build a strong and unified nation, it must do so in large degree on ethnocultural foundations. The crucial question then becomes *what* and *whose* ethnocultural traits should be chosen as the basis for national cohesion and distinction. The two main alternatives prominent in current political discourse in Ukraine for this ethnocultural content of Ukrainian national identity may be termed Ethnic Ukrainian and Eastern Slavic.

Before discussing these alternatives, however, it is necessary first to analyze the ways that the foreign policy of a state can influence the ethnocultural content of its national identity. There are two basic routes.[30] First, foreign policy may substantively alter the cultural characteristics of the state's population through processes of cultural diffusion. Foreign political, economic, and other ties are conduits through which ideas, values, and language cross state borders and modify the cultural landscape inside a state. The unifying and distinguishing cultural characteristics of the citizenry that form the qualitative basis for national unity therefore are altered by foreign cultures. Additionally, because cultures inside a state often are perceived as similar to or different from the cultures outside, import of foreign cultures can either degrade or strengthen ethnic cultures in a state. This shift in the cultural balance of power can change the cultural image of the nation (at home and abroad) and the traits it stresses as those that unify the majority of its citizens. Ethnic groups in a state that compete with each other over what culture should serve as the basis for the content of national identity thus will have different foreign policy preferences when foreign ties are seen as altering the relative strength of their cultures.

Second, foreign policy symbolically conditions national identity through its effect on the in-group/out-group boundaries driving identity.[31] Close relations between a state and foreign countries that members of the state perceive as culturally similar (positive reference groups) symbolically erode boundaries and cement together the members of the state into a nation on the basis of the cultural traits shared within and between the countries at hand. Reducing the distance between the state and its positive reference groups is an act of cultural self-definition specifying the cultural character of the nation: "we are similar to X." Similarly, weak ties with foreign countries perceived by the nation as culturally distant (negative reference groups) symbolically sharpen boundaries and strengthen national identity on the basis of the distinguishing traits that members of the nation share among themselves. By increasing the distance with such out-groups, the nation again engages in an act of self-definition specifying its cultural character: "we are not like Y." If the state is split into multiple ethnic and regional groups that differ in culture, forging foreign ties with culturally similar countries and breaking ties with dissimilar countries can symbolically strengthen one group's identity and its claim to be the basis for the state-wide national identity. Thus, ethnic and regional groups will push for close foreign ties between their state and states they perceive as culturally similar and weak ties with culturally dissimilar states in an effort to promote their identity in the domestic competition with other groups over whose identity will form the content of national identity.

In light of these influences of foreign policy on identity, what are the two main options for the ethnocultural content of Ukrainian national identity and what policies do they demand for their actualization? The *Ethnic Ukrainian* identity is founded on the claim that what does or should unite and distinguish the majority of the population of Ukraine is Ethnic Ukrainian language and culture. Domestically, this content of national identity requires policies that recognize the special position of Ethnic Ukrainians as the core and indigenous group of the Ukrainian state, and that seek to spread Ukrainian language and culture throughout society, displacing to some extent Russian language and culture. An important example of such a policy is assigning Ukrainian as the sole official language of the state. The Ethnic Ukrainian content of national identity does not necessitate a coercive and undemocratic ethnocratic state motivated by "integral nationalism" that gives members of ethnic minorities few rights. The overwhelming support in Ukraine for civic elements of national identity calling for an inclusive notion of citizenship with equal civil and political rights precludes such an option. Rather, the Ethnic Ukrainian content simply calls for the state to give official preference and support to the symbols, traditions, language, and history of Ethnic Ukrainians.

In the foreign policy sphere the Ethnic Ukrainian national identity calls for breaking economic and political ties with Russia and focusing on integration with Europe and the West. Such a foreign policy orientation will hinder diffusion of Russian culture and facilitate diffusion of European culture into Ukraine.[32] The Ethnic Ukrainian identity is predicated on fundamental differences between Ethnic Russian culture (in Russia) and ethnic Ukrainian culture and fundamental similarities between Ethnic Ukrainian and European culture.[33] Consequently, stronger diffusion of European culture and weaker diffusion of Russian culture into Ukraine promote the rebirth and development of Ethnic Ukrainian culture and its ability to serve as the basis of the Ukrainian nation. Additionally, because the Ethnic Ukrainian identity considers Russia as a negative reference group and Europe as a positive reference group for Ethnic Ukrainians, a western orientation symbolically enhances the Ethnic Ukrainian component of Ukrainian national identity by sharpening the state's boundary with Russia and eroding its boundary with Europe. This boundary sharpening with Russia is especially critical for the Ethnic Ukrainian content of national identity due to its role in countering the widespread image among foreigners (and many Ukrainian citizens themselves) of the absence of meaningful cultural distinctions between Russians and Ukrainians. Breaking ties with Russia is a powerful symbolic statement of Ethnic Ukrainian uniqueness. A western orientation is a declaration by the state that, overall, the people of Ukraine are similar to Europeans and different from Russians. Finally, the Ethnic Ukrainian content assumes that Ethnic Ukrainian and Ethnic Russian identities are to some degree mutually exclusive, and that loyalty to Russia competes with loyalty to Ukraine. Consequently, close ties with Russia should be avoided lest they fuel Russian loyalties and identities among the citizenry at the expense of Ukrainian identities and loyalties.[34]

The *Eastern Slavic* national identity, on the other hand, is grounded in the claim that what does or should unite the majority of the people in Ukraine is a common Eastern Slavic heritage and culture. Ethnic Russians and Ethnic Ukrainians both in Ukraine and Russia are for the most part considered by this identity as peoples with common roots in Kyivan Rus', with very similar languages, values, and worldview. Domestically, this identity calls for official recognition of both Ethnic Ukrainian and Russian culture and language, seeking to treat both equally in the pursuit of a fundamentally bicultural and biethnic nation. In the foreign arena, an Eastern Slavic identity requires close and friendly relations with Russia, in either a bilateral scheme or a multilateral one with Belarus and other former Soviet republics. Although it does not exclude the development of close ties with other regions, such as Europe, priority would be placed on integration with Russia. Through diffusionary processes such an orientation would help maintain the strength and position of Russian language and culture in Ukraine. Moreover, such a foreign policy degrades the boundary with what is asserted to be a positive reference group for *both* Ethnic Ukrainians and Ethnic Russians in Ukraine—Russians in Russia. In this manner, both groups' common (Eastern Slavic) culture is reinforced as the basis for Ukrainian unity. Finally, in contrast to the Ethnic Ukrainian content, the Eastern Slavic content is based on the compatibility of Ethnic Ukrainian and Ethnic Russian identities, of loyalty to Russia and loyalty to Ukraine. The promotion of mixed identities and loyalties through bilingualism at home and close ties with Russia is no threat to the image and status of Ukraine; rather, such identities and loyalties further emphasize the common Eastern Slavic culture of the people of Ukraine.[35]

To a considerable extent the Ethnic Ukrainian and Eastern Slavic identities and their implied domestic and foreign policies are mutually exclusive. Either Ethnic Ukrainians and their language and culture have a special place in the Ukrainian nation or they share equal status with Russians. Also, greater state support for the spread of Ukrainian language perforce erodes the position of Russian language. Similarly, one cannot pursue simultaneously both closer ties with Russia and weaker ties with Russia. Ukrainian citizens will perceive any substantial movement by Kyiv away from Russia/CIS as support for an Ethnic Ukrainian national identity, while any move toward Russia/CIS will be perceived as support for an Eastern Slavic national identity,

The preceding discussion makes it clear that the foreign policy debate in Ukraine in great part derives from conflict over national identity content. The ethnically and regionally based foreign policy dissension resulting from conflict over the content of national identity is likely to be long-lived, while dissension based only or primarily on economics and politics can be more easily reduced or eliminated. The reason here is that culture and preferences for identity are far less subject both to variation over time and to policy manipulation than are political and economic variables.[36] For example, consistent evidence that Russian leaders in Moscow respect Ukrainian statehood and are unwilling to use economic leverage to humiliate Ukraine, and that economic relations within the context of a some kind of union with Russia and Belarus are helping to revive the Ukrainian economy, would have a powerful effect in reducing the foreign policy controversy in Ukraine if economic and political considerations were paramount. The controversy would likewise largely evaporate in the face of evidence that breaking ties with the Russia and integrating into European economic and security institutions with generous extensions of aid and technology on behalf of the Western powers are bringing peace and prosperity to an independent Ukraine. Similar scenarios in which the outcomes are negative for Ukraine hold the same potential for reducing foreign policy dissension. The political and economic variables in the Ukrainian case are subject to change by developments and leaders both in Ukraine and abroad, potentially defusing in a relatively short period of time the controversy over foreign policy orientation. If, however, the less malleable factors of culture and identity are at work to a significant extent in the debate, then this debate and its negative consequences for Ukraine will likely persist for a long time.

USING CONTENT OF NATIONAL IDENTITY TO BUILD STRENGTH OF NATIONAL IDENTITY: THE FOREIGN POLICY DIMENSION

The previous analysis demonstrates that in formulating foreign policy, politicians in Kyiv confront the task of choosing among alternate ethnocultural contents of national identity. In so doing, one of their challenges is to reduce as far as possible the negative effects on the strength of national identity of the debate over foreign policy and the mismatch between the policies implemented by the state and the policies preferred by the population. Foreign policy preferences and thus the debate over foreign policy are relatively stubborn, since they are rooted in cultural and identity-related differences among the people of Ukraine that are themselves resistant to easy and quick manipulation. Therefore, the main available course of action is to substantially reduce the difference between state foreign policy and public preferences. Accordingly, the survey data suggest that Ukrainian leaders interested in strengthening national identity should pursue a content based on Eastern Slavic identity. In the foreign policy sphere, this means that integration with Russia/Belarus/CIS should take precedence over integration with Europe. Thus, instead of the Ministry of Foreign Affair's current declared policy of "integration with Europe—cooperation with the CIS,"[37] an orientation of "integration with Russia and Belarus—cooperation with Europe" would more likely strengthen national identity.

In more concrete terms, a Ukraine interested in strengthening national identity should at a minimum move from being a participant in the CIS to being a full member, by ratifying the CIS Charter. In March 1999 Ukraine joined the CIS Inter-Parliament Assembly, and should further its integration by joining the CIS Customs Union and Payments Union and pushing for a free-trade zone in the region. Furthermore, national identity would likely be solidified by Ukraine's entry in some capacity into the Union of Sovereign States currently being negotiated by Russia and Belarus. Regarding the West, to maintain good relations with Russia, Ukraine should renounce any intention to enter NATO, and should declare its opposition to further enlargement of the alliance. It must be stressed that placing priority on integration with Russia does not mean that the popular desire for development of good relations with the West cannot be fulfilled. Just as the North American Free Trade Agreement does not hinder Canada from maintaining and cultivating close political and economic ties with Europe and other regions, Slavic and CIS integration does not necessarily impede Ukrainians from integrating with Europe.

The figures presented earlier in this chapter testify to the great support a high degree of integration with Russia enjoys for every region except Kyiv and the West. Of particular import is the widespread rejection of Ukrainian statehood by so many inhabitants of eastern and southern Ukraine, and by so many Ethnic Russians. This crisis in national identity would almost certainly be aggravated by a westward orientation that entailed the further breaking of political and economic ties with Russia/CIS, and can be ameliorated by an eastward shift in foreign orientation. Every multiethnic state faces a great challenge in cultivating the devotions and loyalties of ethnic minorities. When an ethnic minority is a diaspora, then relations with the historic homeland of the diaspora community take on great importance for the strength of national identity in a state. Previous work using the 1994–1995 elite survey in Donets'k and L'viv shows that large numbers of ethnic Russians and mixed Ukrainian-Russians in Donets'k say that Ukraine's development of close ties with Russia and Belarus would *increase* their support for Ukrainian statehood.[38] The devotion of ethnic Russians and inhabitants of eastern and southern Ukraine more generally to the Ukrainian nation is critical for the strength of national identity given their demographic and economic importance. Especially in light of the fact that the long-term economic success of Ukraine will depend on the ability of policy makers in Kyiv to implement painful reforms to eastern Ukraine's aging and obsolete industries and mines, the satisfaction of fundamental eastern and southern Ukrainian preferences regarding the content of national identity and foreign policy will go a long way in buying the feelings of unity with other regions and support for statehood necessary to survive a long and potentially politically destabilizing economic transition period.

The great popularity in Ukraine of integration with Russia is part and parcel of a general pattern of attitudes that reveal an overall popular preference for an Eastern Slavic content for national identity over an Ethnic Ukrainian one. In addition to foreign policy, the other major issue that fundamentally divides these two contents is language policy. The Ethnic Ukrainian identity implies a policy giving Ukrainian language official status throughout the country's government apparatus, while the Eastern Slavic identity calls for Russian and Ukrainian to enjoy equal status in the conduct of state business. A compromise position is one giving Russian official status at the level of local government where Russians and Russian-speakers predominate. Public opinion data reveal the great popularity of the option most consistent with the Eastern Slavic identity over the option most consistent with an Ethnic Ukrainian identity. In a 1997 survey, 49% of respondents wanted to make Russian an official or second state language, while only 10% wanted to remove Russian from official relations. The compromise position of allowing Russian to be an official language where the local population so wanted was chosen by 35%. As with foreign policy, western *oblasti* distinguished themselves from the rest of the country, with half of all respondents calling for the removal of Russian from official discourse hailing from Galicia.[39] Actual language use in Ukraine also makes an Ethnic Ukrainian content for national identity potentially destabilizing. Data from the Kyiv International Institute of Sociology demonstrate that only 44% of adults in Ukraine use Ukrainian for day-to-day communication, compared to 56% using Russian.[40]

Moreover, the cultural self-identification of the citizens of Ukraine and their perceptions of cultural affinity with other peoples favor the Eastern Slavic content over the Ethnic Ukrainian content for national identity. When asked how they would describe themselves to foreigners, 67% of respondents in a 1996 survey said "Slavs," an identity consistent, naturally, with the Eastern Slavic content, while only 7% said "European," an identity consistent with the Ethnic Ukrainian content. Some respondents (11%) would use both terms. Importantly, Ethnic Ukrainians and Ethnic Russians expressed very similar levels of self-identification as Slavs—65% and 75%, respectively.[41] This strong Slavic identity in Ukraine is complemented by the widespread belief that Ukrainian, Belarussian, and Russian cultures are very similar to one another. This can be inferred from a statewide survey conducted by Ukraine's Institute of Sociology in 1997 that asked respondents to assess the degree of their cultural affinity (in terms of traditions, customs, values, and art) to twenty-six ethnic groups using a seven-point scale ranging from 1 ("very close") to 7 ("completely different"). Overall, the three groups that respondents felt most culturally similar to were Ukrainians, Russians, and Belarussians. Average scores for these groups on the seven-point scale were 1.43, 1.87, and 2.40, respectively. Only 3% of respondents assigned to Russians scores of 5 ("more different than not"), 6 ("quite different"), or 7. In contrast, such groups as Poles (3.47), Frenchmen (4.39), Americans (4.50), and Arabs (5.22) were seen as considerably more culturally distant.[42] The idea, propagated under both Tsarist and Soviet regimes, that Russians, Ukrainians, and Belarussians are but three branches of a common Eastern Slavic people apparently maintains great popularity in contemporary Ukraine, and renders the construction of an Eastern Slavic national identity considerably easier than an Ethnic Ukrainian one. Thus, in contrast to many multiethnic countries, Ukraine's main ethnic groups believe they share a common culture. Foreign and domestic policies that capitalize on this nation-building resource have great potential to emotionally unite the population.

Of course, a move toward greater integration with Russia, Belarus, and the CIS more generally would contradict the preferences of many Ukrainians regarding the content of Ukrainian national identity and foreign policy, particularly those living in western Ukraine. Indeed, whereas the key problem for an Ethnic Ukrainian national identity is how to maintain the devotion and loyalty of inhabitants of eastern and southern Ukraine to the Ukrainian nation, the key problem for an Eastern Slavic national identity is how to maintain the devotion and loyalty of inhabitants of western Ukraine. For too long scholars have focused on only the first problem. It should be recognized that the greatest obstacle to a strong national identity based on Eastern Slavic content may be the attitudes of western Ukrainians, especially Galicians, toward Russia and Russian culture. Some accommodation to western Ukrainian sentiments must therefore be made, as moves toward eastern integration that are too extreme and that abrogate too much sovereignty risk alienating the region and weakening national identity. However, several points must be kept in mind. First, the population of southern and eastern Ukraine far outstrips that of western Ukraine.[43] Second, as mentioned above, the economic import of southern and eastern Ukraine is greater than western Ukraine, and the successful modernization of the country requires that inhabitants of this region endure very painful changes and sacrifices.

Assuming equal amounts of alienation from the Ukrainian nation among residents of these regions from the mismatch between state foreign policy and individual foreign policy preferences, these two points mean that the price (in terms of weakened national identity) to Ukraine of not satisfying eastern and southern Ukrainian foreign policy preferences is higher than that of not satisfying western foreign policy preferences. And third, western Ukrainians have fewer alternatives for their identifications than Ethnic Russians and Russified Ukrainians living in eastern and southern Ukraine. Ethnic Russians and Russified Ukrainians can more easily be alienated from the state and the nation it represents precisely because they can identify powerfully with the Russian people and culture in Russia and ex-USSR, whereas the only state in which ethnic Ukrainians form the numerically dominant and titular group, and where Ukrainian culture is widespread, is Ukraine. Thus it is likely that even with a stronger eastern foreign orientation of the type advocated here, western Ukrainians will still on the whole remain devoted and attached to the state and its people. If their protests against this orientation do become too extreme, however, Ukrainian policy makers can consider devolving some economic and political decision-making power to western Ukraine so that it may concentrate on developing its foreign ties with Europe somewhat independently of the rest of a more eastward-leaning Ukraine.[44]

Finally, there is a strong historical basis for both an Eastern Slavic national identity and eastern orientation. Throughout Russian-ruled Ukraine in the late eighteenth and nineteenth centuries, Ukrainian ("Little Russian") and Russian identities were commonly seen as fully compatible.[45] Additionally, the Ukrainian nationalist movement of Russian-ruled Ukraine in the nineteenth and early twentieth century was dominated not by the goal of drastically severing with ties with Russia and integrating into Europe, but by the goal of Ukrainian autonomy within a democratic, federated state that included Russia. In contrast, the desire for full political independence was relatively quite weak. For example, the first by-law of the Brotherhood of Saints Cyril and Methodius reads, "We hold that the spiritual and the political union of the Slavs is the true destiny to which they should aspire."[46] One of the Brotherhood's founders, Mykola Kostomarov, wrote about the Ukrainian people:

No one among us thinks about tearing South Rus' [Ukraine] from its connection to the rest of Russia. On the contrary, we would like to see all other Slavs unite with us in one union, even under the sceptre of the Russian sovereign, if that sovereign will become a sovereign of free peoples and not the ruler of an all-devouring Tatar-Germanic Muscovy.[47]

Other leading figures in the early Ukrainian nationalist movement expressed similar convictions. Panteleimon Kulish looked back at "the moral inevitability of the merger into one state of the south-Russian community and the north-Russian."[48] Mykhailo Drahomanov drew up a constitution that would reorganize the Russian Empire into a democratic state with a considerable degree of regional (ethno-national) and local self-government.[49] Even the great historian and politician Mykhailo Hrushevs'kyi, in the aftermath of the collapse of the Tsarist government in 1917, proclaimed as head of the Central *Rada*: "Autonomy—Federation! A broad autonomy for Ukraine within her ethnographic boundaries in a federal union with a democratic Russian republic. This is our platform, our slogan."[50] Only with the Bolshevik seizure of power and invasion of Ukraine did the *Rada* declare independence from Russia. But this declaration still stressed the possibility of "federative ties with the People's Republics of the former Russian state."[51] In short, the ubiquity of multiple Ukrainian/Russian identities and loyalties, and the predominance (in the non-Galician regions of Ukraine) of preferences for federation with Russia over independence from it constitute important historical resources that current state elites could harness in their effort to strengthen national identity on the basis of an Eastern Slavic content. By stressing this history, the state can reassure moderate ethnic Ukrainian nationalists that tighter integration with a democratizing Russia does not amount to a betrayal of Ukraine.

Some readers will object to this chapter's argument by countering that although preference for an Eastern Slavic national identity and tight integration with Russia/CIS are strong now, they will become increasingly weak as generational change replaces older citizens socialized in the Soviet period with younger ones. It is true that support for close ties with Russia varies somewhat by age. In response to the question analyzed earlier on whether unification of the Eastern Slavic states is important for the successful development of Ukrainian society, 61% of respondents 56–70 years old said yes, compared to 59% of those 36–55 years old, and 43% of those 16–35 years old. However, even for the youngest group, more respondents thought Slavic unification necessary for successful development than did not (43% versus 35%).

Other survey data as well demonstrate that young people are very positively disposed toward integration with Russia/CIS. A survey distributed in 1998 to youth 15–30 years old in Russia, Belarus, and Ukraine asked respondents: "The creation of a political and economic union of the separate states/former republics of the USSR, and their unification into a single country is. . ." followed by various options (Table 6.5).[52]

Surprisingly, *more than half* (53%) of young Ukrainians either want unification of the ex-USSR states into a single country as soon as possible, or want it but do not think it is possible. Just 40% think that it should never occur or is not desirable even if it is possible. Surprisingly, Ukrainian youth express very similar levels of support (in one form or another) for the foundation of a new country made up of the former Soviet republics as do youth in Russia (57%) and Belarus (57%). On the domestic front, too, the attitudes of young people do not seem to be compatible with the Ethnic Ukrainian national identity. A 1998 survey shows that young people are more likely than old to speak Russian at home, and that young people are more likely to support making Russian a state language.[53] This strong support of Ukrainian youth for Russian language and an extremely high degree of integration (common statehood) with Russia and other former Soviet republics is inconsistent with the claim that with time the popularity of an Eastern Slavic identity and the domestic and foreign policies it implies will weaken.

Table 6.5
Attitudes of Youth in Ukraine, Belarus, and Russia toward Unification of the Former Republics of the USSR into a Single Country

"The creation of a political and economic union of the separate states/former republics of the USSR, and their unification into a single country is . . ." (in Percentages)

	Ukraine	Belarus	Russia
Necessary as soon as possible	18	17	17
Desirable, but not possible	35	40	40
Possible, but not desirable	15	19	17
Should never occur	25	11	17
Other	6	5	4
No answer	1	7	5

CONCLUSION

The argument made in this chapter contradicts the views of many observers who assume not only that Ukraine's foreign policy is destined to turn westward, but that it must. Volodymyr Zviglyanich, for example, writes that political stability in Ukraine requires that "Russia cannot be [its] major strategic political partner." He claims that "the political future of Ukraine is in Europe," and that Ukraine should avoid "the path of Belarus—a quasicomic/quasitragical example of colonization at the end of the twentieth century."[54] Similarly scornful of Ukraine's tight integration with Russia is David Marples, who asks: "Do the answers to Ukraine's problems then lie in a new union with Russia? It is time to place such conceptions where they really belong: on the garbage heap of history."[55] The problem with such views is that they so disregard, and even belittle, the preferences of the majority of citizens of Ukraine.

To the extent that Ukrainian leaders seek to strengthen national identity, they must choose a content of national identity that best maximizes this strength. A fundamental drawback of an Ethnic Ukrainian national identity is that it demands substantial state-directed reshaping of values, cultural patterns, and policy preferences of the population. This process of engineering social change is difficult, long-term and potentially conflictual. Ukrainian leaders who instead capitalize on the existing panoply of values, cultural patterns, and policy preferences will more easily achieve their goal of strength of national identity. As the data in this chapter suggest, current mass attitudes, especially in the sphere of foreign policy, reflect an overall preference for an Eastern Slavic content of national identity over an Ethnic Ukrainian content. Implementing foreign and domestic policies consistent with the already dominant content of national identity (such as establishing closer political and economic ties with Russia and the CIS) will more likely promote national unity than pursuing less popular policies and identities.

Those observers who, for normative or other reasons, want to rectify historical injustices and construct an Ethnic Ukrainian national identity and the policies it demands must confront the very real possibility that this content of national identity will weaken millions of Ukrainian citizens' loyalty to and identification with the state of Ukraine and the nation it represents. Furthermore, the increased alienation from the Ukrainian state that would likely follow from further breaking ties with Russia and other unpopular policies would greatly intensify the difficulties involved in the marketization and democratization of Ukrainian society. These processes can occur only if the people of Ukraine follow state laws, pay their taxes, participate in the political process, and patiently and peacefully endure many years of further economic deprivation. A strong national identity will catalyze all of these behaviors.

Whether the government in Kyiv pursues an Eastern Slavic identity and the foreign policy course it requires depends much on the individuals and parties that control the executive and legislature. In any case, state leaders fearful of losing power in the face of Slavic integration and weakened Ukrainian sovereignty must remember that their political power derives not only from their prerogatives to make policy in various issue areas, but also from the legitimacy of the state, the cohesion of the population, and citizens' willingness to comply with governmental directives. Available evidence suggests that a stronger eastward foreign orientation will promote the latter.

NOTES

1. See, for example, Ilya Prizel, *National Identity and Foreign Policy: Nationalism and Leadership in Poland, Russia, and Ukraine* (Cambridge: Cambridge University Press, 1998); Vlodymyr Kulyk, "The Search for Post-Soviet Identity in Ukraine and Russia and Its Influence on the Relations Between the Two States," *Harriman Review*, vol. 9, nos. 1–2 (Spring–Summer 1996), pp. 16–27; Victor Stepanenko and Sergei Sorokopud, "The Construction of National Identity," in Christopher Williams and Thanasis D. Sfikas, eds., *Ethnicity and Nationalism in Russia, the CIS and the Baltic States* (Aldershot, England: Ashgate, 1999), pp. 184–210; Paul D'Anieri, "Nationalism and International Politics: Identity and Sovereignty in the Russian-Ukrainian Conflict," *Nationalism and Ethnic Politics*, vol. 3, no. 2 (Summer 1997), pp. 1–28; Taras Kuzio, "European, Eastern Slavic, and Eurasian," in Jennifer D. Moroney, Taras Kuzio, and Mikhail Molchanov, eds., *Ukrainian Foreign and Security Policy* (Westport, CT: Praeger, 2002), pp. 197–296; Roman Laba, "The Russian-Ukrainian Conflict: State, Nation and Identity,"

European Security, vol. 4, no. 3 (Autumn 1995), pp. 457–487; Stephen R. Burant, "Foreign Policy and National Identity: A Comparison of Ukraine and Belarus," *Europe-Asia Studies*, vol. 47, no. 7 (November 1995), pp. 1125–1144; and Charles F. Furtado, Jr., "Nationalism and Foreign Policy in Ukraine," *Political Science Quarterly*, vol. 109, no. 1 (Spring 1994), pp. 81–104.

2. Prizel, *National Identity and Foreign Policy*.

3. Myron Weiner, "Political Integration and Political Development," *Annals of the American Academy of Political and Social Science*, vol. 358 (1965), pp. 52–64; Philip E. Jacob, "The Influence of Values in Political Integration," in Philip E. Jacob and James V. Toscano eds., *The Integration of Political Communities* (Philadelphia: J. B. Lippincott Co., 1964), pp. 209–246; Karl Deutsch, *Tides Among Nations* (New York: Free Press, 1979), chap. 15, pp. 269–296; Leonard Binder, "National Integration and Political Development," *American Political Science Review*, vol. 58, no. 3 (September 1964), pp. 622–631; and Arend Lijphart, "Cultural Diversity and Theories of Political Integration," *Canadian Journal of Political Science*, vol. 4, no. 1 (March 1971), pp. 1–14.

4. According to C. W. Cassinelli, the nation is a group of people who believe that they share common interests, that "these interests require for their promotion the active support of government, and that a government is justified only if it can be interpreted as an agency of the group." C. W. Cassinelli "The National Community," *Polity*, vol. 2, no. 1 (Fall 1969), p. 29.

5. For discussion of the ways in which state policies can fuel ethnic/regional grievances and conflict (and thus weaken national identity), see Paul Brass, ed., *Ethnic Groups and the State* (Totowa, NJ: Barnes and Noble Books, 1985); and Ted Robert Gurr, *Minorities at Risk* (Washington, DC: United States Institute of Peace Press, 1993).

6. The survey questioned 3,135 respondents in twenty-four *oblasti*, Crimea, Kyiv, and Sevastopol.

7. For this survey regions included the following *oblasti*: West: Volyn', Rivne, Ternopil', L'viv, Ivano-Frankivs'k, Trans-Carpathia, and Chernivtsi. Center: Khmel'nyts'kyi, Vinnytsia, Cherkasy, Kirovohrad, and Poltava. North: Zhitomir, Kyiv, Chernihiv, and Sumy. East: Kharkiv, Donets'k, Luhans'k, Dnipropetrovs'k, and Zaporizhzhia. South: Odesa, Khersona, Mykolaiv, and the Crimean Autonomous Republic.

8. The data for this survey are taken from M. I. Beletskii and A. K. Tolpygo, "Natsional'no-kul'turnye i ideologicheskie orientatsii naseleniya Ukrainy," *Politicheskie issledovanie*, no. 4 (1998), pp. 74–89.

9. West: Volyn', Rivne, Ternopil', L'viv, Ivano-Frankivs'k, Trans-Carpathia, and Chernivtsi. West-Center: Khmel'nyts'kyi, Vinnytsia, Kirovohrad, Cherkas'y, Zhitomir, Kyiv, and Kyiv city. East-Center: Poltava, Sumy, Chernihiv, and Dnipropetrovs'k. South: Odesa, Kherson, Mykolaiv, and the Crimean Autonomous Republic. East: Kharkiv, Donets'k, and Luhans'k.

10. Stephen Shulman, *International and National Integration in Multiethnic States: The Sources of Ukrainian (Dis)Unity* (Ph.D. diss., University of Michigan, 1996). The written questionnaire was distributed to educated elites working in seventeen occupations at twenty-seven organizations in Donets'k, and at twenty-three parallel organizations in L'viv. Occupations included university professors, schoolteachers, government administrators, factory managers, lawyers, doctors, musicians, artists, museum administrators, librarians, and others.

11. A good brief overview of Ukrainian foreign policy can be found in F. Stephen Larrabee, "Ukraine's Balancing Act," *Survival*, vol. 38, no. 2 (Summer 1996), pp. 143–165. For more extensive treatment, see Lubomyr Hajda, ed., *Ukraine in the World:*

Studies in the International Relations and Security Structure of a Newly Independent State (Cambridge, MA: Harvard University Press, 1999).

12. *USIA Opinion Analysis*, "Ukrainians Draw Closer to Russia after NATO Air Campaign," M-172-99 (2 September 1999), pp. 2–3. Remaining respondents chose the answers "Strike a Balance" (22%) and "Hard to Say" (7%). Such data contradict the assertion by Kuzio that "There is little support anywhere in Ukraine for political and military integration within the CIS," in his *Ukraine: State and Nation Building* (London: Routledge, 1998), p. 82.

13. *USIA Opinion Analysis*, "Ukrainians Seek Security in Diverse Ways," M-55-96 (15 March 1996), p. 2.

14. The figure for ethnic Ukrainian support for merging Ukraine with Russia would be even higher if respondents in the survey had not had the opportunity to declare a dual Ukrainian-Russian identity, as is the case in most surveys.

15. Kuzio, *Ukraine: State and Nation Building*, p. 49.

16. The results of the 1 December 1991 referendum, according to which 90% of the voters supported Ukrainian independence, are increasingly obsolete. In particular, the strong backing for independence in the eastern *oblasti* in the 1991 vote (83 to 90%) can be seen as an anomaly due to the unique historical circumstances associated with the failed August coup attempt and the delegitimization of the Soviet political order in the late Gorbachev era. Indicative of the disillusionment with Ukrainian independence are the results of a national survey conducted by the Center for Sociological and Political Research and Technology. The July 2000 poll asked respondents whether they would vote for independence if the December 1991 referendum were held today. Just 41% said they would, while 48% said they would not. *Den'*, No. 152, 23 August 2000.

17. For works on the foreign policy debate, see Taras Kuzio, "The Domestic Sources of Ukrainian Security Policy," *Journal of Strategic Studies*, vol. 21, no. 4 (December 1998), pp. 18–49; Taras Kuzio, "Slavophiles versus Westernizers: Foreign Policy Orientations in Ukraine," in Derek Muller, ed., *Ukrainian Foreign and Security Policy Since 1990/91* (Zurich: Center for Security Studies and Conflict Research, 1999); Paul D'Anieri, "Dilemmas of Interdependence: Autonomy, Prosperity, and Sovereignty in Ukraine's Russia Policy," *Problems of Post-Communism,* vol. 44, no. 1 (January–February 1997), pp. 16–26; Ilya Prizel, "The Influence of Ethnicity on Foreign Policy: The Case of Ukraine," in Roman Szporluk, ed., *National Identity and Ethnicity in Russia and the New States of Eurasia* (Armonk, NY: M. E. Sharpe, 1994), pp. 103–128.

18. Zenovia A. Sochor, "No Middle Ground? On the Difficulties of Crafting a Consensus in Ukraine," *Harriman Review*, vol. 9, nos. 1–2 (Spring-Summer 1996), p. 58.

19. Kuzio, "European, Eastern Slavic, and Eurasian."

20. In May–June 1997, 54% of respondents in a poll by the Democratic Initiatives Foundation felt "positively" or "mostly positively" about joining the union of Belarus and Russia (Center for the Study of Democracy, "An Archive of Ukrainian Public Opinion" [Online]. Available: http://csd.queensu.ca/ukarchive). As noted earlier, 53% of respondents in March 1999 believed that unification of Ukraine, Belarus, and Russia is necessary for Ukraine's the successful development.

21. Walker Connor, "Eco- or Ethno-Nationalism," in *Ethnonationalism: A Quest for Understanding* (Princeton: Princeton University Press, 1994), pp. 145–164; and Milton J. Esman, "Economic Performance and Ethnic Conflict," in Joseph V. Montville, ed., *Conflict and Peacemaking in Multiethnic Societies* (Lexington, MA: Lexington Books, 1990), pp. 477–490.

22. Also undermining the supposition that economic factors are dominant in the pro-Russian position is the finding by Valeri Khmelko and Andrew Wilson, based on a sur-

vey in December 1993–January 1994, that support for unification of Ukraine and Russia into a single state only very weakly correlates with views on how standards of living have changed since independence (coefficient of determination = 0.07). "Regionalism and Ethnic and Linguistic Cleavages in Ukraine," in T. Kuzio, ed., *Contemporary Ukraine: Dynamics of Post-Soviet Transformation* (Armonk, NY: M. E. Sharpe, 1998), p. 71.

23. In this version of the question Belarus was omitted since most people in Western Ukraine harbor few negative feelings toward this country.

24. For a discussion of the distinction between political and cultural nations, see Peter Alter, *Nationalism* (London: Edward Arnold, 1994), pp. 8–10; and Anthony D. Smith, *National Identity* (Reno: University of Nevada Press, 1991), pp. 8–14.

25. The March 1999 survey by the Ukrainian Institute of Social Research and Social Monitoring Center found that 61% of respondents trusted the armed forces ("completely" or "partially"), with much smaller figures for the judiciary (31%), police (29%), Supreme Council (12%), and cabinet of ministers (government—11%). Another source finds that confidence in state institutions is lowest among young Ukrainian citizens, and increases with age (*USIA Opinion Analysis*, "Growing Pains in Ukraine's Political Culture," M-48-96 [14 March 1996], p. 2). This suggests that the civic elements of Ukrainian national identity content will not automatically increase in strength with time.

26. A June 1999 survey found that 58% of respondents did not think the October 1999 presidential elections would be fair and honest, compared to only 24% who thought they would. Additionally, 71% of respondents thought that they have "little or no influence on the ways things are run in Ukraine." International Foundation for Election Systems, "IFES National Surveys" [Online]. Available: http://ifes.ipri.kiev.ua/Surveys/index.html.

27. The June 1999 survey cited in endnote 26 shows respondents approximately equally divided among support for a market economy (27%), a centrally planned economy (30%), and a mixture of both (25%). A 1997 survey reveals similar disagreement over multiparty democracy. It found that 36% of respondents think a multiparty system in Ukraine is not necessary, 29% think it is necessary, and 36% found it difficult to say. "Ukrain'ske suspil'stvo 1994–1997," *Politychnyi Portret Ukrainy*, vol. 20 (1998), p. 19.

28. For a good, brief analysis of the variegated history and characteristics of the lands that constitute Ukraine, see F. D. Zastavnyi, *Ukrains'ki ethnichni zemli* (L'viv: Svit, 1993).

29. According to a 1998 survey, when asked, "Who do you most of all feel yourself to be?" the majority of respondents said an inhabitant of either their city or district (*raion*) (53%) or *oblast* (7%). Only 21% felt that they primarily are citizens of Ukraine. Other responses were citizen of the CIS (5%), European (5%), and citizen of the world (8%). Ukrainian Institute of Social Research, *Monitoryng hromads'koi dumky naselennya Ukrainy* (vol. 10, no. 23), p. 38. At the same time it is important to stress that, outside Crimea, support for the territorial integrity of Ukraine is strong (Kuzio, *Ukraine: State and Nation Building*, pp. 69–99).

30. For derivation of the theoretical statements that follow, see Shulman, *International and National Integration*.

31. For the importance of boundaries in ethnic identities, see Fredrik Barth, "Introduction," in Fredrik Barth, ed., *Ethnic Groups and Boundaries: The Social Organization of Cultural Difference* (Oslo: Little, Brown, 1969), pp. 9–38.

32. For further discussion of the effect of cultural diffusion on ethnic and national identities in Ukraine, see S. Shulman, "Cultures in Competition: Ukrainian Foreign Policy and the 'Cultural Threat' from Abroad," *Europe-Asia Studies*, vol. 50, no. 2 (March 1998), pp. 287–304.

33. Consistent with the Ukrainian nationalist tradition, the ethnic Ukrainian identity posits that Ukrainian culture is much more individualistic, freedom loving, and democratic than Russian culture, and on that basis is similar to European culture. For further discussion of cultural comparisons and their relevance to national identity in Ukraine, see S. Shulman "The Cultural Foundations of Ukrainian National Identity," *Ethnic and Racial Studies*, vol. 22, no. 6 (November 1999), pp. 1011–1036.

34. For analysis of the debate over the compatibility of Ukrainian and Russian identities in Ukraine and its relationship to foreign policy, see S. Shulman, "Competing versus Complementary Identities: Ukrainian-Russian Relations and the Loyalties of Russians in Ukraine," *Nationalities Papers*, vol. 26, no. 4, (December 1998), pp. 615–632.

35. Kuzio writes, "For state and nation building to proceed in Ukraine . . . Ukrainian and Russian identities have to be disentangled from one another; that is they have to return to the more clearly defined separate nationalities which existed prior to the first half of the nineteenth century." However, this is true only for the ethnic Ukrainian content of national identity, not the Eastern Slavic identity. Kuzio, *Ukraine: State and Nation Building*, p. 154.

36. The relative tenacity of ethnic and national identification and culture is demonstrated by the great difficulty states have had in pursuing policies of assimilation. See Walker Connor, "Nation-Building or Nation-Destroying," in *Ethnonationalism: A Quest for Understanding* (Princeton, Princeton University Press, 1994), pp. 29–66.

37. Kuzio, "Domestic Sources of Ukrainian Security Policy," p. 29.

38. Shulman, "Competing versus Complimentary Identities," pp. 627–628.

39. Beletskii and Tolpygo, "Natsional'no kul'turnye," p. 83.

40. Khmelko and Wilson, "Regionalism and Ethnic and Linguistic Cleavages in Ukraine," p. 74.

41. *USIA Opinion Analysis*, "Growing Pains in Ukraine's Political Culture," M-48-96 (14 March 1996), p. 2.

42. Anatolii Ruchka and Liudmila Skokova, "Vidkrytist' Ukrains'koho suspil'stva: etnokul'turnyi vymir," *Rozbudova Derzhavy*, nos. 7 / 8, 1998, pp. 102–107.

43. Based on the regionalization scheme in endnote 7, the population of the West in 1991 was 9.8 million, while the population of the East and South was 25.2 million. Calculated from F. D. Zastavnyi, *Heohrafiia Ukrainy* (L'viv: Svit, 1994), p. 121.

44. Such a move would have to weigh the risks of increasing "asymmetrical international integration" in Ukraine, a term referring to the asymmetries in foreign ties of western Ukraine and eastern Ukraine. This asymmetry itself hinders national unity. See S. Shulman, "Asymmetrical International Integration and Ukrainian National Disunity," *Political Geography*, vol. 18, no. 8 (November 1999), pp. 913–939.

45. Zenon Kohut describes how in the nineteenth century it was widely accepted that one could be both a Russian and a Little Russian (Ukrainian). "The Development of the Little Russian Identity and Ukrainian Nation-Building," *Harvard Ukrainian Studies*, vol. 6, nos. 3/4 (1986), pp. 559–576. Orest Subtelny writes that with the rise of the intelligentsia in the nineteenth century, "Most educated Ukrainians, as members of the imperial establishment, remained enamored of the all-Russian idea and its Little Russian variant." Orest Subtelny, "Russocentrism, Regionalism, and Political Culture," in Vladimir Tismaneau, ed., *Political Culture and Civil Society in Russia and the New States of Eurasia* (Armonk, NY: M. E. Sharpe, 1995), p. 191.

46. Prizel, *National Identity and Foreign Policy*, p. 310.

47. Mykola Kostomarov, "A Letter to the Editor of Kolokol," in Ralph Lindheim and George S. N. Luckyj, eds., *Towards an Intellectual History of Ukraine: An Anthology of*

Ukrainian Thought from 1710 to 1995 (Toronto: University of Toronto Press, 1996), p. 144.

48. Panteleimon Kulish, "Epilogue to *The Black Council*: On the Relation of Little Russian Literature to Common-Russian Literature," in Lindheim and Luckyj, *Towards an Intellectual History*, p. 121.

49. Mykhailo Drahomanov, "Draft Constitution for the Ukrainian Society in the Free Union," in Lindheim and Luckyj, *Towards an Intellectual History*, pp. 171–183.

50. Mykhailo Hrushevsky, "A Free Ukraine," in Lindheim and Luckyj, *Towards an Intellectual History*, p. 232.

51. Prizel, *National Identity and Foreign Policy*, p. 324.

52. "Upravlinnia vnutrishn'noi polityky Administratsii Prezydenta Ukrainy," *Suchasna politychna sytuatsiia v otsintsi hromads'koi dumky*, no. 11 (1998), pp. 12–13.

53. "Ukraine: Survey Shows Support for Ukrainian and Russian Languages," *Radio Free Europe/Radio Liberty Weekday Magazine*, 11 August 1998.

54. Volodymyr Zviglyanich, "The Specter of Integration in Russia: Lessons for the West and Ukraine," *A Political Portrait of Ukraine*, no. 8 (1997), pp. 20–22.

55. "Ukraine and the Russian School," *Ukrainian Weekly*, no. 14, 2 April 2000.

7

Region, Language, and Nationality: Rethinking Support in Ukraine for Maintaining Distance from Russia

Lowell W. Barrington

With the collapse of the Soviet Union, Ukraine—like the other former Soviet republics—was suddenly converted into a newly independent state. This independence was supported by much of the population, though many others were less sure about the former republic's new independent status. As high hopes about Ukraine's economic future, held both by the population of the country and by many Western scholars, were dashed in the first few years of independence, the wisdom of "distancing" the country from Russia was further called into question. By the late 1990s, with nearly a decade of sovereignty behind it, the country's independence appeared to be on solid ground. Yet, with the continuing economic misery, large numbers of people in Ukraine continued to hold the position that it should be, at the extreme, united with Russia in a single state or, at the least, pursuing much closer relations with its eastern neighbor. Those holding these positions felt that, if not an end to independence, there should at least be an end to the policy of distancing the country from Russia.

There has been a great deal written about the possibility of narrowing Ukraine's societal cleavages. Some assert that government-led efforts can heal societal rifts. Others assert that such differences are beyond the government's control, and that efforts to define Ukrainian identity must seek to recognize rather than overcome these problems. For any of these arguments to make sense, however, we must clearly understand the nature of cleavages in Ukraine. In particular, this means understanding the relationships among regional, linguistic, and ethnic components of identity. If Ukraine's cleavages are based more on region than on language, then programs to increase the use of the Ukrainian language, even if successful, may not substantially enhance societal cohesion. This chapter aims to help sort out the relationship among ethnic, linguistic, and regional cleavages, in order to provide a clearer diagnosis of Ukraine's problems.

What kinds of people in Ukraine would be more likely or less likely to support maintaining policies of distance from Russia? Over the last decade, numerous scholars of contemporary Ukraine have contended that the country's population is deeply divided along geographic, cultural, and socioeconomic lines. Arguably, the most discussed cleavage in Ukraine is language. This is partly because of the many Russian-speaking ethnic Ukrainians, especially in the east of the country. Scholars have typically assumed that the language an individual speaks in Ukraine is a highly important factor in shaping his/her attitudes about Ukrainian politics, economics, and independence. Ethnic identity (used interchangeably in this chapter with the term common to post-Soviet studies, *nationality*) is itself considered by many an important cleavage in Ukraine. Ethnicity has been an important political force throughout the former Soviet Union, and the presence of a large number of ethnic Russians in Ukraine (the largest ethnic minority in Europe) would indicate a potential importance of ethnicity in that country as well.

The Ukrainian regional divide has received less attention than it deserves as a factor in its own right, because it coincides somewhat with ethnicity and language use. When it has been focused on, it has often been discussed in simple terms—the east of the country versus the west, with the results of the presidential election in June–July 1994 providing tangible support for this position. For a few scholars, the regional divide has been considered to be more complex, with four or more distinct regions identified. The October–November 1999 presidential elections lend support to the idea of a more complex regional picture. This chapter (as does the chapter by Taras Kuzio) takes the approach that regional divisions in Ukraine are not as simple as east versus west. It employs a modified version of Arel's framework[1] and analyzes attitudes in Ukraine in nine regions—including Crimea and the city of Kyiv—as regions of the country distinct from the other, larger sections.

Language, ethnicity, and region are thus the three main social cleavages discussed by scholars of Ukraine. But what effects do these divisions have on support for maintaining Ukrainian independence from Russia? What is the effect of each when the others are controlled for? Are apparent regional effects simply due to the ethnolinguistic composition of the various areas of Ukraine? Are language and nationality really as important as scholars writing about Ukraine have assumed? This chapter provides answers to these questions, through the analysis of mass survey data from Ukraine collected in the late 1990s.

The statistical analysis presented in this chapter is based on the idea that variation in support for independence in Ukraine originates from basic demographic differences among individuals in the country: where they live, what nationality they are, what language they speak, how they are doing economically, and so on. The literature on mass attitudes in Ukraine has centered on these basic demographic differences as the driving force behind attitudinal variation at the aggregate and individual levels. While such analysis precludes an examination of grand theories of political attitudes in different settings, it is very useful for building a better understanding of attitudinal variation in Ukraine and its implications.

The results of this study indicate that region of residence plays a very important role in shaping support for independence, while other factors commonly emphasized by scholars of Ukraine are less consequential. The effects of nationality and language are generally much weaker than many scholars of Ukraine have assumed, once region is controlled for. Thus, while ethnic and linguistic divisions may, to a certain extent, reinforce the effects of region in Ukraine, regional cleavages are not simply proxies for ethnolinguistic patterns in the country. Instead, it appears that a complex set of regionally differentiated attitudes has emerged in Ukraine about important questions such as the appropriate distance from Russia, even when one controls for other demographic determinants of such attitudes. These results call into question the emphasis in Ukraine on balancing the interests of the various ethnic and linguistic groups in an attempt to develop a unifying national identity. The results indicate that, unlike other former Soviet states but like many countries in the West, the real impediments to unity in Ukraine may be related to where in the country one lives and how one is doing economically rather than who one is ethnically or what language one speaks.

These findings are particularly important today. A great deal has been written in recent years about the possibility of narrowing Ukraine's societal cleavages. Some assert that government-led efforts can heal societal rifts. Others assert that such differences are beyond the government's control and that efforts to define Ukrainian identity must seek to recognize, rather than overcome, these problems. But to make sense of any of these arguments, we must clearly understand the nature and relative strength of these cleavages in Ukraine. In particular, this means understanding the relationships among the regional, linguistic, and ethnic components of identity. If Ukraine's cleavages are based more on region than on language, then programs to increase the use of the Ukrainian language, even if successful, may not substantially enhance societal cohesion. Thus, by beginning to sort out the independent effects of ethnic, linguistic, and regional cleavages, this chapter can help to develop a clearer diagnosis of Ukraine's problems than can be found in the prevailing conventional wisdom about the country.

SUPPORT FOR DISTANCING UKRAINE FROM RUSSIA

To measure support in Ukraine for maintaining distance from Russia, a scale was constructed from the responses to questions in a late 1998 survey administered in Ukraine.[2] The possible range of values of the scale measuring support for maintaining independence is -30 to 30. The mean score on the support for distance from Russia scale was -0.33, statistically indistinguishable from 0. While someone unfamiliar with Ukraine might be surprised that the mean of such a scale was not more strongly positive, this score actually indicates an improvement in support for maintaining independence from Russia.[3] Using similar questions to the ones in this study, a previous investigation of attitudes in Ukraine found weaker support for independence in 1994.[4]

THE EFFECTS OF LANGUAGE, NATIONALITY, AND REGION ON SUPPORT FOR DISTANCE FROM RUSSIA

While support for Ukrainian independence may be stronger today than it has been, such support varies in Ukraine at the individual level. What can explain this variation? What drives one person in Ukraine to support distancing the country from Russia while another opposes it?

The Potential Importance of Language in Ukraine

Much of the discussion of scholars about attitudes in Ukraine has focused on the role of language. In particular, Arel's work has centered on the "linguistic fault line" in Ukraine, and the way that language affects politics in the country. The majority of scholars have taken for granted Arel's claims that "language politics in Ukraine is coterminous with regional politics,"[5] that language differences are "arguably the most important cleavage affecting Ukrainian society," and that "the major cleavage in Ukraine is *linguistic*, and not primarily *ethnic*."[6] Craumer and Clem's statement that the "Russian-speaking population of Ukrainian ethnicity [has] attitudes more like those of Russians than those of Ukrainian-speaking Ukrainians" is a common sentiment among authors of works on contemporary Ukraine.[7]

In most countries, one would find language dividing ethnic minorities—with some in the minority speaking the language of the titular majority group. In Ukraine, however, members of the *majority* are divided by language. Many ethnic Ukrainians in the east, south, Kyiv, and other large cities speak Russian as their first language. Every *oblast* capital city in the east and south of the country has a Russian-speaking majority. In Crimea, 25% of the population are ethnic Ukrainian, but only around 4% are Ukrainian-speaking.

Since independence, the educational practices regarding language have changed, leading to the "de-Russification of schools" in the country.[8] In Kyiv, for example, 80% of students were taught in Russian-language schools prior to independence, but by the early 1990s, nearly 90% of first graders were taught in Ukrainian-language schools. In addition, the language of administration in the country at the national level is now Ukrainian, though regional and local governments in many areas still function in Russian, and Russian remains the spoken language even in many central government offices. Despite the changes, the language policy of the Ukrainian government remains intentionally ambiguous, and still about half of the total population of Ukraine speak Russian as their first language.

Thus, language is an important issue in Ukraine today, and it is certainly possible that language provides a "fault line" in the country, affecting such factors as support for independence from Russia. Again, scholars have assumed that these linguistic characteristics of the population of Ukraine have important implications, even controlling for other factors. Unfortunately, while Arel associates language lines with regional and urban patterns, he has not tested the language thesis by controlling for cleavages such as region and nationality.

The Potential Importance of Nationality in Ukraine

While language lines crosscut ethnic ones in Ukraine (at least in the case of ethnic Ukrainians), the ethnic breakdown of the country supports the idea that nationality could influence attitudes toward maintaining independence. The presence of more than eleven million ethnic Russians, making up more than one-fifth of the population of Ukraine, and their concentration in the east of the country (especially Crimea), makes the development of attitudes along ethnic lines possible. In addition, the existence of Russia as a neighbor and potential external homeland, and the perception among Russians of their bleak economic fate,[9] adds to a possible ethnic divide. Indeed, previous studies have found differences in support for institutions in the Soviet Union along ethnic lines, and attitudinal differences between Russians and Ukrainians, before and after independence.

Yet, nationality has *not* been as powerful in Ukraine as the preceding discussion would indicate. Nationality has been limited as a mobilizing force in the population in part because leaders in Ukraine have emphasized the idea of Ukraine as a multinational state. Ukraine's Law on National Minorities is typical of the Ukrainian government's approach (see the chapters by Taras Kuzio and Craig Weller in this volume). Not only does the law guarantee rights for national minorities, including the use of their native language and exercise of their native cultural practices, but it also calls for state support for national minority groups. During the drive for independence, deputies in the Supreme *Rada* argued that the focus should be on the "people of Ukraine" rather than on a Ukraine for the "Ukrainian people," and this emphasis continued after independence. A few politicians in western Ukraine spoke of a single-nation state, but none of the top leaders (including the "national democrats") were seriously pursuing the idea of Ukraine as an ethnically defined nation-state.[10]

The presidents of Ukraine have taken the lead in fostering interethnic harmony. During his time as president, Kravchuk pushed the idea that Ukraine was a multinational state. In criticizing those labeling the Russians as a potential fifth column in 1991, for example, Kravchuk said:

I want to point out that the Russians in Ukraine should not be compared with the Russians in the Baltic republics. Here they are indigenous residents, they have lived on this land for hundreds of years. . . . And we will not permit any kind of discrimination against them. . . . Our republic, pardon me for saying so, is not Latvia, Estonia or Moldova.[11]

Thus, nationality is hypothesized to be a factor in shaping attitudes toward distancing Ukraine from Russia, though it may *not* be as powerful as others such as region. But, again, until one controls for other factors, it is difficult to assess the role of nationality in shaping attitudes in Ukraine.

"Regionalism" in Ukraine: East versus West, or Something More?

This chapter argues that regional divisions are more important in Ukraine than scholars who focus on ethnicity and language have assumed. The regional divide in Ukraine has not been ignored by scholars, though it is often discussed in terms of Ukraine's east versus its west, with the Dnipro River serving as an abyss which divides Ukraine into two roughly equal parts. And, certainly, it is tempting to think of Ukraine in such a way. From the 1960s to the late 1980s, the Russian population in Ukraine increased by more than 60%; most of these Russians settled in the industrial areas of the east. During this same period a large number of Ukrainians became Russophones. Scholars have focused on the implications of an east/west split for post-independence Ukrainian politics. A favorite example is the 1994 presidential election, in which Leonid Kuchma, running on a platform of closer ties with Russia, won in every *oblast* east of the Dnipro River.[12] The incumbent, Leonid Kravchuk, who supported distancing Ukraine from Russia, won every *oblast* in the west. Unfortunately for Kravchuk, more people live in Ukraine's east than in its west.

While one can make a case for discussing an east/west regional split in Ukraine, there is more to the story of regionalism in Ukraine than a line dividing the country in two. Historical experience, economic and demographic characteristics, and proximity to Russia combine to present a picture of many distinct regions in Ukraine.[13] Seemingly every scholar who has tried to move beyond the east/west framework has chosen a different set of regions. This chapter uses a modified version of the framework established by Arel.[14] Arel's framework was chosen as a starting point because it is one that combines the various elements mentioned above to bring together contiguous *oblasti* into sensible regions.

VARIABLES EXAMINED IN THE INDIVIDUAL-LEVELANALYSIS OF VARIATION IN SUPPORT FOR DISTANCE FROM RUSSIA

Region, Language, and Nationality as Explanations for Individual-Level Variation in Support

To examine the role of region in individual-level analysis, a set of dummy variable terms was created by combining Ukraine's *oblasti* into nine larger regions (west, west-central, central, south, south-east, north-east, east, Crimea, and Kyiv). Likewise, three dummy terms were used for nationality—Ukrainian, Russian, and "other"—based on self-reporting of nationality in the survey.[15] The dummy terms for the language variable came from the interviewer's labeling of the language patterns of the respondent in answering the survey questions, and were composed of three language groups (Russian, "mixed," and Ukrainian). This form of the language variable is preferred to one based on the respondent's discussion of his language use, since it both captures the actual use of language by the respondent and allows for the kind of mixed language use common in Ukraine.

Other Demographic Factors

While this chapter has focused on region, language, and nationality, one must consider other possible influences as well. Other factors examined in the individual-level analysis in this chapter include the respondent's economic situation at present, whether or not the respondent is a religious believer, the sex of respondent, the age of the respondent, the size of the respondent's locality, and the respondent's level of education.

The Exclusion of Attitudinal Explanatory Variables

The variables examined in this chapter are thus all demographic factors. Readers familiar with other studies of mass attitudes in post-Communist states may wonder about the exclusion of attitudinal variables such as support for economic reform, trust, efficacy, and life satisfaction. Such attitudinal factors are not included as explanatory variables in this study. They are taken to be a fundamentally different kind of variable from the variables focused on in this study. Rather than exogenous variables, as the demographic factors are, these attitudinal variables are understood here to be intervening factors in a partially mediated structure. In other words, they are presumed to fall at a different stage of a causal system from the demographic variables—located between the demographic factors and the dependent variable. Modeled in full, such a structure would contain both direct and indirect effects of the demographics on support for maintaining distance from Russia.

The model presented in this chapter thus serves as the reduced form of a more complex causal structure. As a result, the OLS coefficient estimates are estimates of the total effects of the demographic variables. Using the reduced form makes it infeasible to separate the direct and indirect effects of the demographic factors, and it makes it impossible to analyze which of the attitudinal factors that scholars have treated as exogenous in previous studies are statistically significant and substantively important when modeled as endogenous. But the purpose of this chapter is not to examine the mediating role for such attitudes or to estimate the relative strength of the direct and indirect effects of the demographic variables.[16] Rather, given the kinds of factors that scholars have emphasized in works on Ukraine (region, language, nationality, etc.), its purpose is to examine the total effects of these factors, while holding constant the effects of other likely important demographic factors.

RESULTS AND DISCUSSION

Employing data from a nationally representative sample of more than 1,600 respondents collected as part of the November 1998 KIIS (Kyiv International Institute of Sociology) Ukraine Omnibus Survey, the equation for the dependent variable (support for independence/distance from Russia) was estimated. The dummy variables for region, language use, nationality, size of locality, education level, religious believer status, sex of the respondent, and economic situation at present were included in the analysis.[17] As one must do with dummy variables, at least one dummy variable term from each set (the "west" region from the group of dummy variable terms representing regions, for example) was left out of the equation.[18] The effects of the excluded dummy terms show up as part of the value of the estimated equation's constant term, and, more important, an excluded term serves as the basis of comparison for the coefficients of the included dummy terms from the variable in question. Thus, the coefficients on the included terms of the region variable represent the difference in support between that region and the West region, other factors being constant.

The Statistical Significance of the Coefficient Estimates

Table 7.1 contains the regression coefficient estimates and other statistics from the estimation of the effects on the values of the support for distance from

Russia scale using the explanatory variables discussed above. Because arguments exist for either a positive or a negative direction of effect for some of the explanatory variables, significance levels in the tables and in the discussion below are based on two-tailed tests.

Nearly all of the variables are significant at the $p = 0.05$ level. The central region dummy variable coefficient is significant at the $p = 0.1$ level, as is religious believer status. The only variables without such statistical significance are age, and the dummy variable terms for some higher education, and for medium and large cities.

The Importance of Regional Differences

Because most of the factors analyzed are in dummy variable form, it is possible to compare the unstandardized coefficients. In doing so, the coefficients on the regional variables jump out. Compared to respondents in the far west, respondents in Crimea and the east scored more than nineteen points lower on the support for distance from Russia scale, other things constant. Since the scale has a range of only sixty points, this is a notable difference. Residents in the regions of the north-east, south-east, south, Kyiv city, and west-central averaged between thirteen and seventeen points lower. Only those in the central region came close to the level of support of those in the far west.

Not only were the coefficients on these variables impressive, but also the pattern was very interesting. Contrary to the west versus east idea common to works on Ukraine, respondents in the west-central region thought more like those in the east than like the residents to their immediate west. Those in the central region (again, excluding Kyiv City), on the other hand, were more similar to those in the far west than to residents in the regions around them. Residents in the capital city of Kyiv were also closer to those in the east than the far west, though very different from those in the central region (showing the importance of separating Kyiv City from that region in the analysis).

The Relative Weakness of Nationality and Language as Explanatory Factors

While coefficients on the regional dummy variable terms were extraordinary, the results of the nationality and language variables were less impressive. Granted, the nationality variable terms were highly significant, and their coefficients conspicuous. A Russian would score nearly six points lower on the independence scale than a Ukrainian, other things being constant, while a member of another nationality in Ukraine would be even less supportive. Thus, nationality matters, though less than region. Language matters as well, to an extent. Controlling for other factors, Russian speakers and mixed speakers were both about 3.5 points lower on the distance from Russia scale than Ukrainian speakers. But, again, when one compares the effects of the language variables with that of the regional variables, the effects are much smaller on the highly emotional issue of maintaining independence from Russia.

Table 7.1
OLS Regression Results, Support for Distance from Russia Scale

Dependent Variable: "INDSCALE" (Mean = -0.33; Min. = -30.00; Max. = 30.00)

Independent Variables:	B	SE B	T-Stat	Signif
Regions (Comparison Region: West)				
Crimea	-19.38	2.72	-7.13	0.0000
East	-19.59	1.83	-10.65	0.0000
North-East	-17.30	2.32	-7.45	0.0000
South-East	-16.25	2.01	-8.06	0.0000
South	-16.52	2.13	-7.77	0.0000
Kyiv City	-13.60	2.68	-5.07	0.0000
Central	-3.17	1.64	-1.93	0.0537
West-Central	-13.56	1.74	-7.76	0.0000
Language (Comparison Language: Ukrainian)				
Russian	-3.57	1.57	-2.27	0.0231
Mixed	-3.50	1.53	-2.29	0.0222
Nationality (Comparison Nationality: Ukrainian)				
Russian	-5.79	1.26	-4.60	0.0000
Other Non-Ukrainian	-7.20	2.20	-3.28	0.0011
Locality Type (Comparison Locality Type: Village)				
Very Large City	7.52	1.50	5.00	0.0000
Large City	1.40	1.36	1.03	0.3014
Medium City	0.81	1.46	0.55	0.5795
Small City	3.71	1.62	2.30	0.0219
Education (Comparison Education Level: Completed Higher Education)				
Low Education	-4.88	1.48	-3.30	0.0010
Completed Secondary	-3.14	1.27	-2.47	0.0135
Some Higher Education	-1.38	2.81	-0.49	0.6229
Personal Economic Standing (Comparison Standings: Medium, High, Very High)				
Low	-4.38	1.73	-2.54	0.0112
Very Low	-7.20	1.77	-4.06	0.0001
Other Demographic Characteristics				
Religious Believer	1.76	1.00	1.76	0.0786
Male	2.58	0.92	2.79	0.0053
Age	-0.03	0.03	-1.23	0.2185
(Constant)	20.48	2.57	7.97	0.0000

$R^2 = 0.273$; Adjusted $R^2 = 0.262$; Standard Error = 17.26; $F = 24.19$; Sig. $F = 0.0000$

Ethnic Groups and Language Groups, or "Ethnolinguistic Groups"?

Given the assumption by scholars of the importance of ethnic and linguistic differences in Ukraine, the relatively weak effect of the language and nationality variable coefficients will come as a surprise to many. Yet, the findings are similar to some previous findings after region and other factors are controlled for.[19] At the same time, one could claim that the separation of nationality and language misses the point. The power of language in Ukraine, the argument goes, comes precisely when it is combined with an opposing nationality—such as Russian-speaking Ukrainians or Ukrainian-speaking Russians. While there are hardly any of the latter in Ukraine, there are many of the former, especially in the east, south, and Kyiv. Thus, one could argue that rather than entering language and nationality into the equation as separate sets of dummy variables, they should instead be combined into ethnolinguistic groups. If the argument for the importance of language is correct, one would expect that those of the same ethnic background but different languages (Ukrainian-speaking Ukrainians versus Russian-speaking Ukrainians) would have significantly different attitudes.

The "ethnolinguistic groups" idea was tested by replacing the language and nationality dummy variables with dummy terms representing various ethnolinguistic categories: Russian-speaking Russians, Russian-speaking Ukrainians, Russian-speaking "others," mixed-speaking Russians, mixed-speaking Ukrainians, mixed-speaking "others," Ukrainian-speaking Russians, and Ukrainian-speaking "others." Ukrainian-speaking Ukrainians were excluded from the equation to serve as the comparison group; thus, the coefficient estimates on the ethnolinguistic dummy variable terms are the difference on the support scale for each group compared to Ukrainian-speaking Ukrainians.

The primary concern in this version of the model is the pattern of the coefficients of the ethnolinguistic dummy variable terms. The other coefficient estimates (and other statistics such as R^2) would be nearly identical to those of the previous equations, since language and nationality are still controlled for when estimating these coefficients, but in a different form.[20] As a result, while the other variables were included in the estimation of the three support scale equations, Table 7.2 contains only the coefficient estimates for the ethnolinguistic dummy variable terms.[21]

The coefficient estimate on Russian-speaking Ukrainians achieves statistical significance at the $p = 0.1$ level, but its (negative) value is minor compared to the very large and highly statistically significant negative coefficients on the Russian-speaking Russian and Russian-speaking "other" variables. On the issue of maintaining distance from Russia, *Russian-speaking Ukrainians think a lot more like Ukrainian-speaking Ukrainians than like Russian-speaking members of other nationalities.* Further evidence for the strength of nationality over language on this issue is the statistically significant, large, and negative coefficient on the mixed-speaking Russian variable.[22]

Thus, employing the ethnolinguistic groups approach confirms that the language spoken by an individual in Ukraine is less important than many have assumed, once other social cleavages are controlled for. This finding strongly challenges the prevalent claim in the literature that Russian-speaking Ukrainians think more like Russians than like their Ukrainian-speaking coethnics. Together, the two versions of the model show the danger of not controlling for region when examining nationality and language (either as separate variables or as combined ethnolinguistic groups) in the case of Ukraine.

Table 7.2
Coefficient Estimates for the "Ethno-linguistic" Dummy Variable Terms, OLS Analysis of the Effects of the Demographic Variables on the Support for Distance from Russia Scale

Dependent Variable: "Indscale" (Mean = -0.33; Min. = -30.00; Max. = 30.00)
Independent Variables: Ethno-linguistic groups
(Comparison Group: Ukrainian-Speaking Ukrainians)

	B	SE B	T-Stat	Signif
Russian-Speaking Ukrainians	-2.64	1.60	-1.65	.0986
Russian-Speaking Russians	-8.70	1.67	-5.21	.0000
Russian-Speaking "Others"	-11.98	2.53	-4.74	.0000
Mixed-Speaking Ukrainians	-2.96	1.57	-1.88	.0599
Mixed-Speaking Russians	-9.63	2.87	-3.36	.0008
Mixed-Speaking "Others"	-1.61	8.75	-0.18	.8544
Ukrainian-Speaking Russians	-2.22	5.06	-0.44	.6601
Ukrainian-Speaking "Others"	0.06	5.53	0.01	.9915

CONCLUSION: IMPLICATIONS FOR UKRAINE AND ACADEMIC STUDIES OF THE COUNTRY

It is clear that the population of Ukraine is still far from united in its attitudes toward the country's appropriate distance from Russia. Investigating such variation through individual-level analysis of demographic differences, this chapter surveys the social, economic, and geographic "fault lines" in Ukraine. For those who study Ukraine, the analysis indicates that both linguistic and nationality factors in Ukraine have been somewhat overblown. In addition, the results suggest that the idea that Russian-speaking Ukrainians think more like ethnic Russians than like Ukrainian-speaking Ukrainians needs to be reconsidered by scholars within the Ukrainian studies community.

This analysis also strongly supports the vision of "region" in Ukraine as less exact than the east-versus-west image so common in works on the country. The far west is clearly more supportive of independence than other parts of the country,[23] but one must avoid what could be called the "Dnipro River trap" of thinking in dichotomous (west-versus-east) terms when discussing regionalism in Ukraine. Finally, while the regional story is more complex than many assume, the results presented in this chapter demonstrate that the power of regional differences in Ukraine is considerable. It is even more so since the factors scholars tend to associate with regional differences in Ukraine (e.g., language, nationality, urbanization, and standard of living) were controlled for in the statistical analysis.

For Ukraine itself, the picture painted by this analysis of support for distancing the country from Russia is a mixed one. During the mid to late 1990s, there was an apparent increase in support for independence from Russia, which is consistent with both Kravchuk's and Kuchma's distancing policies, as well as reflecting the reality of separation from Russia. In addition, the regional divisions are not perfectly complementary of ethnic and linguistic cleavages, and these latter divisions do not appear to be as strong as many scholars of Ukraine have taken for granted.[24] One's personal economic situation appears to have a greater impact on support for distancing Ukraine from Russia, for example, than either nationality or language. Thus, the prospects for a successful regional separatist movement in Ukraine along ethnic or ethnolinguistic lines seem remote (see also the chapter by Craig Weller).

But the large numbers of people who continue to oppose independence, and the statements of Communist Party officials in Ukraine about it, mean that the policies of distancing Ukraine from Russia, and even the maintenance of Ukrainian independence, are still not guaranteed.[25] That differences in Ukraine remain as strong as they are along regional lines means that the country will face a certain degree of political instability in the near future.[26] As Agnew argues, the state-building process involves linking regions of a country to the center.[27] In addition, a central feature of nation building is creating a population that is relatively unified in its support of the political community. There is no better measure of a population's sense of unity as a political community in a newly independent state than its unity on the issue of maintaining the new independence. Thus, if mass attitudes signal difficulties in the large nation- and state-building projects, one could expect difficult political fights on a variety of fronts in the near future. However, those fights may not be based on ethnic or linguistic cleavages, as is commonly expected, but rather on regional cleavages, about which there seems to be little concern. As Taras Kuzio points out in his chapter, there is little disagreement among Ukrainian elites about the proper relationship among the regions.

During its first decade of independence, Ukraine has struggled with both the state-building and nation-building processes. Hoping to link ethnic Ukrainians to the state, the Ukrainian government has pursued certain policies designed to enhance "Ukrainianness" in the country. Yet, Ukrainian leaders have repeatedly stressed that Ukraine is a multinational state, and their fear of fostering discontent among ethnic Russians has led to unequal enforcement of language and education laws in different parts of the country and a quite inclusive Ukrainian citizenship policy. The results of the March 1998 parliamentary and October–November 1999 presidential elections in Ukraine suggest that such a tightrope act will continue. The findings of this chapter indicate, however, that the Ukrainian government's emphasis on ethnic and linguistic issues is likely misplaced. The government would be better served by finally becoming serious about fixing the country's economic problems and by adopting a regional approach to dealing with discontent in the country than it would by continuing to search for ways to balance the desires of the main ethnic and linguistic groups.

NOTES

1. Dominique Arel, "Federalism and the Language Factor in Ukraine," paper presented to the annual meeting of the American Association for the Advancement of Slavic Studies, Phoenix, 19–22 November 1992.

2. Due to considerations of space, the Appendix containing the specific questions and coding used to create the support for independence scale and the explanatory variables has not been included within this chapter. The first question used to help create the scale focused on the respondent's view of independence ("How would you describe your attitude towards the independence of Ukraine today?"), while the other two asked for the respondent's views of statements about Russia and Ukraine ("Ukraine should join with Russia in one government"; "Ukraine should develop independently with minimal ties to Russia"). The wording of the other questions used in the analysis and variable coding are included in the Appendix of the larger study: L. Barrington, "Examining Rival Theories about the Effects of Demographic Factors on Political Support: Linguistic, Ethnic, and Regional Divisions in Ukraine" (2000). The manuscript is available from the author.

3. The questions relating to support for Ukrainian independence tend to focus on independence from Russia. This is reasonable, since, as Szporluk puts it, "Ukraine does not have to make a 'choice' between Russia and Poland; Poland has given up any claims to Ukraine and recognizes Ukraine's independence." See Roman Szporluk, "Ukraine: From Imperial Periphery to a Sovereign State," *Daedalus*, vol. 126, no. 3 (Summer 1997), p. 113.

4. See Lowell W. Barrington, "The Geographic Component of Mass Attitudes in Ukraine," *Post-Soviet Geography and Economics*, vol. 38, no. 10 (December 1997), pp. 601–614.

5. Dominique Arel, "Language Politics in Independent Ukraine: Towards One or Two State Languages?" *Nationalities Papers*, vol. 23, no. 3 (September 1995), p. 599.

6. Arel, "Federalism and the Language Factor in Ukraine," p. 6. Italics in the original.

7. Peter R. Craumer and James I. Clem, "Ukraine's Emerging Electoral Geography: A Regional Analysis of the 1998 Parliamentary Elections," *Post-Soviet Geography and Economics*, vol. 40, no. 1 (January 1999), p. 18. One scholar who has certainly not accepted the conventional wisdom about the linguistic cleavage is Taras Kuzio. See especially chapter 4 in *Ukraine: State and Nation Building* (London: Routledge, 1998), pp. 69–99.

8. Arel, "Language Policies in Independent Ukraine," p. 603. See also Catherine Wanner, *Burden of Dreams: History and Identity in Post-Soviet Ukraine* (University Park: Pennsylvania State University Press, 1998).

9. Prior to Ukrainian independence, Russians were doing noticeably better than Ukrainians (if wages are used as the measure), especially in the larger cities. See Evgenii Golovakha, Natalia Panina, and Nikolai Churilov, "Russians in Ukraine," in Vladimir Shlapentokh, Munir Sendich, and Emil Payin, eds., *The New Russian Diaspora: Russian Minorities in the Former Soviet Republics* (Armonk, NY: M. E. Sharpe, 1994), pp. 59–71. See also the chapter by Mykola Ryabchuk in this volume.

10. For survey results of Rukh delegates on this issue, see Vladimir Paniotto, "The Ukrainian Movement for Perestroika—'Rukh': A Sociological Survey." *Soviet Studies*, vol. 43, no. 1 (January–February 1991), pp. 177-181.

11. *Pravda*, 16 July 1991. Cited in Roman Solchanyk, "The Politics of State Building: Center-Periphery Relations in Post-Soviet Ukraine," *Europe-Asia Studies*, vol. 46, no. 1 (January–February 1994), pp. 47–68.

12. Shulman interprets some of the support for close ties with Russia in the East as a desire to keep things Russian. There is more fear that a sharp break with Russia will open the door for other parts of a Ukrainian nationalist agenda than there is a genuine desire to unite with Russia into a single country. See Stephen Shulman, "Cultures in Competition: Ukrainian Foreign Policy and the 'Cultural Threat' from Abroad," *Europe-Asia Studies*, vol. 50, no. 2 (March 1998), pp. 287–304 and his chapter in this volume.

13. For two excellent overviews of the different experiences of the various regions of Ukraine, see Sarah Birch, "Interpreting the Regional Effect in Ukrainian Politics," *Europe-Asia Studies*, vol. 52, no. 6 (September 2000), pp. 1017–1041, and Ihor Stebelsky, "The Topony of Ukraine," *Post-Soviet Geography and Economics*, vol. 38, no. 5 (1997), pp. 276–287.

14. Arel, "Federalism and the Language Factor in Ukraine." His framework, however, differs from those of Zimmerman and Melvin. See Neil Melvin, *Russians Beyond Russia: The Politics of National Identity* (London: Royal Institute of International Affairs, 1995); and Wiliam Zimmerman, "Is Ukraine a Political Community?" *Communist and Post-Communist Studies*, vol. 31, no. 1 (1998), pp. 43–55. Hesli actually employs several different regional patterns, testing contrasting regional divisions based on Russification, industrial development, social development, and agricultural development. Such differences in approaches are not confined to Western scholars of Ukraine. See Vicki Hesli, "Public Support for the Devolution of Power in Ukraine: Regional Patterns," *Europe-Asia Studies*, vol. 47, no. 1 (January–February 1995), pp. 91–121. Melnyk, writing in the Ukrainian journal *Derzhavnist*, comes up with eleven regions (or "statistical areas") in his analysis of nationality and language issues in Ukraine. See Ihor Melnyk, "Natsionalny sklad naselennia ta movna situatsiya v Ukraiini," *Derzhavnist*, no. 2 (1992), pp. 44–50.

15. Pirie has strongly criticized the use of ethnic categories in Ukraine given the high rate of intermarriage. My 1998 survey did allow respondents to state more than one nationality. What is labeled nationality in the regression analysis is the *first* nationality of the respondent. While Pirie's point about the complexity of nationality is well taken, one should not take the argument too far. In addition, his solution to create categories that employ parents' nationality as well is at best a partial solution. It relies on the respondent's perception of his or her parents' nationality, and it only pushes the intermarriage problem back one generation. See Paul Pirie, "National Identity and Politics in Southern and Eastern Ukraine," *Europe-Asia Studies*, vol. 48, no. 7 (November 1996), pp. 1079–1104.

16. Were one interested in these things, the options include two-stage least squares (2SLS) and the estimation of the complete structural equations model (SEM), employing a statistical program such as LISREL or Amos. The latter is more powerful, but also more sensitive to specification error or quirks in the data. For a more detailed discussion of these issues, and a comparison of the OLS and SEM approaches, see Lowell Barrington and Erik Herron, "Understanding Public Opinion in Post-Communist States: The Effect of Statistical Assumptions on Substantive Results," *Europe-Asia Studies*, vol. 53, no. 4 (June 2001), pp. 573–594.

17. Other researchers have tended to avoid using dummy variables for things such as size of locality. Instead, they have a single size of locality variable, with an ordinal scale representing the different categories of cities, towns, and villages. This kind of variable is technically an ordinal variable, but OLS assumes that it is an interval variable. In other words, the statistical program assumes that the difference between each step of the scale is the same. But the difference between a village and a small city may not be the same as the difference between a small city and a medium-sized city. Even those using dummy variables will often have a single urban/rural variable, which stretches credibility. The idea that a small city is similarly different from a village as a very large city is different from a village is hard to believe. A similar argument can be made about numerous other demographic variables. To take education as an example, the use of a scale rather than dummy variables in OLS assumes that each step on the scale is equal. But the difference between not graduating high school and graduating may not be the same thing as the

difference between graduating college and receiving a Ph.D. The only nondummy variable in the models in this chapter is age, since its intervals are truly comparable.

18. One cannot put all the dummy variables of a particular type into the equation without violating the assumption that the explanatory variables are not exactly linearly related. See Eric Hanushek and John Jackson, *Statistical Methods for Social Scientists* (San Diego: Academic Press, 1977), p. 104.

19. Barrington, "The Geographic Component." In addition, analyses of other levels of support (for the government and for the regime) found even weaker effects for language and nationality. See Barrington, "Examining Rival Theories."

20. The coefficients are not exactly the same. While all Ukrainian-speakers and all ethnic Ukrainians provided the baseline with which to compare the language and nationality dummy variables in the first estimations, in the second set of equations (with ethnolinguistic groups replacing the language and nationality variables) the baseline comes from only Ukrainian-speaking Ukrainians.

21. The full table is available from the author upon request.

22. The only support for the role of language in the ethnolinguistic analysis comes from the lack of statistical significance of the coefficients on the Ukrainian-speaking Russians, Ukrainian-speaking "others," and mixed-speaking "others." Given the small number of Russians who speak primarily Ukrainian and the prevalence of Russian language use by other nationalities in the country, these results are more likely due to the small numbers of respondents who fell into these various categories than to similarities between these different groups and Ukrainian-speaking Ukrainians in the population at large.

23. Electoral evidence presented in Holdar shows most forcefully the division between the far East and the far West, with less well-defined differences in the Central part of the country. Similarly, Craumer and Clem discuss the poor showing of leftist parties in the West, and the poor showing of nationalist parties everywhere else. See Sven Holdar, "Torn Between East and West: The Regional Factor in Ukrainian Politics," *Post-Soviet Geography*, vol. 36, no. 2 (February 1995), pp. 112–132; and Craumer and Clem, "Ukraine's Emerging Electoral Geography."

24. One possibility is that the regional differences become linked to new identities, such as the Russian-speaking population discussed by Laitin (see David Laitin, *Identity in Formation: The Russian-speaking Populations in the Near Abroad*, Ithaca, NY: Cornell University Press, 1998). Recent analysis of the strength of the Russian-speaking population label in Ukraine, however, indicates that this identity group option has little value as a mobilizing tool for anti-state elites. See Lowell Barrington, "Russian-Speakers in Ukraine and Kazakhstan: 'Nationality,' 'Population,' or Neither," *Post-Soviet Affairs*, vol. 17, no. 2 (April–June 2001), pp. 129-158.

25. As Solchanyk argues, while the earlier ideas that Ukraine was destined to collapse were obviously exaggerations, the claim that it is an "anchor of stability" in Eastern Europe is also an overstatement. R. Solchanyk, "Ukraine: The Politics of Reform," *Problems of Post-Communism*, vol. 42, no. 6 (November–December 1995), p. 46. Nahaylo adds, "But five years after achieving independence, Ukraine was still not out of the woods: numerous economic, social, political and security problems were the trees that blotted out the light." See Bohdan Nahaylo, *The Ukrainian Resurgence* (London: Hurst, 1999), p. 549.

26. For a discussion of various political consequences of the regional divide in Ukraine, see Paul Kubicek, "Regional Polarization in Ukraine: Public Opinion, Voting, and Legislative Behavior," *Europe-Asia Studies*, vol. 52, no. 2 (2000), pp. 273–294. For a counter-argument downplaying the implications of regional divisions, see Kuzio, *Ukraine: State and Nation Building*, pp. 69–99.

27. See John A. Agnew, *Place and Politics: The Geographic Mediation of State and Society* (Boston: Allen and Unwin, 1987).

8

Nation Building in the Ukrainian Military

Andrew Fesiak

When Ukraine gained its independence in December 1991 it inherited more than 780,000 Soviet troops located in its territory.[1] Since it was necessary to make this once-Soviet military into a Ukrainian military whose servicemen would patriotically defend Ukraine, a Ukrainianization campaign was put into action. The program immediately ran into problems, however. Although switching from the use of Russian to Ukrainian was part of the Ukrainianization program, the most important aspect of the program was to instill in the troops a sense of patriotism toward Ukraine by using historical examples of the military traditions and heroes of Ukraine. The Ukrainian population, however, is relatively divided in terms of (among other things) ideology, language, and historical perceptions. This divide basically runs between the more nationalistic Western Ukraine and the more "slavocentric" Central, Southern and Eastern Ukraine. Those groups or individuals considered heroes in Western Ukraine are often not considered heroes to people living in other parts of the country and vice-versa. Creating an all-encompassing patriotism based on historical examples of military traditions and heroes thus has been next to impossible.

The effort to instill Ukrainian patriotism in the armed forces is an important test of state-led nation building efforts in general. Systematic Ukrainianization has been pursued with more resolve in the military than in any other aspect of Ukrainian society. By looking at this program, we can evaluate the validity of the assumptions that underlie most of the arguments about nation building in Ukraine. Is it the case, as many assume, that a thorough nation-building program can overcome the nation's ethnic, linguistic, and regional divisions? To what extent is it true, as others assert, that such a program is likely to exacerbate rather than heal Ukraine's societal cleavages?

Evidence from the military's Ukrainianization program supports the assertion that an assertive nationalization campaign is likely to backfire. Initially the Ukrainianization campaign in the military alienated many non-Western Ukrainians due to its glorification of such anti-Russian and anti-Soviet military formations as the SS Galician Division and OUN-UPA (Organization of Ukrainian

Nationalists-Ukrainian Insurgent Army). More recently, Western Ukrainians have felt alienated due to the continuous celebration and glorification of Soviet historical events and heroes. Since the Ukrainianization program in the military is used not only for instilling loyalty in the troops but also as a nation-building tool, anything that happens in the military will, and is intended to, affect society.[2] The result so far thus has been a further polarization of not only military servicemen but also Ukrainian society in general. This signifies not only a failure of the Ukrainianization program but even its backfiring, which is having an adverse effect on Ukrainian nation building.

CIVIL-MILITARY RELATIONS AND NATION BUILDING

Inculcating Ukrainian Nationalism

When Ukraine became independent, the work of instilling the troops with patriotism which the Main Political Administration (MPA) of the Soviet Ministry of Defense had conducted was taken over by the Social Psychological Service (SPS) of the Ukrainian Ministry of Defense. The idea for the SPS was originally developed in 1986–1987 by a civilian philosophy professor, Volodymyr Muliava, a member of Rukh. Following Ukraine's independence, Muliava was made an honorary major-general. Originally the SPS was not intended for use in the armed forces but rather among the Ukrainian population in general.[3]

A central aim of the Union of Ukrainian Officers (UUO) program was a need to carry out a Ukrainianization program in the military. As a result, Muliava's SPS program was put into action. The SPS was implemented on 5 March 1992 with Muliava as its first head after the Ministry of Defense and the Supreme *Rada* came to an agreement regarding the direction and objectives the SPS was to assume. Part of the objectives of the SPS read as follows: "To rally the servicemen around the ideal of an independent Ukrainian state, instilling in them a consciousness of the historical development of Ukrainian independence . . . and a deep sense of respect and love for Ukraine, its people, culture, traditions and churches."[4]

Major-General Muliava defended the SPS against accusations that it was exactly like the MPA:

The idea of self-sufficient value of human individuality, respect of the solitude and dignity of every person, have always been a component of the Ukrainian "national idea," which attracted and naturally included in to the Ukrainian *socium* representatives of other nations, peoples and ethnic groups, who lived on the territory of Ukraine and sincerely took part in the national-liberation struggle of the Ukrainian people. And the Social-Psychological Service strives to realize exactly this idea.[5]

Historiography, Nation Building, and the Military

However, Muliava's SPS, which was also supposed to teach "nonrepressive relations" and "non-violent conflict resolution," did more to create conflicts and repression in the Ukrainian armed forces than any other organization since independence. Under Muliava's control, the SPS was instructed to espouse the Ukrainian "national idea."[6] Furthermore, the teaching of the "national-liberation struggle" meant that the SPS was to teach a Ukrainian nationalist version of history and glorify all the anti-Russian and anti-Soviet military formations that had existed until then. There was a legal basis for their actions. The UUO interpreted section 11 of the Law on the Armed Forces of Ukraine that "the military-patriotic education of military servicemen is to be realized using the national-historical traditions of the people of Ukraine" in its own manner. This included the Organization of Ukrainian Nationalists (OUN),[7] the Ukrainian Insurgent Army (UPA),[8] and the SS Galician Division.[9]

Muliava believed that the best way to implement the Ukrainian "national idea" was through the ideology of the Ukrainian Cossacks:

We don't look at the Cossacks as simply a military formation or a social entity, but as a state of the soul, as a way of life and a method of behavior. Through analysis we have found that Ukrainians are in essence a Cossack nation. The Cossacks were the highest embodiment of "national patriotism."[10]

Muliava also extended his Cossack myth to include the *Sichovi Striltsi* (Sharpshooters from the Austrian army who became the backbone of the Ukrainian People's Republic armed forces of 1917–1920), the OUN-UPA, and even the SS Galician Division, all of which he has said were Cossack military formations. Muliava considered all of these military forces to be heroic military formations in the national liberation struggle.

His treatment of the UPA was especially antagonistic to some sections of society who had been instilled for decades by the Soviet state with hatred for these "Nazi collaborators." Muliava glorified the UPA for its desire for the: "complete liberation of the Ukrainian people from the *Russian-Bolshevik* yoke and for their wish to unify all ethnic Ukrainian lands in an independent Ukrainian state without wealthy landowners, capitalists, and without Bolshevik magnates, KGB spies and Communist party parasites."[11]

Muliava also glorified the OUN-UPA for its "multi-ethnic character" and belief in the "equality of all nations inhabiting Ukraine;" and for its "democratic ideals" and "humanitarian principles."[12] Muliava portrayed the OUN-UPA as an organization with highly democratic principles, regardless of its integral nationalist ideology.

The SPS went out of its way to support and glorify nationalist military organizations of the Second World War. For example, the SPS was the initiator and organizer of a fiftieth anniversary celebration of the UPA in Kyiv in 1992 to which UPA veterans from the West were invited. The UPA veterans were overjoyed at their treatment as heroes by the SPS.

The SPS's relations with Ukrainian nationalist émigrés were quite close. Ukrainian nationalist organizations in the United States and especially Canada actively supported the SPS by donating various books, literature, and even computers. Much of the donated literature and books portrayed their idealized nationalist view of Ukrainian history, which typically demonizes the enemies of Ukraine, glorifies their own exploits, and omits their excesses. Muliava said: "I would not be able to name one Ukrainian organization in Canada which did not strive to help the Ukrainian armed forces."[13] However, Muliava also admitted that many people in the Ukrainian armed forces were against this help and did not want to accept it, an attitude which he claims he removed.

In the Vanguard of Ukrainianization: The Union of Ukrainian Officers (UUO)

At this point it is necessary to comment on one organization which was closely linked to the SPS and its Ukrainianization campaign: the UUO. The work of the SPS was aided by the UUO because it was favored by the first defense minister of Ukraine, Konstantyn Morozov. In fact, most SPS officers were members of the UUO, including Muliava himself, and the UUO itself had close ties to center-right political groups, such as Rukh. Morozov openly admitted that he would support and cooperate with the UUO, a statement which certainly added to its initial growth and popularity. The UUO claimed a membership of 20,000[14] individuals throughout Ukraine, most of whom were middle-ranking officers between the ranks of major and colonel.[15]

The ranks of the UUO became filled with ethnic Ukrainians, and from the outset it included anti-communist and anti-Russian sentiment. Over 85% of its members were ethnic Ukrainians.[16] However, a more telling statistic is that over 70% of its members were Western Ukrainians, the main base of Rukh and other national democratic parties.[17]

One of the UUO's goals was to eliminate from the ranks of the Ukrainian armed forces any servicemen considered to be disloyal and unpatriotic to the Ukrainian state. At the time, the UUO claimed that 90% of the Ukrainian armed force's higher officer corps and 70% of the general officer ranks were composed of non-ethnic Ukrainians, most of whom were ethnic Russians.[18] The UUO was highly suspicious of the loyalty and patriotism of the officer corps and felt that many officers who swore allegiance to Ukraine were insincere. According to one survey, 60% of officers who had sworn allegiance had done so because of the promise of housing, the stable social situation, and better access to foodstuffs in Ukraine.[19] Even Morozov complained that some officers had sworn allegiance believing that eventually the armed forces of Ukraine would be united again with Russia in the Commonwealth of Independent States (CIS).[20]

Unofficial surveys confirmed that the majority of officers would not fight in a conflict with Russia.[21] The UUO claimed that only 30% of Ukrainian officers were prepared to defend Ukrainian independence while another poll which asked "Are you ready to defend Ukraine with arms in hand?" was answered positively by only 8% of respondents.[22]

Morozov, with a mixed Russian-Ukrainian ethnic background from Luhans'k, became quite involved with the UUO and even took part in its congresses. The defense minister, following in Muliava's tracks, also promised Ukrainian nationalist émigrés that the Ukrainian military would learn, among others, the glorious traditions of the armies of the Ukrainian People's Republic (UNR), the UPA, and the SS Galician Division.[23] Morozov also made membership in the UUO a precondition for any promotion in the Ukrainian armed forces, a move that was bound to cause dissent among the officer corps.[24]

The way in which the UUO tried to realize its goal of eliminating what it felt were disloyal officers from the Ukrainian armed forces' ranks resembled a witch-hunt. It gathered intelligence on units considered hostile to Ukraine, conducted political campaigns, and tried to control personnel policy and appointments. In reality, the UUO used tactics that were rather similar to those used by Soviet political commissars during the Stalinist period. People could be denounced and thus removed because of what the UUO considered disloyal.[25] The UUO even began pressing then-President Leonid Kravchuk and the Defense Ministry to launch a purge of non-Ukrainians and former high-ranking communists from the Ukrainian armed forces.[26] Though no such purge took place, discrimination against non-Ukrainians—and especially ethnic Russian officers— did take place.[27] The UUO's actions led to the undeserved dismissal of many ethnic Russian officers and prompted more than 200 officers of various ethnic backgrounds to file applications for voluntary dismissal from the Ukrainian armed forces.[28] The union was also known to defend its members against disciplinary actions regardless of whether the person in question was at fault or not.[29]

Another goal of the UUO was to replace ethnic Russian officers with ethnic Ukrainians who were serving in other parts of the former Soviet Union, although this policy seems largely to have failed. Many Ukrainian officers serving in the Russian military decided not to return due to the inferior economic situation in Ukraine, and especially due to the relatively higher standard of living enjoyed by officers in the Russian armed forces.

Throughout the Kravchuk era the UUO became increasingly politicized, moving from the far-right to the extreme right and came to be criticized for being a war party. It criticized the Ukrainian government for giving up the Soviet nuclear weapons on its soil and for making concessions to Russia with regard to the Black Sea Fleet, the Commonwealth of Independent States (CIS), or any other issues.

The UUO's anti-Russian orientation has been strengthened by its close relations with Ukrainian nationalist émigré groups. The British-based Association of Former Ukrainian Combatants, which is mainly composed of UPA and SS Galician Division veterans, actually wrote the UUO statute and provided it with financial and educational support. At least twenty UPA veterans even officially joined the UUO[30]; as have an unspecified number of SS Galician Division veterans.

The UUO also had close contacts with other Ukrainian nationalist émigré organizations in North America and Europe who provide funds and supplied the UUO with office equipment. The greatest help has come in the form of nationalist literature of which it received a large amount. A large amount of this literature consisted of books and journals that glorify the SS Galician Division and the OUN-UPA. This orientation was consistent with the view that the official ideology of the Ukrainian armed forces should be Ukrainian nationalism.[31]

One of the UUO's goals was to promote Ukrainian nationalist military traditions by which it aided the SPS through distributing this nationalist literature. The UUO was also heavily represented in the various Ukrainian military newspapers and journals which would publish articles glorifying the nationalist views of history along with their various military formations and nationalist ideology. However, the UUO's demand that former Soviet *Zampolits* (Political Officers) be forcibly retired was not implemented.

Growing Dissension toward the Use of Nationalism in the Armed Forces

Many members of the SPS staff were former Soviet army officers who had been discharged for nationalist activity. The other officers who were to carry out the work of the SPS were former *Zampolits* from the MPA who, instead of taking guidance from MPA headquarters in Moscow, would now take orders from the SPS in Kyiv. However, this practically ensured that there would be problems because the leadership of the SPS was the most staunchly Ukrainian nationalist component of the Ukrainian armed forces and the *Zampolits* were formerly the staunchest Communists and Soviet patriots. Not all *Zampolits* were openly opposed to the SPS, because Defense Minister Morozov had made it clear that membership in the UUO was a precondition for any promotion, and therefore many *Zampolits* also became "nationalists" overnight.

In essence, the MPA method of using "otherness" as a tool to instill patriotism into servicemen was used by the SPS, though in a slightly more subtle way. By glorifying the Ukrainian "national liberation struggle" the SPS accused Russians of having been the enemy and a negative "other." But if that were not enough, the SPS and UUO espoused an anti-Russian ideology that had limited appeal outside Western Ukraine. Since Russians are not, and have never been, considered the enemy by the majority of Ukrainians, the policy eventually backfired.

These efforts to instill a particular notion of patriotism caused a great deal of dissension within Ukrainian military and political circles. The SPS's Ukrainianization program was therefore bound to fail. In early 1993, 155 left-wing parliamentary deputies officially complained about the growing politicization of the UUO, including its glorification of the OUN-UPA and depiction of Russia as Ukraine's main enemy.[32] Muliava was often criticized by the left for turning the SPS into an organization resembling the Gestapo and inculcating *Petliurite* and *Banderivtsi* (supporters of past nationalist leaders Simon Petliura and Stepan Bandera) ideology into the Ukrainian armed forces.[33]

The last straw came in October 1993 when, after facing increasing opposition in the Supreme *Rada* and openly criticizing President Kravchuk and the Massandra Accord signed between Russia and Ukraine, Morozov was forced to resign.[34] Morozov was replaced on 8 October 1993 by Vitaliy Radets'kyii, the Commander of the Odesa Military District, who quickly acted to defuse the problems with the UUO and SPS. Radets'kyi agreed that the SPS was a very important component of the armed forces and thus wanted to make it more professional. After meetings with SPS staff, Radets'kyii finally replaced Muliava with Anatoli Kobzar and renamed the SPS the "Main Administration for Educational and Social-Psychological Work of the Ministry of Defense."

According to General Muliava, the real reason for restructuring the SPS and his replacement was that "anti-Ukrainian" forces could see that he and the SPS were establishing "real" Ukrainian Armed Forces and this scared them. Muliava believes that another reason was because he attacked Communists who were serving in the Ukrainian armed forces and had them removed. However, it is more likely that the most important reason for Muliava's dismissal was that his nationalism, anti-Russian views, glorification of nationalist armies, and attack on Soviet army traditions were alienating the officer corps. Radets'kyii made it clear that the process of "Ukrainianizing" the armed forces would be slowed down.

The nonnationalist Radets'kyii also pursued the radical UUO. Officially Radets'kyi was opposed to military personnel involving themselves in politics and thus began to clamp down on the UUO. According to UUO sources, the union barely survived Radets'kyi's term in office as defense minister. The once-powerful union began to rapidly lose members until its numbers hit approximately 4,000 people. The UUO claimed that people dropped out of the union for fear of losing apartments, jobs, and retirement pensions.[35] However, other sources state that the union had already begun to lose members prior to Radets'kyi's appointment because it failed to pursue the protection of the social, economic, and legal interests of military servicemen.[36]

After the June–July 1994 presidential elections, Radets'kyii was replaced by a civilian by newly elected President Leonid Kuchma. The new defense minister, former Deputy Prime Minister Valeriy Shmarov, was as critical of nationalist policies as his predecessor and is said to have even removed the portraits of famous Cossack Hetmans from the walls of the General Staff's headquarters.[37] Although Shmarov did a great deal to enhance Ukraine's cooperation with the West through NATO's Partnership for Peace program, he, like Radets'kyii, was criticized by nationalists for having also brought Ukraine closer to the CIS. According to former Defense Minister Morozov, this "halted the processes of Ukrainianization of the Army, and . . . is depriving the Ukrainian Army of the possibility of becoming Ukrainian."[38]

The UUO was highly critical of Shmarov for his "anti-Ukrainian" attitude and the "selling out" of Ukraine to Russia. The UUO was even more critical of Shmarov than it was of Radets'kyii who they believe "at least confronted the Russian Ministry of Defense."[39] The UUO even attempted to organize an officer's rally in mid-July 1995, but it failed to attract more than a few dozen listeners.[40] It was obvious that the UUO was no longer the force it once was.

In February 1995 Shmarov replaced Kobzar, the head of the SPS's successor, the "Main Administration for Educational and Social-Psychological Work" (MAEW) for "misconduct" (he had also supported Kravchuk during the 1994 presidential election campaign). His replacement was Major-General Volodymyr Sytnyk, who maintained his position until the beginning of 1998, when he was replaced by Lieutenant-General Oleksiy Protsepko.

Shmarov himself was unpopular within military circles and especially so among nationalists both in the armed forces and the Supreme Rada. His plans to reform the armed forces were viewed by nationalists and by many in the military as too "dovish." It did not help that he was the first civilian minister of defense, and many considered him unqualified to deal with military issues. In July 1996, Shmarov was removed and replaced by the commander of the National Guard, Lieutenant-General Oleksandr Kuzmuk.

THE UKRAINIANIZATION PROGRAM

Ukrainianization and military-patriotic education have continued in the Ukrainian military under every defense minister, although the levels of officially sanctioned nationalist education have varied. From 1994 the Ukrainianization program has slowed and become less radical and divisive, placing less emphasis upon nationalist military formations. The MAEW determines what is taught in the military educational system. The Ukrainianization work by the MAEW is carried out through "humanities preparation," lectures, museums, *svitlytsi* (reading rooms), and the military media.

"Humanities Preparation"

During the Soviet period, the MPA held centralized control over everything that was taught in the military, and every military unit in the Soviet Armed Forces received the same education regardless of its location. The "Military Publishing House" prepared and produced most of the materials used by the *Zampolit*. Today, Ukraine's situation is quite different. The Ukrainian military has its own publishing house, *Varta*, which, instead of publishing educational materials, is used by the Ministry of Defense to publish military-legal handbooks. These include volumes such as *Military Legislation and Laws of Ukraine: Short Reference-Book for Officers* and *Acting Statutes of the Ukrainian Armed Forces*. Financial difficulties inhibit the Ministry of Defense and the MAEW from publishing a history textbook that could be used in its Ukrainianization, although there is also some reluctance to publish officially what would certainly be a controversial history text. What is taught in the military can—and is—affected by outside interest groups providing their own materials for use in propaganda in the military. Therefore, nationalists especially concerned with patriotism in the military can attempt to exert their influence on the Ukrainianization program.

The work of the MAEW covers all branches of the Ukrainian security forces—the Ukrainian armed forces, Border Troops, and National Guard. In theory, all branches should be taught the same subjects. Humanities preparation is carried out by giving lectures and conducting seminars and through individual study. Twice per year, the MAEW publishes a *Thematic Plan of Humanities Preparation of Military Servicemen and Workers of the Ukrainian Armed Forces* in the various publications of the security forces.

The *Thematic Plan* is divided into sections for each category of military servicemen in the following manner:[41]

1. General and Staff Officers (eighty hours of study per year);
2. Officers of Formations and Units (eighty hours of study per year);
3. Warrant Officers and Contract Military Servicemen (eighty hours of
4. study per year);
5. Workers of the Ukrainian armed forces (twenty hours of study per
6. year);
7. Conscripted Military Servicemen (136 hours of study per year).

Five main subjects are studied:

1. History of Ukraine;
2. History of the Ukrainian Armed Forces;
3. Military Law;
4. Pedagogy and Psychology;
5. Theory of State Independence.

Each subject area in the *Thematic Plan* contains various themes and questions that are to be studied. Thus, according to the plan published in a June 1998 edition of *Vartovi Neba*, the official newspaper of the Air Defense Forces, the questions and themes for Conscripted Military Servicemen for the summer period were as follows:

1. History of the creation and development of the Air Defense Forces of contemporary Ukraine (in honor of Air Defense Forces Day) (six hours of study).
2. Courage and heroism of the defenders of the Fatherland during World War II (two hours of study).
3. Social protection and the main directions of its actualization. (two hours of study);
4. You are the hope of the Fatherland, people and President. Love of Ukraine, of your own people, is the source of the spiritual strength of a soldier (two hours of study).
5. What do you know about the culture of mutual relations and military etiquette? Do you know how to conduct yourself in society and in your collective? (role training: two hours of study).
6. Undivided Authority—an important principle in the recruitment and development of the contemporary armed forces of Ukraine. The educational meaning of disciplinary practice (six hours of study).
7. Statutory interrelations—an important condition in the solidarity of military collectives, the strengthening of highly moral humane norms in the interrelations of military servicemen (six hours of study).
8. The international legal regulation of military conflicts. The code of conduct of participants in military activities (six hours of study).
9. The main periods in the formation of the Ukrainian nation, stages in the formation of statehood, and the molding of the modern territory of Ukraine (in honor of Ukrainian Independence Day: six hours of study).
10. History and the contemporary situation of Ukrainian Cossacks (two hours of study);
11. The Ukrainian Revolution. The Ukrainian People's Republic (UNR) and its military formations (four hours of study).
12. Ukraine and Ukrainians in the Second World War. The fight against fascism and contribution to victory (six hours of study).
13. Historical influence of contemporary material culture of the Ukrainian people: cus-

toms, trades, economy, ecology (four hours of study).

14. The Ukrainian language—basis of the spiritual and artistic culture, science and education of the Ukrainian nation (two hours of study).
15. History and prominent cultural monuments of the region where you are serving (two hours of study).
16. Religion and the church in the history of the Ukrainian people (two hours of study).
17. Fine arts of Ukraine: history and its contemporary status (four hours of study).
18. Medical enlightenment work in the military unit. Prophylaxis of drug addiction and AIDS sickness (two hours of study).
19. Examinations for the winter term (two -hour exam).

Once per year, students are given a test related to these themes and questions in which a commission from the MAEW takes part. Since the days of the SPS, the themes and questions have changed considerably, are now less provocative, and contain considerably less nationalist history. An example of SPS historical questions during 1993 included:

1. Kyiv Rus', and its role in the historical fate of the Ukrainian people. The Galician-Volhynian state—continuing the traditions of the Kyiv state.
2. The military campaigns of the Kyivan princes.
3. Objective and subjective reasons for the origins of Ukrainian Cossacks as a separate societal state. The Cossack army and its martial arts.
4. The Ukrainian Cossack state.
5. The Western Ukrainian lands between 1900 and 1919. The creation of military formations. The Ukrainian *Sichovi Striltsi*. The Ukrainian Galician Army.
6. The military forces of the Central *Rada* and Hetman P. Skoropadsky. The Ukrainian Navy.
7. Interwar Ukraine under the rule of the totalitarian regime. The Famine Years, 1932–1933. Stalinist repression in Ukraine. The socioeconomic situation of the Western Ukrainian lands.
8. Ukraine in the plans of the totalitarian regimes and the development of the Ukrainian national idea during World War II.
9. The UPA struggle for a Ukrainian state independent of German and Communist occupation.
10. Ukrainians during World War II in the Soviet Army and the armies of the Allies.
11. Ukraine after the war (1945–1985). The renewal of Ukrainian statehood in 1991.

The MAEW also publishes articles in the various Ukrainian military newspapers under the heading "Aid to Humanities Preparation Group Leaders," that deal with the previously mentioned themes and questions. Each article begins with the stated theme or question. A short bibliography is provided at the end of the article for each Humanities Preparation Group Leader or, as they are more commonly referred to, Educational Work Assistant. This is supposed to be used in formulate lecture and seminar notes on the given topic. Often, much of the background information that is used by the Educational Work Assistants comes from other sources published in either a variety of newspapers or journals on the initiative of their editors or from books that are found in libraries located on military bases.

This is where the greatest problems begin. During the Gorbachev era, the government admitted that much of Soviet history was tainted with omissions of facts, or were even utter falsifications of the truth. This led to a backlash in which all Soviet historiography was criticized and assumed to be false. For this reason, Soviet history books have, for the most part, been discarded. Because neither the Ukrainian government nor most academic institutions have the financial resources available to publish new literature to actually replace the Soviet books, the outcome has been to rely on foreign sources of information. With few exceptions, the majority of these books are supplied by Ukrainian nationalist émigrés living in the West who, for the most part, have some connection to the three branches of the OUN. The result is that the Soviet falsifications of history have been replaced by a Ukrainian nationalist version that glorifies the exploits of the UNR, the OUN-UPA, and the SS Galician Division. Leaving aside questions of historical accuracy, such works are considered controversial and even offensive to many in Ukraine, and hence tend not to build national unity, but to deepen existing divisions.

Émigré Literature: Its Influence on "Humanities Preparation"

Among the organizations sending literature to Ukraine is the journal *Visti Kombatanta* which is the official bimonthly published by the veterans of the SS Galician Division (or, as they now prefer to be called, the "First Ukrainian Division of the Ukrainian National Army"). The journal itself is funded by advertisements from a wide range of some of the most well-known and successful businesses in the North American Ukrainian émigré community. Not only the journal but also books on the SS Galician Division are sent either directly to the libraries of Ukrainian military units or to nationalist organizations in Ukraine such as the UUO, which then distribute the materials to the security forces throughout Ukraine. However, the literature sent by *Visti Kombatanta* can hardly be considered academic let alone unbiased. Most of the literature is actually written by former veterans and tends to glorify the SS Galician Division as a heroic military formation which took part in the "national liberation struggle" for independence against the Soviet and German occupation of Ukraine.[42] Such views are bound to be divisive in Ukraine.

A considerable volume of Ukrainian nationalist historical literature is distributed and sold in Ukraine by nationalist émigré organizations. In fact, as happened during World War II, the various nationalist groups compete for historical and political influence in Ukraine. Everyone from supporters of Hetman Pavlo Skoropadsky (1918) to World War II figures, such as Hetman Taras Bulba-Borovets, and the Andrii Melnyk and Stepan Bandera factions of the OUN attempt to glorify their own heroes. The most powerful organization is the Bandera faction of the OUN (OUN-B), which has also been the most successful in publishing books that glorify Bandera, the OUN-B and UPA.

The great majority of books that are used in teaching history by the Ukrainian military are published by the Ukrainian diaspora. Because the Ukrainian economy is in a poor condition, most Ukrainian scholars are hard-pressed to find funding and thus the Ukrainian military is forced to rely on foreign sources and their version of history. However, some books which have been published in Ukraine recently deal with certain periods of Ukrainian history differently than foreign nationalist publications. Various interviews conducted by this author have confirmed that the majority of books that are used or have been written by foreign nationals are viewed in a quite negative manner by many Ukrainian servicemen.[43] Some educational assistants still use Soviet history books in the preparation of their lectures. How often this is the case and whether this is due to opposition to nationalist literature are not known.[44]

THE MEDIA OF THE SECURITY FORCES AND NATION BUILDING

One of the most important sources of information for the educational assistants is the military newspapers and journals, which often publish their own historical materials which are not submitted by the MAEW. In fact, most articles related to Ukrainian history are published on the initiative of the editors themselves. Following is a list of the most important Ukrainian military publications available to educational assistants, with a short description of their viewpoints.

Narodna Armiya

This daily is the most important, influential, and widely distributed military newspaper and was previously known as *Leninskoye Znamye*. It was renamed *Narodna Armiya* on 1 October 1991 when it was established as the central organ of the Ministry of Defense of Ukraine. The creation of *Narodna Armiya* was Defense Minister Morozov's very first directive. When *Narodna Armiya* was first published, it was entirely in Russian. This was also the language stated in its application for registration. However, it now publishes articles only in Ukrainian.

Narodna Armiya has published articles that have glorified various nationalist military forces such as the OUN-UPA and even the SS Galician Division, though most historical articles initially dealt with the Cossacks, Ukraine's borders, and Ukrainians in the Crimea. Ukrainian nationalist émigrés have been influential in what is published and have often been the authors of articles that deal with World War II Ukrainian nationalist military formations. As with most émigré publications, these articles do not address negative concerns about the history of these formations. Nationalist émigrés, in a manner similar to everywhere else, have also been very helpful in providing *Narodna Armiya* with financial aid, nationalist literature, and office equipment.[45]

Although *Narodna Armiya* was initially ardently nationalist and was initially edited by a member of the UUO, its position changed under Kuchma to a more liberal form of nationalism. A large number of the historical articles that have been published under Kuchma for the most part deal with less controversial subjects, such as the Ukrainian Cossacks or even Ukrainian participation in the Russian Imperial army during Napoleon's attack on Russia. *Narodna Armiya* has harshly criticized not only the actions of the Russian government in relation to Ukraine but also the Ukrainian government itself. One article stated that Russian citizens were being "psychologically prepared for war" with Ukraine and criticized the Ukrainian government for being too soft on Russia.[46]

Regardless of the still somewhat nationalist perspective of *Narodna Armiya*, the overwhelming majority of historical articles that are published deal with the heroic exploits of the Soviet armed forces and Ukrainian servicemen during World War II, which, in fact, is the case with most Ukrainian military publications. This does not mean that the articles give the Soviet view of the war by glorifying Jozef Stalin or making any excuses for his mistakes. A great variety of articles deal with lesser known heroes involved in the liberation of Ukraine from the Nazis. *Narodna Armiya* has even begun to publish articles by authors who have criticized the OUN-UPA for its activities during the war.[47]

Flot Ukraiiny

This is the official newspaper of the Ukrainian navy and is published in the city of Sevastopol, Crimea, on a weekly basis. The newspaper publishes some articles in Ukrainian and some in Russian, most likely because it is located in the Russophone Crimea. There is an information war between Ukrainian and Russian military newspapers (i.e., *Flag Rodiny*) who seem to be trying to influence not only each other's military personnel but also the local population.[48] *Flot Ukrainy* has often carried the most nationalistic articles relating to twentieth-century Ukrainian nationalist military formations of all Ukrainian military newspapers. Because the Russophone population of Crimea is located in a place where the exploits of the Red Army were among the most heroic during the Revolution, the Civil War, and World War II, any glorification of Ukrainian nationalist militaries or criticism of the Soviet army is seen as especially provocative.

Flot Ukrainy is also extremely critical of the Russian government and the Russian Black Sea Fleet and often publishes articles attacking both. The newspaper typically attacks the stationing of the Black Sea Fleet in Ukraine and often publishes articles to suggest that by doing this Russia is breaking international law and is therefore imperialistic. *Flot Ukrainy* is also known often to publish articles that attack the record of the Communist Party of the Soviet Union and the USSR itself.[49] One issue of *Flot Ukrainy* featured a front-page interview with Ukrainian nationalist émigrés who visited Sevastopol and complained about the usage of the Russian language in Crimea and in the Ukrainian navy.

Prykordonnyk Ukraiiny

This is the official weekly publication of the State Committee in Affairs of the Protection of the State Border of Ukraine, more commonly known as the Border Troops. Though most articles are published in Ukrainian, Russian is also frequently used. The Border Troops were among the most elite troops among all Soviet military formations and were a division of the KGB.

With this in mind, it is understandable that the official newspaper of the Ukrainian Border Troops is also among the least nationalistic. According to its former editor, Vasyl Klymenko, it would be impossible to change the minds of people who worked in such an elite force as the Border Troops for so many years overnight. The newspaper therefore refrains from publishing any articles that glorify nationalist armed formations. In fact, under its old editor, S. F. Volkov, who retired in early 1995, *Prykordonnyk Ukrainy* often published historical articles that criticized the OUN-UPA as traitors, Nazi collaborators and war criminals.

Prykordonnyk Ukrainy, like most other security force newspapers, also publishes articles that glorify the exploits of the Soviet armed forces, especially the Soviet Border Troops. However, whereas during the Soviet period these articles would mention "nationalist bandits" who illegally tried to cross the Soviet border, now the articles speak of "border trespassers."

Vartovi Neba

This is the official weekly newspaper of the Air Defense Forces, which is published for the most part in Ukrainian. *Vartovi Neba* does publish articles in relation to certain episodes of nationalist history such as the Ukrainian revolutionary period, though the articles are more factual than propagandistic. Furthermore, it is not typical of *Vartovi Neba* to engage in political debates criticizing Russia, Ukraine's communists, or other groups. The most important indicator of where *Vartovi Neba* stands in regard to Ukrainian nationalism is displayed directly on the front cover of every issue where it proudly displays the diploma of honor with the hammer and sickle emblem of the Ukrainian Soviet Socialist Republic.

Surma/Viysko Ukraiiny

Surma, formerly *Viysko Ukraiiny*, was the official journal of the National Guard. The journal is no longer in publication, though its back issues are still widely used. In 1995, after *Viysko Ukraiiny* was transferred to the Ministry of Defense to become the main magazine of the military, the National Guard briefly launched *Surma*. As the journal of the National Guard, *Viysko Ukrainy/Surma* was nationalistic and went much further in glorifying Ukrainian nationalist militaries such as the OUN-UPA and the SS Galician Division than any other official military publication in the country.

The journal not only received financial support from the Ukrainian nationalist émigré community but also initially even had nationalist émigrés on its editorial board, which could at least partially explain its political outlook.[50] Among the organizations that sponsored the journal were the U.S.-based Society of UPA Soldiers and the UUO (the editor, Colonel Volodymyr Korkodym, was a UUO member). Among the three non-Ukrainian citizens who were on the editorial board were two retired U.S. military officers of Ukrainian origin and Rutgers University Professor Taras Hunczak, author of a volume in Ukraine on the SS Galician Division.[51] The journal tended to publish articles in support of keeping Ukraine's nuclear arsenal, about the evils of the Soviet Union and Russia in general, and other highly nationalistic views.

In general, the Ukrainian military press is rather varied in its ideological and political viewpoints. This suggests that there is little control by official organs over what is published and that the military press is not used to its full potential as an instrument of nation building or to propagate the views of the Ukrainian government. This may be a potentially destabilizing factor for Ukrainian nation building, since some of the more nationalistic views of these newspapers may be accepted as the official government viewpoint (which they are not) by military servicemen and the population at large. The nationalistic views of some of these publications are not widely supported and might alienate large sections of the Ukrainian population, which would have an adverse effect on Ukrainian nation building.

THE MILITARY AND NATION BUILDING UNDER KUCHMA

From the SPS to the MAEW

The educational assistant's job in offering an objective view (as is supposed to be the case according to the MAEW) is extremely difficult. The reactions of the educational assistants to what they are supposed to teach is quite varied. Since many educational assistants do not believe in the content of the lectures, they either simply briefly mention the topic in passing without comment or make comments with harsh remarks to the historical information which is presented. However, it is clear that the security forces, like Ukrainian society in general, are quite divided about what is taught. This division has a great deal to do with where the educational assistant was raised.

According to Alexander Besedin, head of the Department of Psychology at Kharkiv's Armed Forces University, because Ukraine is multiethnic the Ukrainian Armed Forces University teaches patriotic and internationalist education. This, Besedin believes, is one and the same goal: "you cannot teach people patriotism and to also hate other nations . . . practice has shown that this approach leads to fascism."[52] Instead, Besedin states that they teach people to respect the traditions and cultures of the many peoples of Ukraine.

However, in Western Ukraine the situation is somewhat more complicated. At the Military Institute of the L'viv State Polytechnic University, the local city council and nationalist organizations constantly attempt to influence the affairs of the Military Institute, which, as the sole center in Ukraine that produces educational assistants, gives Western Ukraine a great deal of influence over Ukrainianization efforts in the armed forces. The result has been to provide a more nationalistic look to the institute, with museums and posters depicting nationalist military groups such as the UPA. The institute also invites both Soviet Army veterans and UPA veterans to give lectures on their activities during the war to military cadets. Nationalist groups also play a very active role in supplying the institute with historical literature. According to some of the Institute's officers, representatives of the L'viv City Council also inspect the institute to make certain the institute is fully "Ukrainianized." Although the institute does not take orders from the L'viv City Council per se and therefore does not even have to allow them access to the institute, the institute nonetheless prefers to maintain good relations with the city and thus allows itself to be influenced by it.

Reactions by students to the MAEW lectures vary from those who are genuinely interested in and accept what they are being taught to those who find the nationalist history and viewpoint humorous and those who are outright hostile to the glorification of nationalist history. Major-General Hryhoriy Temko, the former deputy head of the MAEW who was in charge of formulating its program, recalled giving a lecture in Odessa on the OUN-UPA and the audience reacting in a hostile manner.[53]

There is a struggle being conducted among various individuals in the Ukrainian military over influence in the military-patriotic education program. Although the UUO has lost influence and is now almost invisible as a player in the Ukrainian military, it still has many members in influential positions, including the editors of some of the security force publications and Major-General Temko himself.

Temko believes that the OUN-UPA and the SS Galician Division were heroic formations in the Ukrainian "liberation struggle" and that the history of the Soviet army should not be taught. According to his interpretation, any teaching of Soviet traditions would be contrary to statute 11 of the Law on the Armed Forces of Ukraine, which states that the education of the armed forces should be based on the "national-historic" traditions of the Ukrainian people. Temko admits, however, that his interpretation is not supported by the Ministry of Defense or by many members of the Supreme *Rada*, though this had not stopped him from continuing to glorify Ukrainian nationalist military formations.[54]

Temko also admitted that the MAEW in 1995 had prepared a textbook on Ukrainian military history, though the Ministry of Defense refused to publish it officially due to a lack of funds. Temko believed that the real reason for not publishing the textbook was the ministry's "opposition to the teaching of national-historic traditions."[55] Temko also claims that the large number of ethnic Russians in the ministry is an important source of opposition to the textbook.[56] A more likely reason for the Ministry of Defense's refusal to publish the textbook was the fact that it deified organizations such as the OUN-UPA and the SS Galician Division while omitting the Soviet army's place in Ukrainian history.

Other Forms of Ukrainianization

After the Ukrainian military was initially created, among the first things changed were the names of various military objects, military symbols, and medals. In order not to offend anyone, many of the names in the Ukrainian armed forces were changed to reflect the Cossack period, with the most common name used being that of Hetman Bohdan Khmel'nits'kyi. Although the government has attempted to be as balanced as possible in the use of names and symbols, Ukrainian nationalist symbols of the World War II era are completely omitted. This is not the case when it comes to Soviet names and symbols or even those of the Tsarist era.[57] Defense Minister Kuzmuk more than once awarded the title "Hero of the Soviet Union" to distinguished veterans of the "Great Patriotic War."[58] Kuzmuk also often congratulated such military units as the "24th Mechanized Samaro-Ulyanov, Berdichev Iron, Order of the October Revolution, Thrice Red Flag, Order of Suvorov, and Bohdan Khmel'nits'kyi Division" on the eightieth anniversary of their creation.[59]

President Kuchma also often awards such medals as the Georgi Zhukov Medal for participants of the "Great Patriotic War." All famous dates of the Soviet army's liberation of Ukraine and even the USSR, such as the liberation of Kyiv and the Battle of Kursk, are celebrated annually by orders of the president and the minister of defense. This positive attitude towards Soviet symbol and names has caused many nationalists to complain that the military is not Ukrainian. The fact that the OUN-UPA and the SS Galician Division traditions, symbols, and names are not used, whereas the Soviet ones are, has many nationalists wondering why the Ukrainian military holds these "foreign" traditions so close to their hearts while it rejects "Ukrainian" traditions.[60]

Museums and *Svitlytsi* (reading rooms) are another way in which the Ukrainianization process is being carried out. Outside Western Ukraine, little has changed in the museums themselves, with images of Lenin simply being replaced with images of the Ukrainian flag and the state symbol, the *Tryzub* (Trident). All other exhibits that show the exploits of the Soviet army are largely still intact. However, this is not the case in Western Ukraine, where many museum exhibits now include or are solely dedicated to the "national liberation struggle" of Ukraine conducted by such organizations as the OUN-UPA or even the SS Galician Division.

The *Svitlytsi* are usually decorated with the Ukrainian flag, state symbols, poems by well known Ukrainian poets such as Taras Shevchenko, and images of local war heroes. Of course, books are a major part of the *Svitlytsi*, consisting of the same nationalist publications as in the military libraries. Another way in which the Ukrainianization program has been implemented is through the use of posters and signs found on the grounds of military bases. These posters and signs have been hung up all over bases in place of Soviet posters. Themes include excerpts from the Ukrainian military codes and laws, the Oath of Allegiance to Ukraine, and quotes by Ukrainian authors such as Shevchenko, Ivan Krypiakevich, and the historian and leader of the Central *Rada*, Mykhailo Hrushevs'kyi. Other themes include the Ukrainian national anthem, "Shche ne vmerla Ukraina" (Ukraine Has Not Yet Perished). The themes are always about loving one's country or defending the independence of Ukraine (quotes by Krypiakevich).

When asked whether military people actually read these posters, one officer replied that if they were paid enough and received apartments, maybe they would. Because they have to think about more important things, such as buying food and clothing for their families or paying for living quarters, there is little time or interest to be thinking about these posters.[61] The existence of such patriotic posters and signs depends on the location of the base. There are reports that old Soviet posters and signs still exist on some military bases, though in fewer numbers, and they are now mixed in with new Ukrainian ones.[62]

Language is one of the most important aspects of the Ukrainianization program. The Ukrainian language is no longer being taught in the Ukrainian armed forces since it is supposed to be learned in school before a recruit serves in the military. All lectures and seminars are also supposed to be conducted in Ukrainian. However, because many educational assistants are not fully fluent in Ukrainian, many switch to Russian or use interpreters. Most of the time, Russian is the language used in the Ukrainian military because this is the language most widely known by the officer corps. This has provoked widespread condemnation from Ukrainian nationalists both in Ukraine and among Ukrainian émigrés who often do not consider the Ukrainian military to be truly Ukrainian. One commentator wrote: "Today in the Ukrainian Armed Forces, those who consider their native tongue not to be the Ukrainian language (and therefore it must be understood, nor do they consider the Ukrainian state as theirs) make up 90 per cent of all senior officers."[63]

Measuring the Success of Ukrainianization

The only historical figures that were equally well-received by all of Ukraine's regions and can be considered as promoting national integration are Khmel'nits'kyi, Suvorov, Kutuzov,[64] the armies of Kyivan Rus', and the Cossacks. Almost all other individuals and armies (for example, the OUN-UPA and the SS Galician Division) are viewed differently by Western Ukrainians on one hand, and Central, Southern, and Eastern Ukrainians on the other hand.

A sociological survey from 1994 by Edward Afonin of the Institute of Sociology of the National Academy of Sciences of Ukraine, on order from the Ministry of Defense, brings these divisions to the surface. In a poll conducted among 260 officers and warrant officers, Afonin found that 45.8% of respondents felt that the lack of patriotism in the Ukrainian armed forces was an important problem, while another 37.1% felt it was a very important problem.[65] He also found that 47.7% of respondents felt it was advisable to use the traditions of the Russian Tsarist army in the construction of Ukrainian armed forces, while 27.7% felt it was fully advisable. Only 18% of the officers felt that it was advisable to use UPA traditions while 4.4% felt it was fully advisable. The Soviet army fared far better with 41.1% of respondents feeling it advisable and 13.6% fully advisable to use these traditions. A total of 36.1% of officers felt that it was advisable to use Cossack traditions while 11.5% felt it was fully advisable.[66]

This survey suggests that many Ukrainian military servicemen are not in favor of using the traditions of nationalist militaries in the Ukrainian military. Even Major General Temko, who is a great supporter of nationalist military traditions, when asked whether the teaching and glorification of OUN-UPA and the SS Galician Division can divide the armed forces, admitted that "this can create a 'fifth column' to a certain degree."[67] Temko also agreed that it is possible that by glorifying nationalist traditions, many Ukrainian citizens, especially Russians, will feel insulted and would refuse to defend Ukraine. In fact, he admitted that if Russia invaded Ukraine, "half of Ukraine would defend it and the other half would greet them (the Russians) with flowers."[68] Ultimately, it appears impossible to build Ukrainian national identity on a notion of "Ukrainian" that sees Russia as an "other."

CONCLUSION

The Ukrainian security forces have found themselves in an extremely difficult situation following the breakup of the Soviet Union. There is no money to buy new weapons systems or even to provide housing for the officer corps.[69] Needless to say, morale is at an all-time low. Thus it is quite understandable that the Ukrainianization program is by no means the military's greatest concern at the present time.

Most Ukrainian citizens, including military servicemen, voted for independence believing that their standard of living would improve. Instead, their standard of living has significantly worsened. In addition, the glorification of nationalist armed forces has not only failed to instill Ukrainian servicemen with a sense of nationalism but has actually generated opposition to their policies.

The differences between the regions and especially between Western Ukraine and the other regions are quite significant and may be growing as time passes. Although separatist movements have existed in Southern and Eastern Ukraine since independence, a more recent phenomenon has been the growth of separatist movements in Western Ukraine with calls for Western Ukrainian, or even Galician, independence.[70] Although these separatist groups are not widely supported and are still in their infancy, the fact that such movements have actually taken root should be a cause for serious concern. One of the reasons for the growth of such movements has been the Western Ukrainian perception that Ukraine is not truly independent but simply a Soviet reincarnation that still celebrates Soviet heroes, victories, and events. Thus the Ukrainian state's efforts at nation building seem to be not only failing but also even backfiring.

The most widely supported individuals and periods in Ukrainian history, which could be used in the Ukrainianization program, are Khmel'nits'kyi, Kutuzov, Suvorov, and the Kyivan Rus' and Cossack periods. Therefore it would be wise for the Ukrainian military to focus more on these individuals and two periods and less on the more divisive eras in Ukraine's history. However, whether a Ukrainianization program which is intended to instill patriotism into the troops can omit the Soviet period (which is important for non-Western Ukrainians) and the history of the OUN-UPA (which is important for many Western Ukrainians) and actually achieve its goals is rather unlikely.

The history that is taught as part of the Ukrainianization program must be as objective and truthful as possible and based on facts. Due to its almost total lack of objectivity and truthfulness, Soviet citizens almost always largely disbelieved the Soviet version of history. The Ukrainianization program will not succeed in instilling patriotism into its troops if it is based on half-truths or lies.

Furthermore, the Ukrainian military must take more control over the Ukrainianization program and not allow it to be controlled and influenced by outside interests. This also means that the military must instill more discipline into the military press to follow the official views and policies of the Ukrainian government.

The answers to Ukraine's patriotic problems in the security forces are basically twofold. First, an improvement of the standard of living will give Ukraine's citizens and servicemen a reason to be proud of their country and a will to defend a system that brings them prosperity. Second, a Ukrainianization education program within the military that is less divisive and reflects Ukraine's different regional, cultural, and historical traditions might create a common ground on which national identity can unite, rather than causing further division.

NOTES

1. The study of civil-military relations in Ukraine is still underdeveloped. See Anatoliy S. Grytsenko, *Civil-Military Relations in Ukraine: A System Emerging from Chaos, Harmonie Papers* (Groningen: Center for European Security Studies, 1997).

2. In fact, a very important part of the *State Youth Policy in Ukraine* is the *National Program of Patriotic Education* which is intended to instill patriotism in Ukrainian citizens through the military. See *Armiya Ukrainy*, 22 August 2000.

3. Volodymyr Muliava, personal interview, 31 May 1996.

4. *Narodna Armiya*, 22 January, 1993.

5. *Narodna Armiya*, 25 November 1992.

6. The reason for using the term *national idea* instead of *nationalism* is that the Ukrainian population views nationalism in a negative light. Nationalists argue that this is due to decades of Soviet propaganda against the term.

7. The OUN divided in 1940 into a radical wing under Bandera and a more conservative one under Melnyk. The Melnyk wing was more predisposed to co-operating with the Germans in World War II. After the Bandera wing of OUN (OUN-B) declared independence in L'viv on 30 June 1941, its leaders (Bandera and Yaroslav Stetsko) were arrested by the Nazis and spent most of the war in German camps. In 1952 a second split occurred in OUN-B in the diaspora between the radical right under Bandera/Stetsko and a national democratic wing under Mykola Lebed and Lev Rebet. This third OUN wing came to be called OUN-Z (OUN *zakordonno* or OUN-Z). Only OUN-B and OUN-M are active in Ukraine, particularly the former, which established a political party, the Congress of Ukrainian Nationalists (KUN). See Taras Kuzio, "Radical Nationalist Parties and Movements in Contemporary Ukraine Before and After Independence: The Right and its Politics, 1989-1994," *Nationalities Papers*, vol. 25, no. 2 (June 1997), pp. 211–242.

8. The UPA was created in early 1942 by Hetman Taras Bulba-Borovets and then was forcefully taken over by the OUN-B, which was then led after the arrest of Bandera and Stetsko by Lebed. Lebed went on to become a leading figure in the Ukrainian Supreme Liberation Council (UHVR), created by UPA and OUN-B in 1944 as a surrogate underground parliament. The UHVR established an émigré division led by Lebed, which was backed by OUN-Z.

9. H. Temko, major-general, deputy head of the Main Administration for Educational Work, personal interview, 13 June 1995.

10. Volodymyr Muliava, personal interview, 31 May 1996.

11. *Narodna Armiya,* 25 November 1992.

12. Ukrainian nationalists usually support their claim that the UPA was multiethnic and/or not anti-Semitic by pointing to the fact that the organization had Jewish doctors in its ranks. However, they fail to state that these same doctors were eliminated by the UPA once the Germans retreated from Ukraine. See Aharon Weiss, "Jewish-Ukrainian Rela-

tions in Western Ukraine During the Holocaust" in Peter J. Potichnyj and Howard Aster, eds., *Ukrainian-Jewish Relations in Historical Perspective.* (Edmonton: Canadian Institute of Ukrainian Studies, 1988), p. 417.

13. Ibid.

14. Volodymyr Saladyak, deputy head of the Union of Officers of Ukraine, personal interview, 24 May 1995.

15. John Jaworsky, *The Military-Strategic Significance of Recent Developments in Ukraine: Operational Research and Analysis, Directorate of Strategic Analysis, Project Report No. 645* (Ottawa: Department of National Defense, August 1993), p. 99.

16. Ibid.

17. Volodymyr Saladyak, personal interview, 24 May 1995.

18. Pavel K. Baev and Tor Bukkvol, "Ukraine's Army under Civilian Rule." *Jane's Intelligence Review*, vol. 8, no. 1 (January 1996), p. 10.

19. Taras Kuzio, "Civil-Military Relations in Ukraine," in Karen Dawisha and Bruce Parrott, eds., *State Building and Military Power in Russia and the New States of Eurasia* (Armonk, NY: M. E. Sharpe Inc., 1995), p. 167.

20. Ibid.

21. Baev and Bukkvol, "Ukraine's Army," p. 10.

22. Kuzio, "Civil-Military Relations," p. 167.

23. *Visti Kombatanta,* no. 3, 1992.

24. Alexander N. Besedin, head, Department of Military Psychology, University of the Ukrainian Armed Forces, personal interview, 3 June 1995. Also Baev and Bukkvol, "Ukraine's Army," p. 10.

25. Volodymyr Bezkorovainy, admiral, former commander of the Ukrainian navy, personal interview, 11 October 1997.

26. T. Kuzio, "Ukraine's Young Turks—The Union of Ukrainian Officers," *Jane's Intelligence Review*, vol. 5, no. 1 (January 1993), p. 26.

27. According to one ethnic Russian officer, upon graduation from his military academy in 1992 he was ordered to return to Russia by his SPS officer regardless of the fact that he was born and raised in Kharkiv. Anonymous personal interview, 7 September 1999. Another officer who was to take part in a training visit to Canada complained that once Muliava learned that he was an ethnic Russian, his trip was cancelled. Anonymous personal interview, 1 September 1999.

28. Stephen Foye, "Civilian-Military Tension in Ukraine," *RFE/RL Research Report*, vol. 2, no. 25 (18 June 1993), p. 64.

29. V. Bezkorovainy, personal interview, 11 October 1997.

30. Volodymyr Saladyak, personal interview, 24 May 1995.

31. Kuzio. "Ukraine's Young Turks," p. 25.

32. Kuzio, "Civil-Military Relations," p. 169.

33. *Narodna Armiya,* 25 November 1992. Also Volodymyr Muliava, personal interview, 31 May 1996.

34. *RFE/RL Daily Report,* 17 January 1994.

35. Volodymyr Saladyak, personal interview, 24 May 1995.

36. *STATUT Spilky Ofitseriv Ukrainy,* Kyiv, 1994. Copy in the author's possession.

37. Baev and Bukkvol, "Ukraine's Army," p. 9.

38. On the late Soviet era, see A. M. Rusnachenko, *Na Shliakhu Do Natsional'noii Armii* (1989–1991) (Kyiv: n.p., 1992); and T. Kuzio, "Civil-Military Relations in Ukraine, 1989–1991," *Armed Forces and Society*, vol. 22, no. 1 (Fall 1995), pp. 25–48. On the post-Soviet era see T. Kuzio, "Nuclear Weapons and Military Policy in Independent Ukraine," *Harriman Institute Forum*, vol. 6, no. 9 (May 1993); *The Military Tradition*

in Ukrainian History; Konstantyn Morozov, "The Formation of the Ukrainian Army, 1991–95," *The Ukrainian Review*, vol. 43, no.1 (Spring 1996), pp. 8-17; and chapter 8, "Ukrainian Defense Policy and the Transformation of the Armed Forces," in Paul D'Anieri, Robert Kravchuk and Taras Kuzio, *Politics and Society in Ukraine* (Boulder, CO; Westview, 1999), pp. 233–261.

39. Volodymyr Saladyak, personal interview, 24 May 1995.

40. Baev and Bukkvol, "Ukraine's Army," p. 10.

41. For an early handbook on humanities preparation see O. O. Lisna, *Vyvchayemo Ukraiins'ku Samostiyno* (Kyiv: Ministry of Defense, 1992).

42. This is certainly not the official Ukrainian position, which still considers members of the SS Galician Division to have been traitors and many of them as war criminals. See *Visti Kombatanta*, no. 2 (1997) p. 69; and *Visti Kombatanta*, no. 5-6 (1997) p. 116.

43. Vitaliy Nepytaylenko, captain, educational assistant in the National Guard, personal interview, 3 June 1995; and H. Temko, personal interview, 13 June 1995. See H. D. Temko, *Osnovy Formuvannia Systemy Vykhovannia Voiina v Ukraiini u Period Utverdzhennia Derzhavnosti* (Kyiv: Varta, 1997).

44. Anonymous personal interview, 10 August 1998.

45. Vasyl' Bilan, colonel, editor of *Narodna Armiya*, personal interview, 28 May 1995.

46. *Narodna Armiya*, 27 February 1997.

47. *Narodna Armiya*, 29 July 1998.

48. See, for example, *Flag Rodiny*, 20 June 1995.

49. *Flot Ukrainy*, 4 July 1995.

50. According to the editor, Colonel Volodymyr Korkodym, *Surma* decided that the editorial board would consist of only people who live in Ukraine. Volodymyr Korkodym, Editor of *Surma*, personal interview, 7 June 1995.

51. For an example of an émigré professor publishing a book on the SS Galician Division specifically for Ukraine see Taras Hunczak, *U Mundurakh Voroha* (Kyiv: Chas Ukraiiny, 1993).

52. Alexander Besedin, head of the Department of Psychology, University of the Ukrainian Armed Forces, Kharkiv, personal interview, 20 June 1995.

53. H. Temko, personal interview, 13 June 1995.

54. Ibid.

55. Ibid.

56. Ibid.

57. See *Vartovi Neba*, nos. 32–34, March 1998, where President Kuchma awarded the Order of Alexander Nevsky 223rd Rocket Brigade the honorary status of "Terebovlyanska."

58. *Narodna Armiya*, 22 July 1998.

59. *Narodna Armiya*, 25 July 1998.

60. *Visti Kombatanta*, nos. 5–6, 1996, p. 41.

61. Anonymous, personal interview, 18 May 1995.

62. Anonymous, personal telephone interview, 10 August 1998.

63. *Vechirniy Kyiv*, 11 January 1997.

64. Ukrainians played a large role in the victories of Suvorov and Kutuzov.

65. E. A. Afonin, *Stanovlennia Zbroynikh Syl Ukrainy: sotsial'ni ta sotsial'nopsiholohichni problemy*, (Kyiv: Natsionalna Akademiya Nauk, Instytut Sotsiolohii, 1994), p. 211.

66. Ibid., p. 223.

67. H. Temko, personal interview, 13 June 1995.

68. Ibid.

69. This prompted Defense Minister Kuzmuk to sarcastically note that, "after 2005 we may be left with national consciousness and Kalashnikovs" (*Narodna Armiya*, 18 January 1997).

70. See for example, Peter Bejger, "The Restless West," *Ukrainian Observer*, 24 November 1999; Volodymyr Pavliv, "Dev'yatyy misyats' z kryvavym vidtinkom abo Dlya koho ye 'svyatom' 17 veresnya?" *Polityka I Kul'tura (PiK)*, November 1999; and *Vysokyy Zamok*, 5–11 November 1999.

9

Identity Construction and Education: The History of Ukraine in Soviet and Post-Soviet Schoolbooks

Jan G. Janmaat

History has always played a pivotal role in the formation or disintegration of national identities. To promote group cohesion and give citizens a sense of self-esteem, political entrepreneurs emphasize common ancestry and experiences, and exaggerate the significance of certain historical events to such an extent that these assume mythical proportions.[1] To achieve group breakdown the opposite is stressed: inter/intra group conflict, suppression and injustice. Given Ukraine's considerable linguistic and religious differences, it is not surprising to find the present-day authorities turning to history to enhance national unity.[2]

This chapter examines the introduction of a new state-propagated version of history in the school system. What selection of historical events does this version make and how are these events portrayed? How successful is the state in disseminating new teaching materials over Ukraine? Is one standard version propagated, or do schools, teachers, and parents have a certain freedom of choice? Given the potential impact of a new version of school history in educating a whole generation of school children, it is surprising to find so little academic attention being devoted to this issue. Because education is one of the main vehicles by which the state can purposefully seek to alter citizens' notions of national identity, the issue is crucial to the broader question of the state's role in nationalizing the population.

In their use of history strengthen national identity, the authorities may be said to be faced with two major problems. First, the heroic moments or periods in history from which Ukrainians can derive a feeling of pride appear to be sparse. Ever since the collapse of the medieval state of Kyiv Rus' in the thirteenth century, the Ukrainian lands were dominated by neighboring powers and the Ukrainian population subjugated to foreign noblemen and administrators. This is not to say that Ukrainians have nothing to fall back on. Ukrainian historians, for instance, appropriate the legacy of Kyiv Rus' by seeing contemporary Ukraine as the direct successor of that empire. Likewise, the Cossacks of the sixteenth century are considered brave Ukrainians who fought a national liberation war against the Poles and Tatars.[3]

However, it is precisely on these few moments of glory that Ukrainian historiography clashes with the Russian/Soviet one. In the Russian imperial scheme,

Kyiv Rus' was the precursor of the Russian Tsarist empire. It was seen as the first state governed by and dominated by Russians, with Ukrainians and Belarusians not being recognized as distinct peoples. The Soviet view basically endorsed this idea. It only departed from it to the extent that the inhabitants of the Kyiv Rus' state were seen as East Slavs, who consisted of proto-Russians, Ukrainians, and Belarusians. Soviet historians acknowledged these proto-Ukrainians as having been a separate people since the fourteenth century, but asserted that the one and only aim of the Ukrainians was to be reunified with their "elder" Russian brethren. For them, the Pereiaslav Treaty of 1654, in which the Cossack Hetman Bohdan Khmel'nyts'kyi recognized the suzerainty of the Muscovite Tsar in exchange for autonomy, served as convenient proof of this endeavor.[4] In the Soviet view, the Cossack military campaigns of the sixteenth century thus represented merely an effort to re-unite with Russia, not a national liberation struggle.

Second the contradictions between the Ukrainian and the Russian/Soviet view on history place nation-building architects in a dilemma. On one hand, state officials may find it hard to communicate a radical Ukrainian nationalist version of history that could well be unacceptable to the Russian-speaking population of the East and South, who may still feel themselves part of the Russian cultural world.[5] On the other hand, the propagation of a historical scheme much closer to the Russian/Soviet version would undermine the claim that Ukraine is a territory with a history and population distinct from that of Russia.[6] Given the centrality of this claim for the legitimacy of independent Ukraine, it seems that the latter scheme enjoys little popularity among Ukrainian elites.[7]

THE STRUCTURE OF HISTORY EDUCATION IN SCHOOLS

It is important to note that school education has remained highly centralized in post-independence Ukraine, with schools operating on the programs and recommended textbooks of the Ministry of Education. For the obligatory course of history of Ukraine, the ministry offers schools a small choice of two recommended textbooks per grade, books that are also available in a Russian translation for Russian schools.[8] However, all schools—both Russian and Ukrainian—that the author visited on his fieldwork travels throughout Ukraine use one and the same textbook for a certain grade, because only this particular textbook closely follows the program in structure and content.[9] This uniform use of a limited number of textbooks, which is reminiscent of the Soviet era, facilitates the task of a content analysis, because only a few books have to be same time the widespread use of these books underlines the relevance of analyzing them. One has to keep in mind, however, that no matter how uniform their geographical distribution, their dispersal in time may vary, as the Ministry sometimes issues a limited number of new textbooks for trial in specially selected schools in two of Ukraine's twenty-six *oblasti*. After having used these books for a year, the teachers give their comments, which (at least in theory) are taken into account and integrated into the new books. Subsequently, these books are distributed to all schools.[10] It further has to be noted that history teachers are now free to use all sorts of books as additional materials in their lessons. In this respect there has been some structural change.

A COMPARATIVE CONENT ANALYSIS OF HISTORY TEXTBOOKS

Schools in Soviet times also had separate textbooks on history of Ukraine, a subject that was included in the general history course. This enables us to do a comparative content analysis of the old and new textbooks. The advantage of such a comparison is that we can assess the extent to which the current text-books have departed from the Soviet ones in their presentation of historical events. Topics specifically worthy of attention are Kyiv Rus', the Cossack era, the rise of national consciousness in the late nineteenth century, the attempts to establish independence after the February 1917 revolution, the famine of the 1930s, and World War II and the role of the Organization of Ukrainian Nation-alists (OUN) and the Ukrainian Insurgent Army (UPA). Do the new textbooks portray Ukrainians consistently as victims of Russian/Soviet rule? Is the Bol-shevik revolution presented as something foreign and hostile, or is it considered a partly domestically induced turn of events with Ukrainians participating in it? Are Ukraine and its population described as neutral victims of both warring par-ties in World War II, or are they seen as active participants in the Soviet forces and as subjects of German aggression only? Are the OUN and UPA seen as Ukrainian patriots or as Nazi collaborators?

The following textbooks were used in the Soviet era:

- Grades 7–8: V. H. Sarbei, H. Ya. Serhienko and V. A. Smolyi, *Istoriia Ukrainskoi SSR* (Kyiv: Radians'ka Shkola, 1984), 158 pp. This textbook describes Ukrainian history until the twentieth century.
- Grades 9–10: V. H. Sarbei and V. E. Spytskyi, *Istoriia Ukrainskoi SSR* (Kyiv: Radians'ka Shkola, 1987), 183 pp. This textbook describes Ukrainian history during the twentieth century.

The textbooks used in post-Soviet Ukraine are:

- Grades 7–8: H. Ya Serhienko and V. A. Smolyi, *Istoriia Ukrainy: s drevneishikh vremen do kontsa XVIII veka* (Kyiv: Osvita, 1985), 256 pp. This is a history of Ukraine from ancient times to the end of the eighteenth century.
- Grade 9: V. H. Sarbei, *Istoria Ukrainy: XIX-nachalo XX veka* (Kyiv: Heneza, 1996), 223 pp. A history of Ukraine in the nineteenth and the beginning of the twentieth centuries.
- Grade 10: F. H. Turchenko, *Noveishaia istoriia Ukrainy: Chast' pervaia (1917–1945 rr.)* (Kyiv: Heneza, 1994), 340 pp. A history of Ukraine from 1917 to 1945.
- Grade 11: F. H. Turchenko, P. P. Panchenko and C. M. Tymchenko, *Noveishaia istoria Ukrainy: chast' vtoraia (1945–1995 roky)* (Kyiv: Heneza, 1995), 342 pp. A history of Ukraine from 1945 to 1995. [11]

It is to these six books that a comparative content analysis will be applied. Two things come immediately to mind when the books are compared. First, three of the authors (Sarbei, Serhienko and Smolyi) wrote both old and new textbooks. This may indicate the difficulties the Ministry of Education faces in finding experts to write the new textbooks. More important, it may also testify to the ministry's approval of letting scholars associated with the old regime participate in the teaching of a new history of Ukraine. Other postcommunist states were not as tolerant in their treatment of scholars and officials that occupied important positions in the communist era. In East Berlin, for instance, almost all school directors were changed after "Die Wende."[12] Yet, a continuity of personnel need not by itself, of course, stand in the way of a revised content of the history books. Much will depend on the stringency of ministerial prescriptions and on the flexibility of the authors. In view of these considerations, it will be interesting to see to what extent the authors of the Soviet textbooks have adjusted the content of the new books to the new political circumstances.

Second, the study load has increased dramatically. Not only did the number of textbooks expand from two to four in the school period of a pupil, the number of pages of each textbook has also almost doubled.

KYIV' RUS

Beginning with Kyiv Rus', we see that the old textbook for grades 7–8 indeed echoes the Soviet notion of the (pursuit of) unity, brotherhood and friendship of the three East Slavic peoples:

Since the creation of the state [Kyiv Rus'], the differences between the Slavic tribes quickly faded away. Their intensive contacts were greatly aided by the development of the Old Russian language, which was understandable for the whole population of Kyiv Rus'. . . . The Old Russian proto-nation was based on a communality of economic relations, territory, language and culture. In addition to this, certain particularities remained in the language, culture and customs of people living in the northeastern, western and southwestern parts of the territory of Kyiv Rus'. Later these particularities became more pronounced and formed the basis for the evolution of the Russian, Ukrainian and Belarusian proto-nations. Subsequently, out of these old Russian proto-nations crystallized the three brotherly nations—Russians, Ukrainians and Belarusians, who forever retained a feeling of relatedness, communality and historical unity.[13]

This passage was thoroughly revised in the new textbook for grades 7–8. Instead, we now read that:

The main state, political, religious and cultural center of Kyiv Rus' developed, of all places, on the territory of present-day Ukraine, and the Slavic tribes living on these lands founded political alliances, constituted the *Ukrainian proto-nation*, and were at that time the state-building force of Kyiv Rus'. Kyiv, as the historical center of the Ukrainian proto-nation, became the unifying beginning for the other tribes of the Russian lands, as well. For this reason, many scholars consider Kyiv Rus', where the leading role was taken by one ethnic community in particular—the Ukrainian proto-nation, to be a *Ukrainian state*. . . . Each proto-nation living on the territory of Kyiv Rus' developed in isolation and aspired independent state life. Moreover, as we shall see, the union of East Slavic tribal alliances in the state of Kyiv Rus' was far from voluntary: often the Kyivan kings had to subjugate them by means of military force.[14]

Claiming that the Ukrainian proto-nation was in fact the ruling people of Kyiv Rus' and stating that many experts label Kyiv Rus' as a Ukrainian state clearly appeal to modern Ukrainian historiography, which considers Kyiv Rus' to be the forerunner of present-day Ukraine. Moreover, in another contrast to the first extract, not the *brotherhood* but the *animosity* between the East Slavic proto-nations is stressed. The problematic relationship with Russia is also highlighted when the Russian imperialist view of Kyiv Rus' is implicitly attacked: "All this leads to the proper conclusion that the Russian empire in later times did not have the right to present itself as the sole successor of Kyiv Rus' and to subject Ukraine and Belarus to Tsarist rule."[15] To underline the Ukrainian scheme, Hrushevs'kyi, the doyen of twentieth century Ukrainian historiography, is quoted: "Kyiv Rus' appears to be the first form of Ukrainian statehood."[16]

Another difference with the old textbook is the way the introduction of Christianity is evaluated. Although the new book admits that Christianity strengthened the authoritarian power of the king, it generally appreciates it as a positive phenomenon, bringing civilization, literacy, and culture to Ukraine and giving it closer ties with Western Europe. Later in the book, the Orthodox Church is even mentioned as "the spiritual base of the Ukrainian proto-nation."[17] The Soviet book, in contrast, views Christianity as bringing more harm than good. It is said to have contributed to the "exploitation of the popular masses" by the king and the nobles and to have been unable to stop the feudal quarrels, which significantly weakened Kyiv Rus'. Moreover, literacy is claimed to have preceded Christianity.

In addition to these differences, the books also show remarkable similarities. For example, much of the content of the old book was copied literally in the new book, especially—and quite surprisingly—the section on the origin of the names *Rus'* and *Russkaia zemlia* as alternative names for the Kyivan state. Like the old book, the new book (in its Russian translation) simply uses the adjectival form *russkii* (Russian) in, for instance, *Russkaia zemlia*. Although Serbyn argues that *russkii* is indeed the appropriate adjective for Rus' in the Russian language, the term could lead to confusion, because it refers to things ethnically Russian in normal usage.[18] The pupils reading the Russian translation could thus interpret *Russkaia zemlia* as "Russian land," (i.e., the land inhabited by ethnic Russians). Surely this is not the interpretation the Ministry of Education would like pupils to make. Moreover, as Serbyn points out, the terms *russkii* and *rossiiskii* (the adjective for *Rossiia*—Russia) are often used interchangeably in Russian literature, which undermines the distinction between Russia and Rus'.[19] In view of the confusion *russkii* evokes, it seems strange the authors did not choose (or invent) another Russian term as an adjective for Rus'. Incidentally, the Ukrainian equivalent—*rus'kiy*—does not lead to misunderstandings as it only refers to Rus' and not to Russia or Russian ethnicity—the adjective for the latter two being *rosiis'kyi*.[20]

A second remarkable similarity concerns the new book's focus on issues of social injustice and class conflict. Mimicking the old book, the new book asserts that "the king and nobles conquered community land and acres and violently forced the peasant serfs not only to pay tribute but also to work a certain amount of days on their country estates,"[21] and that "the city poor paid the king heavy taxes, fulfilled several duties and had to maintain churches and monasteries. The most cruel exploitation was suffered by the serfs, who did not own land."[22] It continues, "Profiteers and merchants thrived on the destruction and poverty of the people. All this led to explosions of popular rage."[23] These and other excerpts show that the new book was still to a certain extent written in a spirit of class conflict. Given that the authors (Serhienko and Smolyi) of the new edition were also coauthors of the Soviet book, one has to conclude that they certainly did not change all of their historical views with the arrival of Ukraine's independence.

THE COSSACK ERA AND HETMAN IVAN MEZEPA

The account of the Zaporizhzhian Cossacks, the Pereiaslav Treaty, and the controversial Cossack leader Mazepa in the Soviet textbook is predictably in line with the Soviet scheme of Ukrainian history. In brief, it argues that in the sixteenth and seventeenth centuries the Ukrainian popular masses were suppressed by Polish nobles and Tatar warlords, and that due to the courageous military campaigns of the Cossacks (free farmer-soldiers who had fled serfdom) and the unconditional support of their Russian brethren, the Ukrainians managed to cast off the foreign yoke and realize their long-cherished dream of uniting with Russia. Mazepa, the Cossack Hetman who in the early eighteenth century sided with Charles XII from Sweden in his power struggle with Russia's Peter I, is depicted as a traitor who received only minimal support from his own troops. In particular the making of the Pereiaslav Agreement of 1654, which united the Cossack lands with Russia in exchange for autonomy, is exalted as a wonderful display of Russian-Ukrainian friendship: "Along the whole way the population of Ukraine greeted the ambassadors of the brotherly Russian people with festivities and happiness. . . . All the participants of the council unanimously voted for the union of the brotherly nations into one state. . . . The oath [that all forever be one] was supported by the whole Ukrainian nation."[24]

In its discussion of early modern times, the old textbook continues to stress social issues. It contends that only during the war of liberation of 1648–1654 did the "popular masses" of peasants and lower-class Cossacks manage to abolish serfdom and take large areas of land for their own use. Very soon afterward, the Cossack higher circles (the so-called *starshyna*) "began attacking the social conquests of the laborers."[25] With the passing of time, peasants and workers, it is argued, were deprived of more and more rights and were pushed back to serfdom and conditions of slavery. The book considers the destruction of the Zaporizhzhian Sich, the most important Cossack stronghold, by Tsarina Catherine II in 1775, as another lamentable victory of the Tsarist regime over the "revolutionary anti-feudal" forces. No reference is made to the Zaporizhzhian Cossacks or to the several peasant uprisings of the eighteenth century as specific Ukrainian phenomena. Similarly, the book makes no mention of the Ukrainian language, leaving the reader mystified about its fate. Only on two occasions does the book give examples of a specific *cultural* interference by foreign powers: "[in eighteenth-century Polish-held Ukraine] Ukrainian schools, which were persecuted by the Catholic church and the royal powers, led a pitiful existence,"[26] while "German, Austrian and Hungarian nobles introduced languages that were foreign to the Ukrainian people."[27] Thus, if we are to believe this book, only powers other than Russia culturally oppressed Ukrainians.

Understandably, the new textbook has a rather different view on the events of the seventeenth and eighteenth centuries. The Liberation War is presented not only as a social but also as a national uprising, with the Cossacks identified as Ukrainian freedom fighters who attempted to shed Polish rule and found an independent Ukrainian state. It follows that the Pereiaslav Treaty with Russia is described as an unfortunate but necessary event, as it meant that the young Cossack state had to surrender some authority in order to safeguard the attainments of the Liberation War:

The Pereiaslav Treaty and the subordination to Russia was not at all a coincidental step, but a painful decision by Hetman [Khmel'nyts'kyi] after long contemplation. He realized that the temporary respite for the young Ukrainian state could not be long, taking into account the temporary nature of the alliance with the Crimean Khan, the unreliability of the Sultan of Turkey and the still powerful Polish kingdom.[28]

To justify why in particular Russia was chosen as a protector, the book says that "Ukraine and Russia were bound together by long historical ties, the ethnic closeness of both peoples and the orthodox faith."[29]

A similar, rather subtle account is given of Hetman Mazepa. Calling him neither a traitor nor a national hero, the book presents him as an educated man who came to his decision after much deliberation: "restlessness and contradicting feelings tore his soul."[30] The increasing demands of the Tsar on the Hetman to deliver soldiers and food, the high tax burden on the peasants and on the lower-ranking Cossacks and the lack of respect with which the Tsarist governors treated the Cossacks are seen as the direct causes for the switch in Mazepa's allegiance. Yet the textbook does not leave unmentioned that Mazepa received only minimal support from the Ukrainian people and that the population began resisting the pillaging army of Charles XII (as in the old book, there is an account of how bravely the citizens of L'viv defended their city against the Swedes). This rather balanced version of the Mazepa years is surprising if one realizes that nation-building architects could use Hetman Mazepa to present evidence of the "eternal endeavor of the Ukrainian nation to achieve state independence."

Another, perhaps remarkable aspect of the new edition is that Ukraine under Cossack rule is not idealized. In a straight copy from the old book, the social situation that developed after 1654 is criticized, with the Cossack higher circles being accused of enriching themselves at the expense of the lower classes by taking much of their lands and increasing their duties. Similarly, examples can be found of the terminology that can typically be associated with a Soviet account of history: "toiling masses,"[31] "social oppression," "exploitation by entrepreneurs," and "social struggle of the laboring masses."[32]

Yet, in clear contrast to the Soviet textbook, the new book does address the issue of the Ukrainian language. More than once it mentions how in the eighteenth century the Ukrainian language was pushed out of the public domain by a conscious policy of Russification on left-bank Ukraine, and of Polonization on

right-bank Ukraine: "the spiritual state of mind of the community was negatively affected by the policy of Russification, which was enforced by the Tsarist
government"[33] and "Gradually, the Ukrainian language was driven not only
from the administration, but also from literature and from schools. In its place,
Russian was introduced everywhere."[34] Interestingly, by focusing on the introduction of Russian and Polish on Ukrainian territory by neighboring powers, the
book clearly implies that these languages are foreign to Ukrainians and that only
the Ukrainian language can rightfully be called a constituent element of Ukrainian national identity. Although this stance strongly supports the claim of Ukrainian distinctiveness, it may also lead to feelings of estrangement among Russian-
speaking pupils, as they might start to ask themselves whether they are in fact
true Ukrainians if they speak the language of the "elder brother."

THE AWAKENING OF THE UKRAINIAN NATION IN THE SECOND
HALF OF THE NINETEENTH CENTURY

As expected, the old Soviet textbook interprets the growing dissatisfaction
with Tsarist rule in Ukraine in the second half of the nineteenth century as,
above all, a class struggle of the Ukrainian proletariat and peasantry against the
bourgeoisie and the nobility. Nonetheless, the old textbook argues that, as a result of the development of capitalism, the Ukrainian "capitalist" nation came
into being: "Because of the development of capitalism, the accelerated process
of the economic, territorial, linguistic and cultural unification of the population
of the Ukrainian lands created the conditions for the completion of the long
process of the formation of the Ukrainian nation."[35] The book continues by con-
tending that the Ukrainian nation can truly be called capitalist, with all its inherent conflicts, since there were many Ukrainians, either Ukrainian or Russian
speaking, that entered the ranks of the industrial-commercial bourgeoisie. Consequently, it is argued, these Ukrainians found themselves in a class struggle
with fellow Ukrainians of the lower classes. The book claims that local Ukrainian dialects gradually merged into a literary and nationwide language and that
the evolution of this language was greatly aided by the works of the classical
authors of Ukrainian literature. These authors, Taras Shevchenko and Ivan
Franko especially, are portrayed as anti-Tsarist/Habsburg (not anti-Russian)
social revolutionaries.

Quite surprisingly, the old textbook does mention the Tsarist crackdown on
the Ukrainian language and culture: "by means of a special order, Tsar Alexander II prohibited the publication of books in the Ukrainian language, and theatre
plays for a Ukrainian audience could only be performed in Ukraine by special
permission of the governor."[36] Yet, the old textbook fails to note that as a consequence of this Tsarist ban there may have been pronounced not only anti-
Tsarist sentiments among Ukrainian intelligentsia circles, but also a strong desire to separate from Russia and found an independent Ukrainian state. Instead,
the book takes every opportunity to underline the "eternal striving of the
Ukrainian nation to unite with their Russian brethren." In this respect, the
Galician writer Ivan Franko is singled out as a "great revolutionary democrat"
that dedicated his life and works to the unification of the West Ukrainian popu-

lation (which was under Austrian rule) with the Tsarist-ruled Ukrainians "within the structure of Russia." The textbook quotes him as saying that "we love the Russian people and wish it all the best, we love and learn its language."[37]

In contrast to the old Soviet textbook, the new book (for the ninth grade) attributes the awakening of the Ukrainian nation not to the growth of capitalist economic relations but to the abolition of serfdom and the incessant efforts of the Ukrainian intelligentsia to spread the Ukrainian national idea among the peasantry. These peasants are regarded as the "bearers of the ethnic features of the Ukrainian nation,"[38] and the Ukrainian language as the "Cementing force of unity of the national culture."[39] In fact, the new textbook argues that imperialism and capitalism actually frustrated the consolidation of the Ukrainian nation and the creation of a national economy. It states that "The road to a normal development of the Ukrainian nation was closed because of the merciless colonizing exploitation of the national economies of the Russian and Austrian-Hungarian empires."[40] To illustrate this point, the new textbook contends that Ukraine traded at an unfavorable exchange rate with Russia, exchanging cheap raw materials for expensive finished products. Moreover, it is asserted that the trade sector in Ukraine fell almost completely into the hands of Russians, Jews, Armenians, and Greeks, "who often did not operate as civilized merchants, but as barbaric-predatory wholesale buyers and sellers."[41] Thus, the new book refutes the old textbook's claim that Ukrainians participated in the emerging bourgeoisie.

Not surprisingly, the new textbook sees the particular Tsarist policy towards the Ukrainian language and culture as another obstacle to the development of the Ukrainian nation. In a full four pages, the new textbook recounts how the Tsar successively issued orders forbidding Ukrainian textbooks, education, literature, theatre plays, and songs, and how the imperial authorities started persecuting members of the Ukrainian intelligentsia. A last impediment to the full realization of Ukrainian nationhood is seen in the Russian-Austrian border, which separated Ukrainians into two halves and significantly hampered their economic, political, and cultural ties.

Proceeding from the carefully reasoned economic and cultural "exploitation" of the Ukrainian lands by foreign peoples and powers, the new book considers the anti-Tsarist movement of the late nineteenth century to be not only social-revolutionary in character but also, and above all, national-emancipatory in outlook. It provides eleven pages on a discussion of the Ukrainian intelligentsia circles in both the Russian and the Austrian empire and describes how these intellectuals sought to disseminate the idea of an independent Ukrainian state under the threat of deportation. Yet, in an echo of the old textbook, the new volume concedes that the advocates of Ukrainian independence were much inspired by the revolutionary appeal of Marxism. In a similar vein, using typical Soviet phraseology, the new textbook more than once recalls how the Ukrainian peasants and laborers were exploited by foreign nobles and industrials.

Comparing the two textbooks, we can conclude that, despite being written by one and the same author, the old and the new volume show remarkable contrasts in their accounts of the late nineteenth century. As we have seen, these contradictions concern the participation of Ukrainians in "the oppressing

classes" and the particular outlook of the Ukrainian intellectual circles. However, the differences with the old textbook notwithstanding, the new book to a
significant extent continues the Soviet tradition of interpreting historical events
in a materialist way.

THE BOLSHEVIK REVOLUTION AND THE UKRAINIANIZATION OF THE 1920s

In the Soviet textbook for grades nine and ten, the narrative on the October
revolution and the ensuing Bolshevik conquest of Ukraine is equally straightforward. The Bolsheviks are presented as heroes who liberated the Ukrainian
workers and peasants from the tyranny of the bourgeoisie, the nobles, and the
Central *Rada* that took control over most of Ukraine in the months after the
revolution and demanded an autonomous status for Ukraine within a federal
Russia. The participation of the Ukrainian proletariat in the revolution is
stressed more than once. The rebellion of the *Arsenal* factory workers in enemy-
occupied Kyiv is given as a particularly illustrative example: "The Arsenal
workers fought bravely, although there was not enough ammunition and food.
Women and children helped by providing the workers with food and first aid
equipment for the seriously wounded, which were brought in under heavy
fire."[42] Yet the old textbook admits that the transition to Bolshevik power was
not always easy. It even concedes that in a number of city soviets the Bolsheviks
captured only a minority of seats:

In Ukraine the struggle for the victory of the proletarian revolution met with different
rates of success in the various regions, and depended on the actual class relationships.
Thus, Soviet power was established without armed struggle in the Donbas, where the
Bolsheviks predominated in the soviets and the proletariat was more organized. But a
fierce and tense battle evolved in Kharkiv, Ekatarinoslav (Dnipropetrovs'k), Vinnytsia
and Odesa, where the majority of seats in the soviets was captured by Mensheviks, SR's
(Socialist Revolutionaries) and bourgeois nationalists.[43]

There is also an implicit acknowledgment that initially not all of Ukraine's
workers supported the Bolsheviks until they confirmed the right of the Ukrainian people for self-determination up to the point of secession. This was described as "encouraging the workers of Ukraine to take the side of the Bolshevik
party."[44]

Quite noteworthy is the old book's complete omission of the Bolshevik-
induced Ukrainianization campaign of the 1920s. Although there is mention of
the mass-scale operation to combat illiteracy, there is no reference to the indi-
genization of administrative and party executives or to the growing number of
Ukrainian-language schools, *vuzy* (institutions of higher education), and periodicals. On the other hand, the book does report the communist alternative to
the Tsarist "cultural oppression." It discloses that "On the tenth session [of the
Russian Communist Party] much attention was paid to the national question.
The October Revolution had proclaimed the equality of all nations inhabiting
Russia. The task consisted of eliminating the economic and cultural arrears of
the nations that had been oppressed by the Tsars."[45]

The question that comes to mind is why the book fails to address the Ukrainianization of the 1920s when it could serve as an outstanding illustration of the proclaimed endeavor to establish the equality of all Soviet nations. Considering the time the book was published—1987, the year that saw the beginning of national revival movements in the Baltics—one could postulate that the Soviet educational authorities wanted to direct attention away from the sensitive nationality issue. Another reason could be that educational powers sought to make pupils believe that from day one of the existence of the Soviet Union the constituent nations were actually in the process of merging into a larger Soviet nation. A confirmation of this argument can be found:

The common economy and culture, which was international in spirit and character, provided the conditions for an intensification of the friendship and brotherly cooperation of the Soviet Republics. This contributed to the creation of a new historical community of people—the Soviet Nation.[46]

As could be expected, the new edition for the tenth grade presents an entirely different picture of the Bolshevik period. The Bolshevik ideal of absolute equality, social harmony, and economic prosperity is portrayed as a utopian dream for which there was not even enough support among the population of Russia. It is also seen as an ideological movement *foreign* to Ukraine, as reportedly only a small minority of Ukrainians sided with the Bolsheviks. Very cleverly, the book quotes V. Zatonskii, an early Bolshevik leader, as saying that "The Bolshevik party had the Russian or Russified proletariat as its backbone."[47] The book continues by asserting that given these circumstances, Soviet power could be established only by force in Ukraine. To underline this, it is stressed that, "the social base of the Bolsheviks was weak, and their authority insignificant,"[48] with the sole exception of the Donbas where the Bolsheviks captured power peacefully. Moreover, to corroborate the claim that the Central *Rada* was the only political body that legitimately represented the Ukrainian population, the book discloses the results of the November 1917 elections for the first session, which purportedly show that the Ukrainian national parties captured about 75% of the votes, while the Bolsheviks received only 10%.

Yet, the Central *Rada* is also criticized for not addressing the critical issue of land reform. Although it is admitted that a radical redistribution of land would have had disastrous consequences for agrarian productivity, its postponement is seen as the principal reason why the rural poor turned its back on the Central *Rada*. Interestingly, by quoting the historian Viacheslav Lypins'kyi, who "with bitterness stated that the 'notion of Ukraine'. . . was replaced by the notion of the 'desiatina zemli' [a specific measure of land],"[49] the book quite explicitly acknowledges that a Ukrainian national consciousness appears to have been quite shallow among the peasantry. Likewise, it is conceded that most of the *urban* poor chose the Bolshevik side. The textbook even mentions the Arsenal uprising and how it contributed to the defeat of the army of the Central *Rada* in its defense of Kyiv. Taken as a whole, however, the work maintains its position that the arrival of Soviet power in Ukraine is deplorable, accusing the Bolsheviks of eliminating democracy, indulging in cruel terror, persecuting Ukrainian culture, and confiscating food and other products. It ends a section with a strong condemnation: "the establishment of Bolshevik power in Ukraine, by means of deceit, violence and direct interference from abroad, inevitably had to become and became the object of nationwide opposition."[50]

Given the new textbooks' preoccupation with the Ukrainian language—the book for the ninth grade even explicitly states that "the membership of which [the Ukrainian nation] was above all determined by the native [i.e., Ukrainian] language"[51] — it is interesting to see how the Ukrainianization of the 1920s is portrayed. Yet, the book for the tenth grade is ambiguous about this period. On the one hand, Ukrainianization is appreciated, as it "attracted many representatives of the national intelligentsia to the process of cultural rebuilding, who sincerely attempted to serve the nation and to contribute to its social-economic and spiritual revival."[52] In a similar manner, the book values achievements such as the reduction of illiteracy, the increase of Ukrainian-language schools, *vuzy* and publications, and the mass admission of Ukrainians into the student population. On the other hand, it is argued that Ukrainianization was not strong enough to have a lasting impact on the language regime in the most important sphere of public life, the Communist Party bureaucracy, where Russian remained the dominant language. However, the harshest criticism on the policy of Ukrainianization was that its initiators did not see it as a goal in itself:

From the very first beginning this process was subordinated . . . to the construction of a culture on the ideological foundation of Marxism. Ukrainianization . . . was only permitted to the extent that it did not collide with the interests and ideological orientations of the leadership of the highest state and party organs.[53]

THE COLLECTIVIZATION OF AGRICULTURE
AND THE 1930s FAMINE

Obviously, the old and the new textbook completely differ in their narratives of the collectivization of agriculture and its consequences. The Soviet textbook appreciates the collectivization drive as the campaign that broke the last elements of capitalist, anti-revolutionary resistance. It argues that "The socialist restructuring of the countryside eliminated the class stratification of the peasantry, humilation, and poverty,"[54] and it claims that people valued the expression that "people live well on those places where they sow and harvest together."[55] The kulaks are blamed for all the wrongs on the collective farms: the low morale of the workers, the lack of discipline, theft and sabotage of *Kolkhoz/Sovkhoz* property, and even terror against party activists and farm personnel. Yet there is an acknowledgment that the authorities were responsible for certain excesses as well: "In some places, the principle of voluntary cooperation was violated. . . The exaggerations in the *Kolkhoz* campaign led to dissatisfaction among some peasants, which had a negative influence on the solidity of the union of the working class with the peasantry."[56] The book is quick to point out that the Communist Party took appropriate measures to prevent similar mistakes from happening again. However, it is completely silent about the *consequence* of these "exaggerations"—the 1930s Famine.

As would be expected, the new textbook strongly condemns the collectivization and the ensuing famine. It asserts that the former can be equated with a "pillaging of the countryside,"[57] which served to speed up industrialization. Detailed accounts are given of the confiscation of food and private property, of the forceful incorporation of peasants into *kolkhozes*, and of the dramatic decline in production levels. All this is said to have resulted in the artificial famine of 1932–1933, which is characterized as "One of the most cruel crimes organized by Stalinism against the Ukrainian nation."[58] The book even claims that the authorities deliberately induced the famine to crush the resistance of peasants and nationalist forces. To substantiate this statement, the textbook quotes a communist official who reportedly said, "A bloody war is fought between the peasants and our powers. This is a war of life and death. This year was a test of our strength and their endurance. The hunger showed them who is the boss here. It cost millions of lives, but the *kolkhoz* system will exist forever. We won the war!"[59] Nonetheless, the book does not go so far as to accuse the authorities of specifically targeting the Ukrainians with the famine, as it discloses how the hunger affected not only the Ukrainian lands but also other regions of intensive agriculture, such as the northern Caucasus, the Kuban and Volga regions, and northern Kazakhstan.

WORLD WAR II AND THE ROLE OF THE ORGANIZATION OF UKRAINIAN NATIONALISTS (OUN)

In its account of World War II, the Soviet textbook pictures the Ukrainians as a people that greatly suffered from the German occupational regime and who supported and participated in the Soviet army's struggle against the "fascist aggressor." For instance, to give the impression that the people of Western Ukraine welcomed the Soviet invasion of Poland in September 1939, the book reports the local population as saying that "when the Red Army crossed the river Zbruch, the sun started shining over the Galicians."[60] It is stressed that Ukrainians, both on Soviet territory and in other countries, both as partisans and as regular Soviet Army servicemen, courageously fought on the Soviet side to defeat the German occupiers:

Under terrible wartime conditions, the Ukrainian people together with all nations of the USSR honorably fulfilled its holy obligation towards the Socialist Fatherland. For their participation in the Great Patriotic War of 1941–1945, about 2.5 million Ukrainian servicemen were awarded with combat medals and more than a thousand among them were granted the title of Hero of the Soviet Union.[61]

The book pays remarkably little attention to the Organization of Ukrainian Nationalists (OUN), a branch the Stepan Bandera wing of which fought both the Soviet and the German armies. It states only briefly that the German forces relied on, "Ukrainian bourgeois nationalists, former Kulaks and criminals . . . for the pillaging of the Ukrainian lands."[62] The Uniate Church in Western Ukraine, under Metropolitan Andriy Sheptyts'kyi, is singled out as having particularly ardently collaborated with the Germans. According to the book, it played an active role in the creation of the fascist army division *SS-Halychyna*.

The new textbook's version of World War II matches the Soviet version on two occasions. The first concerns the presentation of the Soviet invasion in Poland: in an echo of the Soviet volume, it is argued that the "West Ukrainian population met the Red Army with enthusiasm and hope."[63] However, the new edition is quick to point out that this reaction was quite understandable in view of the preceding period of Polish oppression and the widespread Soviet propaganda, which explained the Soviet attack as a successful attempt to ward off a German occupation of Galicia. It holds that this sympathy quickly turned into hate once the Soviets started disbanding political parties and cultural associations and began persecuting members of the Ukrainian intelligentsia. The second case of resemblance between the Soviet and post-Soviet volumes constitutes the presentation of life in the German occupied zone, which is reported to be full of suffering and hardship: "It [the German occupation] brought such agony, terror on such a scale . . . that the recent Soviet past appeared almost like paradise."[64]

Nonetheless, the pronounced contradictions of the Soviet scheme of events are most conspicuous. One of these pertains to the participation of Ukrainians in the Soviet army. In contrast to the Soviet textbook, the new book is completely silent about the inclusion of large numbers of Ukrainians in the regular Soviet forces, although it does admit that many Ukrainians were active as partisans in the Soviet underground. Similarly, the narrative on the OUN is entirely different. Upon reading it one obtains the impression that the new textbook makes a conscious effort to rehabilitate this organization — and its military wing, the Ukrainian Insurgent Army (UPA) — as it dedicates many pages (eight out of a total of thirty that deal with World War II) to the Bandera-led underground wing, which turned against the German army in the early stages of the war. The volume emphasizes a secret German order of December 1941 that reportedly said that "Except for the OUN-Bandera group, there is not one resistance movement in Ukraine that is capable of presenting a serious danger to us."[65] The book even claims that the OUN-Bandera forces were far more effective in combating the Germans than the Soviet underground. In addition to this, the OUN is portrayed as an organization that embraced democratic values (freedom of speech, press, and religion, and the equality of all nationalities living on Ukrainian territory).[66] In another contrast with the Soviet textbook, no mention is made of any possible collaboration between the Uniate Church and the Germans. The new book only acknowledges that another wing of the OUN, headed by Andriy Melnyk, did cooperate with the Germans, as it mentions that the Melnyk branch supported the creation of the Waffen SS *Halychyna* division.

It is perhaps surprising to find the new account of World War II differing so radically from the old version. The complete lack of any reference to the participation of Ukrainians in the Soviet Army is likely to give these veterans the impression that they are denied a role as the liberators of Ukraine. Moreover, the attempt to rehabilitate the OUN and UPA could give veterans the idea that this new historiography actually portrays them as the "bad guys," who, as servicemen of a foreign army, fought the "good guys" of the OUN and UPA. What is more, this perception of having been part of a foreign army is actually reinforced by excerpts in the book that accuse the Soviet authorities, after their recapture of the Ukrainian lands, of forcefully confiscating food and other products, sending millions of Ukrainian youth to the front as cannon fodder, and reinstituting the totalitarian regime of the past.[67] To make matters even worse, the new book says the following:

After the 20th session of the CPSU (in 1956), it became known that (Jozef) Stalin had very seriously considered a plan to deport all Ukrainians, in addition to Crimean Tatars, Kalmuks and some Caucasus peoples. And, as (Nikita) Khrushchev remarked . . . the only reason that this had not happened was that there were too many Ukrainians, there were no places to send them to, otherwise Stalin would have deported them too.[68]

Clearly, this extract leaves the reader no other impression than that the Soviet army was part of a regime that was alien and hostile to Ukraine and Ukrainians.

CONCLUSION

The Ukrainian government clearly considers history to be a vital tool for the nation-building project. This is a conclusion one has to arrive at judging from the costly but successful distribution of the new history textbooks to the farthest corners of Ukraine and the significantly increased study load these books represent. The standardization of history teaching, with all (types of) schools using the same textbooks, is another sign that education in the national history is a serious matter for the authorities.

The Ukrainian state ideology toward nation and state reveals itself in the content of history textbooks. Five conclusions can be made about this content. First, the new accounts of Ukrainian history are clearly more balanced than the version laid down in the Soviet editions. The new textbooks, for instance, do not hesitate to point to the shortcomings, especially in the socioeconomic sphere, of the regimes that are seen as the predecessors of contemporary Ukraine (i.e., Kyiv Rus', the Cossack state, and the different governments attempting to found an independent Ukrainian state after the Bolshevik revolution). The Soviet editions lack this element of self-criticism.

Second, the Soviet textbooks miss a certain individuality of character. Among the new textbooks, there is a quite a difference between the book for grades 7–8 and that for grade 10. Whereas the book for grades 7–8 dedicates many pages to class conflict and uses some of the terminology and even whole extracts from the old textbook, the book for grade 10 presents a chronicle of Ukrainian history that sharply contrasts with the old version on most points. It appears, therefore, that the educational authorities in postindependence Ukraine granted the authors of schoolbooks more individual freedom of maneuver than the authorities of the Soviet times did. This comparison of books also shows us that Serhienko and Smolyi, as the authors of the new book for grades 7–8, did not change all the content and outlook of the old textbook. One can therefore conclude that the continuity of personnel (remember that both authors also wrote the Soviet textbook) did indeed result in a perpetuation of content and interpretation. In this light, it may not be a coincidence that the present educational authorities ordered that the textbooks dealing with twentieth-century history be written by new authors. They may well have considered the modern period too crucial, and too sensitive for authors associated with the old regime (notably Sarbei) to write them.

Third, the old and the new editions diverge most strongly in their accounts of matters that are related to the sensitive topics of Ukrainian national identity or Ukrainian statehood. The old textbooks, for instance, hardly touch upon the issue of the Ukrainian language, and when they do, it is only to accuse other imperial powers (Poland, Tsarist Russia, and Austria-Hungary) of culturally subduing the Ukrainians. In fact, the old book for grades 9–10 is completely silent about the fate of the Ukrainian language in Soviet times. In the new books, on the other hand, the Ukrainian language is a much-discussed topic. It is asserted that the Ukrainian language is the principal determinant of Ukrainian national identity, and it is implied that Russian and Polish are foreign languages, introduced by neighboring powers bent on eliminating the use of Ukrainian in public spheres.[69]

Fourth, another noteworthy difference of opinion concerns the degree of involvement of Ukrainians in the Bolshevik conquest of Ukraine and in the Soviet army fight against the German invaders. According to the Soviet textbook, Ukrainians fully participated in both struggles, side by side with their Russian "brethren." The message the book sends is clear: the Bolshevik revolution is as much a Ukrainian phenomenon as a Russian one, and it further strengthened the "bonds of friendship between the two brotherly nations." In contrast, the new textbook argues that only a small minority of Ukrainians supported the Bolshevik revolution, and it makes no mention of Ukrainians as regular Soviet army servicemen. Consequently, the new edition portrays the Bolshevik regime as a foreign power, in which Ukrainians had no part. Moreover, its hostility toward the Ukrainians is stressed, as the book seizes every opportunity to discredit the Soviet regime.

Finally, an important contrast can be also found in the narratives on the role of the OUN in World War II. While the Soviet textbook considers the OUN a "Ukrainian bourgeois nationalist" organization that "shamelessly" collaborated with the Nazis, the new book makes a calculated effort to rehabilitate the OUN. Among other things, it presents the Bandera-led wing of the OUN as an underground group that combated the Germans quite effectively and stood up for democratic values and the ideal of an independent Ukrainian state.

To a certain extent, the particular version of history advanced by the new textbooks is understandable. After all, the emphasis on Ukrainian as the sole native language, on the Bolshevik regime as a foreign power, and on the OUN as a genuine national liberation movement firmly upholds claims of Ukrainian distinctiveness. However, at the same time, this version runs the risk of alienating both the Russian-speaking part of the population and people who cherish the Soviet past, such as Soviet army veterans. The former are likely to ask themselves whether they can ever call themselves—and be accepted as—authentic Ukrainians if they continue to speak Russian. The latter may very well take the new historiography as an insult, because it degrades the status of Soviet army veterans. They used to be portrayed as soldiers who "courageously fought to liberate Ukraine from fascist occupation" but are now presented as soldiers who "contributed to the reinstitution of a foreign and oppressive regime that denied the Ukrainian nation its sacred right of self-determination." An intriguing question for further study, therefore, is whether Russian-speakers and people with communist sympathies will accept the new scheme of history (in which their children are being instructed) or will reject it.

NOTES

1. Discussing the structure of Ukrainophile and Belarusophile historiography, Andrew Wilson distinguishes as many as fifteen kinds of myths. See Andrew Wilson, "National History and National Identity in Ukraine and Belarus," in Graham Smith, Vivien Law, Andrew Wilson, Annette Bohr, and Edward Allworth, *Nation-building in the Post-Soviet Borderlands: The Politics of National Identities* (Cambridge: Cambridge University Press, 1998), pp. 23–47.

2. Stephan Velychenko argues that the "poorer, authoritarian" societies "east of the Elbe" assign much greater weight to national historiography than the "wealthier, pluralist and constitutional societies" of the West. In his view, this is because the eastern societies consider national identity, which heavily relies on historiography, an end in itself, rather than a means to pursue their material interests. Thus, "insofar as historiography preserves collective national memory, it becomes essential for group survival [for the societies of the East] (p. 18)." See Stephan Velychenko, *Shaping Identity in Eastern Europe and Russia: Soviet-Russian and Polish Accounts of Ukrainian History, 1914–1991* (New York: St. Martin's, 1993).

The discussion on the use of historiography is a reflection of the wider debate on the distinction between an ethnic and a civic variety of nationalism. According to Kuzio, this distinction serves no empirical purpose since historically both varieties have become intricately intertwined in the nation-building programs of liberal democratic states, homogenizing the societies internally and accentuating the differences between these societies. See T. Kuzio, " 'Nationalizing States' or Nation Building: A Review of the Theoretical Literature and Empirical Evidence," *Nations and Nationalism*, vol. 7, part 2, pp. 135-154 and "Europe or Eurasia? The Ideology of 'Kuchmism': A Review Article," *Journal of Ukrainian Studies* 22, nos. 1–2 (Summer–Winter 1997), pp. 145–163.

3. The early twentieth-century historian Mykhailo Hrushevs'kyi is generally credited for his contribution to the Ukrainian nation-building project. In his framework Ukrainians constitute a separate nation with its own origin and history. See T. Kuzio, *Ukraine: State and Nation Building*, (London: Routledge, 1998), chap. 9, pp.198–229.

4. Zenon E. Kohut, "History as a Battleground: Russian-Ukrainian Relations and Historical Consciousness in Contemporary Ukraine," in S. Frederick Starr, ed., *The Legacy of History in Russia and the New States of Eurasia* (Armonk, NY: M. E. Sharpe, 1994), pp. 123–146.

5. Wilson has argued that "because it [the Ukrainian version of history] excludes or caricatures genuinely complex aspects of the Ukrainian-Russian historical relationship, it runs the risk of alienating the Russian speaking half of the population of Ukraine." Quoted in J. Paraszczuk, "Historical Narrative as a Source of National Identity: The Foundation Myth of Kyiv Rus' in Ukrainian Nation Building," Master's Thesis, School of Slavonic and East European Studies, University College, London, 1999, p. 39.

In a comment on this paper Kuzio argued that it is inappropriate to consider language to be the main cleavage in Ukrainian society. In his opinion, political attitude and generation are at least as important dividing lines, with reform-minded people and the younger generation (who are generally pro-Western, anticommunist, and proreform in outlook) much more likely to support the Ukrainian scheme of events than people with communist sympathies and the elderly. See T. Kuzio, "Defining the Political Community in Ukraine: State, Nation, and the Transition to Modernity," in T. Kuzio, R. S. Kravchuk and P. D'Anieri eds., *State and Institution Building in Ukraine* (New York: St. Martin's, 1999), pp. 213–244.

6. Naturally, the Russian imperial and Soviet versions of history are not any less nationalist than the Ukrainian scheme as they also served to forge specific national identities. I owe this point to Joanna Paraszczuk.

7. In Soviet times, the history of Ukraine was taught as part of a general history course.

8. See *Informatsiinyi Zbirnyk Ministerstva Osvity Ukrainy*, no. 12, 1996. This issue presents a list of recommended textbooks for order.

9. In the years 1996, 1997, and 1998, the author made several fieldwork trips to the cities of Kyiv, Odesa, L'viv, and Donets'k. In each of these cities, he visited twelve schools and simply asked the teachers to show him the books that were used. On one of these travels, Simferopol, the capital of the Crimea, was visited. To the author's surprise, even the schools there had begun to use the programs and recommended textbooks of the Ministry of Education. The efforts to consolidate the state thus appear successful (at least in the sphere of education), which is remarkable given the depth of the economic crisis.

10. *Zerkalo Nedeli*, 26 September 1998.

11. Grades 7, 8, 9, and 10 in the Soviet era equal grades 8, 9, 10, and 11 of post-Soviet Ukraine, respectively. The attentive reader will have noticed that titles are given in a transcription from Russian. This is because the author read the Russian translations. Remarkably, the Russian translation of the grade 11 textbook has a section on the Ukrainian diaspora, which the Ukrainian original does not have. No reason is given for the inclusion of this section in the Russian translation.

12. Interview with Frank den Hertog, Ph.D. candidate at the AGIDS research institute of the University of Amsterdam, February 1999. In Ukraine, the author found significant personnel changes only in the schools in the Western Ukrainian city of L'viv.

13. Sarbei et al., grades 7–8, p. 19.

14. Serhienko and Smolyi, grades 7–8, p. 47.

15. Ibid., pp. 75, 76.

16. Ibid., p. 76.

17. Ibid., p. 97.

18. Roman Serbyn, "Historical Myths and National Identities in Post-Soviet Ukrainian Textbooks," paper presented at the fourth annual Association for the Study of Nationalities (ASN) Convention in New York, April 1999, p. 7. Coincidentally, Serbyn and the author both presented papers on this topic at the convention.

19. Ibid., p. 7.

20. Ibid., p. 7.

21. Serhienko and Smolyi, grades 7–8, p. 49.

22. Ibid., p. 53.

23. Ibid., p. 61.

24. Sarbei et al., grades 7–8, p. 64.

25. Ibid., p. 70.

26. Ibid., p. 102.

27. Ibid., p. 101.

28. Serhienko and Smolyi, grades 7–8, p. 169.

29. Ibid., p. 169.

30. Serhienko and Smolyi, grades 7–8, p. 203.

31. Ibid., p. 195.

32. Ibid., p. 236.

33. Ibid., p. 197.

34. Ibid., p. 243.
35. Sarbei et al., grades 7–8, p. 144.
36. Ibid., p. 155.
37. Ibid., p. 144.
38. Sarbei, grade 9, p. 104.
39. Ibid., p. 106.
40. Ibid., p. 107.
41. Ibid., p. 108.
42. Sarbei and Spytskyi, grades 9–10, p. 48.
43. Ibid., p. 45.
44. Ibid., p. 47.
45. Ibid., p. 74.
46. Ibid., p. 96.
47. Turchenko, grade 10, p. 35.
48. Ibid., p. 36.
49. Ibid., p. 41. The land measure refers to the heated debate on whether estates of less than 40 *desiatina* would be subject to redistribution as well.
50. Ibid., p. 58.
51. Sarbei, grade 9, p. 107.
52. Turchenko, grade 10, p. 194.
53. Ibid.
54. Sarbei and Spytskyi, grades 9–10, p. 87.
55. Ibid., p. 85.
56. Ibid., p. 87.
57. Turchenko, grade 10, p. 221.
58. Ibid., p. 225.
59. Ibid., p. 227.
60. Sarbei and Spytskyi, grades 9–10, p. 105.
61. Ibid., p. 124.
62. Ibid., p. 113.
63. Turchenko, grade 10, p. 278.
64. Ibid., p. 296.
65. Ibid., p. 302.
66. Ibid., p. 316.
67. Ibid., pp. 310, 311.
68. Ibid., p. 325.
69. Motyl asserts that after independence Ukrainian elites began propagating the image of the Ukrainian nation as a multiethnic people that has internalized the Cossack-ascribed values of freedom, equality, and democracy. See Alexander J. Motyl, *Dilemmas of Independence: Ukraine after Totalitarianism* (New York: Council on Foreign Relations Press, 1993), p. 84. Although the spread of this image may have occurred in some policy areas, it certainly, as we have seen, has not touched the teaching of history in schools. Instead, a rather narrow conception of the Ukrainian nation is communicated; it is implied that only those who speak Ukrainian are "real Ukrainians." The new textbooks make no reference to particular Cossack virtues as constituent elements of Ukrainian national identity.

10

Conclusion:
Regionalism and Nation Building
in a Divided Society

Nancy Popson

The chapters collected in this volume present various perspectives on the role of the state in Ukraine's identity politics. They provide a range of answers to questions of the nature and implications of cleavages in Ukrainian society and the role of the state in dealing with those cleavages. As noted by D'Anieri in his introduction, this volume does not attempt to give definitive answers to these questions. Rather, the authors and editors have aimed to provide empirical data and analysis that can be used to clarify the issues at hand and indicate where further research may be necessary. This final chapter will therefore not draw conclusions per se, but will illustrate how the work in this volume can further our understanding of nation building by focusing on one aspect of identity politics in contemporary Ukraine—regionalism.

One of the most salient questions laced throughout the chapters is the nature of the cleavages in Ukrainian society. From the late eighteenth century to the early part of the twentieth, Ukrainians (people living in the territory of what is now Ukraine, regardless of ethnicity) were ruled by two different states centered in Moscow and Vienna. After World War I and the Communist revolution in the Tsarist Russian empire, they found themselves split among the new states of Poland, Romania, Czechoslovakia, and the Soviet Union. The Uzhhorod region was not added to the territory of the Ukrainian Soviet Socialist Republic until 1939; the Chernivtsi region was annexed in 1940, and the regions of Galicia and the Crimea were joined only in 1945 and 1954, respectively. This means that not only do sections of the Ukrainian population have collective historical memories linking them to what are now foreign states, but also, in some cases, individuals remember life in the same geographic location but under different political rule.

The country can be characterized as ethnically divided as well. Although Soviet population policies after World War II included broad exchanges of ethnic Ukrainians with ethnic Poles and other nationalities across the newly formed borders, Ukraine was then, and remains, a heterogeneous state. According to the 1989 Soviet census, Ukrainians made up 73% of the population, with the largest ethnic minority being the Russians, with 22%. Although Russians form a majority only in the Crimean Autonomous Republic (67% according to the 1989 census), they are far more numerous in those districts that were part of the Tsarist Russian empire. Moreover, linguistically the country is split between those individuals who, regardless of ethnicity, speak Ukrainian and those who speak Russian.

There has been a large volume of literature to date that invokes these divisions as critical factors in the development of Ukraine in the post-Soviet era. As several of the chapters in this volume indicate, the debate continues over societal divisions that reveal disparity in the way the population views Ukrainian domestic and foreign policy. These divisions can, at the most extreme, make the process of state and nation building treacherous, if not impossible. Many of the contributors to this volume take up the question of the salience of these divisions and the trends that may exert unifying influences over the territory of Ukraine.

Perhaps the most long-standing thesis on Ukraine's division revolves around ethnicity. In the first years after Ukraine's declaration of independence, the ethnic divide was seen as a likely obstacle to nation-building efforts. It was assumed that the Russian minority would reject Ukrainian independence and would be manipulated by Russian foreign policy aimed at reconstructing some form of empire. However, Russians have been remarkably quiet. They have not mobilized in great numbers against Kyiv's nation-building policies. Crimea, although considered a hot spot prior to 1995, has become a "dog that did not bark." Moreover, there is some suggestion that reidentification may be underway in Ukraine, with more members of the population identifying themselves as Ukrainian and a growing number of children from mixed marriages being registered as Ukrainian.[1]

The chapter by Weller in this volume goes further to show that the ethnic card has not been as contentious as some had predicted, illustrating the absence of ethnic conflict and the very low level of ethnic distance between Ukraine's Russian and Ukrainian nationalities. Using surveys from 1993, 1995, and 1998, Weller has been able to gauge perceived levels of conflict between the two groups as they have evolved over time. His data confirm that ethnic conflict is the exception—rather than the norm—in Ukraine. By comparing survey results across several variables, Weller is able to conclude that regardless of region of residence, ethnicity, or language, Ukrainian citizens do not feel that ethnic conflict is likely. Moreover, Weller's analysis confirms earlier work by Ian Bremmer on ethnic distance, or the perception of a significant divide between those who call themselves Russians and those who identify as Ukrainians.[2] Weller's data indicate that although it may vary by region (see the following), on the whole there is a low level of ethnic distance in Ukraine.

This lack of ethnic distance or mobilization along ethnic lines has led many scholars to argue that Ukraine is divided by more than just ethnic identifications. Riabchuk (in this volume as well as in earlier work) has argued that language use must be assessed as well in order to fully comprehend the divisions of Ukrainian society today. Riabchuk contends that it is the language factor that truly determines public attitudes, and that Ukraine's population can be divided into three groups: Ukrainophone Ukrainians, Russophone Ukrainians, and Russophone Russians. In his chapter in this volume, Riabchuk argues that the number of Russophones and Ukrainophones in Ukraine are more or less equal in number, and that this divide is therefore more salient than ethnicity alone. This is especially true given the post-colonial environment within which Ukraine must determine and implement cultural policy. He points to Ukrainophones as an underprivileged minority and describes the policies emerging from Kyiv as remarkably laissez-faire in the arenas of language and culture. The current government in Kyiv, he contends, implements affirmative action policies that are remarkably weak and unlikely to heighten the status of the Ukrainian language or of its speakers. Given this, Riabchuk characterizes Ukraine as a "creolic state" (one that supports Ukrainian independence but is linguistically and culturally Russian).

Other scholars have found this ethnolinguistic divide to be important in shaping public opinion in Ukraine, especially in the first half of the 1990s. Khmelko and Wilson concluded that it was most salient in predicting voting behavior in the 1994 presidential election, noting that Russophone Ukrainians had the potential to act as a swing group given their mixed identity.[3] In surveys taken in May, April, and June of 1994, Arel and Khmelko found that the ethnolinguistic divide was also important in more general attitudes of the population regarding sociopolitical orientations and Ukraine's relations with Russia.[4]

Some newer studies suggest that as Ukraine enters its second decade as an independent state, observers may be moving away from the view that ethnolinguistic cleavages are most significant. The chapter by Kuzio in this volume goes furthest in this regard, arguing that Ukraine is marked by political consensus rather than division. Through an investigation of elite politics, Kuzio illustrates that the Ukrainian elite, regardless of ethnic background or language spoken at home, has come to agree on most of the fundamentals of Ukrainian nation building. Kuzio's research shows that there is no longer significant debate over the form and content of institution building, the country's territorial integrity, its structure (as a federal or unitary state), the goal of civic nationalism, or the consolidation of a national idea. Kuzio does not discount continued societal cleavages, however. He notes that despite the unity of the elite shown in his chapter, a corresponding mass consensus in Ukraine has yet to emerge.

Other scholars are also looking beyond rifts of ethnicity and language to explain divisions in Ukrainian society. For example, survey research presented by Arthur Miller in December 2000 suggests that the extent of the economic crisis in Ukraine—the fact that a majority of the population struggles to get by day to day in the new economy—has significantly lessened the impact of previously divisive ethnic identities.[5] Andrew Wilson's most recent book, while not discounting ethnolinguistic factors, highlights the historical legacy that has left a wide variety of cleavages in Ukraine, including religious and regional divides.[6] Sarah Birch's volume on elections in independent Ukraine also suggests that ethnolinguistic cleavages have not been most salient in determining voter preferences. Birch's work stresses instead a divide in the population between those who support statehood and those who are against it. According to her analysis, this cleavage overrides issues of ethnicity or language, but may be related to region.[7]

Birch's connection of the pro- versus anti-statehood divide to region supports the work by several scholars in this collection who indicate that regional and local identities are important factors in variations of population attitudes. Interpretation of Ukraine as a country divided into discrete regions is not new. Definition of regions in and of themselves is often tricky, however. Scholars who have focused on the ethnolinguistic makeup of the population, for example, often use ethnicity or language groupings coterminously with regional categories. This should not be surprising, as many of the most easily recognizable regional divisions such as

"East" and "West" correspond with majority populations in either the category of ethnicity or language (or, in some cases, both). For this reason, many scholars who utilize regional categories in their work are using them as another way to group ethnolinguistic communities.

Another aspect of social divisions that is often linked to region, making the situation more complex, is that of religion. The simplistic division of Ukraine's east and west has also been associated with religious conviction: the Ukrainian, Catholic west and the Russian, Orthodox east. Although not covered in this volume, the complexities surrounding religion and the structures of the Orthodox and Catholic churches throughout Ukraine deserve further study.[8] The recently released Atlas of Ukraine indicates that the percentage of Orthodox believers is 30% or greater throughout Ukraine, making up the majority in all *oblasti* except L'viv, Ternopil, Ivano-Frankivsk, and Crimea.[9] Western *oblasti* show higher percentages of believers than those in the east or the south. However, the breakdown of the population by religion is further complicated by a surge in Protestantism: with the exception of L'viv, Ternopil, and Ivano-Frankivsk, Protestants make up between 19% and 50% of the population throughout Ukraine.[10]

However, newer studies are beginning to specifically distinguish local and regional identities from ethnic, religious, and linguistic identities. They suggest that economic, social, and historical variation across region overwhelms ethnolinguistic identification. For example, ethnic Russians living in L'viv may not necessarily have similar sociopolitical outlooks as ethnic Russians living in Kyiv or the Crimea. Local or regional populations may share historical memories and daily experiences that transcend divisive identities. Weller's conclusions about the importance of regional variation in ethnic distance over other variables such as language and ethnicity may support the idea that Ukraine's main divide has been formed through shared historical and lifetime experiences. Weller's surveys indicate that the largest and growing divide regarding who people view as "us" and "them" was found in the Western region, while other regions were far lower.

The findings of Barrington further develop this position. Barrington analyzes mass survey data collected in Ukraine in November 1998 testing the effects of region, language, and ethnicity on support for the Ukrainian political system as an institution, for its leaders in particular, and for Ukraine's continued independent status. Barrington's data indicate that nationality and language are less consequential variables in shaping popular support, while region emerges as a critical factor. Barrington's regressions show that nationality variables were significant for both support of leaders and support of the system writ large (what he terms the "regime"), while language figured prominently only in support for leaders. In both cases regional factors have far more impact than either nationality or language. Barrington shows significant links among nationality, language, and public opinion in regard to perceptions of the importance of Ukraine's continued independence. Even here, however, the regional variable is far stronger.

Barrington's results demonstrate that region is more complicated than has been assumed by many observers, as regional cleavages do not coincide with ethnic or linguistic divides. Barrington uses a nine-region model through which to study regional variation in Ukraine. Other studies have also emphasized this complexity. Several scholars employ a four-region paradigm that includes West, Central, Southern, and Eastern regions.[11] Sherman Garnett has suggested that one could identify seven regions by splitting the Central region into East-Central, West-Central, and Kyiv.[12] While these divisions are in some ways devices to facilitate data manipulation, the very range of possibilities reveals much about regional and local identities: like other forms of identification, they are fluid; moreover, they do not necessarily fit into district boundaries, nor may they always fit into national boundaries.

As noted earlier, the importance of these divisions for the Ukrainian population is a continuing debate and requires further analysis. The lines between region, religion, ethnicity, and language remain blurred. Kuzio is not alone in his conclusion that the regional divide (as well as the ethnolinguistic thesis) may be overcome by growing consensus on many issues. For example, research conducted by Hinich, Khmelko, and Ordeshook on the 1998 parliamentary elections point to the conclusion that these divisions in Ukraine have been overemphasized. Their analysis indicates that although electoral preferences vary, "the eastern and western parts of the Ukrainian electorate perceive things in similar ways and evaluate the alternatives that confront them using equivalent criteria."[13]

However, the suggestion (supported in particular by Barrington in this volume) that regional identities created by shared historical and lived experiences may create stronger "us" and "them" groups than ethnicity or language could have important implications for Ukraine's development. While the possible ramifications of a Ukraine divided by ethnolinguistic variation has been addressed in several of the works cited above, those of regionalism have been less developed. It is those to which this chapter will turn, in particular because the collected chapters in this volume, despite varied perspectives and modes of analysis, lend unique insight into these issues.

IMPLICATIONS OF REGIONALISM IN UKRAINE

If we accept the hypothesis of Barrington and the assumption of Weller that the most important of Ukraine's fissures is that which is formed by historical and lived experience, we must turn to another question set forth in this volume: does this cleavage negatively impact Ukraine's prospects for political stability and development? Regionalism could have significant implications for the ability of the Ukrainian state to maintain its political structure and pursue coherent domestic and foreign policy agendas. Moreover, these divides present important challenges to the creation of a national identity and the role of the state in nation building.

Sub- and Transnational Regionalism

The complexity of regional identity is one important aspect of regionalism in Ukraine. The definition of regional identity employed here draws on both Barrington and on Catherine Wanner[14]: shared experience, both within an individual's lifetime and the historical memories passed down over generations, leads individuals to identify in-groups and out-groups based on region. These identifications in turn lead to shared values and perceptions. This concept of identity is not absolute. It borrows from the work of Paul Pirie and others, who see identity (in Pirie's case ethnic identity) as a dynamic association that is not fixed by birth but is chosen and can therefore be shifted under different circumstances.[15] In this way no one identity is all-encompassing; individuals can and do hold several overlapping identities, and these can also change over time.

Given this definition, it is clear that regions in Ukraine are more complex than just East and West. It is instructive to look at both the larger and smaller scale. As Louise Jackson showed in 1998 in her case study of Zaporizhzhia, there are subtler differences and dynamics that exist on a smaller scale than the more usually high-lighted East-West divide.[16] The importance of this smaller scale—that Zaporizhzhians may not share the perceptions or characteristics of the Donbas, for example—can have both advantages and disadvantages in Ukraine's development. The multiple nature of Ukraine's regional divisions makes the country less polar and therefore possibly more stable. However, without significant leeway for regional and local governments to respond to the demands of their populations, these smaller-scale variations pose potentially difficult problems for the powers in Kyiv. It is therefore important for the unity of the state that individuals who identify with their region are also able to identify with the state as a whole.

In looking at regionalism in Ukraine (or in any state), one must also consider the forces of transnationalism. Patterns of rationalization and regional identity do not always coincide with national borders. Patterns of migration and availability of common economic markets can create a form of "transnational regionalism," where the divides that separate identity, economic groups, or social communities cross borders.[17] According to Hurrell, this form of regionalism can also be based on high levels of social interaction across borders.[18] Regionalism that extends beyond state borders is not necessarily a negative phenomenon. In some cases it has been en-couraged, such as in the European Union and the Carpathian Euro-region. Regional identifications can have a calming effect on international relations and can enhance the overall economy through increased trade flow.

For a state that is attempting to bridge internal divides through state and nation building, the presence of regional identities and networks that extend beyond the state borders also present significant challenges. In Ukraine this was underlined during the October–November 1999 Ukrainian presidential elections, when a sur-vey taken in a border town near Belarus showed many Ukrainian citizens were pre-pared to vote for Belarusian President Alyaksander Lukashenka.[19] Living on the border where they regularly received Belarusian television signals and communi-cated with their Belarusian counterparts, these individuals' ties to the Ukrainian state were weak enough that they were confused over the identities of their national leaders. Ukraine, in attempting to create a shared identity for all of its citizens, must therefore compete with their regional and transnational regional identities at one and the same time.

Foreign Policy Formation and Implementation

The importance of regionalism and identities based on shared experience may also have implications for Ukraine's ability to create and implement a foreign pol-icy agenda. D'Anieri has noted that Ukrainian institutions have been unable to re-solve underlying societal divisions, and are in fact as, if not more, divided than their constituencies. This, in D'Anieri's opinion, has led to a "weak state" that is unable to implement foreign policy.[20] James Sherr has also discussed the impact of what he calls the "cultural factor" on Ukraine's foreign policy—in particular on the decision to pursue a multivector strategy that looks both to Europe and to Russia.[21]

In this volume, Shulman suggests that the conflict over national identity in Ukraine influences and is in turn influenced by foreign policy debates. Shulman stresses that foreign policy affects identity by creating in-groups and out-groups; this leads to the possibility of a state's foreign policy creating an out-group of a country with whom some of that state's citizens may identify. He warns that a state pursuing a foreign policy agenda that is contrary to the values of a large section of the population will weaken national identity. Given surveys showing that a large portion of the Ukrainian population supports some sort of unification with Russia, Shulman concludes that the best way to strengthen national identity is to promote an East-Slavic identity and concurrently provide for closer relations with Russia and Belarus.

Although Shulman notes that region is a factor, his analysis concentrates on the divide between ethnic Ukrainian and Eastern Slavic identities. However, such concerns raise questions that are pertinent to the regionalism paradigm as well. If foreign policy indeed is both shaped by and shapes domestic identities, regionalism (and especially the sort of transnational regionalism noted earlier) can become a significant obstacle to coherent policy making. Foreign policy that creates out-groups will, as Shulman predicts, alienate segments of the population. Shulman suggests that the best exit from this dilemma with both a strong national identity and targeted foreign policy intact is to choose the East-Slavic or Russia-Belarus vector. Although Shulman notes that this would alienate the ethnic Ukrainian identity group, he explains that their strong ties to the notion of an independent Ukrainian state would ensure their continued loyalty to Kyiv. This exit option may become more complicated if, indeed, regional identities are stronger than ethnolinguistic. The problem here lies in those groups whose regional identities and transnational regional identities are close to Central Europe. If their main source of identification is their shared experience and history, it is feasible that they could build enough pride into that regional level identification to significantly challenge Kyiv should closer ties with Russia be deemed unpalatable.

It should be noted, however, that there is some skepticism regarding the influence of such societal groups on foreign policy creation and implementation in Ukraine. D'Anieri, Kuzio, and Kravchuk have illustrated that the policy-making process in Ukraine remains unclear. In particular, the role of public opinion, the media, and interest groups or lobbies are difficult to evaluate.[22]

Another aspect to regionalism has the potential to affect Ukraine's ability to implement a cohesive foreign policy in the future. Should the regional identities remain strong or grow even stronger in Ukraine, it is possible that we will see regions conducting their own foreign policy. This has been the case in Russia, where regional administrations make policy statements normally within the realm of national security and conduct negotiations with foreign trade partners in the absence of strong central control.[23] The current centralized nature of the Ukrainian state makes this unlikely in the near term. Yet there are signs that the desire exists for districts in Ukraine to pursue relationships that can lead to foreign direct investment and increased economic activity, though well within the realm created by the central powers. There are also regional initiatives now supported by the state encouraging regional administrators and legislators to closely cooperate with their counterparts in Central Europe. Should Kyiv decide to shift vectors to one that concentrates on Russia and Belarus, these contacts would be difficult to sever. They would provide access and opportunity for regional actors to conduct their own foreign policy alongside or outside the state.

Regionalism and the Federalism Question

Regionalism may also have serious implications for the very structure of Ukraine. Article 2 of the Ukrainian constitution declares Ukraine to be a unitary state. However, in designing the constitution, Ukrainian legislatures were attuned to the regional variation across Ukraine. Article 132 therefore notes that "The territorial structure of Ukraine is based on the principles of unity and indivisibility of the state territory, the combination of centralization and decentralization in the exercise of state power, and the balanced socio-economic development of regions that takes into account their historical, economic, ecological, geographical and demographic characteristics, and ethnic and cultural traditions." Moreover, the Autonomous Republic of Crimea was given special status, including the right to form its own parliament and council of ministers and to adopt its own constitution with the approval of the Parliament of Ukraine.

This semi-unitary structure is important in that it (in theory) maintains central control while allowing for regional variation. If regional identities are, and continue to be, the prevalent source of identification and of in- and out-group formation among the Ukrainian population, however, there is the danger that regional demands will turn to requests for more autonomy than the center is willing to consider. This has already occurred in the area of language use, with some Eastern Ukrainian cities declaring Russian to be their official language, in defiance of Article 10 of the Constitution.

It seems unlikely that the regional factor in Ukraine will seriously threaten the established constitutional structure of the country in the short term. A federal structure in Ukraine would allow more freedom of decision making and therefore could give regions a greater stake in state building. On the other hand, as Roeder points out (regarding the Soviet context), federalism institutionalizes regional differences and can provide the infrastructure for regional elites to more easily mobilize the population against the central state.[24] This has certainly been the case in Russia, Ukraine's close neighbor and an easy subject of popular comparison.[25]

Ukraine's elite seem to have taken this lesson to heart. As the chapter by Kuzio indicates, there appears to be agreement among at least the elite levels of the population in Ukraine regarding Ukraine's structural integrity. However, given that Ukraine currently is neither a completely unitary nor a completely federal state, regions have some room to exert their authority and demand concessions that take into account their different life experiences. In order to handle these variations and maintain a nonfederal state, the Ukrainian elite must find a way to convince its population to identify not only with their region, but first and foremost with an overarching set of all-Ukrainian symbols and structures.

NATION BUILDING AND NATIONAL IDENTITY

We now turn to the issue of the reaction of the state to the challenges posed by regionalism. How has the state attempted to bridge regional divides? The state in Ukraine has embarked on policies aimed at creating an overarching civic Ukrainian (i.e., nonethnic) identity. By focusing on civic values, polyethnic rights, and patriotism, the nation-building campaign may be able to forge a new layer of identity for citizens of Ukraine. It is important to remember that no single identity is absolute. Nation building therefore does not need to replace existing identities, whether they be regional, ethnic, linguistic, or a variety of other possibilities. Rather, it must only design a mosaic of symbols, structure, and values with which citizens can identify at a level equal to or greater than the regional or local.

Critical in this respect are policies that serve to unite the population despite regional variations in life experience, economic well-being, and social identities. Several of the contributors to this volume investigate the creation of new identities and the process of nation building in contemporary Ukraine. Their research outlines both successes and continuing challenges and can help us to understand the implications of Ukraine's regional divide on the process of nation building.

Regionalism as Challenge to Nation Building: The Case of the Military

As Barrington suggests in his conclusions, the prevalence of regional disparity in Ukraine has the potential to significantly complicate nation-building efforts. The chapter by Fesiak depicts one attempt to create an overarching identity to consolidate the nation's military patriotism. At the same time, Fesiak's chapter points out the severe difficulties in overcoming regional disparity and successfully creating overarching symbols, myths, and constructs with which all Ukrainian citizens can identify.

Fesiak illustrates how the center attempted to utilize the military as a socialization tool, instilling common myths and symbols linked to the new nation that could be accepted by servicemen in the Ukrainian armed forces. In particular, he describes a campaign implemented between 1991 and 1993 that was spearheaded by the Social Psychological Service of the military and aided by the Union of Ukrainian Officers. Fesiak notes that the Union of Ukrainian Officers was made up mostly of officers from the Western regions of Ukraine, and aided by ex-military émigré personnel. His extensive interviews with servicemen and officers in the Ukrainian military show that attempts to focus on the symbols of the Ukrainian "national-liberation struggle" (spearheaded by Western Ukrainian anti-Soviet and anti-Russian organizations such as the Ukrainian Insurgent Army (UPA) during and after World War II) have been largely unsuccessful. In Fesiak's words, these symbols "had limited appeal outside western Ukraine" and were rejected by the majority of military personnel.

Even after 1993, when Fesiak shows a moderation in "Ukrainianization" the success of the campaign to instill patriotism in Ukraine's servicemen, this time with Cossack symbols rather than those of the UPA, was mixed. A lack of textbooks and the question of teachers able and willing to present the material in the same manner regardless of region remains a problem. In effect, Fesiak's research shows that the creation of a military identity that supports Ukrainian state and nation building was made more complicated by regional differences. That is not to say that the endeavor to build a civic national identity has failed. However, the ramifications of regionalism have been instrumental in slowing the process.

Historical Myth and Nation Building: Building Cross-Regional Bridges

While regionalism has posed a challenge to some nation building-endeavors, in other areas the state seems to have successfully navigated the regional maze. One of the most interesting conclusions of the research collected in this volume is what appears to be the lack of division caused by the introduction of a national historiography.

Zenon Kohut has noted that questions of "deimperialization" or "the adjustment of structures and intellectual concepts to the dissolution of an empire" is one of the driving forces in new perceptions of history in the post-Soviet era. These new perceptions of history are in turn essential to the struggles over identity in postcolonial states such as Ukraine.[26] It is not surprising that reinterpretations of history have been central to the process of nation building in the past decade in Ukraine. The two chapters in this volume that deal with history, myth, and the creation of national identity indicate that in this area the nation-building process has not been opposed by regional groups. This is despite the fact that the shared historical and life experiences that make up a regional identity do not fully coincide with the historical narratives being promoted by historians, educators, and the media. This bears further investigation, as it goes against what one might expect given the divisions that exist in Ukrainian society—not only regional divisions, but ethnic and linguistic as well.

The contribution of Kasianov, for example, investigates the new trends in Ukrainian historiography since the fall of the Soviet Union. While in some Western countries we may expect to find less controversy at the level of scholarly historiography, given its removal from mass understandings, in Ukraine historiography is very much tied into historical perceptions evident in more popular histories, the press, and the media. With the lack of national histories in Ukraine, these scholars are being called on to write more popular historical pieces, and their work garners a much larger popular audience.[27]

It is therefore interesting that Kasianov finds the development of historiographic models that emphasize the longevity of the Ukrainian nation as largely harmonious across Ukraine. Kasianov illustrates that Ukrainian social science is intensively involved in the process of nation building: all historians are searching for links to a past incarnation of the Ukrainian nation, all uphold the idea of a nineteenth-century national renaissance (thereby implying an earlier nation), and all agree that the nation has taken shape through a process of organic evolution. Kasianov characterizes the main difference between historians in Ukraine as relating to how far back they look to identify the precursors of the modern Ukrainian nation. Most fall into what he calls the primordialists, who link the concepts of ethnos, people, and nation and trace the evolution of the modern nation back to ancient times. The others, or modernists, identify a premodern and a modern nation, noting that the modern nation's roots extend only to the sixteenth century, paralleling the development of European nations. In his survey, Kasianov does not find significant opposition to these paradigms.

The Janmaat chapter brings the discussion down a level: from that of the science of history to the teaching of it, or its use as a tool of socialization in Ukrainian schools. Janmaat's chapter focuses on the new textbooks for history in the older grades of Ukrainian secondary school and the points at which they differ from those used in the Soviet period. Textbooks are particularly important for socializing a new generation, instilling in them belief in a Ukrainian narrative that can sustain national identification despite different historical memories and myths across region. Socialization through education is often a highly contentious process, as individuals seem more likely to mobilize in defense of values taught to their children than many other issues. Interestingly, Janmaat's research shows that despite the fact that various textbooks are available to schools and that teachers are able to choose from a list of accepted texts, in representative areas of the country the same texts are being used. This indicates that there is little opposition to the introduction of a more national history for Ukrainian youth education.

The set of textbooks studied by Janmaat covers the entire period of Ukrainian history, from the beginnings of Kyivan Rus' through the twentieth century. They therefore include what might be considered more regionally controversial periods of history, such as the UPA movement in World War II that caused such division in the military programs described by Fesiak. Interestingly, Janmaat is able to show that important changes have been made to sections pertaining to the Ukrainian role in the 1917 revolution and during World War II. At the same time, there is much continuity between the texts, two of which were written by the same author in both the Soviet and post-Soviet periods. Janmaat's findings correspond to the work of education scholar Apple, who has noted in Western settings that unless there is a wholesale change of government and elites, as new narratives are introduced into the educational system and very little tends to be dropped from textbooks there is very rarely change in major ideological frameworks. Rather, progressive items are mentioned but not developed, or simply grafted onto old text.[28] This has interesting implications for ways in which new perceptions of history may be able to be introduced successfully in a regionally divided state. Since incremental change does not seem to engender significant mobilization of the society and also is unlikely to contradict the lived experience or garnered historical knowledge of the pupils, introducing minor changes might make it easier to create a new base of agreed-upon knowledge spanning the entire country.

The work of these authors on new historical narratives and historiographic paradigms is instructive in and of itself. If we approach their findings with an eye to determining the implications of a salient regional divide in Ukraine, it is clear that nation builders (in this case this term must be applied to a wide range of citizens, including scholars, politicians, journalists, and teachers) have so far been able to avoid the very real possibility of different regional identities failing to accept new historical narratives and myths. In this sense the history building project has been more successful than attempts to structure a unifying set of military myths and symbols.

Their work also suggests a new question: what will be the effect of the processes of transnational regionalism on mythmaking and on the acceptance of national historical narratives by the society? Regional identities, as noted above, do not necessarily follow border lines drawn on a map. It is conceivable that the shared experiences that made individuals in Eastern and Southern regions of Ukraine think similarly about sociopolitical questions in Barrington's study may also be shared with Russian citizens across the border. The borders are porous and open, making for significant cross-border socialization of the type described by Hurrell in other countries. Therefore, Ukrainian historical narratives are not insulated. They may compete—even among a new generation of pupils—with contradictory myths and narratives prevalent in Russia. The lack of mobilization against the Ukrainian national Rus' myth suggests that this has so far not been the case. As these regional processes grow, it will be interesting to gauge the continued strength of the Ukrainian narrative across Ukraine.

JUDGING THE ROLE OF THE STATE

The debate over whether the policies described above should be considered the agenda of a nationalizing state has raged in the Ukrainian studies field since Brubaker published his well-known study in 1995.[29] Brubaker defined a nationalizing state as one that is ethnically heterogeneous, but whose elites promote the language, culture, and political and economic success of the dominant ethnic group. He noted that the policies of nationalizing states are implemented in a situation where organized and self-conscious national minorities exist and where the minorities' external homelands may seek to protect them. Central to Brubaker's thesis is the importance of *perception*. Brubaker claimed that a state can be perceived to be nationalizing by the minority groups even if it does not actually adopt nationalizing policies.

Several scholars of post-Soviet Ukraine have presented evidence that suggests Ukraine can be considered a nationalizing state of the type that Brubaker describes.[30] While their arguments vary slightly, they all claim that while Ukraine officially endorses the concept of creating a civic, multi-ethnic state, its policies give the impression that the goal is actually quite different. In particular, they point to issues of language policy, the introduction of a national historiography, and Ukraine's foreign policy toward Russia. These policies, as viewed by the Russian national minority, suggest that the state's goal is to build a "Ukraine for Ukrainians" rather than a civic Ukraine.

Many of the contributors to this volume address this debate as well. The chapter by Fesiak suggests that between 1991 and 1993 Ukraine can be characterized as a nationalizing state (or, perhaps, a nationalizing military). Fesiak's outline of the "Ukrainianization" campaign in the military carries overtones of nationalizing tendencies, with the Union of Ukrainian Officers conducting what he has termed a "witch hunt" for servicemen in their ranks who were not sufficiently patriotic.

On the other hand, Kuzio (in this volume and elsewhere[31]) proposes an important question: what exactly is the difference between the nationalizing state and processes of nation building as they are defined in western liberal nations? Kuzio argues that the characterization of a "civic west" and "ethnic east" is overly simplistic and does not take into account nation-building policies in the west that are similar to those in Ukraine. All states are to some extent ethnic and civic, and the attempt to create an overarching cultural identity that includes such factors as a common language, symbols, and historical myths does not necessarily negate regional or ethnolinguistic pluralism.

Weller's work is especially interesting because it asks how the salience of regional identities might affect the potential for Ukrainian elites to pursue nationalizing policies. Given the importance of perceptions in Brubaker's definition of a nationalizing state, the wide variation of lived experiences across Ukraine suggests that we should consider that the way segments of the population perceive nation-building policies may also vary. Weller's research attempts to get at this variable by gauging perceptions of relations between people (i.e., whether ethnic conflict between groups is likely and how much one group feels it has in common with others). However, Weller's research is unable to determine the perceptions of these groups toward state policies in particular. While there may not be a likelihood of ethnic conflict between Russians and Ukrainians in Crimea, the Russian population there may still feel that the elites in Kyiv are attempting to create a nation for Ukrainians that excludes them. Further research into this area, added to Weller's work, would round out our understanding of regional perceptions of the potentially nationalizing state.

For example, the salience of regional identity may mitigate against mobilization by the Russian and Russophone population. Variation in economic position, social situations, and historical traditions may prompt Russians in different parts of Ukraine to view the same policy in different ways. Russians in Luhans'k, for instance, may perceive the state's actions as nationalizing, but their counterparts in Poltava may not. Again, it is the perception here that is most important. Given these regional divisions, the state can pursue policies that some may perceive as nationalizing without risking a widespread uproar from the Russian or Russophone population. Regional differences in perception also suggest that classification of a state as nationalizing is more complex. If only a portion of the minority perceives policies as discriminatory, how would this fit into Brubaker's definition?

The debate over whether or not Ukraine is a nationalizing state will continue as long as there are groups of Russians and Russophones who perceive state policies to be unfair. This volume suggests, however, that important research that moves beyond this debate is underway. By focusing on what can be learned from the state's role in Ukraine in the past ten years rather than trying to characterize it as positive or negative, we might gain insight into state and nation building that can inform political science theory. In addition, the research here indicates that despite questions of perception, a consensus is forming regardless of region, ethnicity, or native tongue around building an independent Ukraine based on civic values and marked by ethnic peace. The salience of regional identities may be important in maintaining that peace by differentiating the perceptions of possible mobilization groups. Additional research into the actual perceptions of the population and how they vary by region may be able to further clarify these issues.

BY WAY OF CONCLUSION

The focus of this chapter on the implications of shared historical and life experiences that create strong regional identities in Ukraine should not be taken to mean that regionalism is the best model through which to view all vectors of Ukrainian domestic and foreign policy. As the preceding chapters in this volume illustrate, the interconnectedness of the many identifications that divide Ukraine remain unclear, and the dynamic nature of identity formation and re-formation can make this type of research a moving target. More investigation is needed to determine the salience of the regional identity in Ukrainian politics and nation building vis-à-vis ethnolinguistic identities.

This chapter has attempted to show that regionalism's rise as a separate factor from ethnicity, language, and religion in the debate over what divides Ukraine has important implications for Ukraine's ability to pursue domestic reform, consolidate a national identity, and conduct effective foreign policy. In particular, it has implications for the way in which the themes of this volume have developed in the past decade and will continue to develop in the twenty-first century. Regionalism and transnational regionalism have the potential to push the limits of Ukraine's semiunitary state structure, especially as local self government becomes a stronger force in Ukraine. These identities as forces may also play a role in the formation of what Ukrainian officials define as the "vectors" of the foreign policy agenda. The extent to which this is the case depends on one's view of the importance of domestic factors in the development of policy in the international arena, but in either case the potential exists. Transnational regional tendencies are a potential weakening force on Ukraine's attempt to build a cohesive civic nation within its present boundaries. At the same time, they may mitigate against ethnic mobilization toward state policies that may be perceived as nationalizing. They also complicate attempts to build overarching national identities in such areas as military symbols and myths.

While the exact ramifications of strong regionalism in Ukraine remain unclear, this chapter has tried to suggest areas in which further research may prove fruitful in determining regionalism's salience and effect on the transition process. Regionalism studies in other countries illustrate the growing prevalence of cross-border relations and the creation of transnational regions and regional identities. The historical closeness of Ukraine to its neighbors Russia and Belarus during the Soviet era and with Central Europe in the nineteenth century and interwar years indicates that Ukrainian citizens may still identify themselves with individuals now living in other states.[32] More research is needed, however, to determine if transnational regional identities at a level below the Central European, Eurasian or pan-Slavic still exist and to what extent these are important to Ukraine's transition and its foreign policy agenda.

Regionalism may also take on increased meaning as Ukraine becomes more and more connected with digital technology and feels the effects of globalization on its ability to govern and maintain identities. Processes of globalization transnationalize the formation of identities and loyalties among various segments of the population, resulting in a shift away from the concept of nation-state as their principal source of identification.[33] Growing globalism may open new avenues to scholars who can study global processes rather than confining themselves to dynamics within individual countries such as Ukraine. Further research into the extent to which Ukraine is feeling the effects of globalism and what this may mean for Ukraine's nation-building endeavor is necessary.

The importance of regionalism in the historical debates and creation of national myths may be an intriguing avenue of research as well. There is an argument to be made for the absence of mobilization of the Russian population against the new emphasis on Ukraine's national history with its roots in Kyivan Rus'. Still, it would be interesting to determine the reasons behind the lack of regional mobilization against more contemporary changes in the historical narrative prevalent in the fields of education, the media, and historiography.

Regionalism as a separate factor from ethnicity and language use may also provide insights into the debate over whether to classify Ukraine as a nationalizing state. Further study into the way in which regional identities affect perceptions of state nation building policies could be informative in two ways. First, such data combined with the work of Weller on ethnic distance and potential conflict would provide a more complete picture of the population's view of nation-building policies across the country. In addition, they could help to explain why the perceptions of discrimination among portions of the Russian minority (detailed by Arel and others) have not caused the expected civil strife or ethnic mobilization suggested by the Brubaker model.

The chapters collected in this volume highlight many of the most important debates now underway in Ukrainian studies. This conclusion has concentrated on the contributions that those chapters can provide to our understanding of regionalism in Ukraine. Beyond this, the volume also makes important additions to debates that were touched on only briefly here—such as discussions over the role of domestic politics in foreign policy decision making and the nature of the nation-building process in Ukraine. The most important contribution of this volume to the field, however, is the breadth and depth of the research included. This research will not only further enhance our understanding of the state's role in Ukrainian identity politics, but will also augment comparative studies of nation building, nationalism, and identity in other environments.

NOTES

1. Stephen Rapawy, *Ethnic Reidentification in Ukraine IPC Staff Paper No. 90* (Washington, DC: U.S. Bureau of the Census, August 1997). The December 2001 census will provide the first clear picture of ethnic self-identification since independence.

2. Ian Bremmer, "The Politics of Ethnicity: Russians in the New Ukraine," *Europe-Asia Studies*, vol. 46, no. 2 (March–April 1994), pp. 261–283.

3. Valeri Khmelko and Andrew Wilson, "Regionalism and Ethnic and Linguistic Cleavages in Ukraine" in Taras Kuzio ed.., *Contemporary Ukraine: Dynamics of Post-Soviet Transformation* (Armonk, NY: M. E. Sharpe, 1998), pp.60–80.

4. Dominique Arel and Valeri Khmelko, "The Russian Factor and Territorial Polarization in Ukraine," *Harriman Review*, vol. 9, nos.1–2 (Spring 1996), pp. 81–91.

5. Arthur Miller, "The Politics of Identity in Post-Soviet Societies," presentation at the Kennan Institute, Washington, DC, 11 December 2000.

6. Andrew Wilson, *The Ukrainians: Unexpected Nation* (New Haven: Yale University Press), 2000.

7. Sarah Birch, *Elections and Democratization in Ukraine* (London: Macmillan, 2000).

8. Wilson moves the field in this direction by including a chapter on religious divides in

his book *The Ukrainians: Unexpected Nation.*

9. Atlas of Ukraine (Kyiv, Institute of Geography of the National Academy of Sciences of Ukraine, 1999–2000), on CD ROM. In the case of L'viv, Ternopil, and Ivano-Frankivsk, the majority was Catholic; in Crimea there was a similar percentage of Orthodox as persons who claimed "other."

10. "Relihijnij vybir naselennya Ukrajiny: za danymy opytuvannya hromads'koj dumky," information from a roundtable held at the Institute of Sociology, Kyiv, 6 November 2000, published by Democratic Initiatives Foundation (Kyiv, 2000), p. 9 and Table 5.

11. For example, Weller's chapter in this volume employs a four-region classification scheme; Andrew Wilson uses a similar classification in *Ukrainian Nationalism in the 1990s: A Minority Faith* (Cambridge: Cambridge University Press), 1997.

12. Sherman Garnett, *Keystone in the Arch: Ukraine in the Emerging Security Environment of Central and Eastern Europe* (Washington, DC: Carnegie Endowment for International Peace, 1997).

13. Melvin J. Hinich, Valeri Khmelko, and Peter C. Ordeshook, "Ukraine's 1998 Parliamentary Elections: A Spatial Analysis," *Post-Soviet Affairs*, vol. 15, no. 2 (April–June 1999), pp. 182–183.

14. Catherine Wanner, *Burden of Dreams: History and Identity in Post-Soviet Ukraine* (University Park: Pennsylvania State University Press), 1998.

15. Paul S. Pirie, "National Identity and Politics in Southern and Eastern Ukraine," *Europe-Asia Studies*, vol. 48, no. 7, (November 1996), pp. 1082–1083. Catherine Wanner also ascribes to a less "fixed" view of identity in *Burden of Dreams*.

16. Louise Jackson, "Identity, Language and Transformation in Eastern Ukraine: Case Study of Zaporizhzhia" in Kuzio, *Contemporary Ukraine*, pp. 99–113.

17. For an examination of the processes of transnational regionalism in Russia, see Michael Bradshaw and Andrei Makarychev, "Globalization and Fragmentation: The Impact of the International Relations of Russia's Regions," in Blair Ruble, Jodi Koehn, and Nancy Popson, eds., *Fragmented Space in the Russian Federation.* (Washington DC: Woodrow Wilson Center Press, 2001).

18. Andrew Hurrell, "Explaining the Resurgence of Regionalism in World Politics," *Review of International Studies*, vol. 21 no. 4, (October 1995), p. 333.

19. "Ukraine Villagers Vote for Lukashenka By Mistake," ITAR-TASS, 14 November 1999.

20. Paul D'Anieri, "The Impact of Domestic Divisions on Ukrainian Foreign Policy: Ukraine as a 'Weak State'" in Taras Kuzio, Robert S. Kravchuk, and Paul D'Anieri, eds., *State and Institution Building in Ukraine* (New York: St. Martin's, 1999), p. 84.

21. James Sherr, "Ukrainian Security Policy: The Relationship between Domestic and External Factors," in Kuzio, *Contemporary Ukraine*, pp. 246–247.

22. Paul D'Anieri, Robert Kravchuk, and Taras Kuzio, *Politics and Society in Ukraine* (Boulder, CO: Westview Press, 1999), p. 228.

23. For more on the foreign policy agendas of Russia's regions, see Bradshaw and Makarychev, "Globalization and Fragmentation." On this trend more generally, see Brian Hocking, *Localizing Foreign Policy: Non-Central Governments and Multilayered Diplomacy* (New York: St. Martin's Press, 1993).

24. Philip G. Roeder, "Soviet Federalism and Ethnic Mobilization," *World Politics*, vol. 23, no. 2 (January 1991), pp. 196–233.

25. See, for example, Kathryn Stoner-Weiss, "Russian Federalism," in Stephen White, Alex Pravda, and Zvi Gitelman, eds., *Developments in Russian Politics, 4th ed.* (Durham, NC: Duke University Press, 1997).

26. Zenon E. Kohut, "History as a Battleground: Russian-Ukrainian Relations and Historical Consciousness in Contemporary Ukraine," in S. Frederick Starr, ed., *The Legacy of*

History in Russia and the New States of Eurasia (Armonk, NY: M. E. Sharpe, 1994), pp. 123–145.

27. For example, Yaroslav Hrytsak, who figures prominently as a "modernist" in Kasianov's chapter, is author of one of two volumes on Ukrainian history aimed at the non-historian audience. Yaroslav Hrytsak, *Narys Istoriji Ukrajiny: Formuvannya Modernoi Ukrainskoi Natsii XIX–XX Stolittya* (Kyiv: Heneza, 1996). In addition, in 1999 a volume on the historical relationship between Ukraine and Russia was published in Ukraine for mass audiences with short articles, colorful graphics, and an introduction by President Kuchma emphasizing the need to study Ukrainian and Russian history closely as each country establishes its independence. See *Rossiia i Ukraina: Vekhi Istorii*, Special Issue of *Rodina*, no. 8, 1999.

28. Michael W. Apple and Linda K. Christian-Smith, "The Politics of the Textbook" in Michael W. Apple and Linda K. Christian-Smith, eds., *The Politics of the Textbook* (New York: Routledge, 1991), p. 10.

29. Rogers Brubaker, "National Minorities, Nationalizing States, and External Homelands in the New Europe," *Daedalus*, vol. 124, no. 2 (Spring 1995), pp. 107–132.

30. See, for example, Dominique Arel, "Ukraine: The Temptation of the Nationalizing State" in Vladimir Tismaneanu, ed., *Political Culture and Civil Society in the Former Soviet Union* (Armonk, NY: M. E. Sharpe, 1995), pp. 157–188; Wilson, *Ukrainian Nationalism in the 1990s*; and David D. Laitin, *Identity in Formation: The Russian-Speaking Populations in the Near Abroad* (Ithaca, NY: Cornell University Press, 1998).

31. See, for example, Taras Kuzio, "Nationalizing States or Nation Building? A Review of the Theoretical Literature and Empirical Evidence," *Nations and Nationalism*, vol. 7, part 2 (April 2001), pp. 135–154.

32. For example, the prevalence of the pan-Slavic identity supports this hypothesis. Reference to the pan-Slavic identity is most often found in work dealing with international relations and the future of Ukrainian-Russian relations. The chapter on foreign policy in this volume is no exception: Shulman refers to it as the "East-Slavic" identity. For an overview of pan-Slavism and other possible cross-regional identities see the paper presented by A. Wilson, "Elements of a Theory of Ukrainian National Identity," the Kennan Institute, 6 December 1999.

33. Saskia Sassen, *Globalization and Its Discontents* (New York: The New Press, 1998), p. xxx. For a general discussion of the relationship between globalization and transformation in the post-Soviet context see Alison Stenning and M. J. Bradshaw, "Globalization and Transformation: The Changing Geography of the Post-Socialist World" in John Bryson, Nick Henry, David Keeble, and Ron Martin, eds., *The Economic Geography Reader* (Chichester: Wiley, 1999), pp. 97–107.

Index

About the Contributors

LOWELL W. BARRINGTON is Assistant Professor of Political Science at Marquette University in Milwaukee and Senior Associate at the Eurasia Group in New York. He has served as Editor-in-Chief of *Analysis of Current Events* and was Vice President of the Association for the Study of Nationalities. Barrington's publications include articles in the *European Journal of Political Research*, *Post-Soviet Affairs*, and *Europe-Asia Studies*, and he is the editor of the forthcoming book *Nationalism after Independence* (University of Michigan Press).

PAUL D'ANIERI is Associate Professor of Political Science and Associate Dean of International Programs at the University of Kansas. He is author of *Economic Interdependence in Ukrainian-Russian Relations* (SUNY, 1999), and co-author of *Politics and Society in Ukraine* (Westview, 1999), as well as articles and chapters on Ukrainian and Russian politics and foreign policy. He has been Visiting Professor at Harvard and at Lviv State University in Ukraine. He is Editor of *European Security*

ANDREW FESIAK is a consultant specializing in the countries of Eastern Europe and the former Soviet Union.

JAN G. JANMAAT is a policy worker in sustainable energy at the province of Noord-Holland in the Netherlands, and is a member of the editorial board of "Oost-Europa Verkenningen", a journal which focuses on political and social issues in the former communist countries. He is author of Nation-Building in Post-Soviet Ukraine: Educational Policy and the Response of the Russian-Speaking Population (University of Amsterdam, 2000).

GEORGII KASIANOV is Leading Research Fellow, Institute of Ukrainian History, Ukrainian National Academy of Sciences. He is author or co-author of several books, including *Theories of Nations and Nationalism* (Lybid', 1995) and *The Dissidents: The Ukrainian Intelligentsia in Non-Conformist Movements, 1960-1980* (Lybid', 1999).

TARAS KUZIO is formerly a Senior Research Fellow, Center for Russian and East European Studies, University of Birmingham; Post Doctoral Fellow, Yale University; and Visiting Fellow, Brown University. He was also head of the NATO Information Office in Kyiv. Currently he is Resident Fellow at the Center for Russian and East European Studies, University of Toronto. He is author of *Ukraine Under Kuchma* (MacMillan, 1997), *Ukraine: State and Nation Building* (Routledge, 1998), and co-author of *Politics and Society in Ukraine* (Westview, 1999).

NANCY POPSON is Deputy Director of the Kennan Institute in Washington, DC. She has been at the Kennan Institute since 1996, where she has coordinated the institute's program on Ukraine. Her research interests include nation building in Ukraine, questions of ethnicity and migration in Ukraine (particularly in Kyiv), women in politics in the NIS, and assistance programs in the NIS. Her most recent articles appeared in *Urban Anthropology* and *Nationalities Papers*.

MYKOLA RIABCHUK is a research associate at the University of "Kyiv-Mohyla Academy" and co-editor of the Ukrainian literary review "Krytyka." He is an author of five books, including a two-volume study on Civil Society and State-Nation Building in Ukraine (From 'Little Russia' to Ukraine, and Dilemmas of the Ukrainian Faustus, 2000).

STEPHEN SHULMAN is Assistant Professor in Department of Political Science at Southern Illinois University, where he teaches international relations, comparative politics, and ethnic politics. His research interests include nationalism and national identity, the relationship between ethnicity and foreign policy, and the role of culture in international affairs. His research appears in journals such as Comparative Political Studies, Europe-Asia Studies, Nationalities Papers, and International Studies Quarterly.

CRAIG A. WELLER was Research Fellow at the Centre for the Study of Public Policy at the University of Strathclyde from 2000 to 2002.